EIGHTEENTH-CENTURY NOVELS BY WOMEN

Isobel Grundy, Editor

Advisory Board

The Recess;
or,
A Tale of Other Times

Sophia Lee

~

Edited by April Alliston

The University Press of Kentucky

Publication of this volume was made possible in part by a grant from the National Endowment for the Humanities.

Editorial and Sales Offices: The University Press of Kentucky
663 South Limestone Street, Lexington, Kentucky 40508-4008

04 03 02 01 00   5 4 3 2 1

Frontispiece: Sophia Lee. Engraved by Ridley from an original drawing by Sir Thomas Lawrence. First published in the *Monthly Mirror,* August 1, 1797. From *The Two Scribbling Mrs. P.P.'s . . . ,* Manuscripts Division, Princeton University Library.

Library of Congress Cataloging-in-Publication Data

Lee. Sophia, 1750-1824.
    The recess, or, A tale of other times / Sophia Lee : April Alliston, editor
        p. cm. — (Eighteenth-century novels by women)
    Includes bibliographical references (p.   )
    ISBN 0-8131-2146-9 (alk. paper). — ISBN 0-8131-0978-7 (pbk.: alk. paper)
        I. Alliston, April. II. Title. III. Title: Recess. IV. Title:
Tale of other times. V. Series.
PR3541.L2R4 2000
823'.6—dc21   99-23224

CONTENTS

ACKNOWLEDGMENTS

For the realization of a long-cherished dream of getting *The Recess* back into print and into the hands of readers, I am deeply grateful to Isobel Grundy for having been willing to place her faith in a younger scholar, and to J. Paul Hunter for his kindness in having put me in touch with her.

Once those in charge of the series had made it possible for me to begin this work, many people contributed to its completion. Isobel Grundy read the entire draft with meticulous care and cheered me on while offering voluminous and detailed suggestions. Betty Rizzo's advice on biographical and textual research proved as valuable as her encouragement and moral support. Claudia Johnson helped me with her editorial experience, while Earl Miner and Julie Peters wracked their extremely learned brains to help identify obscure, unsourced quotations. Carol Barash solved the problem of sources once and for all by introducing me to the information age. Judith Lewin was indefatigable in ferreting out unknown facts about the life of Sophia Lee, and Julie Park was endlessly patient with me, as she was with those recalcitrant bits of fact that were the hardest of all to find. Stephanie Daval and Jennifer Tsien also contributed skilled and invaluable assistance with the biographical and critical research for the introduction and notes. Ellen Brinks was literally my right hand, assisting with copying and marking editorial changes, as well as thinking through some points of editorial policy with me. Chris Ann Matteo and Sejean Sohn were both right and left hands—without their hands, their time, and their patience, the typing could never have been done. Antonio Garcia and Joseph Ortiz, as well as Stephanie Daval and Judith Lewin, helped proofread the manuscript. Andy Stern miraculously retrieved the typed text after a wanton computer had munched it, and Alice Clark produced the microfilm without which no text could have been typed in the first place. Susanne McNatt of Inter-Library Loan Services in the Firestone Library battled well beyond the call of duty with incomplete information and possessive librarians elsewhere to track down rare editions. François Morel provided much needed support, tangible and intangible. To Gregory Maertz, my debt and my gratitude are incalculable.

On an institutional level, I wish to thank Princeton University and its officers for financial support of this project. Deans Brown, Gunning, Gutmann, and Rohrer, as well as the Committee on Research in the Humanities and Social Sciences, generously approved funding from the Class of '59 Junior Faculty Fund and other sources for the transcription of the text in electronic format. Finally, this work would not have been possible without the rich collections of a number of libraries and archives. The libraries of Princeton and Yale Universities, the University of Pennsylvania, and Smith College allowed me to consult the rare eighteenth-century editions needed to establish the text, as well as critical literature and important biographical documents. Further biographical records were found with the very generous assistance of Frances Harris at the British Library; Bruce Barker-Benfield at the Bodleian Library, Oxford University; Colin Johnston and Mary Blagden at the Bath & North East Somerset Record Office; Elizabeth Bevan at the Bath Central Library; and the staffs of the Bristol and Somerset Record Offices. The staff of Special Collections at the University of Colorado at Boulder Library also very obligingly helped me navigate their impressive collection of "Women Poets of the Romantic Period: 1770-1839" during my research for the introduction.

INTRODUCTION

THE RECESS;
OR,
A TALE OF OTHER TIMES

> I must first acquaint you I have read the Recess, and have been
> confined three days in consequence.
> —*Elizabeth Sophia Tomlins (1787)*

The Recess enjoyed enormous popularity for well over twenty years after its
first publication in 1783, not only in the English-speaking world, but all over
Europe. Its success was important in establishing both Gothic and historical
fiction, of which it is one of the earliest examples, as modes that were predominant in England for decades afterward and remain popular to this day.
Sophia Lee sets her "tale of other times" in the reign of Elizabeth I, and weaves
its romance plot around the tragic history of Mary, Queen of Scots. Its twin
heroines and narrators are raised in a mysterious subterranean chamber, linked
to the outside world by secret passages. One of the keys to Lee's success with
her experiment in historical Gothic fiction was her skill in using the form of
the novel to elicit strong emotional responses in her readers, a skill she developed in part through her lifelong association with the theater.

THE RECESS AS A NOVEL OF SENSIBILITY

The heroine of Elizabeth Tomlins's novel *The Victim of Fancy* (1787; quoted
in the epigraph above), an ardent enthusiast of such authors as Goethe and

Burney, is at first skeptical as to whether the upstart novelist Sophia Lee could possibly equal them in touching her readers' emotions. In this ungenerous state of mind she takes up *The Recess,* but quickly finds she cannot put it down:

> From the moment I first opened it, till the last sorrowful scene which closes the overwhelming narration of miseries, I quitted not the book. As I read, I felt all the pains of suspense at my heart, and I know not a term which can convey to you an idea how infinitely I felt myself interested through the whole: I was frequently affected even beyond the power of weeping, and scarcely could prevail on my aunt, with all my entreaties, to let me read the last volume; but persuading her that I should, perhaps, be less affected when alone, I had all the luxury of weeping over it by myself.[1]

The result of this fictional reader's indulgence in "the luxury of weeping" is a fever that keeps her in bed for three days. Such a response portrays *The Recess* as a masterpiece of the literature of sensibility. As such, it participated in an aesthetic and moral code that prevailed in Europe during the mid- to late eighteenth century. One of the keys to the immense popularity of *The Recess* was its power to arouse the "interest," or sympathetic identification, of readers. Sympathy with its characters and situations moved the emotions and the senses, not just of Tomlins's heroine, but of many real people as well.

Critical evaluations of current novels, like the assessment of *The Recess* by Tomlins's heroine, commonly appeared in fiction by women of the later eighteenth century. This strategy allowed female authors in particular an opportunity to "review" works by other women to an extent less often made available to them in the newspapers, and thus to help legitimize the "low" or popular genres (the novel itself, particularly in the modes of sensibility, the Gothic, and the epistolary form) in which the literary women of the time tended most often to work.[2] As Austen wrote, "Alas! if the heroine of one novel be not patronized by the heroine of another, from whom can she expect protection and regard? . . . Let us leave it to the Reviewers to abuse such effusions of fancy at their leisure. . . . Let us not desert one another; we are an injured body."[3] The representation of the weeping and feverish young reader in Tomlins's novel constitutes a "rave" review of Lee's work. When modern readers approach a work like *The Recess,* it must be remembered that, toward the end of the eighteenth century, the only "realism" aimed at by, or expected from, such fiction was located in the reality of the emotions evoked through readers' sympathetic identification with characters, not in any verisimilitude of plot or situation. As Tomlins's heroine writes of her experience of reading *The Recess*, "its language, with all the fire and all the softness of poetry, conveys images the most enchanting to the fancy, and scenes the most interesting to the heart."[4]

Readers today are unlikely to fall ill upon reading this novel, or even, perhaps, to dissolve into tears, because late twentieth-century emotional and physical responses have not been trained in the codes of sensibility to the extent that those of Lee's contemporaries had been. To be sure, the response of Tomlins's heroine is, even within the conventions of the time, an exaggerated one, ascribed to a young and uncritical, though sensitive, reader. Yet even the most sophisticated readers of the period tended to judge the literature of sensibility according to the strength of the emotional response it could and did produce in them. Thomas de Quincey found *The Recess* very moving when he read it in 1803.[5] Hester Piozzi, another author and a mature, sophisticated reader who was given to acerbic observations about contemporary works, occasionally criticized Lee's writing as improbable and romantic. Yet Lee touched even this reader. She came to Lee's defense when a friend criticized her play, *Almeyda, Queen of Granada* (written as a dramatic reworking of the central themes of female inheritance and madness in *The Recess*), as "overstrained." Piozzi writes: "The Play itself half broke my Heart in reading 'twas so tender—and some how I had expected Terror more than Pity would have been produced by Sophia Lee—."[6] Piozzi expected "terror" because of the reputation Lee had gained from her famous Gothic novel, *The Recess*.

Pity and fear, the two emotions that Aristotle said should be evoked by a good tragedy, were also the two primary emotional responses aimed at by novels of sensibility. Samuel Richardson, the first widely successful English novelist of sensibility, explicitly compared his novel *Clarissa* to the drama, as Horace Walpole did his ground-breaking Gothic novel *The Castle of Otranto*. Pity was elaborated during the course of the eighteenth century as "sympathy"; it differs from pity in the classical sense primarily in that a much stronger emphasis is placed upon the audience's identification with the sufferer. Aristotle stipulated that a distance should be maintained through the extreme elevation of the characters to prevent over-identification by the viewers. More recent English usage has adopted the word "empathy" (a term borrowed from the German Romantics) to denote sympathy in its eighteenth-century sense. This is the emotion most generally associated with the literature of sensibility, but its Gothic mode, a somewhat later development, aims at the evocation of both of the Aristotelian dramatic emotions, by adding fear to pity.

Fear, like pity, developed a particular meaning in eighteenth-century aesthetics. In classical times it was said that the representation of the Furies in Aeschylus' play *The Eumenides* was so frightening that their entrance upon the stage caused women to miscarry. The characteristically Gothic "terror" that Hester Piozzi expected from Lee's works was a feeling more of suspense than fright, a dread of the unrevealed and the unspeakable, much more than a shock at anything actually shown or told.

THE RECESS AS GOTHIC FICTION

Its ability to move contemporary readers to terror and sympathy was not the only important achievement of *The Recess*. While working successfully within an aesthetic that Richardson had helped to establish in fiction and Jean-Jacques Rousseau had exploited in his enormously popular *Julie, ou La Nouvelle Héloïse*, Lee also made important innovations. It is chiefly because of these innovations that *The Recess* remains of interest to readers today. Like Richardson and Rousseau, Lee writes in the epistolary form—but she does so in a way that is unique in the history of the novel. *The Recess* is also one of the first English works of historical fiction, and represents a great advance in sophistication over the few that preceded it. It was extremely important in the evolution of that branch of the literature of sensibility known as the "Gothic," which has experienced such a revival in these last decades of the twentieth century. One of the first few Gothic novels ever published, it was the second by a woman, after Clara Reeve's *The Old English Baron* (1777), which was much more domestic and didactic in emphasis than *The Recess*, even though Reeve, like Walpole, chose a male protagonist. It was *The Recess* that ushered in the great vogue of Gothic fiction in England.[7]

In order to understand the role of *The Recess* in the development of Gothic fiction, some explanation of what the Gothic was when Lee began working in that mode is necessary. *The Recess* appeared twenty years after *The Castle of Otranto* (1764), by the antiquarian Horace Walpole. In his 1765 preface to *Otranto*, Walpole explains that the new kind of fiction he has invented is "an attempt to blend the two kinds of romance, the ancient and the modern. In the former all was imagination and improbability: in the latter, nature is always intended to be, and sometimes has been, copied with success."[8] By "the modern romance," Walpole means what is now called the novel.

In order to fuse it with the "ancient" or chivalric romance—a form of narrative whose improbability had already been mocked long before by Cervantes in *Don Quixote*—Walpole locates his "probability" (roughly synonymous with "plausibility" or "realism" in current usage) in character alone, giving free reign to the imagination to invent fantastic events and situations. Thus he "wished to conduct the mortal agents in his drama according to the rules of probability; in short, to make them think, speak and act, as it might be supposed mere men and women would do in extraordinary positions."[9] His explicit comparison of his story to "drama" links his work to Richardson's novels of sensibility. Walpole further states that his sense of "probability" in character is derived from the dramatic work of Shakespeare, "that great master of nature."[10]

The notion of literary probability in general is based on a sense of social norms shared by the audience of a work; thus it tends to be heavily inflected by the frequently stereotyped assumptions of a culture regarding the kinds of behavior expected from various "characters," or categories of people. For Walpole, Shakespeare is a "great master of nature" specifically because he portrays characters whose differences of behavior are determined by differences of class. His servants act and speak quite differently from his noblemen, and Walpole imitates Shakespeare in trying to imitate "nature" in this respect.[11] Gender and nationality are further determinants of social norms for behavior, and thus also of notions of probability. To use the most simplified examples, servants will talk in an unreserved and uneducated way; Frenchmen will be insincere and flirtatious; African slaves may be lazy or fondly devoted; and virtuous young European women will be modest, passive, physically delicate, and highly sensitive to the feelings of others. Given the force of the neoclassical aesthetic norm—again following Aristotle—that the function of literature was to instruct as well as to entertain, such conventions of probability were actually more prescriptive than descriptive. Divergences from the expected norms were considered to be moral as well as aesthetic failings in a literary work. Female authors were by far the most susceptible to such critique, since authorship was in itself potentially a transgression of the norm of feminine modesty.

Lee herself suffered from the extreme vulnerability to moral criticism shared by female contemporaries. Her first and last works, both plays, were criticized on these grounds. The very title of the last, *The Assignation,* was considered shockingly risqué, and the first, *The Chapter of Accidents,* came in for attack because it features a heroine, Cecilia, who does not preserve her chastity, although she is properly repentant. Lee writes in her own defense: "At the time when I produced a frail Cecilia, I was so severely censured by the rigid moralists who directed the newspapers, that I should have thought it due to myself to show immediately, by printing these volumes [*The Life of a Lover*, whose heroine maintains her virtue intact], that I had considered both sides of the question."[12] In spite of the "rigid moralists," *The Chapter of Accidents* was a great success; nevertheless Lee had learned her lesson, and everything she presented to the public after it (including *The Assignation*) conformed more strictly to the codes of late eighteenth-century feminine virtue.

With *The Recess* Lee became a pioneer of what Ellen Moers has termed the "female Gothic," which I would describe as featuring heroines who conform to morally prescriptive notions of probability for feminine behavior, but who are also portrayed as quite literally confined by them. The excesses of feminine frailty and emotion that modern readers may be inclined to read as the height of improbability implicitly critique the notions of probability of their time by the very extremism of their adherence to them. Although the writers of "female Gothic" were careful that their critique of the inextricably linked norms of probability and morality always remain *implicit,* readers of course sensed it, and Lee never escaped entirely from censure. An acquaintance wrote of her contribution to *The Canterbury Tales,* a collection of stories written jointly with her younger sister Harriet, "Miss Lee runs *so wild* in the Fields of tender *Romance* that probability and *Morality* are equally lost sight of."[13]

Lee's grand innovation in the Gothic mode was to combine characters and emotional appeal that were probable according to notions derived, like Walpole's, from Shakespearean and Aristotelian dramatic models, with the avowedly improbable plots of *both romance and history.* (Thus *The Recess* can be called the first important and fully developed text for both the "female" Gothic and the historical Gothic strains in English fiction, despite the importance for her work of one or two predecessors in each of these strains.[14]) In the repeated debates that dominated the earlier eighteenth century over the differences between what Walpole calls "ancient" and "modern romance," a consensus had emerged that the "modern romance" or "novel" was to be defined—and judged—by its probability. It was not enough to tell a true story in a novel, because it was recognized that improbable events occur all the time. Rather, a novel must not violate accepted ideas of the norm and the quotidian. History, while true, could be expected to be a potentially *improbable* narrative of events, unlike a proper novel. Lee takes advantage of this opposition between the true and the probable to create a sense of the truth both of history and of feminine behavior that defies contemporary codes of probability.

THE RECESS AS HISTORICAL NOVEL

In *The Recess; or, A Tale of Other Times,* Lee takes her lead from an already old French tradition whose earliest innovators included the seventeenth-century Madeleine de Scudéry and Marie de Lafayette, by writing the matter of official *historiography* (as opposed to the other nonfictional genres, from devotional works to travelogues, that more commonly informed the early novel in England) as fiction. Discussions of Lee's debt to the French historical novel have regularly emphasized the importance of Prévost, whose *Cleveland* was one of her models, and of Baculard d'Arnaud rather than of the earlier, predominantly female innovators in the genre. Like most writers, Lee was influenced by a number of different precursors, but the importance of d'Arnaud has been exaggerated on the basis of an erroneous attribution to her of a translation of his historical novel *Varbeck*.[15] Lee in fact closely follows and alludes extensively to *La Princesse de Clèves,* whose author had, long before Lee, defied both official historiography and the sense of probable feminine behavior shared by her contemporary audience of seventeenth-century French aristocrats.[16] Set in the reign of Elizabeth I—exactly contemporary with the historical setting of *La Princesse de Clèves*—the romance plot of *The Recess* develops around the history of Mary Stuart, an important character in Lafayette's novel, and a prevalent though controversial Enlightenment and Romantic icon from Lafayette to Schiller.[17]

The critical tradition of identifying Lee's indebtedness to the French novel for her perfection of English historical fiction, however, has failed to recognize an obvious influence closer to home. England already had its own long tradition of poetic elaboration upon history in the drama. History and tragedy were so closely allied in England that a reviewer of Lee's play *Almeyda* observed that "contrary to the common practice of tragic writers, Miss Lee has founded her play upon a fiction, wholly invented . . . by herself."[18] It is thus hardly surprising that Lee, the daughter of two Shakespearean actors and already herself the author of one successful play when she wrote *The Recess,* should have thought of using a standard technique of dramatic composition when she attempted a tragic romance in a genre that, like herself, already had close ties to the stage. Even the primary situation upon which critics have traditionally founded the idea of *The Recess*'s debt to Prévost's *Cleveland*—the shared scenario of the apparently orphaned siblings of secretly noble ancestry raised in a cavern by a foster parent—is already found in Shakespeare's *Cymbeline,* together with another romance element borrowed by Lee, the heroine travelling around Britain and entering on a scene of battle in masculine disguise.

That Lee drew upon her dramatic experience when writing *The Recess* is further indicated by its prose style. Very unlike her earlier-written, though later-published, novel *The Life of a Lover*, *The Recess* borrows the high-flown language of neoclassical tragedy. For this quality it was particularly admired by contemporaries, although some judged the style inappropriate for a mere novel. One reviewer writes that "her powers of description are very great; and there is a richness in her style which shows that her genius is ardent and vigorous." Although he qualifies his praise by adding that "perhaps the language is sometimes overcharged: it is too glaring, too poetical," he nevertheless concludes his evaluation with the highest praise that could be given any writer in a dramatic vein: "the Author [has] studied Shakespear's Lear with much attention, and copied that admirable model with great success."[19]

Reviewers welcomed Lee's historical innovation in English fiction, even though they were made uncomfortable by it at the same time. *The Gentleman's Magazine* in 1786 could not "entirely approve the custom of interweaving fictitious incident with historic truth," and yet, recommending the novel "with pleasure," its reviewer wrote admiringly that "the truth of character is rigidly preserved, for the peculiarities of Elizabeth and James are not delineated with more exactness in Hume or Robertson."[20] This reviewer was not alone in likening Lee's history to those of Hume and Robertson, and a close comparison of her text with theirs makes it quite clear that she had read both.[21] Piozzi similarly appreciated Lee's treatment of historical character, writing that her portrayal of Mary, Queen of Scots left no room for improvement in John St. John's tragedy *Mary*. "After Robertson's History, and [Lee's] Recess, I thought so little more could be done for Mary, that no Accounts of Mr. St. John's Success have hitherto been able to draw me in *her Cause* to Drury Lane."[22]

William Robertson's *History of Scotland during the Reigns of Queen Mary and James VI* (1759) and David Hume's *History of England* (1754-62) in particular were recognized in Lee's own time as historical narratives with which her new form was in competition. So true was this that some naive readers saw no difference between the truth claims of the two forms. Two amusing anecdotes are recounted about ladies who formed their judgments of the characters of the two British queens who appear in it entirely upon information derived from *The Recess:*

> The ingenious defence of Mary Queen of Scots, being mentioned t'other night at a card-table, a maiden lady, who would pardon murder or sacrilege rather than any violation of the laws of chastity, . . . cried out: "Oh! she was an abandoned woman! don't de-

fend her; she had two *bastards* (*natural children* I suppose you'll call them) by the Duke of Norfolk." I said I had never met with that circumstance, even in Buchanan, or any history of those times. "Oh!" says she, "it's very true: I have just been reading an entertaining *novel,* which is *founded* entirely upon *that fact.*[23]

No doubt this extremely credulous response was as apocryphal as the extreme emotional response of Tomlins's heroine, yet another lady, less ignorant of the facts of history, is similarly said to have "confessed that she could not get over a prejudice against the character of our Elizabeth arising from her cruelty to two imaginary daughters of Mary Queen of Scots who never existed but in the pages of a novel."[24] These joking anecdotes, whether or not they are true, reveal a persistent anxiety over the conflation of history and fiction that had been raised as much as a century before by the novels of Lee's French predecessors.[25]

In order to understand how *The Recess* competed successfully as historical narrative, it is crucial to observe the distinction made by the reviewer for *The Gentleman's Magazine* between two different kinds of historical truth: that of "incident" (or plot) and that of character. Lee in fact diverges quite as much from the accounts of Hume and Robertson on particulars of character as she does on those of incident (although she agrees with them, in large part, on both). But Hume and Robertson themselves locate the *probability* of historiography—a form of narrative that might, like romance but unlike the novel, correctly include improbable incidents—primarily in their descriptions of character. Character occupies a central position in their narratives; whenever a major historical figure dies, his or her character is described at length, in a static manner close to what French writers of the previous century had called the *portrait moral.* The implied assumption of the stability of character is crucial to eighteenth-century historiography because whenever doubt arises as to the truth of incident—as to what exactly *did* happen (and for want of conclusive evidence such doubt often does arise)—historians depend upon the truth of character, as they have established it, to make probable judgments of how a particular personage *must have acted.* Thus the truth of character plays an important role in constructing the truth of incident. In this respect Lee operates similarly to the historians of her day, with the exception that she does not use the descriptive form of the *portrait moral,* portraying her characters instead through the more dramatic forms of action and speech. Her conception of character, moreover, like Lafayette's, emphasizes the force of emotions like love and jealousy. These the historians acknowledge but relegate as much as possible to the realm of the private, which they exclude from history. Like

Hume and Robertson, Lee uses her assessments of historical characters to speculate on such of their actions—and thus on "incident" or matters of plot—as cannot be or have not been adequately documented, and these of course fall mainly in that "private" area excluded by other historians.[26]

Even twentieth-century commentators recognize the historical truth of *The Recess* particularly in its portrayal of character. Devendra P. Varma, for example, calls Lee's portrayal of Queen Elizabeth "realistic." Montague Summers says that "the personages for the most part act according to history, but they act from entirely different motives."[27] But J.M.S. Tompkins in the 1930s set the tone for nearly all subsequent critics in judging the novel harshly for those divergences of "incident" that eighteenth-century critics forgave so much more readily. Most commentators in this century repeat Tompkins's censorious wonderment at how "the headmistress of a well-known girls' school could publish a novel in which the Armada preceded the execution of the Queen of Scots and escape censure." Tompkins's best explanation—one also repeated by others—is that Lee wrote "at a period when historical knowledge was partial and thinly spread . . . when education had hung no weights on the dreamer's heels." This rather insulting observation on the state of knowledge in the Enlightenment is completely and obviously belied by the great popularity of historians such as Hume (who before he published his best-selling *History of England* was merely an obscure Scottish philosopher), Robertson, Goldsmith, and Gibbon—to name only the most widely read and respected. Indeed, there is little doubt that the average eighteenth-century reader of *The Recess* was better informed on the subject of Elizabethan history than most who will pick up her novel today. Neither Lee's manipulations of historical incident, including chronology, nor her "escape from censure" on account of them can be the result of ignorance. Rather, the widespread acceptance of her approach indicates that both she and her contemporary audience—including the most serious of her fellow historians—regarded character as the primary focus of truth in historiography. To that Lee was thought to be "rigidly" faithful.

Because Lee's contemporary readers so regularly compared *The Recess* to the histories of Hume and Robertson in particular, the notes to this edition indicate exactly where Lee's novel converges with and diverges from their accounts of the same characters and incidents. In addition to providing basic information about the period for the modern reader, the notes offer a detailed comparison of Lee's version of Elizabethan history with the most learned and widely accepted eighteenth-century accounts of it (including those of Goldsmith and Hurd, in addition to Hume's and Robertson's more extensive treatments). One of the scenes from *The Recess* most relished by contemporaries, for example, was that in which one of Lee's fictional twin heroines, mad with grief, finds her way into the bedchamber of Queen Elizabeth. The Queen takes the heroine for a ghost sent to reproach her for the death of Essex, and is driven to a fatal fit of melancholy. Few took umbrage at the fact that this explanation for the depression of Elizabeth's final days differed from the one, equally romantic, upon which Hume and Robertson were agreed (and which has since been discounted).[28]

POPULARITY AND INFLUENCE

The Recess was enormously popular in Lee's time, and its influence on the subsequent development of the historical and the Gothic novel was important. The first volume of *The Recess* was published in 1783; it was customary for publishers to try the success of a first volume before bringing out the rest of the three that by convention made up a complete novel. The other two duly followed in 1785, all to acclaim from the London critics.[29] The suspense created by the wait for the later volumes itself may have contributed to the work's popularity (each of the first two volumes ended strategically with the heroine falling into a dead faint). The work quickly reached an international audience throughout western Europe and North America. By 1806—twenty years after its original publication—it had gone through five separate English editions and two Irish ones (the latter probably "pirated," or copied from the English editions without permission), and had also been translated into French, German, Swedish, Spanish, and Portuguese. The French translation was even translated back into English in 1809 by Alexander Jamieson, under the title *The Cavern, or The Two Sisters* (from the French title, *Le Souterrain, ou les deux soeurs*). Another French translation with the same title was subtitled *Matilde*, from the name of Lee's primary heroine and narrator. The novel was later published at least twice by houses other than Cadell's in 1824 and 1827, and in condensed form at least four times in various English magazines (precursors of *Reader's Digest*) during the first half of the nineteenth century.

The initial appearance of *The Recess* immediately encouraged a host of imitators. Those whose works are mentioned by Montague Summers as merely "inspired" by Lee's combination of historical data with Gothic romance are too numerous even to mention here; the novels that seem closely and specifically to follow *The Recess* include Martha Harley's *St. Bernard's Priory, An Old English Tale* (1786), Anne Fuller's *Alan Fitz-Osborne, an Historical Tale* (1787), and Rosetta Ballin's *The Statue Room; an Historical Tale* (1790), as well as two novels by Francis Lathom set in Tudor times, *The Mysterious Freebooter; or, The Days of Queen Bess* (1806) and *Mystic Events; or, The Vision of the Tapestry* (1830).[30] George Walker's *The Romance of the Cavern; or, The History of Fitz-Henry and James* (1792) appears to be inspired by Prévost's *Cleveland,* as was *The Recess* itself, but bears the imprint of Lee's intervening novel.[31]

The influence of *The Recess* was not limited to England, to forgotten authors, or even to the novel. A successful play by Christian Heinrich Speiss, *Maria Stuart und Norfolk,* drew largely upon it.[32] The libretto for Rossini's opera *Elisabetta, regina d'Inghilterra,* which opened triumphantly in Naples in 1815 and was performed at the Drury Lane Theatre in London in 1818, is closely based on a French melodrama similarly entitled *Elisabeth, reine d'Angleterre,* which in turn was taken "wholly from Sophia Lee's romance."[33] In a collection of poems by Mary Roberts, adopting the voice of the captive Mary Stuart, the imprisoned queen actually addresses her series of verse letters to her daughter "Matilda"—it seems Roberts expected all readers to know from having read Lee's novel that the Queen of Scots had a daughter by that name.[34] Much closer to our own time, the importance of Gothic literature for the Surrealists has been described by Summers, and the French Surrealist writer, Annie Le Brun, discusses *The Recess* at length in her tribute to Gothic fiction, *Les Châteaux de la subversion.*[35] Still, modern readers are more likely to be impressed with the documented importance of *The Recess* for novelists such as Ann Radcliffe, Jane Austen, and Sir Walter Scott.

Most critics and biographers acknowledge Radcliffe's debt to Lee, and many speculate that Radcliffe may have been Lee's student at the school Lee ran in Bath. There is no proof of that, but there is general agreement that Radcliffe read, admired, and was highly influenced by *The Recess.*[36] In addition to the general and obvious similarity of Radcliffe's writing in Lee's mode of "female Gothic" romance, another less noticed trait that Radcliffe derived from Lee is her habit of making direct intertextual references to earlier works, and to Shakespeare in particular. The difference is that Lee, writing in the epistolary form and thus in the narratorial voice of persons supposed to be living in Elizabethan times, is careful to quote only texts extant at that time (a single exception is a quotation from Blackmore's epic poem, "Eliza," set in the Elizabethan period but written in the early eighteenth century).

Jane Austen's *Northanger Abbey* also alludes to *The Recess,* although its primary reference is to Radcliffe's *The Mysteries of Udolpho* (a more recent best-seller when Austen's parody was published).[37] More importantly, *The Recess* led the way for both Radcliffe and Austen in its innovative play with conventions of probability, implicitly but uncomfortably questioning both gender norms and the status of historical truth. When the heroine of *Northanger Abbey* prefers Gothic romance to "real solemn history," her preference makes sense because of Lee's earlier blurring of the boundaries between them. Austen's juvenile work, *The History of England, by a partial, prejudiced, & ignorant Historian* (written in 1791), further underscores her skepticism of the more aggressive claims to objective truth made by "real solemn" historians such as Hume—and it may also be poking fun at *The Recess* by humorously exaggerating Lee's sympathy with Mary at the expense of Elizabeth.[38]

One of the clearest critiques of Radcliffe's novels to be found in *Northanger Abbey* comes in the famous passage where Catherine Morland realizes that "it was not in them perhaps that human nature, at least in the midland counties of England, was to be looked for. Of the Alps and Pyrenees, with their pine forests and their vices, they might give a faithful delineation."[39] Piozzi had anticipated at least one aspect of this critique when she wrote to a friend,

> Truth is Mrs. Radcliffe might find Scenes to describe in this part of the World without rambling thro the Pyrenees; many detached Parts of the valley of Llangollen are exceedingly fine indeed, very like Savoy; and from the rock above Brinbella heavy with the gathering Winters of a hundred Years is seen Snowdon; frowning in sullen Majesty like the *gros St. Bernard*—but not over as rich a Foreground. Ours is however admirably diversified, we have Cathedral and Castle, and Country Seats and *Sea* which last is inestimable and one *can* contemplate *that* yet, and say tis a subject of England.[40]

What these two very different critiques, Austen's and Piozzi's, have in common is the idea that Radcliffe might have done better not to have strayed so far from home; that both probability and picturesque description would have been more effectively achieved had she focused on national subjects. Lee had already done just that. Like Austen, she found plenty of vice to depict in London and other centers of English power. When she wanted wild landscapes she found them, as Piozzi wished Radcliffe had done, nearer at hand: in Wales, Scotland, and Cumberland.[41] *The Recess* ranges for significant portions of its plot into those very "northern and western extremities" of Great Britain that Catherine Morland would have "yielded, if hard pressed" as belonging potentially, like the Alps and Pyrenees, to the wild and unknown realm of the foreign. But to the more cosmopolitan Lee such regions were not entirely unknown, as she had lived for considerable periods of time in both

Edinburgh and Dublin while growing up, and almost certainly followed her parents to regional summer theaters in their vicinity.

Sir Walter Scott, who imitated far more lady novelists even than those he acknowledges, drew heavily on *The Recess* for his own Elizabethan romance, *Kenilworth*.[42] He took so many scenes and incidents from Lee that later commentators on Rossini's *Elisabetta, regina d'Inghilterra,* writing at a time when Lee had been forgotten while Scott was still read, wondered how the opera, performed over five years before the publication of *Kenilworth,* could have anticipated so much of that novel.[43] Fiona Robertson describes the influence of *The Recess* on Scott's *Woodstock, Redgauntlet,* and *The Abbot* as well.[44] Those who did remember *The Recess* did not think Scott had surpassed it: a reader observed in 1831 that "the great novelist of the north has yet to excite a sympathy equally profound and dignified."[45]

Formal Innovation and Ideological Critique

Perhaps Lee's greatest achievement in *The Recess* is that even as it excites its readers' sympathy, its form creates a subtle and profound critique of the eighteenth-century ideology of sympathy on both ethical and epistemological grounds. It performs this critique by means of a unique and sophisticated innovation in the epistolary form, unmatched either by imitators or predecessors. In Janet Altman's exhaustive survey of the forms of epistolary fiction, she speculates about why there is only one theoretically conceivable variant of which she could find no single eighteenth-century example (and only one example thereafter, in the mid-twentieth century): she imagines a version in which the "type Marianne" (as she calls it, after Marivaux's *Vie de Marianne*), or novel in the form of a long memoir-letter, would include more than one memoirist writing in counterpoint instead of providing only a single retrospective point of view.[46] *The Recess* is that apparently unique, and certainly overlooked, example. Its twin heroines each write such a memoir-letter addressed to the other; the memoir of the elder twin and primary narrator, Matilda, is interrupted, fragmented, and contradicted by that of her sister Ellinor. This structure makes *The Recess* one of the most accomplished and aesthetically interesting examples of a numerous subgenre of the late eighteenth-century epistolary novel, which I have elsewhere named "fiction of women's correspondence," in which female characters establish bonds of sympathy that substitute for or crucially supplement kinship and lineage relationships by exchanging their private histories in letters.[47] In *The Recess,* the closest of female kinship relations—between twin sisters, mothers, and daughters—give rise to sympathetic identifications so dangerously unbounded as to bring about more than one tragic catastrophe.

Lee's formal innovation implies not only an ethical critique of feminine sympathy but also an epistemological critique of contemporary historiography. A dissonance of perspective on the historical figures encountered in the novel is created by the twin memoirs of *The Recess*. This dissonance exposes a contradiction latent in the tendency of eighteenth-century historiography to locate so much of its claim to truth and probability in the stability of character. Hume writes in his portraits of both Elizabeth I and Mary Stuart nearly the same words that he applies to James I (all of whom appear as characters in *The Recess*): "No prince . . . was ever so much exposed to the opposite extremes of calumny and flattery, of satire and panegyric."[48] Yet he goes on to write of them as if these tensions could be resolved in a balanced and quasi-omniscient portrait. Lee instead dramatizes the inevitable partialities of point of view in the perception and construction of historical character.[49]

Montague Summers once lamented that so few readers knew *The Recess:* "this romance is one of the landmarks of English literature, and it is difficult to understand how those who have not read at least *The Recess* and *The Canterbury Tales* can claim any right to be heard when they discourse upon and trace the history of English fiction."[50] Fortunately, knowledge of Lee's classic and of the history of English fiction has increased since Summers wrote those words in the 1930s. With the resurgence of interest, more recently, in the Gothic and in its historical origins in the eighteenth century, literary critics again began to recognize the originality and importance of *The Recess*. It was reprinted twice in library facsimile editions in the 1970s. Since that time, the Gothic imagination has taken a gripping hold on contemporary culture, simultaneously with an ever-increasing interest in early literature by women. Quite aside from its formal sophistication and importance in literary history, *The Recess* still entertains as much as it instructs. It remains to this day a moving page-turner in the best Gothic mode, and still offers "images the most enchanting to the fancy, and scenes the most interesting to the heart."

THE LIFE AND WORKS OF SOPHIA LEE

No full-length biography of Sophia Lee has ever been published, and there are still many gaps in knowledge about her life. Substantial original research, however, has made it possible here to correct several significant factual errors that have long been accepted as truth, and to amplify considerably the information found in modern biographical dictionaries.

EARLY LIFE IN A THEATRICAL FAMILY

The actors Anna Sophia and John Lee had their daughter Sophia Priscilla christened in the church of St. Paul in Covent Garden, London, on 13 May 1750.[51] She was their second child at least; one elder sister, Charlotte Elizabeth, is known to have survived to adulthood.[52] Sophia grew up in a family devoted to the theater, in which both parents had successful careers; they traveled, performed, and resided all over the British Isles.

John Lee was a young but already established actor who, by the year of Sophia's birth, was engaged in an open and bitter rivalry with the most famous actor of the eighteenth century, David Garrick. That year Lee broke his contract with Garrick's company at the Drury Lane Theatre because he felt that Garrick, to whom he compared himself in skill and talent, had deliberately kept him in the shade out of competitiveness over both profit and public recognition.[53] Contemporary judgments of John Lee's acting are highly contradictory, but toward the end of his life he was so much admired by Frances Burney that she referred to him as her "favourite" and would not let anyone speak to her while he was on stage.[54] There is much more agreement about his personality than about his talent. Various sources remember him as a difficult man, vain and quarrelsome. He managed to embroil himself in a series of litigations throughout his life, in which he was often morally, although perhaps not legally, a wronged party. This seems to have been the case with Garrick's treatment of him.

Sophia's mother was also a working actor. During the summer of 1751 she played Juliet to her husband's Romeo, among many other roles played by both in the theater at Richmond. Immediately after the summer season, Anna Sophia Lee went to take up an engagement as the leading lady at the Smock Alley Theatre in Dublin, under the management of Thomas Sheridan. As soon as John finished his contract with Garrick in April 1752 he went to join his wife, where again they played the leads in *Romeo and Juliet*. But after a single performance in Dublin John left for Edinburgh at the invitation of a group of Scottish nobility and merchants. With their financial backing, he became owner and manager of the Canongate Concert Hall. It is not clear where the children were during the year of their parents' separation, but John mentions that during one later separation they divided the children between them, and this may have been their strategy at all such times. In any case, the family was reunited in Edinburgh by September 1752, when Sophia was about two and a half years old. Her mother, not having had much success in her Dublin engagement, now joined her husband's company for the 1752-53 season.[55]

John Lee is credited with having raised the status and morale of the theater in Edinburgh by making a number of improvements: notably, he refused to permit gentlemen to be seated on the stage or to be admitted behind the scenes (Garrick was to follow his example at the Drury Lane Theatre in 1761), and he improved set design. Lee took his company (and no doubt his family, since his wife was in the company) on tours each summer that included engagements at Glasgow, Newcastle, and Scarborough. The first of these tours, in the summer of 1753, was a financial disaster for him, as a result of which he claims to have been out £500 from his own pocket (the rough equivalent of $50,000 current U.S.).[56] Because of this loss he could not make the payment due for the Edinburgh theater in May 1754, and his goods were seized by tradesmen. From this point at least, if not earlier, he seems to have been the victim of a confidence scheme on the part of the investors to use his expertise to make the theater a profitable venture and then repossess it from him by entangling him hopelessly in debt.

Lee's creditors seized his theater on 23 February 1756, while he was on stage. Thus when Sophia was barely six years old her father was thrown into prison, their furniture was confiscated and sold, and she, with her mother and three siblings, was turned out into the street in the middle of a Scottish winter. Anna Sophia took two of the children with her to London, while two remained, as their father described them, "destitute in Edinburgh."[57] At least one of these four children is unidentified and did not survive its infancy. (Another was probably a brother, name unknown, who was close to Sophia and Charlotte in age and died when he was twenty-one.)[58]

John Lee spent two months in jail, and eventually lost a drawn-out legal battle with his Scottish creditors. In the meantime, the family moved frequently, living in Dublin, London, or Bath, depending on the acting engagements of the parents, who also traveled often to the provinces for additional appearances in summer theater. John Lee's predictable quarrels with managers everywhere, and legal disputes wherever he managed theaters himself (as he did in Bath as well as in Edinburgh), ensured that for the first twenty-eight years of Sophia's life her family was never based in one city for longer than six years running. (Six years was the exceptional length of one stay in London, 1762-1768, but even then there was incessant traveling and many separations.)

A biographical sketch published during Lee's lifetime asserts that her mother "died while Miss Lee and her sisters were young," and Lee describes herself elsewhere as "charged early in life with the care of a family."[59] Modern biographers have regularly assumed, probably because of these two statements, that Sophia was still a child when her mother died, and that she had to fill her place for the younger children. The date of Anna Sophia Lee's death has yet to be reliably established, however. Although the two most scrupulous recent sources assert (without citing a primary source) that she died at Craven Hall on 3 September 1770, there is convincing primary evidence that she was in fact still alive in 1776, when Sophia was twenty-six, and practically an old maid by the reckoning of the eighteenth century.[60] Her elder sister was then a venerable twenty-eight, and their younger siblings nineteen (Harriet), sixteen (Anna), and fifteen (George)—all of an age to look after themselves.

If Sophia Lee was "charged early in life with the care of a family," then, it was because she had had a working mother for her first twenty-six years. Nor, having an elder sister, would she have been left alone with the house-keeping and childrearing, as has usually been assumed. Sophia thus left her younger siblings in the care of her sister Charlotte and their mother when she accompanied her father for a time in the King's Bench prison during the summer of 1772.

John Lee was sent to King's Bench as a result of another of his litiga-tions, related to a failed attempt to buy land in Bath to build his own the-ater.[61] After his release from debtor's prison, he worked again in both London and Ireland. The family went back to Bath in 1778. This was their final move to the city that Lee would make her home throughout her professional life. Her father returned to theater management there and performed in a final season of such leading Shakespearean roles as Richard III and Macbeth before his last illness overtook him. He died during the winter of 1781.

FIRST PUBLICATIONS

Not until her thirtieth year does Sophia Lee enter the annals of the family profession with the production of her first play, *The Chapter of Accidents*. It is surely no accident that this was also the first year in which her father was too ill to perform.[62] At what time Lee actually began writing is not known, but clearly she had been doing so seriously for a long time before this public debut. In her preface to the play, she says that it was conceived while she was serving the prison sentence with her father in 1772.[63] In a later preface she states that she had written a six-volume epistolary novel before that (which, however, was not published until 1804, when Lee was fifty-four years old and had almost stopped producing new works).[64] So Lee was certainly writing fiction and drama already in her earliest adulthood, if not before. She made no attempt to bring her work to the public, however, until her father was on his deathbed, her only surviving brother was engaged with a manufacturer in Manchester, and she and her three sisters were living in Bath with no prospect of any provision.

Lee's entry into authorship was not easy. By her own account, she had to overcome strong inhibitions in order to submit *The Chapter of Accidents* to Harris, the manager of the Covent Garden Theatre and her father's employer at the time. She submitted it only anonymously and after long hesitation: "as I had neither a prostituted pen or person to offer Mr. Harris, I gave up, without a trial, all thoughts of the Drama, and sought a humble home in Bath, resolving to bury in my own heart its little talent, and be a poor any thing rather than a poor author." With the help of unnamed friends, she finally overcame these misgivings. Lee was offended, however, by what she called "the most supercilious and unmeaning criticisms" and suspected that Harris had circulated the manuscript without her permission.[65]

After many delays, contemptuous treatment, and unexpected requests for revisions from Harris, Lee withdrew the manuscript and sent it, again anonymously, to Colman, manager of the Haymarket Theatre. Colman was much more receptive, and after further rewriting the play was produced to acclaim on 5 August 1780.[66] Within a year of this first performance, *The Chapter of Accidents* was produced at all the major London theaters, including Covent Garden and Drury Lane in addition to the Haymarket.[67] The play continued to be performed several times a year in London, Bath, and elsewhere through the early years of the nineteenth century: it was produced a total of one hundred times in London before 1800, and at least once a year in Bath nearly every year through 1803.[68] Afterward the play was often reprinted in English and also was translated into French and German. Sophia Lee now had a name to rival her father's in the theatrical world.

FATHER-DAUGHTER RELATIONS

Lee's father died between the first and second productions of *The Chapter of Accidents*. When he died at Bath on 19 February 1781, he had already been too ill to act regularly for over a year. His last stage appearance was as Macbeth in Bristol on 14 July 1780.[69] He died at the age of fifty-six, leaving practically nothing for the support of his five surviving children.[70] But the success of his daughter's play continued apace: it went into a second printing in that year, and the second production opened at Drury Lane on 8 May.[71]

Sophia seems to have had a vexed relationship with her father that affected her literary career. As mentioned above, John Lee's reputation in the theatrical community and beyond was that of a vain, arrogant, and litigious man. She followed him into prison—not the first prison sentence resulting from his quarrels. She still wrote passionately in his defense in that cause shortly after his death nearly a decade later. She had already begun writing years before the time of the prison sentence, but did not bring her work forward until her father was incapacitated. A story was circulated during her lifetime that she had not merely conceived of her first play during the imprisonment she shared with her father—as she herself claimed—but that she had actually written it in order to save him from the debts for which he was imprisoned.[72] This is unlikely to be true, since nine years intervened between the prison term and the play's first performance, but it indicates a general perception of the close connection between father and daughter affecting the start of her career.

A telling hint is dropped by one early biographer, who says that in her beginnings as an author Lee had to contend not only with financial worries and domestic responsibilities but also with "some little discouragement; for Mr. Lee, whose first wish was that his daughters should prove rational and useful members of society, was not without his fears of literary pretension unsupported by real talent; and had also a secret persuasion, that if talent really existed it would force its way without the hot-bed of paternal partiality."[73] Such a "fear" looks more like anxious competitiveness in the light of literary history. One nineteenth-century critic, examining the rumor that Lee had help from her father in writing her first play, judges that "the play is so good that it is not likely he should have written any considerable part of it—Miss Lee's other works put it past a doubt that her abilities were superior to those of her father."[74] From these clues a relationship emerges somewhat like that between Lee's contemporary, Frances Burney, and her father—in which the daughter admires and emulates a father who is distinguished in his literary career but controlling and censorious of his daughter's own efforts and independence.

Mesdames Lees' School and Financial Independence

Lee earned enough money from *The Chapter of Accidents* to finance a joint venture with her sisters, setting up a girls' school with them in the competitive market of Bath, a city renowned at the time for its schools for young ladies. Her elder sister Charlotte contributed her experience in the field of education: she had previously worked as an assistant teacher at one of the most prominent Bath schools, that of Anne Roscoe, whose innovations the Lees imitated and successfully rivalled. Charlotte was running her own modest day school at the foot of Lansdown Road when Sophia's financial success enabled the four sisters to engage in the more ambitious joint venture—while their father's mortal illness and small estate made it a necessity for them to do so.[75]

A 1797 biographical sketch makes a cautionary exemplar of Sophia Lee to all would-be scribbling women by claiming that she began writing only after establishing the school at Bath—even though this assertion contradicts others made in the same sketch (such as that she and her sisters were left without inheritance by their father and thus without other means to establish a school). This notion also contradicts Lee's own earlier statement that she began writing during or before the term she spent in debtor's prison with her father in 1772. But the editors of the *Monthly Mirror* have a moral to deliver with their version of chronology: "May Miss Lee's example and success . . . teach all other females, who are left unprovided for, how preferable personal diligence and professional employment are to the precarious honour and profit of writing for a theatre, or of any other visionary scheme of life."[76] Yet the facts, even as reported by the *Mirror,* reveal that only Lee's persistence in her "visionary scheme" of writing for the theater enabled her so prudently to establish the school that would indeed provide the primary source of income for herself and the three sisters who ran it with her over the next twenty-three years.

The full name of the school was "Mesdames Lees, Ladies' Boarding School." Offering a similar program, but at lower fees, to that of the established Anne Roscoe—including Roscoe's innovation of allowing only French to be spoken—the school grew rapidly, and by 1786 had moved to Belvidere House, "a handsome, spacious, and airy mansion" atop a hill on Lansdown Road, which had been an elegant hotel (and is now an apartment building). In the meantime Anne Roscoe's school lower down the same street had failed completely. "A most sweet situation it is," wrote George James to Hester Piozzi, "and an excellent house for their purpose—besides large rooms for their business they will have ten good bed chamber[s] and every other convenience. They are worthy—clever Women—*and thrive* and deserve it."[77]

From the street, Belvidere House presented a somewhat forbidding aspect, with its heavy green Venetian blinds shutting out the world. Beyond the blinds, however, it was the very antithesis of Brontë's dark and oppressive Lowood School. The other side of the house had large Palladian windows opening onto a terrace and commanding a view, from the hill on which it stands to this day, across gardens (now public, but which the Lees' girls were not allowed to enter), and past St. Swithin's Church and its churchyard. Far on the other side of the river Avon one could see Sydney Gardens.[78] These newly opened pleasure gardens featured frequent fireworks displays, which the boarders would secretly watch through a high window after lights-out, until they heard the steps of Harriet Lee coming up the stairs to see what the commotion was about. At that sound they would give the alarm, trying to get back into their beds and appear to be sound asleep before she could reach the door.[79]

Mesdames Lees was, as one writer describes it, "a concern of magnitude."[80] In 1797 there were seventy-two students there, of which fifty-two were boarders. They were called the "Leevites"[81] by the residents of Bath, which partly served the practical function of distinguishing them from girls enrolled in other local schools, such as the "Colbournites," but was also probably a way of poking fun at the school's reputation for high seriousness. The Lee sisters, with Sophia as their chief, ran the school and presided personally at daily general gatherings for such purposes as prayers, meals, walks, church services, and other outings. One of them at least was on hand at Belvidere at all times, but they did not, it seems, give instruction themselves. They employed two governesses and three female teachers in residence, in addition to masters of both sexes who regularly visited the school to give more specialized lessons in writing, arithmetic, music, drawing, and dancing. Several times a year mothers and female friends were invited to watch the students dance. But the grand event occurred only once every three years, when all the Leevites, ages five to nineteen, donned identical muslin frocks and matching sashes, with wreaths of roses on their heads. Thus adorned, they set out en masse for the Rooms (the gathering place of the fashionable in Bath) to "do credit to Bath"—as their dancing-mistress regularly enjoined them—while such dignitaries as the Prince of Wales and the Duchess of York watched them perform their minuets.

Discipline was strict at Belvidere House, but enlightened. Rules of neatness and orderly conduct were rigidly enforced, but corporal punishment was not allowed. Whenever a student committed any infraction of the rules (which seems to have happened constantly) she would receive one of two "marks" that were always in circulation throughout the student body—eagerly passed to her by whichever unhappy girl had received it last. The unhappiest were those two who were stuck with the marks at the end of each day, for they had to eat watery, heavily salted gruel for breakfast the next morning, while everyone else had tea and ample portions of buttered bread. Infractions deserving such punishment included everything from not putting away one's books properly to sneaking a peek at the fireworks in Sydney Gardens (and getting caught) to speaking English (only French was allowed during school hours).

The Lees fed their boarders well, with plenty of meat at the mid-day meal, cheese and beer for supper, special treats of fruit and cake twice a week (in addition to whatever the students received from their families), and a glass of port wine in the evening (optional, for an extra charge).[82] The Lee sisters may have had a special affinity for port wine, as their mother's family was engaged in the wine business, and their mother herself, although of Scottish ancestry, had been born in Oporto.[83]

The school had a superb reputation and a fashionable clientele.[84] The famed actress Sarah Siddons, a close friend of Lee's, sent her daughter Cecilia there at the age of five in 1798, and she stayed until shortly before the school closed.[85] It is invariably speculated that Ann Radcliffe may have attended Mesdames Lees. Born in 1764, Radcliffe was already seventeen when the school opened. It is possible that she may have attended even at that age, either as a "day scholar" or as one of the very few older "parlour boarders," who received not only instruction but also social introductions and chaperoning services from Mesdames Lees. They were invited each evening to Sophia Lee's drawing room to meet company or would accompany one or two of the Lee sisters to the soirées at which they mingled with Bath society.[86] There were quite a few girls' schools in Bath at the time—so Radcliffe might well have attended another—but Mesdames Lees seems to have enjoyed the highest reputation of all. Application for admission had to be made well in advance, and girls were considered lucky who found a place there.[87]

Lee herself was a beloved and gifted headmistress. One of her pupils later described her as "very impressive in her manner, and very eloquent in her instruction. Her eye was brilliant and searching. She inspired her pupils with a respect that continued through life."[88] Another former student describes Lee at the age of forty-seven (the age at which she appears in the portrait reproduced in this volume) as having an elderly appearance, with grey hair and "rather a stout figure . . . not at all good looking in her features," yet with "perfect benevolence in the expression of her countenance." On leaving the school three years later, the same student "was much grieved at leaving the Misses Lee."[89]

LITERARY CAREER AND LIFE IN BATH

The Recess was published within a few years after the establishment of Mesdames Lees. The success of her first play had brought Lee not only the capital for the school but a national reputation, particularly in the London-centered theatrical world. Her first novel brought her international renown. It was reprinted in a total of five separate English editions, plus several pirated Irish ones, and was translated into at least five different foreign languages through 1806. Tomlins provides a contemporary description of a potential "fan" catching a glimpse of Lee in the crowd at the Pump Room in Bath, where the fashionable set went to see and be seen. Lee is represented at the height of her fame, just after the publication of *The Recess:*

> On my entering the pump-room this morning . . . the intelligent countenance of a lady, who stood near, interested me at the first glance. We were scarce entered before I perceived the universal attention which was attracted, and in a moment the name of *Lee* circulated in a whisper . . . . And this, then, thought I, is the *Temeraire,*[90] whose name has been publicly joined with that of one of the first female writers of our age!
>
> My prepossession for her vanished; since who . . . is there that should be ranked with the writer of Cecilia?[91] . . . I wished, however, to address this celebrated author; but . . . she was so much surrounded, I could not think of breaking through the circle she had attracted.[92]

Sophia Lee's "very uncommon Success" made her "one of the best-known novelists of her day," and at least as much a celebrity in her own time as any of her illustrious acquaintance.[93]

In addition to the time-consuming work of running a school and writing, the Lees kept up a lively social acquaintance in Bath and London. Harriet seems to have been the more sociable of the two literary sisters, if one can make that judgment from the greater amount of commentary about her in the letters of their famous friends. They were acquainted with the much younger Jane and Anna Maria Porter, as well as with Ann Radcliffe.[94] All of these women were influenced by Sophia and became historical novelists like her.[95] In addition, the Lees' literary acquaintance included Frances Burney; probably Jane Austen, who was a fellow resident of Bath from 1801 to 1806; William Godwin; and Hester Piozzi. They first met Piozzi in Bath in November of 1787. "Miss Lees are charming women," she wrote upon meeting them, "and appear to deserve their very uncommon Success."[96] Like Tomlins (and Godwin), Piozzi later compared Sophia Lee as a writer to Frances Burney.[97] By November 1788 Harriet Lee had developed a particular friendship with Piozzi.[98] Thereafter Sophia and

Anna too became regular visitors to the Piozzi home in London at Christmas time, in addition to seeing the family during their regular visits to Bath.

The close friendship with Piozzi occasioned the first in a rapid succession of changes to the Lee sisters' household in Bath. In 1791 Piozzi encouraged a socially impossible match between Harriet and a young Italian nobleman who would have lost half his fortune had he married her. Harriet suffered a great deal from this frustrated attachment. Only a year later Lee's elder sister, Charlotte, ran off with a man well beneath the Lees in station and income, apparently alienating her sisters and giving up her interest in Belvidere House.[99]

Although Sophia Lee herself never married or had children, shortly after her sister Charlotte's mortifying marriage in 1793 she adopted a twelve-year-old girl named Elizabeth (Betty) Tickell (1781-1860). Betty was the niece by marriage of the Irish playwright Richard Brinsley Sheridan and the great-granddaughter of the poet Thomas Tickell, who had been Addison's editor. She had in effect been orphaned three times before she became Lee's ward: by the successive deaths of her mother, the aunt with whom she lived afterward, and her father. He killed himself in 1793 by jumping out of a window in Hampton Court Palace, reportedly because of financial ruin brought on by the "small dowry and expensive tastes" of his very young second wife.[100]

Later that same year, Lee's new tragedy, *Almeyda, Queen of Granada,* was to be performed at the Drury Lane Theatre, with her friend Sarah Siddons in the title role. This was only the second new work she had brought forward in the decade since the publication of the first volume of *The Recess.* Apart from new editions of the novel, she had published only one long poem, "A Hermit's Tale, found in his Cell" (1787), in the interim. The production of *Almeyda* was delayed, projected again for early 1795, but delayed yet again. Apparently Lee blamed these delays on the manager of the theater.[101] A further delay arose in early spring of 1796 because of Siddons's illness. Lee seems to have had high hopes of her new play, as indicated by a remark of Piozzi's: "[Siddons's ill-Health] keeps Miss Lee from Fame and Fortune which She expects to acquire by Almeyda."[102] Indeed the public also highly anticipated its success, but it was not performed until two and a half years after the originally scheduled date.[103] The Kembles, renowned actors themselves and brothers of Siddons, acted with their sister in this production.[104] In spite of these advantages and a positive reception by the public, the play was closed after running only four nights, greatly disappointing Lee.[105] She complained to "the principal proprietor," who agreed that she and *Almeyda* had been maltreated. He promised to have the play performed a fifth time on the last night of the season, which was approaching, and then to complete its run at the opening of the next season. "The promise, in the first instance, was duly performed; the tragedy was acted on the last night of the Drury Lane company's performing that season; the receipt of the house was £400 and upwards, and it has never been performed since." Unable to account for the play's having been dropped after such success, the *Monthly Mirror* writer adds that he does not "believe a similar instance of such conduct of a theatre to an author of established reputation, is to be found in the history of the English stage."[106]

The publication of the first volume of Harriet Lee's *The Canterbury Tales* in 1797, however, to which Sophia contributed an introduction, met with admiration from the most discriminating readers of the age, including the Ladies of Llangollen and William Godwin.[107] Godwin was so impressed upon reading *The Canterbury Tales* that he became more eager than ever to meet both Sophia and Harriet Lee, having desired to make Sophia's acquaintance at least as early as 1786.[108] He did meet both sisters at last on a visit to Bath in March of 1798. Although this meeting occurred only six months after the death of his wife, "he was enchanted with Harriet from the first. The topic of conversation at one of her supper parties was whether it is possible to attend to trifles while engaged on a serious enterprise. . . . Godwin decided at once that Harriet Lee would be a suitable successor to Mary Wollstonecraft."[109] On 5 June 1798 Godwin proposed marriage to Harriet, but she refused him. If at first she was prevented by the fear of what people might say about her marrying an atheist who promoted dangerous Jacobin ideas and had kept up scandalous associations, in the end, after a series of persistent letters from him, she was put off by his rigidity and condescension toward her in the course of their disputes on the subject of religious faith.[110]

At the end of the 1802-1803 academic year, Mesdames Lees closed their school after twenty-three years of operation, when Sophia was fifty-three. There is no direct evidence of their motives, but it is clear that they were by this time financially comfortable enough to live well without continuing to generate income with the school. The three sisters moved to a fine Georgian mansion, Hatfield Place, which still stands on the Wells road a couple of miles outside of Bath, and still commands lovely views of the city on the hillsides opposite. Sophia and Harriet continued writing, now their only profession.

RETIREMENT

The first thing Lee did in retirement was publish the first novel she had written, *The Life of a Lover*, in 1804. Piozzi describes the Lees as looking well and happy at this time, but also notes that "Miss Lees and we have met twice or thrice, but either the Life of a Lover, Sophia's new novel, is not out, or I have not seen it. Holcroft's Paris and Miss Edgeworth's Popular Tales are the only books found in windows, on toilettes, etc."[111]

The year after the publication of *The Life of a Lover*, Lee sustained a heavy personal blow with the suicide of her younger sister Anna on 23 October 1805. Anna and Harriet returned to Bath early that morning from several weeks' touring in Wales, during which they had visited picturesque Llangollen in North Wales and possibly the famous "Ladies of Llangollen," Sarah Ponsonby and Lady Eleanor Butler. Anna refused to come down to breakfast with her sisters that morning, saying she was tired and wanted to stay in bed. When Sophia and Harriet later returned from the morning's shopping, they called Anna again, found her door locked, and had it forced when they still heard no answer. Inside, they discovered her hanging from the upper rail of her bed. She apparently had made a previous suicide attempt during the Welsh tour, while walking by a river. She had approached too close to the bank and slipped in as if by accident, then put up some resistance to being helped out again. A friend reports that she had become unwell a year before, "a slow fever and very nervous—The cause we cannot tell. Report says a disappointment of the Heart, but the person not nam'd." A coroner "with great difficulty it seems brought in the Verdict Lunacy."[112] It is impossible to know Anna's motive, but with the school recently closed, where she had lived and worked all her adult life with her three sisters, one of whom was now married, the other two having achieved literary fame and sharing a strong and probably somewhat exclusive bond—one might wonder what Anna, a spinster at forty-five, had left in her life. Sophia, moreover, seems to have been rather controlling and dominating in her relationships with her sisters; there is reason to suspect that she opposed the marriages of both Charlotte and Harriet, and she may well have done the same in Anna's case. Whatever the motives, Anna's suicide was clearly a rather aggressive act toward Sophia and Harriet. Immediately afterward, they left the house they had shared just outside Bath after closing the school, and went to stay for a time with their brother's family in Manchester.[113]

In the preface to her last-published, first-written work, Lee becomes an elegiac apologist for romance and the literature of sensibility, which by the turn of the nineteenth century was already becoming outmoded. In the process she comments on the "Jacobin feminism" of the 1790s, represented by writers such as Wollstonecraft, which had come to prominence since the publication of *The Recess*. As this preface is the only extant document in which Lee reflects on her own work and its place in the changing world of English letters at the end of the eighteenth century—and in the continuing debate on the "Woman Question"—it is worth reproducing some substantial portions of it here:

> I shall not apologise for having indulged the bias of my own heart in tracing that of woman through almost every tender and silent suffering which is a sad distinction of my sex. I well know, that neither philosophy, wit, nor even ridicule, can stifle in nature its first and strongest feeling. When sentiment is impassioned by situation, it will always find its way to the heart: tears will then as readily attend the unfortunate as smiles the absurd, or rather at the same moment blend, and, by the happy versatility of the human character,
> *"Stream like wat'ry sunbeams through a cloud."*[114]
> During the many years which these volumes have remained in my closet,[115] such changes in nations, manners, and principles have been made, as defy all calculation. The revolutionary system has pervaded literature, even in the humblest of its classes—novels! The rights and character of woman have been placed in lights by which the delicacy of the sex has often been wholly sacrificed to the assertion of a hardy equality with man, that, even if it assured to us an increase of esteem, would cause an equal deduction of tenderness: a bad exchange for the sex upon the great scale. It was, I own, my girlish intention, to draw in my heroine a female, possessing, without a masculine mind or manners, some decided opinions, which, at the time when this work was written, would have been thought new and bold. I have had leisure to compare these opinions with those of other authors; but as I never found myself inclined to come nearer to the late system, I have left Cecilia Rivers as she came first from my pen.
> The sturdy race of female argumentators who have sprung up of late years, raise a cry against that by which they live—romance! and every character which dares to rise above the level of common life, is by them cast out of the pale of existence. But I have lived long enough in the world to be convinced, that it is as difficult to go beyond the merits as the faults of mortality. However chimerical the pictures drawn by authors may appear to persons who move in a narrow circle, those who take a wider range in life will not fail to discover, both among the living and the dead, some informed and elevated beings to whose merits imagination cannot add.[116]

The same preface contains Lee's last (and possibly only) public pronounce-ment on fame and creativity. Like her reflections on "the sturdy race of female argumentators,"—a clear and defensive reference to Mary Wollstonecraft—it strikes an elegiac note even as Lee is embarking on a life to be devoted solely to writing and retirement. Here public approbation is already viewed as too elu-sive to be the object of any rational expectation, and yet as a necessary nour-ishment for the sensitive plant of creativity:

> As an author cannot be certain of pleasing any human being but himself, he must be weak indeed who loses his own approbation, when that may be eventually the sole reward. Yet do I not under-value reputation because I will not court it: perhaps I only affect this philosophic composure to enjoy more fully the applause of the public, should I be happy enough to obtain it.
>
> Ah! remember, readers, that Genius, like some rare plants, re-quires those rays, which scattered ripen all other productions of nature, to be concentrated, ere its fruits can be brought to perfec-tion.[117]

Not long after the publication of this preface Lee lapses into silence. One final play, a comedy entitled *The Assignation,* was produced early in 1807 at Drury Lane, but because of a charge of libel performances were discontinued, and it was never printed.

We might attribute the absence of literary production in the last seven-teen years of Lee's life to the clear insufficiency of recognition for her later works and to her own sense, as expressed in her last published preface, that literary fashion, particularly in women's novels and other works addressing the condition of women, had already moved in a direction in which she could not or would not follow. One thing is evident from the grandeur of her retire-ment residences: she no longer had the motivation of financial desperation to sustain her through the adversities of the theatrical and literary world, adver-sities which had plagued her from the beginning, ever since her often-thwarted attempts to get her first play produced. And yet the single glimpse we have of her in her old age shows that she remained a celebrity to the end of her life, albeit perhaps an unwilling one. Piozzi's last word on her former Bath ac-quaintance was written long after Lee had retired with Harriet to the elegant resort of Clifton, near Bristol. It strikes a note of admiration for "Sophia Lee, whose misanthropism I reverence, while others ridicule it. Why should she let the people in to *visit* her, as it is called? She knows they come for curiosity, not from affection; and I suppose her means of doing good have been curtailed by accident, her powers of pleasing by infirmity and age. Why should she then exhibit the *Skeleton* of Wit?—or Beauty, if she ever possessed it? Is there no time when one may be permitted to die in a corner [after] arranging our little matters for the Journey?"[118] It is clear from the speculative tone of this letter that Piozzi herself had not seen Lee's "*Skeleton*" in a long while. Lee did die in her corner at Clifton only four years later, in 1824. She was long survived by her younger sister, companion, and co-author Harriet. *The Recess,* her most successful, original, and enduring work, was still regularly reprinted in popular publications long after her death. Enthusiasts of the Gothic and of historical fiction have never quite forgotten it.

NOTES

Where not noted otherwise, biographical information is drawn from Philip Highfill Jr., Kalman Burnim, and Edward Langhans, eds., *A Biographical Dictionary of Actors, Actresses, Musicians, Dancers, Managers, and Other Stage Personnel in London, 1660-1800,* vol. 9 (Carbondale, Ill.: Southern Illinois University Press, 1984), and from Sir Leslie Stephen and Sir Sidney Lee, eds., *Dictionary of National Biography* (London: Oxford University Press, 1959-60 [1892-93]).

1. Elizabeth Sophia Tomlins, *The Victim of Fancy* (London, 1787), vol. 1, p. 172.

2. See J.M.S. Tompkins, *The Popular Novel in England* (London: Constable, 1932), pp. 123-24.

3. Jane Austen, *Northanger Abbey, The Watsons, and Sanditon,* ed. John Davie (Oxford: Oxford University Press, 1971), p. 21.

4. Tomlins, *Victim of Fancy,* vol. 1, p. 171.

5. *A Diary of Thomas de Quincey 1803,* ed. Horace A. Eaton (Noel Douglas: London, 1927). Cf. Devendra P. Varma, introduction to *The Recess* (New York: Arno Press, 1971), p. xxx.

6. Hester Piozzi to Penelope Pennington, *The Piozzi Letters,* ed. Edward A. Bloom and Lillian D. Bloom (Newark: University of Delaware Press, 1989-93), vol. 2, pp. 369, 371 nn. 15, 16.

7. See Montague Summers, *The Gothic Quest: A History of the Gothic Novel* (New York: Russell & Russell, 1964 [1938]), pp. 162-64, 186; Tompkins's foreword and Varma's introduction to *The Recess.*

8. Horace Walpole, *The Castle of Otranto,* ed. W.S. Lewis (Oxford: Oxford University Press, 1990), p. 7.

9. Ibid., pp. 7-8.

10. Ibid., pp. 8-9.

11. Ibid.

12. Sophia Lee, *The Life of a Lover* (London: G. & J. Robinson, 1804), p. vii.

13. Bloom, *Piozzi Letters,* vol. 3, p. 116 n. 4.

14. Tompkins, Summers (*The Gothic Quest,* pp. 167-68), and Varma (introduction to *The Recess,* pp. xlvii) all credit Lee with having launched historical Gothic fiction in England. In her preface to Varma's edition, Tompkins writes that in *The Recess* "for the first time, the data of Gothic romance are successfully blended with the facts of history" (pp. iv-v).

15. This attribution seems first to have been given twentieth-century critical sanction by James R. Foster in "The Abbé Prévost and the English Novel" (*PMLA* 42:2, June 1927), p. 458. It is unquestioned by Tompkins (*Popular Novel,* pp. 234-35) and Varma, even though he observes in his introduction that Lee denied any proficiency in French and that her obituary, listing her complete works, warns against false attributions (introduction to *The Recess,* pp. xxx, xxxii, xlvi-xlvii). A biography published during Lee's lifetime, only a year after the English translation of *Warbeck* appeared, issues the same warning and declares that nothing not signed by her should be considered as her work (*Monthly Mirror,* July 1797, p. 11). Harriet Lee mentions Prévost's *Cleveland* as a precursor, as quoted by Summers in *Gothic Quest,* p. 168.

16. See Alliston, *Virtue's Faults: Correspondences in Eighteenth-Century British and French Women's Fiction* (Stanford, Calif.: Stanford University Press, 1996), chapters 2 and 5.

17. See Jayne Elizabeth Lewis, "'Ev'ry Lost Relation': Historical Fictions and Sentimental Incidents in Sophia Lee's *The Recess.*" *Eighteenth-Century Fiction* 7:2 (January 1995), pp. 165-84.

18. *The Analytical Review* 24 (July 1796); quoted in Varma's introduction to *The Recess,* p. xxxiii).

19. *The Monthly Review or Literary Journal* 75 (1786): 135-36.

20. *The Gentleman's Magazine* 56:1 (April 1786): 327. See also Varma's introduction, p. xxv.

21. James Boaden, for example, assumes that Lee was inspired by "the controversy to which Dr. Robertson's History of Queen Mary had given rise." *Memoirs of Mrs. Siddons* (London: Colburn and Bentley, 1831), vol. 1, pp. 212-13. Aline Grant, a biographer of Ann Radcliffe, wonders whether that novelist first became fascinated by the story of Mary Stuart by reading Lee or "the fervent pages of Hume's *History.*" *Ann Radcliffe* (Denver: Alan Swallow, 1951), p. 45.

22. *Mary* was first produced at the Drury Lane Theatre on 21 March 1789 with Siddons as Mary and Kemble as Norfolk (Bloom, *Piozzi Letters,* vol. 1, pp. 292, 293 n. 3).

23. Graves, *Preamble to Plexippus* (London, 1790), quoted by Tompkins (*Popular Novel,* p. 223). George Buchanan was a Jacobean historian, whose perspective in his history of Scotland is hostile to Mary Stuart.

24. Preface to *The British Novelist,* 1810, quoted in Foster, "Abbé Prévost," p. 455 n. 45.

25. On the dispute between Mme de Villedieu and other women novelists of the French seventeenth century with contemporary historians including Bayle, see English Showalter, *The Evolution of the French Novel, 1641-1782* (Princeton: Princeton University Press, 1972), pp. 15-16, 53-56.

26. I call Hume and Robertson "*other* historians" because in their time novels were more often called "histories" than anything else, as the term then denoted any narrative of human action, whether or not it claimed or could be proven to be true.

27. Varma, introduction to his edition of *The Recess*, p. xvi; Summers, *Gothic Quest*, p. 169.

28. The popularity of this scene encouraged Lee to write the play *Almeyda* as a showcase for her friend Sarah Siddons to exhibit her talent for portraying extreme mental and emotional states. See also note 57 to Part 5 of the novel.

29. For dates of publication, see Montague Summers, *A Gothic Bibliography* (London: Fortune, n.d.), pp. 473-74, as well as the bibliography to the present edition.

30. For further titles and for descriptions of plots and specific debts to Lee, see Summers, *Gothic Quest*, pp. 170-79; also Tompkins, *Popular Novel*, pp. 237-38; and Varma's introduction to *The Recess*, pp. xxix-xxx.

31. Deborah McLeod drew Walker's novel to my attention.

32. See Varma's introduction to *The Recess*, p. xxvii.

33. Summers, *Gothic Bibliography*, p. 474.

34. Mary Roberts, *The Royal Exile; or, Poetical Epistles of Mary Queen of Scots, during her Captivity in England*... (London: Longman, Hurst, Rees, Orme and Brown, and Taylor and Hersey, 1822).

35. Ibid., pp. 382-412. See also Margaret Cohen, *Profane Illumination: Walter Benjamin and the Paris of Surrealist Revolution* (Berkeley: University of California Press, 1993).

36. For speculations on Radcliffe's contact with Lee, see *The Annual Register* for 1824, vol. 66, p. 217; Grant, *Radcliffe*, pp. 40-42, 45; Clara Frances McIntyre, *Ann Radcliffe in Relation to Her Time* (New Haven: Yale University Press, 1920), p. 11; E.B. Murray, *Ann Radcliffe* (New York: Twayne Publishers, 1972), 15, 34, 49-50; David Punter, *The Literature of Terror: A History of the Gothic Novel from 1765 to the Present Day* (London: Longman, 1980), p. 62; Varma's introduction to Lee's novel, pp. xvi, xxvii.

37. See Summers, *Gothic Quest*, pp. 169-70; Alliston, *Virtue's Faults*, pp. 238-39, 289 n.42.

38. I owe the observation about the possible connection between Austen's *History* and *The Recess* to Isobel Grundy.

39. Austen, *Northanger Abbey*, p. 160.

40. Bloom, *Piozzi Letters*, vol. 2, p. 189.

41. Lee included remarkable descriptions of Welsh landscapes in her story "The Clergyman's Tale, Pembroke" (1797), her final contribution to *The Canterbury Tales*. See Varma's introduction to *The Recess*, p. xl.

42. See Summers, *Gothic Quest*, p. 169, and *Gothic Bibliography*, p. 474; Varma's introduction to *The Recess*, p. xxx; Fiona Robertson, *Legitimate Histories: Scott, Gothic, and the Authorities of Fiction* (Oxford: Oxford University Press, 1994), p. 7.

43. See Summers, *Gothic Bibliography*, p. 474.

44. Fiona Robertson, *Legitimate Histories*, pp. 74-76, 87-88.

45. Boaden, *Memoirs of Mrs. Siddons*, vol. 1, p. 213.

46. Janet Altman, *Epistolarity: Approaches to a Form* (Columbus: Ohio State University Press, 1982), p. 204.

47. See Alliston, *Virtue's Faults*.

48. David Hume, *History of England, from the Invasion of Julius Caesar to the Revolution in 1688* (London: Cadell & Davies, 1802 [1754-62]), vol. 6, p. 153.

49. Cf. Punter, who observes that "Lee is able to use her modified epistolary technique to give us conflicting viewpoints on events. . . . Lee makes no attempt to resolve this conflict, and we are left with a text embodying attitudinal contradictions and allowing the reader more freedom of realisation, it is fair to say, than any other novel of the period" (*Literature of Terror,* p. 57).

50. Summers, *Gothic Quest,* p. 164.

51. Highfill, p. 210.

52. Rogers (p. 194) and others are mistaken in calling Sophia the eldest daughter. Sophia mentions a sister, Charlotte Elizabeth, as married in about 1802-3. Highfill notes that a Miss Lee, daughter of John Lee, played Lucy in *The Recruiting Officer* at Covent Garden on 8 May 1761, when none of the other sisters would have been old enough for the part but Charlotte could have been fourteen or more. Sophia Lee, undated letter [1802?], *The Two Scribbling Mrs. P.P.'s: The Intimate Letters of Hester Piozzi and Penelope Pennington, 1788-1821,* extra-illustrated, ed. Oswald Knapp, collected and arranged by A.M. Broadley (Bradpole, Bridport, Dorset, England: The Knapp, 1914), 6 vols., vol. 3, pp. 160-61 (Misc. Bound Scripts, Firestone Library, Princeton University); Highfill, p. 195. See also Katharine C. Balderston, ed., *Thraliana: The Diary of Mrs. Hester Lynch Thrale* (Oxford: Oxford University Press, 1942), vol. 2, p. 695 n. 2; Bloom, *Piozzi Letters,* vol. 1, p. 249 n. 7; vol. 2, p. 103 n. 10.

53. *DNB,* p. 800; Highfill, pp. 202-3. John Lee's opinion of Garrick is corroborated by contemporaries. Frances Brooke writes of him, "as a manager, he has, I am afraid, ever seen the dawn of excellence, both in those who aspired to write for, or to tread, the theatre, with a reluctant eye; and has made it too much his object . . . 'To blast each rising literary blossom, and plant thorns round the pillow of genius.'" *The Excursion,* ed. Paula R. Backscheider and Hope D. Cotton (Lexington: University Press of Kentucky, 1997), pp. 84-85.

54. See Frances Burney, *The Diary and Letters of Mme d'Arblay (1778-1840),* ed. Charlotte Barrett (London: Macmillan, 1904), vol. 1, pp. 351, 376, 409.

55. *DNB,* pp. 800-801; Highfill, pp. 203, 205, 209-10.

56. In estimating financial equivalence, I am following the rule of thumb given by Betty Rizzo in her edition of *The History of Sir George Ellison* (Lexington: University Press of Kentucky, 1996), p. 223.

57. *DNB,* pp. 800-801; Highfill, pp. 203-5, 210.

58. *The Annual Biography and Obituary for the Year 1825* (London: Longman, 1825), p. 131. A footnote in the *Monthly Mirror*'s biographical sketch also implies that Sophia once had brothers other than George who were no longer living in 1797. *The Monthly Mirror: Reflecting Men and Manners. With Strictures on their Epitome, the Stage,* vol. 4, second edition (London, July 1797), p. 11.

59. *Monthly Mirror* (July 1797): 7; Sophia Lee, *The Chapter of Accidents* (London: Cadell, 1780), p. ii.

60. In an autograph letter dated 29 August 1776 (British Library Add. MS. 29300,

f. 47), John Lee refers to his wife as living. As there is no reason to believe that he ever had a second wife, Anna Sophia must have been alive at this date.

61. Lee, *The Chapter of Accidents*, p. ii; Highfill, p. 207; Blain, *Feminist Companion*, p. 644.

62. *DNB*, p. 801.

63. Lee, *The Chapter of Accidents*, p. ii.

64. Lee, *The Life of a Lover*, vol. 1, pp. vi-vii.

65. Ibid., p. v.

66. Lee, *The Chapter of Accidents*, p. vi; *Monthly Mirror* (July 1797): 9.

67. For Haymarket and Covent Garden, see Cadell's 1792 fifth edition of the play (unpaginated), which lists the casts for productions at both theaters. *The Chapter of Accidents* opened at Drury Lane on 8 May 1781.

68. Charles Beecher Hogan, *The London Stage, 1660-1800*, part 5 (Carbondale: Southern Illinois University Press, 1968), p. clxxiii; Arnold Hare, ed., *Theatre Royal Bath: A Calendar of Performances at the Orchard Street Theatre, 1750-1805* (Bath: Kingsmead, 1977), p. 235; see also *Monthly Mirror* (July 1797): 9-10.

69. *The Gentleman's Magazine* 51 (February 1781): 95. See also *Annual Biography* (1825), p. 129. *DNB* states that "in 1780 he was too ill to act" (p. 801). His last regular season seems to have been that of 1778-79 (Highfill, p. 208).

70. *Monthly Mirror* (July 1797): 7; Highfill, p. 208.

71. *DNB*, p. 821.

72. Susan Sibbald, *The Memoirs of Susan Sibbald (1783-1812)*, ed. Frances Paget Hett (New York: Minton, Balch, 1926), p. 35.

73. *Annual Biography* (1825), p. 129.

74. John Genest, *Some Account of the English Stage* (Bath: Carrington, 1832), quoted in Varma's introduction to *The Recess*, p. x.

75. Trevor Fawcett, "Leevites and Others," *History of Bath Research Group Newsletter* 23 (January 1994): 5-6.

76. *Monthly Mirror*, p. 11.

77. Ibid., p. 7; Bloom, *Piozzi Letters*, vol. 1, p. 249 n. 7; Fawcett, "Leevites and Others," pp. 5-6.

78. T. Sturge Cotterell, M.B.E., *Historic Map of Bath* (Bath: Spa Committee, Corporation of the City of Bath, 1897).

79. Sibbald, *Memoirs of Susan Sibbald*, pp. 33, 48-49.

80. Boaden, *Memoirs of Mrs. Siddons*, vol. 1, p. 211.

81. Thus likening them to the biblical Levites, the priestly and privileged tribe who were on that very account, in the popular thinking of the day, little better than the Pharisees, represented in the Gospels as a pedantic priestly sect who persecuted Jesus and his followers.

82. See Sibbald, *Memoirs of Susan Sibbald*, pp. 35-82.

83. *Annual Biography* (1825), vol. 9, p. 127.

84. See *Monthly Mirror* (July 1797): 7-8; Hale, *Woman's Record*, p. 389; Rogers, "Sophia Lee," p. 194.

85. Cecilia Siddons was six and a half years old in February 1800 and still at Mesdames Lees; she was removed in 1802, not long before the school closed. See Bloom, *Piozzi Letters*, vol. 3, p. 262.

86. Sibbald, *Memoirs of Susan Sibbald*, p. 40.

87. Ibid., pp. 32, 34.

88. Boaden, *Memoirs of Mrs. Siddons*, vol. 1, p. 210.

89. Sibbald, *Memoirs of Susan Sibbald*, pp. 35, 84.

90. *Temeraire* (French): the audacious one. The narrator considers Lee audacious to aspire to be likened to Frances Burney.

91. The writer of Cecilia: Frances Burney.

92. Tomlins, *Victim of Fancy*, vol. 1, pp. 103-4.

93. Foster, "Abbé Prévost," p. 455.

94. Hester Thrale Piozzi was acquainted with both the Lee sisters and Ann Radcliffe, as indicated in various letters collected in Knapp, *Two Scribbling Mrs. P.P.'s*, vol. 2. See also Jerom Murch, *Mrs. Barbauld and Her Contemporaries; Sketches of Some Eminent Literary and Scientific Englishwomen* (London: Longmans, Green, 1877), p. 135.

95. Blain, *Feminist Companion*, pp. 866, 884.

96. Bloom, *Piozzi Letters*, vol. 1, p. 248.

97. Balderston, *Thraliana*, vol. 2, p. 695. Long before he had met the Lee sisters, William Godwin also listed Lee and Burney next to each other as famous people he wanted to meet. William St. Clair, *The Godwins and the Shelleys: A Biography of a Family* (Baltimore: The Johns Hopkins University Press, 1989), p. 38.

98. Bloom, *Piozzi Letters*, vol. 1, p. 287.

99. Ibid., vol. 2, p. 103 n. 10; undated letter from Sophia Lee to an attorney, in *The Two Scribbling Mrs. P.P.'s*, vol. 3, pp. 160-61.

100. Bloom, *Piozzi Letters*, vol. 3, pp. 97, 99 nn. 11-13; see also E.H. Mikhail, ed., *Sheridan: Interviews and Recollections* (London: Macmillan, 1989), pp. 56, 123.

101. *The True Briton* (15 June 1795), quoted in Bloom, *Piozzi Letters*, vol. 2, pp. 158, 159 n. 15.

102. This remark is tinged with irony; Piozzi seems to have thought in general that the Lees had rather a high opinion of themselves. Bloom, *Piozzi Letters*, vol. 2, p. 326.

103. Ibid., pp. 240, 331 n. 12, 339.

104. Ibid., p. 371 n. 16.

105. *DNB*, p. 821.

106. *Monthly Mirror* (July 1797): 10. Thomas Campbell writes, "though Miss Lee's tragedy has never, to my knowledge, been revived in London since that season, it was respectfully received, and even applauded. Nor, on perusing it, can I perceive why it should not be more popular than many tragedies that keep possession of the stage." *Life of Mrs. Siddons* (New York: Harper & Bros., 1834), p. 188.

107. St. Clair, *Godwins and Shelleys*, p. 201; Bloom, *Piozzi Letters*, vol. 2, p. 478.

108. "The name 'Lee' occurs alongside that of Burney in one of [Godwin's] lists of people he wanted to meet as early as 1786, but he does not seem actually to have met Harriet until he arrived at Bath in March 1798" (St. Clair, *Godwins and Shelleys*, p. 201; see also p. 38). St. Clair clearly thinks "Lee" is Harriet. I am convinced, however, that it refers to Sophia, because Piozzi and Tomlins both similarly associate Burney with her, and because when Godwin made his list in 1786 Sophia's name was already

well known for both *The Chapter of Accidents* and *The Recess,* while Harriet had only anonymously published her first work, *The Errors of Innocence,* in that year.

109. St. Clair, *Godwins and Shelleys,* p. 201.

110. Ibid., pp. 203-4; Bloom, *Piozzi Letters,* vol. 3, p. 273 n. 4; undated [1798] letter by Harriet Lee to William Godwin, Abinger Deposit b. 228/4, Bodleian Library, Oxford University.

111. Bloom, *Piozzi Letters,* p. 267, dated Monday, 16 April 1804.

112. Letters from William Siddons to Hester Piozzi, dated 12 and 29 October 1805, published by Kalman Burnim in the *Bulletin of the John Rylands Library,* vol. 52, no. 1 (autumn 1969), pp. 80-84. See also Highfill, vol. 9, p. 208; Bloom, *Piozzi Letters,* vol. 1, pp. 20, 25 n. 13.

113. Burnim, *Bulletin of the John Rylands Library,* vol. 52, no. 1, p. 83.

114. Possibly paraphrased from Shakespeare, *King Lear,* Act I, scene xvii, ll. 18-20: "You have seen / Sunshine and rain at once; her smiles and tears / Were like, a better way."

115. Closet: any small, private room; often one used for writing.

116. Sophia Lee, *Life of a Lover,* pp. vii-x.

117. Ibid., pp. x-xi.

118. *The Two Scribbling Mrs. P.P.'s,* vol. 5, p. 311, "Begun Thursday Night 24 March 1820."

Chronology of Events
in Sophia Lee's Life

c. 1748	Birth of Sophia's elder sister, Charlotte Elizabeth Lee.
1750, 13 May	Sophia Priscilla Lee, daughter of John and Anna Sophia Lee, both actors, christened in St. Paul's Church, Covent Garden, London.
1751-52	Lee's mother, Anna Sophia, living and working in Dublin; joined late in the season by John Lee.
1752-56	The family resides in Edinburgh, where John Lee manages his own theater and Anna Sophia Lee performs in his company.
1756, 23 Feb.	The Lees are evicted, their goods seized, and John Lee thrown into debtor's prison.
1756-57	The family lives in Dublin, where Lee's parents are both engaged as actors for a season.
1757	Birth of sister Harriet Lee, also a writer, with whom Sophia was to collaborate on *The Canterbury Tales*.
1757-58	The family resides in London while John acts at the Covent Garden Theatre.
1758-61	The Lees live in Bath, where both parents perform at the Orchard Lane Theatre and elsewhere.
c. 1760	Birth of youngest sister, Anna Lee.
1761	Birth of brother George Augustus Lee, later a textile manufacturer.
1762-68	The Lee family resides again in London; both

	parents are members of Garrick's company at the Drury Lane Theatre.
1768, April	The family moves to Bath, where John Lee takes up management of the Theatre Royal.
1772	Lee accompanies her father in the King's Bench debtor's prison.
1772-77	John Lee moves his family back to London, where he is employed mainly at the Covent Garden Theatre.
1777-78	The Lee family settles again in Bath, where John Lee returns to theater management.
1780, 5 August	*The Chapter of Accidents,* Sophia Lee's first play, opens to acclaim at the Haymarket Theatre in London. She publishes it later the same year. John Lee falls ill.
1780, December	Lee and her three sisters open a girls' school in Bath with the proceeds from *The Chapter of Accidents.*
1781, 19 Feb.	John Lee (father) dies in Bath.
1781, 8 May	*The Chapter of Accidents* first produced at the Drury Lane Theatre. A second printing appears this year, as do translations into French and German.
1782, 23 April	*The Chapter of Accidents* first produced at the Covent Garden Theatre.
1783, February	Publication of the first of three volumes of *The Recess* by Cadell.
1785 (late)	Cadell brings out the second and third volumes of *The Recess.*
1786	*The Recess* goes into a second edition in London, and another edition is published in Dublin by Burnet. It also appears in a French translation. Mesdames Lees' school moves to the elegant location of Belvidere House in Lansdown Road, Bath.
1787	Publication of "A Hermit's Tale, found in his Cell." *The Recess* is published in a third, corrected edition by Cadell.

1788	German translation of *The Recess* published in Prague, under the title, *Die Ruinen*.
1791	Burnet reprints his earlier edition of *The Recess* in Dublin.
1792-93, Dec.-Jan.	Charlotte (elder sister) creates a scandal by marrying a poor man in Bristol.
1793	The French translation of *The Recess* is reissued in Paris. Probably the year in which Sophia adopts Elizabeth Tickell.
1795	A Spanish translation of *The Recess*, *El subterraneo; o, La Matilde*, published in Madrid.
1796, 20 April	*Almeyda, Queen of Granada*, a tragedy, produced in London with Sarah Siddons in the title role. In spite of approval from audiences and reviewers, it ran only a total of five nights.
1797	Sophia begins collaboration with her sister Harriet on *The Canterbury Tales*, a collection of novellas. The first volume is published in this year, including an introduction by Sophia.
1797, July	A biography and engraved portrait of Lee are published in the *Monthly Mirror*.
1798	Publication of the second volume of *The Canterbury Tales*, including a novella by Sophia, "The Young Lady's Tale: The Two Emilys." William Godwin proposes marriage to Harriet (younger sister), but is rejected.
1799	Publication of the third volume of *The Canterbury Tales*, including a novella by Sophia, "The Clergyman's Tale."
1803	Lee closes the school at Belvidere House.
1804	Publication of *The Life of a Lover*, an epistolary novel in six volumes written early in life, probably Lee's first sustained literary effort. *The Recess* goes into its fifth edition with Cadell.
1805, 23 Oct.	Anna (youngest sister) commits suicide by hanging.
1806	*O subterraneo, ou Matilde*, a Portuguese translation of *The Recess*, published in Lisbon. A Swedish edition is also published this year.

1807, 28 Jan.	*The Assignation,* a comedy, is produced at Drury Lane without success, apparently because of an imputation of libel, and is never printed.
1824, 13 March	Sophia Lee dies at Clifton, near Bristol, and is buried on 18 March in St. Andrew's churchyard.

NOTE ON THE TEXT

The present critical edition of *The Recess; or, A Tale of Other Times* is based on the text of the second edition, published in London by T. Cadell in 1786. Since the first or last edition of a work is ordinarily considered to have the greatest claim to authority, I explain here my reasons for diverging from that view in this case.

The first edition of the work was published by Cadell in 1783-85. The first volume was printed alone in 1783 and re-issued in 1785, when the second and third volumes were first published. All three volumes contain many errors, both printer's errors and stylistic ones that sometimes render the text unnecessarily obscure. Cadell's later editions incorporate both substantive improvements and corrections.

Cadell's second edition corrects some printer's errors but is most notable for its substantive alterations to the text of the first edition. Judicious improvements are made to the sense and clarity of expression, without any rigid disciplining of the author's use of language or the idiosyncrasies of her style. For example, the Advertisement to the first edition reads, "History, like painting, only perpetutates the striking features of the mind." It is hard to imagine exactly how painting perpetuates features of the mind, and the second edition clarifies the phrase thus: "As painting can only preserve the most striking characteristics of the form, history perpetuates only those of the soul." In the context of the initial delineation of the heroines' strange status as scions of a living queen yet virtual orphans without connections or legitimate rights of succession, the first edition's stock sentimental phrase, "if only sorrow touch our hearts," is changed in the second to "if sorrow only is our portion." This subtle change transforms a cliché into a telling comment on the nature of these heiresses' inheritance, which is one of the main themes of the novel. A third example is one of many errors that persist from the first edition through both of the "corrected" (third and fourth) editions. "He ordered tend us round the gardens and park" obviously makes no sense; only in the second edition does this phrase correctly read, "He ordered them to attend us round the gardens and park." The third and later editions do not always ignore such improvements made in the second, but in addition to missing many they introduce innumerable new changes that are often more detrimental than otherwise.

The third edition (London: Cadell, 1787) is the first one to be labeled "corrected." It does set out to rectify the printer's and stylistic errors of the first edition but also introduces a number of new errors and inconsistencies. After careful collation of all the editions I believe this and the later editions distinctly suggest a non-authorial hand. The editor reveals himself particularly in the regularity with which certain locutions replace others that are characteristic of the author's style and usage as found in both the first and second editions. For example, the first two editions tend to omit the pronoun "that" when introducing subordinate or relative clauses: "From him we learnt there was a terrible large place called the world." The editor of the third edition nearly always adds the pronoun in such cases: "From him we learnt *that* there was a terrible large place called the world." He also regularly changes "scarce," used frequently by Lee in an adverbial sense, to "hardly," and sometimes replaces other words with near synonyms, not always felicitously, in order to avoid repetitive diction. A third type of change made throughout the third edition is the clarification of the referents of pronouns, usually by substituting nouns for the pronouns.

Such changes, although they can lessen ambiguity or render the language technically more correct, are made so mechanically that in some instances the "corrections" betray a lack of basic attention even to the story line. A particularly glaring example appears early on, when the possessive pronoun "her" is changed to "Mrs. Marlow's" in order to make it absolutely unambiguous which character is meant. It is crucial, however, to this tale of concealed kinship relations and shocking recognitions that at this point in the narrative the reader has not yet been informed of the name of the character in question. To name her "Mrs. Marlow" at this juncture shows that the person making the change, concerned only locally with absolute clarity of grammatical reference, never considered that the reader would not yet know who "Mrs. Marlow" was or that introducing her by that name too soon destroys the effect created by the revelation of her true identity later on. This example betrays a carelessness for the composition of the whole of which an author could scarcely be capable. From such instances of awkwardly mechanical corrections I deduce that the third and subsequent editions were corrected by someone other than Lee.

The mechanical "corrections" that mar the text of the third edition throughout are augmented in the fourth edition (London: Cadell, 1792) and conserved in the fifth (London: Cadell, 1804). All further printings of the work before the present one are either pirated, abridged, translated, or unedited facsimile reprints of the first edition (see bibliography for details). Therefore, of all known editions of the work, Cadell's second edition has emerged as the best copy-text, since it includes the most improvements while remaining the most free both of printer's errors and of overzealous editorial corrections. No external evidence has been found as to what role, if any, Sophia Lee had in the preparation of any of the editions of *The Recess* published during her lifetime, but internal evidence indicates that the second edition is the most likely to represent the author's own final version. It contains none of the regular and mechanically applied categories of grammatical corrections characteristic of the third edition and subsequent editions, no changes that are not in keeping with the work's overall style or story line. Moreover, far fewer new errors are introduced in the second edition than in the third. It is clear that the second edition contains the corrections and revisions of a highly sensitive eighteenth-century editor, if not those of the author herself.

I have followed the copy-text fairly strictly in the present edition. In a few instances, however, I have chosen readings from other editions—either the first or third—that seemed clearly preferable. All such changes, with the alternative readings, are indicated in the list of emendations. Obvious printer's errors have been silently corrected. I have amended and modernized the erratic use of quotation marks, where opening but not closing quotation marks appear, or where they appear (inconsistently) at the beginning of each line of a longer quoted speech. I have limited them in such cases to the beginning of each new paragraph of reported speech, closing them only at the end of the entire reported passage. I have not, however, introduced quotation marks in passages of reported speech where none at all appear in the copy-text.

Nor have I attempted to modernize or standardize other punctuation or the inconsistent spelling that characterizes all of the editions published in Lee's lifetime, out of a conviction that it is a significant characteristic of eighteenth-century texts that spelling was not standardized to the extent that it is now. It is important that readers be aware, for example, that English writers of Lee's era freely alternated between spellings that are now considered "British" and those that are now considered "American": *color* and *colour*, etc. In the third edition, the editor or printer seems to make something of an effort to standardize Lee's spelling in the direction of modern British usage, but he also quite frequently changes a "British" spelling to an "American" one, or a modern spelling to one that is now archaic; e.g. sometimes changing "honour" to "honor," "romantic" to "romantick," "Gothic" to "Gothick," even though more often he makes the reverse corrections (and although I call "him" "he," there is no evidence that any *single* person corrected any edition in its entirety). Therefore I have left the spellings exactly as they appear in the second edition. The only exception I have made is in the case of proper names of well-known figures; these have been both standardized and modernized in order to avoid confusion about the identity of the characters.

THE
RECESS;

OR, A

TALE OF OTHER TIMES

> Are not these Woods
> More free from peril than the envious Court?
> Here feel we but the penalty of Adam
> The seasons' difference.[1]

TO

Sir JOHN ELIOT, Baronet.[2]

SIR,

I should but affront a heart which finds its first pleasure in obliging, by asking a formal permission to publish its merits, which alone could induce me to surprize you with this address. Time and distance may have erased the author from your memory, but neither can obliterate from hers the gratitude due to a gentleman, who uniting sympathy with science, and generosity with both, becomes to the suffering a subordinate providence. Indebted to your friendly endeavours till my heart is as cold as those even your skill could not save, I shall always remain,

SIR,
Your highly obliged,
Humble Servant,
SOPHIA LEE.

BATH.

ADVERTISEMENT.

NOT being permitted to publish the means which enriched me with the manuscript from whence the following tale is extracted, its simplicity alone can authenticate it.— I make no apology for altering the language to that of the present age, since the obsolete stile of the author would be frequently unintelligible.— A wonderful coincidence of events stamps the narration at least with probability, and the reign of Elizabeth was that of romance.[3] If this Lady was not the child of fancy, her fate can hardly be paralleled; and the line of which she came has been marked by an eminent historian, as one distinguished alike by splendor and misery.[4]

The characters interwoven in this story agree, in the outline, with history; and if love, or friendship, veil a fault, or irradiate a virtue, it is but reasonable to allow of a weakness all seek in some particular instance.[5] As painting can only preserve the most striking characteristics of the form, history perpetuates only those of the soul; while too often the best and worst actions of princes proceed from partialities and prejudices, which live in their hearts, and are buried with them.

The depredations of time have left chasms in the story, which sometimes only heightens the pathos. An inviolable respect for truth would not permit me to attempt connecting these, even where they appeared faulty.

To the hearts of both sexes nature has enriched with sensibility, and experience with refinement, this tale is humbly offered; in the persuasion such will find it worthy their patronage.

THE
RECESS, &c.

PART I

TO
ADELAIDE MARIE DE MONTMORENCI.[6]

After a long and painful journey through life, with a heart exhausted by afflictions, and eyes which can no longer supply tears to lament them, I turn my every thought toward that grave on the verge of which I hover. Oh! why then, too generous friend, require me to live over my misfortunes? Such has been the peculiarity of my fate, that though tortured with the possession and the loss of every tye and hope that exalts or endears humanity, let but this feeble frame be covered with the dust from which it sprung, and no trace of my ever having existed would remain, except in the wounded consciences of those who marked me out a solitary victim to the crimes of my progenitors: For surely I could never merit by my own the misery of living as I have done—of dying as I must do.

Alas! your partial affection demands a memorial which calls back to being all the sad images buried in my bosom, and opens anew every vein of my heart. Yet consummate misery has a moral use, and if ever these sheets reach the publick, let the repiner at little evils learn to be juster to his God and himself, by unavoidable comparison. But am I not assuming an insolent consequence in thus admonishing? Alas, it is the dear-bought privilege of the unfortunate to be tedious!

My life commenced with an incident so extraordinary as the following facts alone could incline any one to credit. As soon as capable of reflection, I found myself and a sister of my own age, in an apartment with a lady, and a maid older than herself.— Every day furnished us with whatever was necessary for subsistence or improvement, supplied as it seemed by some invisible hand; for I rarely missed either of the few who commonly surrounded me. This Recess could not be called a cave, because it was composed of various rooms; and the stones were obviously united by labor; yet every room was distinct, and divided from the rest by a vaulted passage with many stairs, while our light proceeded from small casements of painted glass, so infinitely above our reach that we could never seek a world beyond; and so dim, that the beams of the sun were almost a new object to us when we quitted this retirement. These remarks occurred as our minds unfolded; for at first we were content, through habit and ignorance, nor once bestowed a thought on surrounding objects. The lady I have mentioned called us her children, and caressed us both with parental fondness.— Blest with every gentle charm, it is not wonderful she fully possessed the affection of those who had no one else to idolize. Every morning we met in a larger room than the rest, where a very venerable man performed mass, and concluded with a discourse calculated to endear retirement. From him we learnt there was a terrible large place called the world, where a few haughty individuals commanded miserable millions, whom a few artful ones made so; that Providence had graciously rescued us from both, nor could we ever be sufficiently grateful. Young hearts teem with unformed ideas, and are but too susceptible of elevated and enthusiastic impressions. Time gave this man insensibly an influence over us, as a superior being; to which his appearance greatly contributed. Imagine a tall and robust figure habited in black, and marked by a commanding austerity of manners.— His features bore the traces of many sorrows, and a kind of early old age, which interested every observer. The fire and nobility of his eye, the gracefulness of his decay, and the heart-affecting solemnity of his voice,

> While on his reverend temples grew
> The blossoms of the grave,[7]

gave an authority almost irresistible to Father Anthony, as we called him from hearing our mamma, to whom we understood he was brother. He usually partook our dinner, and from that time 'till the next morning vanished, for we knew not how or where he went. The interval we passed in little useful works, or in conversation with our mamma, whose only employment was that of forming our minds, for the world we were taught to dread.— *She* was our world, and all the tender affections, of which I have since proved my heart so full, centred in her, and my sister. Time and sorrow had given a wan delicacy to features exquisitely regular, while the soft symmetry of her person united to every common idea of beauty and elegance a feminine helplessness, which is, when unaffected, the most interesting of all charms. Her temper was equal, and her understanding enriched by a most extensive knowledge, to which she was every day adding by perpetual study. Inclined strongly by nature to serious reflection, and all her favorite employments, I used to pass those hours at her side Ellinor devoted to her play-things, or to Alice, whose memory was overcharged with those marvellous tales children always delight in. As our ideas every day expanded, we thought more and more concerning our origin, and our imprisonment. We knew Father Anthony constantly disappeared, but how or where was a secret beyond our comprehension; for in all our researches we had never found a door except those common to the family, and which shut us from the world. Ellinor, whose lively imagination readily imbibed the romantic and extravagant, conjectured we were in the power of some giant; nay, such was her disgust to Father Anthony, that she sometimes apprehended he was a magician, and would one day or other devour us. I had a very different idea; and fancied our retreat a hallowed circle to seclude us from the wicked, while Father Anthony was our guardian genius.[8] Frequently we by agreement interrogated Alice, who though fond to the common degree of an old nurse of both, but more especially Ellen, resisted those little arts nature herself inspires. Our mamma we now and then ventured to sound, but her gravity always disconcerted us, and we retreated from a vain attempt.

She once absented herself fourteen days, and left us to our own conjectures, in a spot truly chearless. Part of the time we spent in searching once more for a door, and the rest in childish lamentations for her loss; which Alice still assured us would be but a temporary one. Inflexible in the discharge of her duty, she still persisted in locking our apartment every day after dinner, at which time all who had occasion, doubtless, passed in and out of the Recess.

Being deprived of my customary resource, books, to amuse a part of our melancholy leisure, we mutually agreed to invent tales from the many whole-length pictures, which ornamented the best room, and to take them as they came alternately. Ellinor readily invented a ludicrous story upon the portrait of an old man, which made us both laugh heartily. I turned my eyes to consider what I should say about the next; they rested on the figure of a man of noble mien; his dress I then knew no name for, but have since found to be armour; a page held his helmet, and his hair, of a pale brown, fell over his shoulders. He was surrounded with many emblems of martial merit, and his eyes, which seemed bent on me, were full of a tender sweetness. A sentiment of veneration, mingled with surprising softness, pierced my soul at once; my tongue faltered with a nameless idea, and I rested my head against the shoulder of my sister. That dear girl turned to me with quickness, and the beam of her eye was like that of the picture. I surveyed her over and over, and found in every feature the strongest resemblance; when she frowned, she had all his dignity; when she smiled, all his sweetness. An awe, I could not conquer, made me unable to form any tale on that subject, and I directed my attention towards the next. It represented a lady in the flower of youth, drest in mourning, and seeming in every feature to be marked by sorrow; a black veil half shaded a coronet she wept over. If the last picture awakened veneration, this seemed to call forth a thousand melting sensations; the tears rushed involuntarily into our eyes, and, clasping, we wept upon the bosoms of each other. "Ah! who can these be?" cried we both together. "Why do our hearts thus throb before inanimate canvas? surely every thing we behold is but part of one great mystery; when will the day come, destined to clear it up?" We walked arm in arm round, and moralized on every portrait, but none interested us like these; we were never weary of surveying or talking about them; a young heart is frequently engrossed by a favorite idea, amid all the glare of the great world; nor is it then wonderful ours were thus possessed when entombed alive in such a narrow boundary. I knew not why, but we lived in the presence of these pictures as if they understood us, and blushed when we were guilty of the slightest folly.

The moment our mamma returned, we flew into her arms, and interrupted her tender caresses with importunate enquiries concerning these favorite pictures. She regarded us with astonishment—her eyes filled with tears, and she bade us leave her to recover herself alone. Shortly after she summoned Alice, and held with her a conversation which restored her tranquillity; but she carefully avoided our enquiries, endeavouring to diversify our hours by music, drawing, poetry, geography, and every ornamental branch of education. Whenever we verged toward an hint about the retreat—"wait, my dear girls," she would say, "the appointed hour—alas, one may follow it, when you will wish yourselves still uninformed."— Impressed with an undefinable melancholy, our years passed on 'till womanhood approached.

Pardon me if I linger over these scenes; I have but few such to relate, and they are all of my life upon which my heart dares to pause. How are we born to invent our own miseries! We start forward from the goal of youth, fearless and impatient, nor know the heights and depths through which we must labor; oppressed in turn by every element, and often overwhelmed with that most insupportable of all burthens, our own dissatisfied souls. How have I wept the moment I quitted the Recess—a moment I then lived but in the hope of! To be always erring, is the weakness of humanity, and to be always repenting, its punishment.— Alas! could we learn wisdom without experience, mankind would perhaps be too happy.

Father Anthony in time ingratiated himself with us, by his continual remonstrances against our being shut up in a place which bounded our ideas so much that he despaired of making us comprehend half of what he taught us. We seconded his advice with endless entreaties. Our mamma, who was persuasion itself in her own person, was not proof against it in that of another. "Alas, my children," would she often say, "by what fatality do you so passionately desire to leave a home you will hereafter remember with a pleasure full of regret? In vain you would return to it—you will lose a taste for the tranquil enjoyments this solitude offers, without perhaps finding any to supply them. Yet far be the selfish weakness from my heart of punishing you, even for your welfare. You shall *see* this admired world. May it ever please you as it will at first sight!"

We embraced her with youthful transport, and then each other—"We shall go at last," exclaimed both together, "we shall see many more like ourselves!"

"What say you, children?" cried she; "ah! you will see few indeed like yourselves."

The next day was appointed for our enfranchisement. We packed and unpacked our little luggage fifty times over for mere employment 'till the appointed hour came; when we were summoned to the chamber of our only friend, who was walking about apparently agitated with a secret.

"Are you grieved, mamma," cried I, "that we are going to be happy?"

"Ah no, Matilda! I am grieved, because I think you are just ceasing to be so. In this peaceful solitude I could supply to you every lost relation—the adopted children of my heart, I stood between you and a fate at once distinguished, obscure, and affecting.— Alas, why do you wrest yourselves and your secret from me? Why do you oblige me to tell you, you must never more call me any thing but Mrs. Marlow?"

"Never more call you mamma!" sighed I, incoherently, "who then are our parents?"

"You have no father: he who gave you existence sleeps in the bosom of God."

"Our mother—"

"Lives—but not for you—enquire no farther; let this specimen of knowledge teach you to fear it.— When the time requires it, I shall disclose your whole story;—weep no more, my lovely, my affecting girls; I have lost but a name; for my nature is unalterable. All who will see us know I never was married, which absolutely compelled me to this discovery. But I dare believe they will rely on my rectitude, and welcome you by whatever appellation I shall give you. Reasons you will hereafter know, induce me always to conceal a retreat, where alone I could have hid you, and both must, ere we leave it, solemnly promise never to disclose the secret."

Chilled with this solemn preparation, our desire of liberty vanished; we felt like links struck from the chain of creation;[9] and still with restless imaginations explored the remainder of a mystery which we wept by anticipation. "She lives, but not for you!" were words whose sound vibrated to my heart, while pleasure danced around me, and the doubt attending the future, often robbed the present of enjoyment.

After we had made at her knees the strict promise required, she muffled our faces, and taking my hand, as Alice did my sister's, led us through many cold passages for some minutes; when unbinding our eyes, we found ourselves in a noble cloister. We flew into the garden it bordered, and how strong was the impression of the scene before us! from the mansion, which stood on a hill, spread a rich and fertile valley, mingled with thickets, half seen or clustered hamlets, while through the living landscape flowed a clear river,

> ————————————and to the main
> The liquid serpent drew his silver train.[10]

The sun was sinking, involved in swelling waves of gold and purple, upon whom we almost gazed ourselves blind: for though we had often read and heard of his effulgence, the author of universal being can alone display it. Imagination, Madam, may sometimes surpass the wonders of art, but those of nature leave all imagination far behind.

Mrs. Marlow led us through the Abbey, which might rather be called a palace: it was erected upon the ruins of a Monastery destroyed at the Reformation, and still was called by the name of St. Vincent. It had all the Gothic magnificence and elegance, and we learnt with pleasure that Mrs. Marlow, the sister of its owner, Lord Scrope,[11] was considered by every servant as its mistress. A noble apartment within hers was allotted for us, and the charms of the new world mingled with our melancholy reveries, alike destroying our repose. The rising of the sun, whose first beams gilt our windows, rouzed us entirely. Methinks, while I expatiate on these trifles, time seems suspended, and the scene still living before me. The rich dew-drops, those jewels with which nature decks her bosom, glittering to the rays that wandered over the grass: the various animals that seemed to derive a daily existence from the return of that glorious orb: the morning hymn of the winged creation,—all united to awaken our gratitude, and humble us before the author of our being. "Accept, oh

God," would we cry spontaneously, "the adoration of two hearts, who know no claim in this mighty universe but thee! oh deign to bless the desire of doing right with the power! and if only sorrow is our portion, sanctify it with resignation: so when time delivers us up to eternity, hope may be our conductor!"

We were delighted with a playful group of fawns and deer, with whom we longed to frolic, and stole through Mrs. Marlow's chamber into the park, by a passage she had pointed out to us the day before. What was our surprize when we saw those with whom we had in idea mingled, were large fierce creatures, and that had they not run from us, we must from them; that every bird feared its natural protector, and that man lived in a continual warfare with every thing in creation, even to his own species!

I am tedious, and must have done with these puerilities, which yet on reflection yield the purest pleasures of our lives. Mrs. Marlow soon procured for us the best instructors in every art and science that remote residence afforded, and, by her own example, gave that elegant finish to our manners, precept never can. Extremely detached, by our situation, from society, we easily discerned Mrs. Marlow was willing we should be so, for she frequently expressed anxiety at the thoughts of Lord Scrope's return; who, I understand, was sent ambassador to the Hague from Queen Elizabeth.[12] Our masters, our servants, and the various rustics who tenanted the estate, met in the chapel of St. Vincent's Abbey once a week, and those were all our intercourse with society. On the evening of every Sunday we regularly went to the cell of Father Anthony, which was a cot[13] raised by Lord Scrope (to whom he stood in the same relation as Mrs. Marlow) on the verge of a large wood which sheltered the mansion behind. Here, while we were indulged with all those simple repasts novelty gives charms to, our minds were enlarged by conversations on every thing sublime or instructive. If benevolence drew Mrs. Marlow abroad, she made us always her companions, and gave her alms but through our hands; ordering us ever to add some mite of our own, in proportion to our means. Avarice is rarely the vice of youth; at least, if I may judge by my own heart; for the chief joy of receiving, to me, was that of giving. Nor could Charity have descended to earth in a more lovely form, than that of Mrs. Marlow. At a tale of distress her eyes assumed a melting benignity rarely seen, and never described; while her approach gave that pleasure to every sufferer, one should feel at the visible presence of a guardian angel.

Three years elapsed in this manner, ere Lord Scrope returned; and when he did, he was so deeply engaged in politics, that the various presents he continually sent from London, made to us the only difference.

Still the sad sound,—"your mother lives—but not for you!" rung through our hearts occasionally; still we equally desired to discover the Recess; and wandered through St. Vincent's Abbey with the same curiosity we once before did through that. The more we reflected, the more we were convinced it must be near us; but the respect we had for Mrs. Marlow's solemn injunctions, sealed our lips to every servant, and we never were allowed to ramble unattended.

Mrs. Marlow, endued with the purest principles, justly conceived happiness the noblest use of understanding; and bent her whole attention towards convincing us, the fate appointed us was the most desirable in the world. "Here," would she say, "in a happy retirement, free alike from the drudgeries of high or low life, peace and innocence becalms your hearts, and blooms on your cheeks. Unenvying and unenvied as now, may that moment find you none can avoid! Ah, how unlike the crimes and miseries of a court! There you can have no vice so injurious to yourselves as sincerity; no merit, like hypocrisy. Love and friendship are unknown, and their names made use of but to entrap the unwary. Women that have beauty are destroyed by it, and all who have not are neglected. The gifts of man take place of the gifts of God, and money alone constitutes merit.— Ah, never! never! my dear girls, can you enough bless that indulgent Providence, which withdraws you from it!"

Shall I confess my vanity? When I looked in the glass, I did not think I should be neglected, even at court. I had no opportunity of forming any just comparison indeed; for the rustics around us, scorched with toil, had only charms enough left to shew what they might have been with care. The clearness of my complexion, and the delicacy of my features, left me no equal, but my sister: Nay, even our habits, though often only of finer camblet[14] than theirs, were made in so different a manner, that they did not appear to be composed of the same materials.

However disposed to profit by the advice of our more than parent, Heaven did not permit us to be happy. The clouds broke at once over our heads; Mrs. Marlow, our only tye on earth, and therefore doubly prized, was seized with a fever; the more dangerous, because it was not violent enough at first to shew itself. To paint our distraction would be a vain attempt. Kneeling on each side her bed, for fourteen days and nights, we by tears and inward supplications persecuted the Almighty. Affectionately attached to us, she struggled for our sakes with the disorder, 'till having worn her down to a skeleton, it began at last to abate; but notwithstanding every effort of art, could never be eradicated. Scarce had we breathed after this distress, when an express from London delivered a pacquet[15] to Mrs. Marlow, which occasioned her instantly to summon Father Anthony; they remained in consultation for some time, when they bade Alice order us instantly to join them.

"My children," said Mrs. Marlow, faintly, "an unforeseen event obliges us once more to retire to the Recess. Every thing is at this moment preparing for our reception. You are now at years to judge of the importance of its concealment, nor will I longer make it a mystery.— But why thus afflict your-selves for a temporary restraint? If I am willing, for your sakes, to be carried thither, like a corpse into a tomb, surely you will not be so ungenerous as to vent one selfish lamentation?"

Effectually silenced by this noble reproof, we collected, in confusion and grief, our clothes and ornaments; when, returning to her room, we found there Father Anthony, an old domestick called James, Alice, and the House-keeper; who, having dispersed the other servants, preceded us to a store-room on the ground floor, and opening a press,[16] unfastened a false back, which conducted us into a closet,[17] dark, but for our torches. She then lifted a part of the floor, fitted very neatly, and discovered a narrow pair of stairs,[18] down which we went, leaving her behind, and effectually secured ourselves, by bolt-ing it firmly on the inside. We past through several subterraneous passages built on arches, and preserved from damps by cavities which passed through every statue that ornamented the garden, 'till at last we reached our prison. But judge of my astonishment, when I found the so often-sought entrance was a door of the size of that portrait which first gave me such singular sensa-tions, and which I perceived was made to fall together, with a spring almost imperceptible.

Father Anthony silenced the exclamations I would have made, and drew me at once to Mrs. Marlow; who, pale and lifeless with the fatigue of this removal, gave additional terrors to the moment. Whether the agitation of her mind had increased her malady, or it was originally beyond cure, I know not; but saw, with speechless affliction, from the moment of our return to the Recess, she would never leave it alive. Enclosed in a spot without sufficient air, attendance, or advice, we saw her finish her generous attachment to us, by resolutely resisting our intreaties.

"Let us quit this dreary place," I would say, "if but for a cottage. Let us not, in losing you, have the cruel aggravation of contributing to so great a misfortune.— Oh! what more can we have to fear, than the loss of all we love?"

"Why, why, my children," returned she, "thus embitter a common fate? Can I, who have voluntarily passed my youth in a tomb, dread to bury my dust in it? You know my opinion is singular, nor do I think man could avert the stroke when God recalls us, however wise or willing. If I had been taken earlier from you, indeed, heavy to all must have been the calamity; but after having taught you to live, there remains this only lesson, and my duty is complete; you now are enabled to judge for yourselves, confide in God, and he will not desert you."

"Alas!" would I cry, drowned in tears, "from your eye alone have we learnt when we did any thing aright; we shall no longer know good from evil when that dear eye is closed."

"Matilda," replied she with a solemn air, "remember only when you are called to any important action, to consult your heart in solitude; God has placed in that heart an unerring monitor, and if we hear not the small still voice,[19] it is because we drown it in the noise of the world; then shall we meet again to part no more; then at the tribunal of the Most High, I shall gladly say, 'these treasures, O Lord, didst thou entrust to my hand unsullied, behold even so I restore them.'"

Rising up as she pronounced these words, she held a hand of each of us to her heart, while her eyes streamed with a kind of glory when lifted toward her Creator. Never did I see such an animated figure; her soul seemed that moment bursting from its beauteous mansion to join its sister angels.

"Matilda and Ellinor, my more than children, you recollect," said she, "I suppressed your curiosity once, by telling you, I would reveal your secret finally when the hour demanded it. That hour has come. Alas! I cannot but weep to remember, that a thousand interesting ideas are now going to detach your affections from her who agonizes over you."

We kissed her hand in speechless sorrow—

"'Tis true," continued she, "my brother might hereafter disclose your story, but there are among its incidents, some that need the gentleness of a woman to teach you to bewail, without imitating. In this little history you will find the full motive of my retreat, and the means by which it was effected.

"You already know I am sister to the present Lord Scrope, but you know not that I derived my birth from the ill-judged zeal of my mother. Bred up a Papist, she no sooner entertained a passion for Lord Scrope, than she formed a design to convert him to the Catholick religion. She was handsome, as I have always heard, and he was young; he affected to be sensible of her efforts, which redoubled her zeal. She thought the love of Heaven alone actuated her heart, but he took advantage of those moments, and she found too late she had sacrificed her own soul's welfare to his indulgence: her relations, who had the more encouraged her, as my father was a great match in point of fortune, exasperated at an error they ought rather to have charged themselves with, shut her up, and treated her with the utmost rigor.

"In this terrible situation she was delivered of me; her relations took me instantly from her sight; they wrapt me in the most disgraceful habiliments, and sent me, with a letter full of the bitterest threats and taunts, to my father. Far, however, from feeling that indifference very young men usually behold their offspring with, he received me as the first gift of Heaven, and, committing me to the charge of proper people, made me of no less consequence than if I had been his legitimate daughter, and heiress of his estate.

"In the mean time my mother was kept in total ignorance of the fate of her child; miserable in her own heart, and eternally taunted for the disgrace she had brought on her family, she at length resolved to make her escape to Lord Scrope;—she effected it, and found in his house the treasure of all her hopes, her child; but as she was not of an age to be independent, on her being discovered by her kindred, she was again torn from his arms, and I was forever bereaved of a mother before I was sensible I had one. How often did my father repent his injustice to her! it hung heavy on his soul in life, and was most terrible in death. In vain he sought her, for never from that hour did Heaven permit the erring pair to meet. A few years afterwards he married, and had by his wife the present Lord; this circumstance, far from lessening his affection, endeared me still more to him; he remembered I had no fortune but from his bounty, no claim but on his heart. His Lady having no more children, began to consider me as her daughter, and the misfortune of my birth was almost forgotten. In this situation I grew up, caressed by all his friends, and admired infinitely more than I deserved; for, from the time my brother grew of an age to appear in the world, Lord Scrope had left St. Vincent's Abbey for the Court. Many matches offered, of which my father often entreated me to chuse. I however saw no man with a preference; and as I was sensible my heart was too tender not to become partial, I wished to evade all proposals 'till then. I had in this interval the misfortune to lose my father, whose senses failing him in his last sickness, he had no power to make a necessary provision for me; yet in this delirium he raved of me and my mother continually. I felt this loss the less sensibly, as I was treated with the utmost generosity and tenderness by my brother and the dowager Lady Scrope; but I found my train of admirers diminish apace, when one appeared, who atoned in my eyes for the loss of a thousand. He was a young West-Indian, possessed of a considerable fortune, and amiable person, and an untainted heart. When I say I loved him, I speak but coldly; you will know how well hereafter. Mr. Colville, for that was his name, was of a character too much resembling the young Lord Scrope's, not to be favoured by him. He proved by the generosity of his behaviour, the sincerity of his love; neither the misfortune of my birth, or want of riches, diminished his ardor; but rather, on the contrary, augmented it. His fortune was independent, and I was not desirous of more than a very moderate competence. The day of our marriage was fixed, and arrived equally wished by both. We were united in the presence of the Lord and Lady Scrope, who had loaded me with noble presents. Our hearts were gay, and a large company assembled on the occasion, invented a thousand diversions. I was sitting after dinner at the head of the table, singing, when a servant entered and whispered my husband; he rose up, and followed him into the next room: my eyes were industrious to find him and as he left the door open, I perceived him, from an opposite pier glass, take a packet of letters from a man; he held them in his hand 'till I ceased singing, and then began reading: he continued to do so for some minutes, when I saw his hand shake with great violence, which soon diminishing, he fell to the ground. I ran to him in the utmost agitation;—he was cold and convulsed. I took up the papers, but had not read half as far, before I was as insensible as himself."

(Mrs. Marlow was so affected at this passage, she had not power to proceed; at last recovering, she held up her hands, while her fine eyes were drowned in tears, and repeated)

"Let me not, oh God, since I survived that moment, sink under the remembrance of it! I must cut short description, my children, on a circumstance which so nearly affects my heart. The letters were from his mother; after telling him she had suffered him to depart with the more ease for England, as she wished to have an opportunity of declaring a secret to him, shame had long suppressed, and which her decaying health forbid her longer to conceal, she related the incidents of her life; a few of which decided our fate, and convinced me the same parents gave birth to both. What a terrible discovery! I shall pass over those events you already know, and only mention, that on being forced by her tyrannical relations from Lord Scrope's house, they sent her under the care of an uncle, in the Spanish service, to the West-Indies. During the passage, she found herself again with child; her kinsman, exasperated at this circumstance, used every means to prevail on her to marry Mr. Colville (a settler whose plantations joined his, and who was a passenger on board the same vessel) without acquainting him with her situation. Persecuted and distressed on all sides, she at last took a resolution on the first occasion, to declare all to her lover. His assiduity furnished her with one ere long, which she did not neglect. As soon as he had conquered his surprise, he assured her she should never repent her generous confidence in his honour, which affected him the more sensibly as his friend would meanly have deceived him. He owned himself so attached, that if she could give up fruitless hopes to partake his fortune, he would marry her directly, without claiming any right from the ceremony, but that of releasing her from the tyranny of her kindred, and hereafter providing in the same manner for her child as he would for any of his own. Overcome with the severity of her treatment, from those who were bound to pity her, and sensible the stranger who could speak so generously on the subject, might make her as happy as she now durst hope to be, she requested time to deliberate on the proposal, which he granted. Some days elapsed, during which, she resolved to secure to herself the privilege of keeping *one* of her children, by consenting. They were united by a holy father then on board, who, at Mr. Colville's desire, gave out that he had married them two months before in London, but concealed it from some motives respecting the lady's friends. Her uncle, under whose care she was, not suspecting the eclaircissement,[20] was astonished how she had brought her lover to consent to this; but, as his authority was at an end by her compliance with his wishes, he affected the utmost satisfaction, and offered them some valuable presents. Mr. Colville, whose ingenuous heart abhorred his meanness, refused with contempt those poor compensations, for a deceit which might have proved so fatal to his happiness, nor left him to suppose he was ignorant of the favor intended him. He painted the infamy of the proceeding in the strongest colours, and on their arrival at Jamaica, carried his bride to his own plantation, without deigning to take leave of her relations. 'Here,' said the dear lady, 'I gave birth, my son, to you, and here I first learnt to be happy. The generous kindness with which Mr. Colville treated you, the unwearied attention he shewed to me, deserved, and obtained my whole heart. It seemed as if the sincerity of my conduct had cancelled its errors; I may truly say, I never saw him caress you, without ardently wishing you had a claim to the name he bestowed on you. You grew up without my ever hearing of your real father, and as it little became me to wound the heart of my husband, I preserved an absolute silence on the subject, nor seemed to remember such a person ever had existed. I will not say I never thought of him; nature taught you to recall him to my mind by a thousand artless gestures.— I gave you, after some years, two sisters and a brother, the loss of whom you doubtless remember. A generous, though silent struggle, continued during their lives, between Mr. Colville and myself; I always attempted to convince him you, though the elder, had not more than a just portion of my love; and he, no less anxiously, sought to satisfy me his own children had not made him forget what he had promised respecting you. Heaven, however, took them to itself, and Mr. Colville divided between you and me a fortune too dearly gained by his loss; though you have paid the tribute of filial gratitude over his grave, my son, remember that is insufficient; you owe him every thing, and can never discharge the obligation. Your youth, and the pleasure Mr. Colville took in being called your father, made it very improper I should intrust to you a secret so humiliating to myself, and distressing to him; yet, sensible of the necessity, I have, since his death, a thousand times resolved on it, and as constantly given up the design. At last, my dear child, you rendered it easier to me, by proposing to visit England, and I suffered you to go with less regret, because I hoped you there would find another parent; one whose claim in you is the same with mine, and one, who I am assured, will proudly acknowledge you. Go then, my dear Anthony, to Lord Scrope; shew him this letter: tell him, for I am not afraid to say it, even to yourself, I send him a son worthier of a nobler name than the weakness of your mother has given you. Tell him, I will not allow him to provide for your sister Gertrude, since the fortune I possess is already destined to her, if living. Do you, my dear Anthony, repair my loss to her, for never, in respect to my husband's memory, will I see again the father of my children; this place shall be my grave, and here, while life remains, I will bless you both, and pray that the sins of your parents may never be visited upon either.'

"Vain wish," said Mrs. Marlow; "the stroke was already given. Judge for me, my dear girls, what I felt on reading such tender sentiments, and remembering the characters were those of a mother!

"We were removed to separate apartments; Mr. Colville, no longer my husband, had strength of constitution, but not strength of mind, to support this calamity; he fell into a deep melancholy, and shut himself from all the world: as to me, Heaven, in mercy, took away my senses by a violent fever; I remained in a dangerous situation several weeks, during which time he formed a resolution, my restoration gave him an opportunity to effect. Each wanting courage to see the other, he informed me, by letter, he only waited my consent to return to his own country, and dispose of his effects, the produce of which might endow the monastery where he should receive the holy habit. He conjured me to support a misfortune, his letter convinced me, he was ready to sink under. The sad choice he had made was already mine; I wrote to inform him of it; I conjured him never to betray to our mother the fatal event of her concealment, but to persuade her we were both happy.— What a vain request! had not Heaven deprived her of ever seeing him, how could he have concealed so exquisite a distress?— A wound in the heart will ever bleed on the slightest touch.

"I recovered my senses, but that disgust with which every disappointment (and how much more so deep a one!) overwhelms a young mind, made every thing odious to me; the hours when I was so pleasingly deceived, were all I reckoned in my life. Before I left my room, my Lord's marriage with the Lady Matilda Howard was concluded; his union with the first Lady in England, both in birth and beauty, gave the greatest pleasure to all who loved him.[21] Little able, and less disposed to assist at festivities, I retired on the plea of bad health to the Abbey. The death of the Dowager Lady Scrope, in the midst of the pleasures, entirely damped them. Lord Scrope conducted his new Lady into the country, to pass the time of mourning; the amiable engaging bride conceived a friendship for me, which, as is frequently the case in noble minds, had perhaps its source in my misfortunes. With all the graces that adorn grandeur, Lady Scrope had the sweet simplicity of a village maid; a heart full of the most exquisite delicacy and sensibility, and features which did justice to her mind. My Lord perfectly adored her, and her rank and charms soon made me find St. Vincent's Abbey no longer a retirement.

"A letter came in a short time from my brother, which informed me, that on his arrival at Jamaica, he found my mother had died during his absence; this was accompanied with bills[22] for a large sum, as my portion of her valuable legacy. There is something so tender in the name, the idea of a mother, although unknown, that in spite of my other afflictions, I found a very sensible one in her loss. My heart had now no resting place. Before, the remembrance that the blow came from her, however unintentionally, gave me a little courage, which I was not sure I possessed 'till it was lost. There is a pleasure to hearts capable of refinement, in sacrificing something to the friends we love; the silence we endured to save her from distress had lessened mine, which now broke forth anew. The amiable Lady Scrope neglected nothing to soften it; she used every effort to prevent my retiring to the monastery,[23] as I had purposed, and her influence over her Lord made her wishes too surely his for him to neglect adding his intreaties; the obligations I owed his family, the esteem I had for his Lady, and the very refinement I have mentioned, made me unable to refuse. I could never make too large amends for such kindness. My sister-in-law, who rather boasted than disowned the title, to gratify me, neglected the amusements natural to her years, and a mind at ease; it seemed as if I had the authority vested in her, and not her will, but mine, directed the family. Our guests departed by degrees, and Lady Scrope's brother, the young Duke of Norfolk, with some other relations alone remained.[24]

"To satisfy my brother Anthony no levity had erased from my mind the tender ties which once united us, and which neither time nor reason could ever entirely dissolve, I laid before him the motives of my conduct, and conjured him to believe, since I could never be his, I never would be another's. Lady Scrope not being able to prevail on me to return to London, departed without me, after extorting a promise, that I would think no more of a nunnery. She had left the Abbey three months, when she gave birth to the present Lord, to the inexpressible joy of her husband. To shew all the gratitude in my power for the favours I had received both from Lord Scrope and his mother, I divided my fortune, and insisted on their accepting half, as a present to the young heir. The generous Matilda would have returned it, but her Lord, more sensible of the value of money, received the gift. She reproached me for it with that kind raillery which friends know how to make so agreeable; she told me she should cease to love me, since the world would now call her attachment interested.

"In the time of her absence, I spent many hours in reviewing the ruins with which this place abounded; the gloomy magnificence of those great remains of art, was more suited to my sadness of soul than the softer and more varied scenes of nature; the liking I had conceived for these places, doubtless first caused the housekeeper to shew me the Recess. She had lived in the family a vast number of years, and knew the secret. How often had I walked through its ruined ailes, without suspecting it could possibly contain one habitable spot! I will now, my dear children, explain its situation and structure:—It was once inhabited by nuns of the order of St. Winifred, but deserted before the abolition of Convents, from its ruinous condition; in this situation it remained many years, shunned by the country people, and devoutly visited by those travellers whom chance or curiosity brought this way. When the Reformation, in the time of Henry, robbed the monks of their vast domains,[25] the ancestor of Lord Scrope obtained this land of the king; he pulled down the monastery to erect a convenient mansion in the same taste, and discovered a secret passage from thence to the Convent; it was blocked up without being generally known, and the ruins left as an addition to the prospect; nor till chance gave the communication a value, was it remembered. The nobleman who could obtain so vast a favor, 'tis needless to mention, professed the reformed religion, but not able to forget that in which he had been brought up, his house became the asylum of many of the unrevenued fathers; this circumstance being noticed, he found his views in the world depended on his expelling them, when the secret passage occurred to his remembrance. He had the stones removed cautiously by the holy fathers, and found the place well arched and paved, and free from damps; it terminated in a room they supposed to have been the refectory, and which still remained entire. They removed, by degrees, such accommodations as were necessary into it, and thither the refugees retired, being supplied with food from the Abbey: but finding themselves shut up in too small a place, and in total want of employment, they began working under ground, and by degrees formed two other passages from the Recess, one of which ends in the Hermit's cave, where the eldest of them lived, and the other in the midst of the ruins. Thus providing against discovery, or rather securing their escape if that should happen. In surveying the ruins, they found several places enclosed, and yet undemolished; from among those, they selected the few we have lived in, chusing them always separated to prevent suspicion. Thus, in a few years, each father had his own cell, and a monastery was hid among the ruins of the convent. At length, the severity of government abating, several of the monks ventured again into the world, and of the eight who made it their asylum, two only ended their days here. Lord Scrope, sensible of the value of such a retirement, carefully kept the secret when its inhabitants were gone; two servants alone knew it, and they were faithful; nor till the house-keeper told me the story, had I an idea of such a place.

"This account appeared to me almost fabulous; the ruin was at least half a mile from the mansion, which then had a view of its rising plantations daily diminished, till the wood became frequented, or indeed passable only on the side near the Hermit's cave: I impatiently desired to explore the whole romantic secret.

"The house-keeper did not delay a moment to gratify my curiosity; she summoned an old servant who knew the way, with torches, to lead me through the windings. The arched roof which was, by some contrivance in the building, kept astonishingly free from damps, echoed to our very feet. The gloominess of the scene accorded with my ideas, and suggested a scheme which I have since thought a providential one, to my mind. The division of the rooms, the bare walls, and holes in the roof for air, displeased me: but since my affection for Lord and Lady Scrope debarred me from devoting myself to a convent, I resolved to fit this place up, and retire to it whenever the owners, with their guests, made St. Vincent's Abbey too gay for me. Three times I visited it, and each time found my desire greater. I discoursed with the old man, who, from a considerable reward I offered him, agreed, with the assistance of his son, who was a builder, to render this a comfortable habitation. I was unwilling to admit a third person into the secret, but soon discovered his son James was already acquainted with it. They directly began lodging their implements in the cave, which was altered to give a face to the whole. Three months made it what it now is; charmed with a device which I little foresaw would be useful to my friends, the house-keeper and my maid Alice, brought, by my direction, every necessary to the dark room, from whence the men fetched them. The time of my Lord's return drew nigh, the place was aired, and my books and clothes already carried there; no sooner had I resigned the care of the family into the hands of my amiable sister,[26] than I acquainted her with my intended retreat. Her surprise was extreme at seeing how commodious we had rendered so sequestered a spot; but being fearful, if she opposed my resolution, of seeming to constrain me, she suffered me to indulge my fancy. Hither then I retired, attended by Alice and James, the latter of whom lived in the cave to secure us from discovery, and furnish us every little convenience. This solitude, so suitable to the sadness of my soul, was inexpressibly agreeable to me; it had all the advantages of a nunnery, without the tie to continue in it; a restriction the most likely to make retirement odious.[27] My brother Anthony (with whom I constantly corresponded) charmed with the description of a spot so well calculated for hearts wounded like his and mine, assured me, instead of shutting himself up in a convent, for which he felt he had no vocation, as soon as he thought he could bring himself to consider me only as a sister, he would fix his residence in the cave.

"I had remained there two months, when a messenger arrived to recall Lord Scrope to Court; the cause could not remain a secret. Mary of Scotland, that beautiful and unfortunate Queen, who had been imprisoned by her subjects as an accessory to the murder of her husband, had found means to escape, and implore the protection of Elizabeth.[28] The jealousy and hatred that princess had long entertained for one so superior in those endowments most admired by herself, made this step excusable in Mary, only from the cruelty of her situation. But did not that very situation entitle her to royal treatment? In Elizabeth many noble qualities are mingled with impatience, caprice, pride, and excessive vanity. Overjoyed at getting a rival into her hands, doubly formidable, instead of offering Mary a princely asylum, till, on the proof of her innocence, she should be restored to her crown, Elizabeth instantly made the Queen of Scots sensible of her power, by dropping those ardent expressions of friendship and esteem with which all her letters had before been filled (most probably to hide the very reverse) and insisting on her consenting to be tried by laws, with which she was unacquainted, and never yet subject to.[29] It was to propose those harsh terms to Mary, the Queen had sent for Lord Scrope; she deputed him in concert with the duke of Norfolk, and several other Lords Commissioners to receive from Mary her justification, and examine into the authenticity of the proofs.[30]

"The deserted, nay, almost betrayed Queen of Scotland, too late found how little the professions of the great are to be relied on. She was now in a worse condition than if she had still remained in her own country, and submitted to laws by which she had governed. Compelled, by the severity of her fate, to bend to a woman but equal with herself; to give herself up a prisoner to a government she had never offended, and over which she was probably destined to reign;[31] as a criminal, to attempt a justification before people too probably ordered to condemn her, and, even if they avoided that, too politic to clear her innocence, and restore her freedom: For the Queen of England had already placed a number of people around her, who watched all her steps so cautiously, that they wanted only the name to become a guard. Amid all these fears and mortifications, submission was Mary's only measure. She had learnt, young as she was, to submit with dignity, and demand a degree of generosity, by not seeming to doubt of finding it. She therefore received the Queen's decision with composure, delivered herself into Lord Scrope's hands, and agreed to defer appearing before her sister Elizabeth, 'till she could appear with honor.

"This great event engrossed the attention of all Europe. Various opinions were formed, and Elizabeth never found Mary more formidable than when in her power. All blamed her errors, but they pitied her youth, and imputed many of them to inexperience and faults in her education. Her uncommon beauty, affability, elegance of manners, and expression, were strongly commended by all who had seen her, and those who had not, listened to the tale with avidity, and reported it with increase. Every word in her praise was a dagger to the heart of Elizabeth, and the unfortunate Mary's greatest crimes with her, were the graces she received from nature.

"Lady Scrope had spent some of her early years in the French Court. Mary was too affable and amiable not to attach every one for whom she had inclination, and the friendship she shewed for the Lady Matilda, would have made the separation the more afflicting, but that Mary, by the death of Francis the second, found herself no longer attached to France, and was obliged, with infinite regret, to quit the kingdom she had been educated in, to govern one filled with domestic jars, and almost ignorant of those softnesses which give charms to society; and which, in a peculiar degree, adorned the court she had hitherto reigned over.[32]

"The troubles in which she had been plunged, from the hour she returned to Scotland, had hardly left her leisure to distinguish those formerly honored with her notice: Lady Scrope had, however, always preserved an attachment to her, less the fruit of gratitude than sympathy. The Queen's present sad situation, of which she heard amply from her Lord, touched her to the very soul. She accused Elizabeth of meanness and injustice; and, without doubting the innocence of Mary, she ardently desired to lighten her captivity, and convince her that misfortune had not robbed her of every friend. These sentiments were too fervently generous not to engage me. I insensibly took part in what interested my sister so nearly, and learnt to deplore a Princess thus treated, whom, in a happier situation, I should doubtless have censured.[33]

"Lord Scrope, to satisfy his wife, who entreated him to the step, represented to Elizabeth, the impropriety of leaving the Queen of Scots unaccompanied by any lady of distinction, and without the attendance, nothing could exempt the place she had chosen for an asylum, from offering her, whether guilty or innocent. To give force to this, he hinted the error of harsh measures, which interested the common people, and by engaging their pity, might weaken their fidelity.

"The last reason, weighed infinitely more with our Queen than the first, for her heart was more full of policy[34] than feeling. She however appointed Lady Scrope to attend upon Mary, and sent orders to treat her suitably to her rank.[35]

"Overjoyed at carrying her point, without appearing in it, Lady Scrope did not delay her journey; but unwilling to leave me, she used all her interest and influence to persuade me to accompany her. She represented, she did not wish to engage me in any gay scenes, the office she was allotted to being that most conformable to the melancholy turn of my mind. The inclination I had to see Mary joined with her, and I consented.

"Bolton Castle, whither Mary had been conducted by the Queen's command, was a strong fortress on the borders of Yorkshire. Without furniture, or accommodations for a royal guest, it declared at once to that Princess, the melancholy captivity to which she was destined.[36] The humanity of Lord Scrope in vain attempted to conceal the fate that awaited her; she gave herself up to an immoderate grief, which was augmented by the news of Bothwell's death, who had taken refuge in Norway.[37]

"We were met at Derby by the Duke of Norfolk, whose ardent desire to see the Queen of Scots had induced him to join us. This nobleman was of an amiable presence, in the prime of life, full of a generous ardor, a captivating vivacity. Without an equal in rank in England, he had formed, long since, the design of espousing Mary, and Bothwell's death had renewed hopes her marriage with him had frustrated.[38] I was amazed at the difference visible in the manners of the Duke; nor did I immediately perceive whence his impatience of any disappointment, and deep reveries could proceed; but the pleasure he took in hearing his sister's commendations of the Queen, the softness that sparkled in his eyes, while he related the events her letters to Bothwell had laid open,[39] shewed me at length that ambition had raised a flame in his heart, he mistook for love.

"We arrived at Bolton, and Mary was not apprized, till Lady Scrope was introduced to her presence, that Elizabeth had sent her a friend so anxiously desirous to lighten her captivity. I would describe the Queen of Scots to you, my dear children, had not nature drawn a truer picture of her than I can give. Look in the glass, Matilda, and you will see her perfect image."

I could not contain my astonishment—"Oh Heavens!" exclaimed I, "is it possible in lamenting the fate of that injured Queen, I have wept for a mother!"

"A short time will explain all," said Mrs. Marlow. "The Queen was in the bloom of youth, and the sorrow which hung over her features gave them an irresistible attraction. Her air of resigned dignity and feminine sweetness, was mingled with innocence and unconscious modesty. If I was inclined to pity her before, how greatly was that sentiment enlivened! Her faults seemed to vanish, or to be atoned by her misfortunes. Nothing could be more interesting than her first interview with Lady Scrope, whose tears alone could express her sorrow and affection.

"How must a scene, which distressed me, touch a heart prepared to love her! The Duke found there was a passion stronger than ambition; her crown no longer engrossed his thoughts, it was herself alone he desired; he lamented the evils it had overwhelmed her with, and from which, even her resignation of it, would not relieve her. Love communicated all its delicacies at once to his heart; and the man who had dared aspire to her, while in prosperity and peace, in this sad moment of humiliation had not presumption to lift his eyes to her, to speak of his affection, or insult her by his compassion.

"Lady Scrope was too quick-sighted to overlook this change in her brother; but far from drawing any ill presage from it, she flattered herself he was destined to restore the Queen, and to find in her gratitude and affection, a reward proportioned to his merit.

"Willing to relieve the tediousness of the hours, that Lady devised amusements of which no one partook, though all, from a just sense of the intention, appeared satisfied with them. The silence and melancholy of the Duke of Norfolk engaged the Queen; she found it a delicate compliment to her distress, and regarded him with an attention too flattering to be overlooked. Charmed with an esteem, which he had rather wished than hoped, the ardor of his soul found words, and Mary discovered, in attempting to attach a friend, she had gained a lover. Considering her interest only, she must have encouraged him; but, remembering how fatal her partiality might one day prove, she conjured him to subdue, while yet in its infancy, a passion it would be cruelty to encourage; to remember her only as an unfortunate friend, and in that light, confessed herself obliged to him for his interest and power in her favor.[40]

"In the first wildness of love, nothing seems impossible; an answer so mild, only animated the hope it was meant to extinguish. He formed a thousand projects, he engaged his sister in his interest, and every hour of his life was filled up by plans for the deliverance of the amiable Queen. But as it was impossible his residence should be a secret, and he justly feared awakening the attention of Elizabeth, before his schemes were ripe for execution, he engaged his sister to make a request, he wanted courage to mention; since she might, with more propriety, represent to the queen, the policy of rendering her fate his.

"In this dangerous conjuncture, the unfortunate Mary listened once more to the partial advice of her heart; which prompted her to yield to so noble, so deserving a lover. She had caught his frenzy, and realized the fictions of his brain with the same facility. His vast estates, numerous vassals, and still more, his extended and noble connections, flattered her with the hope of amply rewarding him, and she thought it but generous to let the recompence rather precede the service than follow it.

"Fatal delusion of a prejudiced mind! Oh Mary, too tender Princess! why were not all the past misfortunes of thy life, which had their source in love, monitors to thee?[41] Why did they not teach thee to avoid this error, which heightened every affliction, and gave new pangs to a long, long captivity?

"The Duke not daring to engage his brother-in-law in an action contrary to his commission, entrusted his intention only to his sister. Too ardent and too amiable an advocate to be denied, the Queen of Scots was persuaded by that Lady to unite herself with the Duke. They were married in the presence of the Lady Scrope and myself, Sir Arthur Forester,[42] and the Duke's two secretaries.

"Possessed in herself of all his wishes, the prison of the Queen became a palace to the Duke; and every hour seemed to add to a passion, which appeared at first incapable of addition.[43] The authority Mary had given him over her, the tenderness with which she regarded him, were powerful arguments against the approaching separation; but Lady Scrope saw with concern, the extravagance of a passion she had encouraged. She knew too well the temper of Elizabeth, not to anticipate her resentment, if this step was discovered, and knew likewise his own safety would be a poor motive, for persuading her brother to leave Bolton; she therefore represented to him, how ill he rewarded the lovely Queen of Scots, by lengthening an imprisonment it was his duty to curtail; and asked him what expectation Mary might form from a husband, who already preferred his own indulgence, to her freedom, happiness, and glory?

"These reproaches were too true to offend the Duke. He lamented, but yielded to the cruel necessity. Mary, as if forewarned that these hours were all the easy ones remaining of her life, used every means to detain him; but the generosity of her affection, awakening his more strongly, he bade adieu to the charming wife, he was never more to meet, and set out for London, to engage all his friends to favor a marriage, no one now could prevent. He flattered himself his interest was so great, that the Queen would be reduced to consent, whether consonant to her inclination or not. Indeed, this was the only rational mode of proceeding; for to imagine Elizabeth weak enough to unite her rival and heiress, voluntarily, to the first of her subjects, would have been an unpardonable blindness.[44]

"Fortune, however, had destined otherwise, and only smiled awhile, to make her frown more terrible. All the great Lords of Elizabeth's Court, who had seen, with regret, the imprisonment of Mary, entered with pleasure into Norfolk's schemes. His letters were filled with the most flattering hopes, and the Queen, who was with child, gave him notice of it. This circumstance added to his joy; he promised, before the time of her delivery, she should have her prison gates opened by all the nobility of England. The Earls of Shrewsbury, Derby, Bedford, Northumberland, Westmoreland, Pembroke, Southampton, Arundel, and Sussex, had warmly engaged in his cause; and their names alone would influence many.[45] But the friend he most relied upon, was the Earl of Leicester, whose ascendancy over the Queen was well known; he had taken on himself the disclosure of the whole to Elizabeth, when that measure became necessary.[46] In the mean time, Norfolk used every means to prevent the Regent of Scotland from accusing Mary to the Queen; nor was his artifice unsuccessful. Murray, after having entered England for no other purpose, suddenly returned, without taking any step in the business; a circumstance, which defeated all the measures of the English Court.[47] But Elizabeth more strongly apprehending from this some plot to release Mary, removed her to Tutbury, and added the Earl of Shrewsbury to Lord Scrope, as her keepers.[48]

"My sister still followed her, nor could I desert her in such a situation. We had hoped, from the information of the Duke, to find the Earl of Shrewsbury inclined to favor her; but whether he foresaw the end of this unfortunate project, or had deceived Norfolk, he kept a strict watch over the Queen's actions, whose condition now confined her to her apartment.

"The Duke, flattered by Murray's retreat, commissioned some of his friends in Scotland, to sound that nobleman on the subject of his marriage; they unwarily laid open more than he intended, and Murray, enraged at having been his dupe, sent notice of the plot to Elizabeth. She was on a visit to Lord Leicester, who was ill when the letter arrived; and confiding to that favorite, the cause of her agitation, he sent, while the Queen was consulting with Cecil, to warn Norfolk to retreat, as Elizabeth seemed bent on committing him to the Tower.[49] Thunderstruck at this unexpected discovery, the Duke set out, with precipitation, for his seat at Kenning-Hall; but, reflecting on the road, that his flight was a stronger proof against him than the accusation of his enemies, he returned directly; he was however met by some officers, sent in pursuit of him, and conducted to Burnham.[50]

"His Secretary posted[51] off to Tutbury with an account of all these proceedings. They sunk the deeper into the heart of the Queen, as she hoped, by this time, to have been at liberty. She was every hour in expectation of an event which must publish her marriage, or load her with infamy. In this hard trial, Lady Scrope suggested to her the only safe way of proceeding: which was, to convey her child, by means of the Duke's Secretary, immediately after its birth, out of the Castle, and concealing the cause of her indisposition, wait a more favorable moment for avowing her marriage. This was the only plan to avoid injuring the Duke's safety, or her own honour. To prepare every thing against the time, I took my leave of the Queen, as returning to St. Vincent's Abbey; and retiring to a neighbouring hut hired on purpose, waited with my maid, to receive the infant she should bring into the world, which was to be carried to the Recess, and placed under my care, till the fate of its parents could be ascertained.

"This sad moment was hastened by a sadder event:—Bothwell, who was supposed to be dead, found means to convey a letter to the Queen, assuring her the report had been spread only to quiet the Scots, who otherwise would never have suffered him to rest; and that he waited in Denmark till the divisions of her kingdom should enable him to raise a powerful party, and attempt her deliverance.[52] Mary, on the first sight of the well known hand, felt all the horrors of her fate; she fell into strong convulsions, which were succeeded by the pains of labor. She gave birth to two girls—for you, my dear children, are the fruit of this fatal marriage, who, scarce had been held to the bosom of a mother, before you were divided from it, I fear, for ever.

"The faithful Secretary conveyed you with the tenderest caution to me. When he repeated this sad tale, oh! how my soul wept for the ill-fated Queen! I vowed ye should be mine, for ye were the children of misfortune, and never,

never have I broke that vow; distress endeared me to you with a parental kindness, and fortune gave you to me to console me all her severity. 'Tis you only have kept alive in my heart the softest impulses of nature. You were cherubs in your infancy, and grew up to chear my days, and embellish my solitude. Full of the great charge vested in my hands, I sought the earliest opportunity of quitting a dangerous place; I brought you safe to this spot, attended by Alice, after having you baptized Matilda, the elder (which you was[53] by a few minutes) after Lady Scrope, and Ellinor after the Duke's mother.

"To return to the Queen of Scots.— She languished a long time between ill-health and despair; but the Duke found means to assure her that this misfortune should not long separate them. He applied now to the Pope to annul Mary's former marriage with Bothwell; the Pope hoping to find some great advantage in the projected union, seemed inclined to grant his request; but the conditions he imposed were so hard, that the Duke had no hope.[54]

"In the mean time, Elizabeth finding an effectual bar placed between Mary and Norfolk by Bothwell's being yet alive, and having some hopes from the ill-health of the Queen of Scots, of seeing an end of her fears, after conveying her to Coventry, she released the Duke, at the intercession of his constant friend Lord Leicester.[55] Sensible of the rashness of his former conduct, he resolved to avoid that fault, and made no attempt to see the Queen of Scots, employing himself in hunting and diversions at Kenning-Hall, till the spies of Elizabeth, persuaded he had laid aside his projects, gave up their employment.[56] The Duke past from the seat of one friend to that of another, to appearance in search of amusement, but in reality to assure himself of their attachment; and, as if by accident, to visit St. Vincent's Abbey, and embrace the daughters of his love. You were a twelvemonth old when I conducted the Duke in the night to this Recess. The captivity and sad situation of his wife arose a thousand times more strongly to his mind when he beheld her children torn from her bosom as if the product of dishonour, and hid in solitude from every human eye; to see, and know he could not prevent this, pierced him to the very soul. He spent the night in viewing you, in recommending you to Heaven, in forming a thousand silent complaints against his destiny, and resolutions, which by shortening his life, perpetuated on you the evils he sought to remedy. But when the dawn of day compelled him to return to his apartment, he again took you both in his arms, and while the tears of paternal affection flowed gracefully down his cheeks, poured on you a thousand blessings; he then gave you to me, and while I was stilling Ellinor, he sat in a deep reverie, when suddenly starting from it, he came and stood by me, and taking my hand—

"'I have yet hopes, my dear Mrs. Marlow,' said he, 'of bringing these infants into life, as the daughters of the loveliest, the most amiable of sovereigns; till when, I commit them to you, as the most sacred of all deposits. Teach them to enjoy an humble rank, and they will adorn a high one; keep them in total ignorance of their birth till able to know its inutility. But if Heaven never allows me to claim them,—if the misfortunes of their parents end but with their lives, act up to the sacred character with which I alike invest you and my sister. Never let them know the Court of Elizabeth, but innocently and happily let them die in the desert where they bloomed.'

"Shades of the honoured Howard and the amiable Mary, I have fulfilled your injunctions," exclaimed Mrs. Marlow, (turning with an enthusiastic action to the pictures I have mentioned with so much respect) "your words have been ever present to my memory, and my cares have not been useless."

"Alas, Madam," said we, dropping with an emotion of awe on our knees, "are these lovely figures the portraits of our parents? Oh! my father, my tender unhappy father! shall we never see you? Were we never to be held in your arms but while insensible of that blessing? and you, my dear mother, who brought us forth in bitterness and pain, shall we not spend our lives in softening yours, and shed our sorrows upon your grave?"

"You interrupt, and distress me, children," said Mrs. Marlow, "let me finish my melancholy tale; you will, alas! have hours enough for complaint.

"The Duke departed the next day, and in a short time, Elizabeth having appointed Lords Huntingdon and Hereford in the room of Lord Scrope, the Queen of Scots was deprived of her only comfort, by the departure of his Lady.[57]

"The Duke, finding gentle attempts ineffectual, resolved on a measure he deemed infallible, and entered into a treaty with a trusty Spaniard named Ridolpho, to engage the Duke of Alva to assist him with ten thousand men, to be landed at Harwich, from whence they were to march to London, to intimidate Elizabeth. The Duke of Alva consented, and even the Pope at length ashamed of neutrality, took a share in Mary's deliverance.[58] Every thing was prepared; Norfolk's friends in England only waited the signal to join him, when one of those trifling accidents which disconcert the wisest schemes, rendered this in a moment abortive.

"To foment the divisions in Scotland so much as to keep the Regent employed, and prevent him from interfering in the affair, the Duke sent many sums to be scattered among the Queen's friends, in that kingdom, at different times;—but now when the crisis approached, he had prepared a large bag of gold, which with a letter he unfortunately trusted to a man quite ignorant of the plot; the carrier, in putting it up, by some accident cut the bag, and the contents filling him with astonishment, he communicated this singular discovery to a servant of Lord Burghley's,[59] who was his brother; this man, through a hope of getting the gold between them, and supposing some mystery was hid in the letter, persuaded him to shew it to his master; the carrier consented, and Lord Burghley easily perceiving the plot, though not its extent, communicated it to the Queen; in consequence of which the Duke was arrested in his bed, and all his servants imprisoned.

"This fatal stroke overturned every remaining hope; betrayed by his servants, all the letters the Duke had written and received on the subject, most of which he had ordered to be burnt, were produced against him; his very benevolence was construed into a crime, and some money he sent to the Countess of Northumberland, who was in exile and distress with her Lord, became an article in his impeachment. He was condemned, and heard his sentence with a fortitude which melted Lord Shrewsbury, who pronounced it, into tears.[60]

"Lady Scrope, distracted at her brother's fate, fell at the feet of the Queen, and left nothing unsaid to move her; but all she could obtain was the deferring his execution, for Burghley had so strongly prepossessed Elizabeth with the idea that the Duke sought her life, that although no circumstances arose to confirm it on his trial, nothing could banish it from her mind.[61]

"But what was the situation of the Queen of Scotland at this completion of her misfortunes! An exile from her own country, a prisoner in another, a wife without a right to that name, and a mother, while a stranger to her children; her fate was wound up in the condemnation of her husband; and she had the poignant affliction of knowing she had raised the axe against him, which all her tears could not avert. Pierced with despair, she conjured the Lady Scrope to assure the Queen she would not only voluntarily consent to remain her prisoner for life, but would give up her claim to the Crown of England, if her sister (as she was compelled to stile her) would free the Duke of Norfolk, and restore him to his honors. This proposal Elizabeth received as a finesse, from which she saw how deeply Mary's heart was linked with his. Even the all-prevailing Leicester's eloquence failed; self-preservation was an unconquerable principle in the soul of Elizabeth.[62]

"The Duke was beheaded fourteen years ago, when you, my dear children, who were bought with his life, were not above two years and a half old.[63] He died as he had lived, with dignity and honour.[64]

"Never was nobleman more lamented: he had endeared himself to the body of the people by his courage, generosity, and affability; and to his equals, by an unconsciousness of superiority, which prevented envy, and an uniformity of conduct, which gained admiration.[65] He was the first victim to the Queen's fears, nor could she have chosen one whose merits were stronger proofs of the value she set on herself.

"Lady Scrope detesting too late the artifices of the Court, and sunk in affliction for the loss of a brother she adored, retired hither with her Lord, who had thrown up his employments. Her body partook of the debility of her mind, and soon gave symptoms of a decay, which reduced her to the grave.

"Her temper too was quite changed. This Recess, which so lately appeared a horrible dungeon, now seemed to her, as to me, a calm retirement from the odious forms and cares of life. She spent many days (and would every one, had it not afflicted her Lord) in weeping over you; in tracing in Matilda the mildly-beautiful features of her friend, and in Ellinor, the captivating graces of her brother. 'Tis to her you owe these valuable pictures.[66]

"Estranged from all society, the Queen of Scots gave herself up to the blackest despair; she had, alas! no hope to soften her captivity, no bosom to receive her tears; with Norfolk died all prospect of release, and at the same time all desire of it; what was the universe to her without he embellished it? Would it not have augmented her affliction to have enjoyed a sovereignty she durst never hope to share with him?

"Elizabeth, whose fears were always awake from this moment, cut her daily off from some comfort or convenience; frequently changed her keepers and prison; and by her severity, taught the captive Queen that hatred may be stronger even than love.[67]

"Lady Scrope survived her brother but a twelvemonth, and left no inheritor of her virtues. She recommended you both in the most fervent manner to her Lord, who solemnly swore to make a provision for you suitable to his fortune, though not your birth.

"Some years past away, when Lord Scrope, whose grief was at an end, finding himself tired of the inactivity of a country life, accepted some overtures the Queen made to recall him. He left to me the charge of St. Vincent's Abbey; which he has not inhabited since.

"Hurried on by other events, I have hitherto neglected to mention the return of my brother Anthony, in three years after I brought you here. He fixed his residence in the hermit's cell, devoting his time to the study of physic, and the care of exhorting the poor, except at those hours you have seen him in; for his life and mine have been uniform.

"I have only two circumstances more to mention; one of which is more afflicting to me, than I once believed, aught respecting money, could ever be.

Lord Scrope, who has been abroad some years in a public character, has become the object of the crafty Burghley's hatred, or suspicion, and is now confined; while his estates and wealth are seized by the Queen, who knows so well the value of money, that it is too probable my Lord will never be able to fulfil the promise made to his wife in your favor.[68]

"The other is, that during several past years, I have not been able to hold any intelligence with the Queen of Scotland, who sent me some letters during the first years of her imprisonment, which, with those she wrote to the Duke, I have preserved, with various other testimonials of your birth. Time may enable her yet to give you the splendor to which you were born; for Elizabeth is now stricken in years, and Mary more worn by sorrow than age.[69] Wait then, my dear children, with patience, when I am in my grave, the destination of providence, and never claim your parent till she pleases to acknowledge you. No virtue is more acceptable to God than patience. To bestow happiness, is only in his power; to deserve it, ever in our own. Oh! if my prayers are heard! if my wishes ascend to the throne of the Most High, he will lead you through this world in peace; he will unite you again to my bosom, in a better!"

Here our generous protectress, our more than mother, ended, clasping us to her heart with an ardor that evinced the sincerity of her words.

But what new ideas; what amazing feelings did her narration give birth to! The impulses of nature taught us to treasure every word she uttered; for what in the history of our parents could be indifferent? Never did our solitude appear so amiable—"the Court of Elizabeth!"— Oh my lamented father, could the sole inflictor of all thy evils, ever, ever attach thy children! Could she who oppressed her equal, and a Queen, innocent at least in all that respected her, only because she was in her power, be capable of alluring two hearts, untainted by that courtly politeness, which sanctifies the errors of a sovereign, and terms her very vices noble weaknesses?

But then, to learn I had a mother yet alive; to believe I might one day be received to her arms, only endeared by misfortune; full of this melting, this heart-expanding idea, I would have sought her prison; I would have been the companion of it:[70] happy, if all my cares could make her forget for one moment, the rigour of her fortune; or call to her remembrance, amidst all her complaints, against the injustice of the world, that it still contained two beings who were willing to return for her the life she gave.

My duty to Mrs. Marlow alone divided my heart: should I desert her, who had neglected every thing for us? What! are the ties of nature to cancel, in one moment, those of inclination, gratitude, and esteem? Oh, no! I owed, it is true, my being to another; but she to whom I owed the best part of that being, the formation of my mind, the instilling those sentiments which alone make us valuable to ourselves and society, had a claim beyond all others, which nothing but death could dissolve. That awful moment was drawing nigh; every one that passed, stole something from the mortal part of Mrs. Marlow. Oh thou amiable saint! thou woman after God's own heart! can I remember the time when thou wert called from us, without floods of unavailing tears? Never—never—selfish as they are, they will flow, even though so often exhausted.

She delivered us a casket, which contained the papers she mentioned, and divers attestations, signed by herself, and the late Lady Scrope, and filled with all the ornaments of her youth. [71] Then, after recommending us tenderly to Father Anthony, she joined in prayer with him, and all her little family; and in the midst, expired.

Oh, Madam, how strange, how terrible to me, was that moment! I saw Death first seize on one dearer than myself: the mansion in which we lived, now became a solitude indeed—a silence—how solemn! prevailed. In the first flow of a rational grief, how vast a vacuum is left in the heart! to hear no longer the voice which led us through life: to see the eyes, whence ours drew fortitude, close, never more to open: the whole frame assume that awful pallidness, every moment increases, and which brings so melancholy a memento to the breast! These touching ideas cannot always arise, for some losses destroy the power of reflection and complaint.

To attempt interring the dust of Mrs. Marlow in the chapel, must have awakened the suspicions of the Queen's officers. The secret of our retirement was in the breast of only three domesticks, and it was highly necessary to keep it concealed. On this account, a grave was made for her in Father Anthony's cell, whither we conveyed her, wrapt in white, and crowned with the fading produce of this world, in imitation of that ever-blooming wreath promised hereafter to all, who persevere in virtue.

Grief makes the most violent impression in youth; but, happily, it is the most transient: a little time abated the acuteness of ours; nevertheless, our solitude being deprived of its ornament, appeared uniform, melancholy, and disgusting. We gradually lost our assiduity in our works, when we no longer promised ourselves the great reward of her praise. Father Anthony, who was never a favourite with us, became every day more unpleasant. Mrs. Marlow had always preserved a sway over him, which softened the severity of his manners: that being now at an end, and his temper still more hurt by his affliction for her loss, he appeared a gloomy tyrant; and the additional carefulness with which he observed us, laid an odious restraint on all our expressions, and made our meals wear an air of sullenness each party was unconscious of causing.

Obliged to hide in our hearts all the little follies and wishes we had been used to reveal to Mrs. Marlow without fear, we conversed with the Father only upon moral and indifferent topics; thus every day was the same, and each of course more tedious, when Ellinor suggested a scheme which promised some amusement. This was to explore the passage leading to the ruins, where we might at least breathe the fresh air, and, for one hour, have the pleasure of a little novelty. I readily came into the proposal, having had a curiosity to emerge from the moment I heard that passage first mentioned. It was the full height of summer, and we pitched upon a long afternoon, when we had no fear of being sought for.

The passage was narrower, closer, and damper than the others, but very short. We took a torch that we might find the way of opening it. When we drew near the mouth, I observed some little holes, made doubtless to give the concealed person an advantage. I made Ellinor keep back while I examined the place, but saw nothing, however, to awaken any apprehension; a long avenue of broken arches, intermingled with brambles and wild wall-flowers, in the paths of which the grass grew very high, was all I could discern—nothing could more fully prove the unfrequentedness of the spot.[72] We therefore examined the fastening immediately, and found it a small square door with two hinges on the top, and fastened across the bottom by a large bar of iron laid on strong hooks. I was unable to open it alone; Ellinor therefore extinguished the light to assist me; but with all our curiosity and courage, the sight of the pile of ruins threw us into an universal trepidation. On turning round, to observe how the entrance was hid, we perceived a high raised tomb, at each corner of which stood a gigantic statue of a man in armour, as if to guard it, two of whom were now headless. Some famous knight, as appeared by his numerous ensigns, lay on the tomb. The meagre skeleton had struck an arrow through his shield into his heart; his eyes were turned to the cross which St. Winifred held before him. Nothing could be better contrived than this entrance, for however rude the sculpture, the ornamental parts took the eye from the body of the tomb. The little door, which dropt after us, was one stone, lined with wood, and so neatly fitted, that even when unfastened, it was not to be discerned. For a long way beyond, the prospect was wild and awful to excess; sometimes vast heaps of stones were fallen from the building, among which, trees and bushes had sprung up, and half involved the dropping pillars. Tall fragments of it sometimes remained, which seemed to sway about with every blast, and from whose mouldering top hung clusters and spires of ivy. In other parts, ruined cloisters yet lent a refuge from the weather, and sullenly shut out the day; while long echoes wandered through the whole at the touch of the lightest foot; the intricacies of the wood beyond, added to the magnificence of art the variety of nature. We quitted, with regret, our new empire, when the sun left his last rays on the tops of the trees.

We resolved to conceal our ramble, lest Father Anthony should forbid us to repeat it. Those, Madam, who would maintain a lasting sway over young people, must, by softening the distance of age, steal into their confidence. Love and respect are united, but if fear once closes the avenues to the heart, no other sentiment ever overcomes it; obedience is then never led by inclination, and we rejoice to escape from haughtiness or austerity, however venerable the form they assume.

From what trifles spring the purest pleasures of life! a prospect, a flower, a song, can dilate the heart, while the passions are yet hid in it, nor have poisoned its simplicity, and curtailed its enjoyments.

Concealed pleasures are allowed to be the greatest; nor can any remark be more just; to deceive the watchful, reflects a compliment on our own sagacity, which renders us insensible to the error.

Almost every day did we visit this darling spot, always, like young birds, venturing one step further; and so often had we ventured without seeing a human being, that, at last, we ceased to fear. On one side the wood shelved down for a considerable way, beyond which the road was cut, and mingled with hamlets that gave a promise of society, which the rusticity of their inhabitants would not allow them to fulfil.

But you reproach me with losing time in uninteresting descriptions.— Ah, Madam! this wood was not always a desert.[73] Chance, or, rather I should say, Providence, led into its solitary windings, the man, of all Elizabeth's Court, the most distinguished and admired; the man to whom nature had been prodigal of every advantage, which art and application had polished to the highest perfection.

One day, in calling my sister, I discovered in the hollow of the wood and building, a very fine echo; delighted with this, I began singing; the notes dying distinctly away, formed a melancholy symphony, when I was interrupted by Ellinor, who quitting some birds that flew tamely to be fed by her hand, ran toward the Recess with great speed, waving to me to follow her. We had so often alarmed each other without any cause, that I hardly moved, when a noise I heard among the trees (which grew extremely thick on that spot) alarmed me. A voice, that sunk at once from my ear to my heart, conjured me in the most earnest manner to stop. Notwithstanding the necessity I found for flying, my eyes longed to claim acquaintance with the features to which that voice belonged, and my head, by an involuntary motion, was turned over my shoulder. The gentleman had now made a way through the shrubs which impeded his passage, and I found it impossible to retreat but by discovering a secret it was highly my interest to conceal. Perhaps I was not sorry to have an excuse to my own heart for a rashness it was too sensible of. The irresolution of my attitude, which was that of a person ready every moment to run, made him approach with profound submission and respect; but finding me attempt to fly, though almost without knowing it, he instantly stopt.

"By whatever chance," said he, "nature has hid in this sequestered spot her fairest productions, permit me, ladies, to derive an advantage from it. Believe me, you see a man who needs too much your compassion and assistance to venture to insult you, were such a thought capable of intruding into a heart never yet inhuman. Let me conjure you, then, to judge of my intentions by your own, and allow me, if you know of an asylum (and are not, like me, driven here by some present distress) to shelter myself from assassins too well prepared to take my life, for courage to preserve it."

The person of him who pronounced these words, made their effect indelible. He appeared something past the bloom of life, but his beauty was rather fixed than faded; of a noble height and perfect symmetry, he would have had an air too majestic, but that the sweetness of his eyes and voice tempered the dignity of his mien. His complexion was of a clear and polished brown; his eyes large, dark, and brilliant; his hair gracefully marked the turn of all his features, and his dress was of a dove-coloured velvet, mingled with white sattin and silver; a crimson sash inwoven with gold, hung from his shoulder with a picture; and the order of the garter,[74] as well as a foreign one, with which he was invested, shewed his rank not less distinguished than his person.

Astonishment—anxiety—a thousand rapid ideas melting into each other, and, defying language, confused and silenced me; when Ellinor, more mistress of her own judgment, took upon her to answer, by directing him to Father Anthony's cell, assuring him at the same moment, that this was all we could do to serve him.— "Ah, Ellen!" cried I, passionately seizing her hand, "he then must return and be murdered!" Struck with the vehemence of my own words, my eyes sunk to the ground, and changeable blushes covered my features, which redoubled when the stranger took my hand, with a grace all his own, and bowing on it.

"To your generous intention, Madam, I shall at least be a debtor—this is not a time or place for deliberation—fly, I beseech you, while you are yet able;

the villains who pursue me, may not respect your youth, your beauty, or your innocence, and nothing could so greatly add to my misfortune as the involving you in it. If heaven lengthens my days, I may, perhaps, be able to convince you, him you wished to save is not unworthy your concern; if, on the contrary, this proves my last, I have only to request you will deliver this (untying and giving me the picture) to the Queen, who will not fail to distinguish the bearer."

How, how did every word penetrate my heart—Ah! how rapid is the progress of passion, and how, in one moment, does it quicken, nay, double every sense and sensibility![75] I could, with the same ease, have exposed my own bosom to the assassins as his. Fear surmounted every prudential consideration, and I was only going to use the caution of enquiring who he was, when the sound of voices, not far distant, put that out of my head. Retaining, in mine, the hand which had hitherto held it, I led him through the most solitary arches to the foot of the tomb; but our astonishment at sight of him, bore no comparison with his, when he found this to be our habitation. The time not admitting any explanation, he assisted us to enter, and followed himself; when leaving Ellinor to watch the approach of those we had heard, I conducted him into the large room of the Recess. With an impatient gratitude, he fell at my feet to thank me for my anxiety, but instantly starting back, he threw me into such a trepidation, that I sunk into a seat without power to look behind me, imagining either that the murderers, or at least, Father Anthony, must be at hand; when looking around him, and at me by turns, he exclaimed,

"Merciful heaven! by what strange ordination of thine do I find, in this desart, two dead portraits of my unhappy friend, and the Queen of Scots, and two breathing ones more lovely than even themselves?"

Imagine my distress at such a speech. I saw in one moment, the whole of a secret preserved with such caution for so many years, committed to a stranger by an indiscretion, which still I could not condemn in myself. Fluctuating with all the irresolution of youth, I now knew not whether I ought to deny the truth of what he had averred, or repose, in turn, a confidence in his honour; but the time I had spent in deliberating convinced him; for my confusion was an affirmative nothing could overcome.

"You are silent, Madam," cried he, "but your eloquent eyes imply a doubt it is my duty to clear. Oh! if I was capable of wronging your confidence, or betraying any secret you wish concealed, heaven would have abandoned me to the fate from which its fairest daughters saved me. Look but at that picture, and you will find an indubitable evidence of my sincerity."

It was the picture of Elizabeth, given by herself to Robert Dudley,[76] as the inscription informed me.

"Ah! have I then," returned I, "been the happy means of discharging the debt long owing to Lord Leicester?"

"How, how have I been so fortunate," returned he, "as to distinguish myself to you? If I durst believe, and yet it must be so—for how should a less lovely mother give being to such children, and how, otherwise, should such matchless beauty and elegance be hid in a desart! Tell me, I conjure you, Madam, whether my past friendship with the Duke of Norfolk, does not intitle me to yours?"

"It does, indeed, my Lord," cried I, (bursting into tears at the name of my father) "to my eternal gratitude. Your frank avowal sets me above all dissimulation; I dare own to you, that you have guessed my birth most truly."

"But, why then were you buried in this solitude? Why not acknowledged in France?"—

"Ah, my Lord! might I not, with much more reason demand, how the favorite of Elizabeth came unattended and alone to seek, in these woods, an asylum from assassins?"

"I will reply to you with candor, Madam," added he, "and thus bespeak your confidence. The favor of a sovereign may easily make us great, but many circumstances must concur to make us happy; and when you hear some events of my life, I dare promise myself your compassion."

Ellinor, having executed her commission, rejoined us at this moment. I will frankly confess I wished her absence, and had imposed a task on her I could never have executed. The presence of Lord Leicester had awakened in my mind a thousand hopes and wishes unknown before. Not recollecting the improbability of his passing so many years without forming tender attachments, almost unconsciously I aspired to his heart; and my apprehension of Ellinor's superior charms had made me meanly cheat her of an opportunity of making a first impression: by submitting to my injustice she rendered me sensible of it in the most generous manner, and the care I then took to display her merit, induced my Lord to imagine I regarded him with indifference. Thus I reaped a double advantage from my return to rectitude.

My sister informed us, she had seen four men examining every part of the ruins: assured Lord Leicester must be hid among them, as one had picked up his hat (which he doubtless dropt when he addressed me) and swearing never to quit the wood till they had found him, they separated to pursue the search.

I turned pale at this terrible intelligence, which made his departure impossible; but as we every moment expected Father Anthony, who might have a share in the alarm the assassins would occasion, we agreed to hide my Lord in Mrs. Marlow's chamber, which had been hitherto deserted, and a place where none but ourselves would seek him.

It was now evening, and as the age and infirmities of our maid rendered her rather an incumbrance than relief, we set before Lord Leicester a repast, perhaps more adapted to his health than his appetite, but all our Retreat at that time afforded; and, withdrawing, left him that we might be ready if our guardian should visit us.

As I would not have you imagine, however we were indebted to nature, the surprise Lord Leicester expressed, sprung only from our beauty, I must observe to you, we drest to the taste of Mrs. Marlow, rather than that of any country; and those habits which covered happy hearts, preserve a long superiority in the fancy. Close jackets and coats, of pale grey, were trimmed round the skirts and sleeves with black bugle fringe; the collars were thrown back from the throat and chest with point lace, and tied at the bosom with black tassels; our hair, which was very thick, covered our necks and foreheads, falling in rings from under cambrick coifs;[77] small beaver hats, with high crowns, and waving black feathers, completed our appearance, at once too rustic and too elegant not to strike every person. Simplicity is the perfection of dress, and Ellinor presents herself in that I have described, more beautiful than when adorned with all the gaudy trappings pride and luxury has invented. She had an arch, a smiling eye, which, while it indicated observation, teemed with good nature; a complexion perfectly fair, and delicately heightened by a bloom which came from the heart, as its changeableness implied; a graceful stature, and a manner which won almost every one to love her half as well as I did. But I need not expatiate on my Ellen's character; though dormant at present, it will soon demand your compassion in the hardest trials of life.

Love, Madam, is the parent of art. When we left Lord Leicester, without declaring my own sentiments concerning him, I sought to penetrate into my sister's, for that constant error of a first passion had infected me, and I fancied the man who had subdued my heart, might those of all my sex; every glance increases a fear so exquisite; I thought constantly I read in her eyes ideas afflictingly similar to my own; yet the lively sense she expressed at our indiscretion, which she easily conceived would put us in the power of Elizabeth's favorite, made me very doubtful; for although the same apprehension occurred to me, the confidence I already had in his honour, and the strong anxiety I felt for his life, made it a faint and distant alarm.

This night I first found my rest disturbed by the reflections of my mind.

I hoped one moment every thing. I flattered myself the simplicity of my education, and the purity of my heart, would, by a contrast with those of the
court, atone for the want of that polish a court alone can give; the obscurity of
my birth, I found too sensibly a misfortune, and withdrawing my compassion
for the first time from my parents, bestowed it on myself. Yet again would I
say, can he despise the daughter of his friend? Will he destine me to suffer for
an indiscretion in which I had no share! Oh! let me judge his heart by my
own, which already feels the sovereignty of the universe would be too little for
happiness, if he was not to partake it.

The calm rest of my sister set my heart at ease respecting her; I told[78]
every moment as it passed, anxiously expecting that in which Lord Leicester
was to begin his narration. I had exhausted the few misfortunes my imagination suggested, without being able to find any which could, in so well-governed a country, reduce a man of his distinction to flight; but how, untainted
with the vices of the world, could I guess at the real one?[79]

Without acquainting Lord Leicester, who had the conduct of our education, we made him sensible we had reasons for concealing him from every
person; he had too much politeness to press for an explanation, and we were
compelled to leave him alone till the departure of Father Anthony should give
us an opportunity to listen to his history.

The Father, always slow and deliberate, seemed this day to have gained
an addition to those qualities; instead of retiring after dinner, as usual, he
began a long discourse (from a momentary impatience I had discovered through
some trifling occasion) on the subduing our passions, every word of which
augmented mine, and the less we seemed sensible of his argument, the more
he became inclined to prolixity, till my impatience having arisen to the greatest height, allayed of itself; and I learnt, nothing but acquiescing in all he
advanced, could put a period to the tedious conversation. This finesse succeeded: he departed, and without staying a moment longer than was necessary to ascertain that circumstance, we released the Earl, and conducted him
to our great room, as we call it.

Lord Leicester did not delay to gratify our curiosity, but began his story
thus: (for to prevent the coldness a relater always gives to events, and as almost
the very words are familiar to my memory, whenever a narration occurs, I, in
justice to the person concerned, shall give him the power of speaking for
himself.)

"Sprung from a family too distinguished to be unknown to you, ladies,
I might pass over the early part of my life in silence, did not one circumstance
in it account for the honours and favours my royal mistress has delighted to

shower upon me. The last of five sons, I was too young to be sensible of the loss when my unhappy family were sacrificed to their own ambition and episcopal tyranny. Without any fortune, and obnoxious to those who had trembled at the very name of Northumberland, no happier fate had awaited me from the persecutions of Mary's reign (a time which will fill the latest with horror) had not the Earl of Arundel generously screened me from her rage. He had me conducted from a seat of my father's, bestowed on him by the Queen, to Hubert Hall, a noble one of his own, where I was educated with his children, without being known to the world.[80] The kindness of this nobleman well deserves commemoration, since to the compassion awakened by my youth and helpless state, nothing was added but a grateful remembrance of a small favour the Lord Guilford[81] had shewn him, at a time when his religion was more feared, though less punished, than ours then was.[82] Sensible of all his generosity, I neglected nothing to prove my gratitude; and habit giving me the same advantage in his affection with his own children, he seemed to take pleasure in numbering me among them, and proposed to unite me to one of his daughters, who had from her infancy entertained a partiality for me. Fate was against him; for of the four lovely children he had when I was added to the number, I saw him without one, before I was fifteen. These losses, far from souring his temper, only softened it; he bent himself more intently on establishing me in all his fortunes, and was not without hopes of obtaining the reversion of his title for me. Miss Lineric, the daughter of his sister, and the heiress of a large fortune, besides what she might hope from him, was the lady he made choice of for me; and the agreement was formed with her father and guardians, without my knowledge; nor did I venture to refuse my consent, when it was demanded; although I had never seen the lady, and found my heart utterly repugnant to a match in which it had no share.[83]

"The princess Elizabeth (whose noble endurance of an unjust imprisonment, will reflect eternal honour on her prudence) was, during the life of her sister, kept in close captivity;[84] various Lords, as various fears obliged them to change, had the charge of her; the Earl of Arundel was for a short time entrusted with the important office, and thus was I early introduced to the knowledge of that pious lady. Far from extending the prejudices she might justly have imbibed against my family to myself, she was pleased to honour me with her notice; to take amusement in polishing my manners and accomplishing my mind. Brought up a Catholic, it was to her I owed the enlightening of my understanding, and the discretion to conceal a difference of opinion from my benefactor, which might have alienated, and perhaps broken his heart.

"My attachment to her was as great as her own goodness; I longed, with the ardour of youth, to signalize myself in her service; nor was it long before an occasion offered. The Earl of Devonshire, actuated, either by love or ambition, flattered himself that the Princess's captivity would make her gladly embrace a proposal of marriage: he engaged many noblemen who favoured the Protestant religion in the scheme, and he imagined nothing was necessary towards obtaining her consent but her knowledge of the design.[85] To effect this, he disguised himself as a gardener, and worked several days in the hope of seeing Elizabeth, but in vain; for the Queen's orders were so strict, that she was allowed for exercise only a long gallery with latticed windows, which joined to her apartment. The awkwardness of the Earl in his new employment, of which I was fond, and consequently a competent judge, caught my attention; I spoke to him, and the involuntary tremor, caused by a fear of detection, strengthened my suspicion; he eluded my questions with too much exactness, to be what he affected; and this I mentioned casually to the Princess, while entertaining her in the gallery: she listened to what I said attentively, and then walking to the window, desired me to point out the man, who was sitting to rest himself, with his eyes fixed intently on the house; Elizabeth remained at the window buried in thought; at last, turning towards me, she demanded, if I esteemed her enough to run some hazard for her sake? I assured her with an eagerness proportioned to the desire I had to serve her, that she could command nothing I would not execute with joy. She replied, 'had not she expected such an answer, she had not ventured such a question;—what I wish then,' continued the Princess, 'is that, when you can find him alone, you will tell that man, I have seen, and know him; and since I cannot doubt but his intention is to render me some service, I request he will signify its nature by you; but as he may doubt the sincerity of a gentleman, whose interest seems so opposite to his own, shew him this jewel, he will remember it, and say I bid you tell him, that it was the gift of his father to me some years ago.'

"The Princess then took from her arm a remarkable diamond, and gave it to my care; I withdrew from her presence, and never did night seem longer than that I spent, before it was possible for me to execute her command; but resolved not to lose a moment, I arose very early, and placed myself in a thicket, through which I knew he must pass. His reluctance to mix with the daily labourers, whose happiness reaches not beyond a coarse meal, and a coarse jest, made him usually come alone, and when the rest were past, I saw him approach. Certain, without knowing who he was, that he must be a man of distinction, I drew near him with respect, and delivered my embassy; the confusion and doubt my address occasioned, vanished at sight of the diamond; he fell into raptures at the goodness of the Princess, and no words seemed sufficient to testify his gratitude for my service.

"Acquainted enough with the world to know the placing a confidence is the surest way of attaching a young mind, he made no secret of his name, and gave into my hands a letter as valuable to him as his life.

"Elizabeth, disgusted at the free hope he exprest, or perhaps unwilling to remove herself still farther from the throne by offending her sister, declined the proposal of the Earl, who neglected no instance to induce her to change her mind, as he could never hope to find a time so favourable for her escape: he fancied at last, I had an interest in her rejecting him, and when nothing could prevail with her, lavished all his reproaches on me, as the capital obstacle. I know not to what extremities he might have carried his resentment, had not Lord Arundel, to whom the head gardener had declared his suspicion of this man, from having found some jewels sewed in his garb, caused him to be apprehended; but his ill health and infirmities, disabling him from an immediate examination, notice was sent to the Court, and the Earl confined with caution. The Princess alarmed at this accident, which she foresaw her enemies would construe to her disadvantage, without giving her a chance to justify herself, forgot that calmness, which constituted in her early years the meritorious part of her character. I too sensibly felt her afflictions, not to participate in this; and to prove my sympathy, formed a design, which the romantic generosity incident to youth alone could justify.

"Intrusted with the charge of the criminal, it was very easy for me, in the dead of night, to set him free; but to render my generosity complete and ensure his escape, I ordered a horse to be in readiness in the thicket as for myself, and furnishing him with some clothes of my own, conducted him to the garden gate, and returned more satisfied with my own conduct than I ever yet had been.

"The consequences of his escape suggested themselves immediately to Lord Arundel on his receiving the information; he sent for me, as my connivance was evident, and enraged at my refusing even a reason for it, save the promise I had made, he ordered me to be confined, and dispatched a messenger to court with the full particulars of the prisoner's enlargement.[86] A short time, however, abated his resentment; he reproached himself for a rashness as culpable as my own, and sent several of his servants to stay the first, but not finding him return, he was pleased at once to forget my obstinacy, and, by coming to visit me, shew he pardoned my fault—He then told me he had nothing to propose, that would ensure my safety, but immediate flight; and not doubting that he could appease the Queen, recommended me to set out immediately for Ireland, to take refuge with his brother-in-law, Sir Patrick Lineric. Overwhelmed with his goodness, I had no way to atone for my error, but obedience, and prepared for my journey without hesitation;—the reluctance with which the Earl parted from me, was a cutting reproach; but heaven did not suffer me to escape unpunished: I was met on the road by a party of guards, conducted by the first messenger, who, ignorant of the change in Lord Arundel's resolution, imagined I was making my escape likewise, and conjured the officer to seize me: astonished at a stroke so unforeseen and unlucky, I delivered up my arms without resistance, and was conducted to the Tower of London.

"Some days elapsed without my seeing any but my guard, when I was conducted before the privy council, and interrogated concerning what I knew of the prisoner and his designs; but refusing to answer, I was remanded back to a closer dungeon and harder fare. This was repeated several times, insomuch that I was astonished at not being tried and sentenced by the law; when one day I was agreeably surprized at seeing Lord Arundel enter my prison. Want of air and proper food had so altered me, that the good man, neglecting his commission, wept like an infant on my neck; but recovering, and remembering he was not sent to console me, and had witnesses attending to report our discourse, he began with conjuring me, by every power he had over me, as a father, a guardian, and a friend, to provide for my own safety by a discovery of all I knew, without which my life would be devoted, in spite of his efforts, and the affliction of losing the only prop of his age, would infallibly shorten his days.

"The gentleness of this address, the concern which wrung every venerable feature, pierced my soul; and, although I could not betray the Princess, I will candidly confess I lamented my rash officiousness; but as repentance was fruitless, I had only to summon patience to endure an evil I had brought on myself; nevertheless, to afflict the benefactor, to whose goodness I owed all, was a trial indeed. I threw myself at his feet, I conjured him only to remember my obstinacy, to cast me from his heart, but never to employ a power I revered, to make me odious and contemptible,—assuring him, an honourable death was, in my eyes, infinitely more to be desired than a life prolonged by treachery and ingratitude.— He regarded me with attention, and after seeming to deliberate for a moment, he proceeded to offer me the most splendid rewards. I stopt him; 'oh, my Lord!' exclaimed I, 'can you think so meanly of the man before you, as to believe, after resisting your intreaties, he can poorly be bribed to do ill; how truly unworthy then were I of the name of your son?'

"'What can I say?' said he, turning to some men present, and drawing his hands from mine to clasp them together in an agony of grief; 'how seek to corrupt a constancy I admire? Adieu, my dear son, I am unequal to the task imposed on me. May the God who taught you principles so just, bless and protect you, whatever your fate; my days may still be fewer than yours, and this is, perhaps, an eternal farewell.— Adieu again, I will never forget you;' saying these words, he caught hold of some persons present, who rather carried than led him out.

"I had before this been supported by pride, but the sense of doing wrong, had never mingled with my feelings till now: my own life had hitherto presented nothing to make it particularly valuable; but that of Lord Arundel, was a blessing to himself and his country: and what right had I to shorten it? I, whose peculiar duty it was to watch over his decay, and smooth his passage to the grave; this remembrance gave me inexpressible grief.

"I found likewise that the court, from my resolution, imagined the plot of much more consequence than it really was; yet after so many denials I could not declare the whole, without bringing an imputation, more terrible than death on my memory: I therefore called together every reflection that could fortify my mind, and waited my fate with composure.

"A very few days after this interview put an end to the life of a Queen, whose cruelty cast a blot alike upon her sex and religion,[87] and Elizabeth being placed on the throne by the voice of the people, made the opening of my prison doors one of her first cares;—she did me the honour of seeing me in the garments I had worn in my confinement, and gave me her royal word that she could find no greater pleasure in her sovereignty, than that of rewarding my fidelity.

"An allay was prepared to this satisfaction; Lord Arundel had expired the night before of the gout in his stomach; but, knowing I might claim my safety from the new Queen, he had left me joint heir with his niece, of his estates, with only one condition, which was, that of marrying her; ordering the covenant should be fulfilled in two years, and if either party refused to comply, his or her share of the fortune should go to the other.— All the advantages I could have reaped, had he left me sole heir of his wealth, would never have recompensed me for his loss. This blow lessened the hopes of my life; I had promised myself in the first moments of my freedom, to convince this nobly disinterested friend, that independence could never lessen my gratitude, but would rather increase an attachment to which the malicious could then assign no motive but the just one.

"The Queen, in the first years of her reign, loaded me with honors, called me her knight, nor entered into any amusement in which I was not a party.[88] The obsequious behaviour of my equals, flattered a vanity latent in my heart, and persuaded me they saw deeper into her intentions than myself. I was much younger than Elizabeth, and involved in another engagement, yet the world thought she loved me; but being little disposed to matrimony, and by the Queen's bounty enabled to indulge myself, I gave up to Miss Lineric the estates of her uncle, without even seeing her, because I would not offend the relation of Lord Arundel, by giving the world reason to believe I did it from distaste. This circumstance no sooner reached the ear of the Queen, than it filled her with gladness visible to the whole Court, which confirmed them in the belief I was destined one day to share her rank. I had reason to be convinced, from many circumstances of the Queen's conduct, known but to myself, that she really had an affection for me, and only waited till some of the elder nobility, who were my rivals, had given up the pursuit, and till my years allowed her to make me her choice, without bringing a censure on her prudence.[89]

"Attached to Elizabeth rather by gratitude than affection, I had patience enough to wait her resolution, and entertained myself rather with the gaieties, than the politics of the kingdom. It was at this time the beautiful Mary of Scotland shone forth (fatally for herself) the rival of Elizabeth, and destroyed that peace which prosperity and admiration had contributed to bestow on our Queen. In the adversity of her youth, she flattered herself with supporting a superiority over her oppressor by a discreet submission; but to meet with so powerful a rival in beauty, talents, and empire, when at the summit of her glory, was a stroke as mortifying as unexpected: Elizabeth ever sickened at the name of Mary, and, by extravagant praises, pointed the severe remarks she continually made on her conduct.[90] She maintained with a rigid exactness the advantages she possessed, from the situation of her kingdom, over her neighbour, and continually affected to chuse her a husband from the handsome and dissolute nobles of her Court.[91] Melvil, the Scotch Ambassador, among other presents to Elizabeth, brought with him a picture of the Queen of Scots; it was done by a French artist exquisitely skilled; this little portrait Elizabeth always wore hanging to her breast: I never beheld it without admiring the finest imitation art could execute of the most finished production of nature. One evening while the Queen was conversing with me, my eyes, by a kind of habit, were fixed on this ornament: she suddenly rose, and retired in great wrath to her apartment. She shut herself up three days before the extravagance of her resentment permitted her to form any resolution; at last the Countess of Somerset came to me with the picture, and an assurance from the Queen, that as she perceived I could never be happy without the original, she should alter her designs, and had directions to the Earl of Bedford to propose me to Mary.

"Thunderstruck at so excessive and ridiculous a jealousy, I neglected nothing to satisfy the Queen; I made a thousand protestations of my indifference to the Queen of Scots in vain; Elizabeth's pride was offended, and that was the hardest to appease of all her passions—she insisted on my keeping the picture, and haughtily forbad me ever to remember her but as my sovereign.

"I retired from her presence piqued by her haughtiness, which, though a quality adapted to her rank, is disgusting in her sex. The picture of Mary was yet in my hand—when I remembered the sweetness and affability she was famed for, the infinite superiority of her charms, and the softness of her character, I was grateful to Elizabeth for her anger; since it broke the ties my gratitude had formed, and left me in hope of a happier fate.— I repented a message I had sent off to the Earl of Bedford to forbid his mentioning my name, and only wished it might arrive too late.— In my union with Elizabeth I saw I must be a cypher, for she was jealous to excess of her power: with Mary I might share a kingdom, and, by studying her humour, render her and myself happy. All our wishes are not, however, to be successful. The Queen of Scots, prepossessed that Elizabeth intended to raise me to the throne of England, believed the proposal a jest, and treated it as such. The Earl of Bedford gave into this, from a conviction that he should oblige me by it, and thus I found myself, after having aspired to two Queens, without hopes of either.[92]

"From the moment of my being neglected by Elizabeth, I had found myself in the condition of those favorites who fall from the pinnacle of greatness to obscurity. After seeing my presence make a circle, and my apartment a Court, I appeared alone, or continued in solitude. Vanity, and not generosity, had governed me, and of those who followed, no one really loved, and all envied me; they rejoiced in my disgrace, and ridiculed my ambition. What shall I say, ladies? shall I give false motives for my actions, or confess faults my youth may excuse? I must be sincere, whether that sincerity interests you in my favour or otherwise.[93]

"Resolved at all events to have the pleasure of mortifying my enemies— I wrote to the Queen, assuring her, the honors she had loaded me with, were incumbrances, since she had withdrawn her favor, and if my offence (unwitting as it was) exceeded forgiveness, I requested to resign my employments and retire to Kenilworth.[94] This letter I took an opportunity of presenting to her in the gardens of Sheen,[95] and, far from pronouncing a severe sentence, she was pleased to shed tears, and tenderly reproach me on the lightness of my attachment; on which I took the picture of the Queen of Scots, and casting it

into the Thames, entreated her to bury with it the remembrance of my fault.—
She gave me her hand to kiss, and I had the pride of leading her to the Court,
re-instated in her favor.

"This disgrace taught me a useful lesson; which was to employ my power
but to serve the worthy, the only way to secure friends and avoid making
enemies. I learnt how to rate justly all who surrounded me, to despise flattery,
and by never elevating myself, put it out of the power of malice or envy in
future to humiliate me. The Queen was pressed by the Parliament to marry;
she had promised to deliberate on the proposal, and my interest in her heart,
made me hope a favorable conclusion to my suit, when an unfortunate chance
overturned all my schemes and hopes, and made me tremble whenever the
Queen opened her lips to me, lest I should hear a resolution which was so
lately my utmost wish.

"Sir Walter, the head of the Devereux family, was lately created Earl of
Essex; he had been sent to Ireland to subdue the rebels, where he married.[96]
He returned to Court to present his bride, whom I had scarce regarded a
moment, when my heart became sensible of a sentiment unknown to it before. I was ambitious of her notice, and envied the courtiers who surrounded
her; I yet trembled to approach her, and the compliment of introduction was
delivered by me with a low voice and timid air; the cold dignity of her manner, and her instantly turning from me to converse with Lord Sands, affronted
me highly. I examined all I had said or done, but not finding any thing excep-
tionable on my part, I condemned her as a flattered girl, vain of accidental
advantages even to folly; I retired with the Queen without taking any farther
notice of Lady Essex. The Queen gave a ball that evening: I drest several hours
too soon, and continually fancied the clock stood.[97] Not doubting that I had
the power of mortifying Lady Essex, I determined to use it; even her Lord
seemed united in her offence, though I had no complaint to make against him
but that he had married her. In short, pleased or angry, I could think of nothing but her, and though I staid at home till quite tired, I found myself the first
in the drawing room.

"The Queen learning I was there, and pleased with my attention, which
she placed to her own account, sent for me to her closet; among other questions, she asked how I liked Lady Essex, and the asperity with which I censured her, was far from displeasing Elizabeth, who had a talent for satire and
was fond of all who excelled in it.

"We entered the room at the same moment with the lovely bride, more
obviously so as more adorned. The Queen turned to me who was leaning on
the back of her chair—'I think,' said she, 'my Lord, I must take the liberty of

appointing you to dance with Lady Essex, that the Court may have an opportunity of admiring how well I have matched her.' 'I thought,' returned I, 'your Majesty had promised me the pleasure of entertaining you; and, surely Lady Essex has matched herself much more happily.' 'Lord Leicester, madam,' said that Lady in an ironical tone, 'is uniform in his opinion respecting me, and for once I agree with him.' Saying this, she gave her hand to her Lord, who honoured the younger Cecil with it. Amazed at a pique, I could no way explain, I remained in a sullen reverie, till the Queen interrupted it by asking, if I did not think Lady Essex's wit inclined to the severe? I replied, 'when I knew whether she had any sense I should judge of her wit, but that at present she was perfectly unintelligible to me.' 'Why, surely my Lord,' cried the Queen, leaning on the arm of her chair and raising her eyes to mine, 'you know she was Miss Lineric?' What a fund of intelligence was conveyed in these few words, and what a revolution did they make in my mind!— To find I had refused, and, in refusing, insulted the woman on whom my happiness must depend, or, rather, from whose resentment my misery was begun.— Pride, anger, and ambition vanished; my heart overflowing with chagrin and love, applauded her just disdain, and owned she could never despise me for my stupidity half so much as I did myself. Insensible to all the discourse of the Queen, my eyes pursued with a vain and late regret the beauteous bride, till the meanders of the dance eluding my sight, I struck my head in a transport against the Queen's chair, and being obliged to excuse myself, complained of a vertigo and retired.

"I was interrupted in the midst of the disagreeable reflections arising from the past scene, by Elizabeth's physician, whom she had graciously ordered to attend me. He easily invented a reason for a malady his art could neither cause or cure, and having directed me to be bled, left me to repose. The Queen sent several messengers to enquire after me, and when I paid my duty next to her, almost gave me a relapse by dismissing her attendants. Perplexed and uneasy, I hardly dared to raise my eyes, or anticipate her determination. I met hers, which seemed equally irresolute, and a pause of a few moments was at last interrupted by Elizabeth.

"She informed me, that after the most mature deliberation, she found, that although she preferred me to all men existing, she could not by marrying make me happy, or be so herself; that in yielding to this weakness of her heart, she should for ever sully her reputation for wisdom, which would always, while single, teach her how to manage other potentates, either by hope or fear; and that such a degradation, in general opinion, would too sensibly affect her.— Leicester, said she, thou seest my ingenuous motives—I know thou lovest me, and to make thee some amends for the grief this must give thee, be assured by our royal word, that we will never marry another man however glorious his rank. Consider, therefore, whatever matrimonial treaties are on foot as tubs thrown out to the whale,[98] and remember Elizabeth's friendship shall distinguish thee almost as much as her choice could.[99]

"I kissed the hand she held out to me with apparent chagrin, but in reality she had relieved my heart from a heavy load. I ventured to admire a fortitude which reduced me to despair, and thus amply gratified that vanity, which in her, takes the lead of sensibility. Nevertheless, I was struck with her demand of a solemn promise on my part, never to marry without her consent, and considered it as a selfish and arbitrary exaction unknown to a tender heart.[100]

"The whole Court learnt I had lost my hopes without losing my influence. The Queen, just to her promise, gave me a palpable superiority on every occasion, and I only desired it to make my homage more gratifying to the fair Lady Essex, who shewed too much anger to rob me of hope. Had she appeared equally indifferent and polite, she would totally have discouraged me, but a man may reasonably flatter himself with the prospect of a pardon, as long as a lady deigns to appear offended. I made every possible concession to her pride, and the pleasure she found in humbling me, interwove me insensibly with her happiness.

"I should spare to your virgin delicacy, ladies, the acknowledgment of a disgraceful and guilty love, were it not absolutely essential to mark the remainder of my story. There was a levity and inconsistency in the manners of Lady Essex, which soon awakened her Lord's jealousy; and as she had always been indulged to folly, she could so ill brook any restraint, that it threw her the more readily into my power. The belief that I was loved alone by her, and had myself reduced her to make another choice, enabled her to preserve a merit with me even in her fall. The few hours we could steal, were lavished in the most ardent affection. I grew almost as jealous of her as her Lord, and blest the caution with which he shut her up more and more, even from me, since it totally excluded all other lovers. The oftener I saw her, however, the more ardently I desired it; and when at last her Lord was appointed to the command of the forces in Ireland, whither he despotically resolved to carry her, my passion and grief kept pace with hers; the Court presented nothing to me worthy to supply the loss of one so amiable, and had not the Queen given me a command in the Low Countries, I know not how I should long have concealed the emptiness of my bosom now its tenant was flown.[101]

"Several years past away in a variety of scenes without my seeing Lady

Essex, when the early death of her Lord left her at liberty to fix her residence in England. I returned home on the first intelligence. The sober widowhood in which she lived, made it difficult for me to gain admission to her presence, which I at last effected by a disguise. Her beauty shone through her sables with new and more touching graces, while my heart betrayed me into involuntary exclamations and caresses. She wept, and retreating from my arms, assured me, the only action of her life she repented was that attachment which had sullied her innocence, and which she was resolved to expiate by eternal seclusion and repentance. All my intreaties were fruitless. She burst from me into an apartment where she told me, her brother, Mr. Lineric, was, who instantly rushed into the room and demanded by what right I had presumed to detain her? I answered truly, by that of a lover alone, and flattered myself with gaining the interest of this young Irishman in favor of my pretensions, by obtaining a considerable post for him the next day. I easily discerned her aim was a marriage with me, which from every reason, and more especially the promise I had made to the Queen, I wished to avoid. Endless negociations were carried on, and these fermented the weakness of my heart to such a degree, that I forgot her error. Vanity but too easily persuades a generous man to pardon a frailty of which he is the cause and the object. Lady Essex listened very readily to an honourable proposal, and gave me at Greenwich an exclusive claim to that hand so long, so passionately beloved.[102]

"Anxious to conceal this event from the Queen, who rigidly maintained over me the rights of a jealous lover, while she disclaimed the title, I visited my bride very rarely, and my affection rather encreased than diminished; in fact, I was the more completely happy when with, because I hourly experienced, in every absence, the impossibility of being happy without her."

To return one moment to the poor Matilda; from the moment Lord Leicester named this Lady, my heart presaged her his wife; the closing evening had luckily prevented the various changes of my countenance from being visible, but the supprest swellings of my heart at last conquered my spirits, and I sunk back at this part of his recital, if not fainting, at least senseless.

Lord Leicester, alarmed, united with the terrified Ellinor to recover me; when fearing my full eyes would betray my heart, I urged indisposition, and besought his excuse for retiring to my chamber. He made many apologies for having fatigued me, to which Ellinor alone could answer. As soon as he left us, giving way to an irresistible impression of sadness, I threw my arms round Ellinor, and wept bitterly; her generous tears streamed with mine, and we seemed fully to mingle souls without exchanging one word.

"I understand you, my beloved sister," said she, "and will spare your delicacy, but you wanted courage to hear the whole, and this lady is not immortal. Think better of yourself and your hopes, my dear Matilda, for Ellinor becomes a prophet in your cause, and says Lord Leicester and you were born for each other."

This little sally could not call the smile she wished for into my cheek. I was the more hurt at this event, because I had, (though I know not for what reason except that we all too readily believe what we wish) overlooked it in my arrangement of suppositions. I past the whole night in walking about my room, and lamenting. "He is married!" I would exclaim; "that invaluable heart and hand are then another's! Oh, just Heaven! have I then inherited my mother's fate with her features? Is a guilty passion ordained to be the crime and scourge of all my race? let me at least bury it in my bosom. Yes," cried I, with conscious dignity, "I may be unfortunate but not censurable: the daughter of Mary shall be worthy the Stuart line. When this admired Leicester returns into the world, he shall remember with reverence this innocent asylum, and the family of Howard shall be still dear to him. Oh may he return in safety to that most happy of wives! while I waste my youth in a solitude only pleasing by its having once been his shelter." Self would then predominate, and floods of impassioned tears wash away every just resolution. Alas, I forget to whom I am writing; the language and thoughts of lovers must be uniformly the same, and I can only excuse these rhapsodies, by observing a tender heart traces its own emotions under the name of another with a melancholy pleasure.

Lord Leicester, at the usual hour, the next day resumed his narrative.

"The wars in the Low Countries carried me abroad half the year; and the remainder I divided between the Court and my Lady. Security perhaps produced carelessness, and the French Ambassador, whose Court was interested in depriving me of the Queen's favor, as the chief obstacle to her appointed marriage with the Duke of Anjou, by some unexpected vigilance traced out the secret of my marriage, of which he immediately apprised Elizabeth. I had the vexation one morning to receive the most marked tokens of her displeasure, for she is but too well known to give an unbounded license to her tongue, whenever her passions are awakened. She ended her virulent reproaches with ordering me immediately to join the army in the Netherlands, and never to return without her permission. Thunderstruck both with the discovery and her conduct, I bowed and retired, without attempting to offer a single word in my own defence. The Queen made me however some atonement for her violence, by refusing the Duke, when every preliminary was settled; which cruelly disappointed the French Ambassador.[103]

"No longer condemned to silence, my retinue escorted Lady Leicester to

Kenilworth Castle, as the safest residence while the Queen's anger continued; and I obeyed her in departing for Holland. I soon learnt that Elizabeth's chief reason for not recalling me, was the being obliged to pardon my wife, to whom, by a most unaccountable whim, she had transferred all her resentment, and whom she hoped to punish by continuing to separate us. The times, and a variety of reasons, made our correspondence uncertain; months sometimes elapsed, and without I sent an express, I obtained no news of one so dear to me. I was unjust enough to impute the difficulties by turns to the Queen and my enemies; and piqued at Elizabeth's ungenerous motive for exiling me, resolved to pass over incognito into England, and conduct Lady Leicester into the Netherlands, or, if she was averse to that measure, endeavour to appease the Queen.

"I executed my design so happily, that my arrival at my own Castle was the first news of my intention to Lady Leicester, whom I found confined to the house by indisposition. It struck me her joy was nearly allied to sorrow; but the thought was momentary, and I imputed it to her malady. Her beauty appeared much impaired, but placing the alteration merely to grief for my absence, it became a new call upon my tenderness. She told me the terror she was under; for Elizabeth had made her almost a prisoner in her own house, where she had passed fifteen months without any company except her brother, who had kindly followed her into this solitude to fix her influence over an ungovernable train of servants to whom she was a stranger. I returned Lineric every acknowledgment, and complimented him with a fine diamond given me by the States[104] on a former occasion.

"A long absence from this mansion where art and nature unite to produce almost the effect of novelty, made it appear a most heavenly retreat from the noise and bustle of a camp. I passed the afternoon in surveying the gardens, and directing many necessary alterations.

"Insensibly fatigued beyond bearing, I consented, at the persuasion of my lady, to retire and endeavour to rest an hour early in the evening. I had slept several, when my valet, Le Val, threw open the curtains, and with a countenance full of horror and intelligence, deprecated the wrath such a rude salutation must necessarily occasion.

"Amazed beyond expression, I bad[105] him recollect himself, since, while thus confused, I could not rely on his accounts, however kind his intention.

"'Pardon me, my Lord,' said he, 'the liberty your safety reduces me to take, of sounding the truth of the grievous intelligence I am obliged in duty to reveal, by first questioning your Lordship: have you remarked that almost all your domesticks are changed?'

"I was struck with conviction by the question, though I had not made the observation.

"'No, no,' said he warmly, 'there was a devilish reason for that.'

"'Beware, Le Val,' returned I, 'of what you would insinuate; for if, without proof, you dare asperse'—

"'I have but too sufficient reasons, my Lord,' added he, shaking his head, 'but they shall never pass this bosom if you give an affirmative to my next demand.— Are you convinced, my Lord, that man is brother to my Lady who is called so?'

"I hesitated.

"'Let us hope not,' said he with vehemence, 'lest we shock humanity; for as sure as one God made them both, they are but too well agreed.'

"Horror-struck with the idea, my heart sickened, and involuntarily admitted a doubt but too many circumstances corroborated.— Her love of retirement might proceed more from such an attachment than regard for me— Nay, even her marriage be but an honourable veil to the loosest connexion. I had neither power nor will to silence the poor fellow, who went on with an honest eagerness—

"'Of all the servants long retained by your Lordship, two only remain, and the rest are a set of ungoverned Irish, attached by country to both brother and sister. The sewer[106] owns he kept his place by silence and submission, and dame Margery, the housekeeper, most probably, by managing all my Lady's secrets. But the sewer will make oath of my Lady's intercourse with Lineric, and, that far from wishing for your return, they are alarmed at it beyond measure, as my Lady expects every hour to be delivered. Nor is this all.'

"'Give me time to breathe, Le Val!' cried I, 'for this horrible intelligence unmans me.'

"'I could not be silent and know you wronged, my Lord, though your sword were to rip out my heart. But I fear the worst—I fear lest something is now hatching against your life, for my Lady is in Margery's room, directing some carp in the manner you used to like so well; and I saw Lineric's servant set out for Coventry, from whence he is this moment returned with a horse his speed has half killed.'[107]

"'Well, well,' said I, 'be assured I shall consider over all you have said, and will avoid tasting the dish you mention.'

"'Ah, my Lord! that will only convince them you suspect their diabolical intention, and the servants of their own placing form a little army in the house. If my Lord will hear the advice of his servant, I have a way to propose, which will have no ill consequence if no ill is meant; if otherwise, it will fall only on the contrivers. Another dish composed of the same ingredients, the sewer can place at the bottom of the table; when the supper is served, I will pretend to be drunk, and making a scuffle in the adjoining hall, my Lady and her brother will naturally take the alarm, and interfere; the sewer can in the interim change the two dishes, by which means my Lady will taste the dish of her own preparing, and must abide the event.'

"This plan was of itself so innocent, and well contrived, that I resolved to authorise it, and Le Val, satisfied with his discovery, retired. He had indeed relieved his mind, but what a weight had he left on mine! The bare idea had filled me with a thousand horrors. Every thing confirms us in either love or hatred.— The silence of my friends when my marriage was discovered; her tears, her altered person, that remissness in writing, for which I had in my own heart censured the Queen—all, in short, I so lately thought inestimable proofs of her love, now rose as terrible presumptions of her guilt; and yet, when I saw her enter my chamber presently after, and tenderly accuse me for so long an absence, I could have received a mortal draught from her hand with less pain than it cost me to suspect her.

"The day was closing, and the table covered when I entered the Hall, occasioned by my long sleep. Le Val began the premeditated uproar, and Lady Leicester with her brother flew towards the door, whence the attendants had before departed, eager to encrease the bustle. The faithful sewer, on whom I kept an eye, exchanged the dishes in the manner agreed, and we returned to the table. I observed to my Lady that she trembled violently, which she naturally enough attributed to the alarm. Assuring me she had herself prepared the carp, she insisted on my doing honor to it, and urging her to bear me company, I accepted her invitation. An involuntary emotion made me every moment ready to prevent her tasting the exchanged dish; but the pleasure with which the infamous Lineric seemed to see me swallow the supposed death, silenced me. Scarce was the table cleared, when Lady Leicester sunk back in strong convulsions. Conscience made Lineric exclaim, 'poison, poison!' Every common antidote was administered in vain; she was borne to her chamber in an hopeless state, and I retired to mine to meditate alone. This terrible conviction of the unhappy fate prepared for me on my return from an exile she alone had occasioned, converted my love into horror and aversion. She raved dreadfully at intervals, and persisting to the last I had poisoned her, expired early in the morning. The blackness of the soul diffused itself over the body, and the proof of her infidelity was too obvious in her person.[108]

"Whether Lineric's constitution was less liable to infection, or that he had tasted the carp more sparingly, it was not till she expired that he found himself affected; but the dose was too deadly for him to escape. Convinced by his sister's example, that there was no effectual antidote, he summoned all his Irish domestics into his chamber. The faithful Le Val chose that moment to enter mine, and inform me of the consultation, which he insisted would produce some fatal event, if I did not consent that moment to mount horses which were ready, and attended by him and Williams set out for London; this step would give me the advantage of first representing the fact, while it secured my person from any savage revenge; the sewer in the interim, by the intervention of the tenants, might seize on the Castle the moment the ruffians abandoned it in pursuit of me.

"This advice had its due weight with me, and quitting the Castle by stealth, I rode off with Le Val and Williams from my own servants as the worst of assassins, and from my home as my grave. It was now day-break, and we had not proceeded many miles, when, from the top of a hill, we perceived a party apparently pursuing; having the fleeter horses, we kept the advantage for near twenty miles, when, by taking some shorter road unknown to us, we saw them very near. St. Vincent's Abbey appeared at the same moment in sight, which Le Val conjured me to seek, giving him my cloak to mislead the assassins. We had no time for deliberation; I struck into the wood, where, finding my horse an incumbrance, I left him to his fate, and was endeavouring to make my way through the bushes, without any certainty of being right, when I had the happiness to meet so fair a deliverer."

Lord Leicester thus concluded his story; but oh! how much of my life had evaporated during the relation! The unconquerable anxiety with which I followed him, united my heart for ever with his; and convinced me, no disparity of either situation or years can restrain the eager sentiments of youth seeking for merit. As the only acknowledgment for his noble frankness, I in turn related the little tale already repeated, of our melancholy birth, and undecided fate. Tears, composed of every melting sensation, seemed to fall from my eyes on his heart. Those fine eyes were teeming with some generous consolation, when a sudden noise obliged us to separate. Hardly could he regain the chamber, hallowed as Mrs. Marlow's, ere Father Anthony joined us: the natural austerity of his air heightened by some present chagrin. He threw himself into a chair, and preserved a long silence; which, fear of his having penetrated into our mystery, prevented my breaking. Confused beyond description, a thousand colours chased each other from my cheek; nor had I power to raise my eyes to my sister, who, accustomed equally to love and honour me, seemed, in holding my hand, to have gained a sufficient protection.

"Unfortunate children!" cried he, with a deep sigh, "Heaven has at last completed the calamitous circumstances under which you were born: destined to an imprisonment as lasting as your royal mother's, you have but the melancholy advantage of chusing it. Lord Scrope is dead in the confinement and disgrace with which Elizabeth rewarded him: his lands, his honors, the very spot on which you stand, all, are the property of a distant relation, and you now see before you your only friend—a feeble, helpless friend; bending daily towards that grave you alone render displeasing to him. The moment may yet come, when the rights of your mother will ascertain[109] yours, and all I can do for you in the interim, is to convey you secretly into France, and place you under the protection of the family of Guise; their prudence or their pride, may equally induce them to secure you an asylum in a monastery."[110]

The terrible alternative implied in these words, froze up my blood; and the beatings of my heart died away:—to become an exile from England—to forget Lord Leicester—or to be forgot by him—to be delivered up a martyr to the family of Guise; perhaps by them tyrannically buried in a cloister, a perjured self-condemned wretch, whose soul was full of an earthly image, while devoting itself to its Maker. All the arguments and entreaties Father Anthony made use of in a long harangue, were lost upon me; I knew him to be speaking but by the motion of his lips, and offered up to God, in my tears, a confutation of all he could advance. He left us not till too late for another interview with Lord Leicester; and I past the night in an anguish time can never erase from my memory—pale, unrefreshed, either by sleep or dress, I met my Lord next morning, more like a spectre than myself. He took my hand, and expressing his surprise but by a glance, kissed it in tender silence. I did not dare raise my eyes to his, and tears stealing from under their lids, fell on the united hands. Oh, how much was expressed in the silence of that moment! I seemed to understand all I wished, and at length respired freely. Ellinor, unrestrained by the tender delicacy which actuated me, declared to Lord Leicester at once the fate allotted us, and her utter detestation of it. The eagerness with which he entered into our interests, bespoke something stronger than friendship. A thousand times he assured Ellinor of his esteem and affection: to me he said nothing, but pressing the hand he still held, its trembling confessed it knew all the distinction. A ray of pleasure once more enlightened my soul: methought at that moment I could have borne every evil fortune can inflict. No, he will never forget me, sighed I to myself, in whatever remote solitude I am again lost to him; this dreary Recess, the daughters of Mary, in their rustic garb and lowly manner, will eclipse all the glories of a court, all the gifts of Elizabeth.

For the remainder of his stay, a serene delight, which neither arose from, nor can be conveyed by language, animated us alike; the intercourse of the eyes and heart took place of that of the tongue, and perhaps nothing was more remote from our thoughts than what we conversed about: till my Lord fixed my attention by declaring he would no longer intrude on our goodness than till the next morning. A sigh accompanied these words, and a sigh was my only reply. Ellinor, who ever treated him with a freedom inseparable from a disinterested regard, insisted he ought not to quit so safe an asylum rashly. He replied, he should bury himself with us, did he not hope to revisit it in a more acceptable manner. Breaking off at these words with an irresolution and timidity which shewed he had not said all he intended, after pausing a few moments he resumed, "Can you pardon, Ladies, a friendship perhaps too officious? But since your natural support, and just hopes have failed, may I flatter myself you will have the goodness to suspend your resolutions respecting the future, till I can appear with honor again before you? A short time is due to clearing my own fame; for ill would it become me to claim the guardianship of the Royal Mary's beauteous children, while loaded with opprobrium." He was proceeding when the cough of Father Anthony startled us. Scarce had Ellinor time to lead my Lord out at one door, ere he entered at another to visit Alice, who had sunk under the fatigue and grief attending the loss of her mistress. With an art I had newly learnt, I snatched up a book, in which I affected to be so absorbed, as not to hear him till at my shoulder. With real perturbation I arose on his speaking; and, as usual, was preceding him to Alice's chamber, when he called me back in haste, and pointing to the ground, bade me give him what lay there. But what words can express the various emotions which ran through my frame, when I perceived it was the picture of Elizabeth, which the Earl had, in retiring, somehow or other dropt! Instead of obeying, I snatched it up, and attempted to hide it in my bosom; when, with a strong arm, the Father wrested it from me, and read in my features half the mystery: the name engraved on it, the date, all put him out of doubt as to the owner, and nothing remained but to learn how I had come by it. Without the finesses of my sex on the occasion, as soon as my terrors and tears permitted, I related the whole adventure incoherently. With his customary sternness, he overwhelmed me with reproaches. "Rash girl," cried he, "could no human prudence save thee? Did not the lost Saint, whom I must ever lament, entomb herself merely to preserve a secret, the folly of a baby's curiosity betrayed ere her ashes were cold? What confidence can be placed in the favorite of Elizabeth, whose interest it undoubtedly must be, to flatter those in whose hands his life now is, and then deliver them up to exalt himself by the total silent ruin of the Stuarts? prudence directs us rather to secure ourselves by retaining him for ever here."

"First, may I perish on the block where my father ended his days!" cried I, in a transport of love and grief: "let me, oh God, rather be a martyr to the sins of mankind, than submit to partake them! What! be more cruel than the assassins, from whom we saved him? Pardon me, Father," cried I, recovering myself; "but you know not the story or the heart of Lord Leicester, who, far from betraying us, is anxious to become our guardian and protector."

"Such a guardian as the wolf is to the lamb," retorted he acrimoniously—"who, oh, who would willingly have the management of youth! Unhappy child, added he, wilt thou inherit the faults with the features of thy mother? an idle weakness like thine sapped all her morals, and left a stain on her life, time never can erase; but if not more virtuous, be at least more prudent."

"Hold, Father Anthony," cried I, with a dignity which awed even him into silence, "nor cancel all the merit of your cares, by a surmise my soul disdains. Far be it from me to censure a parent, but still farther be it to *deserve* the censure of an indifferent person. I may have erred, but only in innocence; and the life that beats within this bosom, can never issue to a nobler purpose, than to save that of Lord Leicester."

Nothing is more dangerous than to judge a generous and youthful mind harshly: it then is too easily acquitted to itself, and rises against suspicions it is unconscious of deserving. The shock the Father's doubts had given me, brought to light, without one idea of shame, that partiality I durst hardly before acknowledge to myself.

Convinced by my manner, that he had lost his influence over me, he commanded Ellinor to re-conduct my Lord into his presence, and requested to be left alone with him. I departed most reluctantly, but I would not entirely exasperate him. The injustice of mankind gave me too much reason to dread lest he should affront Lord Leicester, who might unite the innocent with the guilty, and abandon us entirely: aversions extend but too frequently through families; nay, even descend from generation to generation.

Their conference continued two whole hours, while I counted the moments in painful expectation; at last Father Anthony entered our room, and bidding Ellinor entertain Lord Leicester, desired me to collect my spirits and listen to him.

"However my suspicions may offend you, young Lady," said he, "I will suppose it possible I may know as much of the world, who have passed my youth in it, as you who have yet been confined almost to these walls. Well had it been if you had never gone beyond them. When I tell you this Lord you have saved demands your hand, you will indulge a thousand romantic sallies, and see in his request a love as blind as your own. Perhaps there may be something in that: perhaps too he recollects that your mother is the next in succession to the crown of England—that she may die in prison, and that the aversion the English ever entertain to a foreign sway, may prevail over the prior claim of your brother James, and his ambition may be gratified by a preference given to you.[111] The cruel necessity imposed by your unlimited confidence of attaching Lord Leicester to your interest, makes it needless to enumerate the objections I could reasonably urge against your union: the recent loss of his wife, I find, puts it in his power to marry you: you have left yourself no choice but to marry him: and never will I consent to his departing from this Recess, till the contracts I shall dictate are solemnly signed and the marriage completed in all its forms."

Imagine, Madam, my situation during this speech.— Oh, Anthony, thy dictatorial manner then was happiness! in one moment to emerge from the abyss of despair, and soar into the regions of bliss: to find the generous Leicester was willing once more to sacrifice his safety for love; once more to risque a displeasure from which he was not yet relieved: to raise me from obscurity—ah! to raise me to himself! a height, in my estimation, beyond the throne of my ancestors! The fond hope, suggested by the Father's speech, of one day rewarding my Lord's tenderness, was all I remembered of it. Crowns and sceptres, those play-things in the hands of love, surrounded me in imagination, and impassioned tears rolled down my glowing cheeks, while I said to myself, in the language of Miranda, "I am a fool to weep at what I am glad of."[112]

Reflection and circumstances a little softened Father Anthony, who saw himself on the point of being relieved from a heavy charge, to which his impoverished fortune, and decaying years, rendered him unequal. The amiable Leicester joined us, and every heart being lightened of its load, an evening of such refined pleasure succeeded, that could I wish to live over one of my whole life, I would select that as the happiest.

The interest, the honour of my Lord, demanded his return to Court, and Father Anthony having prepared due contracts, insisted on my compliance. His commands, and the wishes of Lord Leicester, added to these weighty reasons, over-ruled my sense of decorum, and our hands were united.

The peculiarity of the situation can alone excuse such a marriage; but I was born for obedience. Scarce had the transports of finding myself happy given place to reason, when my mother recurred to my mind. Unblest by her matron presence, my nuptials were but half hallowed; nay, unblest with her consent. I compared with grief her fate and mine: a long captivity had impaired her health, and no hope of a release to her spirits. I, although pent in a still narrower prison, beheld it enclose almost every human good, and could have consented to end my days in it.

But the honour, the welfare of my Lord ordained otherwise; every passing hour gave his enemies an advantage. Our servant James had been sent immediately on our marriage to Kenilworth Castle, which he informed us on his return was in the possession of the faithful tenants, who had been able, of all the servants, to secure only Dame Margery. This detestable instrument of a superior's barbarity, more terrified at the idea of an infamous death than any due sense of her crime, attempted to end her days with a remnant of the poison prepared for her Lord; but being detected, it only supplied a new proof of her guilt. Tormented by fear and despair, she at last found means to strangle herself in the night. In her my Lord lost one evidence of his innocence, which made his presence at court doubly necessary. The family of Lineric, having received information of the melancholy catastrophe of both brother and sister, from the Irish servants, who had been their abettors, had carried away the bodies, as if to inter them, but kept them in the hands of surgeons, still undetermined how to proceed.

Involved in one fate with my love, I knew no peace even in his arms; but with incessant admonitions drove him from me, refusing resolutely to accompany him: and although his fondness induced him to urge my departure, his reason must suggest to him all its danger. Would Elizabeth, who had thus resented his marrying an equal, ever pardon his aspiring to her blood? and how could we sufficiently guard from others a secret my very features betrayed to him? Actuated but by the single wish of passing my life near Lord Leicester, I neither asked to be known, or honoured by any one but himself, nor to be greeted by a title only endeared to me, because he bore it.

The strong aversion with which I had been taught to regard the reigning Queen, might perhaps influence me in this case. Before I gave my hand to Lord Leicester, I had made him promise never to carry me to court; a promise readily given, since it perfectly accorded with his wishes. Nay, in this happy union, every wish I could form seemed to be completed; I gained to that dear mother (who never left my thoughts, although I could neither ask her advice or consent in deciding my fate) a powerful friend in the favourite of her unjust rival. I hoped he might yet be prevailed on to attempt her freedom; and I already placed myself at her feet, overcome with the idea of having been the instrument of her deliverance. Alas, Madam, were it not for such vague imaginary joys, how could we exist? All our real pleasures fall infinitely short of these; for the preceding and following afflictions oblige our reason too often to correct them. But fancy, powerful fancy, gains vigour from disappointment; and an infant hope ever arises like the Phoenix from the ashes of the dying one.

A week after my marriage, Lord Leicester departed for Court, promising soon to return, and conduct me to Kenilworth, where he had previously resolved I should reside with Ellinor. He depended less on Elizabeth's partiality, than the justice of his cause, and was far from declining a trial, in which he was satisfied his innocence would become conspicuous. He was sorry nevertheless to convince the Queen he had wronged her confidence, only to obtain the most unworthy of her sex.

From his departure I date my entrance into the world. I had rather, till this period, looked on, than lived in it. Now I began to feel its anxieties, the painful consequences of its tenderest ties. Shall I tell you all, Madam, that passed in my heart? Notwithstanding the proof I had received of a matchless affection, I could not persuade myself Lord Leicester would ever return. If the Queen, finding him once more free, and taught his value by his loss, should at last resolve to espouse him, how could a poor girl, already possessed, and left in a solitude, where even the news of his infidelity could not reach her till too late, how could she weigh against a crown? Where could she hope for justice, when the Sovereign who swears to protect, must find it her interest to condemn her? Overcome with this formidable phantom, I gave myself up for some days to a despair as violent as my love. This imagination was only interrupted by another not less afflicting. How, if his interest in the Queen's heart had expired in his absence; if equally offended at his disobedience and its motive, she should join with his enemies? His proofs appearing less satisfactory to me than himself, I feared it was possible he might be condemned, as a criminal, when he was in reality the devoted victim.[113]

One of these suppositions was as unjust to the Queen, as the other to my dear Lord; and Father Anthony dispelled them all by some letters he brought me. I had the happiness to find Lord Leicester was received by the Queen with kindness, and that the family of Lineric, persuaded of his innocence, would not provoke him to make public the infamous design of his late wife, by calling him to a trial; he had therefore but one caution to observe, which was, to conceal this new union with more care than the last; and to effect this, he must delay our meeting for some little time, lest his immediately retiring from Court should lead the curious to search into the cause.

My doubts vanished with these proofs of his attention. I had only now to contend with the involuntary hatred I had conceived for the Recess. I wandered through every apartment, without finding rest in any: my impassioned fancy followed my love into the court, and the silence and confinement I lived in, became more and more odious. I beheld with astonishment the composure of my sister, and envied her a tranquillity I would not have regained, by being unmarried, if I could.

At last the happy hour arrived when I was to quit my retirement. Lord Leicester had projected the mode of my departure ere he left me. Le Val and his valet were the only persons in the secret. To all others, we passed for young women educated in a Convent, who, not finding a call to the monastic life, came with the consent of our friends, to embellish the retirement of Lord Leicester by our musical talents. This tale we were well able to support, for my voice was a very fine one, and the skill and taste of Mrs. Marlow, added to the tuition of a master, had taught me to manage it properly. Ellinor had not the same advantage, but touched the lute with a delicacy so exquisite, that we became necessary to each other; and as I never sung so well without her accompaniment, she had been so accustomed to adapt it to my voice, that something seemed wanting to either, when the other was silent. The passion Lord Leicester had for music, in which he was a proficient, gave the strongest probability to the whole. He had paid a handsome sum to accomplish the two daughters of his steward in that science, and the young women were taught to expect an addition to their number. The time Le Val remained in the Recess, preparing every thing for our departure, was long enough for him to seem employed in fetching us from abroad. Lord Leicester came several times to direct all, and to support and cheer us with accounts of the care he had taken to render the apartments destined to us, commodious and agreeable.

The Recess, till now, so calm, so tiresomely tranquil, became at once full of confusion and hurry; the family pictures were taken from their frames, and conveyed through Father Anthony's cell, gradually to Kenilworth.

By what strange caprice is it, every thing seems dear to us the moment we know we must lose it! Involuntary tears filled my eyes when the hour of my departure arrived. As much a stranger to the world as if just born into it, how could I promise to myself years as peaceful as I had experienced in the Recess? Long habit has the art of giving charms to places; or, rather, it is the people who inhabit them. It seemed to me, as if in quitting the place where the dust of Mrs. Marlow was interred, I quitted likewise her idea: every spot I looked on was marked by some noble sentiment, or tender emotion of that dear lady: but I was unjust to myself, for I have carried in my heart, through every scene of life, her respectable image, and nothing but death can efface it.

To part with those we love, is the most painful stretch of humanity; but what can make it painful to part with those we do not love? Separation, like death, seems to erase all the individual ever did to displease us, and leaves no remembrance but of his obliging actions. We lost but little in Father Anthony; but could he forget what he must lose in us? His declining years, and ill health, required the tenderest attention; and surely, the care he had shewn in our education gave him a just claim to expect it from us. My feelings in this were superior to my sister's, for he had been the means of my happiness. I joined my intreaties to those of the generous Lord Leicester, to prevail on him to reside in a retirement at Kenilworth: but although he seemed deeply affected at parting with us, he was inflexibly bent on ending his days where those of his sister ended. James still remained to attend on him, and Alice was borne very ill to the carriage which conveyed us away.

We took nothing but the ornaments from the Recess, leaving the furniture ready to accommodate any future unfortunates, whom Father Anthony should think worthy such a relief.

It was in the dusk of the evening we arrived at Kenilworth castle: the steward's wife received us with her daughters. Unconscious of our superiority, they treated us as young people, who sought, from the generosity of their master, a comfortable subsistence. Although I had agreed to confirm this story, I felt myself shocked at the freedom they used from it. I could have fallen to them, but was affronted at their rising to me: A little time however reconciled me. It is Lord Leicester's interest, and shall be my pleasure, was always my argument with myself. Mrs. Hart, for that was the name of this domestick, expatiated on her Lord's person, character, and magnificence; she officiously pointed out the rich ornaments of the gallery and apartments, and looked round to us every moment with the impertinent expectation of seeing us filled with the low awe and surprize of people unaccustomed to grandeur. The indifference with which we regarded every thing, was not a less affront to her consequence: she shrunk before it, and passed the remainder of the evening in a cold and haughty silence. Her daughters, not more amiable than herself, gloomily regarded our dresses, and by whispering, excluded us from joining in the conversation.

Such was my introduction into the family it was my right to govern. My heart sunk within me; I believed myself already fallen to a servant, and neglected by Lord Leicester. Unused to the circumspection necessary, where secrecy is desired, I demanded to be welcomed in his arms. I surveyed the eyes of my Ellinor, fearful they might reproach me for having innocently degraded the daughter of the Queen of Scots; but that dear girl, too delicate to add to my uneasiness, preserved, apparently, her gaiety, and sweetly accommodated herself to the people with whom fortune had mingled her.

The alledging fatigue and indisposition, obliged them to conduct us to the apartment allotted us. I should perhaps have wondered at its richness, but that I saw scarce any inferior. I was no sooner left in it with Ellinor, than I gave free scope to the tears I had scarce been able before to suppress. My face was hid in her bosom, when the voice of Lord Leicester recalled me to myself. I dried my eyes, unwilling even tacitly to reproach him: he entered through a private door, to change the cause of my grief to joy; for in his presence I hardly ever knew any other emotion; and the generous anxiety with which he entreated our pardon for the reception discretion had obliged him to order us, had something in it so graceful, so ardent, and tender, that all the pride of my heart subsided at once, and left it full of gratitude and affection.

We wished my sister a good night, and then passing through a dark passage, the whole length of the grand gallery, came into Lord Leicester's apartments, to which every place I ever saw was mean. He had a noble spirit, a splendid fortune, and an exquisite taste. He had greatly improved this ancient seat, the gift of Elizabeth: its finely chosen situation, elegant architecture, and superb furniture, made it the model of a thousand others. The beauties divided through the rest of the house in this apartment were united; and he gave a proof of the attention inseparable from real love, by omitting nothing to embellish it, he had ever heard me commend. Ah, Madam! these are the mighty trifles that so exquisitely flatter a tender heart, and form its most perfect enjoyments.

PART II

The communication between Lord Leicester's apartment and ours was a profound secret to all the servants but Le Val and Williams, my Lord's valet; in whose fidelity, after the late trial, he had the most perfect confidence. We were, to keep up the farce, presented to Lord Leicester the next day, who soon, by his growing distinction, taught Mrs. Hart and her daughters to observe a kind of deference in their behaviour to us. He ordered them to attend us round the gardens and park, and not to fail shewing whatever was worth observation; and through what a beautiful variety did they lead us! a world in miniature! A magnificent lake presented itself, in whose clear bosom the trees were reflected, and round which the sheep and deer grazed on rich pasture: swans and water-fowls innumerable played on its surface, and an aight[1] in the centre was made highly picturesque by several half-seen cottages, and emblems of agriculture. The late Lady Leicester needed not to have made a merit of remaining within these walls, since nature and art could furnish nothing lovely that was not enclosed here. Several gilded boats, and little vessels, danced on the bosom of the lake, and added, by the various streamers which played upon the surface, to the gaiety and richness of the prospect. When we turned the other way, the Gothic towers, swelling bastions, gigantic statues, and majestic sweep of the building, made that an object scarce less worthy of admiration.[2]

All our allotted employment was to sing to Lord Leicester while at dinner; but as he frequently entertained the neighbouring Nobles and Gentlemen, a curtain of muslin was drawn over the balcony to screen us from observation. In the evening we sometimes fished on the lake; or Lord Leicester, to indulge in our company, joined in the concert we formed: every day brought with it some amusement, and the restraint we lived under, kept up, even in matrimony, all that delicacy, and spirit of affection, which is, by ease of mind, too apt to decay. At last, painful necessity obliged Lord Leicester to return to Court: he, however, would not leave me with more than one equal in the family, therefore directed that I should preside one month, and my sister the next; by this method, rendering it hard for them to fix on his favorite. We likewise, with the steward's daughters, wore one kind of habit, and busied ourselves in the working rich tapestry.

My own happiness could never erase from my mind the opposite fate of the unhappy Queen who gave us birth. She was then confined at a place not far distant from Kenilworth. I had already tried all my interest with Lord Leicester in her favour, without success; and so just was his noble inflexibility, that at the moment my heart was pierced by it, my reason admired it. "Another man," would he say, "in attempting the release of the ill-fated Mary, would only forfeit his obedience, and endanger his life; and were those all, perhaps I should not be able to refuse my Matilda. But remember, my love, to these I must add, the blackest treachery and ingratitude: it would be, viperlike, stinging to death the generous heart that warmed me. Never employ the voice of virtue to charm me to vice; for what seems a duty in you, would be the worst of crimes in me; and what confidence could my wife have in my honor, if I was capable of betraying a partial Sovereign?"

I then would urge, my only wish was to restore my mother's liberty, which nothing but an unparalleled breach of confidence could have taken from her for eighteen years; observing, her crown had been lined with thorns too keen for her to desire to wear it again.

"Ah, my dear Matilda!" he would cry, "how ignorant are you of these terrible emotions, jealousy and revenge! permit me to know your mother's character better than yourself. She had too much pride and pleasure in reigning, to submit tamely to this imprisonment; or even supposing, tired of the evils always inseparable from a Crown, she could master her just resentment, and seeking an asylum with her children, ask only to die in peace, her relations would not suffer it. The ambition of the Guises is become a proverb; they would make use of her name and wrongs to shake the throne of Elizabeth; and instead of guarding the Queen, to whom I owed a perfect duty, I should have the misery of seeing a terrible war devour my country, of which I was the cause.[3] Who knows, my dear Matilda, if amidst these calamities my temper might preserve its equality? I might remember, with regret, the fatal advice which had misled me, and you might lament, too late, the sacrificing your own happiness to a fallacious hope of restoring your mother's.— Remember Elizabeth is now declining, the chances of life may bring about all you wish.— The compassion of the people has been kept alive for Mary these seventeen years; should we lose Elizabeth, her very imprisonment would turn to her advantage, by keeping her in the midst of a kingdom to which she is the lawful heir: my supposition is not vague, for the example of Elizabeth herself proves it very possible."[4]

What could I oppose to reasoning so just? I could only recommend the cause of my dear parent to him who can pull down the mighty and exalt the weak.

Every letter from my Lord was filled with complaints of the tediousness of the Court, and breathed the very soul of love.— He often intreated me to tell him I was happy, and when I complied, reproached me, through a tender caprice, for being so without him.— He required me to enumerate my hourly employments, and although half my time was spent in writing pacquets to him, always complained of the shortness of my letters. He, indeed, gave me no cause to retort; for it appeared as if he withdrew from the Court half of his hours to amuse me with all the little humorous incidents it continually furnished. But even these had not always the power to effect what he wished— my fate never allowed me one hour of perfect happiness, and an evil arose in his absence which filled me with the most terrible apprehensions.

My lovely sister, who was ever my pride and delight, possessed in a peculiar degree, that amiable gaiety which lessens the distance of rank. From her first introduction at Kenilworth, she had given way to an increase of spirits, natural from such a change in our prospects, little foreseeing how great a danger might arise from it.— Williams had been raised by Lord Leicester to the superintendancy of the family on his returning to Court. He preferred this man, believing he would, from knowing me his Lady, take care I was treated with due respect. Williams had been a soldier, and had contracted the authoritative air annexed to petty officers, which made him in appearance peculiarly suited to the post assigned him.— I must confess he was never a favorite with me; nature had been unkind to him, and he had been more unkind to himself, in not softening her severity. He was beyond the meridian of life, his person coarsely made, his complexion swarthy, and his face much scarred; he had besides a fierceness of mien which hardly bent even to Lord Leicester, who, of all men, eminently possessed the art of inspiring as much respect as affection.

This man then, madam, marked out thus by nature, ventured to raise his eyes to the royal, the beautiful Ellinor—the sprightliness of her manner abated his respect, and he had the insolence to declare his passion; call it honourable, and solicit her return. My sister had too much understanding not to feel her own fault, and too much pride to support his insolent freedom. She left him with ineffable disdain, as not worthy of a reply; and came directly to me—a pre-sentiment of some evil consequence arose in my mind at the moment she related the insult. I resolved to give Lord Leicester immediate notice of it, that he might take his measures accordingly, and in the mean while appeared constantly with my sister. But we had to manage a man equally artful and fearless. He had the consummate impudence to open my letter, and (finding its subject) detain it. In the mean time, no advice arriving from Lord Leicester in answer to mine, I remained on the rack of uncertainty; tormented by the confidence of a wretch from whom there was no possible escape, and uncertain even of the nature or extent of our danger. At last, unable, as the wife of Lord Leicester, to endure his insults, and tired of waiting my Lord's resolution, I took an opportunity of representing to him the daring boldness of his conduct, in speaking of love to the sister of his Lord.

Without any emotion or confusion, he pleaded guilty to the charge, but artfully endeavoured to exculpate himself from presumption, by alledging the rank in which we appeared, and the supposition that we were raised from obscurity by his Lord; who of course could only ennoble me.— At this insinuation, all the pride of Norfolk and Mary animated my features, yet fortunately recollecting myself, I replied with moderation; for the villain doubtless aimed at discovering from whom we really sprung, since our habitation had too probably struck him as containing a consequential secret.

I forbad him mildly ever to address my sister in that light again, without the approbation of my Lord, and attempted to retire; when stopping me, he bade me recollect that I talked to one possessed of more authority in the house than myself; that I likewise knew a secret of the utmost importance was in his power, and he was determined to make every use of it, in case I did not persuade my sister to accept him; that I must imagine him a fool by referring him to Lord Leicester; in short, instead of informing him, he was resolved to prevent his arriving at the knowledge of the affair, for which reason he had kept back all my last letters.

How cruel, madam, was my situation! alone, without any means of gaining protection from the remainder of my servants, except by declaring a secret he knew too well I would never reveal; to be thus braved, as well as insulted, was dreadful! I had yet no way of eluding him, since the whole family were under his governance, and had I offered to write to Lord Leicester through any other channel, I had the greatest reason to fear my letters would fall into his hands.

By this terrible dilemma were the days of the wife of Lord Leicester embittered in the midst of affluence; in a spot which might be called the palace of pleasure.— Thus situated, I could only counteract treachery and art by the same. I appeared, after some reflection, alarmed at his threats, and more willing to forward his views: I exacted from him an oath not to betray my secret, and on my side solemnly vowed never to mention his, but to employ my interest with my sister in his favour:—We parted with mutual distrust, and an apparent reliance on each other's sincerity. I performed one part of my promise by conjuring Ellinor to deceive him with false hopes, till Lord Leicester's return gave me an opportunity of consulting him on the safest way of disposing of the traitor. It was with much reluctance she consented, but it would have been a cruelty unlike her character, to refuse to lighten an evil she was the innocent cause of. I had then only to find some means of letting my Lord know it without breaking my word: for once in my life I was guilty of duplicity, and, like Philoctetes, found my equivocation furnished a terrible punishment.[5] I wrote a letter, declaring the whole to Lord Leicester, which I kept in my bosom to give to him whenever he should return; in the mean time I wrote as usual, and delivered my letters to Williams. The profound silence I observed on this subject, probably inspired him with confidence, and although Ellinor refused to marry him directly, the point he aimed at, the complaisance with which we both treated him, lulled him at last into a perfect security.

Worn out with hourly complaints of this wretch's impertinence to my sister, and my fears of the event, I counted, with more than a lover's impatience, the days which must elapse before I could see Lord Leicester. At length the happy one arrived which brought him, and gave me at once joy and sorrow, for who could tell me all its consequences?— Fostered in a Court, where he knew but one superior, Lord Leicester had added a personal pride to that which naturally sprung from the nobility of his birth. The partiality of his Sovereign, who dispensed, through love, with his obedience, had prevented his learning to disguise his foibles; it was the business of every one to seem blind to them, by which means he was a favorite without being a hypocrite. Those who loved him well enough to allow for this error, and a vanity I can scarce term so, when I remember the various and numerous advantages he possessed, might do any thing with him. Impassioned, generous, good-natured, and noble, where once he was attached, his fortune, honor, nay life, would be risked for his friend; but the few who are worthy that name, too often confined his affections. Lord Leicester was too exalted perhaps to be loved. But I digress. Pardon me, Madam, when you consider the cause. This openness of heart gave me just reason to apprehend a guilty mind would read the indignant eye of my love, and induced me to suppress, for some days, the intended disclosure. My precaution succeeded; Williams knew the character of his Lord, and finding by the freedom and confidence he still testified, that I was true, began to rely on my word. A journey on which he was accidentally sent, assisted me highly, in leaving time for my Lord to cool. I laid the letter on his table one evening before I went to bed: Lord Leicester, who was in another room, came in after me, but had not half read it when he frightened me by his rage and indignation. Had the man been in the house I know not how the matter would have ended, but at length my tears and distress softened him; he passed two days after in a thoughtful manner; I knew not, nor ventured to ask him his resolutions: at the end of that time he regained his temper and composure; he saw the apprehensions lurking still in my heart, and bade me take courage, for he had found a way to quiet them for ever. I conjured him at least to conceal with caution his consciousness of the affair, which he promised, and in a great degree performed; but whether it was that knowing he was apprized of it made me fancy his manner would reveal it, I cannot say; certain it is, I never saw him look at or speak to this man afterwards, without feeling my heart sink within me.

Sir Francis Drake, at this time, formed all the conversation of England;[6] he had fitted out a large fleet against the Spaniards, with which he was ready to sail from Plymouth. Many noblemen, and others, engaged as volunteers, and an infinite number of people assembled from all parts to view the fleet.[7] Lord Leicester, who had always been a strong friend to Sir Francis, set out to take leave of him, and enlarged the train of domestics he usually travelled with, for the sake of appearing honorably among numbers who did not know him. So ardent was the desire of all ranks of people to partake the sight, that not a single male servant willingly staid behind.— Williams had so great a relish for these expeditions, that he asked my Lord to take him; Le Val's sickness keeping him at Kenilworth, Lord Leicester complied. A fortnight elapsed before they returned, during which poor old Alice expired: with her died one of the witnesses of my marriage: Father Anthony was still in good health, as James, who regularly came once a month, brought word.

Lord Leicester returned, and returned without Williams.— Struck to the heart, I had scarce strength to enquire what was become of him. My Lord asked me if I suspected him of having murdered the rogue? "I have only sent him," added he, with a gay air, "a long voyage, to teach him to keep a secret. I knew no other way of getting rid of the rascal. Sir Francis has undertaken to provide for him too effectually for my dear Matilda to know any further anxiety on his account: in short, he is shut up in a distant part of the vessel, the sailors are taught to consider him as a madman, and have neither time to listen to his tales, nor sense to understand them.— Thus, my dear love, our fears are entirely over."

"Rather begun," I might have replied, for no rhetoric ever after charmed mine to rest.— A thousand accidents ruin our tranquillity, but it is better to endure their worst consequences, than return evil for evil. However necessary the step, the assuming a right to sentence this man, was too culpable in my eyes, not to make me uneasy; yet, since it certainly was to relieve me, that Lord Leicester executed the scheme, and because nothing could now recall it, I seemed satisfied: Ellinor too persuaded me to be so, from thinking the traitor justly punished.

Before Lord Leicester returned to Court, I gained his consent to a project

I had long revolved; this was, to visit my mother—to have the joy of being held in her arms, and to be acknowledged by her blessing.— He was too anxious to indulge all my wishes, to refuse me in this instance; but, not being able to further it openly, he only gave me a sufficient sum of money to bribe her keepers, and directed Le Val to attend us.

This man proved as faithful as Williams was the reverse—if at first he respected me but as the wife of his master, I afterwards gained an ascendant with him from my own conduct, which attached him to me as much as to his Lord, and made the most essential services seem trifles in his eyes. Eager to oblige and obey, he seemed always ready to fly before he knew whither, and a word of commendation was a sufficient recompence. He was now in the post of Williams, who was supposed to have voluntarily embarked with Sir Francis, and the secret of his fate remained with Lord Leicester, my sister, and myself.

Attended by Le Val, we set out for Coventry with beating hearts. We were to visit, not merely a mother, but an only parent, the sole person in whose arms we could claim a refuge; though now, alas, far more able vainly to offer her one. We were to see that Queen, whose matchless beauty was her least ornament; to behold her graces withered by eighteen years confinement; to share in her afflictions, and prove how dearly the children, who had never known her, could love their mother.

But alas! Madam, we were not permitted to realize these visions.— Le Val found her keepers too honest, or too fearful to suffer any stranger to converse with her, and the only privilege money could purchase, was that of seeing the Queen, through a grated window, take her morning walk in a small garden. Overwhelmed with despair at this news, we yet embraced the only indulgence we could gain.[8]— But what did we not think that faithless woman deserved, who thus treated her equal, her relation, her friend! We were conducted to the window, where we were permitted to remain without attendants; we saw her come down the walk—but oh, how changed, and yet how lovely! Damp rooms had weakened her limbs—her charming arms were thrown round the necks of two maids, without whose assistance she could not move— a pale resignation sat on her still beautiful features: her regal mien could not be eclipsed by a habit of plain purple, nor her fine hair by the veil which touched her forehead.— Her beads and cross were her only ornaments, but her unaffected piety, and patient sufferance, mingled the Saint with the Queen, and gave her charms beyond humanity.[9] Our emotions were too rapid and strong for description; we wept—we incoherently exclaimed—and striking ourselves eagerly against the bars, seemed to hope some supernatural strength would break them. More afflicted at seeing her thus, than not seeing her at all,

I neither could behold her for my tears, or resolve to lose a look by indulging in them.— She drew near the spot where we stood, when our hands, which we had thrust, in supplication, through the bars, caught her attention.— She raised her fine eyes, with their usual divine composure, to the window—I would have spoke, but my lips denied all utterance. Alas! that blessed—that benignant glance, was the first, the last, the only one we ever received from a mother.— When she withdrew her eyes, she carried my very soul with her; all my strength failed at once, and I sunk in a swoon in my sister's arms.

*   *   *   *   *   *

Suspicions of this nature made it dangerous for my Lord, were we frequently to appear there; yet this momentary view had awakened sensations, which, though less strong than love, were equally lasting, and which empoisoned my hours in the bosom of happiness. Bitter tears upon the cheeks of my Leicester, when with fond endearment he would strain me to his heart, alone spoke my thoughts, and I sacrificed the less to the greater duty.— Ellinor, my dear Ellinor, was, on this theme, my only counsellor, and we spent days in forming a thousand projects; weeping every evening at discovering their impracticability. The frequent absences of my Lord, left me too much leisure for this melancholy employment; yet the ardor of his passion made him chuse every opportunity, however short, to be with me, and I trembled lest these incessant journeys should attract the notice of Elizabeth, who had been for some time indisposed, and of course more alive to any inattention of her favorite. But Lord Leicester had not been used to controul, and sometimes imputed hints to indifference which arose from the most generous motives, for my life was without any enjoyment in his absence, but the hope of seeing him again. When he was away, I wandered wearily through every room, and saw only a magnificent solitude: but, whenever he appeared, joy and music animated the whole family; every apartment seemed to have found its guest, and every servant the happy subject of his duty.

To excuse his frequent absences to the Queen, my Lord avowed a passion for hunting, with which his conduct so little agreed, that he shut himself up in Kenilworth Castle, and seldom passed beyond his own walls. Conscious this must in time be observed, we learnt to ride expertly, and often obliged him to accompany us in mere prudence. To prevent our being too much fatigued, my Lord generally ordered a tent to be pitched, with refreshments, in the forest; and one morning, finding myself ill, I quitted the chace almost directly, and went in search of our resting place, guided by a huntsman, as ignorant of it as myself. Among the closest and most intricate paths we encountered a gentleman on horseback, attended by many servants; to make way for us, he ordered his servants to return, and dismounting, bowed, and remained uncovered while we passed.— Addressing the man who attended us, he eagerly enquired for my Lord—the question, I knew not why, alarmed me; I turned instantly to examine his features, and my horse continuing his pace, struck my head against an arm of a tree with so much violence, that the reins dropt from my hand, and the stranger was just quick enough to catch me. I fainted: one of his train opened a vein in my arm, which instantly revived me, and I found myself in the stranger's arms, who pressed, with more than common concern, the hand he held. Confused and perplexed with this accident, I endeavoured in vain to withdraw it, and seeing my hair had fallen in its usual curls over my neck, looked about for my hat, which yet hung on the bough that struck me. Regardless of every intreaty, I persisted in mounting my horse, and returning instantly, after I had rendered him every acknowledgement his active politeness merited. He replied with such peculiar grace and gallantry, as gave me a great desire to know who he was, but his pursuing me with his eyes, rendered it impossible for some time: after which the huntsman informed me he was the nephew of Lord Leicester, Sir Philip Sidney.[10] His appearance confirmed the agreeable impression made by his character,[11] and I only regretted being introduced to him by a vexatious accident which seemed too much to possess his mind. Engrossed by these reflections, although I lay down, it was impossible to close my eyes, when the abrupt entrance of my Lord roused me completely. Extreme vexation and disorder marked his air, and without the least enquiry into my hurts, he threw himself into a chair by me, lamenting the malice of his fortune. Alarmed beyond measure, I started from the bed, and kneeling at his feet, conjured him to tell me in what new instance he had reason to complain.— "Matilda," said he, fixing his eyes on me with a sad intentness, "the Queen approaches."— My heart died within me at the words; his supporting arms alone saved me from falling to the ground, and his caresses from fainting.

"I know her well," continued he, "and have every reason to fear we are betrayed. The subtilty of approaching without an express, convinces me that she suspects at least some charm in Kenilworth I dare not avow.[12] I had always purposed, in compliance alike with my promise and my safety, to convey you to the Recess in case this event happened; but now I fear the appearance it will have, alike to my own servants and Sidney's companions, who are all of the Queen's train, and but too much struck with your beauty.— One expedient alone remains—tell me, my love, may your Leicester hope to triumph over your becoming pride, your just resentment?— Will you condescend to appear before Elizabeth in the same humble light in which you have hitherto appeared; and, forgetting awhile she has been the persecutor of your family, will you consider her only as the patroness of your husband?"

"I will forget every thing," cried I, in a transport of tenderness, "which interferes with your safety and satisfaction; too happy in having something to sacrifice in proof of my love, I will be whatever you wish—as the daughter of Mary, my soul rises against Elizabeth; but, as the wife of Leicester, I ought to know no pleasure except his; nor have I had, till this alarming moment, a merit in submission."

"What are the ties of marriage," said my Lord, (the tears mingling on our cheeks) "to these invisible ligaments of the soul! I can so little bear to be surpassed in generosity, that I can hardly refrain from leading you to the Queen as her hostess, and charming the court with the sight of a wife, who is my sole pride and everlasting pleasure."

Precious, inestimable moment of my life, when the warmth of my heart was so fully displayed, so gloriously answered!— Ah, Madam, Lord Leicester had the rare secret of governing a generous mind.

The same considerations prevailed on Ellinor to give the same consent, and the short hour previous to the Queen's arrival was spent by us in schooling our eyes and hearts, lest the spirit of the injured and pride of the noble should betray all.— Apprehensive too, lest the similitude my features bore to those of my unfortunate mother, might strike some idle observer, I departed from her mode of dress, and letting my hair curl more over my face and neck, enwreathed it fancifully with flowers; then mixing with the villagers in habits resembling theirs, we waited to usher the Queen into the great hall, by strewing that and the inner court with aromatic herbs.

The amazing hurry produced by this unexpected visit, had not subsided, when the cannon proclaimed the approach of Elizabeth. A faint sickness came over me; my limbs were scarce able to support my weight, and my eyes hardly served to guide my steps. My nature shuddered at her, and the spirit of Norfolk trembled proudly within me. Most fortunately confounded with the gay cavalcade, I soon had performed my task, and retired without once fixing my eyes on her face. I struggled much with myself, and regained a tolerable share of composure ere her dinner was served, at which we were, as usual, to sing. Concealed from the public gaze, I had now an opportunity of examining the Queen. She was talking to my Lord, who waited behind her chair. Though the features of Elizabeth retained nothing of her mother's sweetness, they were regular; her eyes were remarkably small, but so clear and quick, they seemed to comprehend every thing with a single glance; the defect in her shape taking off all real Majesty, she supplied that deficiency by an extreme haughtiness; a severe, satirical smile marked her countenance, and an absurd gaiety her dress. I could not but suppose foreigners would imagine that Queen owed much of her reputation to her counsellors, who could disgrace her venerable years by a bare neck, and a false head of hair made in the most youthful fashion.[13] Yet, under other circumstances, the scene would have been charming. The hall enriched and adorned with fine statues, tapestry, and purple fringed with gold, the high arched Gothick windows, which being thrown open, gave a beautiful view of the lake, covered with newly ornamented boats, struck the Queen with admiration; while the immense crowd of royal attendants, and above all, the profound respect of many of the nobles, were sights no less new to me.[14] I turned my eyes round to discover if among them I could find any to compare with Lord Leicester. Where, ah where! could they select his equal! supprest anxiety gave a redoubled glow to his cheek, and his expressive eyes pierced through the veil which hid us from all others. Dinner removed, the music began. The usual pieces played, a silence ensued only interrupted by my voice and the lute of my sister. Amazement seemed to transfix every beholder, and all eyes pursued the bent of Lord Leicester's.—The Queen dropt a peach she was paring, and speaking with warmth to Sidney, he replied with an air so enlivened as shewed his heart was in the subject. Scarce had I reached the conclusion of the air, when the curtain was drawn aside, by the officious Sidney, and we stood exposed to the view of the whole court. Overwhelmed with a thousand sensations, I dropt the book I sung from, and Ellinor bent over her lute with a beautiful modesty. The various exclamations of the noblemen might have flattered our vanity, had we not been continually told any thing can make, to courtiers, the wonder of an hour. That fatal moment was sure the critical one of my life; it awakened dangerous suspicions in the soul of Elizabeth: endless anxiety in the man in whom my life was bound up, and a passion in the heart of another, the cold hand of death alone could extinguish. I mean the amiable Sidney: charmed at finding in the person who charmed the whole court, those features indelibly impressed on his memory, he delivered himself entirely up to his predilection with a generous warmth.

The moment I could recollect myself, I considered the Queen attentively; she sat in the pensive position into which our appearance had thrown her; sometimes surveying us with deep observation, then, with a keener glance, Lord Leicester. I laboured to support the painful examination with composure, but the care defeated itself, and involuntary blushes covered my face, as often as I became the object of her attention. The indifference the Queen expressed towards the music, obliged every one else to be silent on the subject, and we soon obtained permission to retire. Sidney, who was the messenger, overwhelmed us with apologies for the share he had in our confusion, although by the command of his sovereign. I had perpetual reason for resenting his officiousness, but Sidney was not born to be hated. To exalted generosity, and the most manly courage, he joined elegance, refinement, and a temper superior to events.[15] Yes, gallant Sidney, this noble justice Matilda owes thy virtues!—of all her misfortunes, that of becoming thine touched her most deeply.— Our apparent state of dependence never once induced Sir Philip to forfeit that respect a man of merit owes to himself;—it only united to the politeness universally due to the sex, an affecting deference which dignified its object. A husband less adored than Lord Leicester, might with reason have dreaded such a rival—Midnight alone gave us the freedom of comparing opinions, and I saw with unspeakable regret, the peace of my Lord destroyed during this visit. A depression, he could hardly account for, filled up the intervals we passed together; and instead of employing them in forming any reasonable plan, nothing remained of all our mutual tenderness but silence, sighs, and tears.

Elizabeth, in defiance of time and understanding, indulged a romantic taste inconsistent with either; and, not satisfied with real pre-eminence, affected to be deified by the flattery of verse. The Lady of the Lake was the title she chose to be known by here, and nothing art could invent, or wealth procure, was wanting to render the various pageants complete. A boat scooped like a shell, and enclosing a throne, conveyed her to the aight, where I and many more, habited like Nereids, waited to receive her, and ushering her to a grotto inlaid with shells and looking-glass, we presented her, in baskets made of sea weed, pearl, coral, amber, and every jewel of the water; while the place resounded with panegyrics so labored and misapplied, that it was with difficulty we forebore smiling at the gravity with which she listened to them.[16]

I found, with surprize, Lord Leicester feared the eyes of every indifferent spectator would penetrate through a mystery, Elizabeth only had an interest in developing. It is the common weakness of humanity to bend the attention solely to minute objects, while the leading ones come upon us totally unawares.— I, on the contrary, fancied myself every moment surveyed with a harsh air by an inflexible imperial rival.— Every lady of the court, under the pretext of seeking our intimacy, continually sounded Ellinor and myself on our real condition, and the timid incoherent manner in which we answered, gave me the most mortal fears of their employer.— Abject slaves to the Queen's amusement, she kept us continually in her sight, and without deigning to open her own lips, seemed to tempt us to complain by eternal whims.— In those moments, love, shame, and apprehension, spoke a language intelligible in all countries in the features of Lord Leicester; and Elizabeth, having doubtless assured herself, by these artifices, that there must be something to reveal, left her train at one end of the gallery, and retiring to the other with my Lord, interrogated him, as I instantly conjectured.— The fate of my mother now arose more strongly to my mind. "Ah! why," thought I, "did I leave the happy solitude in which she placed me, only to ruin the object of my affections, and deliver myself up to an inexorable tyrant, who can wreak her malice without even being suspected!" While thus lost to the surrounding crowd, I observed my Lord reply to her eager questions with hesitation and anxiety; as he talked, he fixed his eyes on me with the uneasy air of a person who wishes to convey through them what he is hopeless of making you comprehend any other way. I resolved to prevent an error on my part, by a timely retreat; when suddenly speaking aloud, Lord Leicester advanced towards us:—"Mark well all I say," said he, in a whisper, leading me and my sister to the seat of the Queen,—"I shall more surprise these children," said he, "with the knowledge of their origin than your Majesty—it is needless to give them the reasons I have laid before you for this secrecy; it must be sufficient honor and pleasure for them to find themselves daughters of the house of Dudley, and objects of their Sovereign's gracious patronage." Seeing him bend his knee, ours, stubborn and reluctant as they were, gave way, and we kissed the fatal hand she majestically tendered. She informed us, she added us to her train of maids of honor, and should carry us with her on the morrow towards London.— Lord Leicester, charmed with having eluded all her suspicions, dreamt not of the snare he had wound round his own heart in yielding us up to Elizabeth, whose consummate art had induced her to give credit to a most improbable fiction, on purpose to place us beyond his reach, which she could no other way have effected.

The hour of rest enabled him to open all his heart.— I understood that Elizabeth had addressed him in so decisive a manner on the conviction of our being born above our present rank, that he could not hope to save us from the most menial degradations but by a false confidence; Heaven had suddenly inspired him with the idea of a possibility, that his brother, the Lord Guilford, might have married Lady Jane Grey, a twelvemonth ere the two politic Dukes of Suffolk and Northumberland thought it prudent to appear leagued: during which time, he declared the unfortunate Lady Jane gave birth to us both: the same policy had induced them to conceal this event till the Suffolk family should be established on the throne, and that hope being for ever defeated, prudence still buried us in oblivion;[17]—finally, that the secret rested now only in his own bosom, from whence his attachment to Elizabeth would never suffer it to transpire, and that if the Queen still wished to patronize us, he thought it would be prudent to let us imagine ourselves his own illegitimate daughters.—[18] To all this Elizabeth replied little, but suffering him to settle it his own way, persisted only in taking us from him.

Her mode of conduct convinced me at once that she utterly discredited the whole of this fiction; which placed us, by another branch, almost as near to the throne as we really stood. Would not a jealous, selfish soul, like hers, have demanded dates, facts, testimonials and witnesses? Would she not have made us undergo the fate of Lady Catherine, the legal heir of the house of Suffolk, whom, by a barbarous, unfeminine use of power,[19] she had torn from the most near and sacred of human tyes, and condemned, even in the bloom of youth, to a solitary life of imprisonment, only for having dared to become a wife and mother?—[20] Would not, in a word, all the fury of her temper have blazed forth, but that she meditated a more safe and silent ruin?

Unwilling to add to the anguish of this moment by one surmise, I threw myself into his arms, and silent, speechless, strained him to my heart—supplicating, mentally, that God who alone could protect us. No language could have affected Lord Leicester like this conduct.— He accused himself of having meanly considered his own safety; and we were obliged repeatedly to assure him, that we thought he had acted with the most consummate judgment, ere we could reconcile him to himself. "Surely Matilda thinks me a sufficient sufferer," cried he, "in losing the charm of her society?— Can I have forgotten, that I dare no longer indulge even my eyes with her beauty?— Can I have forgotten that all other men may freely adore her, and that her happiness is not more in the power of Elizabeth than mine is in hers?— Did I not know that the Queen would willingly punish her whole race with the celibacy she imposes on herself, I should doubt her protecting the pretensions of Sidney; but she dreads too much multiplying claims to the crown, and I alone shall be persecuted with his passion.— Pity my situation," added he, "and with a uniform coldness, dash his presumptuous hopes.— How do I lament the fate which involves the fair Ellinor in calamities the same motives cannot reconcile her to! but since her choice and affections led her into the world, I rely upon her generous soul to support its evils with prudence and patience.— This will be our last conversation for some time—one only caution let me recommend to you both—make no confidents, cultivate the friendship of Lady Pembroke,[21] and never forget that you constantly act under the eye of a haughty, jealous, and revengeful Sovereign."[22]

Needless admonition! Could a daughter of the Stuart line cease to dread and hate Elizabeth?— Could a wife too, who saw the life of the man she loved depended on her prudence, for one moment dare to shew she did so?

Condemned to mingle with the world, I entered it with presages so melancholy as shewed my future fortune.— Without daring to testify my grief, even by a look, I departed from that hospitable mansion in which I had vainly promised myself long years of unspeakable happiness.— I departed without my Lord, and in so doing experienced every misery of love and dependance. Ah! how weak are those wretches who look up to us with wonder, cried I mentally, as we passed through every town, did ye know the breaking heart this splendid garb covers!—did ye feel the galling chain which writhes round it, and deepens my cheek with destructive beauty, how would you bless the gracious God who gives you peace and ignorance!

Received, acknowledged, and admired, we soon became familiar appendages to Elizabeth; nor had any hopes of seeing our bondage end but with her life. It was not the least of my evils that I involved my Ellinor in this calamity, which love of me could alone render supportable. By a caprice for which there is no accounting, Elizabeth, whose eyes were ever watchful, and heart suspicious, bent both for ever on Ellinor; who endured from her, with silent indignation, a thousand passionate extravagancies. Contrary to Lord Leicester's idea, I plainly perceived she encouraged every pretender to either, obviously to develope the mystery she easily discerned through his false confidence.— Tortured with the passion of Sir Philip, I found all my rigor could not extinguish hopes the Queen patronized, while Lord Leicester's confidence seemed to contract, in proportion as it became difficult for me to partake it.

The fair Pembroke attached herself particularly to Ellinor, and Rose Cecil,[23] Lord Burghley's second daughter, professed an unbounded friendship for me. I had so great a deference to the command of my Lord, as to withhold mine, till time convinced me too feelingly, that she was incapable of abusing it. She was almost a stranger at Court as well as ourselves, and brought up under a mother who abhorred it; the death of that mother leaving her to the care of an ambitious father, he flattered himself her beauty would win her a husband of merit, ere she had gained courage to assert her own choice. He was not mistaken in the first opinion: the tender bloom both of her mind and person, attached to her a thousand hearts, but though in all other instances compliance itself, in the article of marriage, she refused to obey even the Queen, who consequently hated her. This sad conformity of situation, both were at liberty alike to lament, and with the candor incident to youth, I found it difficult to limit my lamentations. Our situations and tempers made us alike cultivate an attachment with Lady Arundel, Sir Philip's eldest sister, who had long since retired to a seat of his on the banks of the Thames, upon the imprisonment of her Lord.[24] With less shining qualifications than her more fair and fortunate sister, Lady Arundel possessed a Roman strength of soul. Beloved from childhood by Elizabeth, she might have remained a favorite, even while her husband was a victim, but she inexorably insisted on sharing his prison, and when it soon after became his grave, retired in an honourable poverty, and owed her little income to her brother's bounty.— Thus, in innocence and hallowed widowhood, passed the days of this amiable woman who now enjoyed that first and last of human pleasures, the seeing herself surrounded with friends, although she had only merit to attach them.

The resentment of Philip the second of Spain broke forth at this period, and employed every one's thoughts; more especially the Queen's, with whom love was ever so subordinate a consideration, that I flattered myself Lord Leicester would chuse this opportunity to plan our future meetings, and a little relieve me from the insupportable tortures of perpetual hypocrisy.[25] When now, to complete my evils, he for whom I renounced every distinction due to my sex and birth, he in whom my soul was treasured, regarded me with coldness and disdain. I examined my own heart. It did not make me a single reproach; but the knowing I was wronged could not restore my peace. I began to dread that satisfied love had given place to ambition; that considering me as the only bar between himself and Elizabeth (who became more and more gracious to him) he vainly regretted he had made me so.— My hatred to the Queen redoubled, although she treated me much better than my sister, as she always conceived Ellinor his favorite, because the vehicle of his sentiments to me: yet, though his displeasure was strongly marked, it did not spring from indifference; for at the same time he carefully avoided my conversation, he incessantly watched my actions, and was always in my view, without ever being in my reach.— It was impossible not to discern he must be jealous; but alas, suspicion soon makes the causes it seeks. My blushes and the disorder of my air, when any supposed lover addressed me, confirmed his fatal prejudice; and the impossibility of finding an opportunity to acquit myself, almost distracted me. Fortune, shortly after, added the only aggravation my fate admitted.

The fair Rose Cecil, whose attachment I have mentioned, had insensibly engaged my affections by the warmth of her own. The pleasure I took in discoursing about my Lord, made me overlook for a time, that she was equally unwearied of the topic; but the eager manner in which she revived it, while increasing sorrow buried his name in my heart, at last opened my eyes. I observed her more closely, I saw the strong affection which impelled her to be near to him, while her heightened colour, and universal agitation, whenever he addressed her, made the secret inclination of her heart but too obvious. There are wives who would have seized this occasion to retort, but she was so innocent I could not distrust her, and was above appearing to do so. Some imaginary slight overcame a mind so delicate, and one evening she indulged in her tears, and unbosomed her whole heart. In vain, she said, did years and circumstances divide her from Lord Leicester, since she took more pleasure in silently admiring him, than in being admired by the whole world—"Ah, madam," cried she, "how barbarous are hereditary hatreds! Exert yourself for me, dearest Matilda, divest my Lord's mind of so narrow a prejudice, assured that this obligation will double an attachment equally produced by your own merit and the family you sprung from."

What a proposal was this to a wife—to a wife, did I say? alas, to a lover—a wild and extravagant lover!— She embraced me, and hid her tears and agitations on my bosom—a bosom which struggled with agonies yet more trying. Affected alike with her innocence and her fate, I returned her caresses, and wept like a mother over her child.— She left me sufficient leisure to consider my answer; I told her, in pitying, I shewed her all the kindness in my power, since the little influence I had with my Lord was obvious enough. I hinted that hers must ever be a hopeless attachment, as the visible distinction of the Queen made it very improbable Lord Leicester should marry any other woman, not to mention the vast disparity between her years and his.

She replied, that she had considered this over so often, that she had reconciled herself to every article.— The Queen thought more of war than marriage, and surely if Lord Leicester could be brought to do justice to her heart, her youth would never be considered as a fault.

In short, I easily understood that what she wished she was resolved to hope. I dropped the subject, but it was with infinite chagrin I beheld this lovely girl encourage a passion, so many causes concurred to render hopeless. In fact, it did not long escape the Queen's notice, and the unfortunate Rose saw every body appear to be acquainted with her weakness but its object, who shewed a coldness towards her, almost amounting to dislike: to me she always flew for consolation, and I frequently administered that I could not find.

On so important an event as the expected invasion, the English were all prepared to take arms: Lord Leicester, as their leader, was already encamped; and I parted with him in common with the other Courtiers, without the liberty of uttering a syllable that might give peace to his heart or my own. The misery of my situation became intolerable, when fear of my Lord's safety was added to every other fear, and I resolved on an explanation, whatever the consequence. The natural ascendancy love and superior years gave him over me when present, vanished with him: I intreated him to suffer me by knowing to repair an involuntary fault, and before it was too late, recover an affection I could not long survive. I conjured him to remember that he was my all in this life, and that if he continued to withhold his confidence, I could only conclude he repented the having ever bestowed it; and should finally give up all care of a being, which was no longer dear to me than while it was so to him.

The equivocal turn of these expressions I thought would secure this letter, even if intercepted, from producing any evil consequence; and while dubious how to convey it, Sir Philip Sidney demanded permission to take leave of me:—not even the pangs I suffered through his love, could rob him of my regard—the disguising it was all in my power. To his care I committed this letter, assured he might be trusted even with the truth; and transported with the least mark of my confidence, he promised all that lovers usually promise.

No sooner was he gone, than I remembered the ill-chosen messenger might render Lord Leicester insensible to the contents of a letter blistered with my tears.— Alas! when once we enter the labyrinth of possibilities, to which jealousy is the fatal centinel, hardly ever can we extricate ourselves. The gentle consolations of Ellinor were all my fate had left me; but for her, sickness must have been the consequence of sorrow; but during the hours of retirement (for one apartment held us) she omitted nothing to soothe or strengthen my mind:—incomparable sister! what a soul was thine! Oh! why were tears my only tribute to thy boundless generosity?

At length Lord Brooke[26] arrived express from the camp, and took the first opportunity to deliver me a letter from my Lord. He said I had found means to convert the accuser into the criminal, and conjured me to pardon a mean jealousy, which punished itself. My too ready obedience to the Queen's command, he added, and the obvious pleasure I appeared to find in his nephew's conversation, had poisoned every moment of his life since I came to Court. Sidney's talents, his equal years, his generous disposition, all conspired to make him a formidable rival. "I am not meanly jealous of your person," continued he—"no, Matilda, it is your heart of which I am a miser; nor do I wish you mine, whatever your loss may cost me, longer than you wish yourself so. Under the cruel circumstances imposed on us, less might excusably alarm a heart which has so severely suffered for its candor; yet, too just in my nature to consider that as your fault, which must have proved our mutual misfortune, I resolved to bury in my bosom its killing suggestions, and cease to persecute you with a passion which you dared not repel, however reluctant your heart. But that which would have made a common mind jealous, has eradicated the weakness from mine; for nothing but spotless innocence could have made you chuse out my imaginary rival as the vehicle of your sentiments. Truth and conviction flash upon my bewildered senses, and love breathes through every invaluable line of your dear letter.— How, how shall I ever recompence you for my injustice?— I can no longer live without humbling myself at your feet, and receiving a pardon I fear I shall never deserve. I have at length resolved to confide our secret to Lady Arundel—sorrow and experience have surely taught her discretion. Her house is the only retired one to which you can come with safety. Appear indisposed, and the Queen will not suspect more in the request of passing some time with my niece, than that of being unable to support the hurry and fatigue of the times. I will prepare Lady Arundel for your reception, and snatch the first moment consistent with my duty to fly and enliven your solitude. The embrace that confirmed you mine was less dear to me, than that which will seal your forgiveness.— Oh! my love," ended he, "who could endure the tortures of doubt, were not the moment of reconciliation so exquisite a transport!"

Ah, true indeed! for all the pleasures of my life faded before that moment! I seemed to tread in air, and had hardly command enough of myself to affect languor and sickness. Elizabeth, who always found herself fatigued with indisposition, because not subject to it herself, readily consented to my spending a month with Lady Arundel, who received me with infinite pleasure. I found she had been apprized of my marriage only, and that my Lord still withheld the secret of my birth. She allotted me a magnificent apartment, which concluded with a saloon opening to the Thames. This noble room was embellished with valuable paintings, some of which were not yet finished, and a painter of eminence frequently attended to complete them. This man was employed by her to take a picture of me, which might fill up the interval of my Lord's absence, as well as agreeably surprise him. While one day dressed gaily for this purpose, and waiting in the saloon, I perceived the man enter, but how was I surprised to see him a moment after at my feet! I turned indignantly towards him; Ah, heavens! it was my Lord, my Leicester himself! who safe in that disguise, which he and Lady Arundel had agreed on, was to forbid the painter whenever he could visit us with safety. We learnt from him news of the utmost importance, that Heaven itself had fought for Elizabeth, and defeated an armada her power could ill have coped with.[27] This intelligence, by securing Lord Leicester, joyed even my heart; and the pride of forgiving being added to the pleasure of loving, life could bestow no more on me.

I had now learnt to be beforehand with suspicion; and as Sir Philip, charmed with the opportunity of seeing me out of the chilling circle of a

Court, was almost a daily visitor, I resolved to end his hopes, even at the risque of an implied confidence. I could hardly sometimes forbear weeping to see him thus pursuing a shadow, and wasting a glorious youth.— Oh Sidney! you was worthy of a better fate, and could I accuse myself of embittering yours, I should be a wretch indeed!—but no, I honored, revered, admired you; nay, had I not already exchanged my heart, it must have been yours— you, whom so many women have loved, and none, no none were ever known to hate.

Having formed my resolution, I permitted him one day to lead me to the terrace. Overjoyed with the distinction, he entertained me with a thousand pleasant sallies.— Ah! is there a more pungent sensation in nature, than the necessity fortune sometimes imposes on generous minds to afflict each other? I opened my lips—the truth hovered on them—but it was not till he himself tenderly pressed me to add language to my expressive looks, and confide to him the sentiments I had endeavoured to suppress, that I could speak. "Alas! Sir Philip," cried I, "why am I reduced to tell you, your merit and your attachment are by a combination of events my only misfortunes?"

"What do you utter, Madam?" cried he,—"is this possible?"—

"A painful truth," returned I, "which the highest esteem for you could alone extort.— I am sensible of the influence of Elizabeth, but believe me, I am among those who cannot obey her."

"*Obey* her!" returned he; "does the fair Matilda know so little of me, as to imagine I would owe her hand to regal authority?— No, Madam, Sidney would not on such terms, he may proudly say, deign to accept even yourself. While my passion was only my own misfortune, I thought myself at liberty to indulge it, but the moment it becomes yours, pride, honor, sensibility, all ordain eternal silence. Yet, surely," added he, in an affecting tone, "a heart like mine might hope to know the fatality which thus wounds it."

"By the love you have professed for me," cried I, seizing his hand in turn with energy; "by the honor which actuates you towards every human being, I conjure you press no farther into a secret I have no right to reveal—if I had—"

"If you had!—ah lovely, generous, candid Matilda—no, I will *not* invade any mystery you think it necessary to conceal. Since my hard fate deprives my youth of its sole charm and hope—yet surely time—may I hope nothing from time?—age would steal upon me unobserved were you but to allow me expectation."

"Why, why," cried I, weeping, "am I compelled to a half confidence in a heart so noble!—but be assured, Sir Philip, time can never unite us by any other bonds than those of esteem; and surely, every day must strengthen those."

"I think I understand you," replied he, fixing his eyes on mine with a melancholy firmness,—"and shall I expose you to the ungoverned passions of the Queen?—no, since I am never—since esteem is to be the only bond between us"—he paused, and kneeling kissed both hands, as if taking an everlasting leave—"when next you see me—though I wring every fibre of this heart—when next you see me, I will feel intitled to all your esteem."

Rising, he quitted me, and walked towards his barge, with sad and irresolute steps, frequently looking back as if he was ready to return, and recant his declaration: but the barge swiftly conveying him toward London, I gave free vent to the tears I had with infinite difficulty suppressed.

The following evening Lord Leicester had promised to pass with us: he arrived with an air of satisfaction it was impossible I could avoid sharing, even while ignorant of its cause. "Who would rely on the constancy of a lover," said he, with a happy smile, "since even my Matilda's charms could not retain my nephew's attachment! He has sollicited the Queen's consent to marry Miss Walsingham; you know her love for him, but his sudden return of it, amazes all acquainted with both. Elizabeth calls him a whimsical fool, but does not care to offend Sir Francis by refusing her consent, however displeased at his thus matching himself—the marriage will be celebrated in a few days, and my Matilda is invited to her rival's triumph."[28]

Ah no, I should have returned, had his jealousy not taught me caution, thy Matilda has a triumph of her own to enjoy. Alas, I now understood Sidney's parting words, and my heart floated in tears tinctured so strongly with every sentiment but love, that I could hardly distinguish whether that had not a share in the sublimity of the moment.

My Lord pressed me to return to Court previous to the ceremony; he even gave out that I meant to do so, and this I only understood by a line which accompanied the formal invitations sent to me and Lady Arundel. "Ah, Madam," added Sir Philip, in the postscript, "is it true that you return ere my sacrifice is compleated?"

"No, I will not return," sighed I, "a husband's claims extend no farther, and humanity resumes its rights."

*   *   *   *   *   *

The dread that malicious observers might once more pry into Lord Leicester's moments of retirement, at last conquered the reluctance I felt at returning to Court. I saw, in defiance of danger, self-indulgence continually increased upon him. At first, a few hours of the evening were all he devoted to me and Lady Arundel; shortly after he came later and passed the night: he then pleaded fear of disgracing one or the other, and lost whole days.— Couldst thou wonder thy former marriage was discovered? said I often to myself, after exhausting all my rhetoric in vain to drive him from me.— Oh Leicester! what was the wrath of Elizabeth then, to that she would feel could she explore the whole of this secret? I entreated Ellinor to write me word my absence was much remarked, and at last returned once more a voluntary victim.

A sad and silent admiration was the only expression of my features at the sight of Sir Philip; he sighed at the compliment indispensably due, which his bride received with cold contempt. To a countenance naturally harsh and inquisitive, however beautiful, Miss Walsingham had always united a temper, proud, passionate, and peevish. Her strong attachment to Sir Philip, had in all instances, where he was concerned, subdued for a time, or, veiled those failings. He could not be ignorant of a passion he had so often been rallied upon, and the moment he found it was not possible for him to make his own choice, he generously resolved to indulge hers. His motives could not be doubted, as all the Court knew she had no fortune, and every body saw it was in her power to become the happiest of women.— But alas, it was not in her nature—far from seeking to win upon his heart, by a silent indulgence of all his little foibles, she wearied him with importunate fondness, and whenever business or weariness drove him from home, employed the interval in fomenting violent passions, with which she seldom failed to overwhelm him on his return. Incapable of bending so noble a mind to the little triumph of conquering a low one, and as incapable of regulating his life by the narrow rules she would have laid down for him, he saw no alternative but the pursuit of glory, and sollicited to be sent to his government of Flushing.[29]

Oh, pardon me, beloved Leicester, the bitter tears I have so often shed for the gallant Sidney.— Why, why had he not chosen my sister? She was free, she had a hand, a heart, a person worthy his; she would have crowned his days with happiness and his grave with honor. Alas, in the weak pride of humanity we seek to new model the distinctions of nature, and insolently oppose our limited faculties to omniscience.

New disturbances in the Netherlands, now obliged Lord Leicester, as commander in chief, to accompany his nephew.[30] I saw them both depart, with a reluctance so extreme as foreboded some calamity. The generous Sidney understood my silence, my conflicts, my wishes. "Rely on my cares—rely on my honor," said he at parting, "and be assured, my breast must be cold as the earth which then will cover it, ere that feels one wound which lodges the fair Matilda's heart.— Oh, let me worship the wise ordination of Providence! If amidst all the evils fate and imprudence have overwhelmed me with, I still weakly feel a regret at pronouncing a last adieu, what must I have endured had I been the chosen! but why by such remembrance disturb her I love!— Yet dear is the sensibility, adored Matilda—Oh let the tears which now enrich your cheeks, be wholly Sidney's!"

And they were wholly Sidney's! A sad presentiment heightened the anguish of this parting, by telling me we never more should meet. It remains not for my weak pen to paint the heroic death of Sir Philip Sidney; it has employed the noblest.[31] Even envy and malice dropt involuntary tears, while friendship was exhausted in vain lamentations. As to me, I set no bounds to my sorrow, and every reason which once confined my esteem for him to my own bosom, dying with him, I mourned as for a darling brother; and thus perpetuated the secret hatred of his widow, who, weak woman, envied me even the melancholy privilege of bewailing him.

Anxiety for the fate of Lord Leicester, which this event must necessarily excite, too soon gave way to a still nearer care. In vain I imputed my continual indispositions to grief: time confirmed an apprehension which had frequently alarmed me immediately after my Lord's departure. I found but too plainly, that imprudent love had produced a new misfortune, and that I bore about a living testimony of my marriage, from which the worst consequences might arise.

Ah, unhappy babe, thy mother's anguish foreran thy birth! Deprived by a sad combination of circumstances of a welcome, throbs of terror were thy first symptoms of existence. This accumulation of misfortune seemed to benumb my reason. I knew not what to resolve on. I saw myself almost in my royal mother's melancholy predicament when I was born. "Alas, perhaps I may to-morrow be entirely so," I would cry to myself; "let me fly then while yet my prison gates are open."— The eye of Elizabeth became yet more dreadful to me; I fancied every moment it dived into my heart, and death for ever seemed to surround me in forms yet dearer to me than my own.

My sister's better sense easily discerned how dangerous and how vain a project flight must prove. "You," she would say, "whose timid heart shrinks even from those it loves: who have hitherto trod the most safe and confined circle; who hardly know what loneliness means; how, in this situation, can you encounter the perils of the road, the insolence of strangers, the dangers of the sea, and the terrors of a camp? Even admitting all these happily past, in following Lord Leicester, you only change the object of Elizabeth's resentment; from which, distance may not shield either you or your Lord.— Oh, by how many ways may she revenge herself!— Leicester it is true loves you; but in you, at present, are centred future distinction, pomp, and a variety of pleasures never yet indifferent to him:—these will be the least of his losses; and, believe me, if the secret transpires, that it is his own may well one day prove your dearest consolation:—and, surely, my dear Matilda will not entirely forget a sister, whose only joy or sorrow she yet has been."

The last tender consideration entirely subdued a spark of displeasure excited by the former. I submitted my wavering resolutions to her direction, and wrote an anonymous letter, descriptive of my situation, which, with innumerable charges, Lady Arundel delivered to Lord Brooke, the distinguished friend of Sir Philip Sidney, to convey into Lord Leicester's own hands. That amiable woman became the confident of my present fear, and with unwearied kindness conjured me to rely upon her conduct—in her house she assured me of an asylum, and in herself of another mother for the unfortunate infant. I felt all the indulgence of heaven in providing me such an unexpected resource; and almost wished I had not made my Lord a partaker in cares, he was so little able to relieve. By her advice I summoned courage to appear again in the Court. "We seldom," said the prudent Lady Arundel, "criticise those we see every day; novelty alone attracts curiosity; and if you are absent any time, some eye of the many your return will attract, may pierce through every veil into the cause. I will carefully watch, and when necessary, warn you to retreat."

I found on my return, the fair Rose Cecil had quitted London by the command of her father, who was highly incensed, alike at her refusal of a very advantageous match, and the passion that caused it. The loss of her society, which at another time I should have lamented, became an advantage in the present delicate conjuncture. I no longer durst wish for companions I could not keep at a distance; and I hoped ere we met again I should be more at liberty to cultivate the attachment she professed to me, while time would have conquered that unfortunate one which alone could interfere with it.

I counted the moments ere a letter could arrive from my Lord—in vain Ellinor assured me the time was insufficient, had Lord Brooke's journey met with no delay. We were talking this over one morning, when a loud knocking at the door much earlier than usual, startled us both; how was I amazed a moment after to see my Lord rush in, booted, and with that disordered dress and air which shewed him just arrived! Pale and speechless, I threw myself into his arms, and made no other return to his embraces than by sighs and tears, while Ellinor, struck with the singularity of his conduct, repeatedly demanded how he came there?— "To see, to save my love," cried he, fixing his eyes on mine with unutterable fondness; "will not my Matilda bless me with another self? and could I be such a savage to leave her to face the pain, the grief, the danger alone? Dry your tears, my most beloved, am not I with you? I, whom you have made the happiest of mankind; I, who was born but to worship you?"— "Imprudent!" cried I, striking my own bosom—"alas, my love, how is it I see you here?" It seemed as if reason, like light, pierced at once through the chaos of his mind. Absorbed in the single consideration of my situation, he had posted to England without resting a moment on the receipt of my letter, nor could find a cause might satisfy even indifferent observers, much more the jealous soul of Elizabeth.— "Ah, heavens! we are now indeed ruined," cried I, wringing my hands, "the implacable enemy of my peace will become so of yours, and every malicious eye will now be fixed on her who sinks under the most casual observation.— Oh that the silent mansion in which I so long vegetated had been my grave, since I quitted it but to become a misfortune to the man I love!"— "Why will my Matilda," returned Lord Leicester, with a noble mildness, "monopolize love and generosity? Perhaps I have yet sufficient influence over Elizabeth, to persuade her, fears for her welfare alone brought me home; but even if not, shall I refuse to bear a single mortification for her sake who has borne so many for mine?— The worst she can discover is our marriage; your birth is beyond the power of malice. Summon your fortitude, my love, and let us concert every measure necessary to our mutual safety, for I will take all the care of myself you would wish me. Never more, I solemnly swear, will your husband leave you. Dreams of fortune and favor fade away before the realities of life; let us, with our darling sister, seek a shelter in France; I want not the means of affluence, independent of the Queen. Let us then avow our union, and thus convert my dear Matilda's tenderness, always her first charm, alike into her virtue and her happiness. There, safe from the vengeance of Elizabeth, we may, without fear or dishonor, quietly await her dissolution. Imagine, my love, the exquisite transport of encircling the Throne of your mother with lovely pledges of our union; so while empire fills every power of her imagination, nature may throb through every pulse to her heart."

The fond, fond vision floated alike through my brain! Lord Leicester, indifferent to the opinion of the Queen, resolved to wait on her without entering into the reasons of his return, which was already known through the Court.[32] Elizabeth had for some time kept her chamber, nevertheless she permitted him an audience ere she left her bed. I knew her capricious temper, and while meditating what line she meant to pursue, several of her ladies then in waiting came out of her chamber; the last of whom told me it was her pleasure, that I alone should witness her conversation with Lord Leicester. Conscience shivered my whole frame, and I entered the apartment as a condemned wretch would that where the rack was preparing. Lord Leicester, equally surprized, pointed out by an expressive glance a place where the closed curtain would prevent her remarking the changes of my countenance; and thither, more dead than alive, I took my station.

"Leicester," said she, in a languishing voice, "thy unexpected return upon the news of my indisposition, is a fresh mark of thy watchful duty and unwearied affection. I have long resisted that tender inclination which distinguished thee in earliest youth; but now, when I have no potent enemy to fear, I may crown thy passion and indulge my own, without endangering myself or the state.— A new plot I have discovered to release Mary, renders it absolutely necessary I should, by marrying, cut off her hopes and those of her party; I shall now, in turn, surprise them. Long have I weighed the business in my mind, and frequently determined to recall thee; but thy unexpected return, by evincing the strength of thy tenderness, demands an immediate recompence.— Take then at last the so-long-withheld hand of Elizabeth, who thus resigns all authority over thee, except that thy heart gives her." She paused, extending a withered hand. Lord Leicester, confused beyond all expression, and expecting me to drop senseless every moment, hesitated a few broken sentences of faint gratitude, and kissed the fatal hand she no longer drew from him, fixing a moment after his eyes on me; and oh, how comprehensive was the look!— "I perceive by thy trembling, my Lord," continued she, "how much I have surprised thee. Recover thyself.— My election of thee is expected by every one, and shall be immediate to mortify Mary. I find myself well enough to quit my chamber; it is my intention thou shouldst lead me hence this evening, and, by taking a regal seat under the same canopy, prepare the kingdom for the declaration I purpose making to-morrow. The ceremony of espousal will demand time and splendor, but never more shalt thou quit her, who finds, after trying every effort, it is impossible to live without thee."

There are instances in nature of timid beings whom darkness merely would deprive of their senses, who yet, on desperate emergencies, encounter the jarring elements without shrinking.— I, who had till that moment been composed of tears and trembling, now found I must no longer hang a helpless weight on the heart of my husband, and blessing the caprice which made her select me as the only witness of her dotage, I leant against the tapestry, and endeavoured, by a self-collected air, to arm him for the occasion. I had the misery to see his fortitude diminish in proportion as mine increased, and that after struggling with his feelings till almost convulsed, he was obliged to quit the presence of the Queen precipitately, and scarcely could his failing limbs convey him thence. The attendants, before dismissed, now entering, the Queen called the Lady Latimer[33] to her bedside, and I followed the footsteps of my Lord.— "Heavens and earth," cried I, on looking round in vain for him, "what is now to become of me!" Even Ellinor, my only comfort, fate had cruelly robbed me of, nor was she to be found throughout the whole palace. Ere the tumults of my mind could subside into recollection, I was informed Lady Arundel's barge waited to convey me to Chelsea, where she was greatly indisposed. Easily imagining this was a feint of Lord Leicester's, to unfold his sentiments to me in safety, I hastened into it, and was conveyed to the fatal saloon on the banks of the Thames, once consecrated to love and pleasure only. I found Lord Leicester alone with his niece, measuring the apartment with unequal steps and a distracted air; he took my hand, and softening with pity for my situation, led me to a seat, and threw himself by me. His tears bedewed the hand he kissed.— "Support yourself still, my soul," said he, "the crisis is come unawares; and fate is beforehand with our intentions. Elizabeth indeed has surprized me, but as her passion, however weak and absurd, is generous, it now stabs me to the heart.— To suffer her to publish it to the world, to stamp with ridicule my Sovereign, my benefactress, would no doubt awaken her most mortal hatred, and rob me of my own esteem.— Matilda, my love, can you support the truth, and all the truth?— Did I not tell you that, one day or another, your anxious wish of seeing your mother free might interfere with your own happiness? It has indeed; for even at the moment the Queen in tender confidence imparted to me a plot to release Mary, she meant to obviate by her own marriage, my secret soul upbraided me as an abettor, if not a principal in that plot.— Happy in the idea of surprising you with its event, and far from expecting so extraordinary a one on the part of the Queen, I find by papers Lord Burghley gave me ere I entered her apartment, that the enthusiastic assistants of Mary pre-meditated the martyrdom of Elizabeth, and have reason to imagine, that she by this time knows the man whom she was willing to level with herself, has been capable of so infamous a concealment.[34] Nay, how do I know how far I may be included in the barbarity? She may be led to believe, the hand to which she gave her own an hour ago, was armed with a dagger, and ready every moment to use it.— My life is at stake, and oh! what is infinitely dearer, every virtue which once I hoped would long survive me, cancelled by ingratitude."— The agitations of his mind almost deprived him of his senses.— I threw myself at his feet.— "Oh! if ever the unfortunate Matilda was dear to you," cried I, "*now* shew it—now struggle to endure for her—has she ever feared to do so for you? It is in vain to hope any thing from Elizabeth, as circumstances appear she must condemn you.— Already I see you in the Tower—I see those gates open to receive you, that have entombed so many alike noble and innocent. If you would have the babe its mother's anguish almost urges into a premature existence—oh! if you would have it see the light of heaven, plunge her no farther in despair.— Fly now, *now*, this very moment while we have yet the power. While you live your innocence may yet be vindicated; and while you live I may perhaps be able to do so."

Lord Leicester, shaking his head, gave a deep sigh—a sigh more soul-piercing than the most violent agitation.— "You know not what you say, my love," returned he—"even now, in all probability, my house is surrounded, and expresses dispatched to close every port in the kingdom, should I attempt to leave it; and hardly is there a rustic in England to whom my features are unknown. One expedient alone remains, and greatly would that soften the stroke. You are neither exposed to my danger, nor like me the marked of every eye—flight is still in your power, and in you I shall still think myself safe—put yourself under the protection"— "Never," cried I, starting up with vehemence; "I am your wife, that holy title I will maintain before men and angels, and nothing—nothing I in turn solemnly swear shall part us. I will, with watchful duty, share the prison to which I shall always remember I have condemned you; and oh! if your fate is accelerated by my means, be assured I alike will share your grave."— "One hope of safety is yet yours," cried Lady Arundel. "How could it escape you that the Recess may still supply a sad and dear asylum till we can judge of circumstances?"— The thought had indeed occurred to me, but I dared not name the memorial of the present misfortune. I examined his eyes in silence. "My gentle love, my sweet Matilda, can I resolve to grieve thee," sighed he, "speak; would you wish me to conduct you thither?" My tears only allowed me to pronounce, "yes." "Yet how," resumed he, "is it possible?— How can you support the inevitable fatigues of the journey, with the addition of its fears in your present situation?" "I can support any thing, every thing," sobbed I inarticulately, "but the idea of your danger." "Yes, my love," added he, kissing away my tears, "I will, if possible, live to reward your unexampled tenderness. Lady Arundel think for us, suggest the mode of our departure." "It should be sudden," cried our generous friend, "and how can either be sufficiently disguised, or how shall we find proper attendants?" "We will have none with us," returned Lord Leicester, "I rely on your care to summon Le Val from Kenilworth Castle; he is master of the secret of the Recess, whither he can follow us, and convey with ease, at different times, the treasure hoarded in the Castle; while with the venerable foster-father of my love, we wait your farther informations."— "Ah, how happy was it," added I, "your fondness obliged me to ride! now can I follow you fearless of any thing but Elizabeth. Supply me, dear Lady Arundel, with the homely garb of a servant;

my Lord must have recourse to the disguise of a painter, invented and worn on a happier occasion, yet if even I hardly knew him in it, who else shall discover him? Oh, haste my darling friend! secure us the fleetest horses—I seem every moment environed with the guards of Elizabeth—when shall we be any thing but a trouble to you?"

The amiable Lady Arundel provided all in the manner required, and we set off immediately. Ere sun-set we reached a peasant's cot near St. Alban's, where my Lord insisted we might with safety take a little rest, which indeed I greatly required. Accustomed to pass and repass that road for ever, he fancied he remembered every face he saw, and I too surely thought all remembered him. Our rustic host and his wife seemed to have just understanding enough to connect the idea of mystery with us, and I roused my Lord ere break of day, secretly resolving no more to enter any house till we reached our asylum. Even the profuse recompence my Lord bestowed on the peasants, rather according with his soul than his appearance, excited their suspicions; they pressed us to stay in a manner which pointed mine, and we departed with a precipitation which I dare say confirmed theirs: pursuing our journey by roads little frequented, Lord Leicester being perfectly acquainted with the ground. I went through incredible fatigues without complaint; riding the whole day with no other refreshment than a draught of new milk, supplied by a girl as we passed along; till as the sun was declining, we reached a brow which commanded St. Vincent's Abbey. At the well known prospect my heart dilated—my eyes wandered over the whole with sensations our first home only can excite.— Nature seemed to tinge the woods with deeper verdure—the translucent stream meandered in majestic silence, undisturbed by noisy bargemen.— Innocence seemed to rest under the shade of the willows which every where fringed its margin, and the empurpled sun diffused the repose he seemed hastening to partake—an invincible charm took possession of my heart, and even the sense of misfortune was for the moment suspended.

"Here," cried I, checking my horse, "here we shall be safe—ah, more than safe, here we may be happy!— Why, why cannot those hours return when first we met? those hours of undescribable felicity?— This landscape then bounded our wishes; in its narrow circle is contained all necessary to existence, in ourselves all essential to happiness: but society, that first of blessings, brings with it evils death only can cure. And the venerable Father Anthony, with what joy—ah! with what sorrow will he receive us—forewarned even by our presence of affliction, he will hardly dare to indulge the rapture of a moment."— Every sentiment and sensation mingling thus in my mind filled the interval ere we arrived at the spot, where my heart recognized the minutest object. Alighting at some distance, Lord Leicester fastened the horses in an obscure part of the wood, and we proceeded on foot to the hermit's cave. Evening began now to gloom over the hemisphere.— I had before agreed not to open my lips, till my Lord had by degrees revealed himself to Father Anthony, whose enfeebled senses might not be able to resist the surprise; but how did that return upon ourselves, when a voice with which we were unacquainted replied to us without opening the door! Heart-struck I caught the arm of Lord Leicester, who eagerly enquired after the hermit. "He has been dead these ten days," returned the man, "and is interred among the Scrope family in the vault of St. Vincent's Abbey: I am placed here to protect the few effects he left behind, till his relations shall direct what is to be done with them."— "And thus vanish our hopes of safety, peace, and pleasure," sighed I, turning disconsolately from the cave. "Oh, sainted Anthony, I have now no tears for thee, and that loss I should lately have shed floods for, is now heard with indifference. Where, wretched wanderers as we are, where now can we betake ourselves? Had we staid in London, friendship, nay interest, might have sheltered us; here I am as well known as you are there, and the possessors of St. Vincent's Abbey will infallibly discover both. Nay we know not who those are, and whether we might not throw ourselves into the power of our worst enemies. Alas, my love, what do you suffer for my sake! it is in vain to affect strength; nature fails, and I must rest if only on the damp earth."— "Gracious God!" exclaimed Lord Leicester, supporting me in his arms, "how have we deserved this accumulation of evils? Let us wind through the wood; who knows, my Matilda, but providence has left the gate of the tomb open to shelter us? It is plain, the peasant who inhabits the cave is not acquainted with the secrets of father Anthony, and in all probability that of the Recess died with him. Oh! struggle a little, but a little, my love, something bids me believe Heaven will yet protect us."

Though faint between want of nourishment and excessive fatigue, I yet strove to follow my Lord, but did it so slowly, that night entirely involved us ere we reached the tomb. Long custom, however, enabled me to lead him aright.— "It is open," cried he, in a transport of joy, "come, my love, and let me assist you to enter."— He did so, but hardly was I within it, ere I found myself violently seized by several persons, who instantly deprived me of the power of utterance had heaven allowed it, but agony and horror so entirely overcame me, that I sunk senseless in their arms.

END OF THE FIRST VOLUME.[35]

PART III

From this temporary death I was at last recalled by a sound that made me wish it had been indeed eternal; the voice, the tremendous voice of Williams. Of what horrors was my soul instantly susceptible! What dreadful images swam before those eyes I hardly durst open! Fearfully at length I cast them around— I saw I had been conveyed into the great room of our Recess; sacred once to piety and innocence, but now, alas! the shelter of rapine, perhaps murder. A number of ill-looking ruffians stood ready to fulfil the worst commands of their ferocious confederate, who with malignant joy contemplated two hopeless victims unpitying heaven seemed to have delivered entirely to his vengeance. I gave myself up for lost—*myself*—I alike gave up Lord Leicester; who thus disarmed and surrounded, collected his soul in silence, and resumed the majestic air which once could awe even this villain to subordination. I every where perceived a variety of instruments, nameless to me, which I considered as the means of torture and of death; and only supplicated the Almighty to spare us the first, since to avoid the latter I supposed a fruitless prayer.

"You see at last," cried the exulting villain, "fortune's wheel has made its circle, and my turn is come, Lord Leicester.— How could you hope to conquer a man whose all was courage? Neither Sir Francis, nor even Elizabeth, could long confine one who dares precipitate himself into the ocean in search of freedom; not," added he in an ironical tone, "that I shall fail to requite my obligation to you."

Lord Leicester replied but with a look; a look so superior, contemptuous, and collected, that it wrought the rage of Williams to a still higher pitch; who turned towards me, malignity burning in every scar of his horrid face, "you are welcome home, fair lady," continued he, "though your visit is an unexpected favor, without the idle train too which once attended this idle favorite. You see we have made a little free with your hallowed mansion, but the saints take all in good part. Do you not enquire after your foster-father? he would tell us no tales, nor will he ever now tell you one." Oh! Anthony, I shuddered for thee, thou venerable murdered friend, in silence! "Monster," burst forth Lord Leicester, "hast thou with unexampled cruelty butchered an Anchorite?"[1] "I always work safely," returned he; "*you* have only saved me the trouble, for never would I have rested 'till by some artifice I had drawn you once more hither, and God, you see, most graciously has sent you."

"Blaspheme not thy Maker, oh cruel wretch," sighed I in a tremulous accent; "just, though severe, are all his ordinations; and lo, with sad submission, I take the death appointed me even from thy hands."

"No," cried he, "though you are not the haughty beauty I adored, yet, as the wife of that imperious lord, you become but a more perfect means of exquisite revenge."

The nature of that revenge blazed in his countenance—my heart turned to marble within me. I raised my eyes towards heaven in speechless agony, then rivetting them on Lord Leicester, found life recede too fast, for my ear to distinguish one word of that bitter indignation, which the voice it loved so loudly uttered.

I almost doubted whether my senses were indeed returned, when I found myself involved in impenetrable darkness. The piercing sigh of some one near me was the only sound that broke the stillness of the night. "If," cried I in a feeble tone, "that is the voice to which my heart was born to vibrate, oh tell me, beloved Leicester, whether the scene which yet swims before my sight was real or a vision?" "Gracious heaven!" returned he in a voice yet more piercing, "you breathe again, my soul's best treasure! the long, long fainting caused by the threats of that execrable monster, and which held during your removal into this dungeon, gave me hopes that you had finally escaped a fate too horrid for reflection. Oh dire extreme of despair and misery when I am con-demned to wish you dead! and yet what else can deliver you?—yet think not, Matilda, I fear to follow;—ah no! the best blood burning in this bosom should joyfully embalm you; but the thoughts of all which may precede that mo-ment, almost urge me to dash my distracted brain against the stones on which I lie, and shorten my own sufferings, since hopeless of averting yours." "Call up your fortitude, your reason, your religion," returned I in a firmer voice; (an emotion which united all those sentiments diffusing itself through my frame) "dare I accuse the Almighty of injustice? Will he, who first gave my helpless innocence a hallowed shelter within these walls, ordain that they should prove its tomb? the shades of those who reared me will surely rise in its de-fence." "Alas, my love," sighed he in a despairing voice, "these visionary hopes may soothe the mind 'till that sad moment nothing can avert—have you for-got that even in happier times you hoped nothing from the villain? and is this an hour to expect a change? Revenge and want have seared his soul to all humanity. How, how could it ever escape my memory, that he was acquainted with the secret of the Recess? how, under such uncertainty, durst I ever ven-ture within it? but short-sighted man, solely employed in weaving snares for others, too late finds his own feet entangled, and falls an easy prey to the ignoble. Not satisfied with heading this set of coiners,[2] for such their appara-tus proved them, his daring disposition breaks forth in acts of plunder and barbarity, and even at this moment he is seeking new victims, though possessing, unsought, those he would out of the whole world have chosen." "Shall we complain Heaven has quite abandoned us," resumed I, "when it has given us but one moment to ourselves? Oh, Leicester! you have hitherto found me a tender, anxious, fearful woman; but alas, I knew not till now the powers of my own soul.— Abhorrent of shame and dishonour, it tempts me to the most desperate deeds; if yours is indeed congenial, it surely understands me; assume a Roman courage, and save thy wife, thy spotless wife, from horrible pollution."³ "So much I agonize at the idea," cried Lord Leicester, "that were these hands free, perhaps—" "and mine too," added I, "feeble as they are, alike are bound; yet surely despair will give me strength to loose them." The violent efforts I made at last broke the slight thong they thought more than sufficient to confine one in my feeble state, and encouraged by my success, I sought Lord Leicester. At the moment I restored his liberty, I half revived, while the sole use the tender Leicester could make of his arms, was to press me a thousand times to his swelled heart, which almost burst with anguish. I struggled against all the sad tenderness which throbbed at mine. "Oh, think no more of love," cried I with increasing heroism, "it has given place to death— to worse than death—rather imagine you hear this dungeon once more open."— "But can I lift that hand, which pledged itself for thy protection, against thy life, thy precious life?" groaned he—"can I deface that angel form, which still illumes my soul through all these complicated horrors? And oh, our dear unborn! for whom we gladly suffered, can I, can I destroy it?" "Think, think my Life," returned I, "we have perhaps this only moment—had these wretches left any means of death in my own hands, do you imagine I would supplicate it from yours? Strangle me now, while darkness favours. Your wife demands of you this final proof of love and courage; hers will at least vie with it; no groan, no struggle, shall issue from a heart which then will return innocent to that dust from which it sprung, devoted alone to the adored husband with whose image it is doubly inhabited." "Oh, matchless, matchless woman!" cried my Lord, flooding my cheek with tears of generous anguish; "never, never, can it be; my sinews relax to childhood; your unhoped-for fortitude totally subdues mine, and melts my soul to woman's weakness.— Oh! thou who gavest me this angel, canst thou have abandoned her to brutality, and me to distraction!"

A peal of thunder, which shook the ruins to their foundation, seemed to reprove his boldness. The livid lightning pervaded our dungeon through many a time-worn aperture. During every tremendous illumination I gazed awe-struck on the pallid face of my love; till suddenly glancing around, I gave a cry which startled even myself—glowing, gasping, transported, yet still unable to speak, I sunk before my Lord, and clasping both his hands, alternately prest them to my heart, and lifted them, with mine, towards Heaven. "What means my beloved?" exclaimed he, in almost equal surprise and agitation, "has pitying providence deprived her of her senses?" "Ah no, it is God himself who has illumined them," faltered I at last; "what dungeon has man yet discovered the Almighty cannot; you have, perhaps, forgot, my love, that you have often heard of one communication from the Recess to the Abbey: closed up on the death of Mrs. Marlow, it was never opened after, nor was it known to that horrible villain; this dismal den contains it, and we tread on the only spot in the creation which could shelter us from those ruffians. In the corner on the right hand, covered with lumber, placed long since on purpose, you will find a trap door; if you have strength to raise it, strong fastenings will secure it on the other side, at least till we reach the Abbey. Oh thou," added I, devoutly raising my eyes, "who alone couldst preserve us, continue those flashes, more welcome than ever yet the sun was."

Impressed solely with the present danger, it was not till we had descended into the vaults, and fastened that blessed door between ourselves and the banditti, that either recollected what we might apprehend at the Abbey. Assured that none but an opulent owner could reside in a seat so splendid, we vainly racked imagination to discover its present possessor; yet persuaded even our worst enemies would rescue us with pleasure from a peril so nearly connected with themselves, we were obliged to defy every other. The housekeeper's room, into which the passage led, was empty, yet scattered furniture, &c. indicated inhabitants. I hailed, with true devotion, that power who gave me once more to see the soft lustre of the moon, which on the subsiding of the storm diffused serenity. Retaining in his hand the bar (which had been one fastening of the Abbey entrance) as the only weapon in his power, Lord Leicester followed my trembling steps; they turned intuitively to the apartment of Mrs. Marlow; ah that there I could have found her! I paused at the door of the anti-chamber, and my heart sickened with despondency—knowing there was an immediate necessity for rousing and arming the whole family, yet convinced we must at first alarm them as preternatural beings, and afterwards, with the conviction our escape introduced a danger to themselves, while ignorant whom we were going to appear before, well might the firmest heart tremble. Engrossed by these various and affecting ideas, I hardly heard a sound, which made Lord Leicester start forward with an eagerness that might easily have deprived me of the little strength Heaven had left me. The anti-chamber into which I immediately followed him was dark, but in the room beyond I perceived a light, and heard the voice of a woman apparently supplicating. Scarcely had I distinguished in that of the man who answered her, the dreaded Williams, ere I saw Lord Leicester start forward, levelling the bar with so desperate a boldness, that the fall of the villain ascertained our safety. Instantly snatching a knife from the wretch's hand, he pointed it at his bosom, but perceived a perforation in the brain, which made his punishment terrible, as his guilt, and his death immediate. "Execrable monster," cried my Lord, dropping the knife, "by unlooked-for means Heaven at last has finished thee."— "Gracious God," cried the lady, "do I hear the voice of Lord Leicester!"— Amazed at this discovery, and the preceding event, hardly could my trembling limbs convey me into the chamber. "Approach, my dear Matilda," cried my Lord, "never more shall this wretch appal thee. Eternal justice is satisfied with one blow, nor need I turn assassin even to him. Happy at the same moment in saving this lady, endeavour to interest her for those misfortunes in which she already seems interwoven."— "Can Lord Leicester ever know a misfortune in which I am not interwoven?" cried the lady; "to have received my life from his hands alone could reconcile me to it." Had I not known the speaker by her voice to be the fair Rose Cecil, such language must have ascertained it: yet to find ourselves under the roof of our most mortal enemy, was a cruel stroke. "Is it possible we should be in the house of Lord Burghley?" cried Lord Leicester disdainfully. She, sighing, replied, "he fortunately is absent, nor can you ever be unsafe in any house where I am mistress." "You know not to whom you speak," cried I, in turn; "alas, Miss Cecil, do you still remember the friendship you have so often professed for the unfortunate Matilda? Ever has she lamented the sad necessity of veiling her fate from a heart so noble; accept then, at this unexpected moment, that confidence I always longed to place in you, and tell me whether you still can resolve to love her who was the wife of Lord Leicester, long ere she saw you? her, who at this moment, renders him a fugitive in his own country?" Her distressful eyes wandered from him to me for some moments in silence, then taking a hand of each, she first kissed, and afterwards uniting them, said with a Spartan firmness, "my friend!" but turning instantly from him to hide her glowing cheeks and impassioned tears in my bosom, sobbed out, "my deliverer!" Her beauty (which was rendered more obvious by her disordered appearance, the ruffian having compelled her to rise and half dress herself) her innocence and her generosity appeared at last a little to affect Lord Leicester, who had hitherto shewn her an indifference almost amounting to disgust. "It remains with you, Madam," returned he in a softer voice, "now to become mine. Miss Cecil no longer sees the worshipped favourite of an imperious Queen. United alike by choice and law to the dear companion of my dangers, a chain of occurrences reduces us to escape by unknown means from England; and with the utmost dispatch. Nevertheless, those even Elizabeth's rage might have spared, were only an hour ago devoted by that lifeless villain. Escaped this moment almost from a den of slaughter, hardly can we tell whether the banditti, of whom this was the ringleader, are not now surrounding us. Summon all your courage and your domesticks, and while providing for your own safety, I need not solicit you to remember ours." "When I forget it, may I be condemned to see you perish!" cried she. Then turning to me, with that innocent candor which eminently distinguished her, sought a pardon in my eyes. Collecting all her thoughts, she continued, in a few moments—"Astonished as I must be, both at your circumstances and your visit, my noble friends, curiosity yields to friendship. With the morning I expect my father, nor is there any safety for you but immediate flight: nevertheless, this danger with which you say we are environed, must be the first consideration." I then explained to her the secret of the Recess; the direful mistake which had thrown us into the power of its present diabolical tenants, and the desperation which the discovery of our escape, and the means by which it was effected, must inevitably cause: except indeed the loss of Williams should abate their ferocity. While I talked, I frequently perceived her mind wandered on another subject. She surveyed the disguised persons, and pale faces of both my Lord and me, a thousand times over; by fits she shook with horror at the story I was relating, and by starts she forgot I had been speaking, and obliged me to go back in my tale. Employed solely in concerting the means of securing our safety, her own seemed hardly a consideration. Such is the nature of love in the mind of a virtuous woman, "I see," said she, (when I had finished) "the necessity for some body's appearing, to account to my servants for the discovery of the villains. I see too, that Lord Leicester cannot be the person, for who can fail to know him?" The inference thus tenderly conveyed was obvious; *one* must be seen, but I could not resolve to be that one without a dismay which surpassed complaint. "Yes, my dear Matilda," added she, "we must part with him for a little time; but you will rejoin him for life. By the ordination of providence, as I could almost suppose, the son of my nurse is now in the house, a young man over whom that circumstance gives me a powerful influence; against the choice of his friends he embraced a sea-faring life, till he acquired enough money to purchase a small vessel, with which he trades between the coast of Devonshire and that of France; but disgusted at the profession he chose, it was only yesterday he arrived here to solicit my interest with my father to promote him in a civil line. Say not then Heaven frowns on your flight, since it plainly points out a secure mode of escape. I cannot but discern that every avenue to Holland must be effectually closed, but who could think of tracing you to the distant and obscure coast of Devonshire? It is true the journey is long, but to compensate for that, you must recollect it is safe. The travels of Arthur have been confined to the road by which he conducts you, and his connexions are doubtless among people who will furnish you with every common comfort, without having curiosity, or understanding, to penetrate through the mystery of your rank. I see too what your expressive eyes, my dear Matilda, would point out—the impossibility of long concealing the share I have had in your fate, since how else can your miraculous appearance here, or the terrible death of my midnight visitor be accounted for? but what of that?" she generously added, after a moment's pause, "much ought to be ventured when our all is at stake." "I have expected every moment," said my Lord, "some dreadful interruption from the rest of these wretches." "No," returned Miss Cecil, "I have every reason to imagine he was alone in this enterprize; when first, by his entrance, I started from the slumber into which I was falling, I began collecting my purse, and every orna-ment near me: he rejected them all, and compelling me to rise, commanded me with terrible imprecations to conduct him to the private cabinet, where my father concealed his state papers: hoping, doubtless, by possessing them to obtain many secrets, which might ensure his own pardon, for that must have been his ultimate object. I knew the character of my father so well as to debate whether I should not rather give up my life than a trust so precious, when the terrible intervention of Lord Leicester released me from the conflict. Yet I agree with you, a moment ought not to be lost; and first let me lock up the room which contains so shocking a testimony, that more than one man has intruded there at midnight." Conscious of her own merit, she encountered even the eye of Lord Leicester without tremor, who could not but admire in her at that moment all the magnanimity and foresight which enobles man, with every softer grace that half deifies woman. For my own part I clasped her to my bosom, declaring I could never love her more than I did long ere this proof of her merit. "This is the only topic dangerous to either," returned she, a tear beatifying her smile, "we will all love one another as well as we can. But now, my Lord, attend to the next step, if you dare rely on my direction; we will conduct you to the door leading to the garden; make your way over the wall on the side farthest from the wood; a mile beyond you will find a bridge; wait near it in silence; Arthur shall first hide a horse for you, and then set out on another, to convey this lady, as if to her home, in some adjacent village; the confusion attending the discovery of the vaulted passage will render the fam-ily, most probably, inattentive either to her presence or departure, and ere they can be enough at leisure to discover Williams, or form any dangerous conjecture, you will both be, I hope, beyond the reach of discovery or pursuit. But oh, my Lord! if you would have either of the trembling wretches now before you survive this night of horrors, use the strictest caution in seeking your appointed shelter, nor leave it till you hear the voice of Matilda."

Lord Leicester promised; and conducting him softly through the house, we reached the door leading to the garden. All the horrors of the past were short of what I felt at that moment. After the dangers I had shared and escaped with my Lord, to see him depart, was to quit my guardian angel, or to deprive him of his: yet convinced Miss Cecil was actuated by the same fearful affection, I yielded to the desperate emergency. The closing of the door after him severed the hearts of both; it was then only we knew the support we had derived from his presence; wan, speechless, helpless, we durst hardly turn our eyes on any object but each other, nor utter a sigh but it swelled into a groan; and the ghastly body of Williams seemed forever to impede our footsteps, floating the path with blood. Miss Cecil took the only possible method to divert our terrors, and soon rousing a few terrified domesticks, commanded them to summon all the family: a command which needed no repetition. A few minutes gathered together eighteen or twenty men, sufficiently armed to secure us from any personal danger. I conducted the whole astonished body to the private door, through which I had entered; I described the place to which it led, and touching slightly on my own danger and escape, recommended to them that profound silence the villains had preserved towards us with such fatal success. During this time, Miss Cecil selected the man she mentioned to us, and retiring into the next room, gave him her orders unobserved; so entirely did both my appearance and strange story engross the attention of every individual belonging to the family. Miss Cecil rejoining us, ordered them to divide, and that while half remained to guard the house, the rest should descend, and passing into the dungeon from whence I came, wait the return of the banditti, and seize them one by one as they entered. This conclusion of the adventure greatly damped the ardour of the group, but ashamed to recede from a place, through which I had apparently escaped alone, they departed in so numerous a body as might almost fill the den in which I was lately enclosed, the few who remained hovering near the entrance, solely intent on the event of the enterprize. Arthur, in the interim, having the full command of the stables, made ready two horses in the manner already mentioned, and Miss Cecil, with her usual foresight, overwhelmed me with refreshments, which a little invigorated my exhausted frame: nor did she forget to provide Arthur with such as might recruit[4] my Lord; selecting from her own wardrobe, linen and every necessary the time and occasion admitted. Impatiently I expected the summons to depart, which was preceded by a message from the Recess, that all was hitherto entirely silent, and the door fastened as when we left it, a circumstance which appalled my inmost soul, as it seemed to leave us still in the reach of the merciless banditti. With mingled tears of grief and hope, I embraced that generous friend I never more might see, and quitting the once hospitable mansion, which seemed of all the universe the only home my heart acknowledged, I seated myself behind a guide, whose sun burnt features softened into a compassion, few indeed could at that moment have denied me. The moon shone forth with resplendent lustre, and our road being in a contrary direction to that which before ensnared us, I recommended myself to Heaven, and anxiously expected the meeting with my Lord. We had not proceeded far when that dear protector (who had in fearful affection for me defied his own danger, and returned almost to the Abbey) started from under a clump of trees, and with a voice that dissipated terror, welcomed my return to freedom, and sprung upon the horse our guide before led for him. Such is the effect of an evil escaped, that I almost forgot my excessive fatigue, and could have fancied myself safe.

Recent circumstances at first occupied my thoughts, and during the intervals of silence, the addition of a stranger must naturally impose, my imagination once more returned to the dungeon: it pictured the fear and horror the wretches themselves must in turn feel, when unknown hands condemned them to a fate like that they had allotted to us. Again I wandered to the Court; I seemed to see Elizabeth burning with embosomed rage, while the helpless noble Ellinor became as its immediate, its only object. I greatly relied on the watchful friendship of all the Sidneys, but hardly could I hope even that could rescue her from the Queen. I knew the letter Lord Leicester had ordered to be delivered to Elizabeth two hours after our departure, would infallibly explain to her the secret of our marriage; which of itself confuted the tale he had advanced concerning our birth: nor could I doubt but every artifice would be practised to unfold the whole mystery; and, alas! ungenerous minds too often fasten on the victim cruel fortune puts most into their power.

Yet in the haste and confusion attending our flight, we had found it impossible to unite my sister in it: neither at that unhappy juncture could she be found, and all the care we could shew for her safety, was to recommend her in the most strenuous manner to those few friends we expected the discovery would leave us. While Ellinor had the resolution to retain her own secret, we knew the power of the Queen could not reach her, and the strength and foresight she had at many times shewn, persuaded me she was equal even to this hardest of trials. Yet could I think of the insolent interrogatories, and contumely she must inevitably encounter, without a bleeding heart? to be the gaze of every eye—the object of every tongue—oh greatly did she need the consciousness of innocence, the pride of royalty, to sustain her!

It had ever been our plan, if fortunate enough to escape safely into France, to remain still in disguise 'till couriers from England could inform us how far the plot of Babington, and particularly Lord Leicester's knowledge of it, had transpired.[5] If it appeared his share in that scheme was undiscovered, my Lord might with safety avow himself; as marrying privately was a crime only in the eye of Elizabeth. And knowing too well her favourites ought ever to consider their influence as precarious, Lord Leicester had long since scattered large sums in the hands of different merchants in various kingdoms, as a resource, he now found his only one: nor was it insufficient. If, on the contrary, we learnt Elizabeth had dived into that dangerous mystery which he was censurable only for concealing, by the charge of treason, she could perhaps affect his safety in France, nay almost in Europe, and to preserve his life some disguise must still be maintained while hers lasted.

Though separated in infancy from every one allied to me, nothing could ever detach my heart from family claims; not daring to look towards my mother, I had always passionately desired to see the sole surviving sister of my father, Margaret Lady Mortimer.[6] Educated with the late Queen in the Catholick persuasion, she had married a general, and with him held many distinguished places under Philip and Mary.[7] The revolution both in politicks and religion caused by the accession of Elizabeth, was fatal alike to her honors and her pleasures. General Lord Mortimer followed the widowed King to Spain, and raised on his favor a fortune that gave him power to fix his own fate, when death suddenly decided it. His relict[8] retired to Rouen in Normandy, where his sister was then Abbess, leaving her younger son in the service of Philip, and her elder in the army of Francis IId. Naturally of an active temper, Lady Mortimer could not resolve to give up the world, though attached to it only by disgusts, and lavished a large portion of the immense fortune her mother and husband had united to bequeath her, in cherishing every exiled enemy of Elizabeth. Elated with the vain hope of one day seeing her ill-fated brother throned in conjunction with the Queen of Scots, she had entered into all his measures while that union was in agitation; and emerging once more from her convent, journeyed to Rome, where she spared neither pains nor money to win friends who might authorize and ratify it. She was among the few who knew the marriage secretly took place; she even knew it was likely to produce heirs of royalty and misfortune; when the discovery, trial, and execution, of the Duke of Norfolk, entirely crushed her last fond project. From that moment she had remained uninformed of the secret soul of Mary, and the fate of her unhappy offspring. The avowed disgust she had shewn towards Elizabeth, made it dangerous for her to return to her own country, and hardly in it could she have arrived at such important intelligence, when once the clue[9] was lost. Aspiring, rich, and restless, she had always affected to appear the patroness of all oppressed Englishmen; and if I found it prudent to avow myself, I might safely rely on a welcome from her who would find with joy every hope so long extinct renovated in me. Our present journey conducted us to a coast almost opposite to that of Normandy. I fancied a pleasure in having it in my power to claim my aunt's cares in the approaching melancholy crisis, and was not without hopes Lord Leicester might safely appear in his own person, when once my sister had escaped to rejoin us.

These various reflections fully occupied my mind till the dawn of day, when our guide assured us we might safely rest in the hamlet to which we were near. Convinced by Miss Cecil's confidence in him that he might fully be trusted, I entered with weary limbs a cottage from whence its laborious inhabitants were just issuing to work. They used their utmost diligence to procure us a homely meal, and we retired almost stupified with intense fatigue to a bed which had only cleanliness to recommend it. Here both sunk into a repose so profound, that the day was closing when we arose. Our watchful guide assured us we must hasten over the dinner which long had waited for us, as we had many miles to journey ere we could find another safe resting place. Earnestly did I wish to remain with our present hosts 'till the next morning, but submitting to necessity, remounted in silence. Arthur well justified the confidence of his lady, having selected horses that never flagged through the whole journey, and always guarding against discovery by conducting us thro' roads very little frequented; among which he found hamlets whose inhabitants were gratified in merely seeing him, and who only attended to his companions in the hope of obliging him. I was astonished at observing how little curiosity we excited, forgetful that the mind is worn down with the body, and that a common laborer rarely considers any thing beyond those common comforts incessant industry alone can procure him.

Insensible to the beauties of the country through which we passed, I was for ever employed in looking for the sea, and when at last I discovered it, strove to extend my sight beyond, and dwell on that shore where I alone could think Lord Leicester safe. The nearer we drew towards the coast, the stronger my fears became. It was inhabited chiefly by men hard by nature, and desperate by profession; accustomed to murder as well as plunder those wrecked on the shore, they sternly examined and defied every passenger. I could hardly persuade myself that some of these were not stragglers from the banditti of Williams, and blessed Heaven as tho' all peril had been past, when we arrived at the homely dwelling of Arthur. It stood on a lonely part of the shore, where lofty cliffs shooting far into the sea, gave safety in the little bay to a few fishing-boats and small vessels. Ah, how do our awakened passions entirely curb every prejudice. Those livid lightnings, at which my nature ever before shrunk, appeared of late but the quivering lamp of love. Now I saw and heard undaunted the encircling sea (once the happy boundary of human pursuits) whose restless waves roar a proud defiance to all who dare approach it; and my sole fear sprung from learning that the wind was entirely contrary, and the watery chasm yet impassable.

Too late we lamented departing unattended. Unable in this sequestered spot to discover any part of what had passed in the court since our flight, and unwilling to trust, as well as unable to spare our guide, or his friends to make an enquiry at the next town, several tedious days elapsed in melancholy and conjecture. Arthur, not being able to go out in his own vessel, without suspicions and examinations we durst not encounter, hired a large fishing smack,[10] in which he stored the few necessaries our limited situation allowed us to provide, and I watched without ceasing the playing of its streamers. On the evening of the third day, I perceived them suddenly point towards France: rest having recruited my strength and spirits, I started up in a transport of joy. The few mariners being gathered at last together, I stept with a lightened heart into a miserable boat, which bore us swiftly towards that destined to convey us over, when two strangers riding full speed to the shore, called to us to put back with the most frantick eagerness. I took the alarm, and offered the mariners imaginary worlds to row on, when Arthur insisting that he knew the voice, turned the boat. I threw my arms round my Lord, as though my heart would have opened to hide him; and regardless of his remonstrances, that we could be in no danger from only two people, however hostile their intention, my senses died away. Recovering at last, I found myself in the cabin of the vessel, reclining on the bosom of Lord Leicester, while a youth who knelt at my feet, prest my hands alternately to his lips—"Look up, my beloved," cried my Lord, "and see whom fortune has united in our exile." "Ah, rather do not look up, lovely Matilda," cried Miss Cecil (for it was that sweet girl indeed in the habit of a boy) "till you have considered what reception you ought to give the selfish friend who has dared interweave her fate with yours. Yet hear, before you judge me," added she, rising with a mild majesty, which gave unspeakable graces to the blushes that every moment visited, and retired from, her cheeks. "I am going to lay my whole heart before you both. It is in vain to attempt veiling a weakness from Lord Leicester, so many circumstances have concurred to betray; it remains with me then to ennoble it. The discovery of your marriage, my amiable friends, quenched the last feeble hope which lingered in my heart. Convinced my partiality could never constitute his happiness, I instantly resolved it should become his pride. Self-love expired before the elevated idea. Ah, what but this could have enabled me to lead him into the garden at midnight, and take a look I then thought a last one, without dropping a single tear? I saw in a moment all the merit, the charms of her character whom he had chosen. Should I hate her then for being all I would have endeavoured to be? for accepting that distinction (which not depending on youth, beauty, merit, or fortune) is the dearest bounty of indulgent Heaven? Ah, no, my heart was juster, and welcomed her as one born to divide it with Lord Leicester. Solely intent on the prosperous flight of both, I almost forgot the servants planted in the Recess, and all the monsters that infested it. I fancied to myself those hours, when all your danger past, you would sometimes think of her who could only think of you. I heard both sigh, and wishing but to be enough remembered to soften without wounding either heart, I sighed myself; and started from these pleasant reveries at the voice of our steward, who rushing abruptly into the room, dismayed my every sense with his recital. 'Rejoice, Madam, rejoice,' cried the man with honest zeal, 'and think this stranger born for your service. Never can we enough adore the astonishing interposition of Heaven! It is not long since when tired with watching in the dungeon, a variety of voices struck our ears, which soon approaching us, every man summoned all his courage; shortly the door was unbolted, and a ruffian darted in, whose daring look was changed to an icy paleness (which lights from behind reflected) when he found each arm seized by one of our people, while a third held a pistol to his head. Uttering a faint imprecation, he alarmed the rest, and both sides immediately fired. We then pushed forward, without any regard for those who fell; and pursuing the rest through the various avenues of the den, secured them all, as we have reason to imagine, astonishment half depriving them of the power of resistance. In the largest apartment of this strange place, we found (guess, Madam, how we were amazed) our Lord, with an unknown lady, and three of our fellow servants, who were newly brought in by the ruffians, and bound; nor do I doubt but a dreadful death was designed them, but for this wonderful event.' Alienated as my affections must long have been from my father," continued Miss Cecil, turning the discourse to herself, "I could not hear of his wonderful escape, without feeling the most lively satisfaction. It was damped, however, by recollecting the body of Williams. I saw too plainly, that I must now account for it to one invested with authority to enquire, and resolution to convict me. Lost in a variety of plans, my father had been some minutes in the house, ere I stirred from my own anti-chamber, where his approach at once confined me. Faint and silent I arose, and bending before him, wept forth my duty and my joy. 'I know all you would say, my child,' cried he eagerly, 'and how this horrible place was discovered; but where is Lord Leicester and his Lady?' Struck dumb with a question, as clear and decisive as if he had been a sharer in the transactions of the night, my eyes were fixed upon him in terror and stupefaction; when my brother, impatient for the discovery, made his way at once into my chamber; whither the loud exclamation he gave collected all present, nor could my father resist hastening, as fast as his infirmities permitted; hoping, as I had reason to imagine, he there should find that enemy, who more engrossed his thoughts than the preservation of his own life, or mine. How were all amazed when the lifeless villain Williams, alone appeared? Some examined his pockets, while others searched the chamber. My father spoke not for some time, when fixing an eye on me falshood never durst encounter, he pointed ironically to the body: 'You killed him, doubtless,' said he, and relapsed again into his meditation. After a time, some faint remembrance glanced across his mind. He drew near, and examining the dead man's features, seemed to recollect, and in recollecting to dread him; for at once he shrunk into himself, and repeated in a low voice, '*that* villain!' Not having, however, any clue to his thoughts, though he had to mine, there rested my idea of the matter. I collected all my courage, and framing the most plausible tale the present situation allowed, resolved to abide by it whatever the event. My father likewise settled his plan of proceeding, and far from regulating the servants, whose every motion fear made wild and eccentric, turned his attention solely on me. Rising at last with a stern air, 'Rose,' said he, 'follow me.' I had of late been but too much accustomed to that harsh voice, and obeyed in silence. Seating himself in an adjacent apartment, he demanded an exact recital of all the horrors of the night. I commenced with the being roused by Williams. I related his design, and the threats which had almost brought my life to the point of a moment, when substituting Arthur for Lord Leicester, I affirmed that it was his providential arrival, guided by an unknown lady, and the desperate courage supplied by the emergency, which rescued me from the knife of that inveterate villain. He interrupted me, eagerly enquiring for the lady. On my assuring him she was gone,—'think well,' cried he, in a terrible voice, 'think well, rash, romantic girl, ere you venture again to answer me. I *know* the cause of Leicester's flight, I know too its companion; I know that he escaped a few hours before from the dungeon in which I was found; I know, if so, who must be his confederate. Stain to the name of Cecil, degenerate wretch, not content with the blind credulity of youth, to embosom, rescue, and abet a traitor, wilt thou conceal his *wife?* Tremble at the vengeance of thy sovereign—tremble alike at that of thy father.' Convinced (by whatever wonderful means he was so fully informed) that I could not hope to delude him, I started up, my complexion changing every moment. 'I indeed find myself, my Lord,' cried I, 'unequal to a falshood, but you will find me equal to the most desperate truth. It was Lord Leicester, I own, whom Heaven itself brought to my relief, and shall I deliver him up to death who saved me from it? Oh never, never! Sheltered in a spot less liable to suspicion than that from which they lately escaped, he with his chosen happy bride can safely wait till the violence of the Queen gives place to justice. Tortures should wring no more from me, and whatever my fate, it will always admit of one sweet consolation, in the remembrance that Heaven allowed me to recompence a benefit at the moment of receiving it.' Why should I repeat," sighed our fair narrator, "all the rage, tears, and altercation, that for a few days made life a torment to me? Totally confined to my apartment, and treated like a criminal, it was even hinted my continued obstinacy would provoke my father into making that horrible den, the Recess, my prison. In one instance alone was I fortunate: my mysterious speech impressed on my father's mind an opinion, he had previously adopted, that Lord Leicester, with his Lady, must be secreted in or near Kenilworth Castle, whither his most trusted spies immediately resorted, and amused[11] him with various suppositions dispatched daily from thence. Oppressed with unkindness and severity, often did my weak, my wavering heart prompt me to follow, and if possible overtake you; but the instant recollection of the obvious track such a rash flight must open to your inveterate pursuers, always subdued so unjustifiable a wish. My father at once changed his measures, and releasing, carried me with him to every suspected place in the neighbourhood; hoping from the alteration of my features he should discover that which contained Lord Leicester. By a fatality which completed my misfortunes, in one of these tours we encountered Irton, that lover who cost me both the Queen's and my father's favour; encouraged by Lord Burghley once more he returned with us. Incapable of love, but infatuated with politics, his ardent desire of holding a rank in his favourite line through my means revived. Regardless of my tears, coldness, and disdain, he had always looked up to my father as the decider of his fate, and still continued to do so. I had the misery of learning a bargain was made, of which I must be the unconsenting pledge, and that almost immediately. I knew my father's inexorable nature; I knew likewise that of Irton; and had reason to dread that the next fit of rage would consign me to legal infamy, unless by a desperation on my own part, I prevented this on theirs. Wonder not that at last I yielded to a measure so long combated. I selected a servant in whom I had a confidence, who procured me this disguise, and offered to protect me. I blest that faith I could never hope sufficiently to reward; and winged alike with hope and fear, pursued your route with indefatigable diligence; having left a letter which spoke of London as my asylum."

To this generous recital, my Lord, and self, replied with reiterated assurances of friendship and protection, as well as the highest encomiums on her courage and conduct. Shortly after which, my Lord quitted the cabin. "You who have long been the confidante, the sole confidante of my weakness," resumed Miss Cecil in a tender tone, while her doubtful eye seemed to search my very soul, "will be less surprized at its effect than its confession. Yet even that, strange as it may seem, sprung from prudence. I had well considered, my dear Matilda, every part of my past and future conduct. I too plainly felt, that while I imagined my Lord a stranger to the impulses of my heart, it might still adhere to him with a dangerous tenderness. By the boldness of this step I have made him a judge over me, and shall act with the severest prudence. I know your generous disposition, seeing only the better part of mine, might have induced you still to wish me near you;—how could I resist so sweet an invitation? Ah, only by silencing the most decisive pleader! Lord Leicester can now never urge me on the dangerous subject. In whatever place you fix your residence, I will retire to a neighbouring monastery as a boarder, where always hearing of, and sometimes seeing both," added she in a voice broken by sobs, "my wishes will be completed: nor do I imagine you will in the interim grudge me a share in Lord Leicester's danger." "Ah little do you know me," returned I, pressing her hand affectionately, "if you think I could grudge you a share in his happiness; never, my tender generous girl, never more will we part; never could Lord Leicester *hope*, or his wife *fear* any thing unbecoming from a soul like your's. Actuated but by one sentiment, counterparts by nature of each other, you and I should violate her laws were we to separate." "To own the whole truth, my sweet friend," returned she, with her usual noble ingenuousness, "I expected this instance of your generosity; but it only confirms my resolution, and my own heart would anticipate the condemnation of yours were it possible for me to waver."

A sense of safety, and of gratitude to my fair friend, diffused itself through my soul as the evening closed, to which I had for some time been a stranger: Lord Leicester pressed us to enjoy the sweetness of the hour. We ascended the deck, and seating ourselves in a little boat lashed to it, every fear, every hope seemed suspended, and the present all of our lives for which any had a sense.

The gentle breezes only played upon the white sails, and the vessel cut with a safe and pleasant motion, through those green waves whose points the full moon exquisitely silvered, as breaking they gave life to the stillness of the night. I turned my eyes with the sweetest satisfaction from my love to my friend, from my friend to my love; the same mild orb delicately illum'd either face; a manly tenderness marked Lord Leicester's attention to me, a grateful deference that to Miss Cecil, while the fair Rose, rich in the applauses of her own heart, and nobly conscious of her claims on ours, forgot there was any thing wanting to her happiness. These sacred pauses in life, which lovers only know, invigorate the soul as sleep does the body, and alone can enable us to sustain the past and coming ills. Prepared by a mental calm for the happiest repose, sleep asserted a claim to those hours fear and fatigue had long possessed, and my Lord insisted on remaining above: the loveliness of the weather, though the autumn was far advanced, made this less dangerous, and Miss Cecil at last consented to share with me the only miserable bed, which nevertheless afforded us that rest a palace had often denied. The next morning entirely reversed the scene, and destroyed at once our comfort and tranquillity; with the moon the weather changed, and the wind becoming entirely contrary, that deadly sickness incident to voyagers, seized alike on Miss Cecil and me, absorbing even the sense of danger. With an exhausted sullenness we surveyed those roaring surges, whose hollows fancy could not venture to fathom, and saw ourselves driven almost back to the shore of England, without strength or spirits even to lament our cruel destiny. My lord, happily, more used to the sea, resisted its influence, and exerted himself equally in comforting the sufferers and assisting the sailors: happily too they were all well acquainted with the coast; while the contrary wind, and enraged elements, constituted in one sense our safety, as every other vessel took shelter in the nearest port, and waited in safety more favourable weather. Tost about for near ten days, we at last made Havre-de-Grace[12] early in the morning, when more dead than alive I was conveyed to the first inn, and instantly put to bed.

Here my fatigues and apprehensions were very near producing a misfortune I from the first had dreaded. I had but too much reason to fear that the poor babe who had been the innocent cause of these calamities would never live to reward us for them, but urged into a premature existence, of all this mighty world would claim only a grave. The grief this gave me increased the danger; I knew the passionate desire of offspring which possessed my Lord. I had often flattered myself this wish, if indulged, would fill up that void in his life the promise had caused. What then should I suffer to see such a disappointment added to the sacrifices and degradations I had already entailed upon him? It was at this crisis all the merit of Miss Cecil shone forth: to the delicate attentions of a friend she united the soft solicitude of a mother. She soothed my mind with the most flattering hopes, and jealous lest in any fretful moment my secret soul should doubt her attachment, she so entirely forestalled every suspicion, that uninformed spectators would rather have imagined me the only source of her happiness, than the sole obstacle to it. At length I conquered the danger, and then my spirits returned faster than my strength. Often I talked of England, of my sister, and the expected dispatches. I wrote to Lady Mortimer, and briefly related those incidents I have here explained in many pages; I claimed her alliance, her protection, explained the present delicate situation of my health, and enclosed my picture in little, not doubting but that would identify my birth: and part of the diamonds we brought with us were converted into money, to establish our rank, if we found it prudent to acknowledge it.

I continued a long time too weak to quit my chamber, yet at intervals a new fear disturbed me. I perceived my Lord absent and anxious; an extreme paleness often overcame the floridness of nature, and traversing the room for hours, he would give way to a chagrin the cause of which not all my tenderest intreaties could wring from him. I often recalled the words of my sister; I fancied he vainly regretted the distinction of royalty, the pride of splendor, and the pleasure of popularity. Accustomed to be the object of every eye, to have every wish forestalled, to be obeyed ere he spoke, I, sighing, owned the change in his fate might well appear dreary. Not daring to hint my ideas, I impatiently expected the return of the express sent to Rouen, hoping it would open new prospects, and disperse the heavy cloud between him and felicity. But oh how delusive is human perspicacity!—insolently vain of our bounded knowledge, we boast of tracing every thought and action of individuals seas divide from us, even at the very moment we misjudge all with whom we are immediately surrounded. My fond attention fixed partially on Lord Leicester, looked not out of himself for causes of grief. Lady Mortimer's answer at length arrived; she acknowledged her relationship to me with surprize and pleasure, and kindly lamented her infirm health did not permit her to pay, in coming to me, that deference my regal birth intitled me to; but that her train waited our permission to escort us to Rouen, whither she urged us to hasten, as well for our own safety as to gratify her impatience. My expectations being fully answered by this letter, breathless with joy I raised my eyes to Lord Leicester, who had been perusing it over my shoulder; they met his full of a sadness so meaning, that it numbed my very heart.

Long used now to dread every day would teem with some horrible event,

I snatched his hand, and in broken accents only begged to know it. He sunk at my feet, and hiding his tears with my robe, swelled with sobs that almost cracked my heartstrings. "You have told me you loved me, Matilda?" said he, in a broken and doubtful voice.— "Told you!" re-echoed I; "heavens and earth, can that, my Lord, remain a question? have I not for you forgot the rights of sex, of rank, of every thing but love?" "Have I not done all man could to deserve these sacrifices?" again demanded he. "Debate no more admitted merits," cried I, with wild impatience; "oh give me the truth, and all the truth at once; nor doubly torture me with this pomp of preparation. Whatever it is, I will remember there might be a worse, since my eyes still behold you: every evil but your danger my soul can surely cope with. You speak not yet: we are then discovered, betrayed, delivered up, condemned—the fatal power of Elizabeth has reached us even here, for nothing else can surely thus affect you?" "It has indeed," sighed he. "Oh why then," exclaimed I, forgetful of all my assurances, "am I unprovided with poison? for death must now be the only mercy hoped. May the ocean, from which we with so much difficulty escaped, entomb us on our return, rather than resign us up to her licensed vengeance." "The power of Elizabeth has reached us," added he, more mournfully, "though not in our own persons. Safe still in my arms, in my heart, you may, my love, long arraign and bewail a misfortune all Europe will bewail with you." His sympathising eyes explained the truth—the agonizing truth—my soul understood him—aghast with horror, my eyes seemed to set, and every limb to stiffen to marble; a sensation, to which fainting is ease, condensed every faculty, and nature, powerful nature, struck on my heart at the thought of my mother, with a pang perhaps equal to that with which she bore me. The radiant sun of Love seemed to dip into a sea of blood, and sink there for ever. Unable to reduce the torrent of my ideas into language, I buried my head in my robe, and pointed to the door, that all might leave me. Happily, my Lord saw a prudence in indulging me, and laying down several letters, instantly retired. A horrible transport for some moments benumbed me;—how multiplied, how complicated, how various, how new, were then my feelings! feelings which ever return with the remembrance! feelings which opened a vein in my character as well as my heart—all sense of gentleness vanished. The first paper I perused confirmed my fears—I saw in the first lines the decided fate of the royal Mary—I seemed to behold the savage hand of Elizabeth, dipt in the blood of an anointed sister sovereign.— I felt she was my mother, my fond, my helpless mother, and my heart floated in tears, which were hours working their way up to my burning eyes. The furies of Orestes surrounded me, and thundered parricide, nothing but parricide, in my ear.[13] What, groaned

I, after so long an endurance, such complicated evils, supported with a patience that left not her enemies a pretence for sacrificing her, that misery was reserved for her daughter? Perhaps even at the moment she laid that beauteous head, so many hearts were born to worship, on the block, every agony of death was doubled, by the knowledge her daughter brought her there.— Why did I not perish in the Recess by lightning? Why did not the ocean entomb me? Why, why, oh God, was I permitted to survive my innocence? In the wildness of my affliction, I cursed the hour, the fatal hour, when I ventured beyond the bounds prescribed me. Yes love, love itself was annihilated, and (could I once have believed it) deeply did I wish I had never seen Lord Leicester. Passing from paper to paper, I saw friends and enemies unite in the eulogium of the Royal Martyr.—[14] What magnanimity, what sweetness, what sanctitude did they assign to her—a bright example in the most awful of trials.— Subliming the idea of revenge inseparable from human nature, she comprized it in comparison.— And what a comparison!—casting off the veil of her mortality, to darken over the future days of Elizabeth, the radiant track of her ascension concentered, while it dimmed the eyes of those surrounding nations, who too late bewailed their shameful inactivity.[15] Spirit of the Royal Mary! oh thou most injured! sighed out at last my exhausted soul, from that blessedness to which the wretch now levelled with the dust, perhaps too early translated thee, beam peace and pardon! Assuage the horrors of the involuntary sin, and oh, receive my life as its expiation; or a little, but a little, soothe its sad remainder.

Yet vain and uncertain were all my ideas respecting the discovery I imputed to Elizabeth. Convinced nothing had ever been intrusted to friendship, I was assured nothing could have been betrayed. In the bosom of my sister our mutual secret rested, and there I imagined every motive must bury it. I reviewed every paper once more; alas, I only added to my affliction, by observing the name of Ellinor industriously avoided. Lost in conjecture, it was some time ere I perceived one letter my robe half covered: I pressed to my lips the writing of Lady Arundel.

"Scarce dare I allow myself time to congratulate you, my most honoured friend, on escaping the deadly rage of Elizabeth, so much do I know you long for news of your sister. Alas, that I could return, in that information, the pleasure yours gave me. Called to visit Lady Pembroke, whose danger was too sudden for me to be apprized of it, Ellinor came back to Court the very hour that my lord and you left it. Filling the place of my sister (who ought to have been in waiting) by this means she was unfortunately present at the time the Queen perused Lord Leicester's explanatory letter. Unbounded in her resentment, Elizabeth levelled it all against the unfortunate Ellinor; and in severely taxing her with treachery and guilt, dropt expressions by which she learnt the dangerous situation your flight had unfortunately placed her in, as well as the evils to which you both stood exposed.— Grief, fear, and indignation almost deprived her of reason; and the Queen insisting her silence proceeded from obstinacy, threw at her a large book she had been reading, which striking the sweet Ellinor on the temple, she dropt senseless at once. The other ladies cut her laces; and the eager eyes of the Queen were attracted by a small pacquet suspended to the black ribbon she always wore round her neck. Not even the surprizing effect its contents took on the Queen, has ever enabled any one to guess at them; colour, strength, and speech, for some moments forsook Elizabeth, when recovering her faculties, she once more perused the memorials; then deliberately tore them into atoms; and summoning Walsingham and Burghley, all her attendants, save the old Lady Latimer, retired. From the Court Ellinor was conveyed that night, though by whom, or whither, is yet a secret. Love and friendship are however incessantly employed in her favour; nor can her prison long remain so when once it is discovered. Were I to name the most ardent and anxious of her lovers I should surprize you, but he shall only be known, when with conscious pride he presents her to you, and claims his reward.

"The profound policy Elizabeth has always preserved with respect to Lord Leicester since his flight, is far from being satisfactory to his friends. She speaks of him only in an indifferent light, and as if employed by herself; while all that passed between them almost every body understands, though no one dares to say so. It seems indeed as if her rage had been diverted from him by another object. I need not name her here. Alas, how severely are you both revenged on the Queen! The galling chain from which she has at last enfranchised Mary, writhes round her own heart; and if it would gratify you to see her tremble, believe me you need only see her. Obliged to avow remorse, to give an example in the severity of her mourning, for a deed only her own will could have authorised, she has the misery of knowing her murdered royal prisoner enthroned in Heaven, and embalmed in the tears of even her own people. Never more will she taste of peace, for that indeed can only dwell with innocence."

The full conviction Elizabeth had incurred the abhorrence of all the world, by this horrible infraction of the rights of royalty, society, and sex, a little gratified my exquisite resentment. Yes, sighed I, Heaven has invented a punishment proportionable to her crime. Counteracting by one stroke the policy of her whole life, she has permitted herself to be known, and of consequence execrated. Destined to survive her youth, her virtue, her fame, and her happiness; although encircled with a diadem, her weary head shall vainly seek one faithful tender bosom to repose on. Those fiery passions, so often destructive to others, wanting now an object, must prey upon the heart that conceals them; till envying the glorious end, as she ever did the distinguished bloom of Mary Stuart, her fate is wound up in fears of her offspring. In vain her cruel care would extirpate them; every crime will but give birth to a new fear, and the martyrdom of the Queen of Scots will multiply the causes of her terror, since she now knows more than one child survives her.

As the evening closed, this billet[16] was given me from my Lord:

"The heart which has long bled by anticipation for your sorrow, demands to partake it with you. Oh! my sole love, deny me not a share in your compassion. Fearful every moment lest I should lose the daughter, the fate of the mother struggled with that grief in my soul, nor durst I communicate it till concealment became impossible.— I do not ask you to be comforted; weep on, my dear Matilda, but weep in my arms, for what have I left in life if you forget to love me?"

This little billet, happily calculated to awaken the softer passions, drew forth my tears in great abundance. I reproached myself with violence and unkindness. Let me not, cried I, while so severely lamenting one error, be guilty of another. Lost to the duties, the claims (oh Heaven that I should be so!) of a daughter, those of a wife ought to assume a double influence. Yes, chosen Leicester, I am yours, am ever yours; if this oppressed heart does not wholly dissolve in sorrow, you will one day be again its only object; and sacred from this moment be the rights of all united with me. I collected my wild afflicted thoughts, and raising them in prayer, a blessed composure overcame the agitations of my mind. Passing into the next room, where I heard my Lord walking, I threw myself into his arms. "Oh you whom I have so fatally loved," faltered I, "you who are now nearly my all, fill up, if possible, every avenue to my heart, and guard it from retrospection." He answered not a word, but pressing his cheek to mine, our tears mingled.

"I see too plainly the truth, the fatal truth," said I, recurring to Lady Arundel's letter. "Lovely, ill-fated sister, it was you then who accelerated our hapless mother's death! That Elizabeth knew me for a daughter of the Stuart line, she took a deadly means to certify, but how she discovered it, must ever have appeared miraculous without this letter; I plainly perceive my sister indiscreetly wore the duplicate proof of our birth, its dearest and best testimonial, while mine is yet treasured in the secret cabinet at Kenilworth; and this in one moment destroyed her own peace, and determined the fate of her mother.

Oh, most inexorable! Could thy vengeance demand more than one victim? Is then the daughter silently sacrificed on the lamented grave of her parent? Never more, beloved sister of my blood and heart, shall I behold thee! never more draw comfort from thy sweet accents, nor with thee pierce through the veil of futurity, and catch gleams of golden days. Doubtless Elizabeth imagines this the only authentic proof existing? Oh, if in consequence of that opinion she touches the innocent life of Ellinor, I will offer incontestible evidence alike of Mary's marriage with Norfolk, and our birth, at the foot of Henry's throne.[17] He is famed for justice and generosity; I am, alas, the helpless object of both. The family of Guise will unite to protect me; perhaps all Europe will aid too late the powerless King of Scots, and save him from feeling his impotence of royalty."[18]

Unable entirely to share, unwilling in the least to controul, my tender feelings for my family, Lord Leicester's life could not at this period be called happy. Miss Cecil again appeared our guardian angel. As an intermediate person she felt for, she soothed both, till my irritated passions meliorated insensibly into sadness. I began to listen to the flattering hopes she continually instilled, that my sister still lived, and some fortunate event might yet restore her to us. My Lord was assured, by the united testimony of his friends, that Elizabeth had no pretence for impeaching him, and Henry learnt with pleasure his design of fixing his residence in France. Thus again our peace seemed re-established on a better foundation than it had yet been: and I devoted my attention, for the present, solely to recompencing my Lord for all he had renounced in my favor.

Overwhelmed with the repeated solicitations of Lady Mortimer, I at last summoned resolution to set out for Rouen; from whence we had been supplied with every accommodation suitable to our rank. That city having long been distinguished as the refuge of every noble exile,[19] my Lord fixed on it for our residence: my relation to Lady Mortimer ensured me every honor, and Lord Leicester's name would soon form us a little court. The crisis[20] now approached very near, which both considered with joy and terror, and it appeared some relief to be in the eye of a Lady, whose experience and tenderness might lessen my sufferings. Lord Leicester's unwearied indulgence and anxious consideration, every hour endeared him more to me, and I gladly on reflection compounded with fortune for all her other severities, since the first object of my heart was still unaltered.

Averse to being known ere we had formed a suite, and selected a habitation, he gave Lady Mortimer notice that we should not arrive till night. As we past through the gates of Rouen, escorted by her train, my heart beat high with the idea of meeting the sister of the noble Norfolk; the only being (my own excepted) allied in blood to me. She met me at the entrance of a saloon; I clasped her hands with emotion; I wept upon, I pressed them to my bosom. She embraced me with extreme composure, and holding me back a moment, ran over my features and person with so keen a scrutiny, as convinced me sensibility was not her characteristic. While due compliments passed between Miss Cecil, my Lord, and her, I, in turn, indulged myself with an examination. Her person was full-sized, tall, and graceful, like all the family of Howard; her features visibly marked both by age, and decayed beauty; her dress simple, being like my own, of mourning, and her manners strongly conveyed the idea of superiority. Dignity tinctured with austerity, marked her conversation; and I felt, to my great regret, I had gained a relation without winning a friend. Two monks, to whom she paid a profound deference; an old officer of the Mortimer family, and his sister, were introduced to us as persons entitled to share our secret; and we saw it indeed lodged with them, ere our consent was demanded. Lord Leicester was struck disagreeably at this discovery, but struggled with his pride, and affected good humour; while finding myself, after all my dangers, under a roof sanctified by alliance, and where my Lord seemed restored to his proper sphere, pleasure dilated my whole soul, and I sat down to a sumptuous entertainment prepared on the occasion, with an appetite I had long wanted.

She avoided, in consideration of my state and fatigues, entering into our affairs, and brought her own before us with a kind freedom; assured us of the friendship of her eldest son, Lord Mortimer, who had preferred the pleasure of liberty in both his religion and actions, by serving in the wars of France, to seeking a precarious fortune in England, under an enemy to the Pope. The landed property, once the inheritance of the Mortimers, her Lord had prudently disposed of ere the return of Philip to Spain, in whose service he had ever continued: and that Monarch, famed as he was for meanness and ingratitude, had shewn a signal sense of the attachment, by a grant to her youngest son of a considerable portion of land in Jamaica, which he had cultivated under such indulgences, as made it every day more valuable. His marriage with a Spanish lady, had united him more firmly to their government and interests: but having lately had the misfortune to lose his wife, he had yielded to the intreaties of his mother to visit France, and was hourly expected. Occupied with her own narration, my aunt no longer remembered I was weary. Miss Cecil however reminded her of the hour, and we were conducted to a magnificent apartment.

Lord Leicester slightly touched on the little disgust he had justly conceived, and indulged a drowsiness which I could not immediately partake. New objects had awakened my fancy, and invaded my rest; images more pleasing than had blest me since the moment I had quitted Kenilworth Castle now enlivened my soul. Yes, my Leicester, said I, softly grasping the hand of my sleeping love, for me thou shalt no more be endangered, and degraded; beyond the reach of our enemies we may now laugh at all their impotent malice. Ah vain and presumptuous! a deadly snare was at that moment winding round my heart, and a punishment prepared which pierced it through the bosom of security. Alas! madam, this night of promised peace proved the æra[21] in my life; and became so by a misfortune which absorbed the sense of every other. How, how shall I recall the scene, and preserve recollection enough to paint it? Dropping into that soft lethargy which foreruns sleep—ah, why had I not been buried in the deepest? but I was born the fate of those I loved. It was my peculiar misery to raise the hand which cut them off from all but my memory, and oh to weep thro' life the errors of too soft a heart!— Sinking, as I have already said, into slumber, I fancied I heard a noise in the room—Starting up with a fear habit had made almost intuitive, I awakened Lord Leicester, who instantly drew aside the curtain. I discerned with inexpressible horror, by the pale light of a lanthorn,[22] many men surrounding the bed with levelled arms, while one with an imperious voice called out to him to surrender to the Queen of England. At that fatal sound my very soul recoiled, but my Lord, not deigning to answer, drew a sword, always laid under his pillow, and haughtily commanded them to leave the chamber. The men advancing, he aimed at the one nearest him, who, by instantly retreating, jarred the arm of his companion. The flash of death, the tremendous sound, the falling of the sword—all, all, confirmed in a moment my fate—Lord Leicester, the worshipped of my soul— my all on earth—alas, almost my all in heaven, sunk into my weak arms in a last convulsion.— That which, at the appointed period, shall annihilate nature, can alone surpass the impression of the moment. Terrible too was the confusion of these wretches at so unforeseen an event. The faint light they carried gleamed over those features so adored. He tremulously raised my hand to his lips, and gave up his soul in silence on my bosom.[23]

But who shall speak the misery of my mind? Precipitated, like the offending angels, at once from heaven to hell, an awful silence took place of lamentation. Oh it was a woe too mighty for complaint! Insensible to fear, I at length desperately urged his murderers once more to unite those they had thus separated. I bathed my bosom in the blessed crimson which still flowed from his, and called alike on heaven and man to end me. Alas, the only object of my hopes, my fears, my cares, my wishes, was congealing before the eyes of the forlorn wretch condemned to survive him. The entrance of Lady Mortimer wrought grief up to phrenzy, and for many days gave that relief to all my agonies.

Reason dawned upon my disordered soul like light through chaos. A dim remembrance of what I had been, preceded that of what I was. Faintly I recognized even the weak hand with which I drew back the curtain. I found myself in a narrow cell, lighted only through an obscure casement of painted glass. Intuitively my lips pronounced the name of Leicester—in vain—Nothing but my own voice returned upon my ear; and the lonely dungeon in which I beheld myself enclosed, overwhelmed me with so deadly a chillness, that the shutting of my eyes appeared a degree of relief. Thought rose tumultuously on thought, till in one moment the terrible whole flashed upon my mind. I seemed once more in that magnificent bed which from the peaceful asylum of love an instant converted into the bier of death—once more I caught that last, last look, indelibly impressed—and felt once more my heart congeal with the life-blood which sprung in torrents from his. I started up once more in wild despair; and wringing my hands, groaned forth his name in accents so piercing, that they roused the withered attendant allotted me, from her undiscovered pallet-bed at the foot of mine. Hurrying towards me, she muttered something I did not understand. "Heavens!" cried I, surveying her habit in amazement, (for 'till then I had never seen a nun) "where am I? surely in the Recess; and the grave has given up its former inhabitants for my relief and comfort?"— "Jesu Marie!" cried she in French, which I very imperfectly understood, "will this poor thing ever recover her senses?" "Ah no," added I, answering myself, "that fatal language confirms every dire recollection: inform me you, who are (I know not why) interwoven in my fate, where, where is my Lord? if all that flashes over my soul be but a wandering of intellect, and he yet lives."— She cast down her eyes muttering, "Yes, my poor child, you are sensible by that question." "Vain, vain hope!" cried I, bursting into tears, and returning to my native tongue; "yet oh! alive or dead, him alone do I require; restore him, but restore him! a dear, a sacred duty attaches me even to his ashes. Lead me to them, since they are all now left me, and allow me to lament at leisure." She shrugged up her shoulders, implying that she did not thoroughly comprehend my language, and crossing herself, denounced eternal perdition on me if I longer thought of a heretic, who seduced me from the true faith, and who of consequence became a dreadful example of vengeance; charging me to adore the holy Virgin Mother, who had by so gentle a punishment recalled me to the Catholick church. Yes, sainted Leicester, in the infatuation of her bigotry she dared to term thy death a *gentle* punishment. Indignation throbbed through those pulses grief had nearly stilled, and I gave vent to all the anguish of my soul: abjured with an aggravated contempt the erroneous faith of my ancestors, bewailed too late the credulity inspired by my own—execrated the cruel, the treacherous Lady Mortimer, and demanded my liberty with a spirit that perplexed and surprized the Nuns. Alas! I perceived at the same moment, by the increasing number who now gathered round my bed, how vain either threats or intreaties must prove in that instance. The Superior approached, and in an authoritative decisive voice informed me, that Lady Mortimer, in right of her relationship, had placed me entirely under their care and protection, relying on their pious endeavours both for the recovery of my reason and my principles: nor could I make so good a use of the first as to apply it solely to the recovery of the latter, instead of idly lamenting a loss which alone could have preserved my soul. They called the noble husband, of whom their illiberal tenets had just deprived me, an heretic; an outcast of society; a wretch not worthy interment. I heard without replying, but my soul was not silent. I appealed to the Most High, and he will not forget me. Oh! in the awful day of retribution, dreadfully will he distinguish the bigotted dictators in religion!

Happily for me, they understood less of my language than I did of theirs; which alone perhaps saved me from a harshness which must have added the ruin of my constitution to that of my peace.

You will be astonished, madam, at my surviving such unceasing complicated misfortunes, and above all, the loss of my beloved. I regard it myself with wonder, and impute my strength both of body and mind solely to the knowing no interval in my sufferings. Driven from one fatigue to another, from one agony to another, lamentation was continually suspended either by amazement, or that necessity for exertion which gives a spring to all but the weakest minds, and counteracts despondency. Grief, I may affirm from sad experience, cannot be fatal till it stills and condenses every other passion.

Left at last with only that miserable companion, my own heart, I ruminated at leisure. Deprived of Lord Leicester, happiness, revenge, name, fortune, every charm in existence, every right in society; entombed alive, ere the ashes of my Lord were allotted a resting place, I reviewed my whole fate with astonishment. Often wearied with suffering, did I meditate giving up a life no longer endeared to me, and quietly pursuing my soul's better part. Alas, the unborn cause of all my late dangers would still recal, still hold me down to suffer! Yes, precious remnant of my love, sole pledge of past felicity; last of the mighty Dudley line, sighed I, I owe thee the painful blessing of existence; I owe thy noble father's memory justice. I know the profound, the execrable policy of Elizabeth, nor doubt her escaping the slightest censure, unless I appear,—and shall I, shall I, oh Leicester, living or dead, forsake thee? shall she who cost thee every worldly good, allow thy honour, thy fortune, thy life, to be annihilated without one effort to retrieve either? No, since revenge is the little all now left me, let me secure that little. Disappoint, oh God! the weak and enthusiastic views of my unworthy relation; permit me to convey from this unhallowed grave, the honoured ashes of my love; let them overwhelm Elizabeth with late contrition and fruitless shame, and then, oh then, allow me to bequeathe to my trembling babe that life, I no longer wish to groan under!

To effect any part of these complicated designs, I found it absolutely necessary to stifle, in a degree, my feelings; and submitting to a dissimulation my soul abhorred, I requested to see that woman who was more terrible to my eyes than any thing human, Elizabeth excepted. This request flattered the Nuns with the hope of my conversion, and a little opened their hearts towards me. I now learnt that the wretches who robbed my days of comfort, imputed the event solely to accident, nor pleaded a commission beyond conveying Lord Leicester to England, and even that in so private a manner as shewed them without legal authority.— The whole had been conducted with so profound a secrecy, that neither the design nor its bloody event had ever reached the knowledge of the police;[24] to prevent which, the body of Lord Leicester had been immediately brought into an outer vault of the Chapel of the Convent, where it had been embalmed ready to send over to England, if such should be the pleasure of the Queen; which, as it appeared, was all they considered. The jewels and money, both Lord Leicester and myself possessed, when we entered the fatal gates of Rouen, seemed to have departed with him, as well as all information respecting the lodgment of those sums I have already mentioned; and I saw myself, for all that fortune once promised me, inheriting only a weed.[25]

As I endured with patience the religious visitations and homilies of the Nuns, as well as those of various Monks, who united with them in converting me, Lady Mortimer in a few days consented to judge of their cares by seeing me. This insolent woman considered the visit as a condescension, and hardly held out a hand mine shuddered again to touch. Unmoved with my paleness, my condition, or my habit, she calmly discoursed with the sisterhood and the Monks, while I continued drowned in tears that no human effort could stifle. A gentleman, who I understood was her younger son, addrest me with the voice of sympathy; uninfluenced by his mother's pious prejudices, he spoke of my misfortune as the first on earth, and of Lord Leicester as the man who most deserved to be lamented; and bewailed the delays in his passage, which had made him unhappily arrive too late to succour either. He spoke too in English. The words, the manner, the language, sunk into my soul, and a faint hope they struck out enabled me to support the ensuing conversation. Lady Mortimer addrest me with an air at once tenacious and haughty; treated me like a mere girl, who to a blind and unpardonable passion, had made perpetual sacrifices of every solid duty of religion and morality; represented me as the sole cause of my mother's martyrdom, a sin no penance could ever expiate; mentioned with horror that union, which wanting the sanction of the Pope, could not by her be termed a marriage: and valued herself on the happy plan she had laid to separate us. It appeared the information of our place of residence had passed from her to Elizabeth, who bargained for the secret delivery of Lord Leicester to her emissaries: a request Lady Mortimer complied with gladly, as the easiest and most effectual means of reuniting me to the Church. The plan of seizing him at midnight, had, she owned, been concerted by herself, as that was a time when he could neither resist, nor I follow him, to create any alarm: a circumstance she dreaded beyond any other thing. From the bloody consequence of this treachery she affected to acquit herself, though without expressing any sorrow on the occasion.

Oh, negative sin! groaned I inwardly; oh, dire collusion! wanting courage to act an ill, are you, when pre-acquainted, less guilty in not preventing it? the laws of England reached not hither; nor was Lord Leicester amenable by those laws; wherefore entice and murder him, beneath a roof alliance and hospitality should have doubly consecrated? Wherefore, but that the commonest inn would have protected him? Tears and sighs being all my comments on her speech, she joined the monks in elaborate exhortations; in high promises of presenting me to all my mother's partisans, and rendering me the head of the English Catholic party, whenever I voluntarily recanted my errors; or if I persisted in them, anticipating the judgment of Heaven, she resolved to punish my apostacy by an absolute seclusion within the walls which at present confined me. Faint, and overcome, I promised to deliberate, and with difficulty obtained the only request I had ventured:—the sad indulgence of weeping over the coffin of Lord Leicester.

I could hardly fail to discover, through this veil of simulation, pride and bigotry, a strong self-interest. The agreement for delivering up Lord Leicester to Elizabeth very highly offended those laws which protected Lady Mortimer, and to which she must have answered, had the intention only transpired; but when to that was added his murder, his midnight murder, in a city chiefly composed of Huguenots,[26] hardly dared she guess at her own danger. The narrow faith which embosomed her among Catholics, proved in this instance her safety, since united in her danger as well as principles, they were resolved to venture the utmost to secure her. Every subsequent day confirmed my opinion, and the absolute necessity of winning me over, or entombing me alive, made the Nuns omit no care or indulgence, after once I seemed to listen to them.

Fearful of rousing all my passions, and reviving every prejudice, by conducting me to the dreary unhallowed vault Lord Leicester was laid in, and not daring to bring his sacrilegeous ashes within their own Chapel, the Nuns amused themselves with decorating his sepulchre with all the pompous insignia of Death.— Ah! vain attempt to sadden anguish! Can midnight tapers, suspended black, or waving plumes relieve those eyes which seek in vain their only object? or gratify a heart writhing under the iron hand of calamity? Can mortal prayers ensure immortal happiness? or can self-sainted wretches bribe the Almighty even with the ore his bounty lavishes? Preposterous blindness!— Such were my mental replies to all their enthusiastic harangues; and this ill-chosen moment of assailing me, only fixed my fluctuating religious principles.[27] On the coffin of Lord Leicester, my secret soul pronounced a vow solemn and irrevocable, to know no heaven but his, nor seek it in another manner. Thou too, oh most beloved! wert present—but not to me—no more my eyes to imbibe pleasure from the lucid beams of thine!—no more my soul was to mingle with thine effusions, which so often had enabled me to sustain the malevolence of fortune! Ah, no! thou, thou, alone wert by a strange transition become my sovereign grief; and the cold lead which seared up dust so precious, enclosed at the same moment the heart of thy sad widow!

I had in vain enquired for Miss Cecil; the Nuns assured me they knew only from my delirium that such a person existed, and Lady Mortimer inexorably refused to inform me, whether she still did so. Deeply I lamented the loss of the only friend who could have soothed by sharing my affliction. Death had hallowed her passion with rights scarce inferior to my own, and my heart too frequently felt none but those who loved could lament Lord Leicester as he merited.

Mr. Mortimer soon became the medium between me and his mother; despairing to touch her impenetrable soul, I employed every moment of loneliness in subduing her son's. Slowly I unfolded my views, and slowly he too listened to them; yet he did listen. Fearful that every hour would add a new inconvenience, by the birth of that poor babe for whom I suffered such unremitting calamity, and dubious whether the pious policy of the nuns might not snatch it, as soon as born, from my feeble arms, as well to ensure my stay as my abjuration, new terrors sprung up in my soul. I could not but perceive an interested motive actuated Mortimer; reduced, however, to owe my freedom to any thing, I appeared blind to a tenderness every circumstance forbad him to avow. A very few days determined him, and he informed me he had secured an English vessel, the crew of which were to be his only assistants. How slowly is hope extinguished, and oh, how swiftly does it revive! actuated with the most impatient desire of escaping, I made even my grief subservient to it; and proposed to the Nuns periodically to watch in the vault with Lord Leicester, (a sad ceremony their religion permitted, and mine did not forbid) being told it would be easier to force a way into this than the interior parts of the Convent. Mortimer had himself directed in conveying thither my departed love, and allowed it to be an easy means of escape, and perhaps the only one.

I past part of several preceding nights in the same manner, accompanied by different Nuns, to lull suspicion, were it possible any should have arisen. What quick, what multiplied, what various emotions foreran the appointed time!— Every eye seemed to dive into my design, and every heart seemed intent to counteract it. I found it impossible to obtain the privilege of watching alone, and shivered lest my deliverers should arrive ere my pale companion was summoned; or I should want strength to prevent her alarming the sisterhood. Fortunately the night proved severely cold, and observing she was no sharer in my penance, I recommended to her to retire to her cell, and rejoin me when the mattins[28] were over. Disgusted with her employment, and already frost-nipt, she sullenly complied, leaving me alone with the coffin of Lord Leicester—Lost husband of my choice! Oh, ever dear, and ever lamented! sighed I, kneeling before, and invoking the senseless lead, not for herself is thy Matilda thus anxious: to vindicate thy honor, to preserve the precious earth which once was part of thee, and that which will soon become so, is all the use she now can make of freedom. An awful silence, which seemed only interrupted by the throbbing of my pulses, succeeded. Regardless of all those emblems of the grave, which harrow up the minds of the happy, I knew no fear but of the living. The bell struck upon my heart the decisive twelve. A jarring in the farthest vault reached my ear; another opened; I heard the feet of men; another yet; I was environed by my deliverers, and one spark of pleasure ran through my cold frame, as I raised my head from the coffin of Lord Leicester. "Fly, fair Matilda," cried the impatient Mortimer, snatching my hand to raise me.— "Stay, generous friend, and hear me," said I, with firmness. "You rescue only half of me, if you leave the ashes of my Lord behind. Would you part a miser from his treasure? rather will he be massacred upon it. *There* is enclosed the whole of mine; bear that likewise away, or entomb me with it; for never, I swear by him in whose presence we were united, never will I, alive or dead, consent to part with my husband." Offended at so unexpected a demand, he urged the difficulty and the danger, with a harshness I thought him incapable of; nevertheless, the place and time allowed not of long deliberation, and finding me inflexible, he at last ordered the sailors to convey away the coffin likewise. An order they only complied with, from taking the metaphorical phrase I had used, "of a treasure," in a literal sense. Attached to Lord Leicester beyond mortality, I always felt protected when he was present, and with ceaseless care watched my deliverers, convinced they would be but too ready to leave so great an incumbrance behind.

They bore me with swiftness to the banks of the Seine, where a boat waited; and the tide favoring, we soon reached a ship of considerable burden, which weighed anchor immediately. Agitated with a thousand remembrances, that of Mortimer hardly occurred to me till the vessel was under the sail, and I still perceived him on board. I had ever understood he was to leave me as soon as I was placed in safety, and reminded him of this promise. "I will leave you, fairest of women," cried he, eagerly grasping my hand, "when you are placed in safety; if you still are cruel enough to desire it. But can I quit you now? or venture to set foot in a country where I have for your sake violated the most sacred law, and exposed myself to condign punishment?" I should have found reason enough in this answer, but that his stifled, short-breathed joy, his ungovernable ardor, impressed my secret soul with terror, and robbed freedom of all comfort.

I found in the cabin, to which he conducted me, a woman allotted to attend me, who strongly recommended that repose my fate had long denied: the misfortunes from which I had escaped, united with those that still threatened me, to fill my whole soul; and willing to avert the fearful anticipation, I entered into some common discourse, with my attendant. I found, with infinite astonishment, that she was a midwife, and provided with every necessary for the expected babe. I should have considered this as the most tender obligation, but that a fatal doubt sprung up in my heart, and suspended every generous emotion. Alas, it soon matured into certainty! The vain and eternal fondness which made me insist on having the coffin of Lord Leicester placed in the cabin, allotted for me, at first seemed to inspire in Mortimer that horror common to weak or guilty minds, at sight of such an awful memento: a few days, however, rendered it familiar to him. A passion he no longer concealed, led him continually into my presence; neither the unburied dead, the black which seemed to envelop my withered heart as well as form, nor the sad circumstances in which I was widowed, any longer operated on his imagination. I too plainly perceived, that he considered me as his own, and only waited my recovery to avow his unwarranted pretensions. What dire vicissitudes of fear did my timid soul experience! I saw myself entirely in the power of this man; forlorn of every human aid! hopeless, helpless, save in the mercy of the Almighty.— Oh, thou supreme! sighed I, hourly raising my streaming eyes to Heaven, thou whose omniscient breath rolls on this mighty world of waters! oh, grant that they may prove my safety or my grave!

A little gallery ran before my cabin, whither I sometimes went for air. Devoured with reveries like those recapitulated, I one evening found them interrupted by the voice of a woman singing. The elegance of her manner, and the sweetness of her tone, convinced me it could not be my coarse attendant; nor did I know the ship contained another female save myself. Rapt in astonishment and curiosity, every sense subsided into ear. I recognized a favourite hymn; a hymn so swelling, solemn, and sublime, that my charmed sense pursued the subject almost to Heaven. She changed to death,—one tone, one deep, one dirge-like tone, struck on my vibrating heart, and almost silenced every pulse. A loud cry, with the name of Rose, burst from me—the noise of a person falling succeeded, and the singing ceased. I ran wildly up to the deck, and loudly demanded my long lost friend of the astonished Mortimer. Confused beyond the power of deceiving me, he opened a cabin immediately over my own. Ah, with what tumultuous emotions did I raise the much-loved, much-lamented partner of my fate! slowly she recovered from the stupor surprize had occasioned; a thousand remembrances endeared the pleasure of the reunion; alas! as many annihilated all sense of pleasure. Embraces and tears at length subsided. As soon as alone, I questioned her concerning the interval, the dire decisive interval.— "Waked by the universal confusion," said the fair Rose with bitter sobs, "which succeeded the fatal accident of the night that parted us, I demanded you, my friend, with frantic ardor, but in vain. A man, I soon understood to be the son of Lady Mortimer, who was concealed in the house when we arrived, shortly after entered my apartment, and ordered others who attended him, to convey me on board the ship which brought him from Jamaica. Tears and intreaties were fruitless, and in the dead of night I was conducted to the banks of the Seine, and rowed to this vessel, in which I found myself imprisoned, without the least hope of meeting you. I soon learnt, from the coarse jests of the sailors, that their owner was an unprincipled villain in all respects, and more especially where women were concerned: every hope of an escape was finally taken from me, by my having the ill-fortune to attach the Captain, whom fear of Mortimer alone has kept within bounds. I understood the vessel was bound for Jamaica, and only waited to take in a new cargo: nevertheless, I saw that completed without our setting sail; and hoped from this the hand of providence would yet interpose in my favor. Alas, little did I imagine that it was involving you in the same hopeless, desperate situation!— Judge then, oh *most* unfortunate," concluded the amiable Miss Cecil, "what fate awaits us both—rescued from the licentious wishes of your cousin, his worthless heart has only exchanged its object, and resigns me as the more ignoble prey to his more worthless companion: the little decency Mortimer has hitherto preserved towards you, this miserable meeting will finally put an end to. He now knows you are infallibly apprized of your destination, and how will you form your mind to it? The island to which we are bound is yet in the hands of a few settlers; power is almost their only law, and he doubtless does not want that, since he ventures to defy every other. Never more shall my aching eyes discern the safe, the pleasant shores of England, those shores they joyed to lose sight of.— Alas, they then were fixed upon an object, offended Heaven has punished me by claiming!"

How, how should we resist the numbing power of desperation, did not the sacred sense of devotion mostly spring from it, and lift the soul above humanity! Although more deplorably circumstanced than my friend, by a courageous effort I resolved to soothe and console her; and gently preparing her tender heart for the fatal object it was destined to encounter, I led her down to my cabin. Ah what affection streamed equal from our hearts and eyes upon the cold memento!

Miss Cecil judged too truly, and the infamous Mortimer no longer deigned to veil his views; perpetually shocking me with free and haughty declarations of his passion. It was but too obvious he knew his power, and considered his intention of marrying me as the most honourable distinction; even at the moment he scoffed at every one custom or nature had established. Miss Cecil was not less importuned, by a wretch rough as the element by which he subsisted, and both so regularly visited our cabin, that scarce could we call it our own, even at the hours sacred to repose. In the eternal conflicts, such a situation must cause, despair would too often prevail; and silently with dubious eyes we fathomed the abyss of waters on which we floated, considering it as the last terrible asylum.

In the midst of these horrors the appointed period revolved, and nature made her agonizing effort. In that awful moment I lost every sensation of fear, and resigned myself into the hands of my Creator; beseeching him to recall the troubled soul which so long had groaned before him, with that of the tender babe, whose first feeble cries pierced my every sense. As soon as my weakness allowed, they gave into my arms a girl, a dear, a fatherless girl, who seemed at her first entrance into existence, to bewail her unknown calamity. An impulse new, exquisite, unexpected, took possession of my soul; an impulse so sweet, so strong, so sacred, it seemed as if I had never loved till then. Feebly straining her to my bosom, I enthusiastically prayed the Almighty to bestow on her every blessing she had innocently wrested from me, while my fond heart baptised her in its tears. Powerful, powerful nature! how did I worship all thy ordinations! No fate can be wrought up to such a height of happiness, but some interwoven sorrow chastens us with the sad sense of imperfection; nor any so steeped in affliction, but some celestial ray streams through this frail mansion of mortality, subliming all our sufferings.

While my eager eyes gazed unwearied on my new-born cherub, and traced in her infant lineaments her father's matchless beauty, even till they ached with fondness, fancy pierced through the veil of futurity to unite each grace of person and of mind, and enduing her with all, every human claim upon my feelings seemed condensed, and revived in this new one. Oh, hope! sweet substitute for happiness, whose mental gildings dawn periodically upon the soul, like light upon creation, awakening and invigorating every active principle of being; recalled by this irresistible influence even from the dark, the dreary grave, each troubled heart arises, and shaking off the heavy dews of sorrow, slowly resumes its wonted habits. The pale converts of experience no longer dare to appropriate the darling object of their wishes, but meekly then receive the appointed pleasure, prepared alike either to enjoy or to resign it. As thus the maternal tye engrafted itself in my soul, I perpetually endeavoured to impress that of my dear unfortunate friend with the same train of ideas. Alas, in vain!— Rather surprized at finding me sensible of consolation, than disposed to receive it, Miss Cecil gradually withdrew a confidence I did not easily miss, and delivered herself up to that cold and sullen despair, which unsettles every principle. Intreaties and arguments soon lost all effect on her. Starting at times from an impenetrable reverie, a broken sigh would overturn all I could urge, while my continued adjurations produced too often a marked disgust. Obliged at intervals to quit the cabin (lest even my present situation should fail to protect it from intruders) and listen to the hateful addresses of her boisterous lover, often did the seat of reason appear shaken in this dear unfortunate on her return, and a vague and extravagant joy would suddenly give place to the deepest gloom and inanity. I saw these fluctuations with horror, and dreaded the moment when a rude demand of marriage should bring her fate to a climax. Ah, not without reason did I dread it! One evening after a conversation of this kind, I perceived her more than usually disturbed. Neither my prayers, nor the pouring rain could bring her from the balcony, where for hours she told her weary steps. I started at last from a momentary slumber on her re-entering the cabin. The dim lamp burning in it, shewed her with a slow and tottering pace approaching the last asylum of Lord Leicester; sinking by this repository of her breaking heart, she clasped her hands upon her bosom with a most speaking sense of woe; while over it her fair locks fell wild and dishevelled, heavy with the midnight rain, and shivering to its beatings. The wet drapery of her white garments floated far over the floor, and combined to form so perfect an image of desolation, as froze up all my faculties. I struggled for articulation. A feeble cry alone escaped me. She started at the sound from her icy stupor, and glanced her eyes every where, with that acuteness of perception which marks a disturbed imagination; then with a long sigh sunk once more into herself. A second cry, followed by her name, my bounding eager heart pronounced. She half arose; the motion of her lips seemed contending with the drear silence of the moment, but not a murmur broke it,—amazement, horror, the wrings[29] of death transfixed me. Springing up with ethereal lightness, even while her feeble frame shivered with agony and affection, she fixed on my convulsed features a long, long look, then waving majestically a last adieu, rushed again into the balcony. Unable to move a limb, my harrowed soul seemed, through the jar of the elements, to distinguish her dreadful plunge into the world of waters. A something too mighty to describe or endure came over me, and sense fled before it.

How long it was ere my careless attendant returned to my relief I know not, but a succession of fits, accompanied with dangerous shudderings, and a raging fever seemed every moment to promise me, from the ordination of providence, that relief my lost Rose had ventured to precipitate. Whether her fatal example, or my sufferings, influenced my tyrant, I know not, but his persecution entirely subsided; in the short intervals of reason my weakness produced, he condemned his own conduct, bound himself by the most solemn promises to convey me home, and conjured me to struggle for life, if not for my own sake, at least for that of my infant. Alas, my babe! when my cheek felt once more thy tender breathings, I accused myself for wishing to leave thee, and acknowledged the sad necessity of living. My cruel malady robbing the cherub of her natural sustenance, it was with difficulty she received any other, and the proposal he made me, of having her baptized, was readily accepted. That ceremony was performed the same evening. Alas, my precious infant, no velvet pillowed thy innocent face! no costly canopies preserved it! no noble sponsors, with ready arms, contended to receive thee! no father's blessing followed that of Heaven; thou wert, alas, given by a sordid nurse, to a more sordid chaplain, and by a dim lamp, within a narrow cabin, thy woeful mother raised her feeble head to see the child of Lord Leicester, a daughter of the House of Stuart, consecrated by the name of Mary.

Recovered a little from the effects, as well as the impression caused by the unhappy catastrophe of my darling friend, I could not fail to adore that gracious providence with whose decrees she had dared to blend her own, on learning that the insolent Captain had, on that fatal evening, by a fall broke both his arms, and lost the power of molesting her. At first this appeared a bitter aggravation, but soon it sunk into my soul, and regulated all my future conduct. Never! ah never, from that moment have I ventured to yield to rashness and despair, but when unable to obey, I have resolved to endure. How severely has this principle been tried? How often, when overweighed by the heavy hand of misfortune, have I been obliged to interpose between myself and my fate, the fleeting form of the beauteous Cecil escaping my helpless will, and rushing, uncalled, into eternity?

The vain hope of returning to England, with which Mortimer had flattered me into health, daily diminished; and the alteration of the air, united with the discourse of the mariners, to prove that the period of my disastrous voyage approached. I heard the fond, the universal shout; and that sweet emotion sailors only feel at sight of land, agitated every heart but mine. Averse and gloomy I turned my hopeless eyes towards a shore where nature's lavish hand had spread a fertility, which seemed to scorn the aid of art. Ah, where are now the barren hills, the chalky cliffs of England? sighed I in silence. I perceived St. Jago de la Vega; and in the idea of interesting the Governor I rested my last hope.[30] I knew not that eager to possess the abundant conveniences my tyrant had brought over I should escape the notice of the inhabitants, or be considered as living lumber not worth enquiry. Confined within the narrow bounds of my own cabin, I had the mortification of hearing the cannon and musick proclaim the arrival and departure of the Governor and Officers, after partaking a sumptuous entertainment; and on the same evening, while intoxication secured the chief people of the island in their own houses, I was landed, and put into a litter, which the slaves of Mortimer bore towards his plantations. The few idlers whom curiosity drew round me, disregarded my adjurations, and with cold insolence examined my features. Their remarks were made in a language I did not understand, and I plainly discerned they did not wish to understand mine. I too late recollected my being unveiled might make them form a false judgment of my character. Meek by nature, and bowed to the earth by misfortune, I lost all power of contending with my fate; and supplicating only the Almighty, awaited its dire completion.

I perceived it was not without reason Mortimer had boasted of his authority: with overbearing insolence he now demanded my hand, and bade me remember he was there a sovereign, nor did I see a being who dared even to murmur at his will. He presumed to rally the anguish he occasioned, and even sacrilegiously to insult the cold remains of that adored husband whose rights he seemed every moment ready to violate. Imagination had long since been exhausted in seeking means of redress. Flight was impossible in a country where I neither knew the roads, the natives, nor whether it supplied an individual willing or able to protect me. Many of his Spanish domestics I was not permitted to see; those that were allowed to approach me appeared haughty, repelling, and silent. I soon found they compounded with their pride for the servile exactions of duty paid to him, by lording it equally over his slaves; who, timid by nature, and subdued by cruelty, seemed to have lost the very wish of any other good than that of existence.

Tears, sighs, and refusals, could no longer avert, or even delay the sacrifice; and having only a few hours of solitude allowed, to prepare my mind for the ceremony, I hushed my smiling babe at my aching breast, and wearied alike with misery and prayer, dropt into a slumber. A dream represented me in the position I really was—sunk on the ground near the coffin of Lord Leicester. Suddenly I perceived the lid was removed. I started up, impatient to behold the chosen of my heart. I saw him once more, tho' wrapt in the garments of the grave—once more I saw rich life mantling on that manly cheek, and those fine eyes, mine never beheld without pleasure, once more beamed brightness upon me. Surprized, entranced, I made a thousand ineffectual efforts to speak, and holding out my newborn Mary, I saw (oh sweet, though vain delusion) a father's arms enfold her. My senses seemed unequal to the ecstacy: impenetrable darkness spread over my eyes, and a burst of ethereal musick absorbed every faculty. Recovering all, however, instantaneously, I looked upward. Alas, Lord Leicester was ascending with his daughter in his arms. I demanded her with agonizing cries; and, catching at a mantle which yet seemed within my reach, it fell upon me like the crash of nature, burying me under an immoveable weight. I awakened at the moment. 'Tis but a dream, cried my scared heart, but such a dream as the horrors of the approaching moment alone could counterpoise.[31]

Scarce had I recalled my shook senses, when Mortimer, attended by his chaplain and domestics, entered my apartment. While the latter were decorating it with Catholic pomp, I summoned the small remains of my courage to address the priest, who stood ready to mock the religion he professed.— "By that awful God, to whom you are consecrated, hear me, Father!" cried I, sinking at his feet, "and oh, that he may graciously impress upon your heart the sad protest of mine! by barbarous hands at once widowed and betrayed, it is no longer possible for every human power combined to make me happy; you, you alone, may make me wholly miserable. If to complete those manifold evils which the Almighty (for ends I cannot judge of) has permitted me to survive, with the violation of every right, both of religion and morality, can be called marriage, and you as the delegate of Heaven dare sacrilegiously to pronounce the ceremony, I stand here a devoted wretch, the hopeless, helpless, victim of my duty! But mark, I adjure you, my last declaration. I have a will, which circumstances can neither alter or bend—delivered up to this abandoned man, it is in his power to make me any thing but his wife, and against that title my soul will ever revolt, and my last breath protest."— "Unhappy, deluded young creature," returned the sordid priest in French, "were my conscience to prevent this marriage, it would be from a different motive than those you adjure me by; and such is the horror your obstinate heresy inspires, that did I not hope time, and a better husband's cares would convert your erring heart, hardly should I venture to unite you with a member of our holy church."— "Submit yourself at once to your fate," imperiously cried Mortimer, "for to end your hopes of the church's interposing in your favor, I will frankly acknowledge she put you into my power." I turned my hands, as well as eyes, in speechless astonishment towards Heaven.

"Hope not, my fair cousin," rejoined he with a malicious smile, "your sentimental innocence can cope with the arts of a sisterhood of Nuns. Wearied with your obstinacy, fearful of your escape, they gladly resigned you to me to ensure their own safety." He paused—my mind took in at once the dreadful truth—My *innocence*, ah rather say *ignorance*, groaned I mentally, that fatal error which ever too severely punishes itself—Hardly could I pardon myself the extravagant credulity. "Scarce could my mother persuade me," resumed he, "that you would be duped by so obvious a collusion; since a single moment's reflection must have convinced you that never man pervaded the last retreat of disappointed women, but by their own connivance: and all the precious mummery of the business but heightened the pleasure of the triumph. How could I fail to smile to see the breathless spouse borne in the train of a living one? who proudly clasped a timid heart which knew not then it throbbed against its master's!" Alike unable to utter, or suppress, the burning indignation this unmanly boast, this elaborate wickedness excited, I fixed my eyes inflexibly on the coffin of Lord Leicester, almost believing heaven itself would effect a miracle in my favor, by renovating my only protector. The ceremony nevertheless commenced; when a new event transfixed not only me, but every person present. A yell, wild, deep, shrill, and horrible, was succeeded by a tumult universal and tremendous. The paleness of death crept upon the cheeks of my late inhuman tyrant, who, with his confederates, turned around his hopeless eyes for some instrument of defence in vain. Impelled by desperation they all rushed out; but were instantly driven back by the tide of exasperated slaves. Appalled by their ferocious eyes, and bloody hands, I sunk into a swoon, but revived as it were by heaven's appointment to see the last, the deadly blow given to Mortimer; who reeling a few paces, groaned his last on the coffin of Lord Leicester: thus signally and memorably avenged. Surrounded with death in every horrid form, I expected continually the completion of my destiny; which I had certainly found, but that a Spaniard, who was united in the plot of the slaves, with the gallantry incident to his nation protected me in consequence of my sex and wrongs, and led me away to their rendezvous; assuring me I should there find safety. Terror almost annihilated my faculties as the ferocious slaves ran backward and forward, heaping in their huts the bloody plunder new murders every moment secured. Having gathered together all they thought it expedient to save, they loaded the horses, and each other, hastening to secrete themselves in those woods, which by narrow passes led to impenetrable retreats in the mountains. Many were the unintelligible disputes concerning me. Many a half-raised arm, and inflamed eye, glared death upon me; but the stroke was as eagerly averted by the interposition of the generous Emanuel. Yet perhaps his utmost interest[32] had been unequal to the occasion, but that one of the slaves they called Aimor, seemed suddenly won over to my party. He was among the ringleaders of this conspiracy, and his decision silenced every murmur. Horses were so precious, that Emanuel could only procure me one by resigning to his confederates his share of the plunder, which it had been allotted him to convey.

Fury now began to give place to fear; and the guilty wretches hastened their departure. The march commenced about midnight. Silent, bewildered, awe-struck, I had meditated on this succession of terrible events, without extending my views beyond the present moment, and scarce dared look towards the future. To see myself and infant led away thus suddenly into slavery, by a wild and unknown people, seared by the oppressions of their murdered master to all sense of humanity, through a country alike wild and unknown, exposed to the insults of two new-made lovers, and only safe in the guard they kept over each other; how strange the transition in my fate! I yet bent my soul to the power, who by such exemplary justice, released me from Mortimer, and thought every other evil less than being confirmed his wife, since that alone was without any remedy but death.

Ere we had made any considerable progress in our fearful journey, the rolling clouds became tinctured with a vivid crimson, and my companions were seized with the consternation incident to guilt. Notwithstanding they had used every precaution to conceal their ravages, on the spot from whence they had escaped, till out of the reach of danger, some unextinguished spark had caught fire, and extending through the range of buildings, I saw the rich, though ravaged possessions of Mortimer, one universal conflagration. The apprehension this diffused through the rest of the wanderers, gave place in me to a nearer and more affecting remembrance. Sad and silent tears streamed down my cheeks, when I considered that the whole riches of his base rival formed but the funeral pile of Lord Leicester. Farewell! a long farewell! sighed forth my oppressed soul. Oh, most beloved! Oh, most avenged! Whatever fate Heaven shall appoint thy persecuted widow, humbly let her obey the God, who so signally interred thee!— Alas! a few hours and no memorial of thy existence will remain, except that poor babe who feebly trembles to the beatings of her mother's heart. No faithful hand shall separate the ashes of the injurer and the injured: Yet let me not complain, since the fiat of the Almighty shall awfully adjudge the souls this fearful moment enlarges.

As Emanuel still walked by me, I sought from him to understand the cause of the present insurrection, and the different motives of himself and companions. "Those of the slaves," said that generous protector, "are like their natures, wild and various—my own, simply justice and love. The tyrannic Mortimer, whose fate no being will ever deplore, established himself in this island, no less by the favour of Philip the Second, than by marrying the sister of the present Governor, Don Pedro de Sylva.[33] In that nobleman he met a kindred mind; mean, mercenary, oppressive, and cruel; in one particular alone they differed; Mortimer was by nature bold and enterprizing; Don Pedro cautious and timid. The enormities of the first, however, always found shelter in the injustice of the latter; and Don Pedro not daring to carry on in his own person that piratical and illicit trade which alone can enrich individuals in the infancy of a settlement, secretly shared with his brother-in-law the purchase and the profit, while Mortimer was the only ostensible person, had any legal enquiry arisen. The arrogance, cruelty, and vanity of Mortimer, received a fatal increase by the accumulation of wealth, and set him above all restraint. Don Pedro, conscious he was in his power, ventured not to question, much less punish his conduct. The intervals between his frequent voyages destroyed the peace, and shortened the days of Donna Victoria, the uncomplaining victim of her brother's and husband's rapacious league. I came with her into the family as her *major domo*, a post, which rendering me a witness of the brutality of Mortimer, soon turned the disgust he generally inspired into hatred. I was the foster brother[34] of Victoria, and attached to her by a reverence so profound, that I insensibly adopted her wrongs as my own. Ungoverned and licentious in every instance, but more especially when women were the objects, force generally was employed by Mortimer, where fraud failed to succeed; and those domestics alone held rank in his family, who were readily subservient to his gross and vicious pursuits. My views died with my lady, and I should gladly have quitted him to return to Spain, but that he meanly retained a considerable sum I had been provident enough to save, as well as a legacy Donna Victoria had bequeathed me. Every complaint, or even solicitation for my own was silenced with the most haughty threats of perpetual imprisonment: a sentence I often saw inflicted for no greater fault. Nor could I hope to quit the island, as the consent of the Governor depended on that of Mortimer. The sense of undeserved oppression thus corroded my very soul, and prepared me for the incident which at last nerved my arm against the tyrant.

Meanwhile the base accomplices of his pleasures and his crimes, assumed a sovereignty over the miserable slaves, which they exercised till invention was exhausted in cruelty and oppression. In vain my nature shrunk at the sight of calamities I knew not how to remedy: unable to quit the island, or recover my money, two years elapsed in fruitless, and sometimes desperate projects. I saw the persecuted slaves ripe for rebellion, and only waiting a favourable moment to rise and sacrifice their train of oppressors; and though I did not purpose to join the confederacy, I concealed it with a sullen satisfaction, till the day which at once determined my conduct. Need I say it was that which brought you thither? When I saw you alike irradiated by innocence and beauty, led into those unhallowed walls—when I saw the tear of misfortune fall on your beauteous babe, like the spring's chaste dews upon the early blossom, I was persuaded your nature intuitively shuddered at the monster; and I swore to preserve you at the hazard of my life; nay even at the moment when hope should be annihilated in your heart. I joined at once in the conspiracy; the hands were ready, the head alone had been wanting. By various artifices I procured arms for the slaves, and fixed the insurrection on the day appointed for your marriage, as that on which Mortimer and his favourites would be wholly occupied, and of course unguarded. The hand of Heaven surely guided all our operations. The various villains have atoned (as far at least as life can atone) for their complicated iniquities. But, alas! Madam, I did not sufficiently consider consequences. It is dangerous to arm the enraged and the ignorant. I know, too late, your life and mine depend on a frail tenure, and only solemnly assure you, while mine lasts, yours shall be safe. The uninformed, desperate wretches, with whom we are surrounded, are not the simple happy beings injurious tyranny first found them. Inflicted cruelty has hardened their hearts, and the sight of untasted luxuries corrupted them. Their own wants have increased with the knowledge of our enjoyments, and what they greatly desire, they have learnt to go any lengths to attain. Why should I conceal from you that your only prospect of safety is the hope of being overtaken, though that to me is inevitable ruin. The fatal fire, therefore, which now these entangling woods almost hide from us, is of all the wonders of the late evening, the most visible interposition of Heaven in your favor."

The nobility of sentiment incident to the Spanish nation, especially in whatever relates to the softer sex, prevented that surprize so romantic a generosity must otherwise have occasioned. To gratify a request made with the highest respect, I entered into a recital of my own hapless story. Aimor, with jealous care, adhered to that side of my horse not guarded by Emanuel, and being ignorant of the language in which I spoke, depended on his rival for translating it; who, no doubt, gave it every construction most favourable to his own views. The information that I was the daughter of a Queen, ran through the troop, and something softened their ferocity: but soon on that pompous distinction, were grounded vain hopes of an imaginary good they were all to derive from me—from me, who was in fact, the most helpless and unprotected of all the miserable wanderers.

I pondered much on Emanuel's remark, that my safety could only be ascertained from our being overtaken; but when I considered the desperate state of all the wretches with me, should that happen, hardly dared I hope it. Still we journeyed onward, through woods the stars of Heaven could scarcely penetrate; and when I recollected the frightful wilds and mountains beyond them, in which myself and babe must infallibly be buried for life, how did my heart die within me! But when to that fear was added the dread of evils yet more horrible, hardly could my senses support the oppression. Aimor, I was convinced, would not want the aid of his whole party, and how could I hope one generous individual would be able to struggle with a tide of combining foes? But even if Emanuel had the address to manage them all, would not expectations in his own favor, hardly less fearful to my thoughts, arise in his heart? Through the chill windings of the desert woods, I raised my soul to him whose eye pervades alike the gloom of midnight and the blaze of noon, and something seemed to assure my sinking spirits, that he rescued me not from the horrors of the Recess, thus to abandon me.— I did not err in that devout confidence. The dawn of day obliging the body to be more guarded in their march, they chose a lone hollow, and halted to send forth scouts, and refresh themselves. Alas, I sighed for the poor wretches, who, seduced by European crimes to a dire imitation of them, had wanted foresight to secure themselves the common comforts, which alone render life endurable, though overwhelmed with gaudy trifles they knew not how to enjoy.

The temporary calm into which they sunk, was fearfully interrupted. The scouts sent out pressed back, with immediate notice that they were intercepted, and so hemmed in that it was impossible to proceed a mile further. Though by this notice my own safety was ascertained, my very soul partook the misery of my companions. The wretched women threw their arms, for the last time, round their despairing husbands, and bathed them with tears so bitter, as might wash out the stains of blood yet recent. The men, thus totally devoted, with a stern and unaltered brow, seized their arms, and resolved to rush upon the broken parties, gracing their own death, by making the loss equal to their enemies. Even some of their wives, rendered furious by the occasion, followed with such scattered weapons as they could collect, and the rest, no less tamed, gathered themselves and hapless children round me, as if I could preserve them; pursuing their friends with a cry that might shake the throne of mercy. Aimor and Emanuel cast a lingering eye towards the foot of the tree at which I sat, apparently the Queen of Sorrow. It was dreadful to make a visible distinction at that moment, and perhaps embitter their last. Laying my babe upon my lap, I tendered a hand to each; the boon was eagerly accepted. Even the savage became humanized, an impassionate tear fell on the hand that shuddered at his touch; while Emanuel, more gracefully obsequious, bowed to the earth, and removing his ardent eye from my face to that of his rival—"Adieu, most worshipped of women! cried the gallant Spaniard, adieu, for ever! How many evils does death save us all from!"

During the horrible interval of blood and slaughter, I endeavoured to close my ears to the sound of the firing, which was echoed by the agonizing groans of the wretches around me. The conflict was short; and bands of Europeans soon pierced through those shades, where a few minutes had made so many helpless widows. Those guilty but unfortunate women, prostrating themselves before the presented pieces, endeavoured, by the most submissive gestures, and offers of their children, to assuage the wrath of the incensed victors. I feebly arose likewise, and pressing forward to the apparent leader, astonished him with the sight of a white among the survivors. I exhausted my little remaining strength in soliciting protection for myself and child, and pity for my companions. He heard, without comprehending me: his very soul was intently fixed on the scattered riches this reduction of the slaves put into his hands, and neither myself, my daughter, or my fate, seemed an object worth regard. The whole party busily employed themselves in collecting the valuables of every kind, and afterwards taking into consideration the human plunder fortune had once more restored to them, they drove off the female slaves, and their children, bending beneath the weight of misery, fatigue, and manacles.

Emerging from the depth of those unwholesome woods, through which I had wandered, I lifted my eyes devoutly towards that rising orb, which seems no less to give light to the mind than the creation: and called on the pleasing prospect of the future, to counteract the horrible impressions of the past. Restored by this extraordinary means once more to civilized society, my heart acknowledged the charm, the simple, the solitary charm of liberty, and springing forward toward England, overleaped every intervening obstacle. Convinced, by fatal experience, at once of the fragility of human happiness, and the persecutions to which nature's dearest gifts too often expose us, the bright forms of love, ambition and glory vanished, leaving no image for my fancy to rest on but Content. I saw her meek eye lifted to her heaven-born sister, Resignation; whose hallowed beams streamed through her earthly cottage, impearling every tear: and my soul sighed after the sad peace of which I found it yet capable. The dear, unconscious partaker of my wayward fate, with many an innocent smile, revived my spirits; and devoted to this only object of my pleasures, I sought in her to lose the sense of every other care.

The curiosity I had at first excited among the whole party, extended not beyond common enquiries, and as I spoke no Spanish, and French was but indifferently understood by either them, or myself, I could hardly hope greatly to interest them in my favor. I had made them comprehend, that I was a near relation of the murdered Mortimer, but that circumstance, far from interesting, seemed rather to alienate and disgust them.

It was night ere we reached St. Jago de la Vega, where we found the inhabitants universally under arms, and eagerly expecting the return of those sent after the rebellious fugitives. Confounded with those persecuted wretches—unsheltered from the taunts, insults, and execrations of an incensed populace, I found myself yet the victim of angry fortune; and overworn with suffering, dropt senseless at the door of a prison, where I understood my journey was to end. I revived on a miserable bed, in a dark room, and without any companions! but conscious of safety, as well as free from guilt, I recommended myself to God, and sunk into the happiest repose I had known since I passed the fatal gates of Rouen.

A black slave brought me some coarse provisions in the morning, nor did I know till the evening that it was meant to sustain myself and child for the day. It proved, however, more than sufficient; for my constitution, which had hitherto resisted every danger, had now received a shock of the most desperate kind. Racked with intolerable pains through all my limbs, I was sensible, too late, that my own imprudence had added a malady of body to all my mental sufferings. During the last awful conflict, when the offending rebels expiated with life the ravages they had committed, I, in common with the females they had left behind, had thrown myself on the ground, alike through weariness and terror. The unwholesome damps arising from a spot which yet the sun never penetrated, stiffened every joint; a rheumatic fever was the cruel consequence. Alone, uncomforted, unassisted, consumed by an internal raging fire, I groaned, I shrieked, with intense torture. The starts and cries of my little one, alone informed me I had done so; I hushed her on a bosom I feared would scorch her, and eagerly swallowing whatever liquid was brought me, had hardly intervals of sense enough to share it with my babe, or sufficiently to provide for her nourishment. The days of this excessive misery were unnumbered—insensibly the fever subsided; but left a lameness happier hours, and incessant care, could never cure.

When returning reason allowed me to extend my reflections beyond the present evil, I recollected from the time elapsed, that my imprisonment must be decided and perpetual. Emanuel had told me the Governor was timid, mean, and avaricious; forgetful of this, I had informed my conductors of the family tie between myself and Mortimer; which rendering me his natural heir, this unworthy Governor, I doubted not, had annihilated my claim to possessions he was resolved to appropriate, by classing me with the murderers, among whom I was found: and by an arbitrary proceeding, (not uncommon there, if Emanuel might be relied on) sentenced me at once, unwilling to venture a judicial enquiry. The languor incident to such incessant sufferings, both of body and mind, as I had for a course of time endured, rendered me less shocked and grieved at this, than many other contingencies. It seemed in my power to die, and disappoint the malice of my oppressors. It was only to remit a little, a very little care of myself, and my constitution would finally give way. Perhaps I should have delivered myself wholly up to this idea, but that the first great tie of nature, still wound round my bleeding heart. My fate, said I to myself, is fully, is finally accomplished. A sad inheritor of my mother's misfortunes, methinks they are all only retraced in me—led like her, a guiltless captive through a vindictive mob, the object of vulgar insult, and opprobrium—like her enclosed unjustly in a prison; even in the bloom of life, a broken constitution is anticipating the infirmities of age. And shall the similitude end here? No, let me like her, extract fortitude from each accumulating injury, and if the will of my Maker shortens the common term of life alotted to mortality, oh let me come into his presence a spotless martyr! and thou, sweet babe, permitted like the palm tree to flourish under oppression,[35] surely for some great end hast thou survived the succession of calamities which foreran thy existence, nor dare thy mother once wish to desert thee!

The days, Madam, thus strangely past on. The female slave I have mentioned appeared every morning, and performing the common offices of life in silence, placed near me the food allotted, and vanished till the next. Imagine not I acquiesced, without attempting at least to ascertain my imputed crime, but I found the poor wretch was so totally deaf, that not one word reached her, nor did she speak any other language than her own, and very imperfect Spanish, to which I was a stranger. Neither could I convey to her by signs, ideas I could find no visible object to represent. The tender graces of my daughter, nevertheless operated gradually on the untaught soul of the Negro, and I had reason to think she would even have connived at my escape, but that such a measure would only have increased my misfortunes, while thus without a friend, a home, or a hope.

One circumstance continually embittered my mind with distant remembrances; the tower in which I was confined adjoined to the fort, and had one window commanding the sea, the other looked toward the inland country. The cannon constantly proclaimed the arrival, or departure of every vessel, and my eager heart irresistibly impelled me towards the window. But it was not for me they came—no hope of release—no well known face to greet me— those ships that departed impressed me with ideas yet more painful and gloomy. The arms of England, *distant* England, often enriched every streamer, and my sick soul groaned under the conviction, that I must never hope to view the port, which would restore those mariners (comparatively careless of the advantage) to the local ties of country, kindred, and friendship; to all that gives charms to existence.— Haunted by a pleasure which was always in my view, without being ever within my reach, I could not subdue the killing emotions thus raised in my soul.

The growth of my child alone marked to me the progress of time. Ah! moment how sweet art thou yet to my memory, when first her little voice strove at articulation! The blessed name of mother at length broke the drear silence of my prison, and hardly the celestial sounds of hovering Angels, had I been launching into eternity, could give me a sublimer pleasure. I saw her walk with a transport scarce inferior. Engrossed by, and devoted to this sole object of my eyes and heart, which the gracious author of universal being permitted her to fill, I no longer repined at my unmerited captivity. Only anxious lest any one should suspect my possession of this invaluable gem, I felt ready to hide her, even when the old slave made her daily appearance. The common raiment with which we were periodically supplied, I became ingenious in fitting to her little form; and by that insensible contraction of our faculties, which extends through nature, although it has been remarked only in the organs of sight, I drew into this narrow bound, those fears, hopes, wishes, and employments, which in rapid succession fill up our lives, and leave behind a remembrance that we always revert to with satisfaction, and often conceive to have been happiness.

Fearful, at some intervals, lest the want of air or exercise should nip my beauteous blossom, I devised a thousand little plans to make her run within her narrow confines; and strengthen a constitution born perhaps to trials, not inferior to those which had blighted her mother's youth. I held her to the window, morning and evening, and found the winds of Heaven blew not less pure through iron bars than gilded lattices. Ah, surely my memory does not err, when I say with the poet, that

> From the children of the first-born Cain,
> To him who did but yesterday suspire,
> There was not such a gracious creature born;
> For nature's gifts she might with lilies vie,
> And with the half-blown rose.[36]

I was one day holding the dear child to the evening air, her little hands now grasped the rough bars, and now were extended through them, while her innocent tongue beguiled her fond mother's attention, when I suddenly perceived a black woman, apparently of distinction, leaning under an awning, raised at no great distance; and while she talked busily to the slaves who were fanning her, the eyes of all were turned intently on my infant. I snatched her away, with an apprehension the most lively I had for years felt; I even absented myself from the window for a long time, then venturing a glance, without approaching near enough to be seen, I perceived her eyes were still fixed upon my prison, and the repose of that night was wholly destroyed by a vague fear the next day confirmed. At the same hour she returned again to the same pavillion, and after watching the window in vain, (as I no longer dared approach it) she shewed manifest tokens of chagrin and disappointment. Alas, this was not all. My old Negro appeared soon after, and delivering me an unintelligible message, demanded my daughter. I prayed, wept, intreated, groaned to the poor wretch, whose eyes alone of all her senses seemed affected by my agonies. After a thousand incomprehensible signs on her part, and resolute refusals on my own, she snatched the child from those weak arms which wanted an equal power of resistance, and left me stretched on the floor from the lameness I have mentioned.

It was long ere I had courage to approach the window; but collecting every power of mind and body, I at length ventured thither. I saw the darling child seated on cushions at the feet of the woman, whose power tore her from me, laden with toys and overwhelmed with caresses. This, however, was but a small relief to my maternal anguish, while uncertain whether I had not lost her for ever: nor did my apprehensions diminish, when I saw the attendant slaves bear their mistress away on a covered couch, with my child in her arms. Ah then my prison became a dungeon indeed! I smote my head against the inclosing bars, and the air echoed to my groans. They were only relieved by the return of my old slave, who leading in my lamented cherub, once more blest my arms with the burthen. My heart rushed so impetuously towards her, that it seemed to extend through my whole throbbing frame. As I surveyed the recovered blessing with added fondness, I perceived that the gentle black I had so injuriously distrusted, had lavishly adorned the tender object of a surprizing attachment. Imagine a girl between three and four years old, slight, graceful, fair, and blooming, whose amber locks the hand of nature had twined into a thousand spiral rings, which fell over a loose vest of silver muslin, girt with roses: her little arms and ancles were encircled with fanciful bracelets, of different coloured beads, while her hand bore a gilt basket, filled with fruits of the country. She seemed a being of another world, descending to bless this— While yet in the arms of her sable conductor, she appeared to me like new-born light, reposing on the bosom of chaos. I took the little luxuries she offered, and while indulging a sense time and abstinence had almost annihilated, I worshipped the hand which thus at length relented.

Ah, Madam, it is only in the early seasons of heavy visitation we dare to repine; when misery once reaches the extreme, it has always salutary effects. Purified entirely from the vain wants and wishes, our pride and our passions for a long time represent, as the very essentials of our being, we then set a due value on the commonest blessings, and soon find in every thing an enjoyment.

When I pondered over the infinite and various advantages my daughter might derive from the partiality of a woman, whose authority was great enough to open the doors of our prison, my heart became sensible of hopes in her favor, I had long ceased to indulge in my own; and resigning myself to the prospect, I sunk into a repose which might almost be called happy. A short time habituated me to periodically parting with, and receiving my daughter, always laden with some little present, conducive either to my health or comfort. Our benefactress too, ever kindly retired to the spot I could command, as if desirous to gratify me, at the same moment with herself; and greatly indeed did she fulfil her purpose. I saw, in spite of that fatality which had long hung over my unhappy family, an exertion of Heaven in favor of my child, which encouraged me to hope a favorable revolution at some (perhaps not distant) period: while in the tedious interval, the means of health and comfort were amply bestowed on her, and the latter, through her means, on her exhausted mother.

At some intervals, weeks, nay a month, would elapse, without my daughter's being sent for, by which I concluded some one in still higher authority, controled the actions of her Negro friend: though the benefits, in a great degree remained to us; wholesome fruits, better provisions, more agreeable cloathing, and a more watchful attendance. I sometimes wondered the woman who thus generously alleviated our sufferings, never once inquired into their origin: but having learnt, by painful experience, the impropriety of judging without information, I still flattered myself with the prospect of a release: which at the worst I considered as only delayed, till I could perfect my daughter in the woeful tale of those later events, which thus unjustly confined us.

In process of time, I understood from my sweet Mary's improved accents, that our benefactress was named Anana; and never from that moment did my soul offer up a prayer, in which that name (however unhallowed) was not included.

The total ignorance in which my daughter's mind yet remained, shocked and grieved me. Being wholly without books, I knew not any manner of supplying their place, and could only substitute principles for modes, and instil into her tender mind the religious and moral documents, which yet existed in mine. I endeavoured to give her an idea of the nature and appearance of books. I every day made her repeat that word a hundred times; I charged her to do so immediately, whenever she visited Anana. But whatever the reason, I saw her near eight years old apparently, without having been able to procure her the advantage, or myself the relief of reading.

Thus innocently and happily employed, I one day saw my prison door thrown open, and the interview so long desired, unexpectedly granted me. Anana entered in mourning. I incoherently blended the dictates of gratitude and sorrow. The amiable Anana told me in broken French, she came to comfort me. Charmed to find it in my power to render myself intelligible to her, I related briefly my story, which her complacency assured me she did not half understand. It was with the utmost difficulty I comprehended from her, that

Don Pedro de Sylva, the unjust Governor, who had condemned me without examination, was at length dead; that she had for some time past been his favorite, and used the influence that title gave her to indulge her fondness for my child, and lighten my captivity: that it had always been as much in her power to visit my prison as now, but not finding any certain crime imputed to me, and sure if I could acquit myself of the suspicion, she should become warmly interested in my favor, (perhaps to the degree of exasperating the benefactor, she might then be obliged to despise) she had wisely forborne to gratify her generous curiosity, and contented herself with bestowing such marks of her attachment as would not interfere with the rights of the Governor, or diminish her own. Finally, that death having snatched away the only man who could restrain her inclinations; who had bequeathed her a considerable portion of his wealth, she bestowed a part of it, to obtain from the new Governor a remission of my sentence; and having succeeded, now came to assure me, I should be at liberty to return to Europe; for which voyage her friendship would amply supply me with means, company, and attendance, as it was her purpose to quit for ever a country, where she had lost her only connexion, and seek in another, protection, religion, and peace.

During this discourse, I thought my senses almost failed me. I made her a thousand times repeat the welcome, the surprizing intelligence, that I was free; and the arrival of her slaves to convey me from the melancholy dungeon, which I believed the day before, would at some future one become my grave, alone gave confirmation to so incredible an event. But when I really found myself at liberty; when I saw the varied Heavens above my head, and the green earth under my feet; when the soft fragrance of the almost forgotten blossoms indulged one sense, and the sweet sounds of congratulating voices blest another, I wonder I did not expire with the tumult of mingled emotions this happy moment revived in my heart. I raised my soul to him who gave those senses, and breathed life into the elements which sustain them, and besought him to moderate my feelings, or condense them all in gratitude.

Blended once more, almost miraculously in the concerns of this world, I learnt with a thousand sensations no words can describe, that Elizabeth had a few months before paid the debt of nature; and that my brother James, as well by her nomination, as the rights of his birth, and the voice of the people, had ascended the throne of England: happily uniting under his sway two kingdoms, so many ages hostile as hardly to leave a hope of the event which was now without bloodshed fully accomplished.[37] Time, grief, and misfortune, had so far allayed the irritation of my mind, that I blessed the ordination of providence which thus left my resentment without an object. Higher, happier, and dearer prospects opened before me, and I looked forward with impatience to the moment, when I should present my smiling Mary to my beloved sister, and in the society of connexions so precious, lose the remainder of my days.

Alas! Madam, I required sentiments like these to sustain me against the conviction that the intense heats of the climate had united with the want of air and exercise to fix the lameness the rheumatic fever had left, and completely debilitate my constitution, which has from that period been subject to a thousand little wearying, nameless maladies, that insensibly absorb the spirit of youth, and bring on an early old age.

Anana, actuated by a fondness for my daughter scarce inferior to my own, shared with me in every maternal care, and earnestly besought me to receive her under my protection on our arrival in England; where I had made her sensible I held a distinguished rank. Solemnly assuring me it was her intention to bequeath to my sweet child the wealth she derived from the Governor, alike to prove her own attachment, and as a compensation for our long and unjust imprisonment. The state in which she had lived with Don Pedro, supplied an objection at which my pride revolted, but that almost instantaneously gave way to principle. I resolved to be above sacrificing the duties of gratitude and benevolence to opinion, and remembering her untaught mind knew no tie in wedlock but constancy, and perhaps in that instance might vie with myself, I sought, by cultivating the wild but solid virtues of her soul, to bury the remembrance of her former error, and fortify her against any future one. Open to the pure impressions of religion and morality, the amiable Anana promised to become an ornament to human nature; but alas, a greater power than I could over-rule shortened her span, and at once determined for us all. The small pox, always so dangerous in the islands, broke out suddenly, and swept off hundreds.— The apprehensions people of Anana's complexion ever entertain of it, contribute, most probably, to render it so fatal. She threw herself into such agonies, that the eruption soon appeared, with the most mortal symptoms. Delirious alike with the dreadful malady, and extreme fondness for my daughter, she called for her incessantly; she strove to break from her attendants, and get out of bed in search of her. She intreated me in the most moving, broken accents, once more to let her hear the little angel she could no longer see; to suffer her to give into her hand the casket she was so soon going to bequeath her. The terrified mother shrunk in silence from such a conflict. Ah, what are the gems she will bequeath her, cried I, to that breathing one herself?—all now left of my promised fortunes.— The dictates of gratitude then prevailing, I would cry, but can I refuse the last request, however wild and erroneous, of her who preserved the being she now would involuntarily endanger? Finding reason ineffectual towards conquering the dying wish of Anana, I acquitted myself to her, by leading to the bed of infection and death, my little treasure, with a resignation I could only compare to that of Abraham, and like the innocent he would have devoted, my child was returned to me.[38] The exhausted Anana, considering this with justice as the highest effort of gratitude and esteem, yielded herself patiently to the will of Heaven, which soon called her hence.

The sincere concern this loss occasioned, gave way to one still nearer; my child sickened with the same horrible distemper, and centred in anxiety every faculty of my soul. It soon, however, took the most favorable turn, and left me at leisure to endeavour to secure the legacy our lost friend had put into my hands. The deceased Governor had converted the principal part of the property he realized into diamonds; a common practice in countries where justice is partially administered; nor did the new Governor know either their number or value: Anana having followed the directions of her benefactor in hiding a part, and bribing his successor to acquiescence by sharing the remainder. I had now gained worldly wisdom enough to adopt the same plan; and having fulfilled every duty, I joyfully embarked for England, accompanied by several slaves, who preferred attending on me to the precarious blessing of liberty under arbitrary power.

Ah, Madam, how different was this voyage from that already commemorated!—from the fallen tree I then continually watered with my tears, a tender, a lovely scion had sprung up; it flourished in the shade; it blossomed in sunshine; with sweet, with gentle hopes, I bore it to its native soil. No barbarous hand was now lying in wait to destroy it; no pestilential wind blew from those cliffs which shot their white arms into the ocean, and hospitably invited us to the bosom of peace. Ah, no! a dear, though small circle of sympathizing friends would receive the forlorn, the widowed wanderer, as one arisen from the dead; would grace my woeful tale with many a lamenting tear.

My sister too, my darling Ellinor—how perfect, how pure, cried my swelling heart, will be our re-union! how will she fondly fold to her generous bosom this dear child of the ocean—this soothing, unconscious fellow-sufferer—this early partner in her Matilda's wayward fortune!— Pause, Madam, over this fair prospect, and let me rest a while my weary fingers and spirits.

Part IV

I struggled with the sad remembrances indelibly impressed on my heart, when my eyes again beheld the shore of England; and folding to my bosom the dear offspring of love and misfortune, I shut up every sense in her. Already alive to the anxious hopes and wishes that so early tincture a being with which alone they expire, my daughter fondly flattered herself with the expectation of an unknown good, and impatiently wished for the termination of our voyage. I landed at Greenwich, because the spot where I could soonest learn intelligence of the Sidney family, as the people who kept the chief inn, I remembered, had been servants to Lord Leicester: alas, I had overlooked the long term of my absence, and the probability that they might either be dead or removed. Greenwich, which I had seen the seat of gaiety, empire, and magnificence, now appeared a dreary solitude. The tide in silence laved the walls of a deserted palace, which verging to decay like its past possessors, seemed but a gaudy mausoleum.[1] I paused over these fragile memorials of human grandeur, as the boat bore me towards the shore; and half surmised the strangeness that might await me there. I was presently surrounded by a set of unknown faces; and after much tedious enquiry, learnt that my tender friend, Lady Arundel, still inhabited her house near Chelsea, whither I dispatched a messenger with a billet.[2] It demanded "a welcome for a poor widowed wanderer, and a babe, for whose existence that dear woman was perhaps responsible, as it was wholly owing to her indulgence. I added, I would not venture one enquiry till I gained fortitude from her presence, but doubted not that I should have as much to learn as to unfold. If, as my flattering forebodings informed me, my darling sister yet survived, I was persuaded by whatever name she was now distinguished she would once more answer to that with transport; and fold to her glowing bosom a weary heart which had long sought in vain a resting place; but I submitted the discovery, and meeting, solely to the care and prudence of our mutual friend."

I waited not long in suspense, for my messenger hastened back with a billet, incoherent as surprize and joy could make it. "Fly," said the generous Lady Arundel, "to my arms, to my heart, to my home—they will ever be open to you and yours—I suspend all explanations till I see you.— Ah Matilda, dear to my eyes will be that lovely face, however changed by misfortune."

Grateful as this invitation proved, my soul was sensible of a damp and disappointment, from the obscurity cast over the interval of my absence, and her leaving unanswered my enquiry for my sister. I hastened nevertheless to obey the request. The sad meditations which would have engrossed my faculties in passing through London, were continually interrupted by the transports of my little Mary; the varying streets filled with gay shops, and thronged with fine-dressed people, were a novelty to her of the most charming and interesting nature. Ere I could half answer her enquiry into each new wonder, it was lost in the next, and that chastened pleasure a mother extracts from blending the sigh of knowledge with the smile of innocence, claimed its turn in my agitated bosom, suspending more powerful emotions: but when my eyes rested on the gates of Lady Arundel's house, those gates from whence I last took my flight so dearly accompanied, a pang so pungent wrung my heart, that my feeble sense sunk under it, and I swooned away. I revived; and it seemed rather by the cries and tears of my little one, than the remedies of the servants who surrounded me. My sweet Mary had climbed up the couch on which they laid me, and clasping her arms round my neck laid her mantling cheek to my pale one, and shed deluges of tears. I comforted her, and feeling my hand pressed by some body who sat almost behind me, turned, and fixing my eyes on the streaming ones of Lady Arundel, I threw myself silently into her arms, and felt my very soul dissolve upon her bosom. Both were half suffocated with feelings too high wrought, and the presence of my daughter proved a fortunate relief; for drawing me fondly down to her, "why do you cry, mama?" said the dear one, "and why does this lady cry? I thought we came home to be happy." "And happy we will be, my darling," cried Lady Arundel, pressing her to a bosom melting in her favor, "who can be otherwise blest with such a cherub? Can you complain, Matilda, when Heaven has left you her?"— "No, my admirable friend, sighed I, I do not complain,—my reason reproves those tears my wounded heart will not cease periodically to pour forth; this house, this room, even your tenderness awakens a train of killing remembrances, I have in vain endeavoured to arm myself against. Here, here, even here has my soul expanded towards her father with a pleasure of which herself, and this weed, are the only memorials."

The entrance of servants with refreshments, suspended a little the agitation of both; and Lady Arundel obstinately refused every kind of information concerning my sister or friends till the next day, insisting I should devote the remainder of the evening to a minute recital of my own story. The astonishment its incidents every moment excited in Lady Arundel, seemed to make it more wonderful even to myself. Having the happy assurance from her that my sister still lived, I gave way to the sweet hope of seeing her, and filled up with her idea a chamber which now appeared more solitary than ever.

My impatience concerning my Ellinor could no longer be restrained, and when we met in the morning, I importunately demanded her story. The visible reluctance with which Lady Arundel granted my request, confirmed my fears of some dreadful catastrophe, and had I not been assured my sister yet lived, I should have concluded her loss the fatal event our friend feared to acknowledge: but satisfied in this instance, and having no tie which could comparatively interest me, I fortified my mind against the impression of inferior sorrows, by the deep sense of those I had already survived.

Whatever courage I had collected, I needed it all, when with that fearful pomp of preparation with which friendship ever binds up the wounds of fate, Lady Arundel produced a number of papers, most of which appeared to be written by my sister. I kissed the dear traces of a hand so beloved. Alas, those sheets are yet by me, and I need only subjoin them.

THE LIFE OF ELLINOR, ADDRESSED TO MATILDA.

OH, you! much loved, but little trusted, dear sister of my heart, whom it fondly pursues through unknown climes, where yet perhaps you wander, the victim of a fatal attachment; receive in these papers, if they ever meet your eyes, the greatest testimony of an affection, which as it was the first my soul became sensible to, so surely will it be the last. Oh! you allied to me in destiny, no less than blood, (for we were born alike to be unknown, except to each other) lo, I lay my heart unveiled before you, its passions, its pride, its prejudices; condemn them not my sister, however they may contradict your own.— Estimate duly the silence I have so long preserved; the sacrifices I have made, sacrifices so much the more meritorious, as my soul ever revolted against the mean imposer, and submitted but to you. I knew the delicacy of your mind, and would not add to the weight which hung upon its nobler faculties, by a confidence that might wrong at the same moment your duty. Ah! no, I remembered Williams, and was from that moment prudent, if not happy—yet as I know too well the horrors of mystery, incertitude, and silence, (for have I not spent ages in vainly guessing at your fate?) let me rescue you from a life of surmise, by preserving this sad memorial. Perhaps this astonishing separation will prove eternal.— If then my heart no more shall feel the throb of affection it has always given when yours pressed against it, (and something seems to tell me that pleasure shall never more be mine) receive in this recital a last proof of my tenderness, and oh, my dear, ill-fated sister, may it mitigate the keenness of your affliction, to learn that you have not been the greatest sufferer.

In one part of this story I must ever have been obscure and insincere, but that fate has snatched away the worshipped object, of whose character we judged in so different a manner. Oh, pardon me all-gracious Heaven, if my opinion has been erroneous!— Pause here, Matilda, if your rising soul has taken the alarm, and weigh well the love you bear me, for I shall need it all, unless I falsify the fact.

On the memorable day, when Heaven decided the destiny of the one sister, and perplexed that of the other, by presenting to the eyes of both the favorite of Elizabeth, how diametrically opposite were the impressions each took of his character! Astonishing that two agreeing in every instance till that moment, should for the first time differ in so decided a manner! more astonishing, that every following day only confirmed the separate judgments. The darling alike of art and of nature, the eye, or mind, could demand no more than was comprized in the person of Lord Leicester—but here, in my opinion, the charm ended.[3] His heart, not warm by nature, had been rendered in a great degree callous, from its having expanded in the chilling atmosphere of a Court. Unbounded in his projects, timid and subtle in his actions, tyrannic in his pursuits, the object he could not govern, never long attached him. Ambition, pride, and vanity, those leading traits in almost every character, were in his so exquisitely blended, and corrected by the frost of his nature, that they might often be mistaken for nobler passions. You were presented to his eyes in early youth, a finished pattern of beauty, endued with royalty; in the tender bloom of a newly awakened love. Uniting thus in your own person the strongest powers of charming, with such as were peculiarly congenial to the heart you wished to win, it laid itself at your feet. Oh woeful moment when it did so, as it entailed upon you all the miseries of a mutual passion, without half its enjoyments! Alas, Matilda, had you really been adored—yet what could that have done, more than to severely aggravate all you was born to suffer? and as the apparent passion of Lord Leicester had to you the charms of reality, I am to blame perhaps thus to represent it: but the season of dissimulation is past, and my tortured heart will utter nothing but truth. So fixed was this opinion of his character, that though there was a moment of my life, when my fate seemed wholly in Lord Leicester's hands, I could not then enough esteem him to venture his decision. Yet still a tender pity for your unmerited and everlasting passion should have suppressed this (in your mind) harsh judgment, but that, I once more repeat, my own actions must ever then have appeared eccentric and enigmatical.

How deeply both father Anthony and I regretted the imprudence which introduced into our solitary asylum so dangerous a visitor, it were needless now to repeat. Prudence was for once on the side of passion, and your fate was by the will of your only remaining guardian, for ever united with that of your lover. I soon found it vain to oppose the ascendancy he had gained in your affections; and as my own were yet unoccupied, I looked no farther than the present moment; and followed you to Kenilworth Castle without repining. Nevertheless I admired the delusions of love, which in a moment reconciled you to a situation apparently so obscure and abject; and still more that total blindness to your own exquisite perfection, which could make you fancy that low state would ever appear to observing spectators your natural one. What then must be my astonishment to see Lord Leicester's love impose such humiliations, on an object nature and fortune had placed so far above him, and meanly content himself with monopolized indulgences.

Hardly were we alone, when the presumption of that wretch Williams filled both of us with a terror which required an immediate remedy. Every faculty of my soul revolted against the abject compliances your entreaties exacted from me; but even those only served to strengthen the contempt which began to predominate in it. Lord Leicester's return gave us a temporary relief, but his method of getting rid of the villain appeared to me alike unsafe and mean, and the only proper mode of ending our fears never once seemed to occur to him. I mean, acknowledging his marriage; which perhaps might at that period have been done without any great danger of offending Elizabeth; whose withering heart was becoming every day less sensible of affection, and whose vanity was so highly gratified and possessed by the addresses of the Duke of Anjou. But it was the *interest* of my Lord to break the match with the French Prince, and to that golden idol his every passion bowed.[4] We were again left to work tapestry, and when he had succeeded in his favorite project, he suffered the Queen in turn, to bewail alone the loss of her last lover, and came once more to amuse himself at Kenilworth.

But he was not always to succeed; the jealousy of Elizabeth had now just provocation, and in her sudden arrival at Kenilworth Castle, she at last over-reached her politic favorite. In vain he would have concealed us—in vain he would have represented us as the vassals of his amusement: the scrutinizing eye of the Queen, the universal voice of her more impartial train, pronounced this impossible. Reduced to frame a new story, tortured with the conviction that it had not gained credit, he was obliged to aggravate every disagreeable circumstance of our present situation, by delivering us unwillingly into the hands of Elizabeth. Alas, my sister, I saw, I understood, all this cost you on my account, while not one sigh on your own escaped you. I stifled the painful and proud sensations that swelled at my heart, and ventured into the world under the doubtful and mysterious patronage of the Queen; who, better acquainted with the finesses of her favorite than those now nearly allied to him, never for one moment was the dupe of his fiction, though unable to disprove it.

Ah, how visionary seems on recollection our new situation! seen without being known; adored, without being esteemed; punished without being guilty; applauded without being meritorious, we were all an illusion. Yet while surrounded with spies, and acting for ever under an eye disposed to condemn, ere it could half discover, how difficult was it for us to avoid suspicion and censure! One sole advantage had either gained by converging into the sphere of a court; a faithful friend: though even that blessing was curtailed by the eternal policy of my Lord, who would not permit us to confide even to his own amiable nieces, the Ladies Arundel and Pembroke, any part of a secret which might affect, however remotely, his own safety. Bounded as our conversations must of consequence be, the charm of attachment nevertheless seized upon our souls. Mine allied itself to Lady Pembroke, while yours equally inclined to her no less amiable sister, and each took pleasure in passing that portion of her time with the distinct favorite we did not spend together. Ah, here Matilda, I approach the appointed moment, when the paths of life, in which we have hitherto trod hand in hand, begin to separate; and every succeeding step bears us farther from each other, till darkness and distance rob the straining eye of its first dear object—In vain each now turns back, and seeks the accustomed path, a thousand various ones perplex the wearied mind; and while the impetuous passions drag us onward, we give to the sweet memory of early youth a thousand fond and hopeless sighs, then follow with trembling feet those ungovernable leaders.

Lord Pembroke's[5] partiality had long distinguished a noble youth the policy of Lord Leicester still kept abroad. I had seen many of his letters, through the medium of Lady Pembroke; and my heart had learnt to flutter at the name of Essex,[6] ere yet I beheld him. Alas, even while I repeat it, I own the same sensation!— Oh, love! exquisite delusion! captivating error! from the moment the lips find pleasure in that word, till they lose the power of pronouncing it, the charm, the inconceivable charm remains.— Whether cherished by the sun beams of hope, or chilled by the dews of disappointment—Whether the chosen object is faithful, or unfaithful—glowing with animation before our eyes, or seared up in the dark and silent grave; the passion, the powerful passion asserts its eternal influence, and decides the character where it once has reigned. While I dwell on the moment which called to being this finer and more poignant sense, sensibility, memory retraces its dear emotions with a softness time itself can never extinguish.

Tinctured with the partiality of Lord Essex's friends; already acquainted with his sentiments on heroism, glory, and every attachment except that of the heart; I fondly flattered myself the day would come, when he would receive from me that last and liveliest impression which forms and finishes the human soul. I interwove myself insensibly in all his concerns; I deeply lamented the tie of relationship, which subjected his actions to the will of Lord Leicester; and employed some of the little time I spent with my Lord, in endeavoring to bias his mind in favor of the absent hero. Cold and silent on the merits of Essex, Lord Leicester often bantered me on being so sensible of them, and seldom failed to remind me of the family compact, which had bound Lord Essex to wed Sir Francis Walsingham's only daughter: to fulfil which, he purposed soon to recal him; and advised me rather to turn my eyes on Sir Walter Raleigh,[7] whose talents he pronounced infinitely superior, and whose homage was wholly paid to me. As this was a lover he knew I detested, the conversation generally ended when he was named, but a succession of such discourses, confirmed me in the opinion of Lord Leicester's selfishness, and prepared me, perhaps, to decide in opposition to it.

Essex was at length summoned to England. He arrived. An idle, unaccountable apprehension at once overcame my reason. I was persuaded I could not see him with indifference. I feared the keen eye of Elizabeth, and the colder and more watchful one of Lord Leicester. I quitted the Court the day Essex was to be presented, and past it with Lady Pembroke. By a singular chance Miss Walsingham had chosen to do the same. The party enlarged insensibly as the circle decreased. Essex was the theme of every tongue, and while Miss Walsingham's triumphant eyes acknowledged the implied compliments, my yielding heart received them. "He is here," cried Lady Pembroke, in the afternoon, looking out of the window, and kissing her hand. I felt ready once more to run away, but that decorum restrained me. Lady Pembroke indulged one of the gay whims which so often were a source of pleasure at once to herself and her friends, and insisted he should only be told his bride was among the unmarried ladies, from whom his heart must select her. This was an ill-judged project. Miss Walsingham had been contracted to Lord Essex in childhood, rather to ratify a reconciliation between the families, than with any idea of a future affection. The rigid principles of Lady Walsingham had hitherto kept her daughter in total seclusion, and the death of her mother had now given the young lady unbounded liberty. Her passions, naturally violent, had always spurned restraint; but compelled for a time to submit to it, they marked her character even in early youth with haughtiness. The beauty she eminently possessed, soon drew around her a croud of lovers, which elevating her vanity, added coquetry to pride, and united in her person the strange extremes of sour reserve and unbounded levity. Sir Philip Sidney was the only man supposed to have any interest in her heart, but as he had from the first devoted himself to another, she affected to despise him, and wait the return of her allotted husband, with a resolution to accept of him.

Miss Walsingham seconded the proposal of Lady Pembroke, which rather perplexed the rest of the company; and after much pleasantry on the subject of sympathy, Lady Pembroke sent for her Lord and the stranger.— Ah, Heavens, that invincible stranger—born to decide my destiny—his youth had accustomed me to expect to find something unformed and unfinished in his person and manners—how then was I surprised to see the height and majesty of Lord Leicester united with a countenance no less perfect; while every grace of figure, feature, and complexion, were lighted up by brilliant youth, an air at once elegant and ingenuous, and an expression of sensibility which heightened every grace. I have not half described the dear, the deep impression—I would in vain describe it—he looked, and I then first seemed to see—he spoke and I then first seemed to hear.— Fearful lest any marked disorder should betray me, I fixed my eyes upon the ground, but they had already borne the image into my heart: I still saw it within, and my charmed sense retained the sound of that voice, regardless of all others—Smiling expressively at Lady Pembroke's authoritative order, he kissed the hand she had given him, and dropping it, knelt gracefully to me.— Gracious Heaven, how excessive was my confusion at this unlucky mistake, yet how exquisite my silent pleasure! The over-powering mirth of the whole party displeased him—kindly deigning to impute my distress solely to that cause, he solicited my pardon for having united me in the very excellent jest the ladies were obliging enough to make at his expence. Adding in a lower voice, that wherever parental authority had destined him to bow, he should always remember with pride and pleasure the distinguished choice his heart had ventured to make. Then advancing to Miss Walsingham, whose readiness saved him a second mistake, he made her some cold compliment, which awakened every fiery particle of her nature, and passed on to pay the same respect to the rest of the ladies: while his eyes ever and anon returned to me with that passionate ingenuousness which through life has been his characteristic.

I left him behind, and returned to Court; glowing with the same ardent passion I had once dared to condemn in you, and flattering myself he was studying how to break an engagement not ratified by his heart. How sweet were the hours, rich with that hope! ready every moment to acknowledge the truth, and to indulge my passion by reposing it in your faithful bosom, I found you overwhelmed with tears, apprehension, and anguish; for it was at this very period the cruel and extravagant jealousy of Lord Leicester became apparent. Wanting courage to mention an incident remote from the cause of your sorrow, I buried the dear impression in my heart, and devoted myself to soothing a mind so deeply wounded. By a strange transition in my own sentiments, I had learnt fairly to judge of yours, and the increasing similarity interwove our souls every day more and more strongly, though not one word escaped me. Dreams of pride and grandeur, which had sometimes embittered a spirit I will venture to call noble, vanished at once before a stronger passion; which strangely filled up that void in my mind nothing yet had ever been able to fill. I no longer complained of the Queen—I no longer thought the Court a prison—conforming from that moment quietly to my fate, I centred every wish in one sole object.

I even employed myself diligently in developing Lord Leicester's sentiments; and conciliating a difference both of you suffered alike by, though neither would allow it. Lord Essex, during these conversations, was ever near us—with watchful eye endeavouring to dive into the nature of our connexion, and the mystery of our birth; so industriously buried by Leicester and Elizabeth. The disgust your Lord already shewed towards Essex, became on these occasions more apparent, and as its cause, I sought by every little distinction to reward that dear lover's patience: a dislike so unjust, heightened, however, that I already felt towards Lord Leicester, though at the same moment it supplied a still more urgent reason for concealing it, than those which had hitherto influenced me.

The sufferings of your mind sunk into mine; and profiting by the sad example of a passion imprudently indulged, I called myself to account for cherishing so dangerous a weakness, and resolved by a courageous effort to govern, if I could not extinguish it. But ah, how vain is that attempt, when once we are truly touched! Love, my sister, like the enwrithed serpent, only compresses the heart more closely, for every effort we make to shake it off. In vain I turned my contemplations towards the obscurity which had hitherto attended our lives, the dark and mysterious cloud which yet hung over them; love drew a vivid rainbow across it, and every tear due to misfortune fell tinctured with Essex. Ah, wherefore should calamity heighten that passion? without being able to define the cause, I acknowledge the effect. The heart for ever active, perhaps then ferments most powerfully, and where love has once found room, every agitation cooperates to its increase, however distinct its origin.

Yet if the weakness of woman could be justified by the merit of the object, the more I examined Essex, the more reason I had to be satisfied. That noble candor, which resisted through life the courtly artifice he would neither profit by or adopt, was at this period eminently conspicuous: while his warm heart, and polished understanding, made him no less the friend than the patron of genius. Every indifferent spectator admired to see even his youth rich with every promise fulfilled in the riper years of Sidney, and thought Sir Francis Walsingham the happiest of men, in being able to match his daughter with either of these distinguished minds. The generous Essex scorned to deceive her he did not refuse to marry, and paying his deceased father's will the deep respect of appearing ready to comply with it, waited the operations of fortune in his favor, and adored me in silence.

At this juncture the camp claimed Lord Leicester, and the nobility accompanied him. I shared the mortal chagrin with which you saw him depart in silence, and followed you so truly through all your feelings, that I sought to persuade myself Essex might only want the power to treat me in the same manner. This painful idea operated so strongly, as to make me assume a cold-ness at parting, to which my lover was unaccustomed, and which, to own the truth, I did not cease regretting the whole time of his absence.

The dispersion and defeat of the Armada restored gaiety and eclat[8] to the Court. The fullest reconciliation took place between you and Lord Leices-ter. My heart opened once more to hope, to happiness, to Essex; who now took courage to unfold his sentiments to Lady Pembroke. She instantly adopted his cause, and promised to find him an opportunity to plead it. Nor was it long ere she drew me to her house, and telling me, with one of those happy smiles which disposed us to grant whatever she wished, "that from the first moment she saw me, it had been one of the darling objects of her life to unite me with Lord Essex, who alone appeared to her likely to deserve the heart she had so thoroughly studied, she had engaged her Lord to join with her in concerting that mode of introduction which appeared to me so wild a whim. It had fully answered her hopes in fascinating one of the parties, and," she added, "she half believed it was not lost upon the other." Fixing her eyes for a moment on my glowing cheeks, she gaily started up to throw open her closet door, "in short, my dear," cried she, "here is my Lord himself; allow him to plead his own cause, and when I think I can speak more to the purpose, depend on my interrupting him:" plucking her robe from my trembling fin-gers, she ran out of the room. Distressed, irresolute, and overcome with the arrival of a moment so long wished for, I made an effort to follow her, but using the same means to detain me, I had unsuccessfully tried with my friend, Lord Essex grasped my robe more firmly. I turned, and not daring to fix my eyes on the graceful form, the fine face on which they fell, I dropt them, and yielded in silence to hear him. How deep, ah Heaven, how exquisite, is the remembrance of that moment, when the name of love first reached my ear, from the only voice which could render it agreeable!— "I will not imagine, most worshipped of women," said the Earl, "I offer you any new homage in thus bending before you.— The moment my eyes first beheld you, my too-ready knees offered up to you a heart, new to the passion that moment made eternal. The highest sense of duty to a father, whose will in all other instances, was governed by reason, hallowed even the generous error which induced him to contract me to Miss Walsingham. Destined to resign in the flower of his days, every advantage which makes this world dear to man, he studiously sought to secure them all for a son, who watered his pale cheek with the tears of guileless childhood! and to secure me friends at Court, who might supply in some degree his own place, allied me nominally to the politic Walsingham; whose interest alone could counter-balance that of our inveterate enemies, the

Cecil family. The event justified his opinion. A combination of circumstances would have buried me in obscurity, had I not had the support and attachment of Sir Francis. Thus circumstanced, it would ill become me to reject the daughter of the man to whom I owe my safety and distinction; but early learning her character, and fearing to trust my happiness in the hands of a girl whose violent temper destroyed her own, I readily yielded to the pleasure of Lord Leicester in remaining abroad: not without a hope (which time confirmed) that she would in the interim give her heart to some more assiduous lover. I had reason to believe this wish was accomplished ere I ventured to return home. Her partiality for Sir Philip Sidney is indeed too apparent for me to think of uniting with her, were the friends of both willing to complete the match; but as I cannot help flattering myself the determination of Sir Philip will regulate that of the Walsingham family, fain would I learn from your indulgence (if indeed you deign to interest yourself in the fate of a man, born but to adore you) whether Sidney has any thing to hope from your sister. Accept in this explanation, my excuse for presuming to hover near your secret; and do not imagine by uniting myself in it, I seek to intrude on engagements I shall readily yield to, whether I am permitted to understand them or not."

Charmed alike with the accents of that harmonious voice, and the passion it generously avowed—prepared by the openness of his recital to indulge my natural candor, I delivered myself wholly up to the impulse of my heart; and the implied acknowledgment of my affection, made when I condescended to explain your sentiments respecting Sir Philip, lighted up his fine eyes with new softness and gratitude. Insensibly led on to speak of Lord Leicester, I recollected at once the error I was committing; and not daring to violate the silence I had promised, I broke off abruptly, covered with blushes and confusion—a long pause ensued—I raised my eyes, anxious and irresolute, to his— chagrin had dimmed all their lustre—he saw the conflict in my mind, and recollecting the superiority of his own character, he conjured me "to consider well all that I would say, and to believe that confidence would be only a weight upon his heart, which mine should ever reproach me with bestowing." His wounded feelings gave a persuasive tremulation to his voice; that, and the delicacy of mind which made him above profiting by the error of mine—the right a lover instantly acquires over the conduct of a woman, who has once ventured to acknowledge her partiality—alas, the exquisite fear such ever feel at appearing for one moment to distrust the object of their choice, all united to authorise, in my own judgment, that full confession the occasion won from me. The astonishing story of our birth, the secret of the Recess, its discovery by Lord Leicester, your subsequent marriage with him, the feint by which the

Queen was influenced alike to remain silent on every point respecting us, all was fully revealed—the veil of fiction fell at once, and presented me to him the being I was born. This interesting confidence cemented our mutual passion, and gave such charms to the moment, as memory ever returns to with pleasure. I imposed on him a vow of silence and secresy, till your decisive refusal of Sir Philip should fix his marriage with Miss Walsingham; and more fortunate circumstances facilitate our own: nor could the interval, I said, appear tedious to either, while we were daily permitted to meet, though in publick, and read in each other's eyes a passion untinctured with doubt, and which every following day promised to sanctify. Essex found too many sources of wonder and pleasure in the mutual confidence, to oppose her he from that moment looked up to, and we parted so satisfied with the interview, that either would have bought it with life.

Nevertheless, I was far from considering Miss Walsingham as the sole obstacle to our union. The politic Lord Leicester, strongly, though silently, opposed it; nor indeed without reason. Conscious he had reigned so many years without a competitor in the heart of Elizabeth, he might justly dread the progress of a rival, in whom all his advantages were united, with many he never possessed. Not satisfied with the reputation of beauty and elegance, Leicester ever passionately desired that of conduct and valor, and had given the kingdom but too convincing proofs how unequal he was to the military rank he held. Essex was born a soldier. The rough and generous virtues of that character, were joined in him with the polished graces of a courtier, and the most refined taste for literature.[9] A man calculated to shine in whatever light you examined him, could not fail to alarm all who valued and held the favor of Elizabeth. Add to this, that Essex was naturally bold and aspiring; consequently would retain whatever he once possessed. Such were already the fears of all the favorites of the Queen, and who could bound mine, when I recollected the dubious fate of his noble father, and the last warning he had given to this darling son?[10]

The sudden and unexpected marriage of Sir Philip Sidney and Miss Walsingham, revived those hopes in the mind of Essex, I had so long strove to throw at a distance; and with them too revived the vain project of confiding his views to Lord Leicester, with whose approbation of them he still continued to flatter himself. Terrified lest such an unguarded measure should exasperate Leicester to his utter ruin, who would ill-brook that this embryo rival should cross his fate in *every* instance, and dare to contend with him for a share of those advantages he was determined to monopolize, I exerted the utmost care to charm my lover to silence. Alas, every day made that more difficult. The Queen and Leicester, fearful of my finding among the many who professed themselves my servants, one whose views would interfere with theirs, immediately allotted me that weak wretch, Lord Arlington,[11] for a husband; and in countenancing his addresses, threw every other lover at a distance: at the same time giving me but too much reason to apprehend, that if ever I was permitted to marry, it must be as a sacrifice to both. Not daring to consult you on a subject I had so long concealed, and on which we must ever think so differently, and unwilling to blight the little gleam of sunshine love illumined your days with, I resigned myself up to a gloom which hardly the presence of Essex could dissipate.

A very short time rendered the intentions of the Queen and Lord Leicester obvious to Essex. His impassioned soul, fired alike with love of me, and disdain of him I was commanded to love, treated Lord Arlington with so marked a contempt, that nothing but the irresolution incident to weak minds, could prevent his rival from making a mortal quarrel of it. Possessed in my confidence of the means to render Lord Leicester more tractable, the Earl of Essex solicited my consent to insist on that of your Lord, as well as his interest with the Queen, if he valued the preservation of his own secret.

The tender love which attached me to you, alone could induce me to oppose a design of which my happiness was the ultimate object. But convinced an eclaircissement of this kind would embroil me for ever with Lord Leicester, and fill your suffering mind with a trouble beyond all those you had already experienced, I consented to see Essex once more at Lady Pembroke's; and exerting at that interview every power I possessed over his perturbed heart, to moderate his rage, and soothe his love, till the ensuing campaign in the Netherlands should be over, I promised a steady resistance to every matrimonial proposal in the interval, and to decide his fate on his return. Knowing it vain to hope to actuate him by any selfish consideration of his own welfare, I buried in my heart its deepest sources of apprehension, and bound him to patience by a strong representation of the dangers to which any rashness on his part would infallibly expose me. Those inflamed passions no other being could ever control, were regulated by my voice; and when necessity compelled us to part, I seemed to leave in his arms the dearer portion of my existence.

Occupied by feelings and views distinct from each other, and agreeing only in watching the wind, and sending every wish towards the camp, you and I seldom entered into our accustomed confidence and friendship. I had, however, sometimes the relief of a letter, through the medium of Lady Pembroke; by those I learnt your Lord still maintained an outward shew of civility towards Essex, while he secretly made him sensible of all his power; yet with an art so profound, as left him no apparent right to complain. He often reminded me of my promise, and vowed to preserve an undoubted claim to it, by still enduring for my sake. Overwhelmed with anxiety and perplexities, I hardly durst look towards the unravelling of events so complicated, and waited in dreadful suspense the will of Heaven. It broke in thunder over me—the cruel situation in which you soon found yourself, Lord Leicester's abrupt and imprudent return on the news of it—the politick construction he gave that return to the sick and doting Queen—her sudden resolution to marry him, and the immediate necessity for getting out of her power, which rendered both him and you in one hour miserable fugitives, were incidents so strange, rapid, and unsuspected, that I became their victim, ere I could any way account for it.

The fatal morning of Lord Leicester's return, you left him to attend the rising of the Queen, which was on that day your periodical duty. I waited with impatience the event of my Lord's visit to Elizabeth, in which my own safety, as well as yours, was immediately concerned. A servant of Lady Pembroke's, in whom she reposed great trust, suddenly brought me word that a fright had thrown her into premature labor, and the danger was so imminent, that even while we spoke she might breathe her last; nevertheless the messenger, in her name, urged me to hasten to her, if I valued the letters I had lodged in her hands. I gave way to the alarm without reflection, and accompanied the messenger instantly; nor did I meet in passing through the palace any of our women, or friends, to whom I could mention the cause of my sudden absence. Happily the danger of my much-loved friend was over ere I arrived. I prest her hand in silence, and took from it the packet relative to Essex, she had kept ready to give me; which I put into my bosom, and was hastening back, when a stranger, as I passed thro' the outer court, presented me a note. The hand, my fluttered senses owned for that of Essex. But why should he return to England? A confused fear arose in my mind, which hardly left me power to read it. It was anonymous, but I learnt from it, "that he had been at the house of Lady Pembroke, where, shocked at the distress into which her misfortune had just thrown her Lord, as well as the whole family, he found it vain to hope their assistance towards obtaining an interview with me, which, nevertheless, was highly essential to the peace and safety of both. He ended with conjuring me to follow the bearer, if I wished to save him from desperation."— Perhaps on the decision of this important moment depended the peace of my whole future life. Too surely my compliance infinitely lengthened the fatal absence from Court which enthralled me for many painful years; and dearly did I expiate that first deviation from propriety and prudence. But are we always rulers over our feelings? mine were agitated with almost every possible cause, and coward reason too often retreats from the dangerous contest.

I stept into a hired boat the messenger shewed me, which was rowed down the river with the utmost rapidity. During the little voyage, I revolved in my mind every probable reason for this sudden and alarming return of the Earl; but I was at Greenwich, ere I yet had fixed on one. I landed at a solitary garden belonging to Lord Southampton,[12] and was conducted to a pavillion which overhung the water, where I found Essex alone: pale, disordered, and undrest, with every symptom of anxiety and fatigue. Overwhelmed with I know not what agitation, I sunk upon his shoulder, as he knelt before me, and gave way to an uncertain presentiment of sadness, a few hours after so fully verified. Not even the charm of his voice could immediately soothe spirits so many concurring circumstances had deeply agitated: nevertheless, on comprehending surmise, and not misfortune, had brought him thus suddenly to England, I felt my oppressed heart breathe a little more freely. I by-and-by understood that the sole motive of this journey was the sudden one of Lord Leicester; that by means of friends who surrounded your Lord, he had always endeavoured to keep a watchful eye on his actions; and found a packet of letters, brought by a trusty hand from England, had agitated him so strongly, as to make him resolve on leaving his command, and returning home immediately. The communication of this mysterious resolution determined him to follow the steps of his General, which he was enabled to do, as he fortunately acted only as a Volunteer. The impatience Lord Leicester discovered during his hasty journey, authorised the fears of the rival who followed his steps; and persuaded him either that the secret of my birth had transpired, or that some manoeuvre was projected to dispose of me as policy dictated. Rendered desperate by these fears, he had left every thing in train for an immediate return, if fortunately I was still at liberty; or if he could be the happy means of delivering me, in case the whole truth had been discovered; nor could he longer doubt but I would at last consent to follow the fortunes of a man, who had never for a moment put all the hopes he might perhaps justly form, in competition with the single one of possessing me. The generous error of his conduct could not offend me, but persuaded my own situation was not so desperate as he represented it, I accounted to him for Lord Leicester's precipitate journey, by acknowledging the truth; and urged him to leave England directly; that even his having visited it might never transpire. But I talked to one who no longer attended to me. His eyes wandered wildly over my features, while his whole soul was engrossed by his favorite project. Possessed and distracted with the idea, that Lord Leicester would infallibly ruin his hopes, by disposing of me if ever I was again in his power, not all my vows of everlasting love and fidelity to him, nor promises of the most obstinate resistance to every other proposal, could avail. "You are gone, you are torn from me for ever, if once these eyes lose sight of you," was his impassioned reply, a thousand times repeated to all my arguments and intreaties.— "It is the crisis of our fate, my love," would he cry,—"yield, oh yield to it! Admitting *you* are proof against trials you cannot guess at till too late, how know you but I may be sacrificed? Sir Francis Walsingham already repents consenting to annul the contract between me and his daughter; she is already widowed; a hint would engage Lord Leicester to favor its renewal (for do not his views coincide with that project?) a word from him would determine the Queen in its favor; and a command from her, disobeyed, would exile me for life. Thus, my sweet Ellen, continued this agitated lover, you not only put your own fate in the hands of a man, who will never consent to unite it with mine, but even should you have resolution to resist his will, you deliver up to it a wretch you say you dearly love, and who certainly loves you to madness." Bathing the hands he grasped, with precious drops of tenderness and anguish, he held them alternately to his lips and heart.— What was the distraction of my soul at that moment?— Inexorably to refuse was the hard duty imposed by my reason, while my soul even melted with fondness. But the fear that I should entail misfortune on the dear choice of my heart; obscure at once the brilliant fortune which seemed to spread before his youthful steps, and track them perhaps with blood; a just remembrance of the severe censure I had passed on your conduct, under circumstances not less trying, and a conviction that such a compliance would infallibly endanger your safety, made me resolve to act up to my sense of rectitude, at whatever price. I collected these reasons, and many more, which have now escaped my mind, to prepare Essex for a disappointment, I was sure he would feel but too sensibly; and strove to reconcile him to the refusal, by convincing him his own welfare was the chief cause of it. Perhaps, in truth, it was; for hardly can the sun tinge the dewdrops with more various hues, than the soul will cast upon its feelings. I a thousand times assured him, "that to be the sole object of his heart, did not give me more pleasure, than to see him the admiration of the kingdom. The happy promise of his youth," I added, "had centred every eye, and every hope in him. What then would be my grief and disappointment, if the coming years which ought to crown him with glory, were to bury him in obscurity, or steep him in sorrow—that nature had formed me with a strength of mind to view every situation in its true light; nor could I comprise all human passions in love, though I thought it, perhaps, the leading one. Fill up the interval of our separation, my Lord," cried I, "with a long succession of such heroic actions, as may give to our union, whenever Heaven permits it, the only happiness not comprised in itself—the sacred sense of having deserved it. Gentler virtues of my sex shall not be wanting; time, patience, and fortitude, often conquer fate herself; nor will I ever yield to Lord Leicester an obedience I do not owe him, though for my sister's sake I shall condescend to temporize, in instances of less importance. Plighted to you by every tye, the rites of the church could only ratify a claim, which will from this moment make my acceptance of another, an adultery of the worst kind. Hasten back then, my dear Essex; conceal, if possible, that you have been absent, and beware how you expose to the eyes of Lord Leicester a suspicion of his honor, he would never, perhaps, pardon." I broke from his arms, strengthened, surely by some supernatural aid.— "Yet stay, my beloved, my worshipped Ellinor—Oh yet be persuaded—you leave me for ever—these aching eyes see you for the last time—never, oh never, shall I now call you mine."— Such were the passionate exclamations which vibrated on my quickened sense, as I flew towards the boat, and ordered the men to row to London. My full eyes still sought that graceful form, which with folded arms, and a dejected air, hung over the terrace; and my heart dissolved at the accents which still lingered on my ear. Alas, I knew not then how far they were prophetic!

Such was my conflict, such my determination, during the busy hours fraught with your fate, and mine, my sister. The mind, however, soon recovers all its vigor, when it has dared to act up to its duties, and I had wept away my tender chagrin ere I reached the Court. Ah, let me shorten this part of my recital, lest I rashly pause to question Heaven, why the most meritorious action of my life became the cause of my ruin? I reached London, Matilda, two hours after you and Lord Leicester quitted it; and fearful of the appearance my long absence might have even in your eyes, did you know how the time had been spent, I resolved to tell you that I had passed the day at Lady Pembroke's bedside; and to avoid the enquiry of indifferent persons, stole at the close of the evening through the back courts: thus fatally eluding the watchful care of Lady Arundel, who had planted assiduous friends in every other avenue to the palace, ready to intercept me when returning, after she had caused London to be explored in vain to find me.

Ah, gracious Heaven, what were my emotions when entering our apartment, I saw the Queen's women and officers in possession of it! The disorder of our cabinets and chests;—every thing indicated a dangerous discovery—a terror, for which there is no name, came over me. A joyful exclamation on the part of those into whose hands I had fallen, and a dispatch to the Queen, gave me reason to fear alike for my Matilda. To the enquiries I made, no other answer was given, than that they were employed to guard, and not inform me; and an officer of the Queen's immediately appeared to conduct me to her presence. Unable to command a single moment of solitude and silence to regulate my thoughts or actions, the past, the present, and the future, presented only one wild chaos to my mind, which hardly the breath of Heaven seemed able to bring into order. Pale, horror-struck, and speechless, I was dragged like a criminal into the closet of the Queen; whose burning cheeks and enraged eyes, told me in one killing look all I had to dread. My conductors were ordered to retire, and Lord Burghley, with the old Lady Latimer, were the only spectators of this dreadful interview. Scarce could my trembling limbs support me, or my sunk soul utter a single word. Death—death in the most terrible form glared upon me—What do I say, death? Oh, that I had feared no other evil!— Grief, insult, obloquy, all that can add horrors to the grave, promised to forerun it. The packet of letters, the testimonials of my birth, whatever was wanting to confirm the doubts of Elizabeth, or redouble her rage, were all to be found about me.— Matilda, Essex—those forms so dear, glistered before my tearful eyes; and I seemed in this perilous moment to drag down to the earth every human being I loved and valued.

Elizabeth gave way to that coarse violence which marks her manners.[13] Is there a vindictive or opprobrious epithet she did not exhaust? Lord Burghley, apprehending this ungoverned passion, would rather *give* than *gain* information, solicited her permission to examine me, which she sullenly granted. To all his artful and insidious enquiries I replied with truth, veiling only such particulars of your life and my own, as malice might construe into a crime; always referring myself to Lord Leicester, in whose bosom the secret of our fate was, as the Queen well knew, deposited. "Ah, ha! then, traitress," cried Elizabeth, no longer able to contain her rage, her very eyes flashing fire, "so thou wouldest artfully feign ignorance of thy detested sister's marriage with that villain thou glossest over so rarely; that information, I thank him, he has thought proper to give me under his own hand," (pointing to a paper lying on the table near her) "take that truth from me, and now unfold the rest, or tortures shall wring it from thee."

She continued to speak, but I had ceased to hear—breathless, mute, astounded, my feet seemed to take root on the spot where I stood, and my tears alone proved I was not marble.— Lord Leicester's marriage acknowledged—authenticated at such a juncture—and by himself too—Heavens, what a chaos did this news make in my mind!— "Speak, Jezebel!"[14] (exclaimed the exasperated Queen, in a tone almost as inarticulate through passion as mine was through fear) "thou art still in my power—though the perfidious villain I had raised from the dust, and loaded with benefits, though he, I say, and his minion, have escaped my vengeance, thou art yet within my reach—tremble lest thou shouldst answer, shouldst suffer for all."

Alas her utmost rage could hardly have added a pang to those which at that moment overwhelmed me. Another killing truth had unwarily escaped her—Lord Leicester himself then thought there was no safety but in flight—he was gone, and my sister, it was plain, had accompanied him—both had surrendered me up a hopeless, helpless victim, however unoffending—even tears, as well as language, now failed me, and my brain shot through with fire. Oh, Essex, in this moment I yet remembered thee. Thy last words yet rung in my ears, and my soul struggled with the deep regret I felt for having scorned thy project, through a vain, vain generosity. Elizabeth finding threats and interrogations alike lost on a girl whose absent senses seemed to have wholly retired into her heart, now gave way to one of her violent transports; she threw a large book of devotion which lay by her on the table, with so good an aim, that it struck me on the temple, and I sunk senseless to the earth. The attendants were all called in, and my laces cut, as if I had fainted, the Queen not chusing to avow a resentment so grossly expressed. A ribbon from whence hung the dearer part of my existence, those testimonials of my birth, which were one day to fix my rank in life, attracted the eye of Elizabeth. The ready attendants disengaged and presented them to her hand, together with the packet containing my correspondence with Essex. I was insensibly reviving when she perused the first, but surely that moment half avenged me.— Never did mind or body undergo a greater revolution—rage evaporated at once—surprize, grief, confusion, silence succeeded; with a face pale as my own, trembling hands, and failing eyes, over and over again did she examine the incontestable proofs of so surprizing an event: then wildly glancing over my features, she tore the papers into atoms, she never thought small enough.

During this interval I had so far recovered myself as to be capable of speaking; but scarce had I uttered a sound, ere she started in her turn, afraid to hear, "take her away on your lives," cried she, in a broken and inward voice; "convey her into my little closet, nor let one soul see or speak to her, as you value my favor." The servile slaves of her will executed this order with the utmost alacrity; and the room was guarded by two officers, who took from me every means of escape or death. Alas! I thought not of either. Yielding to the desolating flood which had in one hour encompassed me, I braved the future.— Betrayed, delivered up by Lord Leicester,—neglected, forgotten by my sister—the pair for whom alone I seemed hitherto to have lived; had fate another blow in store? Yet even if so, it must sport with human misery to level it at me, when those already given were mortal. A stern and sullen despair succeeded the keen vicissitude of emotions which had marked the last hour of my life; I considered myself as the devoted of Heaven and man, and resolved to oppose a heart rendered callous by injury, to every future stroke of fortune.

Elizabeth forgot not her usual policy even while overwhelmed with surprize; the room in which she had ordered me to be confined, had another door, which led to private passages through the palace, and from this entrance a guard approached at midnight, and informed me it was the pleasure of the Queen that I should follow them. I obeyed in silence, and getting into a litter I found at the garden gate, enquired not even my destination. I travelled almost without resting for two days and a night; care having been taken to provide relays, which were every where ready. During the first day's journey, a guard attended, but all prospect of my being released by human assistance then ceasing, I found myself delivered into the charge of Lord Burghley and his servants. My deep perturbations began now to subside, and my soul inclined to its wonted habits: though to have been betrayed by Lord Leicester and my sister, was a recollection my wounded feelings had not yet courage enough to cope with. Alas, how should they? When the passions are permitted to decide our conduct, however heroic it proves, we claim not those returns reason tells us are due to every instance of virtue, which had no other incentive than reason. Ah, Essex! dear prophetic Essex! sighed my heart at some moments, why, why, did I inexorably reject thy generous proposal? that ungrateful sister to whose safety I sacrificed the sweetest hopes of my life, manacles thy devoted love; and flies far away to take shelter in that country I dared not seek even under thy protection.

At the turn of the night, a dreadful storm of thunder, lightning, wind, and rain, broke over us; and the terrors natural to my sex on such occasions, were doubled on finding the whole party were set on by banditti. A moment before, and I should have affirmed I had nothing to dread, yet so lively was my new fear, that even the vengeance of Elizabeth became a trifle in the comparison. The servants of Lord Burghley made a desperate but vain resistance; and the whole were at length led away by the ruffians into a wood adjoining: where all, no doubt, like me, expected to be murdered. The storm now began to abate, and the moon sometimes forced its way through the volumes of black clouds which yet hung over it. My quickened senses caught its transient gleams to examine if any habitation, or other hope of rescue was in view. In vain I strained my sight. The wood involved us entirely, and every feeble hope died away, when my eyes suddenly rested on—ah, gracious Heaven!—our own Recess.— Yes, the well-known entrance of the tomb presented itself, and a thousand vague ideas of safety and danger mingling in my mind, as the robbers approached the litter to take me out, I screamed and swooned away.

Alas, my sister, call to mind your own feelings, and guess at mine when I once more opened my eyes in the great room of our Recess—that room once hallowed with the prayers of father Anthony, and the presence of Mrs. Marlow—that room where once the portraits of our parents smiled peace and security on their now desolate offspring—how hideous was the change!—its bare walls, grimed with a thousand uncouth and frightful images, presented only a faint picture of the present possessors, on whose hardened faces I dared not fix my fearful eyes.

Considering me but as accidental plunder, they were wholly engrossed by the old Lord Burghley; in whom some important view seemed to centre. I shrunk from the terrible scene, and called upon the awful shades of those most dear to me, to appal, in turn, the desperate wretches who made the time-struck walls resound with threats and execrations. My shocked eyes sought the ground as a relief, and fixed upon a well-known object—It was the ring of Mrs. Marlow's, with which father Anthony wedded you to Lord Leicester, and well I remembered that ring was on your hand when last we parted. I stooped impatiently for it—my senses more fully recognized its setting.— The dreadful truth flashed upon my mind. "Alas! my sister and Lord Leicester are alike ensnared, groaned I forth, without any consideration—well I know they must be here—Oh, in what dungeon have you hid them?" "Your sister, fair lady," returned one of the villains, with an odious grin; "comrades, our Captain will thank us for this prize, this must be she he talked so much about when the other travellers threw themselves into our hands.— Make yourself easy, mistress, your sister is locked up as safe as cords can keep her."

All the anguish I had before felt became nothing at this moment. "My sister in this dungeon?" cried I; "oh, born to suffer with me, dear Matilda! how will that soft frame, always unequal to the trials of life, and now entirely debilitated, support these horrors! Alas, Sirs, if there is yet in your hearts one touch of human pity, conduct me to this tender sufferer, and let her die in my arms." "All in good time, young woman," replied another, with an air so surly, as awed even my convulsed soul to silence.

Lord Burghley still was their great object; threats, and oaths were exhausted on him: when, to consummate the terrors of that moment, the name of Williams reached me. That name expounding both the past and future, wrought my fears up to frenzy. I cast my wild eyes around in search of any means to die, and could in that terrible moment, like Portia,[15] have swallowed fire; when a tumult without the room, at once suspended that within it. The sound of pistols, the precipitate entrance of such of the robbers as were not already round us, followed by many unknown persons, instantly convinced me Heaven had delivered us from our oppressors, by some means less shocking to humanity, than those despair had filled my thoughts with. A dreadful contest ensued, but our deliverers prevailing, immediately began to unbind Lord Burghley; who, almost mute with excessive surprize, found in them a train of his own domestics from the adjoining Abbey of St. Vincent, which I understood was now one of his seats. Nor was their amazement less at meeting with their Lord in this newly-discovered den. I comprehended the whole in a moment; and plainly perceived the servants of Lord Burghley must have come through the subterraneous passage, that communicated with the Abbey; I recollected that it was unknown to Williams, and flattered myself that you and Lord Leicester had escaped through it. Overwhelmed with the blessed events comprized in this deliverance, I forgot I had any thing still to fear; and not considering Lord Burghley as my keeper, I saw in him only a fellow-sufferer. I rose with alacrity, and led the way to the dungeon which communicated with the Abbey; those who newly came from thence following me in silent astonishment. I perceived the cords with which you and my Lord had been bound, and demanded you of the servants with a joyful impatience. Lord Burghley learnt from my incoherent transports, a circumstance I had refused before to inform him of: that chance had imprisoned us in the very spot where you and I were bred. Wholly taken up with my own exclamations, and regardless of the silence of my followers, I hailed the entrance of the Abbey, so long our happy asylum. Ah, Heavens, how cruelly were these lively emotions repelled and extinguished, when by the command of Lord Burghley, his servants once more seized me as a prisoner, and attempted to lead me towards a remote apartment.— With a heart humbled and broken by so many successive frights and afflictions, I sunk at his feet, not disdaining the most submissive attitude, and only solicited to see you. I reminded him of the dangers he and I had shared together, and conjured him to remember you alone could have opened the passage which led us all to freedom,—unless he basely resolved to become to me a murderer, as dreadful as those from whom we had just escaped.— Inexorably cold he replied, "my unguarded acknowledgments only gave him stronger reason to imagine much was yet concealed! and that whenever I would resolve to be wholly sincere, I should not want his interest with his royal mistress." Breaking from those trembling hands, which every moment more enfeebled, he ordered his servants to bear me into the grated room at the end of the eastern cloister. You cannot but remember the dismal place. Half sunk in ruin, overhung with ivy, and trees of growth almost immemorial, it ap-

peared the very cell of melancholy. Alas, her pale representative took possession of it in myself. The massy bars no sooner gave assurance that I was imprisoned, than my conductors impatiently flew to rejoin the rest, and learn
the news of the family. To me that small relief was barbarously denied. So near
the cause and partaker of my sorrows, they were destined to flow in solitude;
nor could imagination decide whether you were yet enthralled, or had again
escaped. How terrible are the vague suspicions of an impassioned mind, when
deprived of every means of certitude! The pale gleams of the moon seemed
every moment to people the dungeon they glanced through—my pulse beat
with redoubled strength and quickness—the whole cloister resounded the long
night with distant feet, but they came not to me—fearfully I often started
when sinking into a lethargy, rather than slumber, by the echo of some remote
voice, which fancy continually told me I knew, but it died away ere memory
could assign it an owner; and though my fertile brain exhausted possibility,
the dawning day realized no other objects, than those dreary ones my chamber presented. The bats and owls began to retire to their haunts in my
neighbourhood, and the short visit of the rising sun, only shewed me the
limits of a dark and dismal room.— By this time both mind and body were
alike exhausted, and a mist appeared to envelop my senses, which still recall a
thousand fleeting forms, by turns surrounding me, till fatigue threw me into
a deep sleep.

It was at length interrupted by a maid who brought me breakfast, and a
message from her Lord, "That if I would inform him what was wanting to my
comfort and accommodation, his orders should immediately supply it." I cast
my eyes expressively around, and bid her tell him in one word, "every thing."
The woman seemed affected; I snatched the fortunate moment, and putting
my purse into her hand, asked in return only to know the fate of Lord Leicester and my sister. I learnt, to my inexpressible relief, both had, by some incomprehensible means again escaped, and that Lord Burghley's generous daughter was confined as their abettor. A hasty summons to the maid left me once
more alone; but the news she had communicated, and the idea that the amiable Rose might hereafter be alike ready to relieve my distresses, gave a new
turn to my spirits, which now gathered courage to retrace the past, and look
into the future.

Although unable to comprehend what the urgent motives could be which
impelled Lord Leicester and my sister to so precipitate a flight, every thing
implied that they were desperate: for that it was sudden and without preparation, their intention of taking shelter in the Recess strongly indicated; and
whenever I recollected the dangerous situation of Matilda, I shared with her

that compassion self is but too apt to engross. Was there a spot of St. Vincent's Abbey, however gloomy, which did not call to my mind some instance of that integrity, affection, and nobility of heart, which distinguished my Matilda? and could I remember these, yet doubt that by whatever chance I was deserted, your will could have no share in it? Believe me; my sister, the first prayers I addressed to Heaven in my prison were for your safety.

When time and solitude restored me reason enough cooly to consider my own state, I saw no immediate danger it could teem[16] with. Though a victim to the fears of Elizabeth, and the policy of Lord Burghley, I had not yet learnt to consider them as mere murderers, and if they were not so, imprisonment was the only evil I could have to apprehend, nay even that might perhaps be short, as it was undoubtedly both illegal and unjust. Malice itself could affix on me no other crime than that of being daughter to the Queen of Scots; a fatal truth which Elizabeth would gladly forget, but surely never publish. Could I resolve, therefore, to endure with patience the punishment so unworthily imposed on me, I might in time emerge unsullied to distinction. I called upon the example of her who gave me being, to support my drooping spirits, and should perhaps have vied with her in fortitude, but that one cherished grief wound round my aching heart, and often wrung forth its dearest drops. Essex, the most beloved of mankind; that faithful lover, whose ardent prayers, whose generous proposals, I had obstinately resisted, when his irritated mind seemed daringly to lift the veil of futurity, and pierce through those complicated dangers which followed our parting—Ah, what should guard him, when my loss was discovered, from giving way to his injured and exasperated affection? If fortune should even separate him and Lord Leicester, how could I be certain Elizabeth herself would be safe from his reproaches, and who was ever safe from her vengeance, when once thus desperately awakened? The premature fate of my much-honored father, the noble Norfolk, returned upon my memory—the tower, the dismal tower, scaffolds, axes, a bleeding lover, and a broken heart, daily passed in long array before me, and peopled the solitude to which I was so unjustly condemned.

The decency with which I was attended and served, proved that both Elizabeth and her Minister had still terms to keep with me; but the servant who had ventured a reply was impeached by those who waited without the door, and my purse being found upon her, no doubt became a sufficient proof of guilt. Certainly I saw her no more, and the women deputed in her place, were either too guarded or too ignorant, to inform me on any subject, had I left myself money to try their fidelity.

I had once been so accustomed to seclusion, that it would soon have lost its horrors, had my misfortunes rested here: resolved, however, not to augment them by vain and fruitless repining, I demanded such books as might strengthen and amuse my mind: thus opposing the wisdom of ages to the pangs of the moment. By sharing a part of my food with the birds which inhabited the over-hanging trees, I drew around me some mute associates, who more grateful than the superior beings that ventured to look down on them, are always attached by benefits.

This lethargic tranquillity was soon interrupted by a visit from Lord Burghley. With the fair language of an experienced courtier, he "commended my resignation to an inevitable fate, and admired the wise use I made of confinement, in thus applying myself to enrich my understanding; assuring me he had exceeded his orders for my accommodation, but that an express which arrived over-night from the Queen, had at last put it in his power to restore that liberty, he had by her command deprived me of." My heart leaped at so unhoped an alteration in my fate, but he intercepted the transport ere it reached my lips, and sent it back a dead weight into my bosom. "Think not therefore, fair lady," said he, "that her Majesty's indulgence is unconditional—She wills, if ever you pass these walls, it is as the wife of Lord Arlington."— "They will then be my grave, my Lord," returned I, in bitterness of spirit; "shame on her indulgence, inhuman tyrant!"— "Moderate your wrath," resumed he in the same equal tone, "after your bold attempt to impose on her by forged testimonials of an impossible marriage, and supposititious birth, you ought rather to imagine she treats you with lenity."— "*Forged testimonials?*" retorted I with great acrimony, "why then did she so carefully destroy them? but she destroyed them, my Lord, in vain—look down blest spirits of those who once owned this noble mansion! look down thou dear departed sister of the murdered Norfolk!—look down too, reverend Mrs. Marlow, thou gentle guardian of our youth, and say to whom we owe our being?—but why do I call the blessed from their reward, to authenticate those rights the malice of Elizabeth cannot annihilate? Oh, Royal Mary, dear unknown mother, how would the tender yearnings of thy bosom justify the assertions of thy persecuted daughter, did not a cruel tyrant, by a double injustice, enclose in separate prisons the mother and the child?—bring us but together, and you shall find"— "I am not commissioned to parley on so delicate a subject," replied the crafty Lord Burghley,[17] you give way to these violent transports, remember how fatal they may prove— over the head of the Queen of Scots, the sword has long hung only by a single thread—it is now put into your hand—consider well ere next I see you, *who, and what you will be*;" with these tremendous words he rose and left me—left me—ah, how? Convulsed, annihilated, a terror hitherto unknown seemed to fix every feature, and freeze every sense. Oh, thou, whose awful will alone could authorize this nameless infliction, give me strength to bear it, sighed forth my shocked soul! Can I then deserve the title of daughter only by renouncing all claim to it?— My mother, my gracious royal mother, who even when overwhelmed with woes, didst take such tender care of the little unfortunates to whom thou gavest being; ah, were their lives preserved but to shorten thine? Meditations like these almost shook the seat of reason: and I resolved to conform to the most inhuman command of Elizabeth, rather than suffer the horrible scene his last implication presented, to pass another hour before my bewildered senses.

It was surely at this tremendous crisis in my life, my fermented blood first adopted and cherished those exuberances of passion, which ever after warped the equality and merit of my character; that blood now boiling in my veins, joined with a disordered imagination to call around me a thousand visionary inconsistent forms, to whose voices my burning heart responded— now slowly retreating to every vital source, the very powers of being seemed to congeal, and I remained for hours a breathing icicle. Whenever the first sensation actuated me, the strong desire of saving my mother still returned; and in these dire revolutions of constitution, four and twenty dreadful hours elapsed.

Lord Burghley, at the same time the next day, came once more to learn my final resolution. Scarce able to reply, or raise my heavy eyes from the ground, in which they sought, and saw, only a grave, my whole appearance strongly indicated how I had passed the interval. The desolate acquiescence my silence bespoke, encouraged him to produce a paper. He began reading it, while riveted with a new surprize I listened to the incredible and disgraceful forgery, as if I had lost every other sense than that of ear. It was called, as I think, "the voluntary confession of Ellinor, on behalf of herself and sister Matilda; and set forth, that soon after Mary Queen of Scots sought shelter in England, (under the protection of her sister Elizabeth) for divers politic and ambitious reasons, (as first, in case her only son should die, and leave her without issue, on which to support her claim to Great Britain, as well as to the kingdom she had lately abandoned; next to attach to her interest the disloyal persons into whose charge she was given) she resolved to pretend to have made a marriage with Thomas Howard, Duke of Norfolk; and by the aid and confederacy of his sister, the Lady Scrope (whose Lord was her keeper), together with that of divers Scottish servants, as well as of one Gertrude Marlow (the bastard sister of Lord Scrope) the said Queen of Scots did feign a pregnancy, and in process of time a delivery of two daughters, who were, with the assistance of the said confederates, brought up in secrecy by the said Gertrude

Marlow, till such time as Mary should judge fit to produce them; and that sundry testimonials were invented, drawn, and witnessed by said parties, tending to legitimate said surreptitious offspring at the pleasure of the Queen of Scots, by the names of Matilda and Ellinor. The said Ellinor understanding, in process of time, the above plausible collusion, and sorely repenting the offence against Elizabeth, Queen of England, her lawful Lady and Sovereign, doth on behalf of herself and sister Matilda, freely acknowledge, and solemnly affirm, that they do not believe themselves born of the said Mary Queen of Scots, but have reason to know their parents of a low degree, who, for the lucre of gain, resigned them for ever, to be done with as the said Queen of Scots, and her confederates, thought best. This declaration is made and signed on the spot where Ellinor owns herself and sister were thus secretly brought up, to wit, the Abbey of St. Vincent, the seat of the late Lord Scrope, in the presence of, &c." Having concluded this notable memorial of villainy, he summoned several domestics, and put a pen into my hand. My unsubdued, indignant soul, spurned at the idea of villifying both myself and mother, even to save her life. I would have spoke, but ere grief and rage could be converted into language, he transfixed me with a look; and holding before my eyes an order for the execution of the Queen of Scots, signed, dated, authentic, complete in every form, my shuddering nature could not endure the conflict. I rashly scrawled my name, and snatching that tremendous mandate he yet held before me, tore it into a thousand atoms, and sunk upon the ground in the most violent convulsions. They were so rapid and dreadful, that to have left me alone had been little else than murder. His domestics attended me with a humanity unknown to their Lord; and these fits at last gave place to a frenzy fever. Alas, during its raging paroxysms, I doubtless continually confuted the infamous tale I had witnessed; for every affecting remembrance pressed upon my confused and weakened mind.— My mother, my sister, and my love, by turns bled before my eyes; and death presented himself in every form dear to me, while I vainly invoked him to take my own.

Exhausted nature seemed to rest on the very verge of the grave—Ah, had I then sunk into it, how many pangs had I been spared!—the care of my attendants so far recovered me, as to enable me to quit my bed, when pronouncing me well, they left me to my own meditations—a hideous train, my sister—to add to their bitterness, fancy had now thrown a new colour on my fate—how if this infamous forgery had been extorted from me, only to stigmatize my sister and myself?— A still more aggravating idea sprung from that—What should prevent Elizabeth from presenting to the eyes of the unfortunate Queen of Scots a defamatory declaration, which must give her a stab no less mortal than the blow it saved her from, though perhaps more slow? how indeed, if so, could I hope she would ever forget or forgive an instance of depravity, apparently as unaccountable as it was shocking? finally, (oh grief yet more pungent) might not the Queen take pleasure in wringing the haughty soul of Essex, by shewing him the unhappy object of his dearest affections for ever stigmatized by her own hand?—This painful assemblage of ideas and objects, was too much for my hurt brain—I groaned, I shrieked, I relapsed, and very nearly obtained the relief I so much longed for.

Impelled thus by tyranny down the precipice of fate, my swift course seemed ready to bury me in the gulph it overhangs, when another projecting point interposed, and suddenly stopped me.— I recollected that in thus resigning myself to the stroke, I rendered the last fatal blot my own hand had fixed on my character indelible; that while I lived I had yet a chance of justifying my intention, in an act which reflected alike on myself and all dear to me. By a weakness for which I cannot account, I suddenly became more willing to support all the evils of a life thus prolonged, than the idea of an unknown end, and unhonored grave.

My constitution, destined to struggle with still greater calamities, sunk not wholly under the impression of these; but the period of recovery was marked by a gloom and dejection I can never forget. Silence was now no less my habit than inclination, and I often fancied myself incapable of speaking. Lord Burghley, by a second visit, called together every enfeebled power remaining. Regarding my altered countenance with an air of insidious pity, he lamented the painful duty imposed on him by the Queen. Estranged from sympathy so long, that the least mark of it affected me, I sunk into languor and tears. "Unhappy young creature," resumed he, "destined every way to condemn yourself, hear all I am commissioned now to say, and finally decide your own fate. I need hardly inform you on whatever grounds your connexion with the Queen of Scots is founded, a due regard for herself, and the peace of the kingdom of England, will not allow my royal mistress to enlarge one whose high spirit and distinguished understanding must so greatly aid whatever cause she is a party in. But when the attachment between you and the Earl of Essex is considered, (whose ambition and daring temper sufficiently alarm the prudent part of the Queen's counsellors, unassisted as he yet is by any imaginary rights) it is obvious that one way alone can you hope for freedom."[18] At the dear name of Essex, to which my ear had been so long estranged, every emotion that had gathered slowly toward my heart, spread in wild perturbation through my frame. I faintly repeated it, but Lord Burghley motioned me to silence, and I confined to contemptuous glances my opinion of the remainder of his speech.— "I shall not conceal from you," returned he, "that Essex has had influence enough over the Queen to make her for a while suppress her sentiments on this error in his conduct. Perhaps she would have trusted to time for otherwise matching you, but that this hot-headed, rash young man"— I groaned in impatient silence—he cast on me an attentive eye and pursued his subject.— "After finding it vain to hope he should discover your asylum, (for which I must tell you he spared neither threats, intreaties, money, or assiduity) he completely irritated Elizabeth by uniting himself in a plot to release the Queen of Scots. Providentially for my royal mistress it transpired in time, and the traitors are taken.[19] The chief object of her indignation must of course be him she so greatly favored. Convinced you are the only cause of his rebellious practices, nothing but your making another choice can save him from expiating them on the block. A fond weakness renders Elizabeth still anxious to preserve him. For my own part I confess the safest remedy I shall always think the best"— "Ah, let him live," groaned I, adopting at once the train of ideas he so artfully arranged, "though not for me! Even Elizabeth is merciful, and shall I then condemn him? Rob the world of an unequalled ornament, only because I am not permitted to possess it?— I will no more haunt her slumbers—I will no more gild his—of what consequence is the name I am called by during the few days I linger in this miserable world? Inform me, my Lord, but how I can save him."— "The same reasons that concur in obliging the Queen to separate you and Essex," said the insidious Burghley, "will equally prevent her from matching you with any man gifted with his aspiring qualities: yet as it is not her wish wholly to debase you, Lord Arlington was to me the messenger of her will;" (I shuddered at the fatal name) "the bounded capacity he possesses is one motive for her chusing him, as it ensures her own safety; and his titles and fortunes another, as those are distinctions she is not willing to deprive you of. You marry him, or he returns directly, and his return is the signal for Lord Essex's execution."

Yet weak and unrecovered, my mind wanted firmness to enter into all the reasons which should regulate my conduct. Alas, I saw no more of my own fate, than was inseparably interwoven with that of my lover.— Urged by the generous excesses of which I knew his heart capable, he has for my sake then endangered his honor, liberty, and life. Perhaps that danger is exaggerated, hinted prudence—but oh, if not—if actuated by fear and rage Elizabeth should condemn him to the block, as she already had my father, for no greater crime—my wounded soul shrunk from the bare idea—long faintings and delirium followed—fancy realized every image fraud had presented; I seemed to behold every moment the chosen of my heart tried, sentenced, executed; I drenched the maimed, yet beauteous form my eyes for ever worshipped in my tears, and hardly could be persuaded, during my lucid intervals, that he yet lived, and that his fate still depended on my determination.

Lord Burghley, faithful to the ungenerous trust reposed in him, and weary of the task of confining me, took a willing advantage of the weakened state of my intellects, to wring from me a compliance with the wish of Elizabeth. I was now released from my prison, and the Chaplain and family being assembled, Lord Arlington was introduced, the contracts signed, and a tearful midnight marriage abruptly solemnized, during which my abstracted mind pursued a thousand distant ideas.

*　　*　　*　　*　　*　　*

Wedded—lost—annihilated—the woful mistress of a magnificent solitude, where my inward eyes traced for ever the revered steps of those who were no longer to be found on earth, one only consolation could my exhausted heart supply. "I die, that Essex may live—I sigh, that he may breathe freely."— But oh! such sighs, they seemed to tincture with blackness and melancholy the very air that received them. Lord Arlington wanted judgment alike to subdue the deep regrets of silent sufferance, or to yield to them. My mind could never hold any correspondence with his; and by this means alone was I ignorant, for a time, of a calamity, which, when known, totally overwhelmed me:—Alas, my sister, by a refinement in barbarity, our sainted mother was led to execution, almost at the very moment I was defaming you and myself to save her.[20] This climax of grief and misfortune was too mighty for my reason—I had passed from fear to fear, from sorrow to sorrow, in such rapid succession, that there were only intervals enough of time to render each more poignant. In one short month to behold myself deceived, defamed, and sacrificed. How could I avoid blending the bitter tears of self-love with those of filial duty and affection? The idea of Essex remained engrained on my heart, and doubled every agonizing sensation. Lord Arlington, however, returned to Court, which gave me the little relief of solitude.

Severed at once from every tie both of nature and of choice, dead while yet breathing, the deep melancholy which had seized upon my brain soon tinctured my whole mass of blood—my intellects strangely blackened and confused, frequently realized scenes and objects that never existed, annihilating many which daily passed before my eyes. I sometimes observed the strong surprize of my attendants when I spoke of these visions, but much oftener I remained lethargic and insensible. There were moments when I started as from a deep sleep, (and oh, how deep a sleep is that of the soul!)—turned my dubious eyes around with vague remembrance—touched my hand, to be convinced I yet existed—trembled at the sound of my own voice, or raising my uncertain eye toward the blue vault of Heaven, found in the all-chearing sun a stranger.— Alas! my sister, look no more in this sad recital for the equalminded rational Ellinor you once saw me; sensations too acute for either endurance or expression, from this fatal period blotted every noble faculty, often substituting impulse for judgment. Always sensible of my wandering the moment it was past, shame continually succeeded, and united every misery of madness and reason.

Spring reviving all nature, extends its genial influence even to the withered heart. My intervals became more calm and frequent. I gathered strength to walk into the garden—there I slowly retraced to myself the fatal whole, and began to find, or fancy it more supportable. That I had been a dupe to Elizabeth and her minister, was too obvious; but I was willing to acquit the weak man, perhaps sufficiently punished in a wife like me, of having been a confederate in their plots. I had long been the object of his choice, and it is a common error among his sex to be careless of the means by which their views succeed, provided they attain them. But my feeble efforts toward recovery requiring every indulgence, I wrote to Lord Arlington, assuring him, "I would make the best use of my returning reason, in forming my heart to the future performance of those painful duties, a combination of fatal circumstances had imposed on it; but that the task was too difficult not to claim every allowance on his part; and concluded with hoping, solitude would enable me one day to meet him with feelings less embittered."

With my intellectual powers too returned my affections. The mystery of your fate, my sister, and that of Lord Leicester, racked my weary imagination in vain. I enclosed in the letter to Lord Arlington a billet to Lady Pembroke. It contained only an enquiry for you.

When these letters were dispatched, I bent my every thought to fulfilling the promise made in the first. A thousand times on my knees I besought the Almighty to confirm those upright sentiments he alone could inspire; I strove to obliterate every remembrance of the human means by which his will was effected, and considering it only in the light of *his* will, tried meekly to submit to it. Alas, the answer of Lady Pembroke shook every just determination—astonishment, terror, and affection were obvious in every line of it— eagerly she solicited news of myself, and the incomprehensible means which first restored me to St. Vincent's Abbey, as well as those which fixed me there by so extraordinary a marriage.

From her letter I at last understood a part of your motives for so suddenly absenting yourselves. I found too you had happily arrived in France, by the accounts many had received from you; when all at once (she added) the correspondence broke off, and every effort at renewing it only increased the sadness and perplexity of your friends. That Le Val, having obeyed the orders left by his Lord in hastening to Kenilworth, came on from thence to the Recess; which he found thrown open, as well as that his Lord had infallibly been there. Not able to gather any farther information, he came back to London, there to wait Lord Leicester's directions; but none arriving, this extraordinary and alarming silence induced the faithful Steward to return to his native country, in search of his Lord. Fear and grief having however seized upon his heart, a bad passage wrought both up to a crisis, and he died immediately on his landing. That every other messenger and friend had been equally unsuccessful; though many had traced you as far as Rouen. Nor had the mystery of *your* fate ever yet transpired, though Lord Leicester was admitted to be dead by every body. It was given out he expired in his way to Kenilworth Castle. Certainly he was there laid in state, and afterwards interred at Warwick: but notwithstanding this report was apparently believed, as having the weight of the Queen's credence, the strongest doubts arose in the minds of his friends and relations, upon her seizing Kenilworth Castle, and various possessions of his, as a security for sums due to her: a conduct little agreeing with the indulgence she had for so many years shewn towards him. In fine, having bribed the servants employed in blazoning this pompous fiction, the family were indubitably assured, the body buried under the name of Lord Leicester, was one procured for the purpose.[21]

Almost petrified by this mysterious and affecting recital, I strove in vain to expound it; that Lord Leicester was dead could hardly be doubted, but when, where, or how, imagination could not fathom. Yet the conduct of the Queen proved her too well informed. Ah, where then is now my Matilda? Where then that more unfortunate being, than even myself? Convinced, by a comparison of circumstances, that your death would alike have been published, but that by some undiscoverable event you survived your Lord, I was led to conclude some convent in France still supplied you a grave to groan in: yet even if so, why bury with you that information, for want of which so many affectionate hearts have been racked?— Alas, my darling sister, year after year have I vainly repeated to myself this one affecting question:—Emerge, I beseech you, if yet an inhabitant of this world, and satisfy a fearful heart which achs with fondness. Nay, if translated to a better, and yet sensible of aught sublunary, oh deign to inform me! How often, in the depth of midnight, when the happier world are at rest, have I called upon thee, impelled by an affection incapable of fear—but all was awful silence—no voice replied to me—no form obtruded on the deep gloom where sight itself is lost—yet the days that elapse in incertitude, pass not in vain; they insensibly urge forward one ordained to clear up every doubt.

* * * * * *

I dreamt of Essex—Ah, what did I say? I dreamt of Essex?— Alas, I have dreamt of him my whole life long!— Something strangely intervenes between myself and my meaning.— No matter, I am too stupified now to explain it.

* * * * * *

Oh, these cruel wanderings!—but I dare not attempt to correct or avoid them, lest in the very effort reason evaporate, and one inconsiderate stroke should confuse my whole story.

* * * * * *

Alas, Lady Pembroke, how could you venture to tell me that Lord Essex was married?— And to Lady Sidney too?—[22] Gracious Heaven! I made myself a wretch then only to crown her future days with unspeakable happiness!— At this idea, overwhelming passion breaks the feeble boundaries of reason and religion, sweeping away inferior sorrows—my mother—my sister—alas those ties so dear, so revered, serve only to swell the flood that sinks them.

Hence, agonizing sensations!— I have drawn them up, Matilda, in one weighty sigh.— Ah, surely my heart escaped unawares at the same moment, it has left such a fearful void within.— Yes, my sister, Essex is indeed married; that very Essex for whom I more than died,—and privately too—the sacred, tender union, had every charm but honor—for Lady Sidney he incurred the anger of the vindictive Queen.— Gracious Heaven, I thank thee for that thought—it was not for *me*.— No, I was dying, withering at the heart far from the most false—Ah, still the most beloved of his sex,—that little thought strangely consoles me—rather indeed would I have died, than have been a spot upon that radiant sun, my dim eyes no more must look up to.

* * * * * *

I perceive I have in the wild colourings of a disordered imagination, unfolded a truth my heart almost burst with—this thunder stroke concluded Lady Pembroke's second letter.— How deep, how dreadful was its effect!— tranquillity, health, reason all fled before it—to the evils fate imposes, however grievous, our nature insensibly accommodates itself, but oh, when the arrows of calamity are winged by love, and dipt in poison by friendship the wounds they make always gangrene. The idea of deceit, ingratitude, and unkindness, irritated and preyed on me continually.— It brought on another Greenland winter's night, which lasted many lingering months; and in recovering I seemed to acquire a new disposition.— I had lost with my equanimity all sweetness of temper—revenge seemed the only principle which supported my being, and I nourished a project in secret long ere I could bring it forward. Wonder not at this alteration, my sister, misfortune serves but to soften the soul, injury alone can render it callous. Ah, strange! that we should at the very moment imbibe the vice by which we suffer.

Lord Arlington early in the spring revisited St. Vincent's Abbey. My resentments being levelled at a dear and distant object, I behaved towards him, when mistress of my intellects, with a melancholy graciousness which made him fancy them restored; and proposed taking me with him to London, when necessity obliged him to return. I acquiesced with readiness, as this was the very point to which I wished to bring him, and my unexpected compliance, flattering the egregious self-love that marked his character, he was charmed with the effect, without examining into the cause. He was easily persuaded that decorum would demand my being presented at Court, and undertook to propose it to Elizabeth: while Lady Pembroke, amazed alike at all she heard, and all she saw, steadily opposed a project fraught with so many painful uncertainties. But it was the passion of Lord Arlington to mortify Essex, and conceiving that in his power only by presenting to his eyes, the dear object fatal circumstances had robbed him of, and others yet more fatal had wedded to himself, he soon became as interested in my wish, as if his own heart had dictated it. The Queen heard it, as I foresaw, with surprize, and declined it with scorn; but she soon found I had skill enough to manage even the fool she had selected for me; who persisted in quitting the Court if she denied him the compliment due to his birth. Elizabeth had now put her peace so far into his power, that she dared not entirely break with him: and fearful lest the black history hid in my heart should be published to the world, were she to urge her imprudent refusal, she at last reluctantly consented to receive me. I heard this with a bitterness of spirit I once thought myself incapable of, and brooded over the dreary triumph I had so long projected.

I deferred appearing at Court from time to time, till certain Lord Essex was returned from the camp. Alas! the universal pleasure that return excited, aggravated my deep and increasing resentment. Distinguished now with the same partiality Elizabeth once shewed to your Lord; loaded with honors in his own person, and the chief medium through which others obtained them, Essex conducted himself with such nobleness as endeared him even to those whom he failed to serve: while the happy few who won his confidence, looked up to him as to a being of a superior kind.[23] I, I alone dared silently to impeach his generosity, his honor, his integrity. Wearied with an everlasting discussion of his merits in all companies, and not daring to utter one syllable on the subject, lest groans should take place of language, I often testified an impatience Lord Arlington construed into an extinction of that fatal passion I once entertained for his rival, and a due regard for the rights which he had acquired over me. Charmed with this idea, he became lavish in the jewels, and other customary ornaments; and the tranquillity with which I prepared to appear, lulled every suspicion to sleep. Alas! while they were adorning me with the costly habiliments selected for the occasion, I took a malicious pleasure in tracing the ravages grief had already made in my features, constitution, and figure; the first, shrunk, wan, and withered, the latter emaciated beyond all concealment. I knew, however, those who saw me every day might deceive themselves, in presenting this shadow to his eyes, whose ardent heart once touched with colours yet more glowing, a form then rich with the gifts of nature, youth, and hope—Oh, well I knew that volumes of reproaches were contained in a single look!

I entered the Presence Chamber with an air of determination, grandeur, and composure, astonishing even to myself. My soul found him she alone sought in a moment. Essex was resting one arm on the back of the Queen's chair, in the same familiar, gay, and graceful attitude I had so often seen Lord Leicester assume. His dress, bold, magnificent, and martial. His features (oh, those fatal features! destined to subdue alike my wise and erroneous resolutions) lighted up by every emotion youth, softness, pride, and pleasure ever blended. His fine eyes lightly glancing over each surrounding object, fixed at last on me—*fixed*, I may well say,—how deep, how deadly, was the effect of that single look!—his unfinished speech to the Queen became annihilated, while his quivering lips, in broken sounds, breathed forth unutterable anguish.— Surprize, tenderness, grief,—ah, more than grief!—agony—chased away the bright expression of happiness from every perfect feature, and flooded his eyes in a moment.— No longer remembering the place, the Queen, the circle, he started forward, and almost in the act of kneeling, felt the absurdity, and vanished—with him too vanished every trace of that misapplied reason which had so strongly impelled me to this strange revenge. They told me, I suffered myself to be led to the chair of the Queen, who no sooner in the common form presented me her hand, than I haughtily repelled it, and fixing my eyes on her with a dreadful meaning, gave a deep groan, and sunk senseless at her feet. Elizabeth started up in high indignation, and reproaching Lord Arlington as not less mad than myself, in thus obtruding me upon her, retired precipitately to her closet. Not much more sensible than myself, through astonishment at a conduct so unexpected on my part, he soon so far recovered his faculties, as to take the advice of his friends, in trying to appease the Queen: committing me to the care of those around me. By this means alone he escaped witnessing a scene which touched the sensibility of every spectator. My friends bore me through the great gallery, as the way most convenient; in the anti-chamber leading to it, the unhappy lover I had taken a barbarous satisfaction in wounding, had thrown himself on a couch to recover at leisure. A presentiment of the fact as the croud approached, made him eagerly start up, and resigning himself to the impression of the moment, he rushed through them all, and snatching me with impetuosity from those who held me, placed me on the couch, and kneeling beside it, sought to re-animate my chilled senses with burning tears, and agonized embraces. A thousand times, he called me "his dear betrothed love—his murdered, precious Ellinor,—here is some black artifice, some diabolical villainy in this business," would he cry, starting up haughtily, and throwing his inflamed eyes around, in dreadful search of him who happily was absent: "Oh, if I find it so," added he, "they shall not 'scape who severed us!" By vague and rash exclamations, he thus published the chief incident in our unhappy story; while I alone, still insensible, heard not the well-known voice I once fancied the grave only could close my ear to.

This scene, which every following moment threatened to make fatal, was at last interrupted by the appearance of Lady Pembroke. The excellent understanding of that amiable woman, had made her from the first consider my desire of appearing at Court (even while unapprized of its motives) as the wild start of an unsettled mind: she had employed intreaty and argument in vain to make me give it up; finding the project alike agreeable to Lord Arlington and myself, she became silent on the subject, but declined accompanying me, and dreading some strange event, retired to her own apartments in the palace, to tremble for it in secret. The news of my having frightened the Queen, and broke up the Court, immediately reached her there. However offended at my obstinacy, she was shocked at its effects, and readily emerged to serve and save me if possible. Pressing through the astonished croud, the fond extravagance of Lord Essex continually increased, she beheld me in his arms, and heard his lamentation. Amazement in her collected mind is but a momentary emotion. "What are you doing, my Lord?" said she, with an air which recalled even him—"is this the way to recover the senses, or reason of this dear unfortunate? remember the respect due both to her and yourself, and leave her entirely to my care." Neither prayers nor anger warped her from rectitude: she commanded her servants to bear me to her barge, and followed me herself. The distracted Essex held her by force, and vainly solicited leave to attend me. With a dignity which eminently distinguishes that charming woman, she chid him for a madness not less extravagant than my own, though far more censurable, and requested her Lord to pay him an equal attention.

The women who followed me into the barge sprinkled me with water; that and the open air gradually revived those faculties, so long dormant, they seemed gone for ever. I feebly lifted my head from the bosom of Lady Pembroke, and wondered awhile how I came there. A thousand gloomy uncertainties occurred to me, and a flood of tears at last so far relieved me, as to suffer my mind to fix on the fact. Lady Pembroke, perceiving I was capable of attending to her, spared me the trouble of enquiring into the past scene by relating it; with such comments as an enlarged mind and tender heart, would naturally dictate. My pulses were yet low, and her gentle admonitions made a due impression. "Review the whole of this wild scheme, my dear Ellinor," said she, "and I think you will unite with me in calling it so. The Queen, (beyond your revenge in this world) can amply retaliate on every one dear to you, for the temporary alarms and vexations you cause her. From the eyes of the noble Essex you have snatched away a bandage, which saved both him and yourself from danger. I have hitherto suffered you to imagine him unfaithful and guilty, because anger in your situation, must be a much less dangerous emotion than love. His whole soul is once more awakened, and I would in vain now affect to deceive either—he will be heard—he will even be seen, if to the rash ardor of his temper you do not oppose the most inflexible prudence—Alas, my sweet friend, what direful conflicts do I see before you!—conflicts, the strong and untried soul would wish to shrink from—how then shall your wounded spirit"— "Fear not," answered I, nerved by the occasion, "my dear, my watchful monitress; born for conflict, I seem only to exist by that mental action, and though I lament, with you, the invincible obstinacy which has once more thus involved me, yet believe me I seem better able to bear every evil which may result from the vindication of Essex, than the dreadful weight of his supposed ingratitude. For every other evil I had been accustomed to prepare my heart.— That heart, cherished by tears and softness, started not into excess and insanity, till those sources were dried up. Ah, open again every sluice of pleasure!— Tell me Essex is indeed innocent, unaltered!— Tell me he is still the incomparable being my youthful fancy first worshipped!— Tell me, in short, the whole truth, and see if my soothed senses are not equal to the confidence."— "How little reason do these eager exclamations, these impassioned tears, and glowing cheeks, give me to think so," wistfully replied the sweet Lady Pembroke; "perhaps were it yet in my choice, I should still resolve to deceive you, but in now revealing all, I am only before-hand with him, who, in tenderly urging a just vindication of his conduct, would effectually re-establish himself in your affections, to the utter ruin of the little peace Heaven has allowed you.

"The desperate state of my health at the time when yourself and sister so unaccountably vanished, made my Lord guard against my obtaining that information with the utmost caution; and the first alarm I received, was from the sudden return, and perpetual visits of the Earl of Essex. These were often at odd and improper hours, and generally began or ended with a private conference. A continuance of this conduct, even after I was able to quit my apartment, gave me a disgust to your lover, I did not conceal from my Lord. He pleaded the affliction of Essex, as his only, and indeed sufficient excuse, and thus laid himself open to my enquiries, which soon obliged him to own the whole truth. Its deep effect on me made Lord Pembroke congratulate himself on having thus long concealed it. My agitation and affection soon reconciled me to Essex, and united me in his views. Wholly engrossed by the hope of finding you, every day gave birth to a new project in one or the other. How many disappointments did we experience! yet the fertility of his imagination being only equalled by the warmth of his heart, no toil discouraged him; and adopting all his aerial plans, I urged him to perseverance, taking pleasure in heaping fuel on a flame, prudence should rather have stifled. News happily arrived of Lord Leicester and Matilda, which renovating every hope in both him and me, I joined the deluder self in assuring him he was destined to restore you to the noble exiles, and in receiving your hand, to unite himself at once in their happiness and fate.

"The romantic heroism interwoven in his character, made him readily listen to these pleasing delusions; till a strange rumour reached us one day, that you had been married to Lord Arlington, in the presence of Lord Burghley, and left by him at St. Vincent's Abbey. Impressed with the strongest reliance on your faith, Essex asserted it in the warmest terms, and seemed ready to fly to the spot where it was reported you yet existed. The paleness of my countenance reproved his implicit confidence. The name of Burghley, the remembrance that Arlington had lately quitted the Court, that intuitive sense which arranges and combines a thousand important nothings, tending to stamp a sad conviction more instantaneously than one can pronounce a sentence, now proved the truth of this.— Lord Pembroke proposed going to the Minister, and thus deciding the point. We gladly consented, and Essex traversing the room in great agitation during the interval, found a thousand reasons to justify his opinion; so cautiously collected, as shewed he was not without a secret fear. Lord Pembroke at length returned, and confirming the fatal news, added, Lord Burghley had shewn him the contract, signed by both. But what was the paleness impressed on my countenance, to that which spread over the florid complexion of your lover at this fatal confirmation! The silent struggle in his soul, surely combined every pang of death, without affording its relief.— Speech and colour at last returned; his complexion now glowed with indignation, while his lips trembled with transports of bitterness and grief. He quitted us precipitately, and my Lord devoting himself to assuage my sorrow, was not immediately sensible of the departure of our friend. Alas! could either of us possibly have suspected the fate, the untoward fate, that awaited him!

"The moment Lord Essex thus abruptly quitted our house, he hastened to that of Sir Francis Walsingham; where he found only Lady Sidney, who, secretly as sensible of his merit, as she had before been of my brother's, received him with equal surprize and pleasure. Without entering into the motives which influenced his conduct, he eagerly tendered himself to her acceptance. Her objections were those of one who wished to be persuaded, and he would neither hear of demur or delay: his own Chaplain was quickly summoned, and the marriage solemnized in a manner, almost as sudden and solitary as your own.— Ah, fatal marriages both! beginning and ending in tears!— This news broke upon us with the morning. Lord Pembroke was astounded. I recommended to him to hasten to the wretched bridegroom, and reconcile his mind to the unlucky choice he had thus precipitately made, ere rash expressions of grief or disappointment should rouse that turbulent spirit which had made my amiable brother's philosophy so soon give way to disgust. Well we knew the fiery soul of Essex would spurn at such a bondage, however voluntary.

"The contempt and coldness both Lord Pembroke and myself had always shewn to this imperious woman, who first introduced discord into a family, before distinguished by unanimity, rendered this a great effort of friendship. The time lost in reconciling our feelings to the condescension, made it wholly useless. My Lord found Sir Francis almost annihilated with surprize, and understood at once that his daughter was in fits, and Lord Essex gone. Unable wholly to conceal the anguish that preyed on his spirits, and flattering himself a generous confidence in his bride might in time cement their union, by the charm of esteem at least, Essex had laid open his whole heart to her. The mortal hatred she ever entertained both for yourself and sister, she wanted judgment at this period to stifle. The melancholy Essex, who sought for pity, not passion, now incautiously defended her he had unwarily arraigned. The vindictive temper of his bride, blazed forth in all its littleness, and the quarrel rose so high, that early the next morning he ordered his horses, and calling her at once "his error and his punishment," he took his leave, with the bitter remark, that "he followed in all things the fate of Sir Philip Sidney." A reproach like this might well shock the most callous heart: it threw Lady Essex into fits.— Regardless of this, her Lord mounted, and departing with the utmost swiftness, was soon out of the reach both of friends and enemies.

"The Queen, who was every day more partial to Essex than she had been the former one, insensibly had suffered him to take, both in her heart and court, the place of Lord Leicester. It was the opinion of many, that she intended to marry him, and the rage this step of his excited in her, lent force to the extravagant conjecture. Deeply resenting alike his hasty marriage, and abrupt departure, she banished his Lady the Court, nor did Sir Francis escape a reprimand, however undeserving it.

"Essex soon fitted out some ships, with which he joined Drake and Norris,[24] and his fame daily endearing him more to the Queen, she could hardly support that appearance of resentment she thought due to his temerity, and incessantly languished for his return.

"We soon had letters from the Earl, acknowledging the rash step he had taken in marrying, and that to avoid blushing for it in our presence, he had thus exiled himself. Though pride made him still speak of you with acrimony, it was obvious from the tenor of the whole letter, that he had quitted England, no less to avoid seeing you, than living with the woman he had invested with a legal right to make him unhappy. The generous anxiety he shewed for your sister in sending, even at this juncture, Sir Walter Curtis[25] once more to Rouen, with directions to spare neither trouble or money to discover Matilda, was another new instance of that nobility of mind, which always graces even his faults.[26] Consecrating his cares to a more noble pursuit than love, he thus sought to fill up the void, the aching void, that blighted passion had left in his heart.

"He was not born for inaction; and soon his daring spirit employed the thoughts of the whole nation; when Elizabeth, who knew too well its present exertions were but the wild efforts of disappointment and despair, relaxed at once from all her apparent rigor, and recalled him. Disgust had sunk so deep, that he still hesitated, and nothing but her peremptory command could induce him to return. While in daily expectation of him, I received your first letter. It contained not a word that could inform me of your real situation, or the motives of an action so eccentric, as your acceptance of Lord Arlington. Your long silence, your obscure and laconic epistle; the strong desire I had to see tranquillity restored to yourself and your lover, though happiness had escaped both, made me resolve to shew him the letter, in which he was not even named, if once the subject arose; from this I guessed that he would most probably conclude the union with your own free will, as well as the retired stile of your present life. An opportunity soon offered; nor was I mistaken in my judgment. Lord Essex perused your epistle in silent astonishment, and the conviction it conveyed produced a surprising alteration in his mind and manners. No symptom of either pride, passion, or disappointment, from that moment, has been visible in his conduct. Conforming at once to his fate, he profited by the indulgence of the Queen, and resolved to live decently with his wife, if not happily. Never since have I heard your name from his lips—I knew not that it lived even in his heart; and finding this artifice so successful with one, I resolved to try it with the other. When you related to me the cruel fiction by which Lord Burghley wrought upon your feelings, what purpose would it have answered to inform you, that Essex was never concerned in any plot—never imprisoned, much less condemned. The high sense you entertained of a sacrifice, apparently unvalued by him, made it improbable any explanation, or even conversation, should take place between minds thus deeply and justly offended with each other. How then was I chagrined to see you, on your arrival in London, fondly nourish some unfathomable project, which threatened wholly to defeat mine! Finding all advice ineffectual, I thought it most judicious to leave your mind to its own workings; hoping the gentleness of your nature would counteract the irritation of your passions. Alas, my dear, this fatal day shews me my error, and its extent. In how many ways will you now wound the noble heart of Essex!— Tortured at once with the anguish of disappointed, injured love, the narrow doubts of his untractable wife, and the arrogant vigilance of the Queen, his life will, from this moment, be as devoid of comfort, as it has long been of hope."

The tender motives which dictated this late confession, as well as the past concealment; the melancholy inference with which Lady Pembroke concluded, all made a deep impression, and opened every sluice of tenderness, to the great relief of my oppressed and burning heart. "No, my generous, amiable friend," returned I in a more equal tone than Lady Pembroke expected, "I cannot misconstrue conduct which has ever had the most upright intention; and in doing justice to that of the afflicted Essex, you supply me motives for an exertion I should otherwise sink under. The necessity for preventing a part of the evils my imprudence may occasion, will recal me to reason, honor, and myself.— Oh, thou!" cried I, melting into tears, "too dearly beloved, too deeply lamented, pardon me if I pass a dark and dewy cloud over the bright star of thy distinguished fortune: soon will it emerge with undiminished splendor, while I alone shall drop in tears, enriching the earth that hides me.— And thou too, most favored among women, in being born to share his fate, endeavour but to make it happy, and she who has no use for life, but to weep thy lot, will join to crown it with every earthly felicity. I find my fluctuating mind unequal to entering farther on the interesting subject," concluded I, on arriving at home. "Adieu, my dear Lady Pembroke, be this embrace the pledge of mutual pardon; and if you have not blushed for the last, as well as first, time for your poor friend, her better self must again desert her." She strained me to the purest bosom that ever beat, and left me once more alone with that unstable counsellor, my own erring heart.

The return of Lord Arlington, exasperated by the rage of the Queen, and the surmises of the Court, tried my firmest resolutions: perhaps even those would have been unequal to the conflict, but that I remembered my promise to Lady Pembroke, and was determined to supply a bright example to that noble lover, I now considered as equally unfortunate with myself. I remained from this period wholly at home, yet not without expecting some intelligence from Lord Essex; though I knew not how he could possibly convey it. It reached me at last in the most extraordinary manner. Lady Pembroke seized the first interval of loneliness to address me. "Perplexed circumstances make strange emissaries," said she, sighing,— "who would have imagined that I should request to convey the letter of Lord Essex to you, Ellinor? but finding him determined on thus addressing you, I voluntarily undertook the trust, as well to judge of all that passed, as to prevent his humiliating himself and you to whatever servant he could bribe, and perhaps, if he erred in his choice of a messenger, it would be to the ruin of your peace and reputation."

Hardly hearing this generous preamble, my eager eyes were fixed on the letter, and I gave the fair hand that held it the spontaneous kiss I was at first tempted to bestow on the precious paper.— Ah, how affecting were the emotions produced by the sight of that well-known hand! His language was impassioned, and incoherent—he accused himself, me, the friends of both, and the over-ruling fate which actuated all. He seemed assured fraud, mystery, and a thousand yet unknown execrable arts had been combined to separate us. He conjured me to discover both the persons and the means. He spoke of Lord Arlington rather as a weak tool in the hands of his more crafty enemies, than the object of that deep and eternal resentment, which only slept till I supplied it one. "Scorn," continued he, "the narrow prejudices of custom, and your sex, nor be wholly the sacrifice of situation. Dare to be sincere, and think an adherence to your first sacred vows (vows dear as inviolable) the true point of honor, of religion, and morality. Oh, call to mind the fatal moment when you tore yourself inexorably, from arms that beauteous form no more, perhaps, shall fill.— A little confidence, a little faith, had then made both happy; now, alas, they can only make us less miserable. Yet speak, my betrothed love," concluded he "—tell me all—Once more I conjure you, by those rights your falshood, or death alone can annul, tell me all; and by your care of the life which throbs within this agitated bosom, give me a motive for wishing it to linger there."

As I perused this touching transcript of his soul, mine melted within me.— Nevertheless, I resolved to act up to the idea I had formed, and snatching a pen, I thus replied to him:

"In giving you my heart, my Lord, I own I gave you a right, in every action of my life, which though events may suspend, they cannot annihilate.— Alas, the only right I reserved to myself, was that of concealing aught which might render you unhappy. Suffer me then, to bury in this bosom, the combination of fatal events which tore us from each other. Need I tell you, they have wrung it even to phrenzy; for nothing less could have justified the premeditated shock I cruelly gave you. The deep effect of my presence—perhaps (for why should I conceal it?) that of your own, join with a severe duty in telling me, while thus circumstanced, we must meet no more. The world, a busy, partial judge, delights in beholding the execution of those painful sentences it imposes. Ah, chosen of my soul! remember its afflictions can only be completed by your failing in the arduous trial, I am otherwise resolved to sustain. Rob me not of the melancholy pleasure fortune still allows me, in whatever solitude I am henceforth buried, of thinking him I selected from all mankind, was every thing but an Angel.

"Above the slavery of opinion, I know no guide but rectitude: *that* tells me, Heaven itself will approve the efforts I yet make to charm you to life, to greatness, and to glory.— Oh, awful father of universal being! whose will alone could snatch from each the only object in creation, sanctify to the noblest purpose these dictates of my reason; and form both for the separate lots appointed us. Elevate the passions of my Essex above the little motives of revenge, or malice—sublime his love into philanthropy, his rage into heroism.— And oh, on the frail heart which now bleeds before thee, bestow patience and resignation, so to pass each long day as if the next were to unite me to him. I solicit not strength to expel him from that heart—no, rather may he ever continue its sole object; but be his conduct so ennobled, that when both are called with the whole world before thy dread tribunal, I may look down on the misjudging part of it, and truly say,—Father, it is not Essex I have loved, but Virtue in his person."

This passionate apostrophe, however highly wrought, in the cool judgment of Lady Pembroke, was even in her opinion entirely calculated for the romantic spirit to whom it was addressed. I earnestly besought the amiable Essex to suffer this to end the correspondence, which admitted not an indulgence beyond those conveyed in the letter; and gave it into the hands of my friend, with that sweet sense of self-applause, which ever attends the consciousness of having gone beyond a painful duty.

Yes, still this dear sensation remains to me—it irradiates at intervals the deep gloom which steeps my soul, and annihilates my senses.— I fear I begin again to wander, for my hand-writing appears to my own eyes that of Essex.— Oh, how tight my head, my heart seems bound!—will no one loosen the shrunk fibres?— Hark! Is not that the Queen?— No—It was but the deep voice of the Winter's wind.

* * * * * *

Poor Essex!—and did my letter thus deeply affect him?— Did he so fondly press it to his lips?— Did he blister it with his tears?— Those I have shed for thee, my love, would have drowned thee had they been treasured.— "Unequalled Ellinor—Oh, most adored!— Yes, I will pursue the bright wanderings of the pure mind I have assisted to unsettle, and be all she wishes me from this moment."— (Who told him I wandered then, I wonder?— I am sure I always strove against it before him)—Ah, dear and precious sentiments! how my soul imbibes the charm!— Have you not a penknife, Lady Pembroke, to write these words in my heart—on my very heart?— Oh I would have them sink deep—deep—would feel as well as see them.— And thou too, memory, treacherous memory, for once do thou retain the pleasant tone of the voice that repeated them—not even Lady Pembroke's own is so harmonious.

* * * * * *

Married to Lord Arlington did you say?— Oh, such a marriage!— What did he gain by villainy and fraud? the insupportable society of a wild wretch, whose weary spirit threatened every moment to escape, and leave in his arms the vile dross he thus purchased.— And yet they tell me it is so—he drags me about with him still, and calls me his—*his*, Oh Heavens!— But I am nobody's else, mark that—mark that, or we shall perhaps have murder; and I not there to step between the fatal swords, and see which will befriend me.

Matilda, I have not told you about that I think—but I am not very able just now, such a heavy sleepiness seals up every faculty—and yet if I don't now, I never may wake more you know—but I *have* waked over and over again now I recollect, till I am quite tired, and so for once I will sink quietly into a slumber and dream of you.

*　　*　　*　　*　　*　　*

Let me snatch a moment of reason and recollection to forward my story.—In pursuance of the good resolutions I had formed, I requested leave of Lord Arlington to reside for the future wholly at St. Vincent's Abbey; to which he readily consented. If my offered retirement did not wholly obviate his suspicions, it left him at least no pretence for tormenting me with them. His character I ever found of a common stamp; credulous and mutable, yet self-willed and passionate: vain of the rights of his rank, without merit to distinguish them, he always conceived himself injured when another was preferred; and the partiality of Elizabeth towards his rival, offended him almost as much as that I had so obviously expressed.

The generous Essex respected my peace and virtue so far, that after another fruitless effort to persuade me to see him, he consented to pursue the path I had traced out; and satisfied of my fidelity, swore sacredly to cherish the sentiments I had permitted him to retain. It was needless to ask partial intelligence of a man who employed the voice of the kingdom. I had fortunately distinguished one, fame had adopted. I therefore took a tender leave of Lady Pembroke, and mingling my parting tears with a thousand unspoken blessings, by an effort of virtue I admired in myself, I boldly encountered my fate, determined to use every effort to render it as supportable as might be.

St. Vincent's Abbey again received me. This mansion Lord Arlington had purchased at the time of his marriage, less for any charms he perceived in it, than the advantages of the country round, which supplied him every variety of rural diversion. Here I at last began to breathe, and forming my mind to that melancholy repose, a decided destiny however deplorable, allows, I called to my aid the sustaining principles of religion and morality. I turned my feeble feet towards every dwelling misfortune had passed over, and raising both with gifts and soothing the sad wretches she had depressed, reflected back into my own bosom the comforts I had bestowed. I gathered into the Abbey such of their children as were weakly and deformed, and while those blessed with florid health pursued the track of labour, the others were instructed in tapestry, point, reading, writing, and music, according to their sex and age.[27] Surrounded by these affecting objects, who thus found in the liberality of art, a counterbalance for the unkindness of nature, I sometimes touched my lute with sensations so sublime, that fancy dispersed every bodily imperfection in my little auditory, and lighting up their cheeks with the softest tinge of the morning, I seemed to see the human robes of wretchedness drop off, and the light pinions of immortality wave towards Heaven.— Striving by such, and indeed every means in my power, to shut out the fruitless wishes for lost happiness, which still beat fervently at my heart, I filled up with unceasing employments the long, long year. Often, did my feet wander towards the cell and the Recess. Often, in the well-known windings of that wood, where once we carolled together notes as careless and pleasant as those of the birds around us, have I paused, my sister, and watered with embittered tears the precious memorial of days that never could return.

Conscious I could ill brook the least doubt or enquiry into my conduct, I made it an invariable rule never to pass the gate unaccompanied; yet Lord Arlington conceived an antipathy to this solitary asylum every day increased: I did not compliment him with a total forbearance of the few amusements innocence and retirement allowed. Alas, I soon learnt from his conduct, that jealousy, the most restless and insatiate of all our passions, mingles in the habit, even when driven out of the heart.— Had his love known the refinements common to that passion in a generous nature, he would have felt that an unhappy attachment is nourished by solitude and home: and that the person who once resolves to venture abroad, shews a noble resolution to contend with it. A thousand times he haunted my footsteps; he broke in upon my loneliness. You would have thought he had taken pleasure in beholding the tears and regrets he first occasioned.

The dotage of the Queen became every day more manifest; and even the blow, she in one of her wild transports gave Essex, more disgraced herself than him.— His intrepid resentment—his uncourtly sincerity—his haughty retirement—every action of his life confirmed that admiration I still thought myself entitled to cherish. The unbounded power he afterwards possessed when reconciled, shewed the extravagance of her attachment; and Elizabeth, cruel, inexorable to me in every other instance, crowned to her own disgrace in this, the only wish she had permitted me to retain.[28]

After several ineffectual efforts to gain distinction at Court, Lord Arlington conceived himself injured, and by retiring wholly into the country, persecuted me the year round with his company. But not having a taste for the sciences, nor any of those resources a strong understanding involuntarily supplies, even to the unfortunate, he existed only while employed. Hawking, hunting, and fishing spun out the tedious years, and a rustic company often closed the evening with intoxication. That apathy my exhausted passions had now sunk into, appeared to his undiscerning mind content; and as his own love abated, he fancied mine increased; till he made a discovery that his most needy parasite never seconded—that we were at length entirely happy.

To confirm this surprizing happiness, (which existed only in his own fancy, and perhaps owed its creation to continual inebriation) he resolved to exterminate those ruins where I had owned I passed my childhood, and which, he thought, still kept alive embittered remembrances time would otherwise erase. His Steward suggested that the materials were wanted to erect a manufacture in the neighbourhood, and that the cutting down the surrounding woods, now grown to valuable timber, would more than answer to the expence incurred; while new plantations would at once open the prospect on that side the Abbey, and deprive me of an inanimate object of affection, of which Lord Arlington still entertained a jealousy as excessive as preposterous.

This proposal met the strongest opposition from me on every account; it was dreadful to think of annihilating every trace of my youth; every object which could remind me I had ever been beloved or connected. To disturb the sacred ashes of my early protectors, and leave them exposed to the winds of Heaven, and the hands of the laborer—But it was yet more dreadful to me to risque the little peace I had been able to collect from the wreck of all my hopes—to wake wishes, which were perhaps torpid, only because vain—to tempt Lord Essex to break the promise I had wrung from him—in short, to take the most remote chance of again beholding him—for to prevent the daily regret I might experience at being a spectator of this disagreeable metamorphosis in my favourite spot, Lord Arlington was determined to take me for that time to London. In vain I remonstrated; the stronger my disgust appeared, the less he imagined he had to dread; nor among his whole round of suppositions, once thought it possible I could fear myself. Painful experience now reminded me that the least hint on this subject would be ruin, and every other reason rather strengthening his design, I was compelled to yield to it.— How readily, with every passing mile, recurred the dear habitual impressions! My quickened pulses were again animated by my heart, and I beheld even the palace without disgust, because Essex reigned there. Lady Pembroke met me with an embrace neither time or absence had chilled. She surveyed my amended looks with infinite satisfaction, and flattered herself, because I was no longer a spectre, I was happy. Ah, much erring friend, the embers of that fatal fire tears had almost quenched, again were gradually relighting!— I felt almost disappointed at hearing Essex was still on the seas; that crowned with victory at Cadiz, his valour had only been surpassed by his conduct.[29] The sensation this news excited, rendered me sensible of the precipice on which I stood, and thanking Heaven most devoutly for his absence, I acknowledged in it my safety.

The few friends fortune had left me welcomed my return with ardor, and in their society my subdued spirits might have found some relief, had I been permitted an unlimited share of it; but Lord Arlington saw the world in a different point of view when mingling with it, and at a distance. The habit of being informed of every employment of mine he did not witness, had now grown upon him so strongly that he laid an embargo on my time, and suffered none of it to be passed out of his own house, without he was of the party. Indignation was by nature the marking feature of my soul.— Alas, what sufferings had it already entailed upon me!— This glaring insult at once shocked my feelings, and struck at my principles.— Those traits of bitterness and wildness I had strove to obliterate in solitude and silence, again appeared in my character. I became sullen and impenetrable—for my own sake I forbore violence and error, but I no longer cared whether I was supposed to do so.— Perhaps Lord Arlington was not so culpable as he at first appeared; for the hatred of the Countess of Essex inexorably pursued me.— From the fatal moment when I fainted at Court, she believed herself licensed in her injurious surmises: they had long known no bounds, and expecting her Lord home daily, she by remote and artful insinuations poisoned the mind of mine, to secure her from any danger should Essex arrive.

Weak and misjudging woman!—had she generously sympathized in the cruel events which robbed me of happiness, to cast it away on her, my melting heart would have spent its last breath in wishing that happiness perpetuated. The purest mind alone attracts the venom of the world, as the ether the vapors of the earth; but like that, unless agitated to a storm, soon recovers its clearness, and insensibly returns in blessings the grossness it exhaled. Far from meditating any injury to the Countess of Essex, I respected too much the peace of her husband's mind voluntarily to recall to his remembrance, a wretch born but to destroy it.

Nevertheless, I did not think virtue herself would refuse me one little satisfaction, I could not but desire; a picture of the storming of Cadiz had been drawn by a Spanish painter taken there, and sent by Essex to Lord Pembroke. Among the many portraits it preserved, his own was the most conspicuous; and every one pronounced it the finest ever drawn. It attracted the curiosity of all ranks of people, and the gallery it was placed in was scarcely ever empty. It was so much the topic of discourse, that fashion must have excited a desire in me to see it, had my heart been uninterested. Yet the unreasonable jealousy of Lord Arlington condemned me to silence; nor dared I propose visiting Lady Pembroke at this crisis, lest the desire should be construed into a proof of mental guilt. My nature spurned at the constraint to which I found myself subjected; and my amiable friend (fearful I should suffer in my intellects more severely for the self denial, than I possibly could for the indulgence) planned a method by which she thought the ill-effects of either guarded against.

The Queen gave an entertainment at Greenwich, on the marriage of one of her favorites, to which she invited the whole Court; and a variety of masques, and other entertainments were projected.— Lady Pembroke could not dispense with appearing there, nor could Lord Arlington. Convinced he must for once be safely absent, she proposed calling in her barge ere she went to Greenwich, and conveying me to her house, to leave me in the gallery, with orders to her servants to attend me home whenever I pleased.

In this project there was nothing dishonourable or unsafe; and I embraced it readily. Lord Arlington, I knew, was to be at Greenwich in the morning, as the bridegroom was his relation, and I waited for the appointed moment with an impatience those only who live like me whole years upon a look can judge of.

Lady Pembroke executed this design with as much facility as she had formed it; and passing on to Greenwich, committed me to the care of her family, who were told it was my intention to copy a beautiful drawing of their Lady, fixed up in the gallery. How disdainful of mystery is a truly noble soul! I stopt short on the threshold, and could I without singularity have ventured immediately to return, I had not entered the house. It was silent and solitary; all but the inferior domestics having followed either their Lord or Lady. The servants who conducted me locked the door by which I entered, to guard me from intruders, to whom this picture had accustomed them.— Ah, how lively was my emotion, to behold the features indelibly impressed on my heart, perpetuated with almost the same strength and truth! In the act of wresting a sword (the inflamed eye of him who held it, shewed had a moment before been pointed at the English General's bosom) Essex proudly looked down on the surrounding Spaniards; whose impassioned gestures supplicated for the life of him who had thus immediately attacked the conqueror.— "Ah, Heaven," cried I fearfully bursting into tears, "have I thus long dreamt of glory—honor—immortality—nor considered the dangers by which thou must acquire them?"— "Waste not those precious gems on senseless canvas," said a voice to which my heart was born to vibrate,—"behold thy Essex himself, thy faithful Essex; as truly thine, as when this soft hand first returned his ardent pressure."— Alas, my sister, what a vicissitude of powerful emotions took possession of my soul, and set every feature at an event so unexpected! Fear and horror were however prevalent, and seemed to check the sweetness of again beholding him; for though my eyes surveyed his form, my heart for the first time seemed to shut him out, and fold itself up in utter darkness.— "You speak not, my beloved," added he, "oh, satisfy my agonized heart, and let me think you know me!"— "Know you? Ah Essex," faltered I, redoubling my tears, "can aught but the grave obliterate those features from my memory?— Perhaps even that wants the power—but a thousand nameless miseries make me shrink from the moment—make my terrified soul shrink even from you."— "Collect yourself, my worshipped Ellinor," resumed he, "believe me I come not an artful, black seducer—chance, and chance only has crowned wishes so long submitted to your will. It would not suffer those sacred sighs to become common air, those lovely tears to fall upon the earth; it sent me here to profit by indulgences you were willing to bestow on my shadow."— "If I with-hold them from yourself," returned I, endeavouring to collect my fluttered thoughts, "impute it not to my will, but to the over-ruling fate which has torn us from each other.— Oh, Essex, let us not venture once to look behind, but consider only the present—the time, the place, the person, would stamp me with ignominy if discovered, and rob me of the only pride, the only consolation fortune has left me.— I have long ceased to live to the world, and to myself; but to my God, and you, I yet owe an exertion of the principles he gave, and you called into action."— I rose deeply disordered, and attempted to draw away my hand; but his firmer nerves obstinately retained the trembling prisoner; and my heart yielding to his piercing solicitations for a few minutes, I sat down once more with him by my side.— Good Heavens, while I relate this it appears a mere vision!— Did I really see Essex?— Were my senses really revived by that voice so long forgotten, except when fancy recalled it?— Ah! I have had but too sad a conviction that this *has* been, however strange and impossible it appears.— "Wrong me not with supposing I would entrap you, my sweet love," said he, "I am even now arrived in England; nor did I foresee in yielding to pique in a secret return, how great a happiness I should ensure to myself—disgusted with the injustice of the doating Queen, (who has graced Howard with the laurels won by me) I resolved to call my friends secretly together, and Pembroke is just gone to collect them—at midnight all are to meet here, and agree on the way most likely to punish her unfair decision.[30] By a happiness in my fortune, unguessed by him, and unforeseen by myself, we walked in this gallery while consulting, and when left alone, the fatigue of my journey made me throw myself on the couch in yon window, and draw the curtain to indulge the drowsiness with which I was seized. How sweetly was my slumber disturbed, by her who has broken so many with sorrow! Dear was the surprize with which I saw her enter; I saw the careful servant, as if actuated by love, enclose her, and retire. Entranced with a pleasure which almost took from me the power of motion, I beheld her lovely eyes fixed on my inanimate portrait. I saw, or rather I felt, the tender expressions her unguarded soul uttered.— What dreary ages have elapsed since my eyes have been thus permitted to fix themselves on hers—since in this dear hand I grasped the blessing that *was* to have given value, as well as happiness, to my future life!"— "Alas, my Lord," resumed I, "recollect that those pleasant days, those flattering hopes, those dear wishes, a higher power has annihilated:—nor while the tie which robbed you of this trembling hand subsists, can I suffer it to be thus pressed in yours. Yet recollect at the same moment, the influence you still have over my heart—an influence virtue alone contests with you—Ah, gentle Essex, fix not an angry eye upon me—you know not the wound you give—the horrors you may occasion."— The wild accent of my voice struck even my own ear, and not daring to trust it with another syllable, I strove to bury my agitation and sensibility in silence.— Alas, nature was too highly wrought.— A suffocation more painful than fainting ensued, and agonized with surprize, tenderness, and fear, Essex would have called loudly for assistance. I retained just sense enough to prevent him, and throwing open a window, he then sought to recover me by vows of implicit obedience. My faculties were almost restored, when a noise at the door made me wish them for ever annihilated. No longer able to consider the just or proper, I threw myself for shelter into those arms that gladly opened to receive me, and buried my face in the sattin cloak of Essex. The voice I dreaded rushed upon my ear, and increasing my terror, caused me to grasp my safeguard more closely.— A danger too pressing for apologies obliged that generous lover to throw me from him.— I opened my fearful eyes, soon fixed by horror, to behold the swords of Lord Essex and Lord Arlington pointed at each other's bosoms. Why did not my frail and erring reason at this perilous moment forsake me? Alas, I was never more sensible of agony and terror! I thought the cry I sent forth must be mortal, but perceiving it insufficient either to kill me or prevent the bloody conflict, I started up, and forcibly flung myself between their swords: that of my husband pierced my shoulder, while his more skilful adversary wounded and disarmed him. Inured to every kind of misery, save this, I beheld my streaming blood with a dismay unknown before, and from the faintness it occasioned, never doubted but that I approached the period so often wished for, and pronounced myself dying:—Then raising my eyes to the pale statue of

204 / Tʜᴇ Rᴇᴄᴇꜱꜱ

Essex, who resting on the two swords, hung in silent agony over me, I adjured him to vindicate my fame, and beseeching the Almighty to receive my guiltless spirit, and crown his future days with that honor and happiness I alone had interrupted, I turned towards the erring wretch beside me, with whose flowing blood mine mingled, and having attested in broken accents my innocence, deigned to request his forgiveness. I had no longer, however, power even to receive it. Extreme weakness blended for once objects ever before so distinct, and I ceased to feel for the lover, or dread the husband.

END OF THE SECOND VOLUME.

When the sick languor of the faintings gave place to reflection, I found myself in my own bed; whither I understood I had been conveyed by the orders of Lord Arlington, as soon as the wound was staunched:—his proved so slight that it left him no pretence for apprehension. Eagerly I enquired for Lady Pembroke, when to my inexpressible rage and astonishment I was informed, that she had been turned from my door, whither friendship led her to venture a repulse. The immaculate character of that admirable woman I thought even Lord Arlington would have respected; but without deigning to inform himself of the real circumstances of the unforeseen interview he had so dreadfully interrupted, by this rude implication he treated two of the most estimable and distinguished persons in the kingdom as abettors, if not contrivers, of his dishonor.— The little blood left in my veins turned to gall at the idea. I watched an opportunity to tear away the bandages; and disdainfully resigning myself to a premature fate, I endeavoured to forget the generous hearts this rash action would pierce.— The awful God, whose justice I thus questioned, still extended to me his mercy—my dangerous situation was discovered in time by my careful attendants, who, infinitely more attached to me than their Lord, used every means to prolong the life he, perhaps, wished at its period.

In the cruel state of mind which dictated this desperate resolution, it proved a melancholy advantage; as the injury now fell on my constitution only, and my intellects escaped. It was many months ere I had strength to cross a room, or spirits to venture a question—during this memorable interval I called together every enfeebled power, and placing my conscience as umpire between myself and Lord Arlington, fixed and ascertained the rights of either. Convicted even by my own heart of imprudence, I wondered not he construed error into guilt; and while thus cool offered him every vindication

of my innocence he could reasonably desire: but Lord Arlington was the slave
of passion and caprice, and not having firmness of soul to form, or fix, a
judgment, he followed through years with invincible obstinacy the impression of the first moment.— From this period he ever treated me as an artful
woman, whose licentious conduct had obliged him to risque his life in vain
defence of that honor already sullied, and lost in my person; nor did he affect
to assert his legal rights from any other reason than to separate me from Essex.
This conduct, and the misrepresentations of Lady Essex, blazed the fatal incident throughout the Court, and fixed a stain on my character time could
never erase—happily that stain reached not my person or my heart, and an
injustice so aggravating on the part of Lord Arlington entitled me to forgive
the little error in myself which occasioned it.

In this conjuncture I once more turned my tearful eyes every way around
in search of a protector to interfere between me and a fate alike unmerited and
severe.— Alas! there was not a human being virtue allowed me to call to my
aid; and I exercised the faculties Heaven had so unexpectedly blessed me with,
by resolving to suffer with patience.

Elizabeth Vernon[31] (our old companion), the fair and gentle cousin of
Lord Essex, resolved if possible to see me—she addressed Lord Arlington, and
demanded that privilege; the favour she held with the Queen hindered him
from denying a request he granted with the utmost reluctance. That sweet girl
bathed me in the tears of innocence and affection—she told me, "that the fear
lest his presence should incense Lord Arlington to further brutality, had induced Essex, when I lost my senses, to withdraw from a scene which rent his
very heart—and the same reason still obliged him to remain at a distance.—
That during the long and dire uncertainty attending my illness, he had scarcely
breathed—his own soul continually told him how pure mine was. Fancy presented me to him for ever, pale, speechless, expiring, my sad eyes rivetted on
his with a tenderness death itself could not extinguish: however guiltless of
my blood, every drop which oozed from my veins seemed to congeal on his
heart; in fine, that almost deified by my sufferings, and his sense of them, I
reigned alone in his affections, which were from this moment consecrated to
me by a most convincing proof. Having used the utmost art and diligence to
discover how Lord Arlington so soon became apprized of his secret return to
England, and a meeting so unplanned, and sudden, as to interrupt it almost
immediately, though supposed to be as far off as Greenwich, Lord Essex learnt
that his Master of the Horse, being among the domestics he brought with him
to Pembroke House, had quitted it as soon as he alighted, and hastened to
Greenwich in search of a girl attending on Lady Essex, of whom he was enam-

ored; through whose means her Lady became likewise acquainted with his secret arrival without knowing its motive. That suspicious woman had already remarked that Lord Arlington was among the bridal train, and in his hearing published the return of her Lord, with all her own injurious surmises—ill fortune for once had given them the color of truth, and Lord Arlington needed no more than the hint to make him mount the swiftest horse and fly to satisfy himself.— Lady Essex was quickly informed of an incident she ought to have foreseen, and giving way to another extravagance, passionately conjured every friend she met to follow, and prevent the conflict to which her Lord now stood exposed—but when could friendship keep pace with love and vengeance? The straggling mediators arrived only time enough to witness the event no human power could guard against. Incensed beyond all bounds at the conduct of his Lady, the rash Essex took the only step wanting to my ruin. Determined to make her share the misery she had occasioned, he parted with her at once and forever—in vain were all her subsequent vows of sorrow and repentance—in vain had she from that moment indulged hopes of his cooling and conciliating—his temper, till this fatal period, no less yielding than fiery, now assumed a cold and philosophic sternness; in fine, that the grief and disappointment to which Lady Essex resigned herself would severely punish her unjust suspicions, and ere long release her Lord from the ill-judged bondage he had hitherto groaned so impatiently under."

The fair Elizabeth thus ended her recital, which was so clear, concise, and affecting, that I could not avoid taxing her with being the emissary of her cousin; her blushes acquitted her, and bespoke a secret time soon explained. She was secretly beloved by the gallant Southampton, that heroic friend who was only less attached to Essex than myself, and from him had learnt the various particulars public report could not apprise her of.— I held myself infinitely indebted to her friendship, and through her means sent that farewell to Lady Pembroke I was not allowed to pronounce.

It had been but too obvious through her whole recital, that I was totally the victim of calumny, nor could any human power now justify me.— I had been found in the arms of Essex—the fact was indubitable, the true cause of that fatal impulse not likely to be credited, even when repeated. My youth, my wound, and my past conduct, blended the rash judgment of the many with compassion, but the most liberal-minded ventured not to acquit me. Those impassioned vindications the conscious soul of Essex offered, were always considered as a mere point of honor in him, and no less necessary to his own justification than mine; they therefore only served to stamp guilt on both.— Oh, misjudging world, how severely on the most superficial observation dost thou venture to decide!—let the barbed arrow of misfortune rest in the bosom it has wounded, nor, by inhumanly tearing it out to discover whence it came, rack the heart already broken.

Defamed, dejected, and forgotten by all but the generous sisters of the Sidney family, I followed, once more, my fate in Lord Arlington; and reached again that Abbey destined alike to entomb me in playful childhood, and in blasted youth—the same imperious will which had destroyed me, had deprived that venerable mansion of its sweet, its solitary charms—the hallowed spot where once the ivied trophies of time bound up the defaced ones of religion, presented nothing now but a bare and barren level; and the lofty woods, which so long protected alike the living and the dead, had wholly given place to infant plantations, through the thinness of which the weary eye every where pierced: I returned with disgust from the desolated scene, and locking myself up in the remotest, and most gloomy chambers of the Abbey, spent my life in meditating on my every loss.

Lord Arlington now valuing me only as the appendage of his pride, consoled himself for my undissembled aversion, and cared not what employed me, provided I was yet his legal prisoner.— Alas, I had no longer resolution to rest my hopes on any object—to form any subordinate design, or to reap any subordinate pleasure. The poor children still supported by my bounty, no more touched the lute in my presence—that over which my own fingers once wandered with the wild elegance of untried youth, now useless and unstrung, hung up, an emblem of the discordant soul of its owner. Taste, genius, and science, those rich columns with which enthusiastic fancy erects in peaceful minds a thousand light aerial structures, deep sunk, and broken in my heart, presented to the mental eye a ruin more terrible than the noblest speculation ever paused over.— Misanthropy, black-visaged misanthropy, reigned there like a solitary savage, unconscious of the value of those treasures his rude hand every day more and more defaced.

I was roused one night with the information that a favorite servant of Lord Arlington's, who had long languished in a consumption, now found himself at the point of death, and importunately demanded to speak with me—but ill-disposed at this season even to the gentle offices of humanity, and convinced he could have nothing to impart I should think of consequence, I rejected the request; but finding his Lord was inebriated beyond the power of comprehending aught, on being again solicited, I rose, and accompanied by a maid who loved me, entered the sick man's chamber.— I cast a harsh and cold glance round, and hardly heard the thanks he gave me—having dismissed all the servants, except the maid I mentioned, I prepared to listen to him, imagining some matter relative to his office of chief bailiff and surveyor, alone, could thus disturb his last hours.— "Lady," said he, in the hollow broken voice of approaching dissolution, "I could not have departed in peace had you not bestowed this indulgence—pardon me, I beseech you, for proposing to my Lord the destruction of those ruins I have since seen too plainly your heart was ever wrapt in—alas, that proposal costs me my life.— Condescend too to listen to a secret which continually drags back my soul when striving to quit her dungeon—my crime perhaps brings with it a sufficient punishment.— In removing the rubbish of the artificial hermit's cell, in compliance with the directions of my Lord, I one day saw a common laborer turn up something which tried his whole strength, when casting a quick and fearful glance around, he covered it with earth. I despatched the men in hearing to another part, and seizing the arm of him I had watched, I insisted on seeing what he had endeavoured to conceal—it proved to be a small iron chest strongly fastened— I agreed with him to convey it away till the evening, when he might rejoin me, and we would open it and divide the contents together. He yielded rather to necessity than choice, and I took the casket with a purpose God has severely punished—the many keys intrusted to my care supplied one which immediately opened it; under a number of papers and trifles of no value, I found a large sum in gold, and a few jewels—as I knew my partner in the discovery had remarked that the chest was heavy; in the room of the gold and jewels, I substituted an iron crucifix and many rusty keys; then locking the casket, waited anxiously for the evening. The poor laborer seeing me return, wistfully examined my features, but not daring to express the doubt visible in his own, expected in silence the deciding hour. I suffered him to take infinite pains to break open a chest I was conscious would not repay the labor—great was the poor wretch's disappointment when he emptied it—I affected the same chagrin; but turning over the papers, I offered to give him twenty nobles;[32] a sure proof, had he reflected a single moment, that I must have wronged him: he readily accepted this proposal, and at my desire, promised never to mention the incident; then with much apparent gratitude departed. Eagerly I replaced my guilty gains, and secretly resolved to take an early opportunity of quitting my Lord to commence builder in London; but fear did not suffer me for a time to venture this measure; alas! I have wanted health since to do any thing— from this moment, peace, appetite, and rest have fled me—if worn out with watching, I dropt into a slumber, the idea that my treasure was stolen, has made me often start up, and regardless of the cold sweat produced by the mere apprehension I have flown in the dead of night to convince myself it was safe—imaginary whispers have ever been near my bed, and uncertain forms have glided through my chamber—the dawn of day never gave me relief, every eye seemed to dive into my secret, and every hand to be intent on impoverishing me—in a word, Lady, to this sad moment it has prematurely brought me; for many months doubtful whether I should survive, I have been considering how to bestow that wealth I could no longer hope to enjoy—the poor man I so basely defrauded of it perished a short time after by the fall of a pillar, and restitution to him can never be made. It came into my head this evening, that you were said to have been brought up in these ruins; certainly I had often seen you walk and weep on the very spot where this chest was found; perhaps in giving it to you I only restore it to the right owner; accept it, Madam, and swear you will never discover the gift to my Lord."— This request appeared a needless injunction, if the treasure had not been obtained by defrauding Lord Arlington; and though perhaps I should have been silent through choice, I thought it beneath me to engage to be so—finding me pause, he continued, "fear not any ill design in this request, Madam, you will one day be glad you complied with it, and for your own sake alone is it proposed; the hand of my Lord is grudging—yours bounteous as that of heaven.— Do not rob yourself of the means to be liberal which are now offered to you— yet on no other condition than the vow of silence will I give it up." A strange desire to examine the papers, more than any I felt for the money, made me at last acquiesce. My maid, by his direction, drew the iron chest from an obscure corner, and emptied it of both gold, jewels, and papers, which she and I divided, and with some difficulty concealed till we reached my apartment—he seemed only to have lived to make this discovery, and a few hours after expiated his sin with his life.

While he strove to impress my mind with the necessity of concealing the adventure, I pondered deeply over it; not easily discerning how I should interpret this strange ordination of providence; it at last occurred to me that the treasure might be put into my hands for the assistance and comfort of my sister—how did I know whether she was not even then hastening towards me, perhaps impoverished, certainly distressed?— Oh, how consolatory should I find it to minister to her external wants, though those of her heart should be beyond my power of comforting? The contempt I felt for Lord Arlington was rooted too deep to admit of my thus applying his fortune, had I been the unlimited mistress of it; I therefore saw a degree of wisdom and propriety in receiving and secreting a gift heaven seemed so strangely to put into my hands, as if it were to forerun some yet unknown incident.

The papers consisted chiefly of the correspondence between Mrs. Marlow and Father Anthony, while yet they were lovers, and after the cruel discovery which annulled the nominal union—I perused these invaluable epistles with pulsations of tenderness I lately thought myself incapable of; they recalled me to life and sensibility, and I gathered fortitude from those who now were dust; I raised my eyes to heaven in search of their pure translated souls, and wandering from planet to planet, fancied there must be one peculiarly allotted to lovers now no longer unhappy—A thousand trifles whose value must ever be ideal and local, were preserved with these letters:—cyphers, hair, sonnets, dear perpetuators of those bright hours of youth we look back on with pleasure to the latest moment of decaying life. I kissed the innocent reliques of such an unhappy attachment with devout regard, and held them not the least part of my legacy.

Time dissipated the flattering illusion which led me to expect my sister—my mind sunk into its usual inertitude, and the acquisition remained, if not forgotten, at least neglected.

From this profound stupor I was at last roused as by an earthquake—Lord Arlington in hunting fell from his horse, and breaking some blood-vessel, was brought home to appearance lifeless—conscience and humanity called on me to forget my wrongs; and I made every effort to save him, and for a time he appeared to mend; but the incurable habit of inebriety he even at this period indulged, defeated both care and medicine; and, after enduring a series of sufferings which annihilated my sense of injury, he expired in the prime of his days.

Good heaven, what a transition did this event make in my life!—habituated to slavery—accustomed to suppose Lord Arlington destined to survive me, I beheld this incredible revolution with mute surprise—the horror of his sufferings gave way, when they ceased, to the sweet idea of liberty—liberty, sighed out my weary heart, ah! to what purpose is mine now restored? I beheld myself in the situation of a criminal, whose shakels are struck off only to launch him into the immense ocean in a little boat without a rudder, oars, or sustenance—where could I find a hope to rest on? alone in the vast universe, I turned around in vain in search of one generous hand, whose aid I might receive without fear or shame.

The relation of Lord Arlington who succeeded to his title and estate was an illiterate rude sea officer, whom his illness alone had detained in England. He came on the news of his decease; escorting the late Lord's two sisters, to whom the personals were all devised. I waited only the reading of the will to quit the melancholy mansion I meant to abjure for the future.— Gracious heaven! how deep was my indignation and rage to find myself mentioned in it as an insane wretch to whom he bequeathed a mere maintenance, and left to be confined under the charge of his sisters in St. Vincent's Abbey, which as a purchase of his own, descended to them![33] Never, in all the trials I had hitherto experienced, had I felt a transport like that this usage excited—to extend his tyranny beyond the grave!— Mean, execrable wretch! even at the moment I was exhausting the little constitution his cruelty had left me in unwearied attendance, deliberately to condemn me to an imprisonment so shocking, and render it perpetual!—human nature could not resist so pungent a pang— it *made* the misery it punished; and I sunk into the dreary gulph once more from which I was lately emerging—my brain still fires but to remember it.— Oh, my sister! whatever the inflictions of your mysterious fate, those of mine may surely dispute the woeful pre-eminence.

The overjoyed Essex dispatched an express, as soon as the news of Lord Arlington's death reached the Court, conjuring me to quit the melancholy prison I had so long inhabited, and retire to a seat of Lord Southampton, in Herefordshire; whither that nobleman's bride would immediately repair to meet and comfort me. Lady Southampton was the fair cousin of Lord Essex I formerly mentioned, who by marrying privately had wholly lost the favor of the Queen.[34] The declining state of Lady Essex's health, he added, daily promised him that freedom, made doubly desirable now I had recovered mine. It had always been the intention of Lady Southampton to follow her Lord to Ireland; and he besought me to give him the sweet satisfaction of knowing I was safe in the company and protection of his cousin, solemnly promising not to obtrude himself on me ere the laws of society authorized the avowal of those sentiments which had so long lived in his heart.

The relations of Lord Arlington, possessing by his will an absolute power, intercepted and opened this Letter—far from pouring the balm it contained into my bleeding heart, they kept the dear testimony of an unequalled attachment; and sent back the messenger with the melancholy news of my insanity and confinement: but Lord Essex had been already duped, and could not easily credit this information. He deputed Henry Tracey,[35] a young officer, much in his confidence, to ascertain my real situation; commanding him not to be dismissed by any other mode of conviction than being admitted into my presence.— Alas! ere this was resolved on, resentment had again fired my bewildered brain, and Lord Arlington had little to apprehend in allowing Tracey to enter my apartment. Buried in a profound stupor, I replied not to his questions, but drawing my mourning veil over my eyes, sat like a self-devoted Persian, the voluntary victim of despair.[36] The faithful Tracey, still fearful of being imposed on, insisted on having my picture, as well as a lock of my hair, to prove to his Lord that it was indeed *myself* he had beheld in this deplorable state; and having obtained this request, he departed.

But what became of Essex when Tracey returned with this melancholy confirmation?—the testimonials his confidant had brought added force to the eternal passion of his soul: a thousand times he made Tracey describe the apartment—my dress—my looks—and sometimes fancying even that cautious friend had been deceived; at others, that the wretches in whose power I was left, had, for the short period Tracey was permitted to behold me, stupified my senses; he created a thousand delusions to counteract the fearful impression of the truth.

Distracted with these ideas, Lord Essex set out for Ireland, invested with absolute powers, and heading an army attached to him alike by gratitude and expectation—he had not marched far ere he formed the bold resolution of committing the conduct of the troops to Lord Southampton, and turning off he posted to St. Vincent's Abbey, determined to judge from his own senses of the state of mine:[37] he arrived there at midnight, and requiring the unwilling owners to produce me, in a tone which admitted neither denial or delay, they conducted him to my chamber—a dim lamp alone glimmered in it and closing my eyes as the stronger lights approached, I waved my hand in stupid silence to have them removed. The transports of grief and surprise which overcame the generous Essex at this terrible conviction, threatened his own intellects—by some wonderful ordination of providence my cold and apparently uninformed heart waked at that well known voice—day broke once more upon my soul, and my eyes once more opened to behold their darling object. This surprizing effect of his presence would have persuaded him that reason had never deserted me, but that my poor maids expressed a joy at this unexpected revolution too unfeigned to be misconstrued; they entreated him to leave me time to strengthen my faculties ere he again absorbed them, and he confined to stifled exclamations, and silent homage, all the passion and projects with which his bosom swelled.

Alithea, who had for years been my favorite attendant, informed him (as soon as he could be persuaded to withdraw, and leave me to repose) of the cruel and unjust will, which, by rendering me a prisoner for life, had occasioned this dreadful relapse. Negligent at all times of prudence, and now perhaps of propriety, he boldly told the Arlington family, that he would perish ere I should again be left in their power; and having planted some of his most faithful domestics to guard my chamber door from every one but my own maids, he retired to the apartment allotted him, to meditate on the mode of proceeding least likely to endanger my newly recovered intellects.

Alithea very prudently had me bled, and I sunk into a sweet and sound sleep, the comfort I had long most wanted. I waked late the next morning with intellects entirely clear, though weak; I remembered I had seen, or fancied I had seen Essex; Alithea imparted to me the truth, and shed tears of joy to find I answered her rationally—I yielded to her intreaties in delaying till the afternoon a meeting so dear and affecting, and took the medicinal cordials and other nourishment she offered me; a few hours strengthened me surprizingly, and I was at last allowed to receive the generous lover my soul so much desired. While he poured forth the most ardent vows of unremitting affection and surveyed, in tender sorrow, the ravages grief and disappointment had thus early made in my wan countenance, and emaciated form, I beheld with surprize the advantages he had acquired in both instances; his graceful flower of youth was settled into firmer manhood; his fair and florid complexion, sunned over by his military exploits, had gained strength without losing delicacy, and his eye, now no less accustomed to command than charm, seemed to employ its first power on all the rest of the world, while its last was solely reserved for me. Ah man, happy man! how superior are you in the indulgence of nature! blest with scientific resources, with boldness, and an activity unknown to more persecuted woman; from your various disappointments in life ever spring forth some vigorous and blooming hope, insensibly staunching those wounds in the heart through which the vital powers of the feebler sex bleed helplessly away; and when relenting fortune grants your wishes, with unblighted powers of enjoyment you embrace the dear bought happiness; scarce conscious of the cold dew-drops your cheeks imbibe from those of her, permitted too late to participate in your fate.

It was some days ere I dared trust myself to converse long with Essex, who employed that sweet interval in amusing my mind with lighter topics, while he arranged his future plans; but finding I still appeared calm, he ventured at last to unfold to me the mighty designs which floated in his imagination. "Inexorably opposing choice to fate, my dearest Ellinor," said he, "never from the moment in which I first beheld you, have I formed a project distinct from yourself, this I am about to unfold has been for years the child of my dotage[38] —collect your spirits, listen without wonder, and, if possible, approve it: from the moment I knew the base arts that must have been made use of to separate us, I clearly comprehended we should never unite with the consent of Elizabeth; but, however indebted to her partial distinction, it was a point in which even she could not controul me; it is not the posts or advantages I derive from her favor, on which my soul values itself; elevated on a more solid foundation, it has taken every road to glory, and I may proudly say, given a grace to dotage; yet as that dotage, however unbecoming her years and her rank, has been uniform and generous, I have sworn to yield Elizabeth, to the latest moment of her life, every homage but that of the heart; and sacrifice to my fealty all but my happiness.— It is hard to reconcile duties and inclinations so entirely opposite, yet I think you will own I have done so.

"To a blind partiality for me, and her own egregious self-love, the Queen ignobly sacrificed your youth, your hopes, your happiness; but alas, she forgot in so doing, that she would only make them more perfectly mine—without any consideration for the husband she had given you, a wretch I could at any time look into insignificance, I studied solely how to extricate you from a bondage not more insupportable to you than myself.— Among a thousand other projects, I resolved to apprize the King of Scots of your existence and situation, soliciting from his fraternal regard a safe asylum, and that peace and protection my youth and circumstances would not allow me to offer you. I found means to convey to his knowledge your whole melancholy story—but how shall I declare to you his ungenerous conduct? Fool that I was, to think the man who could tamely submit to the murder of his mother, would be interested by any other tye! Far from exerting himself to rescue the dear un-happy sister I conjured him to compassionate, he affected to disbelieve the story of his mother's marriage with the Duke of Norfolk; though the Count-ess of Shrewsbury solemnly assured me he had, through her hands, received from the Royal Mary the most authentic proofs of it as soon as he escaped from the power of the Regent, and was allowed to act as an independent Sovereign. Anxious without doubt to centre in himself every right of his mother, he voluntarily renounced all regard for either her ashes or her offspring, igno-miniously submitting to kiss the hand which had shortened her days.—[39] What after this is to be hoped from the king of Scots? and why should you sacrifice to a brother, by whom you are disowned, those bright prospects which now dawn before you? Born of the first English Peer, and the Princess imme-diate in succession to the Throne—a native of this kingdom;[40] there is only one thing wanting to establish rights from whence you may justly form the highest hopes—authentic testimonials of these facts; and that such still exist, I have certain information—it is true they are dispersed among the Catholick relations and friends of Mary, yet do I not despair of obtaining them.— The English, ever disposed to be jealous of their national rights, dread the remot-est chance of their annihilation, and already turn their eyes towards the family of Suffolk in preference to receiving a foreign monarch.— That unhappy branch of the royal line, by turns the martyrs of fear and policy, have bled through succeeding generations, till reduced wholly to females; among whom there is no one endued with courage or talents to venture a contest, had they even the priority of birth which rests with you.[41] Let us then adopt the views of Lord

Leicester, who certainly meant, by the most watchful policy, to pave the way for your sister's succession, whenever Elizabeth should expire. Your fate is bound up with that of a man much more capable of effecting whatever views he shall adopt. Elizabeth daily totters on the verge of the grave—disposed to hate the Prince she has irretrievably injured in the person of his mother, she still refuses to acknowledge the King of Scots for her heir;[42] and has fully invested me with every power that may enable me to profit by the popularity I have honorably acquired. My own birth, though it does not give me a lineal claim to the Crown of England, is yet noble in many generations, and princely in some. Circumstances and merit thus entitle me to match with you—nor need you doubt the success of this project.— Born as you are for empire, endued with beauty to adorn, and majesty to dignify it—with incontestable evidence of your birth (which I will employ every art to procure) I will boldly present to the people of England another blooming Queen—they will with joy adopt you; nor can the feeble attempts of the boyish Scotch pedant[43] against an army won by my munificence, endeared to my command, and relying on my valor, affect a claim so strongly supported. How many instances does our own history supply where courage and popularity have dethroned monarchs in full possession of every other advantage!—[44] You now are informed of what has long been the ultimate object of my life; every action and view has had a secret reference to it, and far from idling away my youth in the various pleasures the gay court of Elizabeth offered to her favorite, I have continually ranged the seas, watched in camps, disciplined armies, and by every possible means studied to increase my military fame, knowledge, and popularity, as what must one day decide more than my own fate. It is this that has made me eager to conduct the Irish war—In that country I shall be at the head of an army, which will easily enable me to profit by the death of the Queen, without alarming her declining years with the appearance of cabal, mystery, or rebellion.—[45] Boldly resolve then, my love, to accompany me to Ireland, as the only place on earth where you can be entirely safe; I will lodge you in some impregnable fortress with Lady Southampton; I will remain in the camp, and never approach it but by your permission—I demand this instance of your confidence, of your love; and swear in return inviolable honor and obedience—Oh! answer me not rashly, sweet Ellinor—rather recall the fatal moment of obstinate prudence which once before brought on both so tedious a period of suffering, and remember you again have the power of deciding my fate and your own."

Essex rose from my feet, and left me absorbed in the deepest reflection; my mind however instantaneously adopted the aspiring project he had presented to it. Through the dark and heavy cloud which had long hung over my soul, the sun of love now pierced at once, and turned it all to ambient gold.— To mount a throne; to share it with the choice of my heart; to give to him that sovereignty I owed to his valor—I was astonished that the idea should so long have escaped me: yet such a train of misfortunes had succeeded my birth, as might well obliterate my sense of its rights. "Base and unworthy son!" sighed I, "ungenerous, cruel brother! why should I sacrifice to thee my only chance on this side the grave?" The mean acquiescence of James, under a blow which almost nerved my arm against the royal murderer, had already sufficiently shocked my feelings, and shut him out of all my plans; alas, I could only excuse his misconduct by supposing he was yet subjected to his mother's enemies, though even then, a generous soul would resolutely have protested against the evil it could not prevent; but to learn he sacrificed an inviolable duty, and every social feeling at the shrine of that bloated idol, *self*, robbed him of all claim to the feelings, the duties, he renounced. The determined plan of the generous Essex had every thing in its favor, nor was my concurrence so necessary to his success as happiness—but wherefore should I hesitate, when not to unite in it was to deliver myself up to an implacable enemy? yet, as avowedly to depart with Essex, or even after him, would awaken dangerous suspicions in the mind of Elizabeth, and confirm all the slanders of the world; I pondered much on a singular idea that arose in my mind, by which both might be obviated; indeed the situation of my health would have sufficiently opposed my going with him, had no other objection occurred.— I perceived an air of stifled anger in Essex when he returned, which I conjured him to expound:—"It is a matter of no consequence," said he, with his usual frankness; "fortunately the few friends I have brought with me are tried and valiant, and we have the power in our own hands: the wretches, my love, who surround you, pretend an authority from the Queen, as well as from the late Lord Arlington, for your detention; this will oblige us to use a violence I would rather have avoided; but that is a trifle." "Oh! call not anything a trifle which affects your safety, however remotely," cried I; "in yielding to the bold project you have ventured to form, beware I do not become its ruin—yes, look not on me with so marked a wonder; my soul accords to, adopts at once all your views. I will at last indulge my heart, and thus affiance it to yours— born to pursue your fortune, I will joyfully consent to partake it, so you, in return, swear the confidence will render you but more guarded; in considering my own honor, I am only watching over yours; pledge then your word that you will not interfere with my plan, and I in return will vow, that all I henceforward form, shall have the same tendency with your own."

The generous Essex scarce credited his senses, and gave with readiness the assurance I desired.— Resolved to guard my sister's prior rights, and unable to judge of the motives which might bury her for a time in oblivion, I insisted on his supporting her claim in preference to mine, if ever she should appear; and he perhaps the more readily acquiesced in this request, from a conviction that she no longer existed, as all my opinions on that head appeared to him entirely visionary.

Refusing to confide in this dear rash lover the means by which I meant to rejoin him, I obliged him to assume an air of grief and despair, which persuaded the Arlington family that I had relapsed into insanity. In the interim a maid of mine had been seized with an epidemic fever of the most dangerous kind; I impatiently hastened the departure of Essex, lest the cruel malady should infect him, and conjured him to wait with Lady Southampton at the port, from whence the troops had already embarked, till I should rejoin him.

The air of satisfaction he perceived in me made him comply against his better judgment, and the Arlington race, no less overjoyed at his departure than my supposed relapse, and fearful of the epidemic fever, shut up those who immediately attended on me, in the quarter of the Abbey I inhabited, avoiding it themselves as though the plague were enclosed there.

In this solitude I executed a surprizing project I had long meditated: from the moment I was informed of the mock interment of Lord Leicester, my mind had dwelt on the idea; I saw it was only to methodize the most wild and romantic plan, and, however unfeasible it at first appeared, time might form and bring it to effect—The treasure of the surveyor now became a treasure indeed; reflection convinced me that the bequest originated in his having been the confidant as well as witness of his Lord's ungenerous will, and by thus disposing of it, he enabled me to escape from the despicable bondage it entailed upon me, without betraying his trust.— The maid, who alone witnessed the mysterious legacy, had, by her inviolable silence on so singular an event, sufficiently proved that she could merit my whole confidence; fortunately, she was no less favored by those in whose power I was left, and became of course the properest, and only assistant I could fix on:—by thus turning the artifice of the Queen upon herself, I might at once escape from her power, and that of the guardians under whose care she had placed me; and gratify the first wish of Essex without endangering his safety.

Alithea embraced the plan with joy, and engaged her parents, who were laborers in the neighbourhood, to aid the delusion.— I affected to be seized with the same fatal fever as soon as the maid's symptoms became mortal, and when she soon after died, resigned my bed to her corpse: her hair, height, complexion, and age, so far agreed with mine as to secure me from common observation, and dread of the contagion saved us from a very strict scrutiny; as it was believed the maid expired at the same time with myself, by Alithea's judicious management her supposed body was to be delivered to the parents of that faithful domestic; when placing myself and treasure in the homely coffin, I was boldly conveyed like the Empress Maud[46] through the midst of my enemies, and lodged in their humble cot till enough recovered to pursue the route of Essex.

Alithea now published the news of my death through the family, who heard of it with joy; the unguarded conduct of the generous Essex had suggested to them, that to have acted under the authority of the Queen, might one day be a very insufficient vindication:—this idea added fear to that hatred they always entertained for me, and with pleasure they buried both those passions in my grave.— Having surveyed my wardrobe, jewels, and papers without finding the least deficiency, they prepared for my interment, and discharged my immediate attendants; among them the favored one who had aided my scheme, and her return to her parents restored peace to my bosom.

From the humble cot of that honest creature's parents do I close this period of my memoirs—here, as from an invisible world, have I surveyed the gloomy pageant, with which the erroneous judgments of those from whom I escaped have dignified a low-born female, and by placing her pompously at the side of Lord Arlington, they perhaps have blundered unconsciously on propriety.— As the sable train wound by my window, my soul paused on the solemn vanity—Oh! that in thy tomb, thou quiet sleeper, sighed I, may be interred with my name all the painful part of my existence! that renovated to a new and happier being, I may emerge again into a world which still opens a flowery path before me, with corrected spirits, unfaltering reason, and a temper superior to the shocks of misfortune!—

*   *   *   *   *   *

The soul, ever capricious and uncertain, fully enjoys only the pleasures it makes for itself.— Often do I seem even in this rustic asylum, concealed in the coarse garments of the other sex, and looking towards a distant kingdom as my home, to have hoards of hope and happiness to build on, my youthful, healthful days were never blest with.—

*   *   *   *   *   *

My own fate has once more recalled to my mind that of Matilda—I have meditated much on a sister so dear—alas, too certainly Essex is in the right, and there exists not a being I can call by that name.— Long years have succeeded each other, and still that incomprehensible mystery, that dreadful silence continues; nor is there a circumstance but death that could occasion it.— Farewell then, oh name ever so pleasant to my lips, sink deep into my heart, and remain eternally engraved there—farewell, thou pure spirit! too etherial for a world so gross, I will no more look for thee on its surface, I will no more imagine thee beneath it—no, I will now raise my stedfast eye to that heaven "where the wicked cease from troubling,"[47] and in some yet undiscovered star fancy I behold thee! Ah deign, if so, to guide the uncertain steps of a wanderer, and, if my cruel fate conduct them still toward precipices, irradiate the scene, and deliver me from the danger!— My spirits are highly wrought, and a solemnity too exquisite for description possesses every faculty—I must steep them all in oblivion ere I recover my equanimity.—

*   *   *   *   *   *

Happiness! undefinable good, in what shall I comprize you? no, I will not suppose it can be done in gold, and yet how pure was the transport a little of that vile metal called into the care-furrowed countenances of Alithea's venerable parents! To the earth which gave, I have restored the remainder; it is buried eastward under the spreading chesnut planted by Edward IV.—that popular tree,[48] protected alike from the caprice of its owner, and the spade of the laborer, will hide it safely: but, oh! if ever one noble heart sighs under its shade, oppressed with the sting of penury, may some good angel whisper, "you rest on that which can fully relieve you."

All is now prepared for my flight; I have refused the attendance of Alithea; it will be well supplied in the remembrance that she is happy—indulgent heaven has given to *her* parents who grow old in peace and virtue, a lover who knows not falsehood or ambition, and a soul justly grateful for blessings beyond all valuation—the faithful creature delays the happiness of him she loves till he shall have conveyed this broken narrative into the hands of Lady Pembroke; nor do I fear to trust him with it.— Dear, noble friend, once more my soul fondly salutes you; bestow on my flight those pious prayers with which virtue consecrates our purposes, and believe mine rise ever for you.

LADY PEMBROKE WRITES.

Scarce had I recovered from the surprise and grief occasioned by the publication of this sweet creature's supposititious death, ere a rustic demanded permission to see me, and mysteriously delivered the wonderful packet—alas, how affecting did I find it! far, however, from drying up my tears at learning she yet lived, I looked with terror on the future, lest every following day should multiply, or terribly finish her miseries. Ah, dear Matilda! I cannot agree with this fair visionary, who so easily adopts the romance of her lover.— Something seems to assure me thou art still alive, and suffering; and for thy sake I will preserve these melancholy memorials: alas! perhaps it were truer kindness to destroy them.

LETTER I.

Dated Drogheda.[49]

From the safe shores of another kingdom, once more do I greet my friend.— Alas! ill can we judge for ourselves, dear Lady Pembroke.

Provided with a fleet horse, I set out to follow Essex, but scarce had I travelled a single day, ere my shattered constitution (no longer able to sustain the least toil) claimed two, to recover the fatigue of the first. During my stay at the inn, my youth, the delicacy of my person and manners, with the air of reserve I found it necessary to assume, excited a curiosity my liberality alone was able to bound, though even that gave rise to suspicions almost equally dangerous. I began to fear that my scheme would wholly fail in the execution; I hired, however, two rustics, well recommended, as a guide, and an escort, yet in travelling on the solitary mountains of Wales, often dared not turn my head over my shoulder, lest in my guards I should behold my murderers. My impaired health rendered the journey very tedious; during its progress, I passed for a poor youth following the steps of my father, and far gone in a consumption—After immense fatigue, I arrived at length at the port; where I understood with inexpressible chagrin that Essex had embarked for Ireland a week before.— Alas! a moment's recollection enabled me to account for this, apparently, strange desertion:—in my eagerness to conceal my favorite scheme, I had forgot to guard against the chance of his being informed of my supposed death ere I reached him. On enquiry, I plainly perceived that he had left spies in the neighbourhood of St. Vincent's Abbey when he quitted it, who, misled by report, had hastened after him with news of the melancholy event. I learnt he had delayed crossing from time to time without giving any reason for it, but on being roused by the arrival of two officers, he ordered the seamen to be called in the dead of night, and embarked the moment the tide favored his departure.

Though this information left me only myself to reproach, it did not lessen my chagrin. I wandered toward the shore to meditate at leisure; it was still littered with soldiers and their appendages; they were indulging with ungoverned licence in drinking and riot.— Every thing I beheld, increased my fears of the voyage: it was indeed a tremendous thought; to embark with a numerous body of licentious men for an unknown country, while wrapt in mystery myself, and without a protector.— How, if actuated by curiosity, or a less excusable motive, they should guess at my sex, and pry into my story? perhaps even the name of their general would want influence to guard me. I turned woman again, and trembled at the bare idea. While irresolute in what manner to dispose of my unfortunate self, I observed a body of travellers approaching, and understood with joy that it was Lady Southampton and her train, escorted by a chosen troop, for whom those I had already seen waited— I blest indulgent heaven, which thus relieved me from the effects of my own indiscretion, and demanded to see her—to see her was enough, for with the penetration natural to her sex, she instantly knew me, and throwing her arms around my neck, reproached me with a generous freedom for having retarded her journey, by obliging her to wait in vain for my arrival: and finally, for shocking her with the fictitious story of my death.— I explained to her my unguarded conduct, and its motives.— She assured me that she dreaded the effect it might have on my lover, as her Lord had not time to write more than that Essex was in dispair for my loss, nor dared he venture to leave him; therefore conjured her to confide herself to the care of the officers he mentioned, and follow with all expedition.— This information doubled the regret which had already seized on me; but to guard against all suspicion and enquiry, I resolved to retain my masculine habit, and pass for one of Lady Southampton's pages, till safely lodged in Ireland.

We arrived here last night, and found a letter from Lord Southampton, lamenting the impossibility of waiting for his Lady, without abandoning Essex to a grief which urged him to rashness and despair; he ended with conjuring her to remain in this town till he had considered how to dispose of her safely.— Oh, fortune, fortune, how unfairly do we accuse thee, when folly alone has led us into error!— I am more miserable than it is possible to express. Lady Southampton would fain persuade me that this oversight may eventually prove lucky, as it will prevent my again seeing Essex ere the death of his Lady.— Ah! what alteration can her loss make in my fate?— "I tell you, my watchful friend, you cannot love my honor more than I do his safety—between him and me there is another bar not less insurmountable.— Did not my sister's marriage with a favorite of Elizabeth cost him his life? Alas, perhaps hers too was sacrificed!"—over her mysterious fate a dark veil early fell, dipt perhaps in the blood of her beloved—rather may I see my own veins opened, than survive such a calamity: but even at this moment it has perhaps fallen on me, and I may be dying in Essex while yet unconscious of my fate—oh, what horrors take possession of my soul at the bare idea!— Lady Southampton has sealed her English dispatches, and I can only say adieu.

LETTER II.

Dated Drogheda.

Bound to this spot, my generous friend, and dreading all which passes beyond it, hardly can my heart feel the congratulation you bestow. Environed by enemies, and rendered rash by dispair, Essex now renounces the glorious visions he possessed my imagination with, and resigns himself wholly up to his command.— Oh, that the arrow which stabs me should have been sharpened by my own hand!— All here is alarm, uncertainty, and confusion—we get and lose in the course of every day a passage to our friends, nor dare we trust to that channel aught of importance. Sir Coniers Clifford[50] with a chosen body of troops was yesterday surrounded, himself and half his men cut off immediately—among the officers was a relation of Lady Southampton's; she has been weeping the whole day for him.— For my own part, conscious I have not a tear to bestow on common inflictions, I gather mine into my heart, which feels ready to pour forth a deluge the moment one of my many fears shall be confirmed—you can form no conception of the wants, the woes, the horrible scenes we witness.— Born and bred in the arms of luxury and prosperity, a distant war but faintly affects our minds; but oh, how tremendous does it appear when once we are driven into its tempestuous seat!—death, ghastly death, assumes a bloody variety of forms; while rapine, famine, sickness, and poverty, fearfully forerun him.

I have hitherto thought my sister's fate more consummately wretched than even my own, but how is every evil lightened by comparison!— Beloved Matilda, born as you were to woe, you saw but one bounded prospect of the infinitude the globe presents to us; the horrors of this were unknown to you— uncomforting is the pillow of her who sleeps within the sound of a drum, and fancies its every stroke is fate.— Is this to live? Ah no! it is to be continually dying.

This country so nearly allied to our own, yet offers to our view a kind of new world; divided into petty states, inveterately hating each other, it knows not the benefit of society, except when necessity combines the various parties against a common enemy; yet, though necessity unites, it cannot blend them; the least cessation of general danger awakens all their narrow partialities and prejudices, which continually break out with bloody violence. The advantages of commerce, the charms of literature, all the graces of civilization, which at once enrich the mind and form the manners, are almost unknown to this people; with a savage pride they fancy their very wants virtue, and owe to their poverty an unregulated valor, which often enables them to contend with well-disciplined troops, whom they sometimes defeat by mere want of knowledge; at others, on the contrary, they obstinately pursue an unequal contest, while speculating reason turns away from the bloody scene, vainly conscious that their mangled bodies strew the earth, only because no benevolent being has yet deigned to attempt the conquest of their minds.[51]

How deeply must such reflections operate on a heart bound up in the life of the accomplished leader! endued with but the common powers of humanity, exposed with the rest, alike to the sword and to the elements, he, even he, must one day perish; and while I weep the wretches every hour deprives of their beloved protectors: I know not but I may at the same moment be added to the number.— Ah, if despair should impel Essex,—his natural heroism needs no such incentive,—should he fall, unconscious of my yet surviving, to that fatal though well designed artifice I should forever impute his loss, and die for having feigned to do so.

A wild fancy has taken strange possession of my mind—Lady Southampton says it is madness; perhaps it really is so, but I can think of nothing else: she, however, is too timid to judge—she will pass her whole life here I really believe.

Were I but for a moment to behold that expressive countenance,—were I by a kind of resurrection again to appear before him!—

Something strangely impels me—a chosen troop are now setting out.— I shall be safe under their protection.— Ah, if this ungovernable impulse should be but a presentiment of his danger—never, never should I forgive myself were I to leave him, wounded and dying, to the care of persons comparatively indifferent.

"Argue no longer, my dear importunate friend, I will go, but depend on my hastening back,"—Lady Southampton would have made a wretched love for Essex; she is the most apprehensive of women; but she was not born to mate with that aspiring hero.

PART V

A Silence so tedious will make you number me among the dead; recover yourself, my beloved friend—born to a perpetual contest with ill fortune, I sink not even yet under the oppression.— I have been collecting all my thoughts to pursue my strange recital, more strange indeed every day.

In our way toward Ulster, we were intercepted by a body of the rebellious Irish, and a desperate skirmish ensued—how shall I own it, and call myself the love of Essex? yet so it was—I, who had been so valiant in imagination, and remote from the field of action—I, who had in fancy lifted a sword with the strength of Goliah,[1] and interposed a shield before Essex, heavier perhaps than myself, shrunk into annihilation at the bare sight of the conflict; and the faintings which laid me among the slain, perhaps alone saved me from being added to their number. I revived in the hands of some ferocious women, who in stripping the dead, had discovered at one moment that I yet lived, and was of their own sex. Induced either by a sentiment of humanity, or the hope of a reward, they listened to my eager supplications for life, and conveyed me to a neighbouring cabin; whither they summoned a priest, who opened a vein in my arm. On feebly reviving once more, I cast my eyes round in speechless astonishment, scarce knowing whether I should think my escape a blessing. I was environed by a set of beings who in complexion alone bore any resemblance to myself, their language, manners, and lives, seeming no more analogous, than those of the inhabitants of the Torrid Zone. I laboured in vain to comprehend them, or to make myself understood, and was in dispair giving up the attempt, when the priest already mentioned came to my relief. Through his means I informed them that the Lord Deputy would redeem me at any ransom, provided they secured me from danger and insult. I should, I believe, have ensured my own safety, had not the victorious party learnt, by some straggler, that an English woman of distinguished rank had been discovered among the slain. They eagerly turned back to demand me, and the hope of reward alike influenced my preservers to keep me in their hands, a dispute no less fierce, though not so bloody, as that I had before witnessed, followed; it was too violent to be compromised, and at length, as the only way to prevent murder, both parties agreed that I should be put into the hands of their general, Tyrone; or, as some called him, O'Neal.[2] Intreaties or resistance would have been equally vain, and I was obliged to rejoice they thought me of consequence enough to act so honorably by me.

During this interval, one of the servants deputed by Lady Southampton immediately to attend on me, having lingered a few minutes behind the English troop, followed to rejoin them at the moment of the onset: the sound of the firing reached him ere he fell in with the scouts, and clapping spurs to his horse, he flew back to the village we all had lately quitted, there to wait in safety the event of the contest: at this place he was informed a band of rebels had issued out from an ambuscade formed in the neighbouring mountain; and while he was wavering what step to take, the news of my sex and capture suddenly reached him; struck with the idea of some important mystery, as well from my disguise as the cautions of his Lady, he hastened back to her with the strange intelligence. The generous but timid Lady Southampton, impressed solely with the idea of my danger, wrote instantaneously to Essex, briefly reciting all he did not know of my story, and strongly conjuring him to exert his utmost influence to preserve me from insult.

But who shall paint the feelings of Essex, when this surprizing intelligence first reached him! intelligence which, in one moment, opened all those sources of tenderness in his soul grief and despair had well nigh congealed. To think I still lived would have been consummate happiness, had I not been thus unaccountably snatched away, even at the very moment of my miraculous renovation: so singular a complication of events almost deprived him of his senses, and wrought impulse up to agony. Perhaps the last untoward incident of my life was necessary to save his brain from partaking the distractions of his mind—sick at the heart of an incurable sorrow—fatigued with the cares of government, and the slavery of command, the news of my existence and capture made him find in distinctions hitherto so oppressive, the sole prospect of recovering a treasure, which alone could give value to his future life.

From the knowledge acquired in his military command, Essex was enabled to decide on the character of Tyrone—he justly believed it unprincipled and ungovernable; how must he tremble then to recollect my fate was in his hands![3] In a conjuncture so dangerous, he resigned himself entirely up to the guidance of an impassioned heart, and dispatched an officer of rank, charging the arch-rebel, by the blood of thousands yet unspilt, not to exasperate the English, and himself in particular, by maltreating the lady fortune had thrown into his power; for whose ransom any sum was tendered her captors should demand.

This rash and impetuous address had consequences only less dangerous than those it guarded against. Tyrone unfortunately discovered at once that he had the happiness of the Lord Deputy in his keeping, and though he flattered him from time to time with promises of noble treatment, he secretly determined, no doubt, that if he ever parted with me, it should be upon his own terms.

It was not till several of these messages had passed, that Tyrone's curiosity led him to pay me a visit: the attention excited by my masculine habit had led me immediately to request one more suited to my sex; and the delicate situation I stood in, obliging me to conduct myself with the utmost caution, I had thought it peculiarly fortunate to escape the notice of the General.

The continual repetition of his tedious visits, when once he had seen me; the lavish supply of such accommodations as that ravaged country afforded—an obstinate silence on the state of my affairs, and the most wearisome discussions of his own, all too soon convinced me, that neither his pride, his ambition, or his ferocity, had been able to guard the heart of Tyrone from that powerful passion which invigorated the being of his distinguished rival—I trembled at the recollection that I was wholly in his power—already misjudged as the voluntary mistress of Essex, unwilling to announce myself, and unable, had I done so, to prove my right to distinction, mine was indeed a fearful situation. I was not allowed to hold any correspondence with the English, and only knew by the watch kept over me, that a human being was anxious for my release.

Whatever consequences might ensue from my appearing pleased with the distinctions lavished on me by Tyrone, I felt every day more sensibly that I had no other means of avoiding the licentious insolence of his officers; who fancied their services so important to the cause they had espoused, as to secure their conduct from too strict a scrutiny.

Tyrone meantime sought occasions to break off, renew, and prolong, the secret intercourse in which he had now engaged with Essex: but a lingering treaty agreed not with the fiery impatience of that unfortunate hero. His divided soul no longer attended to the duties of his command—the business of the war was at an end—Essex was no longer a cool and prudent General, watchful to seize every advantage, and harrass the enemy—alas, he was now only a wild and extravagant lover, ready to sacrifice every consideration to the recovery of one adored individual.— Delivered up to passion, to terror, to agony, to every torturing excess of overstrained sensibility, at this fatal period the generous Essex was gradually sacrificing the whole renown of a life hitherto so glorious. The news of Tyrone's love crowned his misfortunes; and that execrable traitor, determined to bring, if possible, the Lord Deputy to his terms, by various emissaries had him informed of plots he never laid against me, and repulses he never sustained; always speciously disowning such designs, in terms calculated only to redouble the suspicions of his rival.

By artifices like these the warlike talents and dignified mind of Essex were kept in absolute subjection; he no longer dared to exert the valour which burned proudly at his heart, but stifling every emotion love did not excite, he eagerly engaged in a secret and dangerous treaty.— The rash proposal of Essex to confer with Tyrone from the opposite banks of a rivulet, I imputed to the passionate desire a lover ever has to judge of the person and talents of the man who dares to rival him—this interview could not be kept a secret—alas, perhaps it decided the fortune of the Lord Deputy.— Misjudged from that moment by a busy world which sees only the surface of things, to timidity, to avarice, to indolence, to ambition, by turns, has been ascribed an incident, of which love had all the merit or the shame.—[4] Ah! had the erroneous multitude considered but a moment, surely they had discerned a mystery in his conduct.— What could ambition, glory, pride, require, he did not possess already? If to hold the most absolute sway over the most absolute of Sovereigns could gratify those wishes, they were gratified.— Rather, ye busy Many, learn to pity than condemn the generous frenzy of a bleeding heart which boldly sacrificed every thing to an over-ruling, an irresistible passion—a passion mine must break to answer—and it *will* break.— Oh! my shook brain, how wild it wanders!—

*   *   *   *   *   *

Gay visions of a higher, happier sphere, where are ye? ah! deign to gild awhile this gloomy world!—how inexpressibly sweet are at intervals the trances of my mind!—care, sorrow, suffering, mortality itself is forgotten; absorbed in a bright obscure, every high-wrought feeling hovers on the verge of a long eternity—fye on this earthy covering, how it drags down my soul, my soaring soul.[5]

*   *   *   *   *   *

I wake from these day dreams, and return to my subject—in fruitless and tedious negotiations were thus consuming those days we would in vain recall, those important days fraught with the very fate of the noblest of mankind.

The long delays, the eternal disappointments, exhausted my patience; agitated by a thousand apprehensions which no less concerned my lover than myself, misery once more struck her iron fangs through my quivering heart. Compelled to struggle with a soul justly conscious of virtue; to support an apparent tranquillity; to adopt an artificial character; to suffer Tyrone to delude himself into a persuasion the tye between me and Essex was dishonorable, lest an uncertain one should want power to restrain him, how many implicated indignities did I patiently endure!— Persecuted with his base solicitations; overwhelmed with bribes as splendid as they were contemptible, I could ward off his expectations only by a feint my nature disdained. In answer to his unbounded offers, and tender protestations, I one day bade him remember that in those instances he could not surpass the generous lover he sought to rival; for that it was in the power of Essex to give me every thing but his *title*.— Tyrone paused indignantly for a moment, and my heart exulting in its artifice, fondly hoped the spectres of his whole line of royal ancestors would sweep before him, precluding every idea of a union so dishonorable. His whole estimation, and the success of the war depended, I well knew, on his retaining the affections of the people, and how could he hope for those if he disgraced the blood of the O'Neals? He scarce credited the boldness of idea which appeared in this hint of mine, and struck with a persuasion I must be of some superior rank to dare thus to elevate my eyes to him, he once more attempted to dive into a mystery so carefully and obstinately concealed. I was however on my guard, and sunk again into my original obscurity. Still eager to possess a woman he could not esteem, he at last assured me (after having observed that an engagement to a lady of his own family alone held his party together) that he would bind himself in secret by every tye I should dictate. I unwarily replied, that the conduct and love of Essex had been so unquestionably noble, that nothing but a superior and public marriage could vindicate me even to myself, in breaking with him.— Tyrone's look and answer made me sensible at once of the danger of this speech, and that in leaving him without hope, I had left myself without safety. I felt from this moment like a wretch entirely devoted; and under the name of indisposition (of which indeed I had sufficient reason to complain) I procured from a surgeon who bled me, a quantity of liquid laudanum,[6] some portion of which I pretended to take every night, but in reality reserved the whole of it for that fatal one which should confirm my fears.

Such were the sufferings of Essex and myself, while the two camps were in sight of each other, and nothing but the most guarded vigilance could prevent the incensed English from coming to action.— I was one evening alone in the tent allotted to me (for Tyrone would never trust me in any neighbouring fort or town), which, from the ascent it was pitched on, commanded the whole valley, and looking with tearful eyes towards the increasing fires in the English camp, when Tyrone approached me unawares—his complexion was flushed with wine, and his eyes and air shewed a determination at which my nature shuddered—no longer regarding decorum or respect, his manners made me in a moment sensible I had deferred taking my laudanum too long.— An idea, at which I have never ceased to wonder, suggested itself to my mind; and while fluctuating between the possible and impossible, I a little soothed the boisterous wretch at whose profligate vows I trembled— intoxication deprived him of the guard he had so long kept over his lips— imagining himself already possessed of the beloved of Essex, he could not forbear vaunting of the address which secured her to him.— I learnt with equal horror and amazement, that the long delay my capture and the subsequent treaties had occasioned in the war, were all concerted strokes of diabolical policy to ruin the fair fame of the Lord Deputy.— That during these fatal treaties, Tyrone himself had sent the most indubitable proofs to Elizabeth of the misconduct of her General, and had every reason to suppose he would immediately be recalled, and ignominiously punished: nor could she ever select another equally dear to the army, on which every thing in war depended.—[7] I turned with ineffable disdain towards the monster.— Oh, that an eye-beam could have killed him!— Engrossed, however, by his various views, inflated with self-love and applause, and confused with wine, he saw not a glance which would instantaneously have unfolded my whole heart, to the execrable, the ungenerous traitor: unworthy the race he sprung from, and the sword he drew.— He continued to expatiate on his hopes of wholly expelling the English, and ascending the throne of Ireland; but what after this unwary and black discovery could his views be to me? A thousand dangers were pressing upon my soul, and a thousand projects floating in my brain: I had hardly temper or recollection to methodize any—while he continued to charm himself with the disclosure of all his vanity and ambition, hatred and horror nerved my heart with courage to execute a strange design, the desperation of such a moment alone could have suggested. Convinced, by the tenor of his discourse and conduct, that I could escape his licentious purposes only by feigning an intention of yielding to them, I smoothed my agonized features into a smile which almost stiffened to a convulsion, and complained of thirst—a glass of water stood by, of which I drank—inclination no less than gallantry, made him insist on pledging me; but refusing to give him the water without wine, I mixed it with an officiousness perhaps but too obvious, adding the whole quantity of laudanum provided for myself. The haste and tremor attending so dangerous a transaction, might well have excited distrust in him at any time, much more at such a crisis; but not in a condition to observe very strictly, and delighted with a condescension on my part alike new and unexpected, in a transport of gallantry he dropt on his knees, and uniting my name with his own, cemented both with that of happiness: the latter seemed to tremble back into my heart as he eagerly swallowed the beverage. Sleep had before hovered over his eyelids; it was now forerun by stupefaction. The hour of rest arrived; but the women who usually slept in the outer tent came not near it—I could not doubt but that their absence was owing to the previous orders given by the General, and falling on my knees, entreated him who armed the Assyrian with courage voluntarily to dare the situation into which I was brought unconsenting, to bear me boldly and safely through it. A fortitude equal to the danger, seemed to spring from the address and the occasion.— The regimental cloak Tyrone had thrown off on entering served to cover my masculine habit, which I resumed with expedition: it was a cloak so remarkable, and familiar to every eye in the camp, as almost to ensure my safety. I overweighed my throbbing temples with his warlike plume, and finally, drawing from his finger a signet to produce if necessary, I boldly grasped his dagger to decide my fate should I be discovered, and issued forth a second Judith.[8]

I had warily marked the progress of the night; the last watch had now gone by, and the time was past when it was probable any officer should be stirring of note enough to address the General. I had heard Tyrone say it was his common practice to walk the camp at night, and in that confidence ventured to pass for him. Scarce had I gone a hundred paces when the homage of the centinels assured me the counterfeit was undiscovered.

With an agitated heart I passed from one to another, guided only by the distant lights (for Tyrone always pitched his camp on a hill) till near the advanced guard; I then retired behind a large tent, and disrobing myself of their General's accoutrements, put on a common hat I had carried for that purpose—what were my terrors when having reached the confines of the camp, now doubly watched, I presented the signet as a proof I was sent on earnest business.— The guard hesitated, but after tediously debating, while I went through tortures, they judged it prudent to admit a token which alone could have enabled me to reach them, and I was suffered to pass.

I shot like an arrow from a bow when once these dreaded limits were overleaped, scarce daring to address my very soul to heaven, lest one lost moment should undo me.

Whether my eyes had deceived me in the imagined nearness of the English camp, or my trembling and unguided feet had wandered wide of it, I knew not; but sorely were they blistered ere I approached its limits—piercing through thickets which tore alike my garments and my flesh, with spirits fainting even to death, I suddenly heard a scout give the watch-word in English. Overjoyed to think myself safe, I unhappily wanted presence of mind to pronounce a single syllable, and the officious soldier mistaking me for a spy, levelled his piece, and instantly pierced my side—My spirits were no longer equal to contending with danger or with death, and the fear of discovery being the prevailing sentiment of my sex, I feebly conjured the man, if he hoped for pardon, to bear me to the tent of the Lord Deputy. The delicacy of my complexion and clothes had already surprized the inadvertent soldier—he quickly called together some of his companions, who assisted in laying me on a hurdle, and bearing me toward the tent of Essex. The morning was now broke—I saw the early beams of the sun emblazon the golden ornaments of the General's tent—some officers came out of it as I approached.— My heart, from which life seemed every moment ready to issue, made a courageous effort to collect into itself the scattered principles of a being I appeared on the very point of resigning. I fancied ere he yet spoke, I heard the voice so dear to me—I fancied! ah, I indeed *saw* him rush forward on the first hint; but, root-bound as it were, he stopped before he came to me, and sent his very soul forth in a groan.— "Yes, Essex," cried I, extending my feeble hand, "the wretch heaven did not allow to live in thy arms, receives its next indulgence in being permitted to die there."— But how shall I describe the tearful transports, the touching agonies of his recovered intellects! I sunk under the keen extasy of the moment, and long faintings succeeded, occasioned by my loss of blood, that once more brought me to the very verge of the grave.

The amiable Lady Southampton came at the instance of her cousin, and gave, by her presence, a decorum to my situation it had long wanted. Every effort of art was exerted to soothe my broken spirits, and strengthen my exhausted frame. He, who alone could give efficacy to medicine, hovered ever near, and when speech was interdicted, by affectionate looks sustained me.— Ah, how pleasant were even these sufferings! how delightful was it to collect back into my heart those gentle impulses war and terror had driven from their home!— To affiance my soul in silence to its only Lord, and to fancy that whatever fate heaven should hereafter ordain him, mine could no longer be divided from it!

As soon as my amended health allowed, I entered into a detail of all that had passed since Lord Essex left me at St. Vincent's Abbey. He in return informed me, that the lethargy into which Tyrone was plunged by the laudanum I had so hastily administered, was very near being fatal to him, as the utmost effort of care and medicine could only preserve him the faculty of breathing; since to disturb his deep and unwholesome slumbers always threw him into a dangerous delirium. The courageous effort by which I had recovered my liberty, he added, still formed the whole conversation of both camps. I blessed the awful power who saved me the guilt of murdering even a villain, and did not immediately remark that Essex gave me no farther information.

I soon learnt from Lady Southampton the painful truths my Lord sought to hide from me—that Elizabeth had incessantly urged him to prosecute a war which his fears for me had hitherto suspended; but finding at length that both intreaties and commands were lost upon him, she grew cold and disgusted.[9] His friends in England had given him but too much reason to believe that his enemies were gradually acquiring the ascendancy in her heart, he as gradually lost; since all her favors were now lavished on Sir Walter Raleigh, the house of Cecil, and the Earl of Nottingham, a party who had long meditated the downfall of Essex and Southampton, of which they now spoke as a certainty;[10] and that even the common people beheld with discontent the slow progress of the war in Ireland, nor could Essex any longer depend upon popularity.

The unguarded friend who made me this recital, engrossed by her own share in it, forgot how it interested me. I called to mind the information sent by Tyrone to Elizabeth, which but too well accounted for the Queen's anger and disgust, and conceived at once all its probable consequences. Essex, unlike all other favorites, could never be brought to know any claim to superiority but merit—incapable of those little arts by which mean souls attach the insidious train of sycophants a Court always abounds with; he had ever scorned a partial monopoly, and politic distribution, of posts and places.— The mercenary wretches, who had bowed to him in vain, paid their court to his enemies with more success, and instructed by them in every weakness of the favorite, were ever ready to strengthen any prejudice the Queen might conceive against him. A thousand fears incident to age and decaying power were thus cherished in her, which, magnified by passions time itself could never allay, might too probably stamp the base intelligence of Tyrone with the fatal authority of unbiassed truth, and give to the inactivity of Essex the appearance of treason.— Such a train of circumstances could hardly fail to stagger a mind in full possession of the noblest and most impartial judgment; what then might we not fear from a Sovereign always influenced by prejudices each passing day strengthened, by insensibly impairing her reason? Fortunately, through an extravagance of dotage which almost punished the errors of her youth, those prejudices had hitherto united in his favor:—yet while I perceived but a single chance against him, my soul shrunk from the idea of entrusting his life with her.

To give Lord Essex the opportunity of vindicating himself to Elizabeth, I resolved to account for her conduct; and divulged to him the inadvertent acknowledgment made by Tyrone, during our last memorable interview, of his own perfidy and dissimulation. A generous scarlet burnt on the cheek of Essex while he execrated the traitor; but struck immediately with a full conviction of the consequences that might result from this base intelligence, he formed the extraordinary resolution of returning to England to justify his honor.

This determination no less shocked than surprized me; far from imagining my information would lead to so wild a project, I rather supposed it would suggest to him the impossibility of ever revisiting England, unless the reduction of Ulster was fully accomplished.— In truth, I dared not confess my fears that even then to remain with the army alone could ensure his safety.— Every reason I could urge, or Southampton enforce, were in his judgment feebler than his own—his honor was piqued, and nothing could hinder him from vindicating it.— Persuaded a step as bold as this alone would convince Elizabeth of his innocence, and accustomed to regain, whenever he appeared, that influence over her, his enemies had often encroached on in his absence, he persuaded himself he need only be seen to triumph, and concluded a truce, as the preliminary to his departure.[11]

The pride of sex, sensibility, and honor, contended with the leading passion of my nature, and taught me to disdain over-ruling him I could not convince:—nevertheless, I almost sunk under the conflict.— The frightful situation in which I had been placed since my arrival in Ireland, made me obstinately refuse to continue there, whenever Essex should leave it; and the curiosity I had excited alike by my bold escape, and wound, made it hazardous to commit me to the charge of any officer left behind. Surrounded with friends, relations, and dependents, Essex (such is the painful uncertainty ever attending on elevated rank) knew not one to whom he could safely intrust so delicate a care. The generous Southampton, determined to share the fate of his friend by accompanying him, proposed to unite that of his Lady with mine, by shipping us off ere they embarked, with servants they should mutually select; apparently bound for France, but in fact for the coast of Cumberland. In the most romantic and solitary part of that remote county the Wriothesleys[12] had long owned a castle, where malice itself would hardly seek, and certainly never find us; there he assured Essex we might repose in peace, till they should return again to Ireland. I felt all the merit of this project, by which the amiable Southampton robbed himself of the dear society of his wife, merely to do honor to the beloved of his friend; and adopted it with the utmost eagerness, from the hope that if the busy transmitters of Lord Essex's actions had ever mentioned me, this total separation would extinguish all jealousy in the mind of Elizabeth; who I knew would much sooner overlook the loss of an army than his heart.

Although Essex knew not how to place me happily in Ireland, it was with pain he consented to my quitting it; but finding me obstinately partial to Lord Southampton's design, he proposed my resuming my masculine disguise, and selected a vessel whose captain was devoted to him, having ordered a lighter one to be prepared for himself.

So sad a presentiment shivered my soul on the morn appointed for our embarkation, that it was the utmost effort of my principles to suffer Essex to act in conformity to his. I had previously insisted that he should sail at the same moment with myself, to end my fears of that formidable savage Tyrone; and when he entered my chamber to conduct me to the ship, my heart quivered on lips which had no longer the power to utter a syllable.— He besought, he conjured me, to support my sinking spirits; "the highest hopes," he added, with an air of sincerity, "elevated his own; that it had always been his pride, his pleasure, to deserve the distinctions lavished on him by the Queen; and whatever views he had formed when heaven should call her hence, he could not resolve even by ingratitude, much less treachery, to shorten her days who had crowned his with glory. Doubt not," concluded he, "my love, but I shall recover all my influence, and remember when next we meet it is to part no more."

Ill-omened seemed that sentence to me—I fancied too his voice sounded hollow—I fancied!—alas, every dire chimera sensibility presents to an impassioned heart, took full possession of mine; yet, as to exert the least influence at so trying a moment was to render myself accountable for his future fate, I opposed every ennobling sentiment to an ungovernable passion, and heroically resigned him up to his duty.

We quitted the port at the same instant: he steering for that nearest the Irish coast, I for the North of England.— Both by consent remained on the deck with souls fixed on each other, till the beloved individual vanished, and the vessel seemed an object only less dear; that at length diminished to a cloud, the cloud shrunk to a speck, and the speck became invisible.— I threw myself on my bed, and, giving way to the tears I had hitherto stifled, I besought the Almighty to guard him he had so eminently distinguished.

Compassion had induced Essex to consent to our taking on board an old officer who had been desperately wounded. The intense sickness produced by the element, caused his wounds to open, which obliged us to put back and land him, or sacrifice his life to our convenience; and this unforeseen delay exposed us to a calamity as lasting as it was grievous.

Launched a second time on those restless surges to which alone I could compare my own perturbed soul, the next day brought the comparison still nearer.— A dreadful tempest arose, nor were we within reach of any port. The enraged and howling winds drove the vessel at pleasure a thousand times side-long into the deep, and the impetuous and foaming waves threw it up again with equal violence.— We remained stupified with terror; shut down with our women in the cabin, the rapid motions and cries of the seamen, the tre-mendous cracks and groans of the vessel, united with the warring elements to make that fate indifferent every moment brought nearer. To prepare my mind for the impending event, I, however recollected, with due gratitude to heaven, that the light vessel in which Essex sailed, had doubtless made a near port, ere the storm began, and landed him in safety.

I pondered once more on that wonderful character I had so often con-sidered. I saw, however strong the predominant foible of Lord Essex, it still gave way to rectitude; and, fearful the passion which led him towards me might one day affect his safety, I bent to the awful God who thus in thunder called away its weak and helpless object:—not without admiring the singular-ity of that destiny, which by interring me in the ocean, secured the forged death and funeral I had published for myself, from ever being discovered.

Strengthened, if not consoled, by these ideas, I sought to cheer my no less suffering friend; who, rejecting alike food and comfort, resigned herself wholly up to sickness, faintings, and sorrow.— Ah, who shall say we suffer in vain! the feelings of the soul, like the organs of sight, gain strength by use, till we dare to analyze that fate we once could not have ventured to consider; while the refined and exquisite sense of mental anguish which renders us su-perior to common evils, often gives an apparent sublimity to efforts which are little in our own estimation.— Lady Southampton, yet distinguished by na-ture, fortune, love, clung to those rich possessions, and shrunk from the awful immortality which threatened every moment to take place of them.— She listened to me with wonder, and this instance of fortitude impressed her mind with a reverence for my character, time could never obliterate.

The sudden abatement of the storm contributed little to our safety; as the ship, ill calculated for such a conflict, had bulged[13] upon a rock, and now filled so fast with water, that the utmost diligence of the crew could hardly save us from sinking.— The sight of land, ere the evening closed, had scarce power to cheer, for a moment, wretches who no more hoped to behold the dawning of the morn.— To the uproar and turbulence of the storm a silent horror and desolation had now succeeded scarce less shocking. Midnight was hardly turned ere a dismal universal cry informed us the vessel was sinking—

Lady Southampton threw her arms helplessly round me, and the unprincipled part of the crew, bursting into our cabin, increased the horrors of the moment by opening our coffers, and gathering together their most valuable contents: an officer followed, who taking our hands in silence, led us toward the deck:— two boats were now preparing—the last melancholy chance we had of surviving.— The captain, who happily owed every thing to Essex, informed us, that as the larger boat had the better chance, he had fixed on placing us in that, ere the scattered crew could collect, and by pressing too numerously upon us, rob us of a last hope.— We were conveyed into the boat while he was yet speaking, and the sailors so impetuously followed, regardless of the captain's remonstrances and commands, that our danger seemed hardly diminished by the removal.— A hope nevertheless arose which encouraged each individual to an exertion from whence the general safety was ascertained. Entirely enveloped in the only watch-coat which had been taken from the wreck, Lady Southampton and myself (who were the only women saved) knew but by the voices of our companions whether life or death was to be expected—the sea ran high, and the grey dawn presented to our eager eyes a coast, which we were informed was that of Scotland, at no great distance; an old castle appeared, on a sharp projection of the land, whose solid battlements seemed proof against every attack of art and nature; but the shoals, rocks, and surf that intervened, threatened to make us ever behold it at a hopeless distance, unless we could interest the compassion of its owners.

Every signal of distress was made for hours apparently in vain, till the turn of the tide; when two fishing boats appeared, slowly working their way towards us. A discordant shout of joy on the part of our companions split the ears of my sick friend and self, who inly worshipped the power that preserved us.— The benevolent strangers approached, and their garb no less than unknown language proclaimed them natives of the Scotch coast. To the men around us they offered biscuits and whisky in abundance, and bestowed on me and Lady Southampton a draught of cold water, which seemed as much more refreshing as it was innocent.

Revived by this unexpected revolution in our fate, we by joint consent shook off the heavy watch-coat which had a little saved us from the incessant spray of the enraged sea, and when the boat was at length drawn towards the flight of rude steps leading to the castle, we both quitted it with no less celerity than thankfulness.— Our progress was for a moment impeded by surprize— at the gate of the castle stood two beings who seemed of some superior order; so singular were their dress, beauty, and benevolence.— A youth and his sister waved us towards them with graceful courtesy—the latter wore a light vest and coat of Scots plaid, with a belt of green sattin clasped with gold; the rude wind had carried off the covering of her hair and caused her long auburn locks to stream on the bosom of the morning, exposing to view her slight ancles half booted, and tinging her cheeks with that pure cold colour, youth, health, innocence, and heaven, alone can give.— The youth, who in features strongly resembled his sister, was habited as a hunter, with a spear in his hand, and a dagger hanging in his belt.— Both with smiles of hospitality ran forward to receive us; and while the young lady took the arm of my friend, the youth with an impassioned pleasure shook my hand, casting a look of mingled wonder and disdain at the soiled, though rich, habiliments I had on; which indeed originally rather agreed with my own sex than that I intruded upon.[14] The antique hall into which they conducted us, was hung with tattered banners, mouldy coats of arms, and every proud remnant of war and ancientry. Refreshments suitable to our past distress were busily set before us, nor, with that intuitive politeness superior minds always possess, did either venture to express a curiosity till they had frankly satisfied ours.— From them we learnt that the spot fortune had thrown us on, was an island on the coast of Scotland, and the place which sheltered us, Dornock Castle, held by the Laird of that name;[15] that they were brother and sister to that Laird, who was now absent on a family concern of no small moment; in short, that their elder sister, Mabel, famed through the country for her beauty, having unhappily shewn it at Court, the King would not suffer her to return; and their brother, fearful she should yield to his licentious wishes, had hastened thither to claim her.[16] The young people who made this artless recital, were formed to grace it—when the fair Phoebe spoke of the charms of her sister, her own were heightened by a softer, fuller bloom; and when she mentioned their dangerous effect, the proud blush of a generous shame gave manliness to the boyish features of her brother Hugh.— Accustomed as my friend and self had long been to every worldly charm and advantage, we saw in this remote spot, and these untutored children of nature, a simple and noble grace art only refines away.

When it came to my turn to narrate, I used every artifice to guard against the possibility of danger.— Adopting the name Lady Southampton had lately quitted, I called myself Vernon; a youth employed till lately as a page in the train of the Earl of Essex, and now his secretary—the lady with me, I said, allied to the Earl of Southampton, was lately wedded to me, and both were following these noblemen when overtaken by the tempest which had thrown us upon their shore, and rendered us debtors to their humanity. Finding we came from the seat of war, and were conversant with the Court of England, they both asked a thousand various questions suitable to their sex, age, and simplicity, respecting the one and the other; and our descriptions, to their unformed conceptions, comprized every charm of magnificence, glory, and gaiety.

The happy device of a pretended marriage enabling me to share the chamber of Lady Southampton, we chose the hour of retirement to consider our present situation, and the mode most likely to restore us once more to the country and connexions from which the storm had separated us.— My friend justly remarked, that the sailors wrecked with us, and its natives, were all the people likely to visit this remote and solitary isle, and that if we failed to take advantage of the departure of the first, we should throw ourselves wholly upon the generosity of the Laird of Dornock, of whose character we could not venture to decide from those of the amiable young people, who had so warmly embraced our cause.— After the application of Essex to my brother in my favour had been rejected, I had every thing to fear if any circumstance should betray me into his power, and the strictest secresy on our names and condition alone could give us a hope of liberty;—how under such restrictions we could clearly explain our present situation to the two noblemen whom alone it concerned, neither of us could discover; nevertheless, necessity obliged us to come to some resolution; and persuaded the writing of each would be known to him to whom the letter was addressed, weary as we both were, a part of the night was spent in preparing two epistles for the sailors to convey.— The morning came and with it the mortifying information that we were a few hours too late; the men saved with us having hired a fishing smack in which they sailed away at the turn of the tide: nor did the owners know their destination till the vessel returned. I was not without an idea that our youthful protectors had voluntarily concealed so material an event in the hope of detaining us; but certainly had that really been the case, it was not half so inexcusable as our own imprudence and neglect.— We hired a boat to pursue them with the letters, but after several days spent in painful expectation, the packets were returned to us with the mortifying information that all enquiry had proved fruitless. We had now no resource but in the generosity of the Laird of Dornock, and endeavoured to fortify ourselves with patience to wait his return.

The youthful brother and sister expressed a generous concern for our situation; but wholly without power, they could do no more.— Prisoners at large, as we were, effectually bounded by the roaring ocean, and depending solely on contingencies for freedom, the days to us crept heavily away—I sometimes remembered with a sigh that I was in Scotland—that kingdom where by inheritance I might claim a rank that would enable me to decide my own fate, had not a combination of events, forerunning even my birth, made every advantage of fortune and nature alike useless to me. I endeavoured to discover the real character of their King, but even from the report of his friends, to be able to term it good, I was obliged to think it weak;[17] and in that case knew he would inevitably be surrounded with artful politicians ready to profit by his foible; in short, I found that, however near he and I were allied in blood, we were born to be distinct beings in creation, and to meet would endanger the safety of the weaker. When I turned my anxious soul toward England, it brought me no relief.— As far from the reach of intelligence as if in the wilds of Arabia, I in vain sought to discover the reception Essex had met with at Court.— That name, which in the vanity of my heart I often thought the world resounded with, I found, with checked pride, was scarcely known in an adjacent country, till my lips so often repeated it; and even when most anxious to oblige me, those of others only echoed the sound so dear, so beloved! I had but too much reason to fear doubts of my safety would make him careless of his own, and often would have resigned every brilliant prospect fancy ever spread before me, to ascertain the life of the Earl. Too late I regretted the pride of heart which had made me resist the desire I felt to detain him in Ireland; and could not but acknowledge it was rather that than principle which reconciled me to his departure; yet, in a situation so delicate as ours, to wish was to command; and the sacrifice his own soul did not dictate, mine disdained to suggest.

My mind now daily passed through such a chaos of ideas and emotions, as would have prevented the time from appearing tedious, had not its prolongation been the origin of most of them.

Often sitting on the rude battlements of the castle, while the surges beat against their base, have I tuned the lute of Phoebe, and while she warbled a few wild airs of inconceivable melody in a language unknown to me, my full soul has wept over the mysterious fate of my sister.— Ah, how easy is it to be unknown!—to be entombed alive!— If I, even in a civilized adjacent kingdom, in effect the country of all my ancestors, can be thus helpless, what may the poor Matilda have been?— Turn, busy imagination, from the fatal supposition.

The oversight we had committed in suffering the sailors to leave us, became every day more and more regretted.— Lady Southampton soon found herself in a situation that required the tenderest indulgence, and would forbid removal, even if our asylum should be traced by anxious love. We spent our lives in fretting, and had we not possessed an unlimited intimacy, I know not how we should have endured the incessant chagrin.— Deprived even of the usual resources; a scanty library, a lute, some rustic airs, and a pedigree as old as the creation, bounded the possessions and knowledge of our young friends, and could not add any thing to our own.

The Laird of Dornock, however, returned at last.— Ah, how unlike his gentle kindred!—phlegmatic, self-willed, crested, and imperious, his aspect presented a correspondent harshness; and we instantly felt it vain to rest a hope on his friendship; he no doubt reproved his brother and sister for having lived on such familiar terms with strangers, avowedly subordinate; and though he often made us sensible our company was a burthen, he took not a single step to relieve himself from it. Phoebe had begun to improve herself in music ere his arrival; it was his pleasure she should continue to do so; but his presence threw a coldness and constraint over the whole party, which made what I had once thought a relief, an inconceivable toil. The ingenuous noble girl saw her brother's insolence with a grief which prevented her from profiting by the lessons so much desired—her gushing tears would often relax the strings of her lute, while low-warbling tales of hopeless love, and her sad eyes fix themselves on mine with an expression too strong to be misunderstood. I perceived while unconscious of the danger, because possessed with the remembrance of my own disguise, I had won the gentle heart I only sought to form.— Circumstanced as I was, this could not but be a dangerous acquisition; and by a fatality yet more alarming, her elder brother soon after became enamoured of Lady Southampton; nor did he conceal that inclination—he had from his arrival regarded me with an eye that indicated doubt on the subject of our marriage; but the increasing size of my friend, and our habit of living together, appeared to controvert a suspicion which nevertheless remained in his mind.

Anxious to profit by the only hour in the day which could favor his views, he was obliged to give the advantage he sought; and permit me to teach his sister with no other guard than his younger brother, Hugh, while he passed the interval with Lady Southampton.— All equally rejoiced at an incident all had equally desired; as to myself, determined from the moment I had been convinced of the passion of the fair Phoebe, to seize the first opportunity of intrusting her with my disguise, ere shame for the mistake should disgust her with the object, I was not sorry to confide it to her brother: as, if it did not more attach him to my interest, it would at least obviate every fear he might entertain on his sister's account, whom he could then safely leave at any time. This just candor produced more consequences than one. The sweet Phoebe started, blushed, and first lifting her swimming eyes toward heaven, then covered them with her hands—when I ceased to speak she timorously raised them to my face.— "Ah! why had you not been thus sincere at first?" cried the generous girl, "the power was then in our hands—*now*"—she shook her head, and in that emphatic gesture strongly finished her imperfect speech. Alarmed and anxious, I conjured her to confide to me those reasons which made our situation in her opinion so hopeless. She could not resist my entreaties; and at length acknowledged, "that from the moment her elder brother returned, Hugh no less than herself had observed a haughtiness and severity in his air and language more forbidding than usual; at last they had discovered that their sister, Mabel, far from listening to virtue and the Laird of Dornock, had yielded to the King; and to protect herself from her family, had been compelled to publish her shame, by claiming her lover's protection. To reconcile the Laird of Dornock to so cutting a disgrace, a title had been offered him, with any post about the Court he should fix on: and that at length the fair Mabel had consoled herself for the forfeiture of every rational distinction, by the temporary honor of reigning in the heart of her King, and being called a Countess." I enquired with surprize, how an event should affect us in which we apparently had no concern? Hugh answered, "that his brother, far from accepting the splendid coverings offered for infamy, had retired from Court in great indignation; that at first they had both been compelled to scorn and return every letter and present sent by their sister: yet of late some view, inexplicable to them, had made a singular alteration in the Laird of Dornock's sentiments.— Several couriers had been dispatched by him to the favorite Countess, but neither their commissions, nor the answers, ever transpired; yet many circumstances had given them reason to conclude that our pacquets had never been forwarded, as we were taught to believe."— I changed colour at the idea of this deliberate treachery, thanking heaven I alone had been informed of it; as Lady Southampton, often unable to govern her feelings, by some imprudent speech would infallibly have betrayed her knowledge of it. The young Hugh, observing my uneasiness, assured me, "though hopeless of finding a faithful messenger, he held himself answerable for the release of those whom he had contributed to enthrall, and that I might depend upon his own services if I would deign to confide in him, nor should we be suspected as the causes of his disappearance, since the Laird of Dornock well knew his sister Mabel's particular fondness for him, and would naturally imagine he was determined to profit by the high favor she held at Court."— Is there a charm on earth so touching as generosity?— The noble youth paused with an air that indicated his ardent desire of having his offer accepted, lest it should be mistaken for a vaunt. I took a hand of each young friend, and returning acknowledgments suitable to the occasion, declined embroiling them with their sullen brother;

who could not want power to render our situation much more intolerable, if once he suspected us of alienating his family from their duty.— I persuaded them, as well as myself, that our own friends would with unwearied diligence search us out the moment they discovered that any part of the crew survived the wreck; of which the Captain would certainly inform them, unless he sunk with the ship.

Yet day after day proved this hope vain and fallacious.— A dreary winter passed away in this remote Castle, through every aperture of which the keen and howling wind poured unrestrained; and the wild ocean swelled with frequent storms, while our affrighted senses often mistook the roar of the tempest for the groans of the dying.

I had almost ceased to hope, when one day, while our host was hunting, I wandered to the battlements as usual, and descried from thence a small vessel approaching, better built, and more clean, than those I was accustomed to see; as it drew nearer the land, I perceived English dresses.— My heart took the alarm, I leant impatiently forward, straining the keen sense whose imperfection I complained of.— The boat drew near. I discerned the regimental of Essex; I gave a groan of exquisite delight, and reeling forward, should have plunged into the ocean, had not the young Hugh, who stood behind, held me fast.— The officer looked up, and I instantly perceived him to be Henry Tracey, the favorite aid-de-camp of Lord Essex, once before deputed in search of me.— Disappointment mingled with the various and interesting emotions of the moment.— I pointed to the stranger, sighed, and fainted away.

They bore me to lady Southampton, who thunderstruck at seeing me lifeless, and unable to guess the cause, seemed little better herself. Hugh, who clearly comprehended from my impassioned gesture, how interesting the arrival of the stranger was to me, hastened to bring him to our apartment, while yet his brother was absent; when instantly retiring, he left us full liberty— "Tracey?" cried both of us at once, "Essex?" "Southampton?" echoed each heart, "sum up all in a word."— "They live," returned he, "and need only behold you to be happy."— "Ah, gracious heaven!" cried I, lifting my eyes thither, while I presented my heart with my hand to the faithful messenger, "receive my transport; we now can breathe freely; give us the relief of knowing the events which followed the dangerous voyage of Essex and Southampton." "I should hardly dare to do so, had I not first assured you of their safety," resumed Tracey, "for sorrow I see has been preying already on your bloom; it would not perhaps have been more spared had you passed this trying interval in London."

Apprehensive every moment of an interruption from the Laird of

Dornock, we besought the worthy Tracey to dispense with all preface, and hasten his recital.

"With terror and anxiety," continued he, "I followed my Lord into the vessel selected to convey him home, nor were these emotions diminished when I perceived the Lord Deputy full of fits of doubt and reflection, which at times were obvious even to himself; often would he affect to drown them in gay society and wine, and, for the first time in his life, he assumed a false bravery.— At the hours of retirement, far from indulging that intimacy so long established between him and Lord Southampton, of which I had sometimes been a greateful and humble partaker, he sunk into an absence of mind, and total silence, no less alarming to his beloved friend than myself; in effect, that Nobleman saw that he had '*set his fortune on a cast, and he would stand the hazard of the die*,'[18] as I conjectured by his turning to me one day, and by an expressive motion of his head, leading mine towards the side of the vessel, where the General leant; his thoughtful countenance apparently fixed on those rolling waves which yet perhaps he saw not.— 'All is not well in the heart of thy Lord, Tracey,' said his noble friend, then pausing a moment, he added, in a lower tone, 'Ah Essex, *aut Caesar: aut nullus!*'[19] The Lord Deputy happily advanced, and saved me the necessity of corroborating sentiments it gave me pain to adopt.

"It was not with the customary greetings we beheld the pleasant shores of our native country—doubt and anxiety had thrown a gloom over those lively and spontaneous emotions, which often suspend even the sense of suffering. Lord Essex lost not a moment, but posted toward the Court, with such expedition, that he outwent all information, and was his own harbinger.— We arrived one morning ere yet the Queen had left her chamber; but alas, it was no longer the Court we had left—every face around appeared strange to us; and we saw too plainly that the invidious Cecils reigned there triumphant. Lord Grey,[20] a favorite of theirs, whom we had met on the road, had presumed to pass the Earl of Essex without notice—that Nobleman gave him only an eyebeam, and hastened on to decide his fate.— Form was annihilated by circumstances, and he rushed into the presence of Elizabeth the moment his arrival was announced—accustomed to behold him with complacency, to receive him with kindness, she yielded through surprize to the habits of so many years, and granted the private audience he requested.— She listened to a vague and weak vindication of his conduct in Ireland, and the dotage of her soul was transiently gratified with the idea, that he had preferred the recovery of her affection to that of his reputation in arms. After a long conference, the Earl rejoined his friends; pride and pleasure had flushed his cheek, and the idea of reassuming his accustomed influence, diffused through his mien that benignity and graciousness which are at once its nature and its charm.[21] Resentment and rage never constituted any part of his character but at the moment he suffered by those passions: such galling sensations were already forgotten.— Overwhelmed with the congratulations of his friends; encircled even by his overawed enemies, the heroic Essex rose above the triumph he could not but desire—every face was instantaneously changed, and those who knew not an hour before whether they should recollect him, now with servile adulation hallowed his very footsteps.— This fatal interval of short-lived power was, however, the last heaven allowed him.— The crafty Cecils and their faction seized the moment he injudiciously quitted the Queen, to persuade her that this indulged favorite had not only acted contrary to his commission, in venturing himself to return, but that he had brought home with him all his chosen adherents, as well as every aspiring spirit likely to strengthen his sway, and circumscribe hers.— They touched the soul of Elizabeth where it was most vulnerable, and having thus opposed to each other the two leading weaknesses of her nature, by throwing the weight of party into the one scale, it soon preponderated. She was unhappily in that declining age which renders every human being in some degree capricious and timid.— Already tinctured with fear, she soon yielded to the various informations officiously brought her by factious confederates.— She was told on all hands that Lord Essex was holding a Court even in her Palace, and insolent and daring as this conduct could not but appear, it was of less consequence than the unbounded influence he ever maintained over the people—an influence he would more than recover the moment he was seen in London. 'For *themselves* they heeded not— willing martyrs to their integrity and fealty; but for their Queen, they all trembled at the prospect.'— It was too hazardous to be risqued by Elizabeth; fear and resentment conquered the tender prepossession which still struggled faintly at her heart, and she determined to ascertain her own safety, as well as that of her kingdom, by imprisoning her favorite; nor is this resolution to be wondered at, since even her love conduced to it, when irritated by the imaginary sting of ingratitude.[22] She had set the Earl up in early youth as an idol for her own heart to worship; but he was not born to be satisfied with unmerited admiration—the more he acquired the more he sought to deserve; till having established his favor on innate nobleness, he rose above partial distinction, leaving her to lament at leisure the very elevation she had given. From this period she had been weak and irresolute in every instance where he was concerned; at intervals lavishing honors to which he had no title; at others, withholding advantages he had fairly won. The motive of this inconsistency he could not fail to discern, but persuaded an attachment which thus powerfully coped[23] with her judgment, was unconquerable, he forgot that she was sinking fast into the vale of years, when the noblest passions insensibly condense into self-love.[24]

"You who so well know the heart of my Lord, Madam," cried Tracey, turning to me, "will better imagine than I can describe, his deep sense of an indignity entirely public, and apparently premeditated. So unexpected a manoeuvre mastered his judgment, and giving way to the most passionate extremes, he drew his sword, and would have returned it by her messenger, beseeching her 'to reward his services by adding a more decisive blow to that she once before bestowed on him, since both seemed to him less shocking and ignominious than such open and unmerited contumely.'— In vain his friends sought to moderate his wrath; in vain his enemies drew near, eager to catch and treasure the rash expressions he should unwarily utter, and convert them to his ruin.— Touched on the tenderest point, his honor, the world combined would have wanted power to silence him—he gave full scope to his indignant and wounded feelings, and, with a severity of truth more galling and dangerous than the greatest exaggerations, declared aloud, 'that the Queen had outlived all her nobler faculties, and that her soul was grown as crooked as her body.' The cutting sarcasm was too faithfully conveyed to Elizabeth, who, regardless of his pride while her own was thus wounded, committed him to the charge of the Lord Keeper, whose house was in effect his prison.[25]

"Oh heavens! what wild vicissitudes, what transports of passion took possession of my Lord, at recollecting the imprudent readiness with which he had delivered himself helpless and unguarded into the hands of his enemies! struggling like a lion in the toils,[26] every vein would sometimes swell almost to madness, nor dared I leave him a moment alone.

"I had no other hope of assuaging his irritated passions, than by recalling to his mind the beloved image of the fair voyager, to whom the news of this event, and the fear of what might follow it, would be little less than death. I averted one storm however only to give free passage to another; the tear of tenderness proudly trembled on the burning cheek of anger, and a grief it split my heart to behold, took possession of his.— 'Spare me the killing remembrance,' he would cry—'disgraced—defamed—imprisoned; how shall I ever lift my eyes to that fair, that noble sufferer? I tell thee Tracey, rather would I have died than known this shameful moment.'— Impressed by the unwearied attachment I had ever shewn him, and overweighed by the sense of his own situation, my Lord at length condescended to lighten his own heart by unfolding to me its dearest views; well he knew they would never pass beyond mine—no, every vein of it should crack ere I would wrong so generous a confidence, which I acknowledge but to prove my fate wholly dependant on the Nobleman I serve: I would have it so, and heaven could afflict me only by separating them.

"The faithful Lord Southampton was his daily visitant: though not himself a prisoner, the consciousness that every action of his life was watched and reported, bound that nobleman to a most cautious observance. The Cecils had now no wish ungratified, for the imprudent bitterness of Lord Essex had supplied the only fuel to the Queen's resentment which could long keep it alive; nor did time, in cooling the passions of my Lord, incline him to submission—convinced in his own mind that he was the injured person, reflection only settled rage into disgust and contempt; nevertheless, his constitution suffered severely by this variety of passions; when one seized upon it which annihilated all the rest, and completely undermined his health—a grief more touching than glory or ambition could occasion suddenly overcame him.— The time was now elapsed which ought to have brought to him and Lord Southampton the welcome assurance that the partners of their souls were safe in Cumberland—the time was come I say!—alas, it was gone!— Afraid to communicate to each other a terror which preyed alike on both, Lord Southampton dispatched express upon express in vain.— The days that lingered so tediously away, however, matured doubt into certainty. Lord Essex no longer contended with the nervous fever which obliged him to take to his bed; where reaching out a languid hand to his overpowered friend, he broke, at last, the fearful heavy silence. 'They are gone, for ever gone, my dear Southampton,' cried he, in the low accent of incurable dispair; 'heaven has spared to souls so gentle and susceptible those trials our stouter minds can perhaps better contend with.— Oh, thou dear one! yet do I regret that this bosom did not receive thy last sighs! that entombed with thee even in the ocean, death had not consummated a union fortune ever frowned on—but I hasten impatiently to rejoin thee, oh Ellinor! my first, my only love!'

"The killing remembrance which distracted his mind soon rendered a malady, slight at first, desperate; he was even given over; the Queen for a long time withstood the accounts given by his friends of his situation, so deeply had his enemies impressed her with the idea that this was only a refined artifice to tempt her to humiliate herself. Nevertheless, by one of those passionate emotions with which nature sometimes overreaches the most elaborate finesses of art, she suddenly determined to ascertain his real situation, by sending her own physician to visit him.— The report of that gentleman convinced her of its danger—he was ordered to watch over the Earl with the most anxious care; and even to hint to him that every distinction would be restored with his health.—[27] But, alas! sympathy itself had no longer any charms for him, and the presence of Lord Southampton seemed the only relief his fate admitted. That amiable Nobleman, no less sensible of the mutual calamity than his friend, had not the same reasons to bury his affliction in silence.— Repeated messengers were sent alike to Cumberland, and the port you embarked from, ladies: those who returned from the latter only confirmed the fears which had hitherto fluctuated—they informed the lover and the husband, that the wife of the Captain mourned for him as dead, nor was it doubted but that the crew and passengers were alike victims to a storm so sudden and tremendous. The active and enlivened soul frequently exhausts its most acute sensations by anticipation.— Certainty could not add to the grief occasioned by surmise; and the extinguished hopes of the friends gave them alike up to that cold and sullen despair, which is the worst of all states, because frequently incurable. Those late hopes the Queen was willing to revive her dying favorite with, made not the least impression on him; and the Cecils learnt with surprize, that, neither their views, their conduct, nor even his own disgraceful imprisonment, any longer touched Lord Essex; nay, that not even his recovery was able to revive those habits the world were taught to think hitherto uncontroulable. His friends, on the contrary, blest the skilful physician who prolonged a life so valuable, and saw with the happiest hopes, that those romantic flights in his character his enemies had almost wrought up to his ruin were at once extinguished; leaving it without any other distinction than a melancholy sweetness which rather turned his thoughts toward philosophy than war. The people, ever naturally disposed to side with the unfortunate, cried out, that he was the innocent victim of the Cecil party; who by some odious strokes of policy, added popularity to their depressed rival, in diminishing their own— Elizabeth herself could no longer support the idea that the man she still loved was obscurely breaking his heart, while yet in the flower of youth, in an unmerited and disgraceful prison.— She yielded to the information of the physician that his amending health required air, and sent him her permission to retire to any of his seats in the country; but forbad him to attempt appearing in her presence: a restriction perhaps more agreeable to him, than herself, could she have seen the desolate situation of mind in which he departed.

"From the country he addressed a letter of thanks to the Queen, which displayed at once his eloquence, gratitude, and languor: in truth, the latter gained ground daily in his character. Lord Essex was born capable of uniting in his person every various and generous pursuit, had fortune allowed it, but not even he was equal to living without one.— I frequently trembled at beholding his gloom and inanity. Wholly withdrawn from the sphere in which he had hitherto moved, and the pleasures he had once enjoyed, the rude society of his neighbours, and the boisterous amusements the country afforded, rather offended than employed an enlightened and susceptible heart. He wandered all day in the woods alone, and returned every evening spent and unrefreshed, only to recover animal strength enough to enable him to pass the morrow in the same melancholy manner.[28]

"In this situation I fancied a false hope could not add to his danger, and might perhaps rouse those active faculties every hour seemed more and more to absorb. I one day ventured to repeat to him an imaginary dream, tending to prove you still existed.— Not even the firmest mind can resist the subtle attacks of superstition when labouring under depression.— His soul so eagerly adopted the fiction of my brain, that I was a thousand times tempted to acknowledge it to be such, but dared not venture to shew him I had played upon his wounded feelings. Revived with the most vague and distant hope, he impatiently drove me away on a search my own soul foreboded to be fruitless. I even debated after I set out, whether I should not loiter out the appointed time in England till I could decently return from my imaginary peregrination, when a dream, more pointed and singular than that I had feigned, awakened in myself those hopes I had communicated to my Lord, and led me from isle to isle enquiring for you: but I will not call it a dream, since surely the event proves it a visitation.— Oh, gracious God! what joy will my return pour into the hearts that now ach for either! How pure will be the satisfaction derived from their acknowledgments!"

During this long recital, my tumultuous feelings pursued my love through every desperate situation.— My woe-struck heart hardly dared to breathe, till finding him at last free and well, it gave a deep sigh, and respired without pain. Essex insulted, endangered, imprisoned;—I cast my eyes round those gloomy walls, I so late thought my prison, and raising them to heaven, adored the power who there confined me, unconscious of the conflicts I could not have supported. Ah, Essex! what were the warring elements, the midnight wreck, the long, long solitude, the dire uncertainty I had so bitterly bewailed, to the single idea of seeing thee one moment at the mercy of Elizabeth, one moment in the power of thy enemies! And yet, for me thy generous soul lost all sense of even these inflictions; pride, vanity, and grandeur, in vain assailed thee: a true and noble passion beat unalterably at thy heart, condensing in one favorite sorrow, those mighty powers, which once fulfilled every various and active duty of humanity.

But this was not a moment for impassioned reveries. Lady Southampton recalled my attention to the present moment; and we employed it in informing Tracey of the name, character, and situation, we had thought it prudent to assume, as well as those of our host. Scarce was he master of these important particulars, ere the Laird of Dornock returned, and broke in upon us with an abruptness and anger he took no pains to disguise. The sight of an English officer a little abated his wrath. Tracey, according to the plan we had agreed on, called Lady Southampton his sister, and, with every testimony of gratitude for the hospitable shelter our host had so long given us, offered a recompence still more agreeable; with which happily he had had the forecast[29] to provide himself.— While the Scot stood irresolute respecting his answer, the wary Tracey turned to us, and, in an authoritative voice, said, he must answer to the Queen for his absence, did it exceed the appointed time; and therefore, we must quickly take leave of our friends, and hasten our departure for England. This decisive speech increased the perturbation and disappointment already obvious in the features of our host; nevertheless, our going was to him so unforeseen an event, that, not being able to find a sufficient reason for detaining us, he tacitly consented to it.

My heart bounded at the unhoped-for liberation, and I would have sailed that moment, despite of wind and tide; but, as the sailors declared this impossible, our departure was delayed till the next morning. Whether the various incidents of the day accelerated the hour appointed by nature, or, that Lady Southampton, contrary to her own idea, had reached it, I know not; she was seized at midnight, however, with the pains of labour, and suffered so severely, that her life was despaired of. In the course of the ensuing day she was delivered of a dead child, and I was obliged to console myself for the long delay this event must necessarily occasion, by the pleasing idea that the partner of my fate was not prematurely divided from it—in truth her vexation was so great, that I was reduced to stifle my own, lest I should contribute to her illness.

The fate which hope yet gilds, though but from the verge of the horizon, is never quite insupportable. We found, in the protection of Tracey, and the idea of rejoining the world, to which he seemed our immediate link, the means of beguiling many a tedious hour; nor was this consolation superfluous; for the Laird of Dornock became, from the moment of Tracey's arrival, more sullen and impenetrable than ever.— Self was, in him, the prevailing principle. Early invested with that bounded, but absolute, authority, which oftener produces and shelters tyranny, than a more extensive field of action, he had hitherto known no opposition.— How often has a blind passion warped the noblest natures? nor was it perhaps unnatural that he should stretch his prerogative, to retain in his hands a lovely and beloved woman, over whom he could claim no right.— Long inured to fear, suspicion, and anguish, they readily returned to their throbbing habitation, my heart. I often fancied I read murder written in dark, but legible lines, on the knit brow of our host; and though Tracey slept only in an outer chamber close by us, scarce could I persuade myself that he was suffered to rest peaceably there, or yet lived for our protection: nevertheless, I strove at times to reject those black chimeras a lively imagination perhaps too readily adopted. The Laird of Dornock no longer interfered with us, or our fate; neither did he withhold from us the company of his sister.— That sweet girl, new to society, with a romantic happiness peculiar to youth, gifted every object with her own graces and virtues: impressed at once with the merit of Tracey, she transferred to a heart which could return it the passion I had unwarily inspired, nor was her second choice unpropitious. Tracey, whose soul had expanded in a camp, was yet to learn the inconceivable charm of love: it took full possession of him. With a sweet, though sad pleasure, I witnessed pure and innocent vows, which continually reminded me of those days, when like Phoebe, I looked enraptured on the varied landscape of life, yet glowing with the early beams of hope; unconscious of the showers which often would fall, the heavy nights which must wholly obscure it. Tracey, no less delighted than his mistress, no longer hastened his departure to England, and looked astonished that we did not find every charm of existence in this dismal exile.

I, however, anxiously waited, with Lady Southampton, the day when her recovered health should enable us to depart.— It came at length, and we were eagerly preparing for the voyage, when the Laird of Dornock sent us an order to read, by which the King of Scots impowered him to detain us. I know not any shock, of all fate had imposed on me, I ever felt more sensibly: nevertheless, I had presence of mind enough to observe, by the date of this order, that it had been obtained during the confinement of my friend. The disappointment and despair this incident occasioned, was only alleviated by the recollection that in abusing the authority of the King, to indulge an unworthy inclination, the Laird of Dornock had made himself responsible to the laws of his country for our safety, by admitting that such persons were in his custody. Tracey gave him notice of this immediately; and though he moderated his rage in consideration of the fair Phoebe, he warned the Laird of Dornock to treat us nobly, as he would answer it to his own King, and the Queen of England, in whose name we should soon be demanded. To this indignant vaunt, for in truth it was no better, the haughty Scot coldly replied, "that he should take his chance of incurring an old woman's anger, who perhaps had already resigned all her rights to his master." Tracey could no longer controul the feelings of his generous soul, and replied with acrimony. The Laird of Dornock bade him profit by the occasion, and be gone immediately, if he did not mean to be included among the prisoners. There wanted only this stroke to consummate our wretchedness, and, however reluctantly we lost our only friend and protector, Lady Southampton joined me in urging him to go: till over-ruling all his objections, we hastened him alone into a bark, which an hour before we seemed to see ourselves in. He comforted us with the assurance of soon returning, being fully persuaded the King of Scots would never authorize so unjust and illegal a procedure, when once the whole circumstance was impartially stated to him. I sighed, at remembering I knew him better; but as an explanation at that moment was vain, I urged not the unbounded influence of the fair Mabel, through whose illicit connection with the King this order had doubtless been obtained. How should that Monarch be convinced of a remote act of injustice, who even at the moment of committing it, was wronging every moral and religious duty? The man who once voluntarily errs, must either be weak or vicious; in the first instance, he resigns himself up to the passions of others, in the latter to his own; and in either case scarce ever recovers the narrow but even boundary of virtue.

It was not by such means I hoped for freedom—ah, no! my views all pointed toward the lover to whom my heart like the needle ever vibrated, though far divided.— Let Essex be once informed, sighed I—let him once know where to find me, and he would cross the globe to ensure my safety. When the chagrin of this trying moment abated, I called to mind the infinite relief the visit of Tracey had given our spirits, and the change it had made in our situation, by acquitting us of those petty obligations which always humiliate a noble mind, unless it finds a congenial one in the bestower.

I soon observed that the Laird of Dornock had not courage to profit by the base injustice he had committed. The subservient situation Tracey placed himself in, when we were present, and the profound deference with which he obeyed our every wish, neither agreeing with the rank we avowed, nor the regimental he wore, a vague idea of mystery had taken possession of our host's mind, which wanted vigor and activity to attempt developing it. Conscious too late, that he had, in releasing Tracey, set a spy on his own conduct, he vainly regretted the timidity which prevented his detaining him. He nevertheless, at intervals, still talked of love to Lady Southampton, offering to buy a return by imaginary worlds of wealth: for to us, accustomed to elegance and luxury, all his possessions appeared but a gaudy poverty. As these ostentatious and absurd offers were one day made in my presence, I could not but take some notice of them; he silenced me however, by replying, that I must be cautious how I exerted a spirit so likely to make him transfer his attachment, and be satisfied with protecting one of the two; since I could neither think so ill of his discernment, or my own beauty, as to believe him the dupe of my disguise. As it was the first time a doubt on the subject had ever transpired, my confusion gave him a full conviction: I could not recover myself sufficiently to reply for some moments: at length I told him that he had guessed the only part of our secret which did not lie too deep for his knowledge; nevertheless, that all he had discovered, was but the least part of the mystery; and finally, that the day which informed him of our names and rank, would call him to a severe account, if his conduct were in the least unworthy either of us or himself.— I boldly added, that the only thing wanting to our safety, was, to have the Court of England informed of our asylum, and now that was by Tracey's means ascertained, we were not without noble friends to claim us. The grandeur of air natural to me when insult roused my pride, astonished and awed him—his mind laboured with vague and indistinct apprehensions; and as all attempts at diving into a secret locked up solely in the hearts interested in retaining it, must be vain, he half repented having exerted an unjustifiable influence, he could no longer hope to profit by.

Lady Southampton acknowledged her obligations to my firmer spirit; and both having no farther reason to affect subordination, resumed the habits of rank and distinction; hiring domestics of our own till the moment of enfranchisement should arrive.

Heartily weary of us both, I often thought the Laird of Dornock meditated proposing to release us; and while I was one day insensibly guiding him to that wished-for point, an order from Court was delivered into his hand. Convinced it would liberate us, I cast an eye of triumph on him, while he opened it; and saw his countenance confess the same idea; but a moment caused a visible change in it. He read the order aloud, and we found with inexpressible astonishment that it contained the strictest charge to guard his English prisoners, as he would answer it to his King: yet with all due deference.— I eagerly caught at this article without seeming to notice the first, which nevertheless sunk deep into my heart; nor was his insensible to the latter.— The weariness and disgust he had begun to indulge, increased; and his pride revolting at the idea that his castle was become a state prison, and himself only a jailor, he felt every way irritated, humiliated, and offended. No human being submits to power with so ill a grace as him who has unjustifiably exerted it; and when its restrictions fall heavily on such, mere retribution becomes in effect a severe revenge.

A tedious interval had again elapsed without any news from England. The tender, timid Phoebe often persuaded herself her lover had never reached it; and the singularity of finding ourselves apparently forgotten, sometimes inclined my friend and self to unite with her in that opinion—yet, how many other causes might we reasonably assign for the neglect—causes, so much more afflicting, that we recalled our thoughts to the isle for consolation.

Whether the infinite variety, the eternal transitions my own life had already afforded, inclined me to hope on; or, whether the incessant prayers I addressed to him who alone could relieve me, endued my mind with fortitude, I cannot say; but, I certainly found in it resources hitherto unknown. Every passing day seemed to refine and settle its powers and perceptions, till those turbulent passions, which of late rushed like a cataract through my frame, now, with a gentle, healthful current, gave motion to my pulses.

We learnt from Phoebe, that many letters came from Mabel to her elder brother, the contents of which he so cautiously concealed, as made it obvious we were their subject. This news only confirmed us in the belief that Tracey had reached England safely; and afforded us at the same time the flattering idea, that our friends were anxiously labouring to recover us; however their progress might be impeded by obstacles, we could neither guess at, nor decide upon: nor were these suppositions vain. An order at length arrived, that we should be delivered to the officer who should present its counter-part. Oh, what joy, what gratitude, what anxiety, did this prospect of a deliverance afford us! From the dawn of the morning till night blackened the ocean, did one or the other watch with eager expectation the promised vessel.— We beheld it at last, and hardly could Essex himself have been more welcome to my eyes.

Tracey once more landed, and glad was the greeting on all sides.— He presented each of us letters—dear and precious characters! my soul poured through my eyes when I again beheld them! With lavish tenderness Essex hailed my second resurrection, and vowed to shew his sense of the blessing by an implicit submission to my will.— "You shall no more complain of the terrors of a camp, my love," continued he, "I turn for ever from the bloody scene.— A court no longer has any charms for me: inspired with juster sentiments, alive to purer pleasures, in your heart and my own will I henceforth look for the wayward straggler, happiness. I am no longer, my sweet Ellinor, the Essex you have known! I am become an absolute rustic, a mere philosopher. With you I will abjure the world, and in some solitary spot, devote myself to love and the sciences.[30] Oh! shut your heart, like me, my love, to the past, and look only towards the future. I wait with impatience the news of your safe arrival in Cumberland, and date from it our happiness."

These words were to my soul, what the balmy breath of spring is to the frozen earth: the winds at once cease to blow, the snow sinks into her bosom, the buds put forth their verdure, and nature forgets she has suffered.

Tracey came fraught with gifts rather suited to the spirit of the donor, than that of the accepter; yet, they opened the heart of the Laird of Dornock, who listened to the avowal of Tracey's love without repugnance; and at length promised him his sister, if, at the expiration of two years, his rank in the army entitled him to claim her.— The tears of the young lovers for ever cemented those vows his will thus authorized. Joy having disposed my heart to receive the soft impressions of every gentle passion, extinguishing all that were not so—I remembered, with astonishment, the moment when I readily adopted the ambitious projects of Essex.— Rank, riches, glory, what are ye?— Gay ornaments which lend splendor indeed to felicity, but which only incumber and weigh down the soul when struggling with the waves of misfortune: gladly we lighten ourselves of such adventitious goods, and grasp in tranquility and love, the unenvied, but rich essence of all our fortune.

In life, as in a prospect, we can long enjoy only a bounded view; and all which present, either to the mind or eye, a multiplicity of objects, however great or beautiful, overstrain the faculties, and destroy the repose. Rejecting at once every gaud[31] vanity delights in, from the distant throne, and the mighty multitude, ready perhaps in turn to conduct me to it, my soul called forth the beloved individual, and seating him at my side in a safe and humble solitude, asked what we should lose by the change?—lose! Ah! rather what might we not gain?— How sweet was it then to find Lord Essex himself at length cherished ideas wholly similar; that, weary of war, ambition, envy, and all the turbulence of life, in renouncing the court of Elizabeth, he left, with the power, the wish of possessing it!— That time, solitude, reflection, disappointment itself, had rather refined than extinguished his taste, which thus regained its true bias; seeking in the powers of the mind, and the impulses of the heart, a happiness not to be found on earth, when those sources fail to supply it.

In leaving for ever the dreary scene of my exile, I could be sensible of only one regret: but flattering myself, Tracey would ere long restore the sweet Phoebe to my friendship, I soon dried up the tears due[32] to the floods that charming girl bestowed upon our parting. The rapid motion of the vessel bore no proportion to my impatience; whenever I looked, that detested isle was still in view; I thought we should never lose sight of it.

Oh! how I anticipated the sweet repose which awaited us in the green solitudes of Cumberland! I flattered myself Essex would already be there; though

Tracey assured me, spies still followed his steps, from which only a long confirmation of his peaceful intentions could relieve him.

At length the pleasant shore of England was descried; welcome to my heart was the shout which proclaimed it! Our very souls shot through our eyes once more, to hail our native country. We found at the port, servants, and every accommodation that might render our journey easy. Ah! how beautiful was that journey!—a thousand various objects of simple majesty united to form one perfect whole, and a new delight stole on every sense, as we wound through varying vallies embowered by hanging woods, reflected in many an expanse of clear water, dim shadowed at intervals by mountains, whose arid heights defied the sun they seemed to swell to.

Far in these green labyrinths we came at once upon the Castle from whence I now write.— It is in fact only an elegant ruin, and might rather be termed the residence of the anchorite, Solitude. In tearful gladness the fair owner threw her arms round my neck, and blest the power which permitted us at last to rest here.

From this antique mansion do I date my narrative; and, in arranging it, seek only to fill up those hours yet unblest with the presence of him born to fill every future one. Dear Lady Pembroke, I cannot express to you the divine repose which hushes at last my overworn faculties.— I look back with wonder on all the past griefs, the mortal conflicts, my shattered frame has contended with. So pure, so perfect, is now my grateful tranquillity, that it seems proof even against misfortune itself.— No more shall my beating heart—my burning brain—but why should I revert to such dismal recollections?

Embosomed in the maternal arms of nature; safe in the obscure and solitary situation of this ivied asylum, here my affrighted soul, like a scared bird, faintly folds up its weary wings! delights to be alone, and joys in mere safety. I think I can never be happy, be grateful enough, and while my heart exhausts itself in enjoyment, I still call on it for ebullitions to which it is unequal. Pride, passion, vanity, all the grosser particles of my nature are at once exhaled, and every pure, every social virtue, unfolds and blossoms to the vernal sun, forerunning even the snow-drop.

Oh! that radiant, glorious luminary! how new to me seems its influence!— Dark have been the films through which I have hitherto viewed it. Pardon, my darling friend, these flights of fancy: how playful does the mind grow when at peace with itself!

Hasten, generous Tracey, hasten to my love, and inform him of our arrival. But is not Tracey already gone? Oh! hasten then, my Essex; quit that busy scene, where virtue incessantly hovers on the verge of a precipice a thousand ready hands would plunge her over,—partake with me the deep repose of this solitude—no longer heed Elizabeth herself; not even her power can reach us here. Nature's gigantick phalanx, impassable mountains present their formidable summits in long array, overawing every inferior guard; while, in their vivid hollows, happiness reposes on the bosom of her mother, Nature.— Oh! come then, and in

> "*A life exempt from public haunt,*
> *Find tongues in trees, books in the running streams,*
> *Sermons in stones, and good in every thing.*"[33]

* * * * * *

A thunder-bolt falls on my brain! avenging heaven, why does it not wholly split it? Tried—sentenced—condemned—while I, entombed in a now detested solitude, gaily dreamt of endless happiness.— Oh! let me once more rush madly into the world, overwhelm my agonized senses with the shouts of armies—the groans of the dying—fountains of blood—rivers of tears—find if possible a horror in nature may counteract that now raging in my soul.— The wreck of the universe alone can equal it.— But let me give the ruin scope—wherefore, wherefore should I wish it lessened—Oh! Lady Pembroke!

LADY PEMBROKE WRITES.

The trembling hand of the friend last invoked, takes up the pen to finish the woes of a fair unfortunate, who will never more be her own historian.— Alas, they had now reached their climax.

The eccentric turn of mind which made the sweet Ellinor form a plan so extraordinary as her supposed death and burial, excited an astonishment in me, its artful execution alone could increase. Nevertheless, the regular pursuit of a single idea was far from persuading her friends, her intellects had recovered their tone, or equality.

When this heart-breaking narrative came to my hands, I could not but observe that the sweet mistress of Essex had a very partial knowledge of his character, or information of his actions.— Blest with the most equitable and generous heart that ever actuated a human bosom, his virtues often took a false colour from the selfish views of those who once found the way to it.

Credulity was so much his fault, that even his enemies profited by it, whom he always ceased to consider as such, the moment they deigned to deceive him with a false protestation of regard.— In fact, the lenity of his nature continually counteracted that ambition, which was its only vice; and irradiated his character with the milder glories of humanity: a lustre, more soft, pure, and lasting, than mere conquest can bestow. Nevertheless, the early habits of power and distinction had seized on his affections, and even his love co-operating with that indulged foible, they increased together. The daring project he had formed was no way unfeasible, had he managed it with address; for he possessed the hearts of the whole kingdom, a few envious individuals excepted. But art was unknown to Essex; and those his superiority offended, were proficients in that science: unhappily too, they were so immediately around the Queen, that they could convert the suspicions she sometimes entertained of his conduct, into certainty. Yet so rooted was her love for this unfortunate favorite, that it long contended with that she bore herself; and tears of ill-judged fondness have often absorbed the bitterness his enemies would have wrought to his ruin. Such a weakness alone could induce a sovereign, wise and experienced like Elizabeth, to delegate a power scarce inferior to her own, into the hands of a Nobleman, valiant, popular, and aspiring. In consenting to Essex's command in Ireland, the Queen made an absolute sacrifice of her own inclination (which was only gratified when he was near her) to his; or, perhaps, in effect, both unconsciously yielded to the secret policy which invariably sought to separate them.— Convinced she had bound him to her by every tie of gratitude, honor, and confidence, how must so high a spirit as that of Elizabeth be shocked, wounded, and irritated, to see her favorite loiter away his days inactively in Ireland, regardless alike of her admonitions, and the censures of the people!— Insensibly she imbibed the prejudices of the Cecil family, the inflexible enemies of the Earl; to whom she submitted the government of the state, less from any esteem for their talents, than the latent desire of piquing the negligent Essex, to whom they were equally obnoxious. Time confirmed to the Cecil faction, the influence they at first owed solely to resentment. The wearisome supineness of the Lord Deputy was at once succeeded by a suspicious, and mysterious conduct. His secret treaties with the arch-rebel, Tyrone, the anonymous captive who seduced him into these—all was reported with aggravation to Elizabeth. The resentment occasioned by the error of his conduct, was doubled when she knew that of his heart: jealousy took full possession of hers, and she determined to make him severely sensible of her power; but she was told it was not safe, at that period, to recall him. Obliged for the first time in her life to controul herself, and meditate how to get him again into her power, her temper became absolutely intolerable. Her Ladies preserved a melancholy silence, save the artful few won over to foment, and profit by, her irritated passions. The fate of Essex seemed wholly to depend on the event of a war, hitherto unprosperous; when to the astonishment alike of friends and enemies, without performing any considerable exploit which might secure him a welcome, the Earl posted suddenly home, and presented himself before Elizabeth, with the dauntless air of unblemished innocence. Whether the surprize of the moment really revived that powerful passion of which he had so long been the object, or whether fear for her life made her dissemble the bitterness and rage swelling at her heart, is a circumstance which never reached my knowledge. It is certain the Queen received him graciously, and listened to a very imperfect and incoherent defence of his conduct. They parted friends; and Essex instantly giving way to that credulity, which so often made every talent art and nature could unite in his person abortive, considered himself as effectually re-established in her heart, and indulged all the exultation such a triumph over his enemies could not fail to occasion.

What a thunder-stroke then was his immediate disgrace! a disgrace he could not but impute to his own imprudence; since in returning without advice, he had delivered himself voluntarily into the hands of his enemies. To the mortification of a long and humiliating imprisonment was shortly after super-added a killing grief, in the supposed loss of the beauteous Ellinor. Resigning himself to a sullen and silent despair, Essex no longer condescended to offer Elizabeth any further vindication of his conduct, nor could be persuaded to make the least submission. This concussion of feelings, however, shivered his animal, no less than his mental, system. A fever followed, which soon rose to a dangerous height. Obstinately rejecting all medical advice, he declared a thousand times that he wished only to die: nor had the wish been vain, but that the Queen, unable wholly to subdue the sentiments of tenderness which had so long reigned in her heart, sent her own physician to attend him, with offers of peace and pardon. The desperate state in which he found the Earl, was faithfully reported to Elizabeth; who, touched to the heart, hesitated whether she should not revive him by an immediate visit; so hard will it always be to counteract by political manoeuvres the genuine impressions of nature. The Cecil party suddenly found themselves on the brink of ruin; and every argument, fear, pride, or prudence, could suggest, was enforced to delay this interview. Elizabeth yielded to the powerful combination of reasons in that instance, but could not deny herself the pleasure of corresponding with Lord Essex as he grew better; and soon suffered him to vindicate his conduct:

nay, even condescended to reproach him with the unknown lady who had so fatally influenced it. To this perplexing hint, he replied, his grief alone must answer; and the melancholy tenor of his life so exactly agreed with this declaration, that Elizabeth pressed no farther into a secret it was plain the grave now veiled: rather seeking by kindness to invigorate a mind ill-fortune had been too hard upon.[34]

It was now the shining time in the life of Essex. The purple torrent of successful war had hitherto swept away, or sunk, those sweet humanities, those social virtues, time at length cast up in the vale of adversity.— Endued with eloquence, taste, science, sense, and sensibility, he now resigned himself to the charms of philosophy, poesy, and the mathematicks. Innocent and tranquil resources, to which the mind must ever turn when disappointed, if blest with powers capable of relishing them.[35] The Cecils never thought Essex more dangerous. Age and infirmity now made Elizabeth anxious for peace abroad, and tranquillity at home, and there wanted only a meeting between her, and the much altered Earl to re-establish him in her favor: but that meeting his enemies entered into a league to prevent; and began, by winning Elizabeth's physician to order the Earl of Essex into the country.— An artifice so refined as his liberation was not immediately discovered to be policy by any party;[36] and the Queen, lulled into a belief that she could honourably receive him when he should return, suffered him to depart without an audience.

Wearied of wars, camps, and political jealousies, and discussions, the melancholy Essex desired in freedom only the solitude he found; when Tracey returned with the astonishing news that the mistress he still adored yet existed.— Fatal news to his future repose!— The impossibility of openly claiming Ellinor, revived with his passion all his dangerous and precarious projects.— Every other effort to obtain her was made without success, ere he secretly applied to the King of Scots; who always knew his own interests too well to grant any favor without having secured an adequate return. James ardently desired to be nominated as the successor of Elizabeth by herself, and had not spared bribes, promises, or flattery, to interest those around her whom he thought likely to influence her choice.[37] The unhoped over-turns of the man whose courage and ambition James most feared, was a circumstance of importance. Uninformed of the real name or characters of the prisoners Lord Essex so eagerly desired to recover, the King of Scots sent the Laird of Dornock notice to guard them more strictly. The impetuous temper of Essex made him always resign to the prevailing object, every other interest: but a treaty like this could not be carried on so secretly as to escape the suspicious eyes of the ministers. With what malignant joy did they silently watch its progress till the moment when its publication would inflame the Queen to their wishes!

Essex now once more thought it his interest to be busy, admired, and popular: he relapsed into all his old habits, and, having gained the Queen's permission, returned to London. Far, however, from profiting by this indulgence, to re-instate himself in her favor, he remained at home; throwing open his doors to all impoverished officers, and clergy, among whom a number of spirited adventurers appeared, whose lavish praises seemed to render his popularity greater than ever.[38]

Elizabeth, with disgust, beheld him assume the distinctions she perhaps intended once more to bestow; and kept in silence a strict watch upon his conduct. By a refinement, known only in politicks, his enemies scattered among his partizans many creatures of their own, instructed to dive into all his intentions, and spread abroad seditious and treasonable projects, as though intrusted by himself with such. This malice was but too successful.— Inflated with the adulation of misjudging friends, the extravagant admiration of the multitude, and the insidious attacks of his enemies, the self-deluded Essex sprung the mine himself which destroyed him.

The mischief commenced by a broil between the Lords Southampton and Grey; the last assaulting the former in the street; and, though the offender was ceremoniously punished, the spirit of party broke out in a thousand little daily quarrels.[39] The Queen, already persuaded that Essex, ever haughty and impetuous, scorned her power, despised her person, and only waited a favorable moment openly to insult both, was irritated beyond all endurance by the artful discovery (at this cruel crisis) of his secret treaty with the King of Scots.— Its real cause was unknown to her, and the offence, though trifling in itself, of a nature most likely to exasperate a Sovereign whose eyes were ever turned from a successor she refused to acknowledge.— The discovery proved decisive—Elizabeth instantly resolved to deliver the ungrateful favorite up to the laws of his country, and authorized a judicial enquiry into his conduct. The Cecil party desired no more; for well they knew, Essex would rather die than brook the deliberate indignity. The commissioned Lords assembled at his house on a Sunday, as the time when they should be most safe from the insults of the partial populace.— They found the Earl sufficiently inflamed, who, swearing he never more would become a voluntary prisoner, shut up the Lord Keeper, and the rest, in his own house, rushing forth armed, and followed only by a few friends and domestics, to claim the protection of the people.[40]

By a fatality not peculiar to himself, the bubble, popularity, which had so long swelled and glittered before his mistaken eyes, burst at once, and left to him a vacuum in nature. The sacred day was but too judiciously chosen by his enemies.— Without preparation—almost without a friend, the unhappy Essex rushed through the streets of London, crouded only with peaceful and humble mechanics,[41] who emerged from every close lane environed by their wives and children to enjoy the weekly holiday.— To people of this stamp the gallant Essex was almost unknown—certainly indifferent: with stupid and curious eyes, they turned to gaze on those warlike steps none ventured to follow—steps which bore the noble Essex so fast toward ruin. Distress, however, only increased his desperation, and the citizens being spirited into making an ineffectual effort to prevent his return, a skirmish ensued. The amiable Tracey had the fate he desired, and fell at the side of his Lord; who, even in this cruel moment, dropt a tear on a youth so beloved. Fame, honor, happiness, nay, even life, were fleeting fast from Essex; and however careless of these goods, friendship still asserted her rights over his feelings—In compassion to the few generous adherents who must have fallen in his cause, had he longer resisted, the Earl at length surrendered his sword.[42]

All was now over with this admired, and erring favorite.— Imprisoned in the Tower he had ample leisure to re-consider the events which brought him there.— The desertion of the people had opened his eyes to the realities of life.— He too sensibly found, that, while he ministered to their necessities, their pride, or their pleasures, the multitude could rend the air with acclamations; but that the moment a claim is in turn made on their feelings, they always become cold, torpid, and inanimate. He perceived with vain regret that he had been duped into this outrage on the laws of society, by the manoeuvres of his enemies, no less than the credulity of his heart. But he was not formed to profit by these humiliating discoveries; they impressed a nature so generous, only with the deepest disgust.— He was, however, consoled with remembering self-preservation was the sole motive for his daring attack, and that no action of his life had yet violated the duty he had sworn the Queen. He resolutely prepared himself to meet the judgment of his peers, and only lamented the friendship which involved the generous Southampton in his fate; who shared without regret the prison of a friend so dear.[43]

The Queen, meanwhile, experienced every emotion such a painful contrariety of passions must necessarily occasion.— The imprisonment of her favorite, as usual, seemed to cancel his offence: but he was now beyond her jurisdiction, and the victim of the laws. She had unhappily surrendered him up to them, and robbed herself of every prerogative but that of pardoning; a prerogative she feared so high a spirit would never solicit her to exert.— She regretted, too late, having driven him to so dangerous an extreme, and while his fate was yet uncertain, suffered more, perhaps, than he did in its completion.[44]

The friends of the Earl, persuaded no kind of influence would be spared to bring him to the block, were unanimous in intreating him to win over the Queen by an early repentance and submission: but they knew not the grandeur of the heart they would have humbled.— Born to distinguish himself most eminently when outward distinctions were withdrawn, it was then only Essex seemed to use his better judgment. "Can any one call himself my friend," would he indignantly exclaim, "and yet wish me poorly to petition for an obscure, an ignominious life? What! to pine away the flower of manhood in infamy and solitude! shunned by all, yet unstigmatized by public justice, and shunning, in turn, the exalted characters I dare no longer emulate.— Shut up with those tormenting companions, my own thoughts, till led, perhaps, by desperation, to inflict that fate upon my self, I have meanly evaded receiving from the law.— No, my friends, I am enthralled here as a traitor—if proved one, it is fit I expiate my crime; and if acquitted I know the value of a life ventured hitherto only for my country."— Neither arguments, or intreaties, could shake his resolution; and he heard with unequalled firmness that public sentence, from which, he still persisted, there was no appeal. In vain every dear and affecting image was pourtrayed in the strongest colours before his active imagination.— From that of the woe-struck Ellinor, liberated too late, and weaving in a distant solitude a thousand fairy bowers for love and happiness to dwell in—from her alone his nature shrunk. "You may wound my heart," would he sighing say, "through every vein; but my reason is still inflexible, nor is even that sweet creature an argument for my submitting to disgrace.— No! when I raised my eyes to thee, dear Ellinor, my conscious soul beheld in itself all that could intitle me to mate with thee.— I cannot resolve to look up even to the woman I adore.— Better she should weep me dead, than secretly despise me while yet existing.— Pure and precious will be the tears that fall upon my grave, but never could I behold one which would not secretly reproach me.— Leave me, my friends, to my fate; honor has hitherto been the invariable rule of my conduct, nor can I now adopt another."[45]

From the moment the condemnation of Essex reached the Queen, peace and rest were strangers to her.— The chosen of her heart was now the victim of the laws, and that heart must bleed through his, unless he could be induced to throw himself on her mercy. A thousand emissaries assured him of a ready pardon—a word, a wish, would have obtained it.— To these he ever replied with the same collected air, "that had the Queen earlier shewn him this indulgence, his life had never come within censure of the law; but as even her utmost bounty now could only prolong to him the liberty of breathing, he was willing, as well for her safety as in submission to his sentence, to resign a privilege, which became a burthen the moment it was his only one."[46] An answer thus calculated to touch the most indifferent heart, stabbed that of Elizabeth: yet as, unasked, to grant him a pardon, would stamp her declining life with inexcusable weakness, she underwent every hour the most trying conflicts.[47]

Ah! why do I say the most trying? alas, there was a fair, and forlorn one, buried in Cumberland, who more than died when this cruel intelligence reached her. As the sentence of Essex extended to his friend Southampton, the relations of the latter dispatched an express to his wife, hoping she would arrive in London time enough to solicit his pardon of the Queen. The messenger found the unfortunate Ladies buoyed up with safety, solitude, and many a gentle hope. When the approach of horses echoed through the remote valley, no other emotion was excited in either, than the fond and latent flutter arising from the idea that it might be one or both of the condemned Earls.— How terrible was then the transition in their minds, when fully informed of their desperate situation; and bereft of every resource expected misery supplies! The unhappy wife of Southampton, engrossed by her own share in the affliction, observed not its deep, its deadly effect, on the intellects of her equally suffering friend; till the stupefaction of Ellinor became intense, and obvious, and the evil irremediable.

The human mind, even when most elevated, is not equal to the influence of two opposing passions—a sacrifice must be made, and friendship yields to love. Lady Southampton posted away with unremitting diligence, intrusting her friend to the care of faithful servants, who were directed to bring her forward more leisurely.— The deep gloom of the sweet Ellinor's mind, in the course of the journey, gave way to a vague and irregular gaiety; but as this had sometimes forerun her recovery, so might it then, had she been surrounded with such persons as knew her disposition.— Those who had her in charge, uninformed of her name, situation, and wounded spirit, could not reasonably be expected to guard against events they could not possibly foresee. It happened, one day, while they were resting, Ellinor cast her eyes upon an extensive building, full in sight, and her wandering imagination called it Kenilworth.— An officious attendant informed her it was Fotheringay Castle.—[48] She wildly shrieked, stretched forth her arms expressively towards the fatal mansion, then tearing those lovely tresses once before devoted to her calamity, and scarce grown to their usual luxuriance, threw herself on the ground, and relapsed into total insanity.

But when Lady Southampton entered the prison of her Lord, upon whose aching bosom she poured forth all her grief and passion, his disturbed friend found every fibre of his heart wrung; and turning a fearful, eager eye toward the door, felt a horror not to be expressed, at finding no one followed her.— The afflicted wife wanted presence of mind to conceal a truth which consummated the fate of Essex—a truth so terrible, that fain would he have believed it invented by his friends to reconcile him to his sentence.— Convinced at length—"now indeed do I feel the weight of my bonds—now indeed am I a prisoner," would he exclaim.— "Oh, Ellinor, matchless Ellinor, that I could fly to thee! recall once more that unequalled soul, which always, like a frightened bird, forsakes its home when misery hovers over it.— Thou, thou, hast broken a spirit equal to every other affliction—thou hast made a coward of me—to save thee, my love, I could almost resolve, poorly to condition for a disgraceful life, and wish to survive my honor." Persuaded his presence would have the same effect it once before took at St. Vincent's Abbey, he passionately solicited to see her.— This single idea seized upon his mind—it even became his solemn request—his dying wish.— In the hopeless state of her disorder, the effect of their meeting was dreaded only on his account; but as all intreaty and argument proved vain, his friends at length resolved to yield to his passionate, his only solicitation. The day was now appointed for the execution of Essex, and the pardon of Southampton granted, which alone he desired;[49]— as all his friends were freely admitted to his person, there was no difficulty in leading thither the darling of his heart, in the habit of a youth, accompanied by Lady Southampton.— Worlds could not have bribed *me* to witness such an interview.— Ah, dearest Ellinor! were those senses they so eagerly desired to restore to thee, in reality a loss? How, had they been perfect, wouldst thou have supported the trying scene, expiring love, and officious friendship, dragged thee to witness?— How wouldest thou have fixed thine eyes on the gloomy tower, or those guarded gates through which thy lover must so soon be borne, but never more should pass?— How must thy soul have bled to behold those fine features, a few hours were to separate from the heart which then gave them such agonized expression! But that superlative misery was not ordained thee.— Retired, beyond the reach of love itself, were all the various powers of that susceptible soul!— Thy vague eyes confessed not their everlasting object—thy ear caught not his voice—nor did thy bosom answer with a single sigh, the bursts of grief which struggled at that of thy lover, still exquisitely alive to every human affliction! To thee his parting soul yet clung; and when his eyes beheld thee no longer, they willingly shut out creation. He saw not, from the moment of Ellinor's departure, friend or relation; but turning all his contemplations towards the awful futurity in which he was so soon to launch, died to this world even before his execution.

On the night which preceded that event, this billet, equally addressed to my sister (with whom the dear unfortunate resided) and myself, was delivered.

"Dear, generous guardians of the lost angel, my soul yet bleeds over, receive in this my parting blessing; and pardon, oh, pardon, an incredulity but too severely punished by conviction! a conviction so terrible as reconciles me to the death to-morrow will bestow. Yes, these eyes have been blasted with beholding the pale statue of my love, dead while yet breathing—speechless—insensate.— To the gathered multitude—the fatal scaffold—the axe which seperates soul and body, I turn for relief when this remembrance presses upon me.

"Adieu, ye faithful sisters of the gallant Sidney—Oh! if intelligence too late should visit the fair form bequeathed to your friendship, with sympathy soothe every aching sense.— Yet wake no more to woe my worshipped Ellinor!— Still may thy pure spirit slumber in its breathing tomb, till that appointed hour which at length unites thee to thy

ESSEX."

TOWER.

It seemed as if in this epistle were enclosed every lingering weakness of mortality: for the remaining hours of his life were devoted solely to the duties of religion.— In the flower of manhood, at the age of three and thirty, this envied favorite resigned every earthly distinction, and ascended the scaffold with a composure innocence and Heaven alone can bestow. The melting multitude too late bewailed to see his glorious youth set thus in blood.— His ear caught the general murmur of sorrow and applause; he cast a look of corrected knowledge on the spectators; then lifting his eyes to Heaven, serenely submitted to the executioner; who severed a head and heart, which, had they acted in unison, might have awed the world.[50]

Of her so much beloved, so generously, so fatally faithful, little more remains to be said.— Neither time, care, or medicine, ever availed toward the restoration of those intellects which might only have proved an additional misfortune—Yet even in this state of insanity, Heaven permitted her to become the instrument of a singular and exemplary vengeance.

A year or more had elapsed, during which her calamity took all those variable and dreadful forms peculiar to itself.— The desire of having every medical assistance made me bring her with me to London; where one evening, with a degree of reflection and art often blended with insanity, she eluded the care of her attendants; and well knowing every avenue of the palace, passed them all with wonderful facility.

The Queen wholly sunk in the chilling melancholy of incurable despair, and hopeless age, resigned herself up to the influence of those evils.— Her ladies were often employed in reading to her, which was the only amusement her chagrin admitted.— One memorable night it was my turn—Elizabeth dismissed every other attendant, in the vain hope of finding a repose of which she had for ever deprived herself. I pursued my task a long while, when the time conspired with the orders of the Queen to produce a silence so profound, that had not her starts now and then recalled my senses, hardly could my half-closed eyes have discerned the pages over which they wandered.— The door flew suddenly open—a form so fair—so fragile—so calamitous appeared there, that hardly durst my beating heart call it Ellinor. The Queen started up with a feeble quickness, but had only power to falter out a convulsive ejaculation. I instantly remembered Elizabeth believed her dead, and imagined this her spectre. The beauteous phantom (for surely never mortal looked so like an inhabitant of another world) sunk on one knee, and while her long garments of black flowed gracefully over the floor, she lifted up her eyes toward Heaven, with that nameless sweetness, that wild ineffable benignity, madness alone can give, then meekly bowed before Elizabeth.— The Queen, heartstruck, fell back into her seat, without voice to pronounce a syllable.— Ellinor arose, and approached still nearer; standing a few moments, choaked and silent. "I once was proud, was passionate, indignant," said the sweet unfortunate at last, in the low and broken voice of inexpressible anguish, "but Heaven forbids me now to be so—Oh! you who was surely born only to chastise my unhappy race, forgive me—I have no longer any sense but that of sorrow."— Again she sunk upon the floor, and gave way to sobbings she struggled in vain to suppress. The Queen dragged me convulsively to her, and burying her face in my bosom exclaimed indistinctly,—"save me—save me—oh, Pembroke, save me from this ghastly spectre!"— "Essex—Essex—Essex!" groaned forth the prostrate Ellinor, expressively raising her white hand at each touching repetition. The violent shudderings of the Queen, marked the deep effect that fatal name took on her.— "Somebody told me," continued the lovely wanderer, "that he was in the Tower, but I have looked there for him till I am weary—is there a colder, safer prison, then? But is a prison a place for your *favorite*, and can you condemn him to the grave?— Ah gracious Heaven, strike off his head—his beauteous head!— Seal up those sparkling eyes for ever.— Oh, no, I thought not," said she with an altered voice.— "So you hid him *here* after all, only to torment me.— But Essex will not see me suffer— will you, my Lord? So—so—so"—the slow progress of her eyes round the room, shewed, she in imagination followed his steps.— "Yes—yes,"—added she, with revived spirits, "I thought that voice would prevail, for who could ever resist it?—and only I need die then; well, I do not mind that—I will steal into his prison and suffer in his place, but be sure you don't tell him so, for he loves *me*—ah! dearly does he love me, but I alone need sigh at that, you know." And sigh she did indeed.— Oh! what a world of woe was drawn up in a single breath!— The long silence which followed, induced the Queen once more to raise her head—the same sad object met her eyes, with this difference, that the sweet creature now stood up again, and putting one white hand to her forehead, she half raised the other, as earnestly demanding still to be heard, though her vague eyes shewed her purpose had escaped her.— "Oh, now I remember it," resumed she, "I do not mind how you have me murdered, but let me be buried in Fotheringay; and be sure I have *women* to attend me; *be sure* of that—you know the reason." This incoherent reference to the unprecedented fate of her royal mother, affected Elizabeth deeply.—[51] "But could not you let me once more see him before I die?" resumed the dear wanderer.— "Oh! what pleasure would it give me to view him on the Throne!— Oh, I *do* see him there!" exclaimed she in the voice of surprize and transport. "Benign, majestic!— Ah, how glorious in his beauty!— Who would not die for thee, my Essex!"— "Alas, never, never, never, shall *I* see him!" groaned forth the agonized Elizabeth.— "Me married to him!" resumed our friend, replying to some imaginary speech,—"oh, no, I took warning by my sister!— I will have no more bloody marriages: you see I have no ring," wildly displaying her hands, "except a black one; a *black* one indeed, if you knew all—but I need not tell *you* that—have I, my Lord?—look up—here is my love—he himself shall tell you." She caught the hand terror had caused Elizabeth to extend, but faintly shrieking, drew back her own, and surveyed it with inexpressible horror. "Oh, you have dipt mine in blood!" exclaimed she, "a mother's blood! I am all contaminated—it runs cold to my very heart.— Ah, no,—it is—it is the blood of Essex; and have you murdered him at last, in spite of your dotage, and your promises? murdered the most noble of mankind! and all because he could not love you. Fye on your wrinkles!—can one love age and ugliness?—[52] Oh, how those artificial locks, and all your paintings sickened him!— How have we laughed at such preposterous folly!— But I have done

with laughing now—we will talk of graves, and shrouds, and church-yards—
Methinks I fain would know where my poor sister lies buried—you will say in
my heart perhaps—it has indeed entombed all I love; yet there must be some
little unknown corner in this world, one might call her grave, if one could but
tell where to find it: there she rests at last with her Leicester—he was your
favorite too—a bloody, bloody, distinction."— The Queen, who had with
difficulty preserved her senses till this cutting period, now sunk back in a deep
swoon.

The distress of my situation cannot be expressed.— Fearful lest any
attempt to summon a single being should irritate the injured Ellinor to execute any dire revenge; for which I knew not how she was prepared, had not
Elizabeth at this juncture lost her senses, I really think mine would have failed
me. I recollected that the Queen by every testimony was convinced that the
unhappy object thus fearfully brought before her, died in the country long
since; nor was it wise or safe, for those who had imposed on her, now to
acknowledge the deception. "So—so—so," cried Ellinor, with a start, "would
one have thought it possible to break that hard heart, after all? and yet I have
done it—She is gone to—no, not gone to Essex."— "Let us retire, my sweet
Ellen," said I, eager to get her out of the room, lest the Queen should suffer
for want of assistance.— "Hush," cried she, with increasing wildness, "they
will say we have beheaded her also.— But who are you?" fixing her hollow
eyes wistfully on me, "I have seen you somewhere ere now, but I forget all
faces in gazing on his pale one.— I know not where I am, nor where you
would have me go," added she, softly sighing, "but you look like an angel of
light, and may be, you will carry me with you to Heaven." I seized the blessed
minute of compliance, and drawing her mourning hood over her face, led her
to the little court, where my servants waited my dismission; when committing her to their charge, I returned to wake the ladies in the antichamber,
through whose inadvertent slumbers alone, Ellinor had been enabled to pass
to the closet of the Queen; a circumstance which combined with a variety of
others to give this strange visitation the appearance of being supernatural.

Every common means were tried in vain to recover the Queen, and the
applications of the faculty[53] alone could recall her senses; but the terror she
had endured has shook them for ever. Shuddering with apprehensions for
which only I can account, she often holds incomprehensible conferences; complains of an ideal[54] visitor; commands every door to be shut; yet still fancies
she sees her, and orders her to be kept out in vain. The supposed disregard of
those in waiting incenses a temper so many causes concur to render peevish,
and her unmerited anger produces the very disregard she complains of. Rage

and fear unite thus to harrass her feeble age, and accelerate the decay of nature. When these acute sensations subside, grief and despair take possession of her whole soul;—nor does she suffer less from the sense of her decaying power. Unwilling to resign a good she is unable to enjoy, she thinks every hand that approaches, is eager to snatch a sceptre, she will not even in dying bequeath.[55] Oh, sweet Matilda! if yet indeed thou survivest to witness this divine vengeance, thy gentle tears would embalm even thy most mortal enemy! thou couldst not without pity behold the imperial Elizabeth, lost to the common comforts of light, air, nourishment, and pleasure; that mighty mind which will be the object of future, as it has been of past, wonder, presenting now but a breathing memento of the frailty of humanity.—[56] Ah, that around her were assembled all those aspiring souls whose wishes centre in dominion; were they once to behold this distinguished victim of ungoverned passion, able to rule every being but herself, how would they feel the potent example! Ah, that to them were added the many who scorning social love, confine to self the blessed affections which alone can sweeten the tears we all are born to shed!— Gathering round the weary couch where the emaciated Queen withers in royal solitude, they might at once learn urbanity, and correct in time errors, which, when indulged, but too severely punish themselves.[57]

*   *   *   *   *   *

Absorbed and blended in the busy and woeful scenes this heart-breaking history presented to my mind—an anxious partaker in each succeeding calamity—I seemed to live over again the melancholy years we had been separated, in the person of my sister.— My own misfortunes—my darling daughter, the whole world vanished from before my eyes—deep-fixed on objects no longer existing, or existing but to double my affliction: remained almost the statue of despair; every sense seeming rivetted on the manuscript I held; and buried in so profound a reverie, that Lady Arundel judged it prudence to interrupt it. The consolatory reflections her friendship dictated, died on my ear, but reached not a heart which deeply pursued the sad chain of ideas thus presented to it.— Starting as from a frightful sleep, I, at last, sunk on my knees, and raising my eyes, with the manuscript, at once toward Heaven— "Oh, mighty Author of universal being!" sighed I, "thou who hast lent me fortitude to struggle with almost unequalled trials, support my exhausted soul against this last—this greatest.— Let not the killing idea that it is a *human* infliction, trouble the pure springs of piety, whence alone the weary spirit can draw consolation.— Rather strengthen me with the holy belief that it is thy visitation for some wise end ordained; so shall my enemies sleep in their graves uncursed, and my heart remain in this agitated bosom unbroken. Alas, who knows but by thy divine appointment, I may be at last permitted to recall the scattered senses of this dear unfortunate? to soothe that deeply-wounded, that embittered spirit! Ah, Ellen!— Ah, my sister!" groaned I, deluged at last with salutary tears,—"changed—lost—annihilated as thou art, my unaltered affection must ever desire thee.— I need not enquire whether she is here—your sympathizing, generous tears, dear Lady Arundel, inform me that the same roof shelters the twin heirs of misfortune."

Although Lady Arundel acknowledged that my sister was under her protection, fain would she have persuaded me to delay a meeting so touching, till more able to support it; but, deaf to the voice of reason, nature, powerful nature asserted her rights, and my soul obeyed her impassioned impulse. The deep, the eternal impression of this agonizing meeting, recurs even now with all its first force. I had shuddered at the murder of my mother—I had groaned on the coffin of my husband—I had wept a thousand times over the helpless infant who trembled at my bosom—but all these terrible sensations were combined when my sad eyes rested on those still so dear to me.— When I saw all their playful lustre quenched, and set in insensibility—when I felt that heart, once the seat of every feminine grace and virtue, throb wild and unconscious against one which I thought every moment would escape from its narrow boundary.— But let me quit a scene too trying for recollection—too touching for description. Oh, Ellinor—my sister!

PART VI

Time, which inures us to every kind of suffering, at length strengthened my mind against the heavy sadness impressed on it by the fate of this dear unconscious sufferer. It was with true gratitude and concern I learnt Heaven had called to itself the amiable and accomplished sister of Lady Arundel, who caught a cold during her attendance on the sick Queen, which ended in a consumption, and carried her off a few months after Elizabeth. Actuated to the last by the sublimest sympathy and friendship, Lady Pembroke had added, to the moiety of the surveyor's treasure (which she had caused to be dug for in the spot specified) a sufficient sum to secure the dear unfortunate every comfort her forlorn state admitted; placing with her Alithea, the favorite maid she had so tenderly commemorated, and committing both to the charge of Lady Arundel; who with equal generosity received so anxious a trust.[1] A virtue thus consummate sanctifies itself, and can receive neither glory or grace from the gratitude of humanity; yet surely the incense of the heart arises even to heaven! accept it then, oh, gentlest of the Sidneys, although insphered there!

The strange and unaccountable difference in my sister's opinion and my own, respecting Lord Leicester, supplied me a source of endless meditation: yet, as this difference became obvious only from the time we arrived in London, I could not help imputing her blindness to the same cause she assigned for mine.— Certainly she imbibed the unreasonable prejudices of Lord Essex; whose ambition (however fatally expiated) always inclined him to dislike a Nobleman born to supersede him. I saw but too plainly from the irritation and vehemence to which her temper from that period became subject, how much a woman insensibly adopts of the disposition of him to whom she gives her heart. I had not however looked on her choice with the contemptuous asperity with which she regarded mine.— Lord Essex, I will frankly own, ere yet he rose into favor, was gifted like herself with every captivating advantage of nature.— The fire and ingenuousness which afterwards marked his character, then lived only in his eyes: and the cultivated understanding he possessed, pointed every glance with elegance and expression. One must have loved Lord Leicester to see Essex with indifference—one must have loved him to the excess I did perhaps, not to remark the attachment my sister avowed.— Innumerable instances of it now flashed on my memory, I was astonished could at the moment escape me. If *she* was indeed more clear sighted than myself— But why do I enter on so vain a discussion?— Alas, dear Ellinor! beloved Leicester! I have no right but to lament ye.

I had likewise gathered another painful doubt from the story of my sister. England had gained a King in the son of Mary Stuart, but her unfortunate daughters must not hope to acquire a brother. From the moment I had been informed that mine had acceded to the throne, the tender mother's heart had fluttered with the idea of presenting to him the lovely girl so nearly allied to his blood. Although regardless of distinction in my own person, I could not turn my eyes on the fair daughter of Lord Leicester without coveting for her every human advantage.— Unwilling to be swayed by prejudice, I separately consulted with the few friends fortune had left me; who all concurred in giving me an impression of the King, degrading, if not contemptible. They represented him as national,[2] vain, pedantic, credulous, and partial: wanting generosity to bestow a royal funeral on the body of the martyred saint, his unhappy mother; yet daily impoverished to meanness by favorites and parasites. Enslaved by the imperious spirit of a Queen he neither loved nor valued; and only endeared to the people he governed through the fickleness of their natures, which are always gratified by change. As those who spoke thus could have no possible interest in vilifying or depreciating him, I could not but give some credit to their account; and made it my first concern to see the King; anxious to read in his countenance a confutation of every charge. How unaccountably was I disappointed when my senses took part with his enemies!— I beheld with astonishment, in the person of James, youth without freshness, royalty without grandeur, height without majesty—an air of slyness and a secret servility characterized features, which, though devoid of the graces of either distinguished parent, wanted not regularity; and a stooping slouch gait gave an invincible awkwardness to a figure nature had endued with symmetry.[3] Offended and repelled, my heart sunk again into its own little mansion, nor claimed the least alliance with his.— I determined to watch at leisure his real character and conduct, nor ventured to confide to his care the single treasure Heaven had permitted me to retain, of all it once bestowed. Resolved to educate my daughter suitably to the fortune she was born to, I thought it wise to bury in my own bosom, at least for a time, the secret of her right to it; and the eccentric turn of mind every succeeding day rendered more obvious in the King made me continually applaud the moderation and foresight which had guarded me on this interesting occasion.

I, however, judged it necessary to assume a title no human being envied, or offered to dispute with me; and to support it properly without encroaching on my daughter's valuable acquisition, I found I must resolve to re-visit Kenilworth Castle, now the property of another family.— In the building were contained cabinets so secure and unknown, that Lord Leicester always deposited there, ere he journeyed to London, such papers, jewels, and other valuables, as he thought it unsafe to take with him. On the memorable night when last we quitted that pleasant dwelling, I had assisted him to place in the most curious of these reservoirs several caskets, for which he seemed more than commonly anxious; and I added to their number, that containing Mrs. Marlow's papers, and the testimonials of my birth. As if actuated by some sad pre-sentiment that he should never more re-visit this spot, my Lord took great pains to familiarize me to the management of the springs, and gave into my hands duplicates of the keys. By a singular chance, amidst all the transitions of my fate these keys remained, and seemed continually to remind me, how important to my daughter's welfare it might one day be to recover the caskets.— Such a motive alone could conquer the reluctance I felt again to behold a spot sacred to the memory of a husband so beloved. You will call this perhaps, a childish weakness, after all I had borne; but alas, the mind feebler and feebler from every conflict, sometimes sinks under a trifle, after repelling the more powerful attacks of ill-fortune with magnanimity.

Lady Arundel, with her usual kindness, proposed accompanying me; and we sorrowfully measured once more those miles which so strongly revived in my mind the most interesting remembrances. At Coventry we rested to enquire into the character of the present owner of Kenilworth Castle. We were told that this magnificent mansion, which I had left fit for the reception of a Sovereign, had long been in the hands of a miser, whose avarice had induced him to strip it of its princely ornaments; not less from the desire of converting those into money, than to deprive it of every charm that might tempt the enquiring traveller to knock at the inhospitable gate. Yet, even when this ruin was effected, the structure itself was so complete a piece of architecture as to attract a number of unwelcome visitors; to exclude whom, he had now let it to some manufacturers, and resided himself in a remote apartment. The chagrin this extraordinary revolution could not but occasion in my mind, was increased when I recollected how hard it would be, perhaps, to gain admission; and even when that was obtained, we knew not whether the only room I wished to lodge in was now habitable. Lady Arundel, with her usual foresight, advised me to seem to have no other motive for this visit, than a desire to re-purchase the Castle; and when shewn through it, to appear to be struck with so severe an indisposition, as soon as I reached the chamber which contained the cabinets, as should render it impossible to remove me; leaving it to her to reconcile the owner to so troublesome an intruder, by the most lavish generosity. A finesse of this kind alone could ascertain me any success, and the sickliness of my aspect, I was sure, would sufficiently corroborate such an assertion.

We set out immediately, that by arriving in the evening we might have a pretence for passing the night there.— My soul turned from the well-known scene, and sickened alike at sight of the reviving verdure, and the splendid mansion, to me alas, only a gay mausoleum. Humbly I solicited entrance at a gate which once flew open whenever I appeared; but, ah, though the exterior was the same, how strange seemed the alteration within!— No more did the liveried train of assiduous domestics assemble to the distant winding of the huntsman's horn.— No longer did I rest in gilded galleries, whose pictured sides delighted one sense, while their coolness refreshed another. No longer could I, even in idea, behold the beloved, the noble owner, whose gracious mien endeared the welcome it conveyed—a change which jarred every feeling had taken place. A numerous body of diligent mechanics were plodding in those halls in which Elizabeth had feasted, and their battered sides hardly now informed us where the rich tapestry used to hang. My ears were suddenly stunned with the noise of a hundred looms;[4] and the distant lake once covered with gay pageants, and resounding only to the voice of pleasure, presented us another scene of industry not less busy, strange, and surprizing. By incidents of this kind, one becomes painfully and instantaneously sensible of advancing into life. When first we find ourselves sailing with the imperceptible current of time, engrossed either by the danger of our situation, or enchanted with its prospects, we glide swiftly on, scarce sensible of our progress, till the stream revisits some favorite spot: alas, so visible is the desolation of the shortest interval, that we grow old in a moment, and submit once more to the tide, willing rather to share the ruin than review it.

Among the few servants retained by the meagre master of this desolated mansion, one appeared who immediately recalled himself to my mind by the name of Gabriel. I recollected his having been warden of the outer lodges. The title by which I was announced—the weed I still continued to wear, overcame a wretch already bowed to the earth by age, infirmity, and penury: and when to these circumstances was superadded the remembrance of the plentiful and peaceful days he had known under a Lord ever munificent to his domestics, gratitude became agony, and the poor old man sunk in a fit at my feet. An incident like this might well have affected an indifferent spectator.— I was scarce more sensible than himself: and the alarm soon spread through the laborious mechanics, till it was conveyed to Sir Humphry Moreton.[5]— Timorously he emerged from his apartment, and, as the humble croud made way for him, he measured me afar off with his eye, and seemed lost in conjecture on the subject of my visit.— My purse was yet in my hand, and part of its contents in those of some persons who had lent a ready assistance. Whether this, or the wan delicacy of my looks interested him, I know not; but every care-furrowed feature gradually relaxed as he approached me, striving in vain to soften into the smile of benevolence. I rose to return his courteous salutation, and informed him, that when last I past the walls of this Castle, I was its mistress, the dear and happy wife of Lord Leicester; but perceiving uncertain apprehensions of some remote claim began again to contract his brow, I added that sensible I had lost every right in a spot yet dear to me, I came to enquire whether he was disposed to part with it, and to rescue from poverty such worthy servants of its late noble owner as had alike outlived their labour, and him who should have recompensed it. What heart is insensible to that virtue in which we alone can resemble our Maker?— Benevolence, like religion, awes even those it cannot win. The miser loudly applauded my liberality: and by a greater effort on his part, allowing for the difference of our characters, invited me to spend the night in the Castle. The chamber I had been accustomed to inhabit he called his best, and thither was I conducted; I was not unprovided with the means of ensuring my own welcome, and my servants having spread the cold viands we brought, Sir Humphry's spirits grew light over luxuries he was not to pay for. A temptation so agreeable prolonged his stay, and I at length discovered the only way to shorten his visit, would be to compliment him with all that remained: seeing my servants, in compliance with the hint, were about to convey it out of the room, fear lest any should be lost by the way, prevailed over the hilarity of the moment, and he departed with the wine.

With an impatient beating heart I raised the tapestry, which providentially had been preserved in this room, less from its beauty than antiquity; as it was so worn that it had long been pannelled in many places.— Behind the bed we discovered the secret spring of the cabinet, which I opened without any difficulty; and with the assistance of Lady Arundel took down the well-remembered caskets, pausing at intervals, to weep over all the tender ideas the sight of them recalled so forcibly to my memory; then raising my eyes toward Heaven, while devoutly thanking the God who thus prospered my remaining wishes, I almost fancied I beheld the beatified spirit of him who concealed these treasures.

Lady Arundel would not rest without inspecting their contents. The largest was filled with family papers, bonds, contracts, mortgages, many of which were to me unintelligible, and all useless. The next contained letters and little ornaments, less precious from their intrinsic value, than their analogy to particular events—under these was a gilt casket filled with jewels of great value, and what was of infinitely more, the authenticated bonds and acknowledgments of all the sums Lord Leicester had informed me he had providantly deposited in other countries; and of which I knew not any memorandum remained. This was so noble an addition to the bequest which already enriched my sweet Mary, that it seemed to me, as if her father even from the grave delighted to endow her: while the Almighty, gracious even when we think him most severe, had thus secreted, for her advantage, treasures it would have been impossible for me to have preserved through so many desperate vicissitudes.

The next casket was a gift from the fond mother to the darling of her heart: it contained all the testimonials of the Queen of Scots, and other parties concerned, on the subject of my birth, with the contract of marriage between Lord Leicester and myself. I felt rich in these recovered rights: and though prudence might never permit me to claim alliance with King James, yet to bequeath to my daughter the power of doing so, at whatever period it should appear advantageous, was a great consolation to me.

Lady Arundel and I past part of the night in packing these valuables in empty trunks brought for that purpose; then, closing the secret cabinet, and leaving no traces of our search for it, we retired to rest. We departed early the next morning, carrying with us that ancient domestic of Lord Leicester, on whom memory had so powerfully operated, and two others, who, long since expelled from the Castle, sought a miserable subsistence in the hamlets around it. It joyed my very heart to supply to these poor wretches a loss irremediable with respect to myself, and the profound attachment of their few remaining days amply rewarded me.

Through the intervention of the friends I yet possessed, some eminent merchants in London undertook to get the bonds, notes, &c. duly acknowledged: and, in process of time, such considerable sums were of consequence recovered, as ascertained to myself and child our accustomed affluence. Years and misfortune had only cemented the ancient friendship between me and Lady Arundel.— I added my income and family to hers.— Her house was fortunately so near London as to allow me the advantage of procuring the first instructors for my daughter; and the infirm state of Lady Arundel's health, rendering her as much a prisoner from necessity, as I was from choice, both insensibly found, in the improvement of my daughter, a mild and growing satisfaction, which more than made amends for the world we shut out.

Ah! could I desire a greater pleasure? Pardon, madam, the fond extravagance of maternal love, and allow me to present to you the darling of my heart in her sixteenth year. Already something taller than myself, to a form that united the strictest symmetry with the wild and variable graces of glowing youth, my Mary added the perfect features of her father, exquisitely feminized by a complexion transparently fair, and a bloom alike delicate and vivid; her hair, of the golden brown I have described as peculiar to his, fell below her waist in a profusion of artless ringlets, heightening her beauty even to luxuriance.— If she had borrowed any thing from me, it was the collected modesty of her mien; and from my sister she had stolen that penetrating, fascinating smile, those two alone of all I ever saw were gifted with:—alas, it was now wholly her own.— Although lightness and elasticity characterized her figure, every limb was rounded even to polishing, and never did I contemplate the soft turn of her white arms when raised to touch the lute, without thinking those more perfect than even her face.— Her voice was no less sweet in speaking than singing; with this difference—that in the first she softened the soul to pleasure, in the last, elevated it to rapture.— Her understanding was strong and penetrating, yet elevated and refined.— Her sensibility (the first formed of all her feelings) was rather deep than ardent. Maternal experience had moderated the enthusiasm incident to youth, nor was it obvious in any instance but the love of knowledge. Incessant, unremitting, in her studies, books were her only extravagance, and musick her only relaxation. To compensate for the worldly pleasures I judged it prudence to deprive her of, I was lavish in indulgencies to which her taste naturally led: I kept musicians on purpose to accompany her, and found, in the years filled up by herself and her employments, that sweet though saddened pleasure parents only know, and which, perhaps, more than makes us amends for all the more lively ones it recals to our memory. In effect, the more lovely she grew, the more necessary I found it to hide her; and, offering her daily up to God, I left her wholly to his disposal; determined neither my pride, vanity, or ambition, should interfere with the happiness I supplicated for her.

On perusing this description, I perceive at once the impossibility of your crediting it; yet, far from accusing myself of partiality, I could call on all who ever beheld my daughter to attest my candor.— How readily would Lady Arundel have done so—entendered to her by a love only inferior to my own, that faithful friend found in declining life a new tye wound round her heart, for which she daily thanked me.

As nothing robs us of the confidence of youth like the appearance of mystery, when time called reflection to being in her tender mind, I slowly and by degrees confided to my daughter the painful events you have thus obliged me to commemorate. This indulgence secured to me her whole heart, and I trembled only lest her deep sense of past misfortunes should affect her health; for sensibility was the leading feature in her character. Far, however, from seeking to expound the future in her own favor, the flattering prospects her distinguished birth, and yet more distinguished endowments, might well spread before her, passed away like a shadow, and she saw only her mother. A thousand times has she bedewed my hand with a reverence the most endearing: and the tears with which she often embalmed the memory of her father, almost recompensed me for his loss. From that period her expressive eyes were fixed ever on mine with such blended sadness and admiration, as proved she thought me almost sainted by misfortune. More studious henceforward of my pleasure, more submissive to my will, more solicitous for my repose, it seemed as if, in learning she was my only remaining tye on earth, she conceived that the various affections and duties of all I had lost devolved to, and centred in, herself. But sympathy was the genuine impulse of her nature; for with equal care she watched over her unhappy aunt.— Whenever that dear creature's incurable malady assumed the appearance of melancholy, she was extravagantly fond of musick.— At those intervals my lovely Mary would lean over her lute with the meek benignity of a descending angel, and extract from it such solemn sounds as breathed at once of peace and sorrow: insensibly soothing the perturbed spirit, and melting only those yet undisturbed. That subtle essence of our natures, sensibility, which madness can only unfix, not annihilate, often paused unconsciously upon the pleasure, and softly sunk into repose.

A child thus eminently amiable at once concentred my affections—commanded my esteem—possessed my whole confidence—actuated, in short, my very being.— Ah, how noble, how affecting is the friendship grounded on the maternal and filial tye; when, unconscious of any weakness in her own heart, the mother dares present it as a pure and unflattering mirror to her child, and, with that self-applause which even Heaven approves, contemplates the upright, the innocent soul it reflects! Sacred and indelible becomes that precept which is expressed but by example.— Happy are those enabled to form such an attachment as inexperience strengthens on one hand, and knowledge on the other:—Neither the gusts of youthful passion, nor the nipping frosts of age, can destroy a plant rooted thus by mutual virtue;—it only gains vigor from time, and, by the peculiar indulgence of the Almighty, our sublimest merit ripens into our most perfect pleasure.

Satisfied that I had already acquired such an influence in my daughter's mind as should enable me to regulate her principles, I left it to time and circumstances to call them into action.— The great business of my life now seemed over; and, delivering my heart up to the flattering presages of maternal love, a thousand visions of almost forgotten grandeur and happiness floated before my eyes, and sometimes half-deluded them.

The fluctuating complaints of Lady Arundel at length settled into a consumption;—It was an hereditary disorder of the Sidneys; nor perhaps could the solicitude of myself and my sweet Mary have availed aught toward her restoration, even if a cruel shock, in which we were all equal sufferers, had not precipitated her fate.

Among the unconscious caprices which by turns actuated my unfortunate sister, was a passion for sitting in the open air.— Neither times or seasons had any influence over her; and she would insist on it alike in the snow of December, and the scorching sun of July.— To this self-will I had no doubt greatly contributed. From the moment of my return to England, I had vehemently opposed the severe controul to which she had heretofore been subject, and habituated her attendants to yield to her in every instance which did not absolutely endanger her safety: fully determined not to render an existence wholly wretched no human being could now make happy. But as uninformed minds never know a medium, the people appointed to watch her gradually suffered her to become sensible of her power, which soon grew into an unbounded indulgence. It was now the depth of winter, and she had sat in the keen air for hours, watching the snow, which fell in abundance.— The most violent shiverings ensued, followed by a fever which settled at last on the nerves, and brought her to the very verge of the grave.— Nevertheless, it appeared to have salutary effects—her spirits were sunk indeed to extreme lowness, but they became more equal; and traces of reason were often discernable in her actions. If she did not remember, she yet strove to know me; and sometimes studied my features in a manner the most touching.— I considered this as the very crisis of her fate—her only chance on this side Heaven, and scarce dared leave her for a single moment. I entrusted the care of Lady Arundel (whose situation, though more dangerous, was not so melancholy) to my daughter, fearful lest her youthful spirits should be injured by constantly beholding an object so affecting. But I had forgot that my own shattered constitution was not equal to the fatigue and anxiety of watching over my sister. I fell one evening into a succession of fainting fits; the servants conveyed me to bed; and the fear of alarming Lady Arundel hindered them from informing my daughter of my situation. My faintings at length gave place to a drowsiness, so intense that I might call it a stupor.— I remained thus for some hours, when I started with an indistinct idea of a heavy fall, and a deep groan. Terror roused, and collected in a moment, every dormant faculty.— I rushed through the chamber which divided mine from my sister's, but I blamed myself for impetuosity when I perceived that all was profoundly silent in hers. The two nurses were in a deep sleep, and the expiring watchlights heavily winked, and revived, before the cold dawn of the morning. I gently opened the curtains of her bed—Ah, gracious Heaven, what did I feel when I beheld it empty!— The agonized shriek I gave, rouzed both her careless attendants, who, impressed with but one idea, flew towards a door I now first perceived to be open: it led to a gallery ornamented with such portraits of our family as had survived the wreck of their fortunes; among them was incautiously placed that (already fatally commemorated) of the Earl of Essex at the storming of Cadiz, an unfortunate legacy bequeathed to my sister by Lady Pembroke.— My soul took in at a thought all the fearful consequences.— I tottered into the gallery—alas only to behold my worst apprehension verified.— The fair spectre, which once was Ellinor, lay prostrate before the picture—one hand had convulsively gathered her disordered garments over her thin chest; the other was still expressively extended towards the inanimate image of him so beloved—Impatiently I laid my hand upon her heart—it answered not the trembling enquirer—its wandering essence was exhaled, and she had ceased forever to suffer. Thy parting prayer, oh Essex! was surely prophetic, for her soul, in recovering memory, had burst its mortal bound, and soared to Heaven.

Scarce were the dear remains quietly interred, ere those of the amiable Lady Arundel followed them. I bore these losses with devout resignation— The tears which fall when Heaven recals the unfortunate still the wild passions of the sad survivor, and deeply wound only the soul yet new to suffering. It was with a quickened apprehension that I perceived the effect of these first afflictions on the tender spirits of my daughter: not that I sought totally to stifle the lively impressions of natural affection;—the tears of youth, like the genial showers of May, serve only to save the planter's toil, and simply ripen the rich fruits of the mind; but when either fall too often, they impoverish the soil, and wash away the buds yet blowing.

My own soul afforded no variety of cheerful images with which I could hope to invigorate the gentle spirits of my Mary; unwilling to form new connections, I rather thought it prudent to change my abode, and by a variety of scenes insensibly amuse her; and my steward was sent accordingly to seek another mansion. I called back the moment when the gloomy aisles of a ruined convent, by possessing the simple advantage of novelty, diverted my mind even at the sorrowful crisis which robbed me of a foster mother. Alas, in yet untried youth, the prospect that is unknown ever adds to its own charms those of imagination; while in maturer life, the heart lingers on all which once delighted it, hopeless of finding in the future, a pleasure fancy can ever compare with those it reviews in the past. To my daughter, however, the whole world was yet new, and, in fixing on a scene habitual to my feelings, I could not fail to delight hers. I hired a mansion near the Thames' side, in Richmond, to which we removed early in the spring.

Perhaps, in this choice, I was influenced, almost without knowing it, by a latent motive: distinct as I had lived from the world since my return to England, the fame of the Prince of Wales[6] had yet reached me.— This accomplished youth had at once rose above the weaknesses of his father, and the prejudices of his rank; devoting his heart to the virtues, his mind to the sciences, and his person to those manly and becoming exercises which, invigorating every human power, prepared him alike for the enjoyment of peace, or the pursuit of war.[7] Delighted to understand a Stuart was rising to redeem the glory of his declining race, I passionately longed to see, know, and be valued by the royal Henry. The King, unworthy a son so distinguished, took no pleasure in his company; but, even in tender youth, resigned him to a court of his own, from the adulation of which merit superior to praise alone could have guarded him.[8] Henry had, like myself, a partiality for the beautiful village of Richmond; he always passed part of the summer in a palace near the Thames; and I took pleasure in thinking a partition of wood alone separated his gardens from mine. With a judgment unequalled at his years, the Prince knew how to be affable without abating aught of his dignity; and, while in the circle of his own court he preserved the authority of a sovereign, to the unfortunate who addressed him, he had the benignity of a brother: such was his character in Richmond, where the people almost adored him, and took pleasure in amplifying on the superior qualities he so eminently possessed. The sweet hopes his merit sometimes infused into my bosom, came accompanied with an equal number of fears, yet could not my heart forbear to cherish them.

The revolving season tinged this sweet retreat with every variety of verdure; the waves of the Thames were more translucent than ever; all nature awakened once more to perfection, when the Prince of Wales took up his abode in the adjacent palace.— This news heightened the soft red of my daughter's cheek, and even faintly coloured my wan one.— Not daring to express to her the eager desire I felt to see the Prince, and not accustomed to venture out without her, day after day elapsed in anxious expectation. My gentle Mary, with a delicacy from which I drew the most happy presages, now always chose to go abroad either so early or so late that it was almost impossible we should ever meet the Prince, and the veil she usually wore was closed with so much care as to ensure her the happiness of being overlooked, even if fortune threw him in our way.

Nevertheless, I took notice that the arrival of the Royal Henry strangely filled up the void in our lives.— What he would do, or what he would not do, constantly regulated our motions, and employed my daughter's thoughts even more than my own. His taste afforded us a variety of indulgences of which he knew not we were partakers.— Sometimes moon-light concerts, or magnificent fireworks; at others, parties on the Thames; where the Prince still took pleasure in beholding a variety of little vessels, built and ornamented for the amusement of his early years, and which were manned by children.— They were often so near, we fancied we heard the voice of Henry, when both mother and daughter would give way to the same impulse, and hastily retire.[9] The summer might have elapsed in this manner, had not chance been more favorable to our wishes, than we could resolve to be.

We were returning home one morning in an ill-contrived carriage, newly invented for airings,[10] the inconvenience of which I bore patiently, from not being able to walk or ride on horseback for any length of time since my memorable fever.— The servant who drove stopt as usual at the brow of the inchanting hill,[11] that we might enjoy for a few minutes its beauties, when the sound of horns approaching near informed us the Prince of Wales was returning from hunting, which at once startled the horses and ourselves. My Mary, actuated only by the impression of the moment, made an eager sign to the man to drive on; and the horses, already frightened, yielded impetuously to the slightest touch of the rein, flying forward with the most dangerous rapidity. The clumsiness of the carriage, and the badness of the road, threatened us every moment with being overturned—for me there was no escape, but could my daughter be prevailed on to leap out, I was sensible she would be safe. Far from obeying my intreaties, or even commands, she threw her arms around me, and protested it was for me alone she feared. The carriage sunk into a deep rut[12] at last, and we were thrown out at a small distance, with a violence that almost deprived me of my senses:—my darling Mary had wholly lost hers.— I perceived the train of Henry approaching, but the favorite wish of seeing him was forgotten in that of recovering her.— I was presently environed by the hunters without regarding them, till their extreme solicitude obliged me to raise my eyes from the lifeless face of my daughter in acknowledgment. I perceived with a surprize even that moment could not conquer, that on either hand stood a young man, adorned with the order of the garter, and so distinguishingly handsome, that I knew not which was the Prince of Wales, but turned from the one to the other with an air of wildness and stupor.— My looks, however, made little impression on the strangers, their whole attention being fixed on the inanimate form of my daughter.— In truth, fortune had contrived to shew her to the utmost advantage. I had thrown up her veil to give her air, and bared her beautiful hands and arms, polished and white as Parian marble; the wild rings of her auburn hair played on her youthful face, as the yellow leaves of Autumn curl over a latter peach; whilst every feature, formed with a truth which might bear the nicest examination, perhaps only appeared more exquisitely regular from the absence of expression; and even her figure and attitude (leaning on her mother's knees) presented a perfect model for a sculptor. The assiduities of the strangers, together with my own, at length recalled her scattered senses.— She opened those eyes so dear to me, and fixing them on the two strangers, a rosy suffusion alone proved she saw them, with such quickness did she turn toward her mother; when, beholding me to appearance unhurt, she lifted her soul to Heaven in a look of gratitude, and throwing her arms round my neck, relieved her overcharged heart by weeping on my bosom. "An angel in soul as well as form!" exclaimed one of the strangers; "assure me, madam," continued he, "that this terror is the only ill consequence of my sudden approach, or I know not how I shall forgive it to myself." This address ascertaining the Prince of Wales, he became the sole object of my attention.— Ah, where shall I find words to endear to you, Madam, the royal youth my heart at once opened to adopt? Henry was yet but in the dawn of manhood, nevertheless his height was majestic, and his figure finished. The beauty of his features was their least charm—virtue herself seemed to sublime every happy lineament, and spare beholders the trouble of developing his character by conveying it in a glance. His manly voice united the firmness of his own sex with the sensibility of ours. A confusion of sad remembrances were at once presented with him to my mind; and the admiration he excited was strangely blended with regret.— I forgot that he had addressed me, and continued to contemplate him in silence; ever and anon turning my streaming eyes wildly from him to Heaven, even then, my dilating heart bids me add, scarce changing the object. The amiable Henry, in whose nature sympathy was the prevailing sentiment, touched with a conduct so mysterious, almost forgot my daughter in turn, so wholly was he engrossed by me.— Informed of my unfortunate lameness by my attempting to rise, he immediately concluded it to be the consequence of the recent accident, and scarce was satisfied by my assurances of the contrary. Oh! as my eyes surveyed the superior soul, living irradiated in the bright orbs of his, how did they stream at remembering that, had his father been born to half his virtues, I might now have been cherished by affection—dignified by rank—unwidowed—unbroken—a stranger yet to sorrow!— My mother too—most unhappy of parents as well as sovereigns! I had a tear for thee at this interesting moment.

The respect due to strangers induced the Prince to conceal the curiosity my conduct could not fail to excite, but having informed himself from the attendants of my title, he addressed me by it, and insisted on conducting me home. I now understood the nobleman who had divided my first looks with the Prince to be the Viscount Rochester: that contemptible favorite of the king, celebrated only for his beauty.—[13] The visible coldness of my air checked a forward insolence I observed in him, and obliged him to quit us on our arriving at home.

With what secret transport did my soul welcome a Stuart worthy that name, glorious for so many ages!— The Prince seemed delighted with his new acquaintances.— The soft reserve of my daughter's air—the deepening roses of her cheek, and the low accent of her harmonious voice, when politeness obliged her to answer the Prince, whose animated eyes reduced hers often to seek the ground, presented to my elated heart every symptom of that passion which alone endears the sufferings it occasions. A flow of happy spirits new to my daughter, almost forgotten by myself, gave chearfulness to the hour which Henry saw elapse with regret.

On this chance introduction was grounded an acquaintance a few days ripened into intimacy.— Led to distinguish the Prince alike by his own merit, and the ties of blood, which secretly allied me to him, it was with the tenderest satisfaction I beheld him cherish the inclination he had already conceived for my daughter: yet the dignity of his mind forbidding him to form an engagement he knew not how to fulfill, it was through me alone he addressed himself to her. Convinced it was in my power to prove her entitled even to such a lover, I suffered fate to take its course, attending only to prudence.

Conscious that Henry had hitherto moved in a very confined circle, I was aware that to extend it must draw much observation on those he favored. To guard therefore against the malice of surmise, I fixed on the hour of the Prince's visit for my daughter to ride out; and always received him alone. His attendants, who saw her regularly depart, were at a loss to imagine what could attach their royal master to the infirm widow of Lord Leicester. The charm was in truth simply affection.— The amiable Henry had early been accustomed to every kind of homage but that of the heart, and had too much sensibility not to feel the want he knew not how to supply. Deeply susceptible of the true regard I had conceived for him, impressed at once by my mind, my manners, and my mien, with the idea of mystery, and the desire of obtaining my confidence, it was only by his own candour he sought to gain upon mine. Slowly and by degrees he deigned to repose with me those regrets and anxieties from which the utmost indulgence of nature and fortune cannot exempt a single individual. He often lamented the dangerous distinction of being the first-born of his father's children, since it cost him every other.— Separated almost in infancy from his parents—surrounded with mercenary sycophants, who sought to make their court to the reigning King by a partial representation or misconstruction of his actions, he had shot up unloved, uncherished, and seen those tender affections he was born to share, gradually centre in that son from whom his parents had nothing to fear.— Nor were there wanting insidious flatterers equally ready to undermine his filial duty, by pointing out the weaknesses of his father, even where they were most likely to wound him. He had punished himself, he added, for yielding to these impressions by an absolute obedience to his authority, but it was with grief he remembered that was now the only tye between them.— Nor would I wonder, he continued, it should be so, if I considered that, born as he was to imperial power, with an ardent passion for glory, he had hitherto been shut up in the narrow sphere of his own court, languishing away the flower of his youth without a choice, a friend, or a pursuit:—Till the infamous Carr should design to decide what foreign Prince's bribe he would condescend to accept, and to what bigoted Papist he should sacrifice the son of his master.[14]

While the admired Prince of Wales, the Idol of the People, the Heir of Empire, the endued of Heaven, thus confided to me the simple and rational griefs which clouded a fortune so brilliant, could I fail to meditate on the equality of providence?—Which graciously allots even to the lowest situation, some portion of happiness, and depresses the highest with the sad sense of misfortune.

It is the fatal peculiarity of youth to throw the strongest light on every secret grief, and waste away under an oppression imagination often doubles. To cure this propensity is therefore the province of experience. I sought to imbue the Prince's mind with the only principle mine had derived from all my sufferings.— That the noblest use we can make of understanding is to convert it into happiness; and that every talent which does not conduce to that great end, ought rather to be considered as a burthen than a blessing to the possessor.— That the mind, like the eye, ever magnifies the object of fear or aversion, which often, on a strict examination, excites no other sentiment than contempt.— In fine, that he was not at liberty to shew any other sense of his father's errors, than by presenting a faultless example in his own life;[15] and that, if he would have it without blemish, he must divert his taste from channels where it would meet with opposition, and turn it into those through which it might flow freely.— That the cultivation of the sciences would at once fill up that void in his life ever so painful at his years, and attach to his welfare all who loved them: a body whose influence was never known unless opposition called forth the powers of eloquence.

The Prince had too much judgment not to see the utility of this counsel, and too much generosity not to value its candour: nevertheless, it was a language yet new to him.— Ingenuity had been exhausted to teach him to govern others, but to subdue himself was a lesson none had ventured to inculcate. How did I lament that a soul so ductile had in childhood been injudiciously delivered up to its own guidance, and suffered every day to imbibe some new prejudice, destined perhaps to mark the character through life; and which an upright and skilful monitor might so easily have eradicated!

The Prince could not be insensible to the maternal caution which induced me to send my daughter abroad whenever he honored me with a visit, yet the observation did not for some time appear to influence his conduct.— Satisfied with merely beholding her as he entered or departed, the desire of opening his heart to me seemed to supersede every other impression. Nevertheless, long reveries would follow the most accidental meeting, and long pauses intervene in the most interesting conversation; rendering it sufficiently obvious, that his mind labored with some project, hitherto suppressed either by pride or prudence.

Perhaps I should ever have wanted courage to open my lips on so delicate an occasion, had not my daughter complained to me that she was now become the universal object of attention; and that the suite who attended her were often rudely surrounded, and sometimes interrogated by such of the Prince's court as had not benefited by his example.— By going abroad unexpectedly with her, I found that she was not offended without reason, and, sensible of my imprudence in thus risquing her safety, I came to the resolution rather to abridge myself of the pleasure of the Prince's society, than purchase it by endangering my daughter.— I desired her to retire for awhile when Henry should visit me next, and ere he could account for the singularity of finding her at home, entered into the delicate explanation. With an acknowledged attachment to him, that I bore my child alone could have over-ruled, I submitted it to himself, whether I could too cautiously guard against a censure or insult she had no natural protector to resent.— The generous Henry paused for a few moments with irresolution, when suddenly collecting courage he broke silence.— "Will Lady Leicester pardon," said he, "those obtrusive visits she has submitted to with so much complacency?— Will she deign to become the confidant of the only incident in my life I have hid from her—will she listen with indulgence?"— He paused a moment, but, ere I could resolve how to answer, pursued the discourse.— "Accustomed even from childhood to the ensnaring glances of the light and the lovely—led to imagine myself older than my years by the continual proposals for marrying me that have constantly succeeded each other, it is not wonderful that a heart naturally susceptible should mature before its time. Among the many beautiful girls, who have already sought to attract me, I soon distinguished one, by whom my peace, my honor, my innocence became endangered: perhaps they had been lost, had I not found her selfish and ambitious. I need hardly inform you that this seducing fair one is the Countess of Essex!—[16] Vain of her influence over me, she took pleasure in publishing it, and taught me early to blush for my choice; but I could not resolve to do so continually. I formed the bold resolution of contending with my own heart, and retired hither to recover it, or die. Lady Essex, enraged and humbled at this conduct, confirmed me in it, by attaching herself to Viscount Rochester: thus rendering it sufficiently obvious she had never loved me.— Besotted with her beauty, that weak favorite is governed by her caprices, and him I was born to obey yields to those of Rochester. Although I do not immediately perceive how Lady Essex means to effect her revenge, I am convinced it is only maturing; and daily expect a blow, from which I know not how to guard myself.[17] Under these circumstances how can I venture to involve your fate with mine?— How can I ask you to permit me to offer to your lovely daughter the heart which ever hovers near her?— Speak Madam—my happiness is in your hands—dare you risque your own to promote it?" While I listened to this sensible, this frank declaration of the Prince's error, and his attachment, my fond heart found its first wish accomplished, and adopted at once the royal youth; solemnly vowing to share, without repining, every evil that might follow an alliance so dear: nor did I fail secretly to exult in my Mary's hereditary right even to this distinction.

To cement the confidence between us, and convince the Prince his present choice was judicious, I resolved to confide to him the secret so long, so painfully, preserved; and related my whole history. As I retraced its affecting incidents, I knew them to be so only by his eager, his generous sympathy; so wholly was my own soul engrossed by the happy prospect he had opened before it.

The Prince of Wales acknowledged with joy the relationship I claimed; to confirm all I had advanced, I presented to him the long-saved testimonials, which he perused with silent reverence: then fixing his eyes, still impressed with that elevated sentiment, on mine, he gave utterance to the dictates of his heart.— "Who could suppose," exclaimed he, "a fortitude so unexampled could possibly be combined with a frame delicate even to fragility!— May the misfortunes you have indelibly impressed on my memory, my more than mother, be the last of your life—may that being who directed my soul to cherish the admiration and esteem inspired by your lovely daughter, and matchless self, suffer the youth before you to supply to your heart, all it ought to have inherited—all it unhappily has lost. Dear will be the moment when to the form of your angel mother my authority shall add the name, and that moment will hereafter, oh! most honoured of women, infallibly be mine."

While I listened to predictions so flattering, I almost believed them accomplished. In thy unblown youth, oh, royal Henry, was comprized every promise that could dilate or fill the heart: mine centred at once in thee, and my daughter: finding, in the mere hope of so glorious a union, a total suspension from suffering and sorrow.

I had now no reserves with the Prince, and leading in my blushing Mary presented her to her royal cousin; who gracefully offered up his unblemished soul on the hand he bowed over. So pure a transport took possession of mine as obliterated every other impression. I snatched the united hands so dear, so beloved, and pressing them to my bosom, sickened with very extasy, and withdrew to recover myself.— Wandering alone by the side of the Thames, I raised my full eyes to heaven; and called the happy spirits of my mother, sister, and Lord Leicester, to sympathize with me in an event which promised to end the persecutions of my family, by thus blessedly uniting the last sprung branches of it. A serenity of the sublimest nature succeeded the sweet trouble of my spirits, and enabled me to rejoin the youthful lovers with the dignity due to my own character.

The situation in which we stood endeared us still more to the Prince, by perpetually reminding him how intimately our welfare was connected with his own. Every hour seemed to unite us more and more to each other. Henry spoke to me with the freedom of a son; conjuring me not to take any step that might create the least suspicion of my birth, or the secret tye formed between us, till he had well weighed every consequence that might ensue: and, to elude the watchful spies, with whom we were alike surrounded, he proposed passing in the evening through his garden to ours, if I would deign for a while to allow him thus to reach the saloon.[18] Our situation was too delicate not to require the strictest caution, yet as I could discover no mode of receiving the Prince, which was not equally questionable, and more dangerous, I acquiesced in his proposal, as well as that he should render one of his gentlemen (Sir David Murray)[19] a confidant of this intimacy, though not of its nature, or extent.

An incident so important engrossing my every thought, my heart returned once more eagerly into the world. It had now an interest in fully understanding the real characters of the King, the Queen, Viscount Rochester, and every individual likely or intitled to interfere at this interesting crisis—I examined, considered, and weighed every thing. I soon discovered that the whole royal family were at variance! That the imperious Queen, unable to wrest her husband from his favorites, or her son from his duties, scorned the first, and neglected the latter: confining herself wholly to a court formed of her own creatures, who assisted her to spoil her younger son; whom she had almost estranged from his brother.[20] Her beautiful daughter, who united in her own person the graces of Mary with the spirit of Elizabeth, alone allured to the court of the Queen the few persons of merit it afforded.[21] Henry was often lavish in the praises of his sister, and, as she was the only relation he ever voluntarily spoke of, I naturally concluded she was the only one intitled by superior qualities to that distinction. King James, who had mounted the throne under happier auspices than almost any preceding sovereign of England, had already lived long enough to lose the affections of his people. By turns a pedant and a buffoon, his solemnity was even more disgusting than his levity. Governed by a predilection of the most absurd and singular nature, to a beautiful favorite he always delivered up the reins of empire; readily submitting to a shameful subjection in all important points, provided he might enjoy a ridiculous supremacy in his hours of indulgence and retirement. From such a weak and inconsistent King, and his profligate Ministers, the wise, the scientific, and the good, had gradually retreated; and, in neglect and silence, contemplated from far the growth of that exemplary Prince, who promised to retrieve the fame of his ancestors, and the glory of the kingdom he was born to reign over. A youth of eighteen capable of uniting the unblemished virtues of that age, with the discernment of a maturer one, was a phaenomenon, and of course either adored or detested—While the body of the kingdom regarded him only with the first sentiment, the worthless favorites of his father were actuated solely by the latter.

To marry and escape the plans of Rochester was the interest of Henry; and to marry without his father's knowledge his unwilling choice.— Yet highly sensible of the slavery imposed by his rank, he had resisted every temptation from beauties of an inferior one:—but, when apprized of my story, he saw, or fancied he saw, in my daughter, a wife alloted him by heaven—one to whom no just objection could possibly be made, one born to give happiness to his heart, and honor to his name. Nor could he doubt, even if his father shut his eyes against the truth, but that he should be able to convince the people of my birth, when the publication of the marriage should give my story the whole weight of his credence.

Success, in his judgment, depended solely on the concealment of the purposed union till it could be accomplished; for, if the intention transpired ere the event, he was satisfied the most desperate efforts would be made to wrest us from him. Yet as at this very period a public treaty was negociating with a foreign Prince, he could not form a tye of such importance without giving his father just case of offence, the nation at large a contempt for his character, and the distant Sovereign thus insulted a mortal disgust. We therefore agreed to wait till this Ministerial project like many others should disappoint itself, and seize that moment to celebrate and publish a marriage, which was to end all our fears, and complete all our hopes.

During this interval I observed with pain that the extreme timidity of my daughter's character prevailed over the enthusiasm incident to her years; and damped with vague apprehensions those moments love and hope might have made so happy. I saw this little feminine weakness with extreme uneasiness. The Prince of Wales was distinguished by a manly firmness, which ever wisely weighed the approaching trial, then calmly dared it. For a soul so noble, I desired to find a faultless bride; and looking fearfully into the future, I sometimes thought my Mary's timid heart would one day throb without cause against that of a sovereign oppressed with innumerable cares, he perhaps sought to lose the remembrance of in her society. Nevertheless, I did not perceive my tender admonitions on this subject had any other consequence than that of inducing my daughter to bury in her bosom those sentiments and emotions, I had so many years delighted to participate.

It was now autumn!—The time of the King's periodical progresses.—[22] The Prince could not avoid following his father, but he lingered in his duty; and having staid a day too long with us, hastened to overtake the King, whom he was to feast at Woodstock. He wrote to me from thence, complaining of fatigue and lassitude; but, with his usual attention, informed me he was in treaty for Kenilworth Castle; where he flattered himself I should again see golden days like those I still remembered with so much pleasure.

Alas, those he had irradiated were quickly hastening to a period! At the first visit he paid me on his return, my soul was struck with a very apparent alteration in his person; which was grown thin and wan beyond conception, considering the shortness of the time. Not all the joy he expressed at our meeting could satisfy me he was either well or happy; but, observing he evaded my questions, and fearful of alarming him without reason, I strove to suppress that maternal anxiety all his assurances of health and cheerfulness could not dispel. I perceived my daughter was impressed with the same idea, for, though she spoke not, it was visible to me that she wept greatly when alone.

The evenings were now too short and damp for me to allow the evening visits of the Prince; and I rather chose to risque every danger by receiving him openly, than subject him to any by an ill-judged caution.— Alas, these cares were vain.— The rapid decay of the royal Henry's health became visible even to indifferent spectators. An affecting languor was the only expression of those fine eyes once so full of fire, and the youthful cheeks every following day should have tinged with a deeper bloom, grew more and more wan and hollow—He could no longer conceal his illness. Alas, it pierced me to the soul! I was miserable at remembering a charge so precious, as his welfare, should be committed to servants of whatever denomination.— No mother—no sister— duties indispensible in every other rank of life, were it seems incompatible with royalty. Oh, Henry!—dear amiable youth! even yet am I tempted to accuse myself for not having better deserved the tender appellation thy filial reverence so often bestowed on me, by daring every thing for thy sake! Slaves to imperious custom, our actions are too often regulated by that idle multitude, whose most lavish applauses would but ill console us for one single reproach from that unerring monitor, our own conscience.

Either not convinced this secret malady was undermining his constitution, or indifferent to the event, the Prince still continued in the pursuit of his usual athletic exercises and habits, till his strength was wholly unequal to them. I once more persuaded him to call in medical assistance, and he promised to attend to himself as soon as his sister and the elector[23] should depart.— Obliged to appear at the celebration of their marriage in London, he came to pay us a parting visit. Impressed, perhaps, with the idea it would be the last, he threw himself into my arms, and shed there the first tears I had ever seen fall from his eyes.— Mine readily overflowed—a grief too deep for utterance pressed upon my soul, and Henry recovered ere I could. His heart missed my daughter, who was gone abroad.— He sighed, sunk into a little reverie, and breaking it, with a faint smile, said, "he ought rather to congratulate himself on her absence." He sighed again, and, after another pause, resumed his discourse in a low and broken voice.— "Mourn not thus, my mother (for I will still give you a title you may justly claim from her who bore me; since who ever loved me as you have done?) I have youth in my favor, and this oppressive malady may not be mortal: for your sake alone do I wish it to be otherwise, believe me.— Already weary, disgusted with this world, I could retreat from it almost without a pang, did I not know my loss would be to you an irremediable calamity. Yet who shall judge of the dispensations of the Almighty?— I might fulfil all your wishes without seeing you happy—I might obtain all my own without ceasing to be wretched. Recal this often to your memory, whatever follows our parting; and remember your name will be ever on these lips while they have power to utter a sound.— For the adored of my soul—but she is surely become a part of it; and if not permitted to possess her in this world, I will expect her in a better."— Perceiving his dim eye was fixed on a picture of my daughter which hung at my bosom, I presented it to him.— "And do you too, beloved Henry," returned I, in a broken voice, "remember that the mother who gives you this, would have comprized in the original every grace, every virtue, to be found through human nature: and having done so, would still have thought her honored in your choice.— Ah! royal youth! resign not a heart so noble to vapourish depression.— Your life, your happiness, are not your own merely—a nation are born to pray for the former, to crown you with the latter.— For myself—upon the sweet hope of matching my daughter with you, of sharing the soft transports of mutual virtue and affection, I have learnt to live, but surely I could never survive its extinction."— My full soul allowed not of another syllable. The Prince fixed his suffused eyes on mine, with a mysterious melancholy, almost amounting to despair; and touching with his lips those hands his trembling ones still grasped, rushed precipitately into the court yard. The sound of his voice drew me towards the window— the graceful youth made me a last obeisance and galloped way; while my partial eye pursued him till beyond its reach, and even then my ear seemed to distinguish the feet of his horse.

With his usual kind consideration, Henry wrote to me the next day, that he found himself better; and, in the pleasure of seeing his sister happy, felt reconciled to the impolitic match made for her.—[24] He even assisted at the various festivals with which the nuptials of the royal Elizabeth were honored; but scarce were they over, when his health and spirits failed at once, and the faculty were called in to his aid. A malady which had been so long engrafting itself on his constitution, left but little hope of his life;—I had ceased to entertain any: yet, far from supporting the idea of losing him with fortitude, my soul mourned as if it then had first known sorrow. Not daring to give free vent to my apprehensions in the presence of my daughter, I strove with cold and watery smiles to flatter those hopes in her heart my own had long rejected, and saw with vain regret, the deep excesses of a sensibility I had laboured to excite and strengthen.

What days, what nights of sadness and suspense were ours, while the unfortunate Henry was languishing away every vital power ere yet they had reached maturity!— Frequently delirious, our names escaped unconsciously from those lips, which at his lucid intervals, uttered only sighs and groans. Murray, his beloved attendant, gave us constant information of the progress of his fever; nor did the amiable Henry fail at intervals to charge him with tender remembrances. Sir David at length acquainted me that, as the impassioned delirium of the Prince pointed ever toward us, the King had been apprized of it;—that he had minutely questioned his son's most favored attendants, and among them himself, on the origin, progress, and strength, of an attachment thus suddenly and strangely brought to light, deeply ruminating on all he heard. "I could not feel acquitted to myself, madam," concluded the faithful Murray, "were I to conceal this, nor dare I add a surmise on so delicate an occasion."

"Ah, of what importance to us are all the late inquiries, the vague conjectures of James!" cried I, folding my daughter to my bosom, "if heaven deprives us of his inestimable son, neither his love or his hatred can greatly affect us.— Beloved Mary—dear inheritor of misfortune!—widowed ere yet thou art a wife, a long obscurity, a solitary youth is all thy portion—a sorrow which can never end thy mother's—But why should I hesitate to avow myself?— Wherefore should I not publish claims which even tyranny can not cancel; but perhaps it will not dispute? The timid, abject spirit of James knows not how to contend with one firm in virtue—immutable in truth.— Ah, had I done so long since, I might at this moment, dear Henry, have hovered near thy couch, and softened the anguish no mortal can prevent!— Perhaps the King already surmises the fact—let him demand it."

Sir David Murray's next letter breathed the very spirit of despair.— "Prepare yourself, madam," said he, "for the worst; perhaps, ere this reaches you, England will have lost its dearest hope, the royal Henry's friends their only one. The most desperate efforts of art have failed, and exhausted reason often now revisits with a languid ray the noble heart she is so soon to quit for ever. The Prince has just ordered me to commit to the flames every letter and paper in which you are mentioned:—a sure proof that he has given himself up.— Alas, he knows not how often names so dear have escaped him; he has called for you, madam, and your angelic daughter, almost the whole night, but frequently recollecting himself, has waved his feeble hand, and sighed out no—no—no."

Three hours after, another express arrived.— "Pardon, madam, the haste and incoherency of scrawls penned at so trying a moment.— Alas, the most sanguine of us has now ceased to hope.— Our royal master's speech entirely fails him—his last effort was hastily and repeatedly to call me—I flew to his bedside; but, though my every sense seemed to resolve into ear, I found it impossible to understand him—either I widely erred or he named France; perhaps I commit a second error in supposing he referred to you, madam, but

I voluntarily risque every thing to fulfil the parting wish of a master so adored. The King, the physicians, all have taken a long leave of the almost beatified Prince; and there is nothing left for those who love him best to wish, but that his pure spirit may pass away in peace."

The agony and stupor this affecting billet occasioned, were hardly abated when another arrived.— "It is all over, madam," concluded the worthy Murray, "raise your streaming eyes to heaven; it is there alone you can now look for the incomparable Prince of Wales.— Fatigue and anguish disable me from saying more."

It was not till the awful moment which restored the unsullied soul of Henry to its omniscient Creator, that I had dared to breathe a wish of which he was not the object, or allowed my thoughts to pass beyond himself.— That exquisite sensibility which lives through all dear to us, had made me severely suffer with him, and consequently pray for that release which alone seemed likely to give him ease, nor did I recollect till he was gone forever, the void his loss would leave in my hopes.— The tremendous calm, by which death is ever followed, now took its turn.— Bereft of a support on which I had long un-consciously rested, I sunk into a desolation which made me almost wish to follow the lamented Prince.— It is at these intervals, madam, we become most truly sensible of all the imperfections of our nature.— How often had I flattered my own erring heart with the vain belief it had acquired strength, purity, and virtue, from its various trials! alas, what but pride, vanity, and ambition, still throbbed unalterably there! time had only altered the object, not the passion, and centred them all in my daughter.

We shut ourselves entirely up, and deeply joined in the general mourn-ing. The sad pleasure of knowing him we bewailed, universally lamented, was yet ours. I perused, I appropriated, with a mother's fondness, the lavish eulo-gies, all sects, all parties, all poets, graced the memory of the Prince with:—it was the only mitigation my grief could know.— A considerable time had elapsed without our hearing any thing from Murray, in confirmation of his conjecture concerning Henry's last wish, and the imperfect accents which lin-gered on his dying lips.— But though I could not resolve to become a guiltless fugitive even in compliance with Prince Henry's will, I had had no other mo-tive for remaining in England than to shew I was not driven out of it. I now determined to quit a country which had been the grave of a hope so dear, and found my daughter entirely of my mind. In gratitude for the unwearied atten-tion of Sir David Murray, I informed him "of my intention to retire into Flanders, not doubting but that the Hollanders would afford an honorable asylum to the widow and orphan of Lord Leicester."— I besought him to accept a ring of considerable value in token of my deep sense of the generous attachment he had shewn alike to myself, and that incomparable Prince whose loss was ever present to my mind; and requested as a last proof of his regard, the restoration of that picture of my daughter I had given to the royal Henry at our memorable parting.

The answer of Murray strangely startled and alarmed me.— "Your intention of quitting England, madam," said he, "relieves my mind from extreme anxiety;—time and circumstances have united to convince me I did not misunderstand the last imperfect accents of my much-loved master.— Lose not a moment in hastening to the asylum you have fixed on.— The picture, madam, is, I fear, irretrievably gone—I cannot by either bribes or intreaties procure any tidings of it.— *Power*, alas, I now have not!— If ever it comes to my hands, rely on its being restored by him who will ever devoutly pray for your happiness."

This inexplicable letter roused every dormant faculty.— Wherefore should my retiring abroad relieve the mind of a person unconnected with me *from extreme anxiety?*— Why should he urge thus my departure? As it was rather pride than prudence which induced me to seek a country where I might fearlessly assert my every right, that project was now rejected from the very motive which first dictated it.— A mystery my nature ever disdained. Resolved to comprehend all the motives on which Murray wished me to act, I ordered every thing to be replaced, and sat down once more quietly at home; resolved to brave the storm, if indeed there was any gathering, rather than ascertain my safety by a disgraceful flight. I once more wrote to Sir David, acquainting him with my present conduct, and its reasons, insisting on being fully informed of those which actuated him to offer me advice so singular and mysterious.— How infinitely was my impatience, curiosity, and disdain, heightened by his answer!— "I hear with admiration, madam, a determination which from a perfect knowledge of your character, I ought, perhaps, to have foreseen; nevertheless, my sentiments are not altered, nor less urged could I divulge the reasons on which they are grounded: but decorum and delicacy give way to your commands, and the occasion. Nevertheless, I find it impossible to commit them to paper.— Dare you give me an admission at midnight?— I shall be near your gate upon the chance, but be wary in the choice of my conductor, as perhaps my life, nay, even your own, depends upon its being supposed you never had any private correspondence or communication with me."

How did my nature take fire at this incomprehensible letter!— Me to stoop to secresy!—to be exposed to shame!— The unknown danger, with which he represented me to be environed, appeared wholly indifferent; so exquisitely sensible was my soul of the imputation of dishonor.— At times I resolved to shut out Murray, and leave the brooding mischief to disclose itself by its effects; but love for my daughter controling the strong spirit of indignation inseparable from innocence, I yielded to the suggestions of prudence, and prepared to admit him.— Inured to every other species of suffering, I knew not how to blush before any human being.

My perplexed and agitated mind passed through the infinitude of possibilities without fixing upon one.— At times I imagined all the caution of the royal Henry had been insufficient, and that the King, by means of some lost or secreted letter, had been fully apprized of his son's attachment to us, and the hopes that were grounded upon it; though even then I knew not why my life should be in the question; still less could I imagine it endangered, had his discoveries reached farther, and traced out the long buried secret of my birth. Involved in busy, vague, and alarming conjectures, I hardly knew how to wait with any patience for the singular hour appointed to ascertain them.

Sensible, by the deep effect this took on my own mind, that it must dreadfully shock my daughter's, and still flattering myself that this indistinct danger might be the creation of a desponding temper in Henry's favorite, I resolved to wait the event of my midnight interview with him, ere I confided more to my Mary than she must already have learnt from the change in my resolution respecting quitting England.— But as to see her was to explain all, (for how could I hope to veil emotions which burnt indignantly on my cheek?) I sent her word that I was seized with a violent headach, which I would endeavour to remedy by sleep; and accompanied this message with a new book she had an eager desire to see, and which I sincerely prayed might wholly occupy her attention at this interesting crisis.

Oh, world! how false, how erroneous are the feelings we imbibe from thee!— Nature ordained shame the companion of guilt, but overbearing custom has broke that tye, and oftener bids her follow virtue. Scarce could I resolve to know my imputed crime, or look with complacency on the amiable man who had ventured to suggest the unforeseen danger.— It was the utmost effort of my reason to govern this unworthy impulse.

The estimable Murray was sensible of an equal constraint, and, by the generous confusion with which he appeared before me, restored my mind to its dignity and composure. His mourning, and the tears which followed the name of his lost royal master, drew forth mine, and at once blended our feelings. Sir David, with infinite delicacy and address, entered into the Prince of Wales's singular illness, as well as the various opinions his death had given rise to:—but how did my soul freeze with horror to learn that there were many (and among them some of his physicians) who believed him poisoned![25] The killing grief such a suspicion must at a more tranquil moment have caused, vanished, however, at once before the confused and rapid sensations his following discourse occasioned.— Oh, let me pause here a moment to adore the indulgence of the Almighty, which alone could have enabled my intellects to support so terrible a shock as the report that it was from my hands he received the deadly present!— I looked at Murray a while in speechless astonishment!— Grief, anger, shame, and horror, divided and tore me in pieces.— I scarce heard his prayers and adjurations, but, pushing him from my feet, shut up every indignant sense in my swelling heart, and only hoped it might burst with the deep convulsion.

A considerable time elapsed ere I was enough recovered to enquire into the origin of so black and malicious a calumny. I then conjured him to inform me who was supposed to be its diabolical author.— To this he answered, that when the equivocal decision of the faculty respecting the cause of the Prince's death first reached the Queen, the vehemence of her grief, as well as that of her temper, made her instantly join with those who pronounced him poisoned.— This doubt was no sooner published than it became general; every domestic of the Prince's household had been by turns the object of suspicion to his fellows, and some of them had been weak enough to ascertain their safety by quitting the kingdom. The rumour was by this means corroborated and strengthened; but, as nothing transpired that could authorize a judicial enquiry, the King became satisfied that the melancholy catastrophe of his youthful heir had been in the common course of nature; when, all at once, by some incomprehensible means, the vague suspicions of the multitude, which were far from extinguished, though wholly unfixed, revived with added force, and centred in me.[26] It was now generally believed that the Prince of Wales, in the last visit he paid me, had tasted some dry preserves (a little refreshment of which he was extremely fond, though fortunately the distraction of my mind at that period had prevented me from offering him any) which most likely were poisoned, as his last illness rapidly increased immediately after.— It was well-known that I had been the constant object of his delirious reveries; and every vague or mysterious expression which had escaped him at those intervals, had been remembered, traced, and applied, with diabolical ingenuity. The singular precaution of his seeing his own papers burnt had served only to persuade the prejudiced multitude that the unfortunate Prince was unwilling to stigmatize her who had destroyed him. By such plausible and base suggestions the eyes of an inflamed and afflicted nation had been led towards the

solitary dwelling, where, unconscious of danger, I remained buried in a grief
the most charitable imputed only to remorse. There wanted but little to incite
the people to anticipate the stroke of justice, by tearing me to pieces, when the
King confirmed the general suspicion by a renewed and more minute inquiry
into the nature of his son's visits to me, their continuance, and design: and no
person being able to satisfy his curiosity, he dropt harsh and ambiguous expressions; that several of his favorites had since urged the propriety of bringing me to a public trial; a measure which had the whole weight of the Queen's
interest. Alarmed and uncertain how to proceed, Sir David had learned at this
very juncture my intention of retiring into Holland; and, by supposing me
pre-acquainted with the slanders of the public, had unwarily reduced himself
to the painful necessity of repeating them.— He concluded with hinting the
prudence of abiding by my former design of immediately quitting England,
as in instances where the prejudices of a nation infected even those individuals
intrusted with the execution of its laws, innocence itself was scarce a protection: biased judges might easily mistake presumptions for proofs, nor have
candour enough to vindicate the honor which had thus been questioned.

While Sir David yet spoke, a new world displayed itself before me.—
Ah! how unlike the paradise pictured by my guiltless mind!— Those countenances in which I yesterday saw only the living image of their Creator, now
glared upon me like so many fiends.— A horrible gulph seemed to open beneath my feet into which a thousand hands sought at once to precipitate me,
and my timid soul retreated in vain from the danger.— To live undistin-
guished—to die unknown, were mortifications sufficiently grievous.— But
the bare idea of being arraigned—dragged as a pre-judged criminal before a
partial judge, had something in it so tremendous, as made every other evil
appear ease. My blood flowed impetuously through my frame, and my bewildered judgment wanted strength to govern the torrent.— A malice so bold,
profound, and diabolical, could have only one author, but where to look for
that one I knew not; nor could I recollect a human being I had injured, or a
villain I had provoked.— Like a wretch awakened by assassins in the darkness
of midnight, I knew not but the hand raised to ward the blow might bleed on
the presented dagger. In this terrible conjuncture I had only virtue to befriend
me: though, alas, virtue herself half withers before the blighting breath of
calumny! While Sir David enforced the arguments he had already urged to
induce me to quit the kingdom, my soul, by one of those violent exertions
great occasions will sometimes produce, recovered all her powers.— Indignation subsided at once into fortitude, and anger into heroism.— "You have
hitherto only seen me, Sir David," said I,—"it is now alone you can know

me;—shuddering with horror at the imputations you have explained, I yet dare not retreat unless I can confute them—no, not even condemnation could induce me to fly, and leave my honor behind me.— What! shall I blight the opening virtues of my child by exposing her with myself to unmerited censure? The pride, the pleasure, of unsullied virtue, was all fortune permitted me to retain of the wealth and honors which once glittered before my youthful eyes—nor did I undervalue the most dear and sacred of all possessions—alas, even that is now ravished from me, and one way alone can it be retrieved.— Desperate as the effort seems, it must be ventured—yes—I will see the King whatever it costs me: surely, the sainted spirit of the royal Henry would appear to vindicate my innocence (heavens! that I should live to know it questioned!) were every other means to prove insufficient.— I will trouble you no farther, respected Murray, unless you will deign to convey a letter to Lord Rochester, requesting a private audience of the King."

An idea so singular had transferred the astonishment Murray had at first excited in me to his own mind; that my intellects were touched then seemed to him very probable, but perceiving that I was mistress both of my senses and temper, he presumed not to contend with a spirit injury had nerved; and, struck with the dignity I assumed, began to believe I had indeed something important to disclose, though quite at a loss respecting its nature. I wrote to Lord Rochester (now newly created Earl of Somerset)[27] according to the idea I had formed; and Murray, having engaged that the letter should be delivered early in the morning, departed with the same caution with which he had entered, leaving me alone.— Alone, did I say?— Ah, gracious heaven, never was I less so!— The shades of all I had ever loved seemed to gather round me on this interesting occasion, and volumes of obscure ideas rushed impetuously through my brain.— I had unexpectedly reached the very point of my fate.— That important moment so often delayed, so eternally dreaded, was at length arrived, and the long treasured secret on the verge of being published.— For *myself* I had long ceased to fear—The fraternal acknowledgment of the King could now add nothing to my happiness; since, alas, that incomparable youth was gone for whose sake alone I desired it: nor could his rejection greatly imbitter a fate which had left me so little to hope.— But, oh, when I remembered his single breath might blight the tender blossom I had exhausted my very being to rear—precipitate my youthful Mary, ere yet her virtues were known, into an obscure and dishonorable grave, where, where, could I gather strength to cope with this idea?

I employed the remainder of the night in collecting and arranging such plausible reasons as should amuse my daughter's mind till the event was known;

thus sparing her all the pangs of suspense.— I gathered together likewise every paper, and proof which could authenticate the rights I was compelled to avow, and, on perusing them once more, found such reason to be assured, not only of safety, but distinction, that a sacred calm succeeded to all the transports of grief and indignation with which I had of late been agitated.

By a feigned invitation from a neighbouring lady, who permitted me to render her house my convenience, I sent my daughter abroad for the day: and scarce had done so ere an express arrived, to acquaint me that the Earl of Somerset would wait on me in the afternoon.

What were my proud emotions when the upstart Somerset littered my court[28] with a princely retinue!— Alas, the only Prince who had ever entered it, with a noble consciousness, despised such idle parade. By oppressive offers of service, the Earl made me sensible of his importance, and sought, by unbounded adulation, to gain upon my heart, and dive into its intentions: but it was not by such a medium I sought distinction. I politely avoided referring either to the slander, or the purport of the requested audience, and only thanked him for having obtained me the ear of the King; half blushing to have gained it by so contemptible an intercessor. I perceived chagrin, curiosity, and disappointment, strongly expressed in his really fine features, but I could not prevail on myself to confide aught to the man Prince Henry had despised. The Earl took his leave with the same profound deference, and assurances of service, with which he entered; having appointed the next morning for presenting me to the King.

As the privacy of the promised audience enabled me to dispence with form, I made no addition to my servants, nor any other alteration in the weeds I usually wore, than that of forming them to the model of my mother's dress; which ever rendered the likeness I bore her from my very birth striking and obvious. A thousand half-forgotten occurrences pressed upon my agitated soul as I past through each well-known apartment 'till all were lost in the present, by my reaching the closet of the King. The assiduous Somerset, drest as elegantly as though he had meant to charm me, advanced on my being announced, and politely offered me his hand—a sudden chill came over me;— I trembled,—lingered—drooped,—but resolved to conquer myself or perish, I shook off the scalding tear which hung upon my cheek, and accepted the favorite's introduction.— The superior air with which I affected to enter was not necessary towards confusing the King, who, always awkward and perplexed, seemed more than usually so; and doubtful, whether he should not fly the moment he saw me, or at least call back Somerset who had instantly retired.— Bending my knee in compliance with custom, I instantly rose, and, retaining the hand he had presented to me, fixed my eyes, strongly animated by the occasion, upon his ever-varying countenance. "Your Majesty," said I, "doubtless, expects to find in me a weak suppliant, soliciting protection, or suing for your pity; but on terms like these I had never bent before you—I come to claim a dear and sacred title hitherto unknown, but never annihilated. Does your heart, oh, royal James!" added I, melting into tears, "recognize nothing congenial to it in these features? this voice! the timorous hand which grasps yours for the first time, in fraternal alliance?— Oh, sainted Mary! dear author of my being, look down from heaven, and touch the heart of your son, in favor of the desolate sister who now stands before him." The King started, receded, gave manifest tokens of doubt and displeasure, and sought to draw away the hand I obstinately retained.— I kissed, I bathed it with impassioned tears. "Shake me not off, reject me not unknown," resumed I in the deep tone of stifled anguish.— "It is neither pride, vanity, or ambition, which induces me now to publish a secret so long buried in my bosom. By the ashes of our anointed mother, I conjure you to hear—nay even to believe me.— Born in obscurity—reared in solitude, the early victim of misfortune, long suffering had reconciled my weary soul to every evil but disgrace: against that she still proudly revolts.— The same blood which flows through your veins, burns in tumults along mine, at the very thought of aught unworthy—it urges me to assert my innocence by indubitable proofs—it *will* be acquitted, before men as well as angels; nor does the claim thus avowed rest on my declaration alone, your Majesty will see in these papers the solemn attestations, the unquestioned handwriting of your royal mother; in *these* you will find the corroborating testimonies of many noble and unblemished persons.— Peruse them cautiously, and oh, beware how you pre-judge me!" Unable to utter another word, I almost sunk at the feet of James, and gave way to the oppressive, the agonizing sensations such an æra in my life could not fail to awaken. The King still regarded me with an irresolute, uneasy air, coldly advising me to compose myself by retiring into the anti-chamber, while he perused the papers on which he had hitherto only glanced his eye; though even that cursory view had deeply tinged his cheek with silent conviction. I was met there by the Earl of Somerset, who, perceiving me near fainting, ordered water, and such essences as are customary, remaining himself by my side, as if ostentatiously to convince me he did not influence in the least the determination of his royal master.— The bitterness of the conflict was, however, over the moment the secret was avowed, and my spirits soon began to recover their wonted equanimity.

The obliging efforts of Somerset to revive me did not pass unnoticed,

though my watchful ear followed the footsteps of the King, who still continued to walk about with an unequal pace, stopping at intervals. He opened the
closet door at length, and Somerset retiring out of his sight, made signs to me
to re-enter it.— The King came forward to meet me with affability, and seizing my hand slightly saluted my cheek.— "Take courage, madam," said he,
"for however you may have surprized us with this sudden declaration, and
wonderful discovery, reverence for our deceased mother's rights, and justice to
those you derive from her, oblige us to acknowledge you as her daughter."

And now I was indeed near fainting, I might rather say dying.— To be
at once acknowledged as his sister, as the daughter of Mary! Scarce in my
happiest hours had I dared to flatter myself with the promise of what was now
so incredibly realized. My susceptible soul indulged the exquisite transport,
and one short moment compensated for ages of anguish.— A thousand impassioned, incoherent exclamations, burst from my lips; and giving way to the
genuine impulse of gratitude and affection I threw myself for the first time
into the arms of a brother, nor remembered they were those of a King. Never
did the most consummate hypocrite counterfeit a joy so pure, so perfect; and
though I could have brought no other proof of my birth, the sacred throbs of
nature might well have ascertained it.

The King sat down by me, and, turning over the papers he still held,
questioned me at intervals respecting those that appeared mysterious or defi-
cient. I entreated his patience while I briefly ran through the wonderful events
of my life, and thus very naturally led his attention toward the sole object of
my cares, my hopes, my existence.— "I have already heard much of your
daughter," said James; "they tell me she is beauty itself—why have you thus
strangely concealed her?" As I could not declare my real reason, which was
simply want of esteem for his character, I pleaded various trifling ones, that
indeed had never influenced me. "Say no more," said the King, interrupting
me, "I easily perceive, Madam, you was not so reserved to every one—I plainly
discern who was your confidant; had I earlier been entrusted with your secret,
it would have been happier for all, and I should then have been able to account for"—He paused ere he came to the dear name of his son, and sighing
dropt the unfinished sentence. As to me, entranced alike with his unexpected
candour, graciousness, and generosity, I severely reproached myself for relying
on report, and not proving the character I ventured to decide upon. I had a
long conversation with the King afterwards, every word of which heightened
my confidence, esteem, and affection. I gathered from many expressions, that
he feared opposition on the part of the Queen, and his favorite; and was
fearful that this late declaration of his mother's marriage with the Duke of

Norfolk would not fully satisfy the minds of the people, or establish my rank sufficiently. He paused upon the whole, with the air of one who is a party in what he meditates; and I thought the least I could do, was to leave the regulation of the important acknowledgment in his choice.— To be vindicated in his opinion, I truly assured him, was the first object of my life, and I submitted my general vindication, in the public acknowledgment of my birth, entirely to his better judgment. That I had been so many years a solitary being in the midst of society, as not to have one friend to whose inclination I need yield my own. In fine, that time had gradually robbed me of all interested in the important secret I had just confided to him, which now rested solely with him, my daughter, and myself. He replied that "this instance of my prudence, as well as regard, infinitely heightened the partiality he had already conceived for me; nor need I fear his delaying the acknowledgment longer than was absolutely necessary, since he could not but look on such relations as inestimable acquisitions: nevertheless, as he had many points to consider, and many persons to reconcile, he recommended to me to continue the same circumspection I had hitherto shewn; but that he could not restrain his impatience to behold the fair maid of whom he had heard so much, and would come tomorrow evening to a seat of my Lord Somerset's, whither he would send for myself and my daughter, and hoped by that time he should be able to ascertain the day for publishing my birth, with a due regard for his mother's honor; after which he could gratify himself by establishing me in a situation that should make me forget all my misfortunes."— Those misfortunes were already forgotten in the unhoped-for transition in my fate.— I took my leave with the profoundest gratitude, burning with impatience to impart this blessed news to my Mary; and, as the King did not offer to return the papers, I thought it better to leave them in his hands, than confirm the doubt my long silence could not but give rise to in his mind, viz. that I wanted confidence in his honor.

I hastened to Richmond, and communicated this surprising, this happy event, to my darling girl.— A thousand times I enfolded her to my delighted heart, and found every transport doubled in her participation. She tenderly entered into all my feelings, and sweetly smiled at the eagerness with which I sought to adorn her for the next day's introduction. Yet, considering the King as the slave of exterior, it was a material point to heighten her beauty by every adventitious advantage. To present her in absolute black, was to recal the most melancholy impressions to the mind of James; I therefore resolved to lighten her mourning with a fanciful elegance. I drest her in a vest of black velvet thrown back at the bosom in the French fashion, with a semicircle of rich lace points, which shewed at once her graceful waist and chest to the greatest advantage. Her petticoat was of white sattin, wrought in deep points round the bottom with black velvet, and richly fringed with silver. A fuller coat and train of silver muslin, wrought with black, fell over the sattin one, and was looped up to the waist at regular distances by strings of pearl, and dragged toward the bottom into points by the weight of rich black bugle tassels and roses of diamonds. Full sleeves of the same silver muslin were braced round her arms to the elbow by strings of jet, and roses of diamonds; and from thence they were bare, except for similar bracelets circling each wrist. The rich profusion of her auburn hair, which fell in natural curls below her waist, required no ornament, but to avoid the affectation of shewing it, she wore a hat of white sattin with a narrow fringe of black bugles, and a waving plume of feathers. This splendid dress, on which the legacies of both her father and Anana were displayed, by some peculiar happiness, either in its make or mixture, became my Mary beyond any I had ever seen her wear. The fond mother's heart anticipated the impression she would infallibly make on her uncle, and drew from her heightened beauty the happiest presages.

Ah, who could have conjectured that this brilliance and parade were only destined to forerun one of the most dismal moments of my life!— That an inhuman tyrant had delighted to employ the trembling hand of misfortune in decking a gaudy pageant, for herself eternally to mourn over!

At the appointed hour, a close carriage came for us with due attendants, and as the King had desired me not to bring any of my own, I rigidly obeyed, nor even hinted whither I was going. They drove us a long way, while engrossed by meditations on the approaching interview, as well as concerning the dear creature by me, I hardly knew how the time passed. My daughter at length observed that it was farther than she expected.— I looked out, but it was too dark for me to distinguish any object, and all I could discern was an increase of attendants. I called out aloud, and one drew near, who to my inquiries respectfully replied, that the King had been detained in London, whither they were hastening by his orders. This information quieted us again; and I strove to recal my fluttered spirits into their usual channel, by turning the conversation on our future prospects. Nevertheless, we went at so great a rate, that I thought it impossible we should not be near London, when all at once I found we were driving through an unknown village. The surprise this occasioned was doubled by my daughter's throwing herself into my arms.— It was not immediately I could comprehend her, when she told me that a light which gleamed from the window of a cottage, had shewn her that we were environed with armed soldiers. From this alarm we were not yet recovered, when, by a sudden rise, and hollow sound, we perceived we had passed over a drawbridge; immediately after which we stopped. As we alighted, I cast my eyes round a large and dreary court-yard, where a few straggling centinels were planted, but neither lights, splendor, or attendants, indicated a royal guest, or a favorite's residence. The gloomy passages through which we were ushered, seemed rather to lead to a prison than a palace.— Arrived at an empty apartment, I gave way at once to the dire, the obvious truth; and arraigning in silence my own egregious credulity, felt, severely felt, its every consequence.

An officer who had preceded us, now offered me a packet, which I received as the sentence of my fate, but made no effort to open it.— Hope, fear, curiosity, every dear and powerful emotion were annihilated by instantaneous conviction, and a stupor succeeded more dangerous and dreadful than the most violent operations of the passions.— My daughter, more terrified by this still agony than even the cruel and unexpected event of the evening, threw herself at my feet.— "Oh, speak to me, my mother!" exclaimed the dear one; "do not indulge the desperation your countenance expresses! do not consummate to your poor Mary the horrors of the moment!" I gazed at her with a vacant air, but nature resumed her rights, and fondly plucking at my heart, the tears I refused to my own fate, flowed lavishly for hers.— So young, so fair, so innocent, so noble,—how could I but bewail her? Surely those maternal tears alone preserved my senses at a juncture when every thing conspired to unsettle them. My Mary, by an expressive glance, requested leave to open the packet, and, starting at sight of the paper it contained, put it eagerly into my hand; a glance informed me that it was that defamatory declaration the crafty Burleigh had deceived my sister into signing, while a prisoner in St. Vincent's Abbey. The King, in sending this, only added insult to injury, since the testimonials I had delivered to him might have invalidated a thousand such vague and artificial falsehoods; yet had it a fortunate effect, for nothing less could have roused my spirits from the cold and sullen torpor which every passing moment seemed to increase—"Insolent Barbarian!" exclaimed I, "not content to imprison the unhappy offspring of the Queen who had the misfortune of giving thee being, dost thou delight in villifying and debasing even her ashes!— Oh, paper! dictated and preserved surely for my ruin; by what singular chance hast thou survived the very views thou wert invented to serve.— Treasured, as it appears, only to effect a ruin your execrable contriver could not foresee.— Yet of what consequence is this single attestation towards annihilating claims all those I delivered had not power to establish in the judgment of a cruel, insidious tyrant, who voluntarily shut his heart alike to reason, virtue, and nature?— Devoted to self-interest, vain of a petty talent at deceiving, contemptible in every rank, but infamous in the highest, he meanly watched the generous impulses of my heart, and wrought out of them my ruin.— Yet why do I name myself?— Alas, of what importance is it to her who no longer wishes to live where heaven or its arbitrary delegate shall have appointed her to die?— It is for thee, my daughter! for thee alone my soul thus overflows with inexpressible anguish.— Rescued, in yet unconscious childhood, from slavery, neglect, and obscurity, fortune at one moment seemed willing to restore all the rights of your birth, when a weak, credulous mother assisted the cruel wretch who was pre-determined to entomb you, and annihilate every trace, every memorial, of our dear and honored progenitors.— Nameless—dishonored—your blooming youth must wither in an unknown prison—blighted by the tears of a parent who can never pardon herself the extravagant error produced by over-fondness.— I knew the King to be mean, base, subtle, yet I madly delivered into his treacherous hands every thing on which our hopes, nay, even our vindication must be grounded."— "Hear me, in turn, my dear, my honored mother," cried my sweet girl, bathing my hands with tears of veneration and fondness. "Alas, the order of nature is inverted, and I am obliged to become the monitor.— Recollect the maxim you have so deeply impressed upon my mind—that the malice of man would in vain strive to make us wretched, did not our own ungovernable passions aid his artful machinations. Oh, let us respect even error when it has its source in virtue.— To have distrusted the King were to deserve to be rejected—leave him then to the contemptible satisfaction of having wrested from the widow and the orphan the last treasure of their lives, and let us examine what he has been compelled to leave us. Have we not yet the power of looking down on his throne, and all its specious advantages, even from that obscure prison where his authority confines us?— Have we not the pride of reviewing our own hearts without finding aught in either unworthy of our Creator or ourselves?— For the vain grandeur of that name of which he has unfairly deprived us, can it be worth regretting while he lives to dishonor it?— Fortunately no favorite view depended on its attainment, consequently no hope is blighted by the deprivation. Have I not often heard you say, a noble mind can become every thing to itself?— Let us then rise superior to our fortune; time will soon calm our spirits—reason will reconcile us to the inconveniences of our fate, and religion elevate us above them.— Mourn not then for me, my much-loved mother," concluded the dear one, sweetly smiling through her tears, "since I shall never think that place a prison which contains you, nor that fate a misfortune I owe to your fondness."

Oh, virtue, how awful dost thou appear, sublimed thus by generosity! When I saw this half-blown human blossom support the storm without shrinking, I blushed to have bowed my head before it.— When I heard her with Spartan courage apply to her own situation the noble tenets I had sought, not vainly, to imbue her mind with, could I fail to profit by the principles I had taught?— From the admiration she excited in my soul sprung that pure and elevated heroism which calms in one moment every human weakness, and turbulent passion; disposing us to turn upon that fate it enables us to judge of.

I now recollected that by a fond vanity in decking my daughter in all her valuable diamonds, I had inadvertently provided ample means to buy the fidelity of our keepers; nor were they aware of our treasure, as the severity of the weather had made me wrap her in a long cloak lined with fur. I hastily stripped her costly dress of its richest embellishments, and secreted them. Ah, with what difficulty did I stifle the tears and anguish which struggled at my heart when I remembered the different views with which I had adorned her!

Scarce had we executed this prudent resolve, ere the man I have mentioned presented himself once more;—he was young—not unpleasing—had an air of integrity, and profound respect, that a little prepossessed me in his favor, even under all the disadvantages attending our meeting. Our countenances were now calmed, and our resolutions taken.— He appeared surprized alike with this transition, and the beauty of my daughter, whose magnificent but disordered dress had a share of his attention.— He was flattered with our civility, and assured us "that every accommodation consistent with the strict orders of the King he should take pleasure in supplying us with; and would, with our permission, make us acquainted with our new home." He then produced some keys which opened double doors at the farther end of the large room we were in, and conducted us into a chamber neat and commodious enough.— The keys, he informed us, were committed solely to his charge; and that whenever inclination or convenience induced us to change our apartment, we had only to touch a spring he pointed out, when he would attend, and unlock the intermediate doors.— The purport of this extreme caution was very obvious; it excluded every possibility of winning over a female servant, as all the domestic offices would now of course be performed in either room while we occupied the other; nor was he suffered to supply us pen, ink, or paper. As the conveniencies of these apartments, and the air of respect in our guard, shewed some attention had been paid to our welfare, as well as the most judicious precautions taken to prevent our enlargement, I neither imputed the one or the other to the King, but rather both to his cunning favorite. Our enquiries were interrupted by the entrance of two servants, who set out an elegant supper, of which neither my daughter or myself had spirits to partake. Resolved however to gather all I could from my attendant, ere another should be put in his place, or suspicion make him dumb, I asked the name of the Castle, and its owner; but to these questions he declared himself enjoined to refuse replying; nevertheless, I conjectured from his looks that I did not err in supposing Somerset directed him. The refined artifice of offering to introduce me to the King, and even remaining by my side, while perhaps my ruin was effecting by his will, seemed entirely consistent with the character Prince Henry had given me of that worthless favorite; though I could find no crime in my own conduct could possibly irritate him to bury us thus alive, unless indeed our attachment to that lamented royal youth appeared a sufficient one.

In the gallery leading to our apartment, I observed a centinel planted, from whom we were shut by double doors safely locked: perceiving we were thus effectually excluded from every hope, and chance of freedom, I desired to pass at once into a chamber, where I did not flatter myself I should find rest.

My first employment on rising was to examine the windows, as well as the view from them; they were so closely grated as to convince me that however comfortable our residence, it was still a prison. The apartments we occupied formed one side of a quadrangle of old buildings, most probably barracks, but now entirely deserted. On making the signal, Dunlop (for so was our guard called) readily attended, and we passed into the other room where we found breakfast ready. Trunks containing all kinds of apparel had been placed there, and Dunlop recommended to us to form our minds to passing the remainder of our days in confinement. I did not submit to hear this without demanding the authority by which he acted. He produced an order, signed by the King, strictly enjoining him to keep us in safety, and beware we neither wrote or received a letter, or indeed held any kind of communication with the world.— While he spoke I examined every lineament of his countenance, but fidelity was written there in such legible characters, that I dared not make any effort to bribe him, lest if it failed he should publish that I had the means, which might in a moment utterly impoverish me.

A few wearisome uniform days only had elapsed when every hope decayed, and my spirits flagged at once.— Alas, my mind had no longer the vivifying ardor, the inexhaustible resources of unbroken youth—its bloom had passed away like a shadow, and all its fire evaporated.— The woeful realities of life had dissipated the bright illusions of imagination.— Every human good was, in my estimation, shrunk into so small a compass, that freedom constituted a very essential part of my little possessions.— I was no longer able to rely upon contingencies, and sunk at once under all the sadness of knowledge.— Not denied the relief of books, I pored over them in vain; every idea was still pursuing an absent good, and my senses would reject the sublimest author, to follow the careless steps of a weary centinel, or listen to his whistling. Whether my daughter had really more resolution than myself, or only assumed the appearance of it to save me from despair, was a point I could not ascertain; but the complacency of her mind and manners was invariable. By a thousand little affectionate artifices she engaged me to work while she read, or read while she worked, nor would perceive those melancholy reveries it was impossible to overlook. I was not, however, thankless for the blessing left me. That my eyes opened on her every morning, still made me bless it; and in composing myself to sleep, I nightly praised the God who yet suffered her to rest by me.

Two tedious months elapsed in undecisive projects.— Dunlop ever present, vigilant, and respectful, precluded alike complaint and temptation; but, as if to guard himself against the latter, I took notice he now never remained one moment alone with us.

The impossibility of forming any judgment of our centinels while divided from them by double doors, and the danger of a fruitless effort to seduce one, had at intervals engrossed my attention; but the mind cannot dwell forever on a single idea, or a remote and uncertain project. Wearied out with this, another suddenly came to my relief. Though yet early in the spring, the weather was uncommonly beautiful, and the lenity with which we were treated left me not without hopes of being allowed, under rigid limitations, the liberty of walking in whatever gardens the castle-walls enclosed. By this means I could examine the countenances of our centinels, and, if I saw one in whom humanity was not quite extinct, I thought I might find some means to shew him a jewel; thus proving I could largely recompense him, should he have the courage to assist us. Nor did my lameness wholly deprive me of the power of walking, though it prevented my enjoying the liberty.— After considering this plan in every possible light, I saw nothing to forbid the attempt, and ventured the request.— A few anxious days elapsed ere I had the satisfaction of finding it was granted, on as good terms as I could hope. Dunlop acquainted me we must walk separately, that the person confined might be a check upon her that was liberated; who should not remain in the garden more than an hour, nor quit his sight one moment. These restrictions were as moderate as I could expect, and I eagerly prepared to profit by the granted permission, ere I ventured my daughter: certain I should at least discover the strength, height, and situation, of the Castle.— Dunlop, followed by two other men, attended upon me. I cast an eager eye on the centinel on the gallery, but saw in him no trace of sense, feeling, or curiosity. I found the little garden in so antique a style, and ruinous a condition, as plainly proved that this dismantled building was now only a prison, whatever its former distinction. The wall around it appeared decayed, and not very high—it looked down on a moat, apparently dry.— From one part of the terrace I caught the corner of a tower I fancied belonged to Windsor Castle, but dared not venture a word which might imply design, and returned without asking a single question. My daughter now took her turn; and, as we continued to claim this relief whenever the weather favored, I fancied it improved her health as well as my own.

It chanced at length, I one day found a centinel on guard whose eye expressed both pity and curiosity.— Mine addressed itself to him in a most pointed manner. Without altering the position of my hand (in which I always carried a diamond for that purpose) I opened it, and the soldier, as I wished, surveyed the jewel.— I turned my head at the instant Dunlop was unlocking the door, and the centinel shook his emphatically. Yet only to have been understood revived at once my spirits, and my hopes; for to escape did not appear so impracticable to me, as to gain an assistant. I saw him no more for a week, but soon found that day was the periodical one for his attendance.— Involved in a thousand plots, the want of pen and ink seemed to condemn them all to inhabit only my brain, when at once I discovered a substitute for those useful articles. From the middle of a large book, which we had unmolested possession of, I took some of the printed leaves, and from the conclusion a blank one; out of the first I cut such words as simply conveyed my meaning, and sewed them on the last.— "Assist us to escape, and we will make your fortune," was the substance of this singular but important billet. To ascertain my ability to realize this promise, I wrapt in it a diamond of some value, and carried both ever in my hand, still hoping fortune would enable me for one moment to mislead the attention of my guards; but, alas, Dunlop, far from relaxing his vigilance, continually increased it. The two men who followed him in the garden now attended to my door; remaining as spies on me while Dunlop opened it. Thus circumstanced, I could not make the slightest overture without being liable to detection, and I dreaded awakening the most distant doubt, lest it should condemn us to a more rigorous confinement.— One favorable omen alone occurred.— The soldier I had selected clearly understood me. I saw his eye ever anxiously fixed on my hand, as if eager to transfer its contents to his own; nor had I ceased to flatter myself I should yet do so, when an unforeseen incident at once annihilated every hope and project, and plunged me in the deepest sorrow.

I had always counted the moments of my daughter's absence, and nothing but the conviction that the air and exercise were necessary towards her health, could have enabled me to support it. What then became of me when one day I found her walk unusually lengthened!— I endeavoured to persuade myself that my fears foreran the danger.— But more than twice the usual time had certainly elapsed; nor dared I venture an enquiry, lest I should suggest a hint to my persecutors which hitherto had escaped them. The hours thus passed on, but Mary returned not—Ah me! While my weak hand repeats this, I almost expire under the recollection.— Every evil my untoward fate had yet teemed with became peace, nay pleasure, on a comparison with this.— Though the turbulence of each succeeding storm had swept away invaluable treasures, something yet remained my weary soul might cling to.— This single gem, this solitary relique of all my fortunes, more dear, more precious from becoming so, a dreadful, a deceitful calm had at length swallowed up even while I was fearless of the danger.— Heart-struck—incapable at once either of distinguishing, or complaining, my respiration became perturbed, and deep.— A still agony, more dreadful than the wildest tumults of the passions, numbed my very soul; every hair seemed to start from, and pierce my too-sensible brain; while drops, cold as those of death, chased one another down my scarcely throbbing temples.— When Dunlop presented himself, I rose not from the earth, I uttered not a syllable; but lifting an eye to him which would have melted a savage, he turned away, unable to support the shock, and offered me some order from the King, bewailing at the same moment the painful duty imposed on him. This roused my torpid spirits—I tore it indignantly into a thousand atoms; resentment restored my speech.— I called for my Mary in the most piercing accents—nothing could suspend, or mitigate my anguish. I bitterly reproached Dunlop with tearing the beauteous innocent from her mother's bosom, only to deliver her up to assassins—In vain he declared himself incapable of such villainy, and acting under the orders of the King—in vain he assured me she was only removed to another apartment, safe, and unhurt.— My soul rejected all his assertions.— Mary—Mary—Mary!—was all my convulsed lips could utter, or my disconsolate soul dictate.

Ah, God! the solitude that succeeded! Food, light, air, nay even life itself, became nauseous and insupportable.— Stretched on the cold ground—drenched in my own tears, I gave way to the deep misery, the tremendous void, this barbarous separation could not but plunge me in.— How long was it since she had been the very essence of my existence! From the sorrowful moment which gave her into my arms, to that which tore her from them, she,

she alone, had occupied my every sense, and enabled me to support every affliction.— Never, though I had led her myself through an admiring nation to the altar, and joined her hand with that of the incomparable Henry, never could even that advantage have compensated to my yearning heart for the loss of her society. What then must it suffer to recollect that a savage had wrested her, for unknown purposes, from my arms!— Nor could I, amidst all the horrors this idea teemed with, fix on any distinct one.

Oh, that melodious voice!— Still it seemed to vibrate on my ear, but no longer could I hear it.— That unmatched form glistered through every tear, but evaporated with it. The most deadly glooms came over me—a thousand times I raised my rash hand to precipitate—the unfortunate Rose Cecil alone withheld me.— I often thought I heard her aerial voice, and despair slowly subsided into resignation.

I now exerted every effort to gain upon Dunlop; but, too faithful to his execrable employers, I never won more from him than that my daughter was still in the Castle, not only unhurt, but treated with distinction and indulgence.— Yet, how could I credit such improbable assurances? or even if they were true, ought not an indulgence so partial to alarm more strongly a mother's feelings? To every solicitation once more to behold her, I received a positive denial; nor was even the liberty of walking now allowed me. I often enquired why I was thus restrained, if no injury was meditated to my unfortunate child? To questions of this kind he never answered, but left me to my own fluctuating conjectures: They were so numerous and frightful that conviction could hardly aggravate the evil. Nevertheless, as Dunlop seemed ever anxious to compose my mind by reiterated assurances of my poor girl's safety, and as there was an air of candour in all he uttered, I began at length to conclude that the contemptible Somerset had aspired to the niece of his master, but from being already married to the divorced Countess of Essex, had not dared to avow his passion.[29] I recollected too late the singularity of his being with Prince Henry when first we beheld that amiable youth;—the assiduous respect he had shewn in waiting on me at Richmond;—the affected offer of his interest with a tyrant whose will he so well knew how to make subservient to his own;—the combination of refined arts by which we had been led to throw ourselves into the prison selected for us;—and, finally, that the prison was probably a house of his own.— Through the whole of this, as well as the manner we were guarded, there was a policy too minute for a King to plan, and too watchful to be the work of an indifferent person.— When by a just turn of thought we insensibly unravel any hitherto inexplicable event, how does the mind disdain its former blindness! I now considered with wonder my long want of perspicacity, and found something every moment to corroborate and strengthen the idea I had adopted.

To fix on any thing certain appears to the exhausted soul a degree of relief; and though, at some moments, I dreaded art and violence might be employed, if gentle methods failed to undermine the virtue of my sweet girl, yet I much oftener flattered myself that she could not inspire a passion so gross and unworthy; and knew her soul superior to every other seduction. From the instant I ventured once more to hope, all my plans for escaping revived; I had no longer, it is true, the privilege of passing beyond my apartment, but misery is ever ingenious, and I was pre-informed of the days when the compassionate centinel guarded the door; nay, I fancied I often heard him draw near, attracted by my sighs and groans.— The note I had formerly prepared was yet in being; I sewed it to a long thin slip of whalebone, and, on the day when he used to be attending, worked it gently under both doors, at a time when I judged no other person near, and softly rapped at the inner one. A sweet hope rekindled in my heart as I felt it drawn out of my hand. I watched in vain the whole tedious day for a reply, and often fancied my effort had been betrayed to Dunlop; but as I did not perceive any alteration in his countenance, I became reassured; and concluded that the soldier could not write, nor perhaps even read; and if so, a whole week must necessarily elapse ere I could learn his resolutions. The expiration of that time verified my last conjecture. With unspeakable satisfaction I at last saw a billet introduced into my solitude, by the same means I had successfully ventured. I was a long time deciphering the almost unintelligible scrawl: "I pity you, lady, from my heart, but I know not how to help you; it is true, you are rich, and I am very poor, but then it is impossible to get at you; if you can think of any way, I am ready to assist." Ah, God! how did I lift up my eyes to thee, who hadst thus strangely opened once more to me a communication with that society from which I had been so unfairly wrested! In moments like this every thing appears possible; already I seemed to see my prison gates open, my daughter in my arms, and our honest assistant rich at once in our wealth and our blessings. Having had the foresight to prepare another billet, I conveyed it in the same manner. "Worthy soldier, is my daughter safe, and yet in this Castle? if so, tear away all but the word, yes, and my soul shall for ever bless you." How pure was the joy with which I received the precious monosyllable!

To prepare another billet, comprehending my plan, was a work of time;— with what perturbation did I undertake it! To condense my meaning to a few words, and yet leave it obvious to a common capacity, was not an easy task.— I thus at last effected it: "Generous friend, win over him who guards my daughter's door, while you are at mine, and I will share with both of you the rich jewels I possess, of which you saw only the smallest. Observe the form of the keys Dunlop brings—buy many as near them as possible, and so various that some may certainly fit.— Procure likewise two regimental suits, that we may pass the gate unquestioned; if you can raise the little money necessary for this, fear not to spend it; I will make your fortune in the moment our doors are opened.— Restore me to my daughter—conduct us to the gate, and we will both beseech the Almighty to bless the riches we will joyfully leave in your hands."

Having dispatched this, I waited the deciding hour with the most anxious impatience; and scarce dared to raise my eyes from the ground, lest Dunlop should read in them aught that might alarm his suspicions.

How to dispose of myself, and daughter, when out of the Castle, was a question I could not decide upon; but I flattered myself that as we should have some hours the start of our persecutors, we might reach London; where it would not be easy to apprehend persons who had been imprisoned without any judicial enquiry or sentence.— A greater fear however than that occurred.— How if these soldiers should not be honest—the reward we must bestow would prove what we possessed, and our lives might be the forfeit. Yet such was my desperate state, that even this reasonable apprehension did not induce me one moment to hesitate.

The appointed time revolved, and I received another billet. "Be ready when all is quiet—every thing is prepared if any of the keys fit. My comrade and self must go with you to secure our own safety, but it will likewise secure yours." Oh, how did my heart bound at this happy intelligence!—my languor, my lameness, all was forgotten. Maternal love, and habitual fear, seemed to wing me with supernatural powers.

As the important moment approached, I knelt and devoutly invoked the assistance of heaven. Ah! not in vain; for the first effort of the soldiers was successful. I reached out a rich and ready hand to each.— They received the contents with extreme satisfaction, and, conjuring me to preserve the most profound silence, locked the doors, and led me to the further side of the Castle. At the threshold of my daughter's apartment they gave into my hand the disguises I had desired, and agreed to wait till we were ready. The tender meltings mothers only know thrilled through my heart, and sweetened every apprehension, as I gently made my way through a dark room towards one where I saw lights still burning: but fearful of alarming my sweet girl, I hesitated at the door. What was my astonishment to perceive that the apartment was gay, magnificent, and illuminated!— I thought at first that anxiety had bewildered my faculties, but their truth became evident when they centred at once on my daughter; who, elegantly habited, had sunk on a couch asleep. A writing table covered with due implements stood before her, on which lay a letter it appeared to me she had been answering. The deadly coldness, the nameless sensations this extraordinary scene could not but occasion, at once suspended even the most powerful emotions of nature. A repulsion so terrible obliged me to rest my head against the pillar of the door, and struggle some time with the sickness and confusion of my soul, ere I could gather strength to penetrate into the fact. She still continued to enjoy a repose, it seemed to me I never should know again, and I had now lost the wish of awakening her; of escaping—alas, even of existing! Slowly at length I tottered toward the table, and catching at the two letters I mentioned, appeared to grasp in them my very fate. The signature of the first made its contents almost needless.

"A few days, a very few days more, most charming of women, and I shall be able to indulge your every wish—every thing is now in train:—pain me not therefore in thus pressing an impossibility. The heart of your mother is inexorable to me—it has ever been so, and I neither dare trust her with the truth, or you with one so prejudiced, till the law shall have annulled my detested marriage, and the King agree to my union with yourself—I live but in that hope; it supports me under all these long and tedious absences. Why will you call the safe home in which you are enclosed, a prison?— The whole world appears so to him who beholds with pleasure only that spot where you dwell. To-morrow I shall steal an hour to pass with you—smile for that hour, my beloved, and bless with a welcome your devoted Somerset."

Of what various, what manifold miseries is the human heart susceptible! None of all the exquisite variety I had hitherto known, ever surpassed this new one. My disdainful soul recoiled from even the dear object of its affections— hypocrisy, that essence of all vices, had stolen into her heart under the name of love, and blighted the virtues yet blossoming—fearfully I perused her letter, to end every doubt.

"What ages of solitude, of suffering does your love, my lord, impose on me! In vain you would fill up that place in my heart, a parent so justly revered must ever hold. But you still talk of to-morrow, and to-morrow—alas, it is a day that may perhaps never come—you think me vapourish, but you know not how strangely my illness increases—it is acute and violent—Oh that I could lay my burning head one moment on my mother's bosom!— Catharine gave me some whey yesterday; I don't know,—perhaps I wrong her, but I have not been myself since. A thousand gloomy images have taken possession of my mind! my eager ear is filled with imaginary knells: I could fancy myself dying: you will laugh perhaps at this weakness, but I cannot conquer it—if I should indeed judge right, release my mother, I conjure you, and conceal forever from her—"

Ah, what? exclaimed I in the most terrible agony, for at this unfinished sentence the letter broke off.— Disdain, suspense, anguish, contended within me, and shook my frame like the last struggle of nature.— Of all the horrors that bewildered my mind, one, one alone, could my senses ascertain.— My hapless girl was indeed dying—wan and sunken were those cheeks late so florid—the icy fingers of death were impressed upon her temples, and the eyes she heavily opened, as her woe-struck mother dropt upon the earth, had no longer either life, beauty, or lustre—Oh, that my soul had escaped in the groan which followed this horrible conviction!— She faintly shrieked, and remained in a kind of stupor; tenderness, however, soon predominated in my mind over every other sensation.— I threw my arms round her in silence, and the tears which deluged her cheeks, alone declared what passed in my soul.— Still she uttered not a word, but griped my hands as though the pangs of death were indeed upon her. I in vain conjured, intreated her to speak; it was long ere she had courage to enter into a detail which she had neither breath or voice to go through. "Condemn me not wholly, my mother," at length cried the dear one, "however appearances may incense you. I ask for only life enough to acquit myself, and will to my last moment thank the God who restores me to your arms, though only to blush away my being in them. Yet have I no other crime to avow than that reserve unconquerably interwoven in my nature.— Alas, yesterday I thought it a virtue.— Heaven will, perhaps, give me strength to go through the story, at least, I ought to make the effort.— Oh, deign to pardon my compelled abruptness, and hear me with patience!

"At the moment which first presented Prince Henry to our knowledge, he was accompanied by the Earl of Somerset.— How my eyes conceived the partiality my reason could never erase I know not, but they decided at once in his favor.— Whether the Earl perceived the involuntary distinction, or was led by an equal one on his own part, is alike unknown to me; but I understood the reluctance with which he gave way to the Prince, whom he left with us— the contempt with which you mentioned Lord Somerset strangely shocked and alarmed me; yet (may I own it) I secretly accused the most upright heart existing of pride and prejudice; and found a thousand reasons for suddenly disputing a judgment which had hitherto been the rule of my own.— During the frequent visits Prince Henry paid you, when prudence induced you to send me abroad; alas, to what a temptation did you unconsciously expose me! Somerset availed himself of those opportunities, and, by distant homage, confirmed the prepossession I had already conceived.— What shame, what sorrow, what humiliation, has it cost me!— Can you ever know a more exquisite misery than to bestow your heart unworthily? to be humbled without guilt—compelled to blush hourly for errors not your own—and reduced to a perpetual conflict with those powerful and natural emotions which form, under more fortunate circumstances, the felicity of youth! Sensible by the curious attention of others, how injurious that of the Earl might in time become, I requested leave to remain at home; and awed, in spite of myself, by your sentiments, boldly resolved to sacrifice the erroneous inclination of my heart, and received the vows of Prince Henry. To see you happy, to flatter him with the hope of being so, for a time elevated and amused my mind; but solitude soon restored it to its favorite object: Somerset still presented himself, and I took pleasure in the tears in which I drowned his admired image. By some means or other I found letters from him frequently in my chamber.— I dared not enquire how, lest I should awaken your suspicions; alas, perhaps that was one of the fine-spun webs with which love ever veils its errors! I found him regularly informed of all our designs;—I knew it was in his power to cross them by a word; and I began to esteem him for daring to be silent. During the last progress of the King, Somerset resolved to profit by the absence of Henry, and, apprized of the interviews we granted the Prince in the pavilion in the garden, as well as of my habit of sitting there, determined to take the chance of pleading his cause. My stay was by the rising of the moon unusually prolonged on the evening he had selected to present himself before me. The pale light served only to shadow out his form—any human one must at such a moment have appalled me.— I shrieked, and was half-fainting when the sound of his voice dissipated my terror. Surprize, perhaps joy, that instantaneous confidence we ever repose in the object beloved, doubtless reassured him. I was scarce conscious I had granted the audience he demanded, till he fell at my feet to thank me. The manner in which he avowed his passion, made me sensible too late that I had ill-disguised my own; I know not whether I should have had resolution to attempt doing so much longer, had not our conversation been suddenly interrupted by Henry. The Prince, to my inexpressible dismay, entered the pavillion.— My voice had drawn him thither, but the sound of Somerset's made him retreat in contemptuous silence. The Earl would have followed, but I caught his arm and obstinately withheld him:—then conjuring him to hasten to his boat, I flew after the Prince. Henry had thrown himself on the seat near the terrace; but, sensible of the necessity of separating him and the Earl at such a crisis, I entreated the Prince to accompany me to the house. The light of the moon enabled me to judge from his bewildered air

of the distraction of his mind. I had not courage to break a silence he voluntarily maintained: yet to part under appearances so equivocal was impossible.
I hesitated at length a faint explanation. 'Could you contradict the evidence
of my senses, madam,' sighed the Prince, in a low and tender tone, 'I might
wish to hear you: as it is, spare me, I conjure you, on a subject so hateful; I
have nothing to reproach you with but a reserve which led me to deceive
myself.— Adieu, I promise you inviolable silence.— He who once hoped to
constitute your felicity, disdains to interfere with it. Yet one truth I ought
perhaps to apprize you of: your happy, your favored lover is married; think
not I wish to reap any advantage from this information—never more shall I
breathe a vow at your feet—Oh, Mary! you have undone me!' He wrung my
hands in an agony of passion, and rushed through the garden to conceal the
sobs which continued to pierce my heart through my ear. What a night did I
pass!—sad prelude to so many miserable ones. I readily absented myself the
next day at the Prince's usual hour of visiting us. I never saw him afterwards
without pain, humiliation, and constraint; though he omitted nothing likely
to reconcile me to myself. During the fatal illness into which he fell, how
continually did my heart reproach me with increasing, if not causing it! and
how deeply was my injustice to his merit punished, in the mortifying conviction that Somerset had dared to deceive me!— What prayers did I offer up for
Henry's recovery—What vows to atone for my error, by a life devoted to him!
Alas, I was not worthy a lover so noble; and heaven recalled his purer essence,
while yet unsullied. The sense of a hopeless and unworthy passion mingled
with the deep grief I could not but feel for his loss. A sickliness and disgust
succeeded—rank, royalty, distinction, every worldly advantage combined,
could not have dissipated the gloom of my mind, or reconciled me for a
moment to society. I took no pleasure in the hopes, you, my dear, my generous mother, cherished for me; but I would not be ungrateful, and therefore
concealed my ideas. Thus impressed, what merit was there in that philosophy
which enabled me to become your comforter under a reverse I scarcely felt?—
Oh, that my errors, my misfortunes, had ended here—that I had breathed my
last on your revered bosom, while yet unconscious of wounding it! When the
vain hope of freedom made you solicit for a limited portion of air and exercise, how could you foresee the fatal consequences of that periodical indulgence! In the first of these solitary walks, Somerset presented himself before
me; not the crested, aspiring favorite; but the self-accusing, the pale, the humble
lover.— My eyes resisted the impulse of my heart, and turned haughtily from
him; but he hung on my robe, he intreated, he conjured,—he *would* be heard.—
I feel I shall not have time to enter into the long explanation of his conduct

which won from me an unwilling pardon: suffice it to say, that he knew every, the most secret, transaction in our house, nor ventured to marry till convinced I was betrothed to Prince Henry. But, oh! the wretch he espoused!— Never may you know the crimes of which she has too probably been guilty! It was to Somerset's interposition we owed the prolongation of those lives, the pride and rage of the King had devoted from the moment he read the papers he took a malicious pleasure in destroying.— Still anxious for me, the Earl owned he had persuaded James to imprison us in this Castle, as well to secure our safety, as to provide us those comforts and conveniencies our royal relation would have deprived us of.

"I could not be insensible to services like these; and, finding my wrath began to abate, he awakened my pity, by describing the domestic miseries an unhappy marriage had imposed on him. The tears with which my wounded soul blotted this picture, induced him still farther to explain himself. His hopes of a divorce seemed rationally grounded, and I could not but enter into his views on that head.— I was not however able to persuade him that you would ever think as I did, and weakly promised a secresy I ought to have seen the danger of.— Yet, the prejudice which induced you to impute even our imprisonment to him, seemed so fixed, so unalterable, that though a thousand times the integrity of my nature tempted me to unfold to you the only secret my bosom ever teemed with, I shrunk before a mind so disgusted, nor dared to utter one syllable might pain you. The delays of Somerset, however necessary, alarmed and distressed me.— I became cold and melancholy; and, too delicate to confide to him the true causes of this alteration, he soon assigned a false one. Peevishness and altercation now robbed our interviews of all their sweetness.— He often reproached me with having opened my heart to you, who alone could thus shut it against him.— Disdain urged me one day to assure him I would do so, the first moment I again beheld you.— He left me in a transport of rage. Alas, my heart became sensible of one every way equal to it.— When I found that I was not permitted to return to your prison, I refused to admit him to that allotted for me, and gave vent to every extravagance so unforeseen an injury must excite.— His answer convinced me that this step had long been meditated. He assured me 'he would sooner die than restore me to a mother who had ever hated, detested, and despised him without any reason, till his claim took place of hers, and he could call me his wife.' The cruel remembrance of what you must suffer, soon reduced me to intreaties, and solemn promises of continued secresy. 'They were now,' he replied, 'too late;—that he could not suppose it possible I should be able to conceal from you the cause of my absence; and this, justly strengthening the unreasonable disgust and hatred you already felt towards him, would make you go any lengths to prevent a union you must naturally abhor.'— To this he added all he thought likely to soothe my embittered spirit, and solemnly assured me your mind was relieved, by a conviction that this separation was only in consequence of a new order from court.— Although I saw in this mode of conduct a chicanery and little art my nature disdained, I was yet glad to imagine it lightened to you the heavy affliction our separation could not but cause. I felt too late the error of mental reservation, and had sufficient reason to think every evil might branch out from that little root. Having in vain contended with the man no less master of my life than fate, I at length was wearied into forgiving him. The divorce was now in great forwardness, and the manifold iniquities of the fiend in human shape he had married such as could not but shock and interest a heart disposed to love him.[30] A thousand busy projects passed daily from his brain to mine, and often intervened between myself and a mother so revered. Every hour that went over my head made it more impossible for me to appear before you but as his wife, and I became as eager as himself for a day which heaven had pre-ordained I should never see. One who pursued her point more effectually, has severely punished all my youthful errors—Oh may my premature death be received by him who made me as an expiation!— How shall I tell you!—and yet I must—I have often thought my food tinctured with poison—yesterday—Alas, my mother, where is now your fortitude?—where is that sublime resignation I have seen you exert?—forget the vain hopes you once formed for me—forget that I am your daughter; oh! think the erring wretch this awful moment recals was born to embitter the days that yet remain to you, and adore, even in this painful moment, the mercy of the Almighty!— If I have not sinned beyond forgiveness, graciously extend yours to me, while yet I am sensible of the blessing."

As she threw herself into my arms, every feature seemed shrunk, and moulded by the fingers of death—Alas! what became of me at this crisis! her paroxysms were scarce more dreadful than those that seized upon my soul—every emotion of love, friendship, and kindred, appeared tranquillity, when compared with the wild, uncontrolable anguish of the robbed, the ruined mother. Perpetually ready to give vent to the tumultuous execrations my heart pronounced against the artful, insidious traitor, who had alienated her affections, and warped the rectitude of her mind, an intuitive conviction that such a transport would vainly embitter the little time remaining to her obliged me to confine to sighs and groans all the miseries of the moment. I drew her fondly to my bosom, and poured over her pale convulsed cheeks a heart-broken mother's solemn absolution.

One horror only could be added to a scene like this, nor was it wanting. The centinels, weary of waiting and startled by our groans, now abruptly entered the chamber.— Scared at the sight of my daughter expiring in my arms, the sense of their own danger soon over-ruled every other; they urged, they conjured me to leave my Mary, now apparently lifeless; but they urged, they conjured in vain.— On her I was so soon to resign to her Creator my whole soul was now fixed.— The dear one faintly revived; but, struck with inconceivable horror at sight of the soldiers, she relapsed into convulsions, griping me still closer. Ah, God, the cold chill that followed! when I found her hold relax at once—the world vanished from before my eyes—they beheld only the fair form, which sought a grave on the bosom where it first found a being.— Inspired with the fierceness of a savage, I grasped her yet closer, shrieking tremendously, and with a strength surely supernatural. The confused and incensed soldiers, having used every persuasion in vain, made the most violent efforts to sever me from the last, the dearest, the only object of my love. Threats, intreaties, art, and force, however, were alike vain—nothing could win, could tear her from me. They presented at length their bayonets to my bosom, and beheld me with surprise dare the blow.— Perhaps they had really pierced it, but that some women, attendant on my daughter, now rushed into the room. Fear for their own safety obliged the soldiers to forbear urging or enforcing me further. They seized the intruders, lest any of them should escape, and, having bound them, sought safety in flight. A terrible calm succeeded my intense desperation—the blood which had tumultuously burnt along every vein now returned in torrents, to choak up, and drown my heart.— The black fumes mounted thence to my brain.— With a grief-glazed eye, I contemplated the pale and precious cheek from whose rich coloring I of late drew life, till ignorant that I either suffered, or existed.

*　　*　　*　　*　　*　　*

Seldom enough myself to distinguish the shadowy forms that flitted round my bed, and always too indifferent to utter a single question, I opened not the curtain, nor cared who was beyond it.— Vague and stifled exclamations alone informed me of the danger of that fatal fire which raged within my veins:—danger did I say?—I ought rather to have called it relief. During the short intervals of my delirium, I voluntarily sunk in silence under the gloom and debility it left. Suddenly I was seized with such flutters, and gaspings, as seemed to indicate an immediate termination of every human infliction.— My weary soul hovered at the gate of its prison, and I felt as if a single word would release it; but I had neither ability or inclination to pronounce that word; and though I perceived every curtain was undrawn to give me air, I raised not my quivering eyelids to distinguish the two persons who anxiously held each hand, as watching for the last beat of the faint and hurried pulse.

While thus in the very struggle and fluctuation incident to parting nature, a voice suddenly reached my receding senses—a voice so mellow, calm, and holy, that life yet lingered on it. I distinguished these words: "Oh, Almighty God! with whom do live the spirits of the just made perfect, when they are delivered from their earthly prisons; we humbly commend the soul of this thy servant, our dear sister, into thy hands, as into those of a faithful Creator, and most merciful Saviour!" A faint effort I made to release my hands, with the design of raising them towards heaven, caused the prayer to cease. An emotion I could not resist made me lift my dim eyes to behold, if not absolutely an angel, the human being that most resembled one. At a table near my bed knelt a Clergyman, whose reverend locks time had entirely bleached, but it had taken nothing from his fine eyes, which seemed to reflect the divinity he served—care and experience had worn traces in every perfect feature; and the pale purity of virtue, chastened alike by sorrow and resignation, had succeeded to the vivid hues of youth, hope and health. I uttered a sigh, and faint exclamation.— A sweet, yet sad, pleasure wandered through my exhausted frame, thus to be assured that I had reached the very point of my being. Some women decently arrayed in black having assisted my infirm and venerable comforter to rise, conducted him to the side of my bed, and retired. With a graciousness peculiar to himself, he adjured me, since the mercy of the Almighty had unexpectedly restored my intellects, to profit by the indulgence in preparing my soul to appear before him. An impulse of gratitude made me raise my hand to take his, that sympathetically trembled over me; but even this trifling motion made me sensible I had on many blisters,[31] which wrung my feeble sense even to fainting. The women, as is usual in desperate cases, gave me some vivifying cordials, and again retired. The reverend stranger once more addressed me, praising the Almighty for the restoration of my intellects—they were indeed restored, for, oh! the recollection of that dismal event which had rendered their loss a blessing returned upon my mind, and made me loathe the succours I could owe only to the detested hand that had consummated my woes! "Oh, you," cried I, in a broken voice, "who thus seek to comfort the miserable, inform me first to whom I owe the benefit?" He paused a moment—his gracious eyes glanced upward, and, having thus consulted with his Creator, he answered me with firmness; "that his name was De Vere; the household Chaplain of the Earl of Somerset."— At that abhorred title I shut my eyes as though I could have shut out retrospection, and waved him to leave me.— "Rash, unfortunate woman," returned he, in a solemn and yet tender tone, "religion does not permit me to obey you—would you bear into a better world the pride, the passions, the prejudices, which have certainly embittered, perhaps shortened, your days in this?— Dare you present to the pure source of good, your great, your glorious Creator, a soul yet sullied with voluntary frailties and human imperfection?— Are you not on the point of ceasing to suffer, wherefore then should you not cease to resent? Religion enjoins you to forget the faults of others, and contemplate only your own.— Attend to truth, and I will impart it to you—resolve to be patient, and I will pour balm into the deep wounds of human calamity—control your passions, and I will elevate them, even under the struggles of parting nature, by hopes which shall surely be realized, because they centre in immortality."— The author of universal being seemed to speak to me through his Minister—the gathering tumult stood suspended. "You address not an ingrate," returned I feebly, "I have walked in peace through life with my God, and fain would I die so: though surely to remember the wretch, who precipitates me into eternity by a grief too pungent for endurance, with charity, or composure, exceeds my ability. If you have aught to reveal that may allay this irritation, be truly generous in unfolding it—if otherwise, present such images only to my mind as may drive from it that of a villain, whose offences you cannot extenuate; nor double the agonies even you cannot relieve." "It is my only intention, madam," replied he.— "Alas, I would not probe your wounds even to heal them!— If it is necessary to suffer ere we can feel, believe me, I want not even that power of sympathizing with you; yet must I reconcile my divine and human character, by vindicating the innocent while I soothe the unfortunate; though even the wealth of nations could not tempt me for one moment to palliate guilt. Have you courage to hear a letter, given me in hopes of the present opportunity?" I controlled myself, and signed him to read.

"In what words, most injured, most unfortunate of women, shall the wretch who has unconsciously destroyed your peace and his own deprecate the wrath his very idea must occasion?— Alas, overwhelmed with grief, horror, despair, every killing sensation, (guilt alone excepted) his punishment is as acute as even malice could wish it.

"To fill up the measure of my afflictions, I am informed that the blow which has robbed my soul of its dearest hope, struck at your life—that even in the wildness of delirium your curses pursue me, and you are ready to sink into the grave with unabated hatred.— If returning recollection should ever enable you to read, or hear, these genuine dictates of a breaking heart, do it, madam, I conjure you, the late justice of an acquittal. By the spotless spirit of the dear

lost angel my fatal love deprived you of, hear, pity—if possible, forgive me.—
Can you for a moment believe that I would have touched a life, dear, precious,
to me, even as to yourself?

"The abandoned woman, to whom heaven, as a punishment for all my
sins, united me, discovered by some unknown means those views I thought
impenetrable; and, foreseeing in their completion her own disgrace and ruin,
she took a deadly means to save herself from both.— Already but too familiar
with poison, and with death, she found, among the maids attending on my
dear lost love, one base enough to aid her in translating an angel too early to
the skies. To say, that I hate, detest, and shun the execrable monster, is surely
needless—I even resign her to your justice, nor do I wish to shelter myself
from it, if you still think me guilty.

"The last words of an expiring saint are not more ardent, more sincere
than those I now utter.— Oh! strive, then to live, madam, nor let my agonized
soul have the additional misfortune of shortening your days, and lingering
under your curse!"

Alas, of what importance are these late convictions? When a ball has
gone through the heart, we are incapable of heeding the quarter it comes
from.—

I could not however refuse credence to this letter, and, accusing myself
of having hitherto perhaps wanted candour towards the author, I acquitted
myself to him, by affording him my forgiveness.

Nature, ever shrinking from dissolution, is easily recalled to a lingering
sufferance; but the exhausted soul no more can recover its powers. The activity which once supported me was gone forever.—

The venerable divine I have mentioned still watched over me, and by
the holiest consolations contended with the apathy into which I was sinking.— But who could heal a heart broken by so many sorrows?— That it *was*
broken alone could console me. Destined to turn my dim eyes around this
vast globe without finding one object on which they could rest, De Vere led
them towards heaven; he bade me remember that my treasure was only removed, not taken wholly from me; and that every passing day brought me
nearer to recovering it.

For the execrable woman who had, to the ruin of her own soul, murdered the only hope of mine, I ventured not to imagine a punishment.— I
dared not trust myself with so dangerous a wish—No, I consigned her to the
God she had offended, and he has, even in this world, fearfully avenged me.[32]

The pious De Vere shewed, by preserving and restoring my jewels, the
equity of his nature, and I made him such acknowledgments as must flatter

his heart, and establish his fortune. As soon as I thought myself equal to the journey, I resolved to retire to France, that I might at least expire in peace, and besought him to accompany me.— Not able without ingratitude immediately to quit his patron, he comforted me with the hopes of soon partaking my voluntary exile.

How unworthy the man who won the innocent heart of my translated angel ever was of it, I had soon another convincing proof. Because I resisted the impulses of despair—because I listened to the dictates of virtue and religion, and deigned to live out the days appointed by the Almighty, his narrow soul began to believe mine susceptible of human consolation; he dared to intrude upon me, in the name of the King, late offers of acknowledgment, distinction, fortune—Heavens! how could either imagine I would owe aught to those I must alike look down upon?— The very idea had well nigh disarranged my feeble faculties, and destroyed the religious composure of my grief. It however convinced me that no opposition would be made to my quitting that prison in which I left, alas, all worth enclosing.— I launched once more into the immense world, unknown—unendeared, and willing to be so.

My fever returned on my landing in France with the most mortal symptoms.— Ah! can I fail here to commemorate the second angel heaven sent to my assistance? The arrival of the Ambassador in his way toward England, though at first an inconvenience, in so narrow an asylum as an inn, eventually prolonged my days. His dear and lovely daughter was informed of my state— she indulged the sublime impulse of humanity, which led her towards the bed, where lay a forlorn wretch who appeared ready to draw her last breath in silent affliction. She summoned her noble father's physician, whose skill relieved one it could not save.— She even deigned to outstay the Ambassador; and, by a glorious principle known only to superior natures, began to love the wretch she succoured. A virtue so exemplary almost reconciled me to the world I am shortly to quit.— Sweet Adelaide, when in this faint portrait you survey yourself, sigh for those decaying powers which cannot render it more striking.

That my decline has been prolonged till this narrative is concluded I do not regret; and by compliance I have evinced my sense of your friendship:— I have now only to die.— Yet, alas, it is with regret I present to your youthful eyes so melancholy a chart of my voyage through life.— Suffer it not to damp your hopes, but rather let it blunt your sense of misfortune: for have I not said already, that consummate misery has a moral use, in teaching the repiner at little evils to be juster to his God and himself?— Glorious though inscrutable are all his ways, and, short as my time now is, he has suffered me to see his righteous retribution. Condemnation, infamy, and solitude, are henceforth the portion of Somerset and his execrable Countess.— A similar crime, long buried in oblivion, has been proved upon them,[33] without my having once disturbed the sacred ashes of my Mary. An act so atrocious has broke the tye which bound De Vere to the Earl, and I every day expect him. I struggle to retain my last breath till I can give it up in his presence, assured that his superior soul will prepare my frail one for a long hereafter, and decently dispose of the mortal frame I soon must leave behind me.

Dear and lovely friend, you are now in England.— Already perhaps your feet have trod lightly over those spots where my happiness withered.— Ah! if sensibility should lead you more thoughtfully to retrace them, check every painful emotion, by recollecting that I shall then be past the power of suffering.— Yet when your noble father reconducts you to the home you was born to embellish, grant a little to the weakness of mortality, and linger once more on the spot where we met: the pious De Vere will there attend your coming.— Accept from his hand the casket I bequeath, and suffer him to lead you to the nameless grave where he shall have interred my ashes: drop on it a few of those holy tears with which virtue consecrates misfortune; then raise your eyes with those of your venerable conductor, and in a better world look for

MATILDA.

FINIS.

Emendations

Note: Numbers given are for the page and line numbers in the present edition. The critical reading of this edition is listed first, followed by the number of the edition from which it is taken (1st or 3rd); a single square bracket separates this from the rejected reading of the copy text (the second edition), which follows it. Obvious printer's errors have been silently corrected and are not listed here.

Part I

10.5: sorrow; (3rd)] sorrow,
12.29: hers (3rd)] her's
26.9: offering (3rd)] paying
34.16: despair; (3rd)] despair,
43.13: suggested, (3rd)] had treasured,
53.23: were (3rd)] was
63.36-38: The peculiarity of the situation can alone excuse such a marriage; but I was born for obedience. Scarce had the transports of finding myself happy given place to reason, when my mother recurred to my mind. (3rd)] The peculiarity of the situation can alone excuse such a marriage; but I was born for obedience. Formed wholly of the mild elements, I wept the disappointment of my wishes ever in silence. Scarce had the transports of finding myself happy given place to reason, when my mother recurred to my mind.

Part II

69.1: Lord Leicester's apartment and ours (3rd)] our apartments
75.21: But (3rd)] But,
76.32: we (3rd)] I
76.37: myself (3rd)] ourselves

Part III

108.16: hers (3rd)] her's
112.27: 'Rose,' (3rd)] 'Rise,'
118.29: conjecture, (3rd)] conjecture
123.21: Lord, (3rd)] Lord
124.30: him alone (3rd)] he alone

126.31: as well as (3rd)] as well
132.1: nevertheless, (3rd)] Nevertheless,
132.11: settlers; (3rd)] settlers,
133.3: as if I (3rd)] as I
138.15: their huts (3rd)] these huts
139.6: possessions of Mortimer (3rd)] possessions, of Mortimer
143.16: earthly (3rd)] earthy
149.18: seek in another (3rd)] seek another
151.28: though small (3rd)] though, small

Part IV

154.7: collected, (3rd)] collected
154.11: subjoin (3rd)] copy
171.17: as if I had fainted (3rd)] as having fainted
183.4: equal-minded (3rd)] equal minded
187.13: selected for the occasion (3rd)] selected on the occasion
215.19: advantage! (3rd)] advantage?
215.34: rashly, (3rd)] rashly
223.12: mangled (1st)] mingled

Part V

249.29: lest (3rd)] least
255.36: itself! (3rd)] itself?
257.27: people! (3rd)] people?
258.14: art and nature (3rd)] heart and nature
259.26: Ellinor, revived (3rd)] Ellinor revived,
263.18: supplies! (3rd)] supplies?
264.4: door, felt a horror (3rd)] door felt a horror,
264.39: departure, (3rd)] departure
268.9: lest (3rd)] least

Part VI

273.14: borne (3rd)] born
274.13: in which (3rd)] were
275.15: conducted; (3rd)] conducted,
275.30: eyes (3rd)] eye
286.3: counsel (3rd)] council

286.24: his example (3rd)] this example
291.37: Yet who (3rd)] Yet, who
308.32: lest (3rd)] least
312.33: led (3rd)] lead
312.38: blindness! (3rd)] blindness?
313.27: hadst (3rd)] hast
315.25: susceptible! (3rd)] susceptible?
318.18: it! (3rd)] it?
322.33: loathe (3rd)] loath

NOTES TO THE NOVEL

Biographical information is drawn, unless noted otherwise, from G.E. C[okayne], ed., *Complete Baronetage* (Exeter: W. Pollard, 1906), and from Sir Leslie Stephen and Sir Sidney Lee, eds., *Dictionary of National Biography* (London: Oxford University Press, 1959-60 [1892-93]). The final authority used for definitions of words is *The Oxford English Dictionary.*

PART I

1. Shakespeare, *As You Like It,* Act II, scene i, ll. 3-6. The exiled duke speaks to his attendant lords as they hide together in the Forest of Arden. Ann Radcliffe frequently uses epigraphs from Shakespeare; she may have derived this practice from Lee. Unlike Radcliffe, however, Lee is careful to preserve the fiction of the Elizabethan-Jacobean narrator by quoting only sources that do not postdate that era (with the exception of Blackmore's *Eliza;* see note 10 to Part I). As Lee grew up in a theatrical family and had her first literary success as a dramatist, it is not surprising to find her quoting dramatic antecedents. John Lee, her father, had acted in *As You Like It* at least four times during her lifetime, in the parts of both Touchstone and Jacques (Highfill, vol. 9, pp. 204-8). But Lee may also have had more literary motives for the choice of Shakespeare, since Horace Walpole had modelled his earlier Gothic novel, *The Castle of Otranto,* on Shakespearean drama (see Introduction, pp. xiii-xiv). Use of Shakespeare is in keeping with the Gothic, pre-Romantic impulse to ground literature in a national, "modern" tradition, as opposed to an ancient or classical one.

2. Sir John Eliot (1736-1786), prominent Scottish physician. Having been a navy surgeon on a privateer, he became physician in ordinary to George, Prince of Wales, established a lucrative London practice, and was created baronet in 1778. Despite his professional success and Lee's praise, some contemporaries, including King George III, thought him not a very capable physician. As Lee's dedication hints, he attended both her parents in their last illnesses. It is just possible that Lee also met Mrs. Eliot, Grace née Dalrymple, the physician's much younger wife and a celebrated beauty, whom he married in 1771 but sued for divorce on adultery charges within three years. She went on to become the mistress of many aristocrats and princes (including both a Prince of Wales and a Duke of Orleans) and to become a writer of a very different stamp from Lee, a courtesan-memoirist whose journal of the French Revolution was published after her death.

3. In Bishop Hurd's Dialogue III "On the Golden Age of Queen Elizabeth," Addison and Arbuthnot debate whether her reign was really a "golden age" in which the moral ideals of chivalric romance prevailed. "To be sure! said Mr. Addison, smiling: or, why not affirm, in the proper language of romance, that the women of those days were all chaste, and the men valiant? . . . . [Dr. Arbuthnot]: Their notions of honour and gallantry were carried to an elevation, which, in these degenerate days, hurts the credit of their story" (*The Works of Richard Hurd, D.D., Lord Bishop of Worcester* (London: T. Cadell & W. Davies, 1811 [Millar, 1759]), vol. 3, pp. 189-92; see also Dialogue IV, vol. 3, p. 248.

4. The reference is to the royal Stuart line; this phrase has not been located in any particular "eminent historian," but the general sentiment can be found in any of the histories of the English sixteenth and seventeenth centuries that were widely read in Lee's time.

5. Lee may have been inspired in her approach to the depiction of character by the historian William Robertson, who remarks of Mary, Queen of Scots: "Humanity will draw a veil over this part of her character which it cannot approve, and may, perhaps, prompt some to impute some of her actions to her situation, more than to her dispositions; and to lament the unhappiness of the former, rather than accuse the perverseness of the latter. Mary's sufferings exceed, both in degree and in duration, those tragical distresses which fancy has feigned to excite sorrow and commiseration; and while we survey them, we are apt altogether to forget her frailties, we think of her faults with less indignation, and approve of our tears, as if they were shed for a person who had attained much nearer to pure virtue." William Robertson, *The History of Scotland during the Reigns of Queen Mary and of James VI* (London: Cadell & Davies, 1802 [Millar, 1759]), vol. 3, p. 67).

6. The addressee is a fictional character.

7. Anonymous, "The Beggar's Daughter of Bednall-Green." Chadwyck-Healey's *English Poetry Database* offers a different form of this "popular old ballad" dating from Elizabeth's reign. It mentions another, "lost" version, of which an informant remembered only one stanza, ending with a variant of the two lines Lee quotes here.

8. guardian genius: a guardian spirit; derived from classical pagan beliefs.

9. The idea of "the great chain" of being pervaded eighteenth-century thought. The universe was conceived of as a hierarchical chain in which all entities, from the inanimate to the divine Creator—with all living beings ranged between—were linked one to the next by similarity. Human beings are created in God's image and so on down the "scale" of creation. See Arthur O. Lovejoy, *The Great Chain of Being: A Study of the History of an Idea* (Cambridge: Harvard University Press, 1936).

10. These lines describing the Thames are paraphrased from Sir Richard Blackmore's epic poem *Eliza* (*The English Poetry Database* [London, 1705]), Book III, ll. 37-38. Set in the reign of Elizabeth I, it is the only work quoted by Lee that was actually written later.

11. Henry Scrope (1534?-92) succeeded his father to the title of Lord Scrope on his majority in 1555. He served Elizabeth throughout his life in border conflicts with the Scots and against the neighboring English Catholic nobility of the north, when they rebelled against her. Mrs. Marlow, like all the inhabitants of the Recess, is a fictional character.

12. Lord Scrope held many high offices but never served as an ambassador.

13. cot: cottage.

14. camblet: any of a large variety of fabrics blending animal hair with other fibers to produce a mohair-like texture. Originally it referred more specifically to a costly fabric from the east made from silk and Angora goat hair, but Lee seems to have a more humble and probably anachronistic material in mind.

15. A "pacquet" or "packet" always refers here to letters.

16. press: cupboard.

17. closet: any small, private room.

18. pair of stairs: flight of stairs, staircase.

19. Elijah heard the "still small voice" of God on mount Horeb; I Kings 19:12 (King James Version). The phrase was quoted so often in the eighteenth century that it became divorced from its context and in general tended to be used to refer to an *inner* voice of conscience—the "unerring monitor" mentioned here.

20. eclaircissement: a revelation or explanation of the truth about a situation (from French).

21. Matilda Howard is "the first Lady in England" as the sister of the unmarried duke of Norfolk, the premier duke of the realm. The duke's real sister, named Margaret (1543-90) became the second wife of Lord Scrope in 1565.

22. bills: promissory notes.

23. monastery: here the house of any religious order, whether of women or men.

24. Thomas Howard (1538-2 June 1572), 4th Duke of Norfolk, Earl Marshal of England.

25. King Henry VIII (1491-1547), father of Elizabeth I, ordered the dissolution of all English monasteries in 1536-40 after breaking with the Catholic Church and founding the protestant Church of England.

26. sister: here, sister-in-law.

27. Lee here echoes Mary Astell's *A Serious Proposal to the Ladies* (London, 1701). Astell invited women to form a Protestant "Monastery," observing that "since Inclination can't be forc'd, and nothing makes people more uneasy than the fettering themselves with unnecessary Bonds, there shall be no Vows or irrevocable Obligations, not so much as fear of Reproach to keep our Ladies here any longer than they desire." *The Pioneers: Early Feminists,* ed. Marie Mulvey Roberts and Tamae Mizuta (London: Routledge/ Thoemmes Press, 1993), pp. 36, 63. Lee repeats this point of view in her other novel: "Monastic institutions . . . if free from vows of perpetual celibacy, or total seclusion, would be a great advantage to single women." *The Life of a Lover* (London: G. and J. Robinson, 1804), vol. 1, pp. 8-9. See Megan Lynn Isaac, "Sophia Lee and the Gothic of Female Community," *Studies in the Novel* 28, no. 2: 208. Sarah Scott's vision of Millenium Hall, described in two of her novels, conjures such an idealized Protestant nunnery, although she never uses those words. Sarah Scott, *Millenium Hall,* ed. Gary Kelly (Orchard Park, Canada: Broadview Press, 1995), and *The History of Sir George Ellison,* ed. Betty Rizzo (Lexington: The University Press of Kentucky, 1996). On the combination of the idealized fantasy of a Protestant nunnery and a negative fascination with Catholic convents in eighteenth-century England (especially in Gothic fiction), see also Katharine M. Rogers, "Fantasy and Reality in Fictional Convents of the Eighteenth Century," *Comparative Literature Studies* 22, vol. 3 (1985): 297-316; and Max Byrd, "The Madhouse, the Whorehouse, and the Convent," *Partisan Review* 45 (1977): 268-78.

28. Mary Stuart (1542-7 February 1587), Queen of Scotland, was accused by her rebellious subjects of being accessory with the earl of Bothwell (whom she later married) to the murder in 1567 of her second husband, Henry Darnley, son of the earl of Lenox. The story of her escape from imprisonment by political enemies, her military defeat at Langside, her flight into England, and her reception by Elizabeth is told in

detail by Hume and Robertson, famous contemporary historians with whom Lee was compared, and more succinctly by Goldsmith in his equally popular history. See David Hume, *The History of England, from the Invasion of Julius Caesar to the Revolution in 1688* (London: Cadell & Davies, 1802 [Millar, 1754-62]), vol. 5, pp. 128-47; Robertson, vol. 2, pp. 256-69; Oliver Goldsmith, *The History of England, from the Earliest Times to the Death of George the Second* (London: C.J.G. and F. Rivington; T. Cadell; Longman, Rees, Orme, and Co.; etc., 1831 [Davies, 1771]), vol. 2, pp. 30-31. Lee's adjectives, "beautiful and unfortunate," strongly echo these historians' descriptions of Mary (e.g. Hume, vol. 5, p. 319; Robertson, vol. 3, pp. 66-68; Goldsmith, vol. 2, pp. 24, 50).

29. Both Hume and Robertson similarly make excuses for Mary's reliance on Elizabeth's protection in her distressed circumstances and blame Elizabeth for failing to offer it, although they contrast the imprudence of Mary's decision with the prudence of Elizabeth's response. Goldsmith excuses Elizabeth by urging that "she acted entirely under the direction of her council." All three also discuss the question raised by Elizabeth's conducting the trial: whether she had any jurisdiction over a sovereign princess of another nation. Friedrich Schiller's later play, *Maria Stuart* (1800) explores the question of jurisdiction in depth. Where the historians diverge Lee particularly follows Robertson, both in her severe judgment of Elizabeth and in her strong emphasis on Mary's entitlement to "respect and compassion." Lee's words closely echo Robertson's on Elizabeth's motives as well as on the sympathy due Mary: "The satisfaction which she felt in mortifying a rival, whose beauty and accomplishments she envied, had, perhaps, no less influence than political considerations, in bringing [Elizabeth] to this resolution (Robertson, vol. 2, pp. 260, 263; see also Goldsmith, vol. 2, pp. 32, 45; Hume, vol. 5, 132-33).

30. Here Lee collapses two events that occurred four months apart: Robertson and Hume agree that Elizabeth meant to put on a friendly appearance by sending first Lady Scrope (see note 21 to Part I) followed by Lord Scrope and Sir Francis Knollys (not the duke of Norfolk, as Lee would have it) to greet Mary in Carlisle on 20 May 1568; these emissaries did propose to Mary that she clear her name of guilt by undergoing a trial in England, but it took months for her to submit to this, and it was not until late September of that year that the duke of Norfolk and others were appointed to try her case (Hume, vol. 5, pp. 131-34; Robertson, vol. 2, pp. 263-74).

31. probably destined to reign: Catholics did not recognize Elizabeth (child of Henry VIII's second marriage with a Protestant) as legitimate and many therefore, including the Catholic rulers of Spain and France, supported the claim of Mary Stuart, daughter of Henry's sister Margaret and next in line for the succession to the English throne. Because of the power of these allies and because Elizabeth produced no other heir, it might have seemed in 1568 that Mary was "probably destined to reign" over England.

32. Mary Stuart's first marriage was to François (1544-60), the dauphin (crown prince) of France. Both spouses were very young, and he was weak in body and mind. He reigned briefly as François II, with Mary as his queen consort and her powerful uncles as his advisers, from 1559 until his death the following year. The accession as regent of his mother, Catherine de Médicis, who saw Mary as a political rival, forced

her to flee the French court (see Goldsmith, vol. 2, pp. 23-24). The death in the same year of her own mother, who had been regent of Scotland during Mary's residence in France, also influenced her to return to her native country. Lee's description of Mary's regret at leaving France particularly echoes Hume (vol. 5, pp. 45-46).

33. Mary was "censured" by contemporaries, mainly the Scottish Protestant clergy and the faction that opposed her rule in Scotland, primarily for having openly taken up with the earl of Bothwell almost immediately after the violent death of her second husband, Henry Darnley. Bothwell, married himself, was widely suspected of having murdered Darnley with Mary's connivance. See Goldsmith, vol. 2, p. 29.

34. policy: political skill, opposed here to "feeling" as a kind of cold calculation.

35. Hume says that Elizabeth, "seemingly generous, but really cautious," sent Lady Scrope to Mary on her first arrival in England (not later, as Lee has it here) on the advice of her minister Cecil (later Lord Burghley), not on that of Lord Scrope (vol. 5, p. 131). See also Goldsmith, vol. 2, p. 31, and note 30 to Part I.

36. Mary was moved by Elizabeth's order on 16 July 1568 to Bolton, a seat of Lord Scrope's, away from the border town of Carlisle where she had arrived, in order to prevent her escape (Hume, vol. 5, p. 134). Here Lee's account is again closer to Robertson's than to Hume's in its emphasis on Mary's suffering, although by comparison with either historian Lee exaggerates Mary's ill-treatment by Elizabeth at this stage: "She now felt herself to be completely in Elizabeth's power, and *though treated as yet with the respect due to a queen,* her real condition was that of a prisoner" (Robertson, vol. 2, pp. 270-71; emphasis added).

37. According to Robertson and Goldsmith, Bothwell was forced to fly Scotland during a military confrontation in 1567 with a confederation of Scottish nobles who coerced Mary into dismissing him in order to continue as their queen. Bothwell fled to the Orkney islands, where he took to piracy in order to sustain himself and his crew. He was chased to Norwegian waters and taken prisoner by the Norwegians during an attack on one of their ships. He died in a Norwegian prison, but not until ten years after his capture. Lee invents the report that Mary's husband Bothwell is already dead so as to excuse her sentiment for the duke of Norfolk. See Robertson, vol. 2, pp. 227, 245-46; Goldsmith, vol. 2, p. 30.

38. Hume describes the duke of Norfolk similarly and guesses that the idea of marrying Mary was first proposed to him by the earl of Murray (see note 47 to Part I) just before Mary's trial in England, in early October 1568 (vol. 5, p. 155-56). Robertson agrees on the timing but attributes the idea to another Scottish minister, Maitland (vol. 2, p. 279). Lee makes it the duke's own, much older plan, and invents the personal interview between Mary and Norfolk.

39. Mary's letters to Bothwell were considered the chief evidence against her in her trial as accomplice in the murder of her husband, Darnley. Love letters and promises of marriage dated before the trial (generally considered a travesty of justice), which had officially "cleared" Bothwell of guilt for the murder, were called the "Casket Letters," after the silver box in which Bothwell had kept them (Hume, vol. 5, pp. 141-42; see also Robertson, vol. 2, p. 282).

40. Hume has Mary respond to Norfolk's first overture with much more circumspection than sentiment: "This princess replied, that the vexations which she had met

with in her two last marriages, had made her more inclined to lead a single life; but she was determined to sacrifice her own inclinations to the public welfare: And therefore, as soon as she should be legally divorced from Bothwell, she would be determined by the opinion of her nobility and people in the choice of another husband" (vol. 5, pp. 156-57). Lee seems to attempt to reconcile this with Robertson's quite different account: "nor was Mary, with whom Norfolk held a correspondence by means of his sister Lady Scroop, averse from a measure, which would have restored her to her kingdom with so much splendour. . . . and many letters and love-tokens were exchanged" (vol. 2, p. 300-301).

41. Contemporary historians similarly blame Mary's sufferings on her having followed her own misplaced inclinations in her marriage choices. Robertson and Goldsmith mention chiefly the marriage to Bothwell, while Hume primarily blames that on Darnley (Robertson, vol. 2, p. 300; Goldsmith,vol. 2, pp. 28-29; Hume, vol. 5, p. 319).

42. Sir Arthur Forester is a fictional character.

43. The secret completion and consummation of the marriage between Mary and Norfolk is Lee's invention. According to Robertson a contract for the marriage was signed in the summer of 1569, but then the scheme was discovered and Norfolk imprisoned by Elizabeth (vol. 2, pp. 306-7).

44. Lee follows Hume in speculating that the duke of Norfolk must have thought he could raise so strong a party to support his marriage to Mary that Elizabeth would be compelled to accept it (vol. 5, pp. 157-60).

45. Lee here adopts the list given by Hume of the noble supporters of Norfolk's conspiracy (vol. 5, p. 158).

46. Robert Dudley (1532?-88), earl of Leicester, one of Elizabeth's favorite courtiers. Lee supposes Leicester might support Norfolk's plan by revealing it to Elizabeth. Hume and Robertson agree that his loyalty was to Elizabeth, not Norfolk, and Robertson thinks he joined Norfolk only to betray him. Both historians date this conspiracy nearly a year later than the events narrated here (summer 1569 instead of fall 1568). Hume, vol. 5, pp. 158-60; Robertson, vol. 2, p. 306.

47. The Regent (whom Mary had been forced to appoint on 24 July 1567 on behalf of her infant son, James VI of Scotland) was her illegitimate half-brother, the earl of Murray. Robertson says Norfolk dissuaded him in October 1568 from openly accusing Mary of being an accomplice in her husband's murder, thus thwarting Elizabeth's plans for Mary's trial (vol. 2, pp. 239-40, 279-84; see also Goldsmith, vol. 2, pp. 30-31).

48. Elizabeth moved Mary away from Lord Scrope (who was after all Norfolk's brother-in-law) on 26 January 1568/69 to the earl of Shrewsbury's castle of Tutbury in Staffordshire. For the same reason that Elizabeth separated them, Lee needs to keep Lord and Lady Scrope with Mary: in order to maintain her communication with Norfolk (see Robertson, vol. 2, p. 285; also Goldsmith, vol. 2, p. 33).

49. Hume and Robertson agree that Leicester, far from warning the duke of Norfolk, first revealed his plot to Elizabeth in mid-August 1569 (before Murray did). Hume, vol. 5, p. 160; Robertson, vol. 2, pp. 306-7. See note 46 above. Lee has to preserve the character of her hero from such an act of betrayal, yet her Leicester is

perhaps the most interestingly and ambiguously portrayed of all the historical figures in the novel. The Tower of London served as the royal prison, where political prisoners were incarcerated.

50. Here Lee follows Hume most closely. Robertson and Goldsmith also recount Norfolk's flight from the court, although Robertson puts his change of heart slightly later than Lee does. Hume specifically mentions Burnham, three miles from Windsor (vol. 5, p. 162). Robertson dates his return on 3 October 1569 (vol. 2, p. 307). See also Goldsmith, vol. 2, p. 34.

51. posted: hastened; traveled quickly (from the system of post-horses available for hire in relays).

52. According to Goldsmith and Robertson, Bothwell's stay in Denmark (or Norway, then a part of the Danish kingdom) was in prison, probably with Mary's knowledge, after his arrest for piracy (Goldsmith, vol. 2, p. 30; Robertson, vol. 2, pp. 245-46). See note 37 to Part I.

53. you was: the form "was" could be used in the eighteenth century (and earlier) for the second person as well as for the first person singular.

54. Robertson relates that it was Mary who petitioned the Regent to have her marriage to Bothwell dissolved but that the privy council of Scotland refused her the divorce because "they imputed it not so much to any abhorrence of Bothwell, as to her eagerness to conclude a marriage with the duke of Norfolk" (vol. 2, p. 300). Hume's account is similar (vol. 5, pp. 166-67). As this marriage had been a Protestant one, it would not have been a matter for petition to the Pope (see Robertson, vol. 2, p. 218).

55. Robertson says Norfolk was released after nine months' imprisonment in the Tower of London, in May or June 1570. Lee's sentimental recuperation of Leicester as intercessor is at odds with his historical role in the betrayal and imprisonment of Norfolk. Hume and Robertson disagree as to the timing of Mary's removal to Coventry for greater security; Hume dates it to the time when Norfolk was first imprisoned, August 1569, Robertson to November 1569, at the time of a separate Catholic rebellion in favor of Mary. Neither historian mentions any infirmity in Mary at this point. Robertson, vol. 2, p. 307, 342-43; Hume, vol. 5, pp. 162, 196-98.

56. Hume, Robertson, and Goldsmith all agree that Elizabeth released Norfolk only after obtaining his promise to hold no further correspondence with the queen of Scots. Hume, like Lee's narrator, portrays Norfolk as essentially loyal to Elizabeth, while Robertson says he thought so little of his promise to her that he was continuing to receive love letters from Mary at the very moment of making it. Hume, vol. 5, p. 196; Robertson, vol. 2, pp. 342-43.

57. Robertson and Hume say that the earl of Huntingdon and viscount Hereford were added to the earl of Shrewsbury as guards over Mary upon her removal to Coventry (Robertson, vol. 2, p. 306; Hume, vol. 5, p. 162). Shrewsbury had already replaced Scrope (see note 48 to Part I).

58. Mrs. Marlow's account here agrees in the main facts but inverts the degrees of initiative assigned by the eighteenth-century historians to the principal actors in the duke of Norfolk's conspiracy. Hume and Robertson agree that the duke of Alva (on behalf of Philip of Spain) and the Pope conspired with Norfolk to land ten thousand men near London (Hume names Harwich specifically) and march on the capital to

impose conditions on Elizabeth, including Mary's liberation and marriage to Norfolk. They both, with Goldsmith, identify the go-between as an Italian named Ridolphi (rather than Mrs. Marlow's "Spaniard named Ridolpho"), an agent of the Pope in London. Lee's narrator makes the plot Norfolk's idea and has him convince the foreign powers to join him in rescuing Mary, who remains entirely passive. Robertson makes Mary herself a primary originator of the scheme; Hume makes her more passive, but both give Ridolphi the role of persuading Norfolk to act, rather than vice versa. Goldsmith, whose account is as usual the least detailed, gives the initiative to Ridolphi and to Mary's minister in England (vol. 2, p. 36). Lee removes any stain of agency in this rebellion from Mary, while making Norfolk more active in the rescue of his lady. See Robertson, vol. 2, pp. 342-44; Hume, vol. 5, pp. 196-97.

59. Sir William Cecil (1520-1598), created first Baron Burghley in 1571, was Elizabeth's secretary of state, one of the most able politicians of her reign, and opposed to Mary Stuart's succession to the English crown.

60. Mrs. Marlow elaborates considerably on the events reported by historians. The assignment of a particular motive for Norfolk's sending money to Mary's partisans in Scotland, the detail about the countess of Northumberland, and the emotional response of Shrewsbury are Lee's own. She mitigates some details of the treachery that resulted in Norfolk's arrest, while essentially following Robertson. Hume, Robertson, and Goldsmith all relate the story of the bag of gold entrusted to a servant who was not in on the secret, but the greedy brother is Lee's addition. The idea that Norfolk was "arrested in his bed" seems to be a displacement of the detail in Robertson's version of the story, that letters from Mary in cipher were found under his bed. Robertson, vol. 2, pp. 343-45; Hume, vol. 5, p. 198; Goldsmith, vol. 2, p. 36.

61. Here Mrs. Marlow's story is closest to that of Hume, in giving details of Elizabeth's hesitations, but follows Goldsmith in making Burghley specifically responsible for Norfolk's death. Hume, vol. 5, pp. 199-200; Goldsmith, vol. 2, p. 36. See also Robertson, vol. 2, p. 345.

62. Eighteenth-century historians do not mention any effort on the part of Lady Scrope, Mary, or Leicester to intercede with Elizabeth on Norfolk's behalf. The characterization of Elizabeth here, however, is typical of them. Robertson writes that with her "the question was not, what was most just or generous, but what was most beneficial to herself, and the English nation" (vol. 2, p. 260). Hurd has Addison echo this: "what she had ever most at heart, [was] her own supreme and uncontrolled authority" (Dialogue IV, *Works*, vol. 3, p. 270).

63. This places the birth of the fictional twins early in 1570 or late in 1569, as the duke of Norfolk was beheaded on 8 May 1572. Mrs. Marlow is therefore telling the story in 1586.

64. "Norfolk died with calmness and constancy; and though he cleared himself of any disloyal intentions against the queen's authority, he acknowledged the justice of the sentence by which he suffered" (Hume, vol. 5, p. 200). Goldsmith copies this sentence verbatim (vol. 2, p. 36).

65. Hume's characterization of Norfolk is again closely followed: "Beneficent, affable, generous, he had acquired the affections of the people; prudent, moderate, obsequious, he possessed, without giving her any jealousy, the good graces of his sov-

ereign" (vol. 5, p. 155). Goldsmith copies Hume's description almost word for word, as elsewhere (vol. 2, p. 34). See previous note.

66. Women of substance in the eighteenth century often had responsibility for the disposal of portraits and jewels. These are frequently inherited through female lines in *The Recess*. See Marcia Pointon, *Strategies for Showing: Women, Possession, and Representation in English Visual Culture, 1665-1800* (Oxford: Oxford University Press, 1997), pp. 31-49.

67. Historians concur that Elizabeth moved Mary more than once and kept her under stricter guard and more rigorous confinement after the execution of Norfolk. Hume, vol. 5, p. 202; Robertson, vol. 2, p. 346; Goldsmith, vol. 2, p. 40.

68. Lord Scrope's confinement and the seizure of his property are Lee's invention, as is his ambassadorship. See also note 12 to Part I.

69. At the time of Mrs. Marlow's narration in 1586 (see note 63 above), Elizabeth would have been fifty-three years old, Mary forty-four.

70. Sophia Lee did accompany her father into debtor's prison (see Introduction).

71. casket: a small box used as a container for valuables. Jewels in caskets, like portraits, represent a characteristic form of inheritance passed on through female lines in this novel (and historically in eighteenth-century England). See note 66 to Part I.

72. The description of the entrance to the Recess is reminiscent of Boccaccio's description of the passage leading to the secret trysting-place of Guiscardo and Sigismunda in the First Story, Fourth Day of his *Decameron*. This tale was a popular literary and pictorial subject in the eighteenth century. Such overgrown subterranean passageways evoke female genitalia and their "exploration." Giovanni Boccaccio, *The Decameron*, trans. G.H. McWilliams (Harmondsworth, Middlesex, England: Penguin Books, 1972), p. 333; Alliston, *Virtue's Faults*, p. 277 n. 8.

73. desart: any deserted place, not necessarily dry or barren.

74. order of the garter: the highest order of English knighthood. Knights of the order wear several ornamental emblems, including, at this period, a pin or pendant of gold and enamel set with diamonds and other jewels, representing a mounted knight encircled by a buckled blue garter.

75. sense and sensibility: the word "sense" here refers to the senses and not to having good sense, as it does in Jane Austen's well-known title. The effectiveness of Austen's title depends upon a pun on this common phrase of the time, which is used by Lee in the way it was generally understood, as referring to keen senses and a sympathetic sensitivity thought to arise from them.

76. See note 46 to Part I.

77. cambrick coifs: close fitting caps covering the top, back, and sides of the head, and tied under the chin. Cambric was a type of fine white linen first manufactured at Cambray in Flanders (now northern France). Coifs were worn outdoors by both sexes in the middle ages, but already by Elizabethan times they were only worn by men as night-caps.

78. told: counted.

79. This ironic treatment of the idea, commonplace in the eighteenth century, that, compared to the Continent, England was "so well-governed a country" that law and order made secret crimes difficult to imagine, became a convention of the "female

Gothic." It was used later by Eliza Parsons in *The Castle of Wolfenbach,* for example, and by Jane Austen in *Northanger Abbey.* See Alliston, *Virtue's Faults,* p. 230.

80. Robert Dudley, later earl of Leicester, was the fourth son of the duke of Northumberland. He was about twenty-one in 1553 when he was imprisoned in the Tower of London and condemned to death, along with his four brothers, his father, his uncle, and others, after the failure of the duke's attempt to place his daughter-in-law Lady Jane Grey on the throne. He was thus not a child at the time nor was he adopted by the earl of Arundel. Hume mentions that Northumberland "abjectly begged his life" from Arundel, who arrested him (vol. 4, p. 372). The succeeding reign was that of Mary I (Mary Tudor), persecutor of Protestants.

81. Guilford Dudley (1534-54), Robert's brother, whom their father married to Lady Jane Grey on 21 May 1553, before supporting her claim to the throne. See previous note and note 17 to Part II.

82. The family of Arundel was Catholic, that of Dudley Puritan.

83. Miss Lineric is Lee's invention; the earl of Leicester married Amy Robsart in 1549, is said to have married Douglas Howard in 1573, and in 1578 married Lettice Knollys, widow of the first earl of Essex, whom he had seduced during her husband's lifetime.

84. Hume relates that Elizabeth was twice imprisoned on false pretenses by her half sister Mary I in 1554 (vol. 4, pp. 390-91).

85. Edward Courtenay (1526-56), earl of Devonshire, was "nearly allied to the crown" and was first thought of as a match for Mary, Elizabeth's elder half sister. But he preferred Elizabeth. "This choice occasioned a great coldness in Mary towards Devonshire; and made her break out in a declared animosity against Elizabeth" (Hume, vol. 4, p. 380). He died in Padua, "not without strong suspicion of poisoning," during Mary's reign (*Complete Peerage*). The romantic story of Devonshire's attempt to rescue Elizabeth from prison and marry her is fictitious. It allows Leicester to portray himself to the heroines in a much more positive light than Hume does.

86. enlargement: release.

87. The queen is Mary I (Mary Tudor), her religion Catholicism.

88. Elizabeth's reign began in November 1558, and she immediately named Robert Dudley her master of horse. After her coronation in 1559 she named him privy councillor and Knight of the Garter. In 1564 she created him earl of Leicester and Baron Denbigh.

89. Hume gives a more cynical cast to his account of the court's expectations concerning Elizabeth's possible marriage choice: "the person most likely to succeed, was . . . lord Robert Dudley, who by means of his exterior qualities, joined to address and flattery, had become, in a manner, her declared favourite, and had great influence in all her counsels. The less worthy he appeared of this distinction, the more was his great favour ascribed to some violent affection, which could thus seduce the judgment of this penetrating princess; and men long expected that he would obtain the preference above so many princes and monarchs." Dudley was in fact the same age as Elizabeth and had been married to Amy Robsart for nearly a decade before she became queen (see note 83 to Part I). The aged earl of Arundel, who by Lee's account has just died, was according to Hume one of Dudley's rivals for Elizabeth's hand (vol. 5, pp. 60-61).

90. Hume and Goldsmith describe Elizabeth's "discreet submission" during the reign of her half sister Mary Tudor and her jealousy of Mary Stuart (Hume, vol. 4, pp. 442-43, vol. 5, p. 87; Goldsmith, vol. 2, pp. 20, 23). In portraying Elizabeth's rivalry with the queen of Scots, however, Lee most closely follows Robertson, who sees Elizabeth not only as a queen but also "merely as a woman" motivated by jealousy of other women more attractive to men. Lee's enterprise as a historical novelist is indeed grounded in Robertson's stated principle for the portrayal of historical character generally: "In judging the conduct of princes, we are apt to ascribe too much to political motives, and too little to the passions which they feel in common with the rest of mankind" (vol. 2, p. 54).

91. The "rigid exactness" refers to Elizabeth's response to Mary's public assertion of her claim to the English succession. Mary repeatedly insulted Elizabeth and the legitimacy of her claims to the English throne by publicly assuming the royal title and arms of England along with those of France while she was queen of that country (Hume, vol. 5, p. 40; Goldsmith, vol. 2, p. 23). Elizabeth wanted Mary to marry "some English nobleman, who would remove all grounds of jealousy, and cement the union between the kingdoms; and she offered on this condition to have her title examined, and to declare her successor to the crown" (Hume, vol. 5, p. 82).

92. Both Hume and Robertson describe Elizabeth's proposal to Mary of a match with Leicester as a calculated bluff rather than the result of an impassioned fit of jealousy. Lee's account follows Robertson's particularly in describing Mary as insulted by the proposal and Leicester as both interested in and embarrassed by it. Hume guesses that Mary alone may have taken the proposal in earnest. Leicester's lament here over having lost hopes of two queens echoes both historians, who say he attributed the marriage proposal to his enemy, William Cecil, as an attempt to ruin his favor with both by causing Mary to feel insulted and Elizabeth to feel jealous (Hume, vol. 5, pp. 82-3; Robertson, vol. 2, pp. 99-103, 109).

93. Here Lee has Leicester bid for sympathy by confessing the very faults attributed to him by Hume: "He was proud, insolent, interested, ambitious; without honour, without generosity, without humanity" (vol. 5, p. 83). Hurd echoes this negative characterization, attributing "fraud" and "rapine," as well as "insolence," to Leicester (Dialogue III, *Works,* vol. 3, p. 176). No historian mentions Leicester's having been disgraced as a result of the marriage proposal to Mary, however.

94. Kenilworth Castle in Warwickshire, built in the 1120s, became a fine palace in the fourteenth century. It was granted to Leicester by Elizabeth in 1563 (it had previously been granted to Leicester's father, the attainted duke of Northumberland). By the eighteenth century it was well known as a picturesque ruin. John Brandard, *Kenilworth Castle Illustrated,* introduction by John H. Drew (Buckingham, England: Barracuda Books Limited, 1982 [1865]), pp. 13-14; John H. Drew, *Kenilworth: An Historical Miscellany* (Kenilworth: Pleasaunce Press, 1969), pp. 2-3, and *Kenilworth: A Manor of the King* (Kenilworth: Pleasaunce Press, 1971), timeline, n.p.

95. Sheen, Surrey (near London): the ancient manor of Sheen was associated with royalty since at least the twelfth century, and the manor house became Sheen Palace in the fourteenth century. Destroyed by fire in 1499, the palace was rebuilt by Henry VII and renamed Richmond. It was very popular with the Tudor monarchs but

was a ruin by Lee's time. *The London Encyclopedia*, ed. Ben Weinreb and Christopher Hibbert (London: Macmillan, 1983), pp. 649, 782.

96. Lee is playing very fast and loose with accepted history here. Walter Devereux (1541-76) was created first earl of Essex by Elizabeth in 1572. That was at least seven years after he married Lettice Knollys, an Englishwoman (see note 83 to Part I), and a year before he went to Ireland on his own initiative in an effort to colonize Ulster.

97. stood: had stopped.

98. tubs thrown out to the whale: diversions created to evade a threatened danger (in this case, the threat that Parliament might try to force Elizabeth to marry).

99. Robertson: "Elizabeth had often declared that nothing but her resolution to lead a single life, and his being born her own subject, would have hindered her from chusing the earl of Leicester for a husband." Both Robertson and Hume say contemporaries marveled at the lapse in this queen's notable wisdom in marking Leicester openly as her favorite (Robertson vol. 2, pp. 100-102; Hume, vol. 5, pp. 60-61, 275). See also note 89 to Part I. The "matrimonial treaties" refer to the proposals made by the French king Charles IX (younger brother of François II, whose early death had left Mary Stuart a widow) and his mother Catherine de Médicis, the queen regent, of two of his brothers. See Goldsmith, vol. 2, p. 39; and note 4 to Part IV.

100. Elizabeth I is known to have punished members of her court who married without her consent. See notes 103 to Part I, note 20 to Part II, and note 34 to Part IV.

101. This passage implies that the first earl of Essex went on a second campaign in Ireland (see note 96 to Part I); historically, he is known to have conducted one only, from 1573 until his death in 1576. See note 10 to Part IV. Hume says the earl of Leicester was first given command of the English forces in the Low Countries much later, in 1585 (vol. 5, p. 273).

102. Leicester did secretly contract a marriage with the earl of Essex's widow, née Knollys (not Lineric), in 1578.

103. Hume relates how the French ambassador "endeavoured to discredit Leicester with the queen" by revealing his secret marriage, "which so provoked her, that she threatened to send him to the Tower." This incident occurred in 1581; according to Hume, Leicester was not sent to Holland until 1585, the year England became involved in the wars there (vol. 5, pp. 240, 273).

104. the States: the States-General of Holland. In 1585-87 Leicester first acted as general of the English forces aiding the Protestant Flemish and Dutch uprising against Spanish Catholic control of the Netherlands (in what is now Belgium and the Netherlands); he was soon proclaimed governor of the United Provinces of Holland, the federation of seven provinces that did not revert to Spanish rule and became the modern Netherlands. As Leicester was extremely unpopular among the Dutch, who tried to expel him, it is unlikely that they really presented him with such a splendid gift. See note 32 to Part II.

105. bad: bade.

106. sewer: a servant who supervised meals, including the arrangement of the table, the seating of the guests, and the tasting and serving of the dishes.

107. Coventry is about six miles, or ten kilometers, northeast of Kenilworth.

108. Contrast Hume: "[Elizabeth's] constant and declared attachment to [Leices-

ter] had naturally emboldened him to aspire to her bed; and in order to make way for these nuptials, he was universally believed to have murdered, in a barbarous manner, his [first] wife, the heiress of one Robesart" (vol. 5, p. 83). Lee seems to be combining a reversal of this unsubstantiated historical rumor connecting Leicester and murder with another one: that he died by poisoning—survived by his then wife Lettice Knollys, the former countess of Essex. See note 83 to Part I.

109. ascertain: make certain, ensure.

110. Mary Stuart was niece, through her mother, to the powerful French family of Guise; thus the fictional heroines would be their relations as well.

111. As elder (and as male), Mary's son James has the prior claim to the throne of England, but a potential legal obstacle is raised by his not being an English native, as Lee's heroines are. (Scotland, James's birthplace and original kingdom, remained a separate nation for over a century after his accession to the English throne.) "The aversion the English ever entertain to a foreign sway" alludes to Hume, who mentions Mary's foreign birth as the main legal objection to her own claim (vol. 4, p. 360). Lee transfers that objection to her male heir (against whom it was not raised) in order to lend greater historical plausibility to her heroines' claim to the succession.

112. Shakespeare, *The Tempest*, Act III, scene i, ll. 74-75. Miranda weeps in response to Ferdinand's declaration of love.

113. The allusion is to the belief "universally" held by Leicester's contemporaries (according to Hume) that he had murdered his first wife, Amy Robsart. See note 108 to Part I.

PART II

1. aight: a small island.

2. This description is reminiscent of the extended meditation on the ruins of Kenilworth Castle in Hurd's Dialogue III, *Works*, vol. 3, esp. pp. 172-73.

3. "Mary's close connexions with the house of Guise . . . was the ground of just and insurmountable jealousy to Elizabeth, who regarded them as her mortal and declared enemies, and was well acquainted with their dangerous character and ambitious projects" (Hume, vol. 5, pp. 81-82).

4. Leicester refers to Elizabeth's having been herself imprisoned and threatened with execution by the previous queen, Mary I; this gained her the sympathy of the nation, which helped her mount the throne upon her half sister's death (ibid., vol. 5, p. 2). The statement that Mary has been imprisoned for seventeen years dates this fictional dialogue to 1585, the year before her execution. Lee's chronology is very flexible, however; historically, this dialogue should have preceded Mrs. Marlow's deathbed narrative by a year.

5. Philoctetes was punished in Greek myth but not for duplicity. For lighting the funeral pyre of Heracles and thereby making that hero's apotheosis possible, he inherited his marvelous bow but also received an incurable wound on his foot (thus he was punished by the goddess Hera, wife of Zeus, for helping Zeus' son by a mortal woman). On the way to the Trojan war his comrades abandoned him on the desert island of Lemnos because of his lameness—but they soon discovered they could not defeat the Trojans without the bow of Heracles. In Sophocles' play *Philoctetes*, the deceitful

Odysseus is given the task of persuading a resentful Philoctetes to rejoin them. Sophocles represents Philoctetes as stubborn but forthright; Lee may be confusing him with Odysseus in the play. I am grateful to Professor Robert Fagles for information about the various versions and sources of this story.

6. Sir Francis Drake (1540?-96) had recently become the first Englishman to circumnavigate the world, in 1577-80.

7. In late 1585 "a fleet of twenty sail was equipped to attack the Spaniards in the West Indies: Two thousand three hundred volunteers, besides seamen, engaged on board it; sir Francis Drake was appointed Admiral." (Hume, vol. 5, p. 274).

8. Hume makes vivid the close watch under which Mary was kept near the end of her life: "Though all England was acquainted with the detection of Babington's conspiracy [to assassinate Elizabeth and place Mary on her throne], every avenue to the queen of Scots had been so strictly guarded, that she remained in utter ignorance of the matter" (vol. 5, p. 291). Goldsmith copies this sentence nearly word for word (vol. 2, pp. 42-43).

9. Compare Robertson's description of the queen of Scots at her death: "with a majestic mien . . . [she] advanced towards the place of execution, leaning on two of Paulet's attendants. She was dressed in a mourning habit, but with an elegance and splendour which she had long laid aside, except on a few festival days. An *Agnus Dei* hung by a pomander chain at her neck; her beads at her girdle; and in her hand she carried a crucifix of ivory" (vol. 3, p. 63). Hume adds that "she leaned on two of sir Amias Paulet's guards, *because of an infirmity in her limbs*," and "her beauties . . . though faded by years, and yet more by her afflictions, still discovered themselves" (vol. 5, pp. 313-16; emphasis added). See also Goldsmith, vol. 2, p. 48.

10. Sir Philip Sidney (1554-17 October 1586), poet, soldier, and courtier, was the son of Leicester's sister, Lady Mary Dudley.

11. character: reputation. Sidney's "character" was that of the ideal Elizabethan gentleman. "This person is described by the writers of that age as the most perfect model of an accomplished gentleman that could be formed even by the wanton imagination of poetry or fiction" (Hume, vol. 5, p. 276; see also pp. 244, 273). "He was, in truth, to speak the language of that time, the very flower of knighthood, and contributed more than any body else, by his pen, as well as his sword, to throw a lustre on the profession of chivalry" (Hurd, Dialogue III, *Works,* vol. 3, p. 198).

12. Hurd refers to Elizabeth's arriving unannounced at Kenilworth in 1575 (Dialogue III, p. 174, n. g).

13. This description of Elizabeth follows Hume and Robertson: "Her attention to dress, her solicitude to display her charms, her love of flattery, were all excessive. Nor were these weaknesses confined to that period of life when they are more pardonable. Even in very advanced years, the wisest woman of that, or perhaps of any other age, wore the garb, and affected the manners of a girl" (Robertson, vol. 2, pp. 53-54). Hume adds that when she was nearly seventy "she allowed her courtiers and even foreign ambassadors to compliment her upon her beauty; nor had all her good sense been able to cure her of this preposterous vanity" (vol. 5, p. 420). No references have been found to any "defect in her shape"; this must allude simply to her lack of a youthful figure. Elizabeth would be about fifty-two years old at this point in Lee's

story (c. 1585). It is apparently true, however, that the white lead make-up she used eventually corroded the skin of her face. Maggie Angeloglou, *A History of Make-up* (London: Macmillan, 1970), p. 52.

14. This again recalls Hurd's fantasy on the ruins of Kenilworth (vol. 3, p. 173), in which reference is made to a sumptuous entertainment given there by Leicester for Elizabeth from 9 to 27 July 1575 (a decade before the other events narrated here), at an expense of about £60,000.

15. "Virtuous conduct, polite conversation, heroic valour, and elegant erudition, all concurred to render [Sidney] the ornament and delight of the English court" (Hume, vol. 5, p. 276).

16. "Where now . . . is the floating island, . . . the lady of the lake, the silken nymphs her attendants, . . . surpassing even the whimsies of the wildest romance?" Hurd, Dialogue III, *Works*, vol. 3, p. 173; see also p. 203.

17. Leicester's father, the duke of Northumberland, fearing a Catholic succession, persuaded Edward VI on his deathbed to exclude by his will both his sisters, Mary and Elizabeth Tudor, from succeeding him to the crown. The succession thus devolved upon Edward's cousin Lady Jane Grey (1537-54), eldest daughter of the duke of Suffolk, whom Northumberland had already taken care to have married to his own youngest son, Lord Guilford Dudley. Jane and Guilford, who were both under seventeen years old, reigned for nine days before Mary overthrew their partisans with an armed force and eventually executed them both. See Hume, vol. 4, pp. 350-94, and Goldsmith, vol. 1, p. 429-vol. 2, p. 10.

18. Hume says some contemporaries suspected that "Leicester intended, in case of the queen's demise, to produce some bastard of his own, and affirm that he was her offspring" (vol. 5, p. 184). The idea appears here in modified form as a strategy to protect the heroines.

19. Historians in Lee's time generally judged Elizabeth's use of power unfeminine. Robertson writes of her treatment of Mary that "she not only laid aside the magnanimity which became a queen, but the feelings natural to a woman" (vol. 3, p. 181). Hume adds, "when we contemplate her as a woman, we are apt to be struck with the highest admiration of her great qualities and extensive capacity; but we are also apt to require some more softness of disposition, some greater lenity of temper, some of those amiable weaknesses by which her sex is distinguished," approving her rather nervously as a ruler even though "we may find it difficult to reconcile our fancy to her as a wife or mistress" (vol. 5, pp. 61-62, 449-50). Hurd has Addison call her manner toward her subjects "unwomanly," and criticize her "strange mix" of negative feminine qualities with "masculine ferocity" (Dialogue IV, *Works*, vol. 3, pp. 255-57).

20. According to Hume, Elizabeth was not only hostile toward her potential successors but also determined "that no one who had pretensions to the succession should ever have any heirs or successors." Henry VIII's two sisters had married the kings of Scotland and France; as a widow the queen of France had married the duke of Suffolk. Since Henry's will had excluded the Scottish branch (Mary Stuart's) from the succession, that left the daughters of Henry's other sister by Suffolk closest to the throne. Lady Jane Grey's younger sister Lady Catherine had become the heir of that family after Jane's execution (see note 17 to Part II). She secretly married the earl of Hertford.

When she became pregnant, Elizabeth imprisoned her and her husband in the Tower of London and declared the marriage illegal, freeing Hertford only after his wife died more than nine years later. Hume attributes Elizabeth's behavior to jealousy of marriage and motherhood as well as to political rivalry (vol. 5, pp. 61-62).

21. Mary Herbert, countess of Pembroke, née Mary Sidney (1561-1621). The sister of Sir Philip Sidney, she was, like him, a notable poet, scholar, translator, and patron of the arts—and thus, like him, she personified the Elizabethan courtly ideal. After her brother's death she finished and published his *Arcadia*, which he had dedicated to her. She wrote the greater part of their joint translation of the Psalms (whose experiments in meter were an important influence on Donne and Herbert), besides other poems and plays. She also conducted chemical experiments in her own laboratory and held a court at Wilton that rivalled Elizabeth's own. See Margaret P. Hannay, *Philip's Phoenix: Mary Sidney, Countess of Pembroke* (Oxford: Oxford University Press, 1990).

22. "[Elizabeth's] caprice, and jealousy, and haughtiness, appeared in a thousand instances. She took offence so easily, and forgave so difficultly, that even her principal ministers could hardly keep their ground" (Hurd, Dialogue III, *Works*, vol. 3, pp. 246-47).

23. Rose Cecil is Lee's invention.

24. Anne Arundel, née Dacre (1556-1630), was not a sister of Sir Philip Sidney but rather a stepdaughter of the same duke of Norfolk who is the fictional heroines' father. "Her Lord" is Philip Howard (1557-95), first (or thirteenth) earl of Arundel and Surrey, eldest son of the duke of Norfolk; he is thus the heroines' half brother and his own wife's stepbrother. Lady Arundel converted to Catholicism in 1582, and her husband converted in 1584. That year he was placed under house arrest upon suspicion of being involved in Throckmorton's conspiracy, another plot to put Mary on the English throne (Hume, vol. 5, p. 257; Goldsmith, vol. 2, p. 40). After an attempt to escape he was imprisoned in the Tower of London in April 1585 and died there in 1595.

25. By 1585 England had entered into a league with the states of the Netherlands against Spain and had sent Sir Francis Drake on the expedition previously mentioned to attack Spain in the Americas. See Hume, vol. 5, pp. 267-74; also notes 103 and 104 to Part I; note 7 to Part II.

26. Fulke Greville (1554-1628), first baron Brooke, was a philosophical poet and a favorite of Queen Elizabeth as well as a friend to Sir Philip Sidney, the earl of Essex, and Sir Francis Bacon. In addition to his poetry he wrote a life of Sir Philip Sidney.

27. The English defeated an attempted invasion by an extraordinary Spanish fleet called "the Invincible Armada" in 1588. See Hume, vol. 5, pp. 332-45, and Goldsmith, vol. 2, pp. 51-54.

28. The frustrated passion Lee makes Sidney feel for Matilda is reminiscent of the historical Sidney's love for Penelope Devereux, the subject of his famous sonnet sequence "Astrophel and Stella," written in 1582. He had fallen in love with her shortly after her marriage to another man. Only a year after composing "Astrophel and Stella" he married Frances Walsingham (1567-1632), daughter of Sir Francis Walsingham (1530-90), one of Elizabeth's most trusted counsellors. Elizabeth did indeed disapprove of this marriage, although probably for political reasons. Hannay, *Philip's Phoe-*

nix, pp. xvi, 52. Lee makes Sidney's courtly love more conformable to late eighteenth-century moral standards by making him unaware of his beloved's marriage to another.

29. Sidney did serve as governor of Flushing in the Netherlands (see Hume, vol. 5, p. 273). He was stationed there not long after his marriage to Frances Walsingham.

30. According to Hume, Leicester was sent to the Netherlands late in 1585 "at the head of the English auxiliary forces" and was greeted at Flushing by Sidney (ibid.). Sidney would not have been able to make this farewell speech to Matilda if Lee had left him already in Holland waiting for Leicester's reinforcements.

31. Sir Philip Sidney died on 17 October 1586 of wounds received while fighting the Spaniards in the Netherlands. His death is described in heroic terms by Hume. It was lamented by Mary Stuart's son James VI of Scotland (in Latin verse) and by Lord Brooke. See Hume, vol. 5, pp. 276-77, and note 26 to Part II.

32. Hume offers very different reasons for Leicester's sudden return to England in 1586: the States of the Netherlands "were much discontented with his management of the war; still more with his arbitrary and imperious conduct," and he left to avoid responding to their appeal for redress (vol. 5, p. 277).

33. Lee may have had in mind Lucy, Lady Latimer (1523/4-1582/3), a daughter of the earl of Worcester who married John Nevill, Lord Latimer, in 1545. She died shortly before the other events referred to here took place, however, and no record of her having been one of Elizabeth's ladies-in-waiting has been located.

34. The reference is to Babington's plot to assassinate Elizabeth and place Mary on her throne. None of the historians ascribes such treasonous motives to Leicester as are implied here; rather Hume and Goldsmith say that after the discovery of Babington's conspiracy Leicester advised Elizabeth to dispatch Mary secretly by poisoning instead of proceeding through a public trial and execution (Hume, vol. 5, p. 290; Goldsmith, vol. 2, p. 43). See also note 5 to Part III.

35. *The Recess,* like many novels of its time, was originally published in three volumes. The first volume was published alone in early 1783, a common strategy to see how sales went before publishing the rest. The other two volumes did not appear until late 1785, however, so readers had to wait almost three years in the suspense of this moment. One reviewer complained of this painful experience: "We may appeal to Miss Lee, and, as giving credit to her '*inviolable respect for truth,*' ask her,—Whether, on the first perusal of the '*obsolete manuscript,*' she did not feel such an interest in '*the Tale,*' as would have made the loss of the concluding events of it a severe mortification? And to us they are as lost; nor are we sure that they will ever be found!" *Monthly Review* 68 (1783): 456. Another critic approved that the heroines "are left in a very interesting situation, when the volume concludes" (*Critical Review* 55 [1783]: 233).

PART III

1. anchorite: hermit.

2. coiners: counterfeiters.

3. Matilda is asking her husband to kill her rather than allow her to be raped by the bandits. Stories of ancient Roman suicides to prevent dishonor were popular dramatic and artistic subjects in Lee's time. Lucretia killed herself to avoid rape and preserve her wifely chastity, and Virginius killed his daughter Virginia to avoid another

rape (and to preserve her virginity). Portia killed herself when she learned her husband Brutus was dead, as Arria did to set an example of courage to her husband. Aphra Behn's character Oroonoko, an enslaved African prince whom she compares to the ancient Roman heroes, kills his pregnant wife after a failed slave rebellion to prevent their child from being born into slavery. Lee's father had performed in Southerne's dramatic version of *Oroonoko* as well as in Shakespeare's *Julius Caesar* (where Portia's suicide is mentioned; see note 15 to Part IV).

4. recruit: refresh, restore.

5. Anthony Babington (1561-20 September 1586) led a conspiracy to assassinate Elizabeth and place Mary Stuart on her throne. He was promised support from the usual forces behind such plots—the Pope, the duke of Guise, and the king of Spain, as well as the discontented English Catholics—but it was detected by Sir Francis Walsingham, and fourteen of the English conspirators were executed. The discovery of Babington's conspiracy led immediately to the trial and execution of Mary. See Hume, vol. 5, pp. 284-90; Robertson, vol. 3, pp. 33-42; and Goldsmith, vol. 2, pp. 41-42; also note 34 to Part II. None of these historians include Leicester in the plot or mention his ever fleeing to France.

6. The Mortimer family described here is imaginary; the title was borne by no one during Elizabeth's reign, although it did belong to an earlier king's favorite.

7. The late Queen: Mary I, Elizabeth's elder half sister, was married to King Philip II of Spain in 1554 and died in 1558.

8. relict: widow.

9. "clue" originally meant "key" or "thread," as in Ariadne's thread, used to find the way out of the labyrinth. In this case the lost connecting "thread" is the deceased duke of Norfolk and his knowledge about the heroines and the Recess.

10. smack: a light single-masted sailing vessel.

11. amused: distracted.

12. Havre-de-Grace: now called Le Havre, a port in northern France on the English Channel.

13. In Greek myth Orestes killed his mother, Clytemnestra, in revenge for her murder of his father, Agamemnon. He in turn was pursued and driven mad by the Furies in divine retribution for the crime of killing his mother. Matilda identifies with Orestes' guilt because she infers that her sudden flight from England with Leicester contributed to the discovery of Babington's conspiracy and thus to the execution of her mother, Mary Stuart. Parricide: the murder (or murderer) of any parent, near relation, or ruler.

14. Hume and Goldsmith say Mary Stuart saw herself as a martyr to the Catholic religion (Hume, vol. 5, p. 302; Goldsmith, vol. 2, p. 46).

15. During her imprisonment Mary had always hoped in vain for help from France and other Catholic nations.

16. billet: a short letter or note, often amorous (from French).

17. Henry III of France (reigned 1574-89).

18. James VI of Scotland was twenty years old by the time of his mother's execution and for most of his reign had been a child puppet, sometimes even a prisoner, in the hands of regents and factions.

19. Rouen, a city on the river Seine west-northwest of Paris, was famous in the late tenth and early eleventh centuries for the number and wide variety of foreigners who traveled there from every part of Europe and the Middle East—including "noble exiles" from England, fleeing the invading Danish king Knut I, among them the future king Edward the Confessor (1003?-66). *Histoire de Rouen*, ed. Michel Mollat, François Gay, et al. (Toulouse: Privat, 1982 [1979]), pp. 42-43.

20. crisis: any important change; here, the approaching birth.

21. aera: the starting point of a new period; an important date or event that becomes a turning point.

22. lanthorn: lantern.

23. Leicester died at his house in Cornbury, Oxfordshire, on 4 September 1588; an investigation was made into the possibility of his having died by poisoning.

24. police: The police force was new in England in Lee's time, its introduction having been long resisted partly because the idea was so strongly associated with the French, who had invented both the word and the thing much earlier. Lee's allusion to the French police typifies this strong eighteenth-century English association. The idea of a police force in the sixteenth century, even in France, however, is an anachronism.

25. weed: a widow's mourning garments.

26. During the sixteenth-century Wars of Religion between French Catholics and Protestants (the latter called Huguenots), the Peace of Amboise (1563) accorded the Huguenots freedom of conscience but limited the celebration of their religious services to a few cities, including Rouen. Its population became largely Huguenot until 1685, when religious freedom for Protestants was completely revoked and many went into foreign exile.

27. Her impatience with Catholic beliefs and practices confirms the previously wavering Matilda as a Protestant, although the daughter of a Catholic queen and educated by a priest. This is not improbable: her father Norfolk, although born into the principal Catholic family in England, was a Protestant, and so were the Scrope family. The anti-Catholic sentiments she expresses are also characteristic of eighteenth-century England in general and of Gothic fiction in particular.

28. mattins: in the Catholic church, a prayer service said at midnight; in the Anglican church, morning prayers. Lee seems to have the Anglican service in mind, but that is not entirely clear.

29. wrings: writhings, torments.

30. St. Jago de la Vega: a city in southeastern central Jamaica on the Rio Cobre, ten miles west of Kingston (now called Spanish Town). It was one of the few European settlements in Jamaica in Elizabethan times and was the capital of Jamaica in Lee's time.

31. A rewriting of Lovelace's dream of Clarissa's ascent to heaven: see Samuel Richardson, *Clarissa; or, The History of a Young Lady,* ed. Florian Stuber, Margaret Anne Doody, and Jim Springer Borck (New York: AMS Press, 1990), vol. 7, pp. 147-48 (Letter XLVIII).

32. interest: influence.

33. Don Pedro is apparently Lee's invention.

34. foster brother: the son of Victoria's wet nurse. In Lee's time, as in the time of Elizabeth, the children of the upper classes were rarely nursed by their own mothers.

35. The palm tree was a medieval symbol of triumph over adversity, from the belief that it always grew erect no matter how it was bent or weighted down. Ernst and Johanna Lehner, *Folklore and Symbolism of Flowers, Plants and Trees* (New York: Tudor, 1960), p. 27.

36. Altered from Shakespeare, *King John*, Act III, scene iv, ll. 79-81. The original lines describe a male child and predict the ruin of his beauty by sorrow.

37. James VI of Scotland succeeded Elizabeth as James I of England in 1603. Matilda's narrative of this event closely follows Robertson, who describes James's legal right to the succession, Elizabeth's confirmation of it on her deathbed, and the satisfaction of "the nobles and people." "Thus were united two kingdoms, divided from the earliest accounts of time, but destined, by their situation, to form one great monarchy" (vol. 3, pp. 181-85).

38. God tested Abraham by asking him to sacrifice his only son (Genesis 22).

PART IV

1. Greenwich Palace or Placentia, a riverbank house on the Thames, was the birthplace of Elizabeth, as it had been of her father Henry VIII. It did fall into disrepair during the English Revolution, well after the time of Lee's story.

2. In the reign of Elizabeth I Greenwich was about five miles distant from London to the east, Chelsea about three miles to the west.

3. Matilda's blindness, according to Ellinor, to Leicester's faults parallels that of Queen Elizabeth as described by contemporary historians. See Hume, vol. 5, p. 330; Robertson, vol. 2, p. 100; Goldsmith, vol. 2, p. 23.

4. Hume relates that despite her policy Elizabeth was so flattered by the marriage proposals addressed to her in 1581 by the duke of Anjou, twenty-five years her junior, that Leicester became alarmed she would accept the match and become less open to his influence. He "spread reports" that the duke's ambassador had used "incantations and love-potions" to influence the queen (vol. 5, pp. 239-40). See also note 99 to Part I.

5. Lord Pembroke is Henry Herbert (c. 1538-1601), second earl of Pembroke.

6. Robert Devereux (1567-25 February 1601) became second earl of Essex at the age of nine. He had accompanied his stepfather, the earl of Leicester, to the Netherlands in 1585 (Hume, vol. 5, p. 273). The story of Essex's rise and fall as Elizabeth's favorite was the subject of several plays popular in Lee's time. Early in his career her father had played the roles of both Essex and his friend Southampton in two performances of John Banks's *The Unhappy Favorite; or the Earl of Essex* (1682).

7. Sir Walter Raleigh (1552?-1618), courtier, navigator, colonizer, writer.

8. eclat: brilliance (from French).

9. Robertson describes Essex as "better fitted for a camp than a court" (vol. 3, p. 165), while Goldsmith says he was "fitted, not only for the foremost ranks in war by his valour, but to conduct the intrigues of a court by his eloquence and address" (vol. 2, p. 54). Hume refers to his "refined taste in literature" (vol. 5, p. 412).

10. Essex's father, Walter Devereux, died in Dublin in 1576 after conducting a series of brutal massacres of the Irish populace and treacherously entrapping and executing several of their leaders. The "warning" seems to be Lee's invention.

11. Lord Arlington is Lee's invention; the title was not created until 1665.

12. Henry Wriothesley (1573-1624), third earl of Southampton from 1581, was an "intimate friend" of Essex (Hume, vol. 5, p. 405).

13. Hume mentions her "sallies of anger" as a flaw in Elizabeth's character (vol. 5, p. 448).

14. Jezebel, the Sidonian wife of Ahab, king of Israel, was a worshiper of her people's god Baal. She defied the prophet Elijah when he murdered the priests of Baal. He then set up Jehu against her son when he became king, because of her "whoredoms" and "witchcrafts." When Jehu killed her son, she "painted her face and tired her head [dressed her hair], and looked out at a window" of her palace to threaten him with revenge. He had her thrown from the window, splattering the palace wall with her blood, trampling on her body, and allowing it to be devoured by dogs (I Kings xvi: 31; xix: 1,2; II Kings ix: 7-37). To this day her name is applied to any woman who talks back, wears makeup, displays herself, or is in any other way wicked.

15. A Roman suicide, used by Shakespeare in *Julius Caesar*, Act IV, scene iii, ll. 151-55. See note 3 to Part III.

16. teem: contain, produce.

17. Robertson describes Burghley as "crafty" (vol. 3, p. 166); Hurd similarly calls him "wily" (Dialogue IV, *Works*, vol. 3, p. 257).

18. Robertson describes the English court at the beginning of the seventeenth century as divided between the rival factions of Essex and Burghley (Cecil). "Essex despised the arts of Cecil as low and base. To Cecil, the earl's magnanimity appeared to be presumption and folly. All the military men, except Raleigh, favoured Essex. Most of the courtiers adhered to Cecil, whose manners more nearly resembled their own" (vol. 3, p. 166). Hume writes of this rivalry, "as Essex's person was agreeable to the queen, as well as his advice conformable to her inclinations, the favourite seemed daily to acquire an ascendant over the minister" (vol. 5, p. 390).

19. The reference is clearly to Babington's conspiracy (see note 5 to Part III), although historians did not associate Essex, any more than Leicester, with this plot against Elizabeth's life.

20. Mary Stuart was executed on 7 February 1587 (Hume, vol. 5, p. 311; Robertson, vol. 3, pp. 58-65).

21. Leicester died at home, although not without suspicion of poisoning. See note 23 to Part III.

22. Essex secretly married the former Frances Walsingham, by then the widow of Sir Philip Sidney, in 1590. Hume, vol. 5, p. 412.

23. Essex "was the most accomplished and the most popular of all the English nobles; brave, generous, affable. . . . He was soon distinguished by the queen, who, with a profusion uncommon to her, conferred on him, even in his earliest youth, the highest honours. Nor did this diminish the esteem and affection of his countrymen; but, by a rare felicity, he was at once the favorite of his sovereign, and the darling of the people" (Robertson, vol. 3, p. 165).

24. In 1589 Sir Francis Drake and Sir John Norris led a mainly private expedition, little supported by the English government, to reconquer Portugal from Spain and place a Portuguese heir on its throne. They were met in Spain by Essex, who,

"fired with the thirst of military honour, had secretly, unknown to the queen, stolen from England" (Hume, vol. 5, pp. 348-50).

25. Sir Walter Curtis is Lee's invention.

26. Hume describes Essex as possessing "many noble virtues" as well as grave faults in the form of "ungovernable passions" (vol. 5, p. 431); Robertson agrees (vol. 3, p. 165), as does Goldsmith (vol. 2, p. 54).

27. Other novels by women of the later eighteenth century also show female characters founding schools for orphans, the poor, and the disabled. See, for example, Sarah Scott, *Millenium Hall,* ed. Gary Kelly (Orchard Park, Canada: Broadview Press, 1995 [1762]), and Sophie von La Roche, *The History of Lady Sophia Sternheim,* trans. Christa Baguss Britt (Albany: SUNY Press, 1991 [1771]), pp. 177-187. See also note 27 to Part I.

28. Ellinor alludes to an argument recounted by Hume but places blame rather differently: "Being once engaged in a dispute with [Elizabeth] about the choice of a governor for Ireland, [Essex] was so heated in the argument, that he entirely forgot the rules both of duty and civility; and turned his back upon her in a contemptuous manner. Her anger, naturally prompt and violent, rose at this provocation; and she instantly gave him a box on the ear; adding a passionate expression suited to his impertinence." Hume further blames Essex for haughtily withdrawing from court thereupon instead of apologizing but observes that the Queen nevertheless pardoned him later and showed him more favor than ever (vol. 5, pp. 390-92). As elsewhere, Goldsmith repeats this passage nearly verbatim (vol. 2, p. 55).

29. At the instigation of Essex, an English naval expedition attacked the Spanish in the bay of Cadiz in the Azores (Atlantic islands far off the Spanish coast) in 1596. Essex led the assault despite Elizabeth's orders that he hang back for personal safety. When he led his victorious men to sack the city, his "generosity . . ., not inferior to his valour, made him stop the slaughter, and treat his prisoners with the greatest humanity, and even affability and kindness" (Hume, vol. 5, pp. 379-80).

30. Charles Howard (1536-1624), second baron Howard of Effingham, was admiral of the fleet in the action against Cadiz. As a reward for the victory Elizabeth created him earl of Nottingham. Essex, having encouraged the attack against the admiral's hestitations, resented this so much that he challenged him to a duel (Hume, vol. 5, p. 381). As second son of Thomas Howard, fourth duke of Norfolk, this man is the heroines' half brother. Confusingly, he is called Howard, Effingham, and Nottingham.

31. Elizabeth Vernon (1573-1656?) was one of Queen Elizabeth's ladies in waiting. A.L. Rowse, *Shakespeare's Southampton* (London: Macmillan, 1965), p. 104.

32. nobles: gold coins first minted in England by Edward III, each worth six shillings eight pence.

33. Lord Arlington's estate is divided according to the legal system of entail, either in "fee tail male" or in "fee simple": the seaman inherits the ancestral land instead of the more nearly related sisters because it has been "entailed" either on male relatives *only* (in fee tail male) or on a male of remoter degree of relationship to the deceased in precedence over, but not necessarily to the exclusion of, females (in fee simple). The "personals" consist of any property that Lord Arlington may personally have bought

or otherwise acquired after the entail was settled—including, in this case, St. Vincent's Abbey—and he is free to bequeath, or "devise," them to his sisters. Ordinarily Ellinor, as the widow, would have been entitled to a life-use of at least one-third of the estate, but she is treated as insane and thus disqualified from inheriting. The system of entail developed in England during the thirteenth century and was in effect among great landowning families in both Elizabeth's and Lee's time. J.P. Cooper, "Patterns of Inheritance and Settlement by Great Landowners from the Fifteenth to the Eighteenth Centuries," in Jack Goody, Joan Thirsk, and E.P. Thompson, eds., *Family and Inheritance: Rural Society in Western Europe, 1200-1800* (Cambridge: Cambridge University Press, 1976), pp. 198-233; Susan Staves, *Married Women's Separate Property in England, 1660-1833* (Cambridge: Harvard University Press, 1990), p. 60.

34. Southampton's affair with Elizabeth Vernon began in 1595 and culminated with their hasty marriage in 1598, incurring the queen's anger and leading to their brief imprisonment (see notes 31 and 37 to Part IV).

35. Hume also mentions "Tracy, a young gentleman to whom [Essex] bore great friendship" (vol. 5, p. 427).

36. The reference is unclear. "A self-devoted Persian" may allude to Scheherazade, the storyteller of the *Thousand and One Nights,* who sacrifices herself for her people by voluntarily marrying the king who has executed a new wife each morning. This was an allusion made frequently by women writers of Lee's day. She may instead be referring to *sati* (or suttee), the Hindu practice in which widows immolate themselves on their husbands' funeral pyres. This custom was known and apparently much commented upon in Britain in the 1780s. A contemporary German novelist records her shock and sorrow at hearing about it during a visit to London. See Sophie von La Roche, *Sophie in London, 1786, Being the Diary of Sophie von La Roche,* tr. Clare Williams (London: Jonathan Cape, 1933), pp. 255-56. An instance of *sati* is described in detail in *The Edinburgh Magazine* (February 1785), pp. 90-92. The woman performing it is described as silent but not veiled. Neither the figure of Scheherazade nor the custom of *sati* is a completely satisfactory explanation for this passage, since Scheherazade was far from silent and *sati* was known to be practiced by Indian women, not Persians.

37. Ellinor supplies a private reason for Essex's preferment of Southampton in defiance of Elizabeth's orders. Essex, sent to Ireland as Lord Lieutenant to subdue a rebellion there and granted "more extensive authority than had ever before been conferred on any lieutenant," left London in March 1599 at the head of a large army, "accompanied by a numerous train of nobility and gentry, who, from affection to his person, had attached themselves to his fortunes." Hume and Goldsmith say that he antagonized Elizabeth by making his friend Southampton (whose recent marriage she had not forgiven) general of his cavalry but do not say that he delayed his departure (Hume, vol. 5, pp. 404-405; Goldsmith, vol. 2, pp. 55-56).

38. dotage: here signifies intense love (as in "to dote on") rather than failure of mental power.

39. Essex here follows Hume, who says that James's "peaceable unambitious temper" enabled Elizabeth to pacify his anger over his mother's execution for "their mutual interest" (vol. 5, p. 326). Robertson gives James credit for considerably more filial resentment (vol. 3, e.g. p. 81).

40. Ellinor's English birth makes her plausibly a better candidate for the succession than her brother James. See note 111 to Part I.

41. See notes 17 and 20 to Part II.

42. Elizabeth would not acknowledge the right of any heir to her throne until she was on her deathbed (Robertson, vol. 3, pp. 165-70, 181-82; Hume, vol. 5, pp. 418-21, 447; Hurd, Dialogue IV, *Works*, vol. 3, p. 251).

43. Hume calls James a "pedant" several times (vol. 6, pp. 57, 63, 153), as does Hurd (Dialogue IV, *Works*, vol. 3, p. 274). See also note 3 to Part VI.

44. Historians agree that Essex schemed rather to seize the throne for James: "Essex was descended by females from the royal family; and some of his sanguine partisans had been so imprudent as to mention his name among those of other pretenders to the crown; but the earl took care . . . to assure James, that so far from entertaining such ambitious views, he was determined to use every expedient for extorting an immediate declaration in favour of that monarch's right of succession" (Hume, vol. 5, p. 421). Robertson also mentions Essex's offer to help James take the English throne by force (vol. 3, 168).

45. Lee follows Hume's account of Essex's military exploits, including his insistence upon being appointed governor of Ireland (vol. 5, 403-404).

46. Maud, or Matilda (1102-67), was the daughter of Henry I of England and became his acknowledged heir on the death of her brother William in 1120. She is called "Empress" because her husband was the Holy Roman Emperor Henry V. On her father's death in 1135 her cousin Stephen seized the crown. The resulting civil war became a popular topic with women novelists in the generation after Lee. During that war Maud/Matilda, in flight from Stephen's partisans, is said to have been carried into Gloucester on 14 September 1141 while bound to a bier as if she were a corpse (*DNB*). Goldsmith tells a different version of this story, in which Matilda escaped, dressed in white, from Oxford Castle over snow-covered fields (vol. 1, p. 111). Although Lee uses the name Maud here (unlike Goldsmith or Hume, both of whom call this queen Matilda), she may have named her heroines in memory of two spirited twelfth-century queens of England: the empress Matilda and her daughter-in-law, Eleanor of Aquitaine.

47. "There the wicked cease from troubling; and there the weary be at rest" Job 3:17 (King James Version). Job is wishing he were dead.

48. The only famous medieval English chestnut tree we have identified was not planted by Edward IV (1442-1483), but was "already known as the Great Chestnut of Tortworth [Gloucestershire] in the days of Stephen" and Maud (see note 45 to Part IV). This tree was alive in Lee's time, and its circumference had been measured in 1720 at fifty feet. Thus it would have been protected from felling both by its fame and by its sheer size. M. Grieve, *A Modern Herbal* (New York: Dorset Press, 1992 [Cape, 1931]), p. 194.

49. Drogheda: a seaport on the river Boyne on the southern border of County Louth, Ireland.

50. Sir Coniers Clifford is mentioned by Hume as having had a command in the attack on Cadiz but not in connection with the Irish campaign.

51. This entire passage on many points follows Hume's description of the state of

Ireland in Elizabethan times, except for his blaming the English for its deplorable condition (which would be implausible in the mouth of Ellinor). He too remarks on their internecine divisions, saying Elizabeth's invasion brought them together in a common cause. He also refers to their lack of "civilization," calling them "a people whose customs and manners approached nearer those of savages than of barbarians." He lays this, however, to the charge of English "tyranny": "Instead of inviting the Irish to adopt the more civilized customs of their conquerors, [the English] even refused, though earnestly solicited, to communicate to them the privileges of their laws, and every where marked them out as aliens and as enemies." The English forces under Essex, according to Hume, were sometimes unexpectedly routed by the Irish, "whom they were wont to despise" as soldiers (vol. 5, pp. 395-97, 407).

PART V

1. Goliah: Goliath, the giant defeated by David. I Samuel 17, esp. 4-11.

2. "Hugh O'Neale, nephew to Shan O'Neale, had been raised by the queen to the dignity of earl of Tyrone; but, having murdered his cousin, son of that rebel, and being acknowledged head of his clan, he . . . fomented all those disorders by which he hoped to weaken or overturn the English government" (Hume, vol. 5, p. 401).

3. Hume on Tyrone's character: "He was noted for the vices of perfidy and cruelty, so common among uncultivated nations; and was also eminent for courage, a virtue which their disorderly course of life requires, and which, notwithstanding, being less supported by the principle of honour, is commonly more precarious among them, than among a civilized people" (ibid.).

4. Hume ascribes Essex's willingness to meet with Tyrone to his troops' fear of fighting the notorious chieftain, together with Tyrone's evasion of combat. He agreed in the spring of 1599 to Tyrone's proposal to meet alone, separated by a river, and arranged a cease-fire to be renewed every six weeks, which could be broken by either side at two weeks' notice. Elizabeth suspected Essex of treachery for receiving peace proposals from Tyrone containing "many unreasonable and exorbitant conditions," when his expedition was "the greatest and most expensive" of her reign (vol. 5, pp. 408-9). See also Goldsmith, vol. 2, p. 56.

5. Compare Clarissa: "I shall be happy. Nay, I am more so already, than of late I thought I could ever be in this life—Yet how this *body* clings!—How it encumbers!" Richardson, *Clarissa*, vol. 7, pp. 234-35 (Letter LXVII).

6. laudanum: an opiate.

7. Hume says that Essex's enemies at court set spies upon him, "the better to make advantage of his indiscretions" and that after expressing her displeasure at Essex's attempt to treat with Tyrone, [Elizabeth] commanded him to remain in Ireland until he received further orders (vol. 5, pp. 405, 409). See also Goldsmith, vol. 2, p. 56.

8. Judith: eponymous heroine of an apocryphal book of the Bible. By predicting victory to the Assyrian general Holofernes, who was laying siege to the Jewish city of Bethulia, she got herself invited into his tent (whereas Ellinor has been brought unwillingly into Tyrone's tent). When Holofernes was drunk and sleeping, Judith cut off his head, thus facilitating the ensuing Jewish victory. By "the Assyrian" Lee can only mean Judith herself, who however was not Assyrian but Hebrew.

9. "The queen was extremely disgusted when she heard that so considerable a part of the season was consumed in these frivolous enterprises" (Hume, vol. 5, p. 407).

10. "Essex heard at once of Elizabeth's anger, and of the promotion of his enemy, sir Robert Cecil, to the office of master of the wards, an office to which he himself aspired" (Hume, vol. 5, p. 409). On Essex's enmity with Nottingham (also called Howard and Effingham) and Raleigh, see notes 18 and 30 to Part IV.

11. Hume relates the story of Essex's hasty return to England in an attempt to regain Elizabeth's favor, "dreading that, if he remained any longer absent, the queen would be totally alienated from him." In imitation of an earlier action of his stepfather, the earl of Leicester, Essex abruptly left his post despite Elizabeth's orders that he remain there (vol. 5, pp. 409-10). See also Goldsmith, vol. 2, p. 56.

12. The Wriothesleys: the family of the earl of Southampton.

13. bulged: had a hole smashed into the hull.

14. The Scottish youth finds Ellinor's elegant English masculine clothing effeminate.

15. The Dornock family and its castle are Lee's invention, although Dornoch is a town on the northeastern coast of the Scottish Highlands.

16. Here Ellinor's account is at odds with Hume's, who writes of James that "he never discovered any tendency, even the smallest, towards a passion for any mistress" (vol. 6, p. 154).

17. Hume similarly writes of James: "all his qualities were sullied with weakness and embellished by humanity" (ibid.).

18. Paraphrased from Shakespeare, *Richard III*, Act V, scene iv, ll. 9-10: "Slave! I have set my life upon a cast, / And I will stand the hazard of the die." Part of the famous final speech in which Richard III offers his kingdom for a horse, the lines are spoken as he is losing the battle of Bosworth Field. Richard III was one of Lee's father's signature roles. He played the title role at least five times during Sophia's lifetime, including one of the final performances of his life, in Bath (see Highfill, vol. 9, pp. 203-8).

19. "Either Caesar or nobody," i.e., "I will attain supreme eminence, or perish in the attempt"; saying attributed to Julius Caesar. H.T. Riley, ed., *Dictionary of Latin Quotations* (London: G. Bohn, 1856), p. 34.

20. Thomas Grey (1565/6-1614), Lord Grey was with Essex in Ireland in 1599 and sat on the Commission in 1600/1 for the trials of Essex and Southampton.

21. "[Essex] arrived at court before any one was in the least apprised of his intentions. Though besmeared with dirt and sweat, he hastened up stairs to the presence chamber; nor stopped till he was in the queen's bed-chamber, who was newly risen, and was sitting with her hair about her face. He threw himself on his knees, kissed her hand, and had some private conference with her; where he was so graciously received that, on his departure, he was heard to express great satsifaction, and to thank God that, though he had suffered much trouble and many storms abroad, he found a sweet calm at home" (Hume, vol. 5, p. 409-10).

22. Lee explains the sudden change in Elizabeth's reception of Essex by emphasizing the influence of his enemies at court, while Hume and Goldsmith ascribe it to Elizabeth's own resentment, giving us her thoughts instead of the words of her courtiers (Hume, vol. 5, p. 410; Goldsmith, vol. 2, p. 56).

23. coped: contended.

24. Elizabeth was sixty-six years old when this event occurred in 1599; she died four years later.

25. This account of the events succeeding Essex's presumptuous visit to the queen's bedchamber follows Goldsmith's in diverging from Hume's version of chronology and in ascribing the conveyance of Essex's disparaging remarks about the queen's appearance to political, rather than sexual, jealousy (Goldsmith, vol. 2, p. 57; cf. Hume, vol. 5, p. 420).

26. toils: a net used to trap game.

27. Tracey's report of Essex's illness concurs largely with Hume's, diverging mainly in the emotional responses of Elizabeth and Essex. Hume reports that Elizabeth always said "that the purpose of her severity was to correct, not to ruin him." He attributes Essex's illness to thwarted ambition and his cure to Elizabeth's renewed encouragement of it, with the company of his wife (vol. 5, pp. 410-11). Hurd also refers obliquely to this event (Dialogue IV, *Works*, vol. 3, p. 247).

28. Essex's letter of thanks to Elizabeth on her permitting him to retire to his country seat mentions a quite different principal pastime there: indulging a shared taste for literature with his wife (Hume, vol. 5, p. 412).

29. forecast: forethought, prudence.

30. See note 28 to Part V.

31. gaud: a mere toy, a gaudy ornament.

32. due: owed as a debt. Generally in literature of sensibility sincere expressions of emotion require a sympathetic return in kind. This is not an instance of the common modern adverbial misuse of the adjective "due": Phoebe's tears *deserve* Ellinor's, but they do not cause them.

33. Paraphrased from the same speech (by a duke exiled from his rightful domain) that provides the epigraph to novel: Shakespeare, *As You Like It*, Act II, scene i, ll. 15-17. See also note 1 to Part I.

34. Lady Pembroke's account differs from Hume's in its portrayal of Elizabeth's feelings towards Essex after his imprisonment and illness. Hume does write similarly, however, that "when the symptoms of the queen's returning affection towards Essex were known, they gave a sensible alarm to the faction which had declared their opposition to him"; so much so that Sir Walter Raleigh fell ill in his turn and had to be nursed back to health by the queen as well (vol. 5, p. 411).

35. See note 28 to Part V.

36. Neither Hume nor Lee's other narrator (Tracey) sees Essex's liberation and retirement to the country as an effect of "policy." See note 27 to Part V.

37. Hume mentions Essex's "secret applications to the king of Scots," who "cast a wishful eye to the succession of England" and negotiated with everyone but Elizabeth herself "in order to ensure himself friends and partisans" (vol. 5, pp. 420-21). Robertson also writes that Essex "determined to redress his wrongs by violence. But . . . he endeavoured to give it the semblance of public utility, by mingling the king of Scotland's interest with his own" (vol. 3, pp. 168-69). See also note 44 to Part IV.

38. This part of Lady Pembroke's narrative closely follows that of Hume, who says that back in London Essex entertained not only "men of the military profession"

but "all desperate adventurers," along with Puritan preachers (vol. 5, p. 419). See also Goldsmith, vol. 2, p. 57.

39. Neither Hume nor Robertson mention such quarrels.

40. The "commissioned Lords," headed by Egerton, the lord keeper, were sent by Elizabeth, according to Hume, simply to see what all the commotion was about at Essex House, where the earl was gathering his confederates. Surprised by them in his plot, he took them prisoner in his house and "sallied forth with about two hundred attendants, armed only with walking swords" (vol. 5, p. 426). Robertson writes: "With two or three hundred followers incompletely armed, he attempted to assault a throne the best established in Europe" (vol. 3, p. 169).

41. mechanics: manual laborers.

42. Hume's and Goldsmith's accounts of Essex's failed insurrection similarly relate how crowds gathered around him rather out of curiosity than a willingness to join him, how they attempted to block his retreat to his own house, and the death of Tracey as Essex attempted to fight his way home. They diverge from Lee, however, in saying that Essex surrendered after returning to his house and finding himself hopelessly besieged there (vol. 5, pp. 426-27). Robertson agrees with them, without mentioning Tracey (vol. 3, pp. 169-70). None of these historians attributes Essex's surrender to a concern for his followers.

43. Again Hume offers a different perspective on the same actions: "Essex's best friends were scandalised at his assurance in insisting so positively on his innocence, and the goodness of his intentions; and still more at his vindictive disposition, in accusing, without any appearance of reason, secretary Cecil as a partisan of the Infanta's title [to the English crown]. . . . Southampton's behaviour was more mild and submissive" (vol. 5, p. 428).

44. Hume and Goldsmith both say that Elizabeth was even more to be pitied in having to condemn her favorite than Essex himself was in being condemned (Hume, vol. 5, p. 430; Goldsmith, vol. 2, p. 60).

45. Lady Pembroke elaborates on Hume: "When sentence was pronounced, Essex spoke like a man who expected nothing but death: But he added, that he should be sorry if he were represented to the queen as a person that despised her clemency; though he should not, he believed, make any cringing submissions to obtain it" (vol. 5, p. 428).

46. Hume contradicts the idea that Essex was informed that he had only to ask for pardon and attributes the misunderstanding between him and Elizabeth to his political adversaries: "Essex's enemies told her, that he himself desired to die, and had assured her, that she could never be in safety while he lived: It is likely that this proof of penitence and of concern for her would produce a contrary effect to what they intended, and would revive all the fond affection which she had so long indulged towards the unhappy prisoner. But what chiefly hardened her heart against him was his supposed obstinacy in never making, as she hourly expected, any application to her for mercy; and she finally gave her consent to his execution" (vol. 5, p. 430).

47. Hume describes Elizabeth's "conflicts" in greater detail: "She felt a perpetual combat between resentment and inclination, pride and compassion, the care of her own safety and concern for her favourite. . . . She signed the warrant for his execution;

she countermanded it; she again resolved on his death; she felt a new return of tenderness" (vol. 5, pp. 429-30).

48. Fotheringay Castle was the place of execution of Mary, Queen of Scots.

49. "Southampton's life was saved with great difficulty" (Hume, vol. 5, p. 432).

50. The earl of Essex was beheaded on 5 February 1601. Lee corrects an error in Hume, who says he was thirty-four when he died. Hume similarly describes his turning toward devout religion in the last period of his imprisonment and laments the contradictions between his "head and heart." Lady Pembroke's version contradicts Hume's, however, in supplying a "melting multitude": "The execution was private in the Tower, agreeably to his own request. He was apprehensive, he said, lest the favour and compassion of the people would too much raise his heart in those moments, when humiliation under the afflicting hand of Heaven was the only proper sentiment which he could indulge. And the queen, no doubt, thought that prudence required the removing of so melancholy a spectacle from the public eye" (vol. 5, pp. 429-30).

51. "This incoherent reference" is to the harsh treatment Mary received from Elizabeth's deputies, who tried to deny her female attendants to accompany her to the scaffold. Robertson, Hume, and Goldsmith all tell how, when one of the executioners "rudely" tried to help her remove some of her upper garments to prepare her for the block, "she said, with a smile, that she had not been accustomed to undress before so many spectators, nor to be served by such valets" (Robertson, vol. 3, pp. 64-65; Goldsmith, vol. 2, p. 49). Hume adds that Mary obtained permission to have a few women to attend her at her execution only when she told the earl of Kent that she hoped Elizabeth, "being a maiden queen, would vouchsafe in regard of my womanhood, that I should have some of my own people about me at my death" (vol. 5, pp. 315-18).

52. "As [Elizabeth's] amorous inclinations, in so advanced an age, would naturally make her appear ridiculous, if not odious, in [Essex's] eyes, he was engaged by an imprudent openness, of which he made profession, to discover too easily those sentiments to her" (Hume, vol. 5, p. 431).

53. the faculty: the doctors of medicine; physicians.

54. ideal: unreal; ghostly.

55. See note 42 to Part IV.

56. "So dark a cloud overcast the evening of that day, which had shone out with a mighty lustre in the eyes of all Europe" (Hume, vol. 5, pp. 445-47); "[Elizabeth's] nature, in the decline of life, was somewhat clouded by apprehensions; as the horizon . . . in the evening of the brightest day, is apt to be obscured by vapours" (Hurd, Dialogue IV, *Works*, vol. 3, p. 253).

57. Hume and Robertson describe the death of Elizabeth similarly, with more and different details (not including fear of apparitions). Robertson says there were "various conjectures" as to the cause of her sudden emotional and physical decline, but "the most common opinion, at that time" was the explanation Hume also offers. It is a story hardly less romantic than Lee's and shares with it the idea of the queen's haunting guilt over the execution of Essex: Elizabeth had given Essex a ring that she said he had only to send her if he ever needed her pardon. When Essex did not send it to her in his final imprisonment as she expected, she thought him obstinate and agreed to his execution. In fact Essex had asked the countess of Nottingham to deliver the

ring to Elizabeth, but the earl of Nottingham (the admiral whose promotion to that title had so enraged Essex) had persuaded his wife not to do so. She repented on her deathbed and confessed her secret to Elizabeth, who became enraged and then went into a severe depression from which she never recovered (Hume, vol. 5, pp. 445-47; Robertson, vol. 3, pp. 177-79). Goldsmith also tells the story of the ring (vol. 2, pp. 60-61).

PART VI

1. The countess of Pembroke died on 25 September 1621 (eighteen years after the death of Elizabeth). Lee's emphasis on female lines of inheritance makes an earlier death convenient.

2. national: chauvinistic.

3. Hume describes James as "awkward in his person and ungainly in his manners" (vol. 6, p. 153); Hurd has Addison call him "the pedant king" (Dialogue IV, *Works*, vol. 3, p. 274). See also note 43 to Part IV and note 17 to Part V.

4. Mechanized textile factories did not exist before the eighteenth century, although mass production of handwoven textiles by large numbers of women working together under one supervisor, and sometimes in assembly-line fashion, occurred even in the ancient world. In any case, Kenilworth Castle apparently never housed a textile factory, but Lee had at least two sources for the idea. By the time *The Recess* was published, her younger brother, George Augustus Lee (1761-1826), had been working for several years for a firm of cotton spinners in Manchester, in which he was later to become a partner noted for his improvements in factory technology, working conditions, and workers' benefits. In addition to Lee's personal acquaintance with textile manufacture through her brother, she may have encountered in the village of Kenilworth "a local legend that the Coventry silk-weavers used the castle as a factory." This tradition was perpetuated in official guide books of the nineteenth and twentieth centuries, which asserted that the weavers occupied Leicester's buildings in the ruins of the castle sometime in the eighteenth century, but the story has since been disproven. Drew, introduction to *Kenilworth Castle Illustrated*, p. 14, and *Kenilworth: A Manor of the King* (Kenilworth: Pleasaunce Press, 1971), p. 23. See also Elizabeth Wayland Barber, *Women's Work, the First 20,000 Years: Women, Cloth, and Society in Early Times* (Princeton: Princeton University Press, 1994), pp. 190-99, 214-22.

5. Moreton is fictional.

6. Prince Henry Frederick Stuart (1594-1612), eldest son of King James I.

7. "[Henry] had not reached his eighteenth year, and he already possessed more dignity in his behaviour, and commanded more respect, than his father, with all his age, learning, and experience. Neither his high fortune, nor his youth, had seduced him into any irregular pleasures: Business and ambition seem to have been his sole passion. His inclinations, as well as exercises, were martial" (Hume, vol. 6, p. 62). Lee adds a taste for learning to this description.

8. Hume reads James's motivation for giving Henry a separate court quite differently: "his indulgence to Henry was great, and perhaps imprudent, by giving him a large and independent settlement, even in so early youth" (vol. 6, p. 63).

9. The boarders at Lee's school secretly watched such entertainments from their

bedroom windows and "hastily retired" to their beds when they heard the approach of the headmistress. See Introduction.

10. It was widely believed that Elizabeth had introduced the covered carriage to England. Although there is some evidence that she was not absolutely the first English person to use one, carriages were a novelty in her lifetime, and she was the first English monarch to use them in state processions (previously the aristocracy rode in chariots, litters, or on horseback). Ezra M. Stratton, *The World on Wheels* (New York: Benjamin Blom, Inc., 1972 [New York: 1878]), pp. 264-66.

11. Beginning in the sixteenth century, wealthy gentlemen built country estates on Richmond Hill, overlooking the Thames Valley. The view was famous. "Heavens! What a goodly prospect spreads around, of hills, dales, woods, and lawn and spired and glittering towns and gilded streams," wrote James Thomson in 1724. *The London Encyclopedia*, p. 684.

12. Unpaved country roads frequently had ruts worn in them by carriage and cart wheels, although this was probably more of a problem in Lee's own time, when there was much more coach traffic than in Elizabeth's (see note 10 to Part VI).

13. Robert Carr (c. 1587-1645) was created Viscount Rochester in 1611. James "seems to have indulged an unlimited fondness for his minion, beyond even that which he bore to his own children" and "bestowed on him the supreme direction of all his business and political concerns" even though "all his natural accomplishments consisted in good looks" (Hume, vol. 6, pp. 64-65). See also Goldsmith, vol. 2, p. 72.

14. Lee imagines an alliance between Prince Henry and a Catholic princess, such as was later arranged for the next heir, Charles.

15. Hume says that Henry "seems indeed to have nourished too violent a contempt for the king on account of his pedantry and pusillanimity" (vol. 6, p. 63).

16. Frances Howard (1590-1632), daughter of the earl of Suffolk, married the third earl of Essex in 1606. (The countesses of the first and second earls, Lettice Knollys and Frances Walsingham, have been mentioned earlier). See Hume, vol. 6, pp. 66-67; also notes 83, 96, and 102 to Part I; note 22 to Part IV.

17. Lord and Lady Essex, married at fourteen, were separated while the earl finished his education abroad. The countess fell in love with Rochester, who engineered her divorce with the king's help and married her on 26 December 1613. The couple was later found guilty of plotting the murder of Rochester's mentor, the poet and essayist Sir Thomas Overbury (1581-1613), who had encouraged their affair but disapproved of the divorce and remarriage (see Hume, vol. 6, pp. 66-70; Goldsmith, vol. 2, pp. 72-74). Prince Henry seems to fear for himself what was historically the fate of Overbury.

18. saloon (from French): a living room or parlor.

19. Sir David Murray (d. 1631) entered the household of King James VI of Scotland about 1578, was knighted by James before he succeeded Elizabeth to the English throne, attended him when he went to take possession of that throne, and was created Viscount Stormont in 1621.

20. her younger son: later king Charles I (1600-January 30, 1649). Hume mentions that King James maintained separate courts for himself, the queen, and the prince of Wales (vol. 6, p. 46; see also note 8 to Part VI).

21. Her beautiful daughter: Elizabeth Stuart (1596-1662). Known as Elizabeth of Bohemia after 1619, she was a writer herself, and much celebrated by women writers.

22. progresses: ceremonial journeys undertaken by kings and nobles through their domains.

23. Frederick (1596-1632), Elector Palatine of the Rhine, married Elizabeth Stuart on 14 February 1613, shortly after Henry's death (Hume, vol. 6, p. 63).

24. "This marriage, though celebrated with great joy and festivity, proved itself an unhappy event to the king, as well as to his son-in-law. . . . The elector, trusting to so great an alliance, engaged in enterprises beyond his strength: And the king, not being able to support him in his distress, lost entirely, in the end of his life, what remained of the affection and esteem of his own subjects" (ibid.). See also Goldsmith, vol. 2, pp. 79-80.

25. "Violent reports were propagated, as if Henry had been carried off by poison; but the physicians, on opening his body, found no symptoms to confirm such an opinion" (Hume, vol. 6, p. 63).

26. "The bold and criminal malignity of men's tongues and pens spared not even the king." Rochester and his wife were also suspected (Hume, vol. 6, pp. 63, 70-71).

27. James promoted Rochester in 1613, about the time of his marriage to the former countess of Essex, "lest the lady should lose any rank by her new marriage" (Hume, vol. 6, p. 70).

28. court: courtyard.

29. See note 17 to Part VI.

30. Hume and Goldsmith blame the murder of Sir Thomas Overbury primarily on Frances Howard's rage at him for having attempted to dissuade Rochester from marrying her (see note 17 to Part VI). Although the truth of her actions and motives remains uncertain, "all accounts of Frances Howard have concurred in the representation of her as an epitome of female villainy, malicious, irrational and lustful." David Lindley, *The Trials of Frances Howard: Fact and Fiction at the Court of King James* (London: Routledge, 1993), p. 2.

31. blisters: anything applied to the skin to raise blisters as a medical treatment.

32. Within two years of Overbury's death, Somerset and his countess were found guilty of his murder and imprisoned, but were spared the death penalty by royal pardon. They were eventually released with a pension from the king. Lee follows Hume's interpretation of their life thereafter: They "languished out old age in infamy and obscurity. Their guilty loves were turned into the most deadly hatred; and they passed many years together in the same house, without any intercourse or correspondence with each other" (vol. 6, pp. 75-78). See also Goldsmith, vol. 2, p. 74.

33. See previous note.

BIBLIOGRAPHY

EDITIONS OF *THE RECESS*

The Recess; or, A Tale of Other Times. 3 vols. London: T. Cadell, 1783-85. The first edition. The first volume was published in 1783 and reissued when the second and third volumes appeared in 1785. The third volume includes a list of errata for the first two volumes. Microfilmed by General Microfilm, Cambridge, Mass., 1971.

The Recess; or, A Tale of Other Times. 3 vols. London: T. Cadell, 1786. The second edition. Contains emendations to the text, possibly the author's (see "Note on the Text"), but is not "corrected," as the third, fourth, and fifth editions are. Microfilmed by Research Publications. New Haven. *History of Women,* Reel 54, 339, vol. 1-342.

The Recess; or, A Tale of Other Times. 2 vols. Dublin: G. Burnet, R. Moncriefe, J. Exshaw, J. Beatty, L. White, P. Byrne, S. Colbert, H. Whitestone, W. Sleater, J. Cash, R. Marchbank, T. Heary, and J. Moore, 1786. A new edition, probably pirated, using smaller print and cheaper paper to condense the text into two volumes. The text exactly follows that of Cadell's first edition except that it introduces additional printer's errors.

The Recess; or, A Tale of Other Times. 3 vols. London: T. Cadell, 1787. The third edition, corrected. Most printer's errors present in the first edition are here corrected, and a few new ones are introduced. Changes in spelling and style are made throughout the text, as described in detail in the "Note on the Text." Microfilmed at Princeton University, Firestone Library, 1995.

The Recess; or, A Tale of Other Times. 3 vols. London: T. Cadell, 1792. The fourth edition, corrected. The text is nearly identical to that of the third edition but makes further corrections to printer's errors missed or introduced in the third edition and a few additional stylistic corrections.

The Recess; or, A Tale of Other Times. 2 vols. Dublin, G. Burnet, P. Byrne, H. Colbert, W. Sleater, T. Heery, and J. Moore, 1791. A reprint of the 1786 Dublin edition.

The Recess; or, A Tale of Other Times. 3 vols. London: T. Cadell and W. Davies, 1804. The fifth edition.

The Recess; or, A Tale of Other Times. West Smithfield, Eng.: Fisher, 1824.

The Recess, in *Popular Tales.* 1827.

The Recess, 1840.

The Recess; or, A Tale of Other Times. Preface by J.M.S. Tompkins, introduction by Devendra P. Varma. 3 vols. The Gothic Novels Series. New York: Arno, 1972. An unedited facsimile library reprint of the 1785 edition.

The Recess; or, A Tale of Other Times. 3 vols. The Gothic Novels Series. Manchester, N.H.: Ayer, 1979. An unedited facsimile library reprint of the 1785 edition.

The Recess, or, A Tale of Past Times. Portsea: J. Williams, [1800?]. The first condensation of the novel, published as a chapbook (33 pp.).

The Recess. A Tale of Past Times. The Marvellous Magazine and Compendium of Prodigies. 1:3. London: T. Hurst, 1802. Another abridgment (72 pp.).

The Recess: A Tale of the Days of Queen Elizabeth. The Novelist. London: J. Cunningham, 1840 (133 pp.). Another condensed version of the novel.

The Recess: A Tale of the Days of Queen Elizabeth. The Novel Newspaper. Nos. 98-100.

London: N. Bruce, 1844 (133 pp.). Probably a reprinting of the condensed version published previously in *The Novelist.*

CRITICISM OF *THE RECESS*

Alliston, April. "*Corinne* and Female Transmission: Rewriting *La Princesse de Clèves* through the English Gothic." In *The Novel's Seductions: Staël's* Corinne *in Critical Inquiry.* Ed. Karyna Szmurlo. Lewisburg, Pa.: Bucknell Univ. Press, 1999.

————. "Of Haunted Highlands: Mapping a Geography of Gender in the Margins of Europe." *Cultural Interactions in the Romantic Age.* Ed. Gregory Maertz. Albany: SUNY Press, 1998.

————. "The Values of a Literary Legacy: Retracing the Transmission of Value through Female Lines." *Yale Journal of Criticism* 4:1 (Oct. 1990): 109-27.

————. *Virtue's Faults: Correspondences in Eighteenth-Century British and French Women's Fiction.* Stanford, Calif.: Stanford University Press, 1996.

Doody, Margaret Anne. "Deserts, Ruins and Troubled Waters: Female Dreams in Fiction and the Development of the Gothic Novel." *Genre* 10:4 (winter 1977): 529-72.

Ellis, Kate Ferguson. *The Contested Castle: Gothic Novels and the Subversion of Domestic Ideology.* Urbana: University of Illinois Press, 1989.

Foster, James R. "The Abbé Prévost and the English Novel." *PMLA* 42: 2 (June 1927): 443-64.

Isaac, Megan Lynn. "Sophia Lee and the Gothic of Female Community." *Studies in the Novel* 28:2 (summer 1996): 200-218.

Le Brun, Annie. *Les Châteaux de la subversion.* Clamecy, France: Garnier, 1982.

Lewis, Jayne Elizabeth. "'Ev'ry Lost Relation': Historical Fictions and Sentimental Incidents in Sophia Lee's *The Recess.*" *Eighteenth-Century Fiction* 7:2 (January 1995): 165-84.

————. *Mary Queen of Scots: Romance and Nation.* New York: Routledge, 1998.

Punter, David. *The Literature of Terror: A History of Gothic Fictions from 1765 to the Present Day.* London: Longman, 1980.

Roberts, Bette B. "Sophia Lee's *The Recess* (1785): The Ambivalence of Female Gothicism." *Massachusetts Studies in English* 6:4 (1978): 68-82.

Robertson, Fiona. *Legitimate Histories: Scott, Gothic, and the Authorities of Fiction.* Oxford: Oxford University Press, 1994.

Rogers, Katharine M. *Feminism in Eighteenth-Century England.* Urbana, Ill.: University of Illinois Press, 1982.

Spencer, Jane. *The Rise of the Woman Novelist: From Aphra Behn to Jane Austen.* Oxford: Blackwell, 1986.

Spender, Dale. *Mothers of the Novel: 100 Good Women Writers Before Jane Austen.* London: Pandora Press, 1986.

Summers, Montague. *The Gothic Quest: A History of the Gothic Novel.* 1938. New York: Russell & Russell, 1964.

Tompkins, J.M.S. *The Popular Novel in England, 1770-1800.* London: Constable, 1932.

Varma, Devendra P. *The Gothic Flame.* London: Arthur Baker, 1957.

————. Introduction to *The Recess; or, A Tale of Other Times,* by Sophia Lee. New York: Arno Press, 1972. Pp. vii-xlviii.